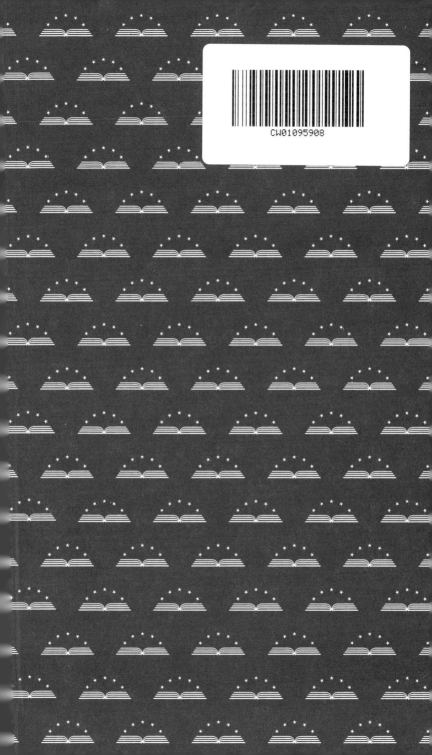

Library of America, a nonprofit organization,
champions our nation's cultural heritage
by publishing America's greatest writing in
authoritative new editions and providing resources
for readers to explore this rich, living legacy.

JACK KEROUAC

THE UNKNOWN KEROUAC

RARE, UNPUBLISHED & NEWLY TRANSLATED WRITINGS

Todd Tietchen, *editor*
Jean-Christophe Cloutier, *translator*

THE LIBRARY OF AMERICA

Visit our website at www.loa.org.

This paper meets the requirements of
ANSI/NISO z39.48–1992 (Permanence of Paper).

Distributed to the trade in the United States
by Penguin Random House Inc.
and in Canada by Penguin Random House Canada Ltd.

Library of Congress Control Number: 2016934976
ISBN 978–1–59853–498–6

First Printing
The Library of America—283

Manufactured in the United States of America

Special thanks to John Sampas, literary executor of the Kerouac estate, for the many ways in which he supported this project.

The Unknown Kerouac:
Rare, Unpublished & Newly Translated Writings
is published with support from

THE FLORENCE GOULD FOUNDATION

and will be kept in print by its gift to
the Guardians of American Letters Fund,
established by Library of America
to ensure that every volume in the series
will be permanently available.

CONTENTS

EDITOR'S INTRODUCTION

THE writings that follow offer a substantial and vital enlargement of the Jack Kerouac canon, tracing the growth of his voice and vision and giving a fresh sense of the wellsprings of his literary art. Hitherto unexplored pieces in a moving and impressive chronicle of aesthetic development, they deepen our understanding of Kerouac's artistry and his evolution as one of the twentieth century's most adventurous writers. These works, which span the course of Kerouac's authorial life, attest to his aspiration to become an enduring American writer—an aspiration that drove him to reimagine the perspectives and cadences of American literature.

Kerouac transformed the materials of his life into a work of art realized across a multiplicity of genres and categories—letters, journals, poetry, novelized prose, and mongrel modes of experimentation juxtaposing and blending these forms. He was a tirelessly prolific and relentlessly ambitious writer, at what often proved a significant personal cost. The writings collected in this book will become indispensable to future appreciations of Kerouac's work, prompting reconsideration of much that has been taken for granted about the intentions and scope of his accomplishment.

Many readers discover Kerouac through *On the Road* (1957), the signature work that seems to position its author as the generational voice of young people breaking free of their inherited past for the immensities of experiential possibility in Cold War America, hitting the road in a literal and figurative escape from crumbling moral conventions and mores. That is, in brief, the Kerouac myth. It has proven particularly hardy; and as myths are apt to do, it foregrounds one aspect of its subject at the expense of others. Kerouac himself resisted the myth. It becomes clear, for instance, from *Beat Spotlight*—an incomplete scroll manuscript Kerouac labored over during the final year of his life—that he came to lament the literary notoriety that followed the publication of *On the Road*, apprehensive that his name had become synonymous with aimlessness, irresponsibility, and criminality. Despite his dedication to the confessional and autobiographical, Kerouac died fearing that he had somehow remained unknown to critics and the reading public.

The Unknown Kerouac presents a more robust Kerouac. In the light of these newly available texts, *On the Road* can be seen as something more than a testament to unadulterated freedom and experiential journeying. In the wake of World War II, Sal Paradise and Dean Moriarty—the novel's dual protagonists based respectively on Kerouac and his close friend and muse Neal Cassady—find themselves torn between the comforting promises of domesticity and their desire to flee conventional visions of the American good life for destinations less certain. Again and again, Sal attempts to slide out of his circumstances and into the possibilities of new experience on the road, into the new intensities that Dean heralds. Yet Sal also backtracks onto more predictable paths, into territories already settled. *On the Road* provides a detailed literary sketching of a generation torn between orthodoxies and unconventionalities, sentimental flirtations with nostalgia and optimistic longings for a world newly pried open.

Sal and Dean inhabit existential predicaments that Kerouac had already articulated in the holograph essays from the 1940s included here, composed while he was living in New York. Kerouac had moved to New York in 1939 from Lowell, Massachusetts, to attend Columbia University and play football—although his admission to Columbia required that he spend an additional year of preparatory work at the Horace Mann School. A talented athlete who also excelled in track and field and in baseball, Kerouac had harbored artistic hopes since his early teenage years. New York bohemian and jazz culture nourished those aims, as did his relationships with Allen Ginsberg, William Burroughs, Lucien Carr, and other members of the nascent Beat orbit revolving around Columbia. In this heady environment—an environment detailed in *I Wish I Were You* (1945), included here as an appendix—the animating conflicts and characteristics of Kerouac's work began to take shape.

In the early essays that open this collection, Kerouac hovers somewhere between despair and triumphalism, seeking a common cultural ground with his generation while retaining his sense of being an outsider. In "On Frank Sinatra," he identifies the "profundity of feeling" evident in the crooner's voice as expressive of the mood of "loneliness and longing" experienced by young men during and after World War II. At times, those longings take on positive hues, as in "America in World History," an affirmative essay in which Kerouac proclaims himself affiliated with his "American brothers" who as yet feel "young and unfulfilled," poised to seek a cultural destiny distinct from the ossified traditions of Europe. Such generational optimism also infuses "On Contemporary Jazz—Bebop." Elsewhere, however, Kerouac retreats into nostalgia, as in "A Couple of Facts Concerning Laws of Decadence," where couched within a critique of city intellectuals is a devotion to "lineal heritage" stirred by a "liberal" New York radio skit.

The tensions between these opposing perspectives would continue to resonate through Kerouac's writing. In the midst of his quest for the new, he often felt the pull of more familiar and consoling harbors. The allure of the quest coexists with what ultimately proves an unresolvable desire to feel rooted. Kerouac's is a literature of roots and routes. Jean-Christophe Cloutier's translations of *The Night Is My Woman* and *Old Bull in the Bowery*—two narratives from the early 1950s originally composed in the French patois of Lowell's Québécois working class, as *La nuit est ma femme* and *Sur le chemin* respectively—bear out the crucial significance of Kerouac's roots in the French-Canadian culture of twentieth-century New England. Both works fill important gaps in Kerouac's autobiographical aesthetic, the multivolume project he outlined in his preface to *Big Sur* (1962) as the *Duluoz Legend*, greatly augmenting the ethnography of French-Canadian life contained in the Lowell trilogy consisting of *Visions of Gerard* (1963), *Doctor Sax* (1959), and *Maggie Cassidy* (1959). The genealogy of the Duluoz clan's migratory history from Québec into New England, as related in *Old Bull in the Bowery*, is an especially valuable addition.

Michel, the narrator of *The Night Is My Woman*, remains, like Kerouac, split down the middle. Michel discloses, "I'm all mixed up in my noggin," ensnared within his desire to write in his native French, while at the same time harboring literary ambitions sparked by American writers such as Twain and Melville, and "their large form which was free and magnificent." While known to generations of readers through the all-American moniker "Jack," the writer was born Jean-Louis Kérouac in March 1922 in Lowell to native Québécois parents, Joseph Alcide Leon Kérouac and Gabrielle-Ange Lévesque. His father, who went by the name of Leo, had been born in Saint-Hubert, Québec, then immigrated with his family to Nashua, New Hampshire. Kerouac's mother, Gabrielle, was born in 1895 in Saint-Pacôme, Québec, and her family also migrated to Nashua. The married Kerouacs settled among the sizable French-Canadian community of Lowell in order to raise a family in a setting in tune with more familiar ways of life. The ultimate distillation of the life of this family can be found in the affecting childhood memoir *Memory Babe*, begun in 1957 and published here for the first time.

Kerouac's restlessness, his interest in road-bound and freight-bound outsiders, was partly grounded in his experience of the French-Canadian diaspora and the imperatives that often sent his own family on the road. Kerouac's portrayals of French-Canadian life in *The Night Is My Woman* and *Old Bull in the Bowery* put his interest in migration or journeying in a more nuanced light. In both texts we meet characters who take to the road not for raw and unmoored adventuring for its own sake, but for the economic motives that send Michel trekking back and forth between Lowell and Portsmouth, or send the Kerouac family to New Haven seeking work, or send the Depression-era Pomerays racing desperately for New York. As many of the works included here make clear, his creative impulses always tapped into something much deeper than the youthful search for kicks.

Kerouac has long been seen as an impetuous writer, impulsively following his instincts wherever they might take him on the page, just as his characters seem to wander aimlessly, without governing principle. Such characterizations fail to take into account the artistic goals expressed, notably, in the document published here as *Journal 1951*, the record of a psychic and aesthetic breakthrough that transformed Kerouac's sense of his mission as a writer. Here, Kerouac makes clear his commitment to creating a literature of lived experience, an expansive body of writing made from the events of his life. Later, in his June 1963 epistolary exchange with John Clellon Holmes (printed here for the first time), he would identify his time in the Veterans Hospital, where the journal begins, as pivotal in his development, observing that "I had time to think at last without interruption and unfolded my secret desire in writing at last."

True to his aims, there appears to be nothing of literary contrivance about this journal. Kerouac's writing here pulses and breathes. When Kerouac is at his best he allows us to partake in his dawning realizations, his wonderment and uncertainties. We get it pure, as Kerouac goes back and forth between sudden bursts of literary confidence and mountainous doubt—between illumination and the psychic pain that often sends him spiraling into demoralizing binge drinking. We share those vacillations with him in a way that feels profoundly true.

Journal 1951 enacts the literary principles it espouses. It is one of Kerouac's most impressive accomplishments, its jewel-like complexities finally tapering into the fine point of its epilogue. Strikingly, Kerouac gains much of his insight while remaining still, lying on his back convalescing in the Kingsbridge VA hospital after an attack of thrombophlebitis. He stresses this correlation between his convalescence and his growing sense of himself as a literary artist, telling us at one point: "Though I'm writing this on my back I feel again like my own giant." As he prepares to leave Kingsbridge he further admits "this is my last day in the Hospital where I have learned at last to think," going on to say that "the solution of my lifework I attribute to the month of pure meditation in the hospital and thank God for it."

Much has been made of the critical role played by Kerouac's journals in allowing him to write while he was on the go, traveling across the states and beyond. The sedentary meditations of *Journal 1951* provide a valuable contrast with Kerouac's road journals, efforts represented here by *Private Philologies, Riddles, and a Ten-Day Writing Log*, a notebook whose hybrid contents reflect Kerouac's peripatetic life as he traveled from New York to Denver and back in 1949 and 1950. Notably, *Private Philologies* features an extended engagement with Chaucer, including the passage from the Prologue to *The Canterbury Tales* in which Chaucer evokes the springtime stirring in the blood that sends people pilgrimaging through the world. Not only is this allusion perfectly at home among the searching experiments of Kerouac's road-worn journal, but it shows that his interests in migratory experience and road narrative have as much to do with long-standing literary archetypes of pilgrimage and quest as they do with the longings of the postwar period, or the history of the French-Canadian diaspora. Allusions such as this abound here and usher us tellingly into the remarkably diverse, and as yet unappreciated, sources of Kerouac's literary art. In *Journal 1951*, Kerouac baldly declares: "It is necessary for me to prove I'm a great writer." Writers such as Joyce, Dostoevsky, Melville, Proust, and Céline provided models for Kerouac's ambitions. The lifework of each developed across an expansive breadth that Kerouac clearly hoped to emulate—and ultimately did.

In his introductory comments to "Doing Literary Work: An Interview with Jack Kerouac," John Clellon Holmes explains that his exchange with Kerouac was motivated by the sense that "proper justice" had yet to be done to Kerouac's "essential gravity and dedication as a writer." Kerouac's discipline, as captured in *Journal 1951*, the act of willing himself toward a lifework of epic proportions, gives the lie to persistent characterizations of his art as purely intuitive and spontaneous. Much as Kerouac himself had done in *Beat Spotlight*, Holmes worries that the easy identification of his friend as the "King of the Beats" had obscured the arc of Kerouac's achievement, suppressing his "stubborn fidelity to his own purchase on the truth." Holmes feared that Kerouac had become ensconced in the public imagination as a reductive caricature of himself, a literary Marlon Brando iconized as ill-mannered, insubordinate, and lacking in artistic principles. In many ways, I have approached the editing of this collection in the spirit of Holmes's concerns.

Kerouac left behind a sprawling, multiform, and multigenre chronicle of his life, much of it unpublished at the time of his death. His dedication to preserving his work has proven indispensable to our evolving comprehension of his accomplishments. The writings in *The Unknown Kerouac* have distinctive shadings and charismatic allures that further enrich our understanding of who he was. The longings and conflicts manifest in his work from its inception could never be truly resolved. True to his abiding aims, Kerouac handled those dilemmas through the unyielding devotion to candor on display here.

Todd Tietchen
University of Massachusetts at Lowell

TRANSLATOR'S NOTE

AFTER the attack on Pearl Harbor in December 1941, a nineteen-year-old Jack Kerouac went out into the "clear dead cold of New England winter" at 2 A.M. to look for "the eye of the war." Young Jack was home for the holidays in Lowell, Massachusetts, shortly after quitting Columbia University, and he recorded this nocturnal trek in the story "Search by Night." The narrator enters an old lunchcart in Lowell's factory district and orders a hamburger, the only thing, he happily declares, that can "satisfy a hunger in yourself which is exclusively and completely American." As the "juicy mess" lavishes his palate, a few nightshift factory workers enter the lunchcart and interrupt his thoughts with their "vulgar and ugly jargon called New England French-Canadian." "Ernest, Calvert, 'tara pas une chris de chance—! Ha ha ha!" one of the men says, and the other replies, "Héh Batège!—Ha! Ha ha ha ha!"[1] With remarkable insight into the profound mutilation this "jargon" has endured to survive on foreign soil, Kerouac describes their speech as "tormented, twisted, severed French." Disgusted by these louts, Kerouac watches them "prattling incoherently, half of the time in coarse and obscene N.E. French-Canadian, half of the time in rowdy, faulty English." The two men, he writes, switch "quickly, effortlessly" between the two languages. "This," Kerouac instructs the reader, "is the language of the New England French Canadian, who is the rarest animal in the various N.E. mill cities, who is the bawdy, rowdy, gustful, and obscene inhabiter of crude wooden tenements, infestor of smelly barrooms along infamous slum streets, crude-handed

---

[1] The American vernacular equivalent of what they're saying would be something like "Ernest, dammit, you wouldn't a had a goddam chance"; and the other man replies, "Well, shee-it!—Ha! Ha ha ha ha!"

laborer of factory, ditch, and field." He goes on to qualify their broken English—phonetically rendered by Kerouac (e.g., "de fella wid de new Cad'lac")—as "heavily, ponderously accented, almost idiotic."[2]

What this narrator—this Jean-Louis Kérouac—never tells the reader is that it might as well be a scene from his family's dinner table. Kerouac is, in fact, describing himself. Or rather, at nineteen, he is desperately trying to distance himself from the "animal-like crudeness" of the *race canadienne-française* to which he belongs.[3] In this early story, we can detect a logic behind his subsequent mastery of English: to never sound so "rowdy, faulty" and "idiotic" in America again. There is almost a sense that, if he eats enough hamburgers—he eats two in the seven-page story—he may finally become "exclusively and completely American." Through such scenes, Kerouac notably renders in written form a type of French that, at the time, only existed as speech.

It's not surprising that Kerouac would be made to feel shame for his ethnic background; as Joyce Johnson underscores in *The Voice Is All*, in the early twentieth century "French Canadians were despised by workers of other nationalities because they were willing to take the worst jobs . . . The Massachusetts Department of Labor called them 'the Chinese of America'."[4] Like their cousins up north in Québec, New England French Canadians were also called "frogs, pea-soupers, dumb Canucks, white niggers,"[5] and often told to "speak white" on the factory floor. Speaking "white," of course, meant speaking English. Henry James, in his essay on "Quebec," had described French Canadian women as "genuine peasants of tradition, brownfaced," and habitually refers to Canucks as "brown" people—in addition to comparing them to field animals with "bovine stare" and "simple, unsharpened faces," speaking a

---

Jack Kerouac, "Search by Night." *Atop an Underwood: Early Stories and Other Writings.* Ed. Paul Marion (New York: Viking, 1999), 173–174.
Ibid., 174.
Joyce Johnson, *The Voice Is All: The Lonely Victory of Jack Kerouac* (New York: Viking, 2012), 22.
Ibid.

"narrow patois, in their ignorance and naiveté."[6] James's preju-
dice against French Canadians reflects what was a widespread
sentiment across the continent among Anglophones.

Kerouac's particular ethnic and linguistic position calls to
mind a passage from Friedrich Schleiermacher's 1813 trea-
tise *On the Different Methods of Translating.* Schleiermacher
writes: "[I]f someone has turned against nature and custom
and deserted, as it were, his mother tongue, devoting himself
instead to another, it need not be affectation or mockery when
he assures us he is no longer in a position to move freely in his
native language; rather, by this justification he is seeking to
convince himself that his nature really is a natural wonder that
subverts all hierarchies and laws, and to reassure others that
he is at least not walking about double like a ghost."[7] In Kerouac's case, he did more than convince himself that he was "a
natural wonder"; he managed to convince the world, becoming
known as one of the most quintessentially "American" authors
of his age. But he never shook the feeling of "walking about
double like a ghost." Kerouac is "doubled" in more ways than
one: open road hitchhiker and reclusive hermit; young anti-
establishment Cold War sexual rebel and aging right-wing
conservative living with his mother; All-American football jock
and bookworm egghead intellectual; melancholy Catholic and
ecstatic Buddhist; native French speaker and internationally
acclaimed writer of English prose and verse, to name just a few.
Kerouac addressed his fundamental bilingualism in the first
draft of *Memory Babe*, a text published here for the first time:
"American writers who write and speak in one language are
lucky. I write in English but I speak French to my family . . .
What I have to do here is transpose the French talk into understandable modern American English, and then add the exact
sound-spelling of the old French behind it, in italics parenthesized, in case any French or French students are interested . . .

[6] Henry James, "Quebec," *America: Early Writings,* in *Collected Travel Writings: Great Britain and America* (New York: The Library of America, 1993),
767–776.
[7] Friedrich Schleiermacher, "On the Different Methods of Translating."
Trans. by Susan Bernofsky. *The Translation Studies Reader, Second Edition.*
Ed. Lawrence Venuti (New York and London: Routledge, 2004), 59.

I want the reader to see what I had to go through and how much work it is to know two languages."[8] In Kerouac's revised typescript he altered the final sentence to read: "I want the reader to see what I had to go through and what fun it was to know two languages." Hiding his pained relation to his mother tongue, Kerouac revises the sentiment to make it more upbeat. This elision is pure Kerouac: the surface of pleasure shown to the public belies the tremendous toil and craft undertaken behind closed doors.

Like other notable twentieth-century writers such as Joseph Conrad, Vladimir Nabokov, and Samuel Beckett, Kerouac wrote literary masterpieces in an adopted language. For years, only John Sampas, Kerouac's brother-in-law and legal literary representative, knew with certainty that Kerouac had written multiple secret French narratives. When he first examined the extent of Kerouac's carefully arranged archive over two decades ago, Sampas discovered *La nuit est ma femme* and immediately commissioned an amateur translation by a local Lowellian.[9] Narrated by one Michel Bretagne, a French Canadian aspiring writer, *The Night Is My Woman* is one of the most candid, moving, and raw texts Kerouac wrote, and is the last story he penned before sitting down to type the 1951 *On the Road* scroll. The narrative consists of an incomplete review of "all the jobs I ever had in this earth of labor and sorrow," as Kerouac himself describes it in *Visions of Cody*, the novel in which he offers the most clues regarding his private French writings.[10]

In a sense we've *always* been reading Kerouac in transla-tion. "The reason I handle English words so easily," Kerouac wrote in 1950, "is because it is not my own language. I refash-ion it to fit French images."[11] This confession is from a letter

[8] Jack Kerouac Archive, 14.2. Henry W. and Albert A. Berg Collection of English and American Literature, New York Public Library (from now on, Kerouac Archive).
[9] The translation was done by Roger Brunelle. Shortly thereafter, a short excerpt from the French manuscript, along with a facsimile of a page, appeared in *La Nouvelle Revue Française* (no. 521), Gallimard, 1996.
[10] Jack Kerouac, *Visions of Cody*. Ed. Todd Tietchen (New York: The Library of America, 2015), 124–125.
[11] Jack Kerouac, letter to Yvonne Le Maître, 8 Sept. 1950, *Selected Letters: 1940–1956*. Ed. Ann Charters (New York: Viking, 1995), 228.

he sent to the French Canadian critic Yvonne Le Maître in response to her review of his first novel, *The Town and the City*. The French-language review had appeared in *Le Travailleur*, a New England paper in which Le Maître had discerned a "curious ancestral lacuna" in young John Kerouac's first novel:[12] the newly fledged novelist had deliberately concealed his true origins. Indeed, John or "Jack" Kerouac was born Jean-Louis Lebris de Kérouac in Lowell, Massachusetts, to French Canadian parents who were born north of the border in the province of Québec, and he did not speak English until he was six years old—even at twenty-one, Kerouac himself admits in the same letter, he "was still somewhat awkward and illiterate-sounding in my speech and writings." Both the Lévesques—on his mother's side—and the Kerouacs were among the approximately 900,000 French Canadians who migrated to New England in search of work and a better life during the second half of the nineteenth and beginning of the twentieth centuries—a period of Québécois diasporic history referred to as the "Exodus" in which the province's French-speaking population was essentially cut in half.[13] As Kerouac put it in *Visions of Gerard*, it was a time when New England saw "the whole troop coming down from the barren farm, to the factories of U.S.A."[14]

Kerouac was thus a native French speaker and child of working-class immigrants, part of what was then considered a "backward" ethnic group known as French Canadians or Canucks.[15] As Kerouac's Lowell-based works reveal—especially *Visions of Gerard*, *Doctor Sax*, and *Maggie Cassidy*—his childhood was steeped in the culture, mores, religion, and language of French Canada. In his earliest boyhood, the sense of group

---

[12] Yvonne Le Maître, "The Town and the City," *Le Travailleur*, March 23, 1950. My translation. Kerouac published his first novel under the name of John Kerouac.

[13] See *Le Français au Québec: 400 ans d'histoire et de vie*. Sous la direction de Michel Plourde et Pierre Georgeault (Montréal: Éditions Fides, 2008); and Edith Szlezák, *Franco-Americans in Massachusetts: "No French no mo' 'round here"* (Tübingen: Narr Verlag, 2010).

[14] Jack Kerouac, *Visions of Gerard*. Ed. Todd Tietchen (New York: The Library of America, 2015), 522.

[15] See Johnson, *The Voice Is All*, 22.

unity and community among New England Canucks was at its peak: "Centerville in Lowell in 1925," he writes in *Gerard*, was "a close knit truly French community such as you might not find any more."[16] Kerouac's lifetime, 1922 to 1969, in fact corresponds to the apex and decline of French Canadian *survivance* in the United States. The deterioration of *survivance*—the name of the Québec diaspora's rallying cry, a mix of survival and resistance—helped foster Kerouac's perennial sense of homelessness and his lifelong contradictory inclinations toward both wanderlust and sedentary life at the side of his mother—the one person with whom he could always speak his mother tongue without fear of being misunderstood or mocked. In his 1951 journal, he formulates this "Canuck dualism" quite pithily: "*Il faut vivre en Anglais, c'est impossible vivre en Français* [You have to live in English, it's impossible to live in French]. This is the secret thought of the Canuck in America. *C'est important aux Anglais*—it's important to the English . . . so the Canuck does it."

Yet Kerouac also took great pride in his lineage, especially at the level of language. As he reveals in a short piece about his paternal grandfather, "The Father of My Father," Kerouac considered his mother tongue to be a language filled with ancient power. "The language called Canadian French is the strongest in the world," Kerouac wrote. "It is too bad one cannot study it in college, for it is one of the most languagey languages in the world. It is unwritten; it is the language of the tongue and not of the pen. It grew from the lives of French people come to America. It is a terrific, a huge language."[17] Unsurprisingly, then, in *The Night Is My Woman* we encounter a Kerouac who vacillates between pride and shame. Take, for instance, the narrator's stint on the construction job in Portsmouth when he hears the other French Canadians speak in English: "The guys told stories—in English, a curse word at each end, as though they were afraid of being sissies speaking French. In two years they were all going to be on the beaches of the South Pacific." The fear of not measuring up to the American ideal

16 Kerouac, *Visions of Gerard*, 513.
17 "The Father of My Father," *Atop an Underwood*, 151.

of masculinity is here associated with their subsequent sacrifice for their adoptive nation in World War II. Or the scene when the narrator's college friends from New York come to pick him up and he confesses: "With them I spoke in English and I was a completely different man." This public "different man" is the Kerouac most readers have known for years; with Kerouac's two longest French narratives, *The Night Is My Woman* (La nuit est ma femme) and *Old Bull in the Bowery* (Sur le chemin), offered here for the first time in translation, readers are finally able to meet the other, unknown Kerouac.

Kerouac's French writings are a testament to his prodigious linguistic genius; steeped in the rhythm of his formative years, they embody what Kerouac sought to attain through his modern spontaneous method, a raw kind of improvised bebop, a musicality set down onto paper. Disorienting at first, the narrative structure of *Old Bull in the Bowery* follows the logic of a jazz session, where each musician has his moment to stretch out, culminating in an ensemble performance. The final "solo" of *Old Bull* is in fact a description of a jazz session in which one of the characters has just participated.

Old Bull in the Bowery is the title Kerouac gave to his incomplete translation of *Sur le chemin*. As others have noted, the original French title gives us a new appreciation of what it really means to be "on the road." To be "sur le *chemin*," as opposed to "sur la *route*"—the word used in the European French translation of *On the Road*—means to be on the way, on the trail or, more literally, "on the path." The French title is protean with spiritual connotations, pointing toward the ritual of the Catholic pilgrimage that fascinated Kerouac, along with the Eastern doctrines of Tao and Buddhism that Kerouac studied for years.

Sur le chemin was composed in five days—December 16–21, 1952—at William S. Burroughs's residence in Mexico. It is the missing link in the evolution of *On the Road*. In January 1953, immediately after completing the manuscript, Kerouac wrote Neal Cassady a letter casting this novel as nothing less than the key to all other versions of *On the Road*: "In Mexico, after you left, I in 5 days wrote, in French, a novel about me and you when we was kids in 1935 meeting in Chinatown with Uncle

Bill Balloon, your father and my father and some sexy blondes
in a bedroom with a French Canadian rake and an old Model
T. You'll read it in print someday and laugh. It's the solution to
the 'On the Road' plots all of em and I will hand it in soon as
I finish translating and typing."[18] Kerouac did try to translate
it—several times. A few notebooks in his papers contain different English versions of the opening to *Sur le chemin*, and
there is an incomplete typescript translation from 1954 with a
little more than half the complete text. The latter is Kerouac's
longest and most sustained effort to translate *Sur le chemin*,
and this typescript, revised in Kerouac's hand, represents the
bulk of *Old Bull in the Bowery* as printed here.

Although this typescript proved invaluable, it is incomplete and the original French manuscript itself was scattered
among several notebooks; *Sur le chemin* took me several years
to reconstitute and can now be read in its original French
patois in the volume titled *La vie est d'hommage*.[19] Yet Kerouac's typescript translation was essential both for translating
the remainder and for reconstructing the original text: as a
sustained example of Kerouac's own idiosyncratic translation
practices, it was at once my guide and my narrative map to
stitching together the scattered pieces of text in the correct
order. The two notebooks listed in the Kerouac finding aid at
the New York Public Library as "Sur le Chemin" and "French
Old Bull" together make up about 70 percent of the complete
novel. The other 30 percent was not listed and needed to be
found. This required an understanding of Kerouac's compositional methodology, the system of symbols and codes he used
for additions and inserts, and immersion in the author's precise
situation at the tail end of 1952. There was also the ongoing
challenge of properly deciphering and transcribing the unique
phonetic quality of Kerouac's French—Kerouac did not write
in standard French but rather wrote phonetically using "sound-
spelling," as he explains in *Memory Babe*.

Once the text for *Sur le chemin* was reconstituted, I studied Kerouac's translation practices, scouring his work for any

---

[18] Kerouac, *Selected Letters: 1940–1956*, 395.
[19] Jack Kerouac, *La vie est d'hommage*, edited by Jean-Christophe Cloutier
(Montréal: Les Éditions du Boréal, 2016).

equivalent or fortuitous moments of self-translation in order to remain as faithful as possible to Kerouac's literary project. *Visions of Gerard* was particularly useful in providing multiple examples of unique French Canadian expressions. I also took note of the few short excerpts from *La nuit est ma femme* that he had translated—about two pages' worth—including the first paragraph and the long final passage. All of Kerouac's extant translations have been kept intact in this volume—my contribution was to finish what he started, hewing as close to his style and literary vision as possible.[20]

The *Old Bull in the Bowery* typescript was a revelation: it demonstrated how Kerouac, as a translator, often chose to foreground rather than bury his linguistic foreignness. His hand-edits disclose moments when he deliberately worsens the spoken English of the characters. For instance, he first had Old Bull Baloon say "Not far from here," but then revises it to "Not far to here," making the character sound much more French Canadian. Kerouac also favors the original French structure of his sentences as he refashions the images into English. In one of the few paragraphs he translated of *The Night Is My Woman*, he translates "*dans le derriere d'un bus*" as "in the *behind* of a bus" rather than the standard "in the *back* of a bus." This practice extends into the narrative voice of *Old Bull* where Kerouac prevents the original French from being completely assimilated into English.[21] Taken as a whole, Kerouac's translation practices become a means of conveying a sentiment he had shared with his closest confidants and with Le Maître in his response to her review of *The Town and the City*: "All my knowledge rests in my 'French-Canadianness' and nowhere else."[22]

---

[20] The only modifications brought to the translation covered by Kerouac's typescript have been made to ensure consistency of the text as a stand-alone piece and, as Kerouac puts it in his "Essentials of Spontaneous Prose," to fix "obvious, rational mistakes, such as names or *calculated* insertions in act of not writing but *inserting*."

[21] For more on this issue and what Hassan Melehy calls Kerouac's "hybrid diction," see Melehy's "Literatures of Exile and Return: Jack Kerouac and Quebec," *American Literature* (Vol. 84, No. 3, September 2012), 589–615.

[22] Kerouac, *Selected Letters: 1940–1956*, 228.

Since, in the early 1950s, the French Canadian language had not yet been given its "laws of scripturality"[23]—as Édouard Glissant would say—Kerouac further faced the challenge of translating uniquely French Canadian words and expressions. The first sentence of *Sur le chemin* gives us such a word: *bardasseuze*, a term that more or less means making an agitated racket.[24] In his translation, Kerouac opens: "IN THE MONTH OF OCTOBER, 1935, in the night of our real restless lives, a car came from the West. . . ." Here, it is "restless," a relatively diminutive word, that translates the more grandiloquent Canuck word. As alternative translations for *bardasseuze*, in a separate notebook, Kerouac also considered "gloomy," "disturbed," and the following neologisms: "behasseled, crawlsome, dawdlesome, bedawdling, folderolsome, botheration."[25] Even the descriptive "a car came from the West" can look demure compared to the full-throttle power of the original's "*y'arriva une machine du West.*" An earlier translation by Kerouac takes a stab at retaining more of that structure: "there then came a car from the West,"[26] but the "there then" stalls the car's arrival even more. So in the final revision, Kerouac brings the *car* in first, making the noun rather than verb the driving force of the sentence. Later in this opening paragraph, he purposefully writes "white line *in* black floor" rather than "on"; and "old suitcases deboxed with their ropes tied around," where "deboxed" translates the Canuck patois word *degarouillez*—all messed-up, out of sorts—and is here used in a manner akin to the standard French *déboîté*, meaning dislocated, broken, no longer possessing its initial rigid structure. This is precisely the effect of Kerouac's translative poetics,

[23] Édouard Glissant, *L'imaginaire des langues: entretiens avec Lise Gauvin (1991–2009)* (Paris: Gallimard, 2010), 23. My translation.
[24] The roots of *bardasseux(ze)* vary: aside from causing din, *berdasser* can also mean to keep busy without clear purpose; *barda* is an older French word meaning heavy and cumbersome equipment; it once referred to the clanging noise marching soldiers made while carrying all their gear. The Breton word *berdadas* means "great noise."
[25] Kerouac Archive, 51.1. Kerouac's various translations for the word hint that he was attempting to capture many of the Canuck word's meanings in a single term (see previous note).
[26] Kerouac Archive, 51.1. This alternate holograph translation covers roughly the first 2,000 words of *Sur le chemin*.

which dislocates American English from its rigid structures to let it stretch out onto new and unknown territories.

A series of notes that Kerouac folded into the first *Sur le chemin* notebook provide clues as to why Kerouac considered *Old Bull* the "solution to the 'On the Road' plots all of em," as he wrote to Neal in that 1953 letter. On a torn piece of now-yellowed paper, Kerouac described how he imagined the bilingual nature of the novel: "For the sake of getting to pure fiction and pure autobiography, I want to dispatch this mixed <u>French</u> *On the Road* (written Mexicay)."[27] *Old Bull in the Bowery* is indeed mixed; Kerouac inserted four sections of varying lengths composed in English, two of them eventually incorporated in modified form into what became *Visions of Cody*. The second longest English section that Kerouac earmarked for *Old Bull* recounts the history of the Duluoz clan, tracing the father Leo Duluoz's ancestry back to Brittany and into the New World. Kerouac, who tried to use this material in many of his works-in-progress during the early 1950s, later reworked this particular section obsessively. It reappears, with slight modification of names and other details like dates, locations, adjectives, and exact narrative order, in multiple narratives that were once part of *On the Road*—sometimes featuring the Martin family from *The Town and the City*, sometimes new families like the Boncoeurs, the Bernier-Gaos, the Loves, and others, all filed away in "the neatest records you ever saw."[28]

In those same notes Kerouac expands on the wider implications of his new mixed *On the Road*: "In French a pithy, short, Balzacian novel, in English a profound American Prose novel . . . converting one to another, first to second, translating, deepening, opening out, continenting, capping, reddening-in, endearing to mind. . . ."[29] Kerouac has to invent a new verb in order to adequately express his literary imagination: one that is "continenting," transcending the boundaries of nations to achieve a wider sense of the terrestrial masses on which we tread

[27] Kerouac Archive, 39.11.
[28] "I've kept the neatest records you ever saw," Kerouac wrote to Ann Charters in 1966. Jack Kerouac, *Selected Letters, 1957–1969*. Ed. Ann Charters (New York: Viking, 1999), 424.
[29] Kerouac Archive, 39.11.

and where we share our polyphonic lives. Canada, the United States, and Mexico are continented throughout the pages of his manuscripts; borders are only there to mark the liminal points of one's continenting travels upon the globe, rather than to enforce geopolitical divisions. Kerouac's road is one that allows readers to create unexpected correspondences across imagined lines, deepening them, opening out our outlook and giving us a taste for adventure and the unknown, endearing us to the Other, even when that other is none other than oneself.

Jean-Christophe Cloutier

Written in Philadelphia,
Shackamaxon, 2016
Ancient Capital
of the United States,
sacred meeting place
of the Lenape

ON FRANK SINATRA

On Frank Sinatra

In his 1968 novel *Vanity of Duluoz*, Kerouac writes of stopping off in New York "just so I could hear Frank Sinatra, and see Frank Sinatra sing in the Paramount Theater, waiting there in line with two thousand screaming Brooklyn Jewish and Italian girls, I'm just about, in fact, AM the only guy in the line, and when we get in the theater and skinny old Frank comes out and grabs the mike, with glamorous rings on his fingers and wearing gray sports coat, black tie, gray shirt, sings 'Mighty Like a Rose' and 'Without a song . . . the road would never end' oww." The Paramount Theater, a landmark venue of the old Times Square that closed its doors in 1966, was central to Sinatra's rise to unparalleled stardom, from his legendary solo performance as a "special guest" of the Benny Goodman Orchestra on New Year's Eve 1942 to the "bobbysoxer riot" of October 1944.

Kerouac lived in New York throughout 1946 and this essay (from a handwritten journal dated May 6, 1946–July 21, 1946) celebrates the authenticity that Kerouac had come to associate with Sinatra's voice, attesting to the crooner's influence over Kerouac's evolving conceptions of voice and style. Kerouac acknowledges Sinatra's ability to vocalize the moods of melancholy and loneliness defining the World War II generation, a disposition that Kerouac would explore in his first published novel *The Town and the City* (1950) and in *On the Road* (1957).

(Notes on a projected essay Sorelian in intent—)

June 5, 1946.

I BELIEVE THE THING that really assures Frank Sinatra's success as a singer in this country is not so much his appeal to teen-age girls, but the fact that he always sings with profundity of feeling, and he himself being a young American from top to toe, the result is always a magnificent expression of young American loneliness and longing. (For male & female alike.)

Other singers who attempt to imitate him are continually affecting technical vocal tricks that impede the natural expression of feeling in spite of their being designed towards that end. In their striving to enunciate musical phrases in the Sinatra manner, something of their own natural feeling is lost, and the result is of course mannered, artificial and hollow.

Sinatra himself is gifted with the perfect average American voice. He was the first "crooner" to sing in his natural voice; his speaking voice and his singing voice are easily recognizable at once. (Minstrel style.)

In many ways, Sinatra's own musical tastes are the musical tastes of young America. He never sings maudlin or shop-worn songs. His favorite songs—"Without a Song," "You Go to My Head," "Old Man River," "Going Home," "Stormy Weather," "I Hear Music," "Night and Day," "These Foolish Things," "Try a Little Tenderness," "Someone to Watch Over Me," "Ghost of a Chance," "If You are But a Dream," and others—represent a cross-section of the absolutely best in popular American songs. (He selects moods of songs.)

Many young men appreciate Sinatra's sense of loneliness and longing, a feeling which Sinatra sensitively assumes from the mood of the generation around him and expresses with a lyrical and sometimes poetical tenderness that has been mistaken by an older generation for "bawling and caterwauling." To young America, serious, sad, and wistful, it is no caterwauling, it is the poetry of its time, and in it, in the longing of Sinatra's soft tones and prayerful sustaining notes, is contained most of their own youthful melancholy.

AMERICA IN WORLD HISTORY

America in World History

From a handwritten journal dated September 3–October 9, 1946, this essay, begun on September 23, echoes the theme of American national exceptionalism formulated by Ralph Waldo Emerson in such essays as "The American Scholar" (1837). Animated by the triumphalism of the immediate postwar period, Kerouac's essay idealizes America as a virtuous alternative to European mores and traditions. At the center of "America in World History" is an enumerated list of singular American achievements, fueled by what Kerouac considers the "unconscious pulse of soul and destiny" propelling national life into the Cold War era. The discussion of jazz is especially notable in this regard, as the budding twenty-four-year-old writer celebrates the jazz idiom for its dynamism and extemporaneous inventiveness—qualities that would guide some of his most impressive writing.

I T WOULD BE MUCH easier for me to assert that America is a separate culture-civilization from "West-Europe"—younger, with an unfulfilled destiny, not in the petrified decadent "late" civilization stage that Europe undoubtedly is in—because I *myself* do not feel "late" and "finished," and because I feel young and unfulfilled. However, it would be infinitely *harder* NOT to separate America from West-European civilization because there happen to be innumerable *facts* that indicate there is actually a deep separation.

Therefore, I hereby separate American culture from West-Europe, I do it as an American, and it is not because this is the *easier* choice: I am impelled by facts, the deepest and most powerful of which is my feeling that I am young and unfulfilled, like 90 percent of my American brothers, and I believe that in this decision beats the unconscious pulse of soul and destiny.

This message will have most meaning to those who have *felt* what I write long before now, to many of those who, indeed, never read as a general rule. This message is directed to those Americans who feel the final culminating Alaska of American meanings beating in their blood.

But before anything of American destiny can be worked out and *hinted*—before that Goethean task, it is necessary for me, as an American versed in world history, as a thinker and novelist, as an intellectual conversant with the summaries of West-Europe (lodged comfortably in all large American cities, but in not *one* Alaskan town), it is necessary for me for the first time in America to formally and consciously disengage my nation from West-European civilization, announcing that it is a young and separate culture, with its own separate age and destiny, and marshalling these facts to prove it to all doubtful Americans.

A LIST OF THE FACTS——

1. Native Americans themselves have always disclaimed any cultural ties with Europe, and ever certain of the immigrant populations of the 20th century, after they have

dispersed among the native culture and civilization, are first to disclaim any such cultural ties with Europe, having experienced that indefinable "American Way" and the deep opposition of it to European ways. Hitherto, it has been only in the classroom of the academician or in the salon of the great intellectual that America has been identified as a transition, a growth of European civilization, in the most matter of fact taken-for-granted manner.

2. Nothing has been accomplished in Europe with the industrial tool that Europe itself developed, to compare with what America accomplished with that borrowed tool—take American mass production of automobiles and planes, on a scale undreamed-of in Europe. The American soul, here, is incalculably *new* in its originality and impulsiveness. A European, Céline of France, was baffled and crushed by the sight of Ford's assembly lines in Detroit, as though face-to-face with a Martian horror. It was only *America*.

3. The deep persistence of capitalism in American ways, despite the socialization of England and Europe, and the Communizing of Eastern Europe and China, is a pure sign of *irreversibility of soul*, a pure sign of American selfhood—("You can't change the spots on a leopard"). The more America swings to the "right"—which is a European word for capitalism—the more America proves its spots. Free enterprise, the root of capitalism, developed in the American Summer of the late 19th century—it is the prime phenomenal direction of American society, the rugged individualism that can only be erased from the American's soul when he is no longer his "own boss." All "leftism" in America is European in origin and in *purpose*.

4. America's literature, from Emerson, Thoreau and Twain on down to Whitman and Wolfe, is one continuous assertion of American *singularness*. Of Wolfe it can be said that he devoted all of his energies in evoking the feeling of the "unuttered American tongue in the wilderness" in all of his huge novels. Twain's *Innocents Abroad*, Whitman's evocations of a fresh West wind blowing over a newly felt land, Emerson's springtime testimonials to a "new man,

a new freedom"—all these are self-evident. All American writers who were not *Americana* in sum, were, like Poe and Henry James, influenced by Europe by their own tacit admission.

5. In passing—(If I myself, in this year 1946, were alive in Europe as a citizen of a European nation, I would have nothing left to write about, and I would not write. As an American, however, I see no end to my subject and to my task!)

6. The "naiveté" of the American, a common complaint made by all Europeans and American Europa-intellectuals, is just one way of their admitting the American's cultural *youngness.* (Adolescence is another charge leveled at the American.)* The peculiar American mother worship and Oedipal complex is responsible for this "adolescence" and for many other singular American traits, all of which is material to be examined in due time, which, I believe, will further substantiate the fact of America's separate age and destiny from that of West-Europe.

7. The "boom town" atmosphere in many American towns, especially during the war in towns where new war plants were springing up, a fact which is more of a reflection of the *spirit* of Americans than the mere presence of the new industries, is something quite different from the weary atmospheres of Europe and England.

8. American music—Native, "unlearned" Americans persistently fail to appreciate "fine" music—which is just another word for European music, from Bach to Schoënberg—because, as it should have been evident long ago to our historians, Americans appreciate *their own music* only. This native American music is as yet unrecognized and uncatalogued. There are the fiddle reels of hillspeople, Negro *and* white jazz, folk music ("Big Rock Candy Mountain," "On Top of Old Smoky"), "cowboy music," and so forth. The prime phenomenal *individualism* of American culture is most vividly apparent in jazz music where each *soloist* extemporaneously creates new melodies in infinitely

*Lions are big babies; intellectuals are mature.

changing progression, so that all the composer supplies is the harmony line, the *true composer remaining the jazz soloist himself.* All formal American composers schooled in European music, are not the true American composers, of course, this including such as Sessions, Harris, et al.

A COUPLE OF FACTS CONCERNING LAWS OF DECADENCE

A Couple of Facts Concerning Laws of Decadence

Kerouac's father, Leo Alcide Kerouac, died of stomach cancer in May 1946. The nostalgic tone of this essay (also from the September 3–October 9, 1946 journal) may reflect the weight of that loss, which also contributed to Kerouac's idealized portrait of Leo (as George Martin) in *The Town and the City*. Kerouac's perceptions of New York—where he lived fairly regularly during the 1940s—always remained complex, vacillating between moral disgust and voyeuristic fascination. In "A Couple of Facts Concerning Laws of Decadence" Kerouac elaborates on his antipathy to "city civilization" in what becomes a condemnation of "city men of the higher cognitive order." The nostalgic pessimism of "A Couple of Facts" stands in stark contrast to the optimism of "America in World History," making plain Kerouac's conflicted views regarding America's future.

HENRY MORGAN, the New York radio comedian, intellectual, sophisticate, "liberal" and whatnot, although being a very intelligent, clever and amusing person in himself, has more or less made his decadent views known on a variety of subjects through the medium of his radio work; and on the subject of family I gather this:

A skit relates the *horror* of having to look through a family album of pictures, very well done, especially in delineating the *horror* which city men of the higher cognitive order have when they go through this routine. I have my sympathies with these high cognizers, but let us see how high it really is: I went through a family album tonight, with a magnifying glass, and heard my aunt relate histories, events, legends connected with the old forebears, and never before have I seen such glimpses into society, changing times, the law of families, lineal heritage and such; in no *book* have I ever seen so much, learned so much about human beings (if I may be permitted the phrase, Mr. Morgan and all ye sycophants). What does this mean, if it doesn't mean that the so-called high consciousness, or complex understanding, or sensitive enlightenment, or whatnot of the city intellectual, is not high enough, or conscious enough, or complex enough, or understanding enough, or sensitive enough, or enlightened enough, or whatnot enough, if it is going to deny its vaunted intellectual powers a thorough and earnest study of the family album, with all the illuminative wonders and secrets therein, and all for the sake of fashionably shrinking back from the "Bourgeois horror" of such an album. Ah! you cliques of the city!—don't you know you had forebears with handlebar mustaches, who came down to the river in the morning bearing masts and booms on their shoulders? who killed their own bulls with a mighty club? who made their own clothes and tilled their own earth? For a million of your clever fashionable phrases, would you exchange one single such accomplishment? I know I would—and Oh God but I'm just as futile as you are, you city vermin; I too am vermin, vermin trying to struggle back to manhood, with small success.

Here is our second illuminative nugget, with no emotions this time: that the fear of the family album is pursuant to the city's general fear of *time* and particularly of the *past* ("Oh the stupid Victorian 19th Century!" they keep crying, as though Victorianism were the whole sum of that great century). Fear of the past *is* in the city, thus a love, a frantic need of the *present*—with all the hedonistic overtones involved, the psychological doctrines of "alertness" and the so-called liberation of sexuality: in other words, giving the moment over to the dictates of sexuality (divorce is such a dictate) and leaving time, the *future*—which is to them equivalent to the past, as a moral factor rather than a hedonistic factor of the "pulsing present"—leaving the future to the dogs, childless marriages, or one-child "families," broken-up families, and thus leaving the future of mankind and the race to the dogs: to the destruction at the hands of a society's inward atom bomb of organic-familial-societal disintegration: in short, the end of a race, as in Rome. This fear of reaching back into the past, into lineality and tradition, and of extending similarly forward into the future, is like a plant drying up, dying. Where I say this, they speak of the "reality of the moment" and the danger of suppressing the urges of the moment for any reason—but I find good reason if it is to spell the continuation of our own cultural mankind. Perhaps that's what they don't want, like children who resent all brothers and sisters burgeoning in their mother's womb, *resenting the future after them*, feeling *they* should be the last, final men, that *none* must follow—a childish emotion. But to give oneself over to childish emotions is the aim of these city intellectuals, they abstrusely find much to "scientifically" substantiate this desire in the cult of psychoanalysis and its subcults, the Orgone "Institute" for one splendid example, and so they go ahead blithely, and I am not the one to oppose their concepts, their march off the ship's plank—since I am marching to a plank of my own, since I do not wish to be reviled as a neurotic and an atavistic neo-fascist, since the other night, when mentioning these objections of mine, a city intellectual had apoplexy right before me.

Oh for an *earnest* sensitivity!—for someone like Sebastian again!—for more of that, and less of this critical malcontented sensitivity all around! And give me one, if miserable, to be sincerely miserable! For more men and women in my life, for the old friends to come back, for me to grow and die among persons I have always known!—this nomadic existence, this irreverent inconsequential time-dripping sun-slanting afternoon in the city suburb no more!—this lack of rich bloody dark life—this unmanly way to live—*No Joy, No Beauty, Nothing!*

ON CONTEMPORARY JAZZ—
"BEBOP"

On Contemporary Jazz—"Bebop"

At the conclusion of *The Town and the City*, Kerouac's alter ego, Peter Martin, flees suburban Galloway for life on the road. Cloaked in a black leather jacket, thumbing beside the highway for a ride, Peter prefigures the 1950s cultural styles that emerged so powerfully along with the popularity of rock-n-roll. Yet, for the most part, Kerouac's musical affinities remained rooted in 1940s culture—especially modern jazz. Jazz supplied an aesthetic model for Kerouac's interests in improvisational and spontaneous aesthetics.

"On Contemporary Jazz—'Bebop'" (from a handwritten journal dated February 24–May 5, 1947) focuses more intently on the effects of speed and virtuosity on stylistic changes in the jazz idiom, as embodied in the playing of figures such as Charlie Parker, Dizzy Gillespie, and Thelonious Monk—all of whom Kerouac had seen perform in New York's Fifty-second Street jazz clubs by the mid-1940s. Flexing his talents as a music writer, Kerouac presents an informed, condensed jazz history of the 1930s and 1940s. He not only recognizes the significance of bebop's modern, avant-garde revision of jazz's compositional vocabulary, but views those compositional developments in rhythm and harmony as the virtuosic equivalent of the European classical tradition. If "A Couple of Facts Concerning Laws of Decadence" displays Kerouac's tendency at times to sentimentalize the premodern, this early essay on bebop valorizes propulsive, forward-looking art, the avant-garde abandon that came to characterize American expressive culture in the decades following World War II.

A N INTERESTING CHANGE has come about in modern jazz music in the past few years, since 1944 and thereabouts. And this, a tremendous kind of step forward in rhythmic and harmonic ideas, has taken jazz, once seemingly so infinite, and yet established, set, and concluded, and given it an astounding new power and beauty that makes everything else in jazz which has come before seem obsolete. Thus it is when an art is in its developing stages: the life of an idea is brief when it does not contain profoundest resiliencies and possibilities. This is why the Ellington idea and the Lester Young idea has lived through 3 jazz eras.

The newest jazz—only a step forward in the development of what may well become a great formal musical system comparable to the European Classical—has been called "bebop" for the sake of popular identification. But this frivolous name is far from serviceable in describing the enormous complexities inherent in the new feeling for rhythm and harmony, and for melodic and contrapuntal expression as well which jazz is now undergoing. It is an explosion of music, an exciting renaissance of musical force, one which has seized the imaginations of all young musicians up-coming, and troubled the minds of all veteran musicians down-going in a swirl of change. Literally, one can feel it in the air—there has not been an authentic excitement of music in jazz since the last great step forward in the late Thirties, in the burgeoning time of arranged big-band jazz, the time of Basie, Lunceford, Goodman, Shaw, Benny Carter, Don Redman.

Troubled veterans and jazz critics ask nowadays: "Where is jazz going?" Some say "swing" is dead, some say jazz has stopped developing, and finally some say "bebop" represents a last incoherent mélange of a music once formal and cogent. The change from pre-1944 jazz to modern progressing jazz is so violent that this confusion of the diehards in the art, and the terrific exhilaration of the new musicians in "bebop," stand side by side in the field, creating an utter chaos probably comparable to any other upheavals in other art-forms of the past.

19

There is here the same force and counter-force reminiscent of the great European change from Classical to Romantic idioms.

"Where is jazz going?" they then ask, those whose conception of jazz is fixed within its former rhythmic, harmonic, contrapuntal and melodic limits. And Dizzy Gillespie, principal founder of "bebop," of modern progressing jazz, answers— "It's going where it's going, it can't go anyplace else." He points out that all young jazz musicians rising out of the struggle and obscurity of study and preparation, are actually falling into the "bebop groove" without forethought or assistance, with a naturalness and an ease that belies a new spirit of the musical time, one that is "in the air" after the fashion of great renascences of feelings.

These are the main features of the modern progressing jazz: rhythm has been subordinated to harmony, and in the process, changed in its function from a simple carrying beat to a coloring of tones. One of the foremost new drummers, 20-year-old Shelly Manne of the Stan Kenton progressive organization, is the first known jazz drummer to actually perform *melodic* functions on the drum by means of intonation and emphasis and by the use of vari-toned drums. It is useful to mention here that one of the major complaints lodged against the new jazz-feeling is that the rhythm no longer predominates, "the beat is lost." Actually the beat is not lost—it is only given a new function and a new life of its own. Manne is also a forerunner of new drumbeats, identifiable as primitive African in variation and freedom.

Harmony is the keypoint of this new jazz. Changes in its structure have been astonishing, in some cases incomprehensible to the old jazz imagination. An example of this is in the big-band arrangements by Pete Rugolo for the Kenton band, the Boyd Raeburn arrangements (assisted by the brilliant Dizzy Gillespie & Ray Brown), the new Mercer Ellington arrangements, scorings for the 1946 Herman band, and so forth. Here harmony, in close cooperation with infinitely new modes of rhythm, melody and counterpoint, is presented in an excitingly new mood and method that can only be described as "exploitable"—that is, it can be exploited and experimented with to the point of dissonance, yet never quite. For what would seem dissonant by itself, now becomes harmonic within strange new melodic interpretations that carry the idea of jazz beyond old boundaries. Music is an unutterable—it's difficult to describe adequately what goes on in these new harmonic reaches.

In the new melodic feeling, ninths are sought after continually. Unheard-of diminisheds are framed, forming the key structure of the NEW scale-idea, also incidentally implying the sound "bebop."

In this music rhythm is no longer the primary vehicle of the musical idea nor the principal impact of expression. Harmony is exploited anew. And melody is made over to conform to a new concept of rhythm and harmony, and to a new mood.

The result is electrifying. The result is also a music which, when understood, produces a "relaxation" of former jazz tension, takes it from monotonous pounding regularity with fugal variations and established chord changes and harmony changes, and leads into a realm of freedom, "relaxed" freedom, with possibilities greatly multiplied.

Timing is one of the keys of this relaxation. The soloists do not depend on the beat, which has been subordinated, rather they understand the beat and do with it what they will—off-beat, afterbeat, "drag." The subtlety is striking, the complexity is amazing.

PRIVATE PHILOLOGIES,
RIDDLES,
AND A TEN-DAY WRITING LOG

Private Philologies, Riddles, and a Ten-Day Writing Log

Kerouac moved in May 1949 to the Westwood neighborhood of Denver, where he intended to settle permanently with his family: his mother Gabrielle, his sister Caroline, Caroline's husband Paul, and their young son Paul Jr. In Denver he resumed work earnestly on what would become *On the Road*, a book that had already gone through a series of partially drafted versions in which the protagonist was successively named Ray Smith and Red Moultrie; while in Denver, Kerouac also considered a further draft featuring Chad Gavin, a talented young football player and petty criminal. At the same time, he began the notebook he subsequently labeled *Private Philologies, Riddles, and a Ten-Day Writing Log*, whose early pages describe his activities in Denver and his impatience for the arrival of his family.

As things turned out, the relocation scheme quickly floundered, in large part because of his family's reluctance to remain in Denver. Kerouac returned to New York in August 1949 with Neal Cassady after a brief stopover in San Francisco, a journey memorialized in Part Three of *On the Road*. The final entries in *Private Philologies* were completed in Richmond Hill, Queens, where Kerouac was living with his mother. The journal testifies to Kerouac's wide-ranging intellectual and artistic interests as he entered his fertile period of the 1950s, among them Shakespeare, Joyce, and Spenser; the section titled "Riddles" makes plain Kerouac's indebtedness to surrealism and Rimbaud.

Log

SUNDAY MAY 22—Took a walk up to Morrison Rd. to buy this notebook and had a beer in a big Sunday afternoon road-house up there on the ridge. How less sad Sunday afternoon is in the West. I sat near the back door and listened to the mid-American music and looked out on the fields of golden green and the great mountains. Walking around the fields with my notebooks I might have been Rubens and all this my Nether-lands. Came home, ate, and made preparatory notes at night. Starting *On the Road* back in Ozone, and here, is difficult. I wrote one full year before starting *T & C* (1946)—but this mustn't happen again. Writing is my work now both in the world and the "moor of myself"—so I've got to *move*. Planned an earlier beginning before the 8,000 words already written in N.Y. first 2 weeks of May. Went to bed after midnight reading a Western dime novel.

MONDAY MAY 23—Got up refreshed at nine, walked to the grocery store, came back and ate breakfast. It's a sin how happy I can be living alone like a hermit. Mailed some letters I had written yesterday. Drank coffee on the back steps, where the western wind in bright afternoon airs hums across the grass. (Why do I read Western dime novels?—for the beautiful and authentic descriptions of benchlands, desert heat, horses, night stars, and so forth; the characterizations are of course non-authentic.) I worked in the afternoon, and till eleven at night, knocking off **1500-words** or so. I sometimes wonder if *On the Road* will be any good, although very likely it will be popular. It's not at all like *T & C*. I suppose that's allowable—(but sad)—now.

TUESDAY MAY 24—Woke up at 9:30 with the first "worried mind" in a week, since I've been here. Just a kind of haggard sorrow—and later some worries about money until my next sti-pend from the publishers. This is a better kind of money-worry

than before *T & C* was bought, for then I had nothing, absolutely nothing. What they call the "proverbial shoestring" was for me then a mad mysticism. Hal and Ed White must feel today what I used to feel then—a loveless existence in a greedy money-world. I still feel that way even though I know I'll have *some* money all my life from writing, and will never starve or have to hole up in a canyon, eating vegetables like H
uescher, or wash dishes in the great-city slops. Someday perhaps I myself will look back on those days (before selling book) with the same kind of wonder that we now look back upon the pioneers living in the wilderness on their wits and grit—someday when some form of social insurance will be in effect for all mortal beings. Because most of the jobs nowadays by which you can earn just enough to live are insupportable to imaginative men . . . like Hal, Ed, Allen, Bill B. and numerous others. It is just as difficult for that kind of man to punch a clock and do the same stupid thing all day as it is for an unimaginative man to go hungry—for that too is "going hungry." I am continually amazed nowadays that an actual Progress is underway in spite of everything. This Progress should aim at meaningful work and social security and greater facilities for minimal comfort for all—so that energies may be liberated for the great things that will come in the Atomic Energy Age. In that day there will be opportunity to arrive at the final questions of life . . . whatever they really are. I feel that I'm working on the periphery of these final things, as all poets have always done . . . and even Einstein in his deepest investigations. "Solving problems," as Dan Burmeister insists, is essential now (and may or may not be a tendency in late-civilization anxiety)—but after that there is the question of the knowable that is now called "unknowable." I feel that the most important facts in human life are of a moral nature:—communication between souls (or minds), recognition of what the Lamb means, the putting-aside of vanity as impractical and destructive (psychoanalysis points there), and the consolation of the mortal enigma by means of a recognition of the State of Gratitude which was once called the Fear of God. And many other things as yet unplumbed.

But these are all sunny Colorado reflections and may not apply in the Dark Corridor where something far stranger is burgeoning (I mean Allen). It may be that Allen is deliberately insane to justify his mother, or that he has really seen the Last Truth of the Giggling Lings. Even if that were so, I, as Ling, could not use it. (All this refers to the fable "Ling's Woe.") Then again, since all of us are really the same man, he may, or I may only be fooling now.

Finally I recognize this at least as an *absorption* of the life-mind . . . which may be the only thing we have, like flowers that have nothing but petals that grow. *All is likely.* "This was life," as I wrote yesterday in *Road.* Ripeness is all.

There is a dynamic philosophy behind the Progress of the 20th Century, but we need to reach the depths of a Static Meta-physical Admission—a Manifesto of Confessions—as well, or the dynamics will just explode out of control like Kafka's penal machine. Perhaps something like this should happen:—after the age of five, every human being should become a shmoo and feed the little ones; shmoos with wings like guardian angels.

There should be no giant shmoos to kick Good Old Gus across the valley. This is not the Lamb, not peace. Even Good Old Gus, at his depths, is standing alone weeping on the plain looking around for confirmation of his tears; and his vanity is his evil. . . . Dostoevsky knew that even about Father Karamazov.

Worked all day, wrote **2000-words**. Not too satisfied, but enough. Retired at night with papers & the Western dime novel. Anxious for the folks to get here, especially Ma:— What a joy it will be for her! Heh heh heh—(a cackle of satisfaction on my part, you see).

WEDNESDAY MAY 25—Went to Denver University and to the home of the Whites. The Denver campus is beautiful and interesting. I walked into the rambling structure of the Students Union just as a jukebox was booming Charley Ventura . . . first bop in weeks. My hair stood on end. I floated in. I realized that the music of a generation whether it is swing, jazz, or bop—(at least this law applies to 20th century America)—is a keypoint of mood, an identification, and a seeking-out. Anyway, I looked for Dan, drank milkshakes, sat in the grass, looked at the gals, visited the buildings, etc., and finally hitch-hiked in the hot afternoon countryside to the Whites' house. This is the house they built themselves, that Ed and Jeffries and Burt worked on all winter. Frank White was there. I was somewhat amazed by him. He is more like Ed than people think . . . the same quick understanding of all statements; in fact, the same fore-knowledge of the trend of what one is about to say. Also he has the some cool, modest ability of much variety. His only drawback is a garrulousness that one can't follow due to his tumbling speech and inward-preoccupation with details. Then the rest of the family arrived for supper. Mrs. White made me feel most at home (like Frank). Of course I was unexpected and shouldn't have crashed in so casually. Jeanne seemed thoughtful about something else. After supper Frank and I drove back to the D.U. campus, where he spoke on cosmic ray research of some kind, to a physics class. They applauded his talk admiringly; I was unable myself to follow the scientific language. Another speaker, on geophysics, was Wally Mureray, friend of Frank's, whom I liked. He was born & raised in Leadville and like his father & grandfather has mining in his blood. Also he is a genuine mining type while being a scientist:—a remarkable combination. We met Dan Burmeister at his social science seminar and there ensued an endless argument between the physical scientists and the social scientist, with much reference to relativity, Oppenheimer, atomic research, etc. I finally announced (in these flood-tides) that it was all a "continuum of ambiguity." Okay?—for relativity is just the idea that one point of reference is as good as another. We got mellow on beer; went home. Frank drove me home.

THURSDAY MAY 26—Then today (while I continued my hermit domesticity in the empty house . . . as a matter of fact tried to fix the wellpump just as it seemed to fix itself) the kid on the street here, Jerry, asked me to accompany him to the amusement park, Lakeside, in the evening. His mother, Johnny they call her, drove us to the park. (Her husband has disappeared somewhere.) It was the Sad Fair again. I took a few rides with Jerry (who seems to be looking for a father of some sort). However a waitress didn't believe I was 21 and wanted proof before she gave me a beer. Jerry (14) drank rootbeer. We rode around a sad little lake in a toy railroad; in the high ferris wheel, etc., and ate hotdogs and ice cream. Still and all, it was a "sinister" night . . . sinister-seeming . . . and I became depressed:—for two days. A park cop threatened to arrest Jerry because he was fooling around with the tame fish at the motorboat dock. Then, when we rode home in an old truck after a Roy Rogers movie, a car almost rammed us in the back. It was strange. In the first place I couldn't understand anything. I doubt if the driver of the old truck knew we were in the back. Between us sat his little son,—mysteriously wrapp'd in a blanket. *No one noticed the fact we almost got rammed by the car* . . . or that is, they didn't care at all. Then, in the dark sinister country night, as Jerry and I walked home, a car of drunks almost plowed us off the road. Everything was sinister . . . like for Joe Christmas.

FRIDAY MAY 27—Depressed all day. Full of my own private hurt and haunt. Jerry brought over a little kitty for me . . . it has sick eyes. It needs meat. It hangs around me mewing for affection. It is somewhat like that lost kid, incomprehensibly lonely. I feed the cat and do my best to achieve a talk with Jerry—and with his incomprehensible mother, who asked me to go riding in a rodeo tomorrow. That is, Sunday. My depression cannot see the light of these things. What did I do all day?—I can't remember any more. Part of my sadness stems from the fact my family's wasting time getting out here. Why? I hated myself all day, too . . . hurt and haunted by hurt.

SATURDAY MAY 28—After a mopey day, I perked up and went to the beerjoints on the ridge. Gad, some beautiful waitresses up there. I really enjoyed the cowboy music . . . ate French frieds at the bar, etc. There are some good people out this way, just as I had guessed. Came home and slept, to be ready for the Ghostly Rodeo.

SUNDAY MAY 29—So I rode in a rodeo . . . of sorts. Johnny picked me up and we drove to a farm ranch, and slicked down four horses. A remarkable woman called Doodie runs the place and dominates immense horses, including a 17-hand Palomino, with fiery contemptuous love . . . in other words, a real horsewoman. Her son Art is a mild, happy kid growing up among horses. We mounted the four horses and started off for Golden, 15 miles west. I have not ridden extensively since 1934, so I was saddle-sore pretty soon . . . but enjoyed it nevertheless. My horse Toppy, a strawberry roan colt, had a tender mouth so I could not rein him up too hard. We joined two other women, one a haughty bitch on an Arabian thoroughbred, and the other a most marvelous woman on an old circus horse . . . an old carnival woman with flaming red hair and no teeth. She said, "I hate women who don't say *shit* when they've got a mouthful of it." We cantered and walked and trotted to Golden. I had a beer in a bar; then we mounted again and the first thing you know we were joined by a whole posse of riders, and first thing you know, on a dirt road, something happened psychologically, I yelled "Woohee!" and off some of us went lickity-cut down the road in a race. My roan loved to run, and "he run." Up in a glorious mountain meadow we raced around while, by arrangement, a photographer took pictures with a motion picture technicolor camera . . . I still don't know under what auspices. We did Indian-circle runs, and Figure-Eights, and galloped *en masse* down a draw, and had a good time. We drank beer in the saddle. Going back to Golden we raced furiously across lots and down into a creek-bed and up out of it flying and hell-for-leather over fields gopher-holes or no gopher-holes. I've never been afraid of a horse falling somehow anyway. After another beer we started back . . . and the kid and I really had a race. He was in the road and I in the field parallel, and it was even. Then he beat me on the road . . . but he's a lighter rider, and used his reins on both flanks, something I didn't bother to do.—Finally we got back exhausted, a 30-mile day. I went to bed immediately . . . with some muscles and one bad blister.

MONDAY MAY 30—And today I was scheduled to ride in the rodeo at Table-Top (ride a bronc for all I incomprehensibly know) but of course I was too sore. I'm sorry I missed this. Meanwhile some neighbors around here are gossiping about Johnny (Jerry's mother) and me . . . an old hen across the street. This sort of thing goes on even here. Best thing to do, is nothing. What does it matter anyway?—No harm in it that's *real* harm (like jail, etc.). Rested all day. Wrote at night. Still and all, consider how horrible it is to have an old woman like that peeking from out her shades all day, trying to figure out what you're doing behind yours, and starting "scandalous" stories about you. Gad! It's *funny* only in a horrible way. (Francis Martin.)

But how I love horses!

Next year:—*mountain ranch.*

And tonight re-examined my literary life and I'm worried somewhat about losing touch with it in these natural-life atmospheres. After all, great art only flourishes in a *school* . . . even if that school is only friendship with poets like Allen, Lucien, Bill, Huncke & Neal.* Well—Hal and Ed White will be back in Denver here this summer. Besides my desk and papers will arrive soon, so I laboured a poem:—

> "The God with the Golden Nose, Ling,
> gull-like down the Mountainside did soar,
> till, with Eager Flappings, above the Lamb
> so Meek did Hang, a Giggling Ling.
>
> And the Chinamen of the Night
> from Immortal Jails did Creep,
> bearing the Rose that's really White
> to the Lamb that's really Gold,
> and offered themselves thereby, and
> the Lamb did them Receive, and Ling."

(I got the idea for "golden nose" while peering around at my own nose, while lying in the cornfield last week . . . in the sun it was "golden." The "god" is a natural rhyme-idea that followed.)

~

TUESDAY JUNE 1—*La Kermesse* de Rubens:—If only my life had been like that, but it has not been. A letter today from Allen misunderstood my mention of Rubens' christening picture . . . which is not an Ecstatic Horizontal Dance beneath the Pipings of the Satyr in the Living Tree . . . but merely a hidden-from-attention view of all the Netherlands countryside, and fowls and greeneries, beneath the church-steps outside.

*And Holmes . . . and Van Doren & Lenrow too, of course.

This is where I've always been, under the steps . . . not dancing with White Arms Sailing over the Void, not even being
christened by Gouty Devout Patriarchs, but just looking, looking—watching for the Lamb. Well—enough of the Lamb now.

I'll review things, and ask no questions. It usually boils
down to how I'm going to write my next novel. I'm thinking of making *On the Road* a vast study of those I know as
well as a study of rain and rivers. Allen expresses weariness
with my "rain-&-rivers" preoccupation now, but I think it's
only because I have not explained manifestly what they mean:
as I did in the notebook "Record" on pages covering "New
Orleans to Tucson." That's clear in my mind.

Now. About the people. People are more important than
rain.

With the "Junkey" of *T & C* I think I'll re-create "Clem."
Based on his "testament written in Pennsylvania Station."

I think I'll bring in the huge elements of the Cannastra-
Ansen gang of 1948 in N.Y., which will someday reappear in
"Christmas in N.Y." (or "The Imbecile's Christmas"). The only
thing to do is to exert the necessary amounts of brain-power
to push it through.

The thing that stops me is Red Moultrie's family. I think
I'll make old Bruce his stepfather, and Bruce's (second) wife
his stepmother. Where is Red's real father hidden?—nobody
knows. His real mother died when he was six or seven or so.
Thus, when Red is coolly received at the end of his great quest,
he realizes that he must himself become The Father somehow. And Red has trouble with women. He is the loneliest of
my characters. Nowhere to turn except to Smitty, Vern, Clem
and all the countless others around the country . . . and Bea
and Mary Lou and the Ginnies. His life a real "continuum of
ambiguity."

Also, he will be intelligent, even eloquent, no Peter Martin.
Laura is just an illusion. Only the past is no illusion. The
future?—a claim.

"True progress shall lie in men's hearts." This is what Lincoln knew, and said.

There is never a real goldstrike, or a real "scientific advance,"
only a revelation in the heart on one day or the next, subject to horrible change and further revelation. "Revelation is

Revolution," as Holmes says, insofar of course, as it is a *change*, miserably from mere day to day.

There is no heaven and no reward, and no judgment either (Allen says his lawyers "will be judged"):—no:—there is only a continuum of living across preordained spaces, followed by the continuum of the Mystery of Death. That Death is a Mystery makes Death acceptable therefore; because Mystery never ends but continues.—

Still waiting for the family.

But then Red does find his gal, after the wreckage of his attempt to straighten out everything *as before*, which is of course impossible. The gal he loves very much finally, when he sees how great she is. Her name will be Bunny? Laura.

WEDNESDAY JUNE 1—Fixed the well-pump at nine o'clock this morning. Got dirt out of the valve and tightened a loose cylinder around the pipe, and raised the pressure to 50. For awhile there I was *enraged* because I thought my one-year-lease was on a house with a dry well. It is okay, I think—122 feet deep. On top of that it rained today. Rain is not only poetic in the West, but necessary. So I say "Rain you bastard!"—and it rains. I've been goofing off those two days just listening to the radio, playing with the cat, playing solitary stud-poker, and thinking up *On the Road* more. *I need my typewriter.* No furniture, no family, nothing. I can't understand all this delay. It took me 60 hours to get out here, and another 48 hours to get a house. It's taken them close to three weeks . . . and all I do is wait, wait, wait. I don't think Paul wants to leave the East actually . . . he is wasting time in North Carolina. His mother has a husband to support her, and a grandchild, and 2 other children in the East; therefore, there's no tragedy in Paul moving out West, inasmuch as he can visit her occasionally also. So I don't understand all this delay. They arrived in N.C. last Tuesday, and here it is nine days later—and the 1650 mile trip is a 3½ day drive. So they're staying there at least a whole week, and here I am in an empty house paying rent. This I don't like . . . a waste of time and money, and a waste of a good thing, and silly. Got a letter from Beverly Burford *Pierceall* today . . . now married, living in Colorado Springs, whose Pikes Peak I can see from the kitchen window. Wrote back at night.

THURSDAY JUNE 2—And tonight the family is finally arriving; got a telegram in the morning. I'm now down to my last actual penny (1¢), excluding the $20 bill I'm hiding for the lawn (part of the deal on this lease is to plant a lawn). So now things will start vibrating and we'll get our home going. Only thing is:—Where is the furniture truck? Hal Chase ought to be home by now. And soon I'll hear from Giroux and decide about June 15, and a job, and my writing-schedule [months] for *Road*.—Last night I went to bed reading the New Testament. My own interpretation of Christ I will write soon: essentially the same, that he was the *first*, perhaps the *last*, to recognize the facing-up of man to life's final enigma as the only important activity on earth. Although times have changed since then, and "Christianity" is actually Christian in method by now (socialism), still, the time has yet to come for a true "accounting," a true Christlike world. The King who comes on an Ass, meek. "True progress shall lie in men's hearts." Do you hear me, Huncke of the Fires?—Also, I planned to write a "Literary Autobiography of a Young Writer" within a few years, preferably while in Paris. I'm full of ideas, yet not of real work. I keep saying I need my typewriter—I do, and my desk, books, papers too. I wish I had the will and energy of ten writers (as I did in 1947). The 1948 work on *T & C* was a Gift from God, for I had long ago gone on my knees like Handel prior to his Messiah-work, and Received that.

But thank God for *everything*. The other night I saw that.

: —*Private Philologies* — :

THE Scythian name for earth, which is "apia," meaning WATERY or WATER-ISSUED (or first ISLE, then
LAND), is a name of great significance to me and undoubtedly
explains a universal feeling concerning water. We never think
of the dry desert as land or earth . . . mere sand. Water is the
soul of earth, that is, that earth should be fertile, wetty, moist.
Here again *rain* is the key.*

It seemed to me today that, while we were crossing the So.
Platte in a bus over the bridge, everyone in the bus was somewhat conscious of their connection with the water in the river.
It would take a fantastical ignorance, or worse, a fantastical
sophistication, to be unaware of one's relation to water in the
river. It is as though a man digging up fat dark soil, seeing
worms so glistening and glutted-up, should fail to recall it is
these moisty sucks that one day will feed on the very muscles
he uses to wield the pitchfork.

Incidentally: What is the meaning of that expression
"There's always room for one more"? It may be that the body
of mankind is always capable of joining a little closer (in a mass)
to admit another soul . . . both symbolically, and actually, in
a crowd—every joint moving nearer to every other joint to
make more room, every arm and leg pressing closer, every body
squeezing nearer to every other body, to the point where the
Universal Unity is recognized (though we are not ready for it
in this life).

Philology need not seek for this Universal Unity in the words
of languages—it's in a crowded bus, in the flesh.

Philologies . . . not *A* philology.

In Sanskrit, "tara" is to SHINE, which is connected to the
Scythian "Targi*tavus*" (a God), SHINING SUN. There is a
philological connection sure enough. But here is what I seek:—

*New recent song: "When it rains it's time to love again."

35

The Latin "familia" (family) is understood to derive from "thymele"—*the sacred center of fire*. We learn from this everything we want to know about the origin of the family—not only the word, the sacred center of the fire, the hearth, and the family there assembled:—in raw darknesses. This reminds me of my one and only investigation in anthropology, which consisted of staring several minutes at an Esquimaux ladle (for cooking). It seemed then also that the mere ladle offered everything I needed to know about the woman who used it, and the women of the culture, and perhaps a lot about the culture itself. I can't hope to disparage great sciences, but for my purposes, and for general later purposes of all men, I think, it is necessary to find some way of pulling out our inner knowledges and putting them to use in our studies of origin: not induction proper, for it is a realm where neither deduction or induction are so important.

It is a realm (Jung touched on it?) approaching a true vision of the universal unity:—and one which will require the work of expressive, word-wise thinkers.

I don't see how a philologist should be unword-wise if he does deign to call himself a "philos-logos," LOVER OF WORDS, which is now aridly known as the SCIENCE OF WORDS. A philologist should therefore be a Spenser and not merely a German hack—a *philomath*.

To turn an expressive study of words and of the inner feelings which they darkly evoke, into a *science*, is perhaps unwise—and I guess impossible. There's no need for a study to be useful in terms of what they call results—in this day when results are referred to a kind of material productivity. So long as there is the productivity and fertility in the imagination, which, like earth, may lead to a harvest if so desired. A lot of good earth goes untilled, and is merely used as a place to walk over . . . and the walker need not necessarily have an urgent destination.

But less of this boring Victorian philosophizing, and more actual philologies. Things to *find*.

There is a Western expression which I heard from Mr. H. Huescher; goes—"It's about to clabber up and rain all over." I thought "clabber" was a phonetically inspired colloquialism describing thunder; but tonight I learned that milk "clabbers" when it sours. So the sky *sours up* to rain—which is still another colloquialism in itself, to *sour up*, as in sourpuss, sour grapes, and so on. This is the farmer's, not the poet's, angle on rain—that it is a sour matter, a clabbering-up.

Another matter, touching in some degree on the larger, final area of any study whether it be philological or not:—it concerns a Celtic legend and the striking relationship of that legend with a thought recently entertained by your distinguished scribbler (a Celt by blood,) (if you do not believe that Kerouac is Celtic, consider the name of old *Kynyr Keinvarvawe*, who said his "son's heart will always be cold and there will be no warmth in his hands."):—

The legend is of Bran the Blessed, who counsels his chiefs to bury his head in the White Mount in London with the face towards France. "And the head (will be) with you uncorrupted, until you open the door that looks towards Aber Henleven and towards Cornwall." Everything is joyous for the chiefs, the birds of Rhiannon singing unto them the while, until one day Heilya said: "Evil betide me if I do not open the door to know if that is true which is said concerning it." "So he opened the door and looked towards Cornwall and Aber Henleven. And when they had looked, they were as conscious of all the evils they had ever sustained, and of all the friends and companions they had lost, and of all the misery that had befallen them, as if all had happened in that very spot; and especially the fate of their lord."

Sitting in the park the other day, musing on something that might modernly be called *spiritual relativity*, I saw that insofar as one point of reference is as good or true as another, therefore the door that might open on melancholy was neither truer nor better—in spite of all worldly circumstance—than the door that opened on joy:—in all factual reality. *I saw the doors*—the doors of Bran, if you will. One was a dark door and one was a golden door, and I could open either one.

The Gaelic "dorch" means *dark*. The Dutch "door" means *fool*. The French "d'or" of course means *of gold* (but the last is facetious). The Golden Horn of Constantinople, the Golden Gate of 'Frisco, the Golden Door of the Sistine Chapel.

No doubt the legend of Bran, with its immense door-like hint, is concerned somewhere with the phenomena of inward renunciation and inward resurrection . . . what I called *mood* when I first innocently approached the subject.

You've heard of "body and soul"—but it appears that its earlier version was "body and bones." Which indicates the depth of the bone, and throws light on Ginsberg's skeleton that laments, "You can do anything to my flesh, my eyes, my love, my et ceteras—*but leave my bones alone.*" Here the bones is the soul, dem golden bones.

An old spiritual:—

> "De head bone's connected to de ear bone
> Jes' to hear de word of God."

> "Lawdy dem bones, dem bones, dem dry bones."

And what about the door-bone? And roll dem bones, the dice, go roll your own bones. In a letter Lucien refers to his girl "woman-bone."

In Chaucer bone is "boon":—

> "We stryve, as dide the houndes for the boon."

And in Chaucer "bone" is PRAYER, from *boon* as we know it now. So that when the spiritual emphasizes bone, or prayer, and Lucien chants "bone bone bone bone . . . BONE!," there is prayer. The god-bone, to which all other bones are connected.

But can I ever investigate *bone* the way Hopkins investigated *horn?*—and the reason "horn" does not appeal to me yet is due to poetic immaturity, perhaps.

"And in a Dongeon deep him threw without remorse." This is what I crave now—the sound of terror—no vague horns; that and the Sweet Poetrie ("O that I were there, to helpen the Laydes their Maybush beare!")

Admiring or regarding are not so strong as *admirant* and *regardant.* It is the poet who bends language to his own use who deserves the name, as Shakespeare did; and admirable Joyce began to do, till it bent him; or did it bend him?

What of these divine lines in Chaucer's "Prologue"—

> *"So priketh hem nature in hir corages:*
> *Than longen folk to goon on pilgrymages—"*

This demonstrates the pity of removing the strong "Y" in English, along with the lolling French "L" and purring "R" (extant in Irish washerwomanhood) and, most dearly, the soft "G"—for if you read the above as it should be, French-like, the glory of pure English, which is so French, dims our present "advanced" English. We now make words like "junket" for *pilgrymage*; "junket" sounds like a Model T Ford; soon, therefore, we will invent a 1950 BUICK word, a speedy word, one with eyes like the snarling headlamp-eyes on new cars, with radiator-sharkfangs. Jaunt?

Here's how that Chaucer-line reads to me, in sounds:—(in spite of the "silent E" rule):—

> "Sau priketh 'em natzur en our cor-rā-jez
> Then loa-gen fok to goan on pill-gree-mā-jez."

—with that wonderful heaviness on the "ā's."

If I were "translating" I'd do this:

SO PRICK'D ALL THINGS IN NATURE'S
COURAGING DAY:
THEN LONG'D ALL FOLK TO PILGRIMAGE AWAY.

But what a farce. (Prick'd as *preen'd*, see?)

For some reason, also, last night, on the brink of "anguished" (for ANGUISHED SILENCE) I chose, rather, "agonized"—AGONIZED SILENCE. This is not important in itself, except insofar as I did it; I wonder why? Rhythm, yes. But what else?

Right now I'm looking for universal images so that I may speak to everybody directly beneath their education-cant. This is in the Mystique of Cities at the end of the first chapter of *On the Road*—in a thing like:—

"Miami, sea, dishes, sink, star—"

"Bakersfield, boxcars, palms, moon, watermelon, gin, woman." Or are these mere American Universals?

How about:—

"rain, manure, night-hay, the Wabash River—"

Well, I guess they're just American, except that in Joyce the juxtapositions, while Irish, are certainly Irishly Universal to this reader, and finally, therefore, purely universal—like in:—

"Before Nelson's pillar trams slowed, shunted, changed trolley, started for Blackrock, Kingstown, and Dalkey, Clonksea, Rathgar and Terenure . . . Rathmount, Sandymount Green, and Ringsend."

Do you think Joyce was only being cute when he listed these *Dublinisms*, these Dublin-names & Dublin-sounds and these Myth of the Dublin Day? It was because he knew . . . (secrets of humanity).

So I, also knowing this, have:—for 'Frisco:—

"Oakland, waterfront dive, sawdust floor, red lamps, Bay Bridge; Turk, Jones, O'Farrell and Annie Street; Fog, Coit Tower, Tarantino's, steak, wine, White Russian Hill."

Why? Is it apparent anyway? "Red lamps" in any case is All Universal, first off . . . I learned this from Alain-Fournier's obviously finely thought-out "naphtha flares" in *The Wanderer*, a perfection of deep image. But "fog" and "Coit Tower" are as one, whether you've seen the Tower or not, for, if I said, "Coit Fog," I think you'd understand. "Turk" is just a street-name; it follows red lamps and a bridge; could not do anything else. "Tarantino's" is only the name of a restaurant, but it is a winey name (because Italian) and a *white* name because of "AN," as in bl*AN*c, thus goes with a white hill, one called "Russian," which is a snowy country, and has a Ukraine, and a history of its own in settling 'Frisco. See?

Chauntecleer Chaucer was French too.

Popular, romantic songs, even poetry, sings—

"The mist around your eyes."

But crazy American satirists like Spike Jones come back with:—

"The bags under your eye-balls."

This too is poetry, since it *recognizes the poetry* of the original; a brilliant *counter-poetry.*—

Listen to this: I had no idea what FIRKIN meant, yet while writing a line in "The Rose of the Rainy Night" I used it because nothing else satisfied me as soon as it inexplicably and implacably entered my bean. "The rose of the rain falls open, / and dropping lights the sky / with *firkins* of softest dew. / " I felt this word was perfect, like Whitman's sudden use of KELSON somewhere, so strange and mysteriously perfect. So I used "firkin" without looking it up; it was *so* right I was convinced the meaning of the word would melt for my purposes.

Well—it's a barrel-measurement, is "firkin," from Old Dutch *vierkin*. Why can't God empty rain from old Dutch barrels, hey? Oh I myself have melted—too many of these sweet things have happened now.

I know now that I "remembered" the word from Melville's great passage on Dutch whaling-vessels in *Moby Dick*, but this has no connection with my choice of the word (not to say that it is a *great* choice). Only the *sound* determined me. Why is that? Because:—I wanted something "filling," that is, which would resound with a fat "F," to indicate abundance of rain—yet soft, soft. "Soft firkin" goes together in itself.

What a strange word I heard today—in connection with Albert Schweitzer's influence on modern theology— "ESCHATOLOGICAL," meaning pertaining to final things: death, judgment, heaven, hell. "Life's final enigma" as "the only important activity on earth," I said was the great contribution of Jesus—years after Schweitzer and 1,000 pale theologians in seminars. Ah well, great minds obviously run the same course. Now, of course, it will be necessary for me to work out a new idea.

Neal and I invented a word for the lost and hidden thread-ends of thought that are still remembered but with no name, and these are TUCKAWAYS.

How to *atone* for one's sins? By being *sorry*. What is it to be *decent* like this? A matter of *form*. When do we break out of forms? When we know what form is for.

This is a philosophical philologizing, flibbergibbet.

I have found wonderful tidbits in Herman Charles Bosman's excellent novel about a prison in South Africa—*Cold Stone Jug.* (Or that is, Robt. Giroux found them).

Here is a list of terms American and terms South African dealing with "underworld" matters:—

AMERICAN	SOUTH AFRICAN
Prison, pen, jug, can	Prison, jug, boob
Tea, marijuana, hemp, weed	Dagga, boom, pappagei
Stick (of tea)	Zol (of boom)
Real Mexican "shit"	Real Swaziland boom
Teaheads, hipsters	Rookers
High, flipped, "crazy"	Blue
Water-smoking	Ground-vaar

In America it is understood that marijuana is smoked by degraded sex-fiends in dens, by Negroes and Mexicans, and members of the hip generation, and jazz musicians, making them crazy.

In Johannesburg and South Africa generally it is understood that dagga is smoked by members of the white underworld, by the most degraded city-natives, and by the Bushmen in the Swaziland Bush, and that it drives them mad.

Translation of parts of *Finnegans Wake*, by "N.R.F."
From James Joyce Yearbook, 1949, Transition Press, Paris

"O, dis-moi tout d'Anna Livie! Je veux tout savoir d'Anna Livie! Eh bien! tu connais Anna Livie? Bien sûr, tout le monde connait Anna Livie. Dis-moi tout, dis-moi vite. C'est à en crever! Alors, tu sais, quand le vieux gaillarda fit krach et fit ce que tu sais . . ."

"Raccontami di Anna Livia. Tutto vo' sapere di Anna Livia. Beh, la conosci Anna Livia? Altro che, conosciamo tutte Anna Livia. Dimmi tutto, e presto presto. Roba d'altro mondo! Beh, sai allorché il messercalzone andò in rovina e fe' ciò che fe' . . ."
JOYCE-SETTANNI.

"Oh! Erzähle mir alles über Anna Livia! Alles will ich von Anna Livia wissen! Du kennst doch Anna Livia? Aber natürlich, wir alle kennen Anna Livia. Erzähle mir alles, erzähl's mir sofort. Lachst dich kaputt, wenn du es hörst. Na, du weisst doch, als der alte Holdrio hopps qins und tat, was du weisst . . ."
GOYERT.

". . . Je me sens vieille comme mon orme même. Un conte conté de Shaun ou Shem? De Livie tous les fillefis. Sombre faucons écoutent l'ombre. Nuit, Nuit. Ma taute tête tombe. Je me sens lourde comme ma pierrestone. Conte moi de John ou Shaun. Qui furent Shem et Shaun en vie les fils ou filles de. Là-dessus nuit. Dis-mor, dis-mor, dis-mor, orme. Nuit, nuit! Contemoiconte soit tronc ou pierre. Tant rivierantes ondes de, couretcourantes ondes de. Nuit.— . . . Par la terre et le nuageux, mais c'est que j'ai bougrement besoing d'une flancterge flambant neuf, pauvre de moite oui pour sur et dodu avec çà."

"Et c'est vieux et vieux et c'est triste et vieux, c'est triste et lourd je retourne vers vous, mon père froid, mon froid père fou, mon froid père fou et terrible, jusqu'à ce que la proche vue de sa grandeur, ses môles et ses vagues, grognant et grognantes m'aient rendu boue de la mer raide de sel, et je me précipite, mon unique, entre vos bras. . . ." BUTOR

JOYCE:—"Loonely in me loneness."
BUTOR:—*"Absurdement en moi solitude."* (!) (Sic)
J.L.K.:—*"Foulie dans mon isolement."* (?)

JOYCE:—"In the name of the former and of the latter and of their holocaust. Allmen."
J.L.K.:—*"Dans le nom du premier et du dernier et de leur épris sang. Aumône."*

JOYCE:—"By the watch, what is the time, pace?"
J.L.K.:—*"En passant-partout, quelle heure est-il, s'il vous paix?"*

⌒

The mad have unkind hearts; there's madness, right there. Paranoia blooms in such aridities.

What comes goes.

: —— *Odd Notes* —— :
March 1950

THE night is atonement for the sins of the day—in America. That is why they want "the end of the night"—complete purgation from sloppy decadent pursuits of noon. Only the hardworking riveter sleeps at night—the television adman gets drunk. The time has come to pursue the day in honest ways.

[Have Champa Gavin wake up in middle of night, much like the Elizur-preacher, wanting "out" from his sins which he cannot name—and talks (confesses he feels like a slob).] And there is love.

* * *

I think the greatness of Dostoevsky lies in his recognition of human love. Shakespeare himself has not penetrated so deep beneath his pride, which is all our prides. Dostoevsky is really an ambassador of Christ, and for me the modern Gospel. His religious fervor sees through the very facts and details of our everyday life, so that he doesn't have to concentrate his attention on flowers and birds like St. Francis, or on finances like Balzac, but on anything . . . the most ordinary things. There alone is proof about the sparrow that falls. It is the crowning glory of such a man as Spengler that he recognizes Dostoevsky to be a saint.

The vision of Dostoevsky is the vision of Christ translated in modern terms. The fact that he is barred in Soviet Russia implies the weakness of that state. Dostoevsky's vision is that which we all dream at night, and sense in the day, and it is the Truth . . . merely that we love one another whether we like it or not, i.e., we recognize the other's existence—and the Christ in us is the premium mobile of that recognition. Christ *is* at our shoulders, and *is* "our conscious in God's university" as Cleo says . . . he *is* the recognizer in us. His "idea" is.

The reason "television admen" get drunk at night, as above, is only because the nature of their pursuits shuts them off from

44

meek love of man, which is what we all want. D.H. Lawrence
is mere masturbation of self. Consider: tonight I went to Lou's
house, looking suave and well-contained in my suit, and spoke
to him "confidently" about my new plans. Nevertheless I was
nervous, and could not help noticing his pale melancholy, even
as his mother laughed and chatted with us. Everything I told
him—everything that happened—is for me overshadowed
by the fact that I *writhed* before this man (famous-young-
author-soon-to-be-wealthy notwithstanding, also prophet-of-
American-strength notwithstanding) and that this was because
I recognized his existence with love and fear, and could not
bear the mortification of my own senses receiving the grace of
his being. Lou is only an intensification of this feeling which
I have for everyone; he is a dramatic example of mankind.
Nevertheless I could not bear seeing him every day, for fear
of boredom, or the fear of boredom—perhaps fear of losing
the fear & trembling which is a dramatization of my being
alive. When I left I sighed . . . "It's always the same . . . My
position with one like that will never change . . . A relationship
is established for eternity . . . This world we walk in is only the
scene, the temporal scene, of eternal realities; this sidewalk only
exists for souls to walk on."

Further than a "dramatization of my being alive" is that such
a recognition of fear and love—or the fear and love itself—
simply the love—is our existence, and mine too, and yours, and
we try to avoid it more than anything else in the world. Thus,
tonight, reading my new books, I find that Kafka avoids it in
a dream of himself; Lawrence avoids it by masturbating (same
thing); and Scott Fitzgerald, though closer to recognition of
love, only wrote his story to make money and omitted certain
things (in "Crazy Sunday"). Then I read Dusty and it was all
there. There is no truth like the truth of the earthly prophet.

I want to become, and pray to be, an earthly prophet.

All the diplomats and statesmen who are obstructing peace
and progress today, and have been doing so for so long, are
simply avoiding the recognition of human love more than
anything else in the world. It is even possible that America the
organic body loves Russia the organic body—allegorically link-
ing them as two living beings on the same dark plain. A war
between the two will only result in further wars of imaginary

supremacy . . . positions of pride in the world. The time to stop war is simply now, 3:19 A.M., Wednesday March 1st, 1950— just as easy as that—by some bold yet strangely meek decision to merely recognize each other's existence with honest eyes. But war is not the real curse. The curse is the reluctance to admit the love human beings have for one another and even for plants, animals, and objects. It's all exceeding simple. What the United Nations need is one bold man who, like Napoleon, realizes there is always something *dared to be done* and no one accepts the dare out of sheer wonderment at the gateways of light . . . specifically out of fear of leaving the lowing herd. In the herd are individuals of love; but the mass of it is a blind propulsion like a storm, without direction.

I don't think "peace" is the solution because of certain terrible laws—[I start with a study of man then on to the state]— The laws are that militant nationalism is the only thing that makes a nation "strong," pacifistic internationalism courts destruction. But if we apply that to individuals?—we have to ask, "courts *what* destruction?—only a destruction of one's system of pride." Proud men are strong destroyers; nationalistic nations have systems of pride, and can lick the humble nation. The thing is to "abolish" the system of prides in nations . . . which is impossible, for the first one bereft of pride will fall. But fall where? All the nations will "fall" eventually into a family of earth.

An Organization and Measurement of the World and the Soul

Sept. 7 '49

The soul receiveth life, because the soul itself is dead, and what life the soul receiveth, and it does not every moment receive, is Grace. And the snowflakes fall like Grace, or Graces, upon our shoulder. Each snowflake and each petal substantial is thereby, through the Mystery of Grace, made spirit. But Beatitude is given only to those who give recognition to Grace and to the mysteries of God.

There are then souls which become so advantaged and arranged, and so subtle, that they receive all Grace and Graces through the agency of one gracious being, as light converges in the prism, and to them it is therefore given to know Beatitude in the form of the Burden of Grievous Love. This is the highest Beatitude when it is also recognized, and always is so, that the Grace of God is also shining in that beloved convergence.

But there are souls of saints so vastly desirous, and so disparate and warm, which receive the Graces everywhere in everything at every moment, as if they themselves were prisms and all light converged to meet there, and in them the recognition is a Beatitude as well, the Beatitude in the form of saintly Love.

For the self is dead, and it were not meet, nor avowable, to trace one's gracious Graces themselves outward flowing, whereat Beatitude which is the knowledge of the receivership of Grace, cannot enter.

All souls are dead, but all souls receive, and all souls give.

And so the love of a being, as described, is Beatitude, but the love of the being's substantial flesh is but a Grace, for the spirit cannot enter and be humbled. It is therefore so that the soul is dead without Beatitude.

God is the Master of Grace who does dispense his gifts to the senses of beast and plant, and he is the Keeper of Man dispensing the Beatific Light.

Bliss—[of Tony Smith in On the Road]

Bliss then follows, when the recognition of Beatitude becomes as the recognition of the Saint seeing all things proceeding from the Source, and without cavil enduring all things in this Light. To cavil is human, and to cavil is to bray and judge and divide matter, whereby Bliss is not possible, or that is to say, the Bliss of Saints is not possible.

Bliss is also the condition of the Imbecile and the child, particularly that of the Imbecile.

When shall the Imbecile show our faces?

The most evil of men is he who gloats among others when the Imbecile walks forth, moaning.

For the soul is dead.

And the serpent incheth . . .

: —*Riddles*— :

ONE has come among us that ate our blood last night as we slept and is now flying in the air like an airplane, and will die next week. But this is an easy riddle.

Out of Singapore, at Tanjong Katong, lives a mosquito in a tree.

The wood has numbers.

The transparence is dimmed by ashes.

My key has a sign.

[ANSWERS:—The mosquito ate our blood, and buzzes in the air, and will die in the first cold snap.

The wood that has numbers is my ruler.

The transparence dimmed by ashes is my ashtray.

My key which has a sign is my typewriter key.]

In these endeavors I seek to come close to the meaning and secret of ambiguity . . . which is "madness," and also our sadness.

I have seen an entire land turn from green to red.

The words you addressed me reached me by means of violent fires and explosions.

I lie prone in the embrace of the Scriptures.

[ANSWERS:—The land that turned from green to red did so when I looked at another map of Arizona. The words reach me through the air mail, an airplane getting motion from the rapid combustion in the piston cylinders. In the Scriptures my poem lies between the pages, prone.]

Answer this:—

Who is it from whose source of life flows blood, yet lives
    and laughs?
What is the beautiful sound that emanates from the house
    of the angels?
How may I encompass a star?

ANSWERS NEXT PAGE.

49

1. A young child whose mother is menstruating.
2. Church music, as a rule.
3. By creating a puddle of my own in which I can catch the reflection of any planet.

— A Sonnet Now —

When Summer softly strays my love afar, as always,
    And turns with hope of home of Autumn dark;
    When yet even Autumn hints of homeless lays,
And sighs at me with leaves and groaning bark,

And signs that even home will poorly cling,
    When I then foresee old elusive Winter
    Shall my Christmas quite deceive, and sense Spring
Again revolving with pretty talk of lover,

Then I see me wandering among the mockeries
    And wonder if seasons think me so foolish
    That I would not love just as eye sees,
In lieu of wily winks in all these trees and swish.

    Moans they merely are in this old groan
    Of all my loves, the rose-tree that's mine own.

O ═══ O

A FURTHER RIDDLE:—

A river that disappears not in the sea but in the antique bottom of the sea.

[ANSWER:—The Humboldt disappears in Carson sink, and even the Western desert was once the bottom of the sea.]

ANOTHER ONE:—

What is the bridge that bridgeth Bridget's mind?

[ANSWER:—Her nose—] That is, her nose begins at the brow and *terminates* [TERMINALATES?] just above her mouth.

The number 729 is one of the holiest of all the heavenly numbers.

[The ANSWER to this riddle is presented as a riddle also:—

Because . . . *Trinity times Trinity to the Trinity power multiplied by Trinity.*

Mathematically: 3×3^3

$$\frac{3}{729}$$

All the preoccupations of man have their source in fact, just as all the crimes of man are committed from out of a source of good:—hate is the fear that love has flown.

Who will go mad by the moon who never thinks of the moon?

Our artistic fancies are but modern versions of old moon-madness.

"Who moans?"

"Not I,—I groan."

"Who groans?"

"'Tis I,—I lied."

"Who moans and groans?"

"I cannot lie—I moan, I groan."

"Who is the liar who moans and groans?"

"'Tis I, 'tis I, the liar who moans and groans."

: —— :

To ride a railroad in the Indian Summer!—

In Indian Summer, the leaves are sadly scattered on the ground, there is no wind, and a heavy-hanging, old, misty moon's up there. The still, dolorous leaves on carpets of earth, all crinkled; the yellow moon; the warm night of ferns. The ghost of summer returns, and quietly lingers awhile; his moans are in the distant winds that have yet to come. Then the ghost departs.

And winter surges up with stark announcements of his purpose. Dead leaves wither and crack.

Riddlic Verses

Tied, to dark-trod earth,
The trembling veil, ascending,
Rent.

Torn, tangled shroud
That the bloody weeper wore,
Go up.

Weary of the valley
His groaning fades below.

Veil of wraiths, loonar sprig,
From gruesome fens arise,
From the common skeleton earth
Go, from the Valley of the Roars
To the Vale of Airs,
And airily hint in Heavens.

Since kindness be the Venus-star
    of friendship,
And that bright star doth light
    the lowest hill,
May praise be worthy of
    the highest good.

Nor deeper peer, nor know more,
Ere mere seething grow roar.
Aumônes!
Allmen!
Almoner!
Alms!
Arms!
Âme!
Ahm!
Ahm jest bone, Ah groan alone.
"When I hear mine I moan."
Tied, to dark-trod earth, alary veil, *vole!*

Ow!

Pome Dedicated
to
N. C.

Warp!
Urp!
Woof!
Uff!
Weft!
Whisht!
Weave!
Grieve!
Wind!
Mind!
Wurrah!
Water!
What!
Wap!
Wa?
Warp!
Urp?
Woof!
Uff?
Weft!
Whisht?
Weave!

Poem

Why all is so
In the bleakness of this realm
I, mortal, as yet still,
Do not know.

(The key is "as yet still.")

For I'm beginning to know *again*.
The mortal realm is only waiting for us to do it.
What is more suggestive than "do it"?

We can all do it in the parlor,
Or do it in the air, anything,
Or do it anywhere, everything.

: —*Rough Work on the Poem with A. G.*— :

Pull my daisy,
Tip my cup,
   All my doors are open.

All my doors
Cannot open
   Lest you open yours.

Hear my songs,
Oh my bongos,
   All my gongs are going.

Tit my tat,
Toll my doom,
   Tuck my luck away.

Your noodle's toodled,
Your heart's all doodled,
   A dirty old soul you've got.

Yet all this,
As we know,
   Is just a goofy sorrow.

Oh dear Allen
Why do you
   Make such crazy music.

Ling my lang,
Bang my dong,
   Ling my banging lang-dong.

Root tee toot,
Just a fruit,
   Bloot bloot tee bloot.

Ope my rosebush,
Pluck my thorns,
   All my loves are there.

   What's the hex?
   Who's the hoax?
   Where's the axe?
   How's the hicks?
   Who's so hincty?
   Itch to inch?
   Bees woo who?

How sweetly the mind shrinks it.
Such bleakness man in infancy hath seen
A nuder think will change thee.
Waste of time is waste of sand.

The bee woos who?
Roosters' hullaballoos.
Who woos bees?
Void-noises and eye-roses.
Boohoo's busy goofing.

. . . The romance of time . . .
The depths of life
The crash of guitars.

The Simpleton's Christmas
: —A 3-Act Play— :

Unalterable lines like: "I say:—be reasonable. Kind is kind."
Who would speak like that?

    The Simpleton Tony, 29, a shoeshine boy, French Canuck
    His Sister, Clara, 31, an office girl
    His Kid Sister
    His friends
    His girlfriends
    His Lost Father

Time: The Anniversary of the Birth of Our Lord
Place: New York
Theme: All overtones of our Bleak Realm.

ACT ONE, Scene One—A Streetcorner
Enter Tony the Imbecile and a fellow Shoeshine Boy

Tony:—Then, when the angels saw the shepherds, they began
    to sing—"Hosannahs upon the King of Kings born this
    day Anna Domini Oleomargarine Amen!" The shepherds
    they raised their eyes to the sky, full of frights and crying—
    "O Lord, watch my little lamb on the mountainside."
Boy:—So this is your corner.
Tony:—(Unpacking box of shine.) Watch our sheep; our sheep,
    our sheep.

And so on so,
And so and so . . .

The Simpleton finds great joy in the fact that all kinds of
people all over N.Y. City celebrate Xmas, and keeps pointing
that out to his bored friends. This is thus like the idiocy of the
artist. "The peoples with the fur collar on Park Avenue; the
peoples in the beer room on Tent Avenue—see?"

Plays I've seen—
   My Heart's in the Highlands, Saroyan 1939, with Frank
      Leahy
   The Beautiful People, Saroyan 1940, alone
   Native Son, Wright (Canada Lee) 1941, with Pa
   Flight to the West, Rice (Betty Fields) 1941 with Pa
   Crime & Punishment, Dostoevsky (Gielgud) 1948, alone
   Red Gloves, Sartre (Boyer) 1949, with Holmeses
   Hamlet, Shakespeare (Evans) 1939, with H.M. class

Further Notes on "The Simpleton's Christmas"

A Canuck, Tony speaks like old "Zouzou" Gene Paquette in
Lowell.

It is only the simpleton who lives as though an angel had
just appeared announcing he has but one hour to live—and
embraces life: yet, by that very token, sees little difference
between good and evil (?)—at least, Tony. Life as the last hour.

Notes of 1950 February

On the Road is my vehicle with which as a lyric poet, as lay prophet, and as the possessor of a responsibility to my own personality (whatever it rages to do) I wish to evoke that indescribable sad music of the night in America—for reasons which are never deeper than *the music*. Bop only begins to express that American music. It is the actual inner sound of a country.

There are saints, and there are scholars; and the difference is always there. Absorbing and/or avoiding.

In Denver last summer all I did was stare at the *plains* for three months, for reasons, reasons.

There's a noise in the void I hear; there's a vision of the void; there's a complaint in the abyss—there's a cry in the bleak air; the realm is haunted. *Man haunts the earth.* Man is on a ledge *noising* his life. The pit of night receiveth. God hovers over in his shrouds. Look out!

More than a rock in my belly, I have a waterfall in my brain; a rose in my eye, a beautiful eye; and what's in my heart but a mountainside, and what's in my skull; a light. And in my throat a bird. And I have in my soul, in my arm, in my mind, in my blood, in my bean a grindstone of plaints which grinds rock into water, and the water is warmed by fires, and sweetened by elixirs, and becomes the pool of contemplation of the dearness of life. In my mind I cry. In my heart I think. In my eye I love. In my breast I see. In my soul I become. In my shroud I will die. In my grave I will change.

But enough poetry. Art is secondary.

Plaintiveness is all.

(In my sleep I referred to myself, in French, not as a "writer" but as *arrangeur*—he who arranges matters; at the same time, I associated this function with eating supper (*manger*). I woke up to remember this.)

FEB. 1—A night at the opera with Bob & Kelly. A banquet for 300 millionaires. Gene Tunney was there. Afterwards

Birdland with Neal; champagne in the lounge of the Yale Club. The past month of January has been crazy . . . beginning New Year's Eve with that fantastic party that ended for me in Princeton, N.J. and the Lyndons. A thousand swirling things all untold.

FEB. 7—Tonight I mused & worked simultaneously on four major projects . . . *Road, Sax, Simpleton* and a juvenile football novel (the latter may be major only in terms of $). (Altho kids in Lowell read it avidly when I wrote it at 17.) Busy day & night. I realize now that if I feel like it, any moment I may start *camping* and decide to be bored & depressed, just for a change. And that's what *that* is, or anything. Tonight I wrote the "serpent of evil" poem . . . "all three sighed the sigh of life, and the serpent inched." Needless to say, I also cramm'd my "Rain & Rivers" travelbook further. That makes *five* projects in all . . . in today's fine range. One of those far-seeing days, when you're your own great-statesman of personal history, and see it all like a prophetic protocol . . . within the dreamlike bleakness.

FEB. 10—Mark Twain's *The Mysterious Stranger* is an undiscussed masterpiece, in some ways more profoundly all-inclusive than Melville's last-work masterpiece (as *The Stranger* is Twain's)—*Billy Budd*. "Life is a dream," says Twain's beautiful Satan, but it is said in a context more terrible than anyone's before. "You are but a vagrant thought wandering forlornly in shoreless eternities."—and—*"All the dream-marks are there."*
   Last night—party at Varda's, to which I took Adele; later, party at Holmeses, which I left and won't return. Adele and I had wonderful warm hours together. The other night, at Neal's birthday party, I also felt like not returning. Next month I'm off with my new map; don't know where.

FEB. 13—Still yet further expansions of *On the Road* occurred tonight as I walked home from a Times Square movie in a sleet-storm. All along I've felt *Road* was not enough for a full-scale effort of my feelings in prose: too thin, too hung up on unimportant characters, too unfeeling. I have the feelings but not the proper vehicle as yet . . . unless this "works," *as*

*I imagine it might if I develop things properly.** Consider: a man wandering on the road in search of his lost daughter, for the wife of his youth is dead and he has lost his kingdom moreover. Just archetypical, in essence, as that. The man has just come from a 3-year stretch connected with narcotics and an unpleasant homicide—"innocent in his complicity." This is no Red Moultrie kid, but a real man of feelings & tragedy. The prison term has ruined his former high position in the world. His wife has died. The daughter has run away wild at fifteen and is somewhere in America. He wants to find her because he loves her, and because he is certain through apprehension and experience that she needs his help. Like an Angel Detective he follows her clues through city after city, beat & destitute, till he finds her. He wants to recall the "Love of God" to her heart, and is intelligent enough to know he himself is not far from that "God." But he is also intelligent to her true benefit, and offers to marry to give her a home (he has chosen a woman en route) after finding her desolate in the sordid hipster nights. This is like my own present mission . . . strangely . . . and not so strangely.

I wish to call him by another, new name I never thought of to date.

He is no *old man*, properly—and perhaps was even a ballplayer recently, and once a jazz musician. *How should I know?* What does it matter? The MAN will stand without accoutrements. I will re-read Carlyle—am now reading Tolstoy & Dostoevsky.

FEB. 15—In fact this man will not be a father at all, but just a resolute & mature young man looking for a girl who loved him in childhood and wrote letters thereafter. It is all the same thing. The point is—"His love is somewhere in America."

And he is "on the road" to it—the raw, harsh road of poverty & troubles, too . . . but he is no Red Moultrie (who, I realized at dawn, is only Al Hinkle my old easy-going Denver friend). This is closer to Bill Clancy, the football-hero-hobo I wrote at sixteen; also closer to Wesley Martin of *The Sea is My Brother*; and closer to a more resolute Peter Martin, even Joe Martin (and Michael Breton, Pete Gaos, all the others).

*Typical will-lessness!!!

There will be families in Calif. and Colo. I'll make preparatory plot-notes in a more convenient place, however.—Just ate molasses sandwich & potato chips. Death is when you don't eat molasses & chips any more. Today wrote to Alan Harrington about his possible acceptance at Harcourt. Walked 2½ miles in sleet storm for ice cream tonight. Where my grandfather's from, Riviere du Loup, properly St. Hubert, near the Gaspé Peninsula, and all my folks there since 1770's, and previously icy Brittany coasts, explains why I love the cold & storm so much and can't stand summers. Some undiscoverable Louis Alexandre le Bris de Kérouac (or Keroac'h) must have left me his hot guts, wherewith I need no coat half the winter in tropical America.

FEB. 17—The hero of *On the Road* is Chad Gavin. I made out a *dramatis personae* and it has marvelous depth and range. I pray to God that this is finally the discovery of my work, after years of meditating it (from the early Oct. 1948 idea of Ray Smith and Warren Beauchamp). This will be a great *T & C* of the nation itself. The only book I foresee beyond it is an "American War & Peace"—*The Sorrows of War*, which I will write after *Sax & Simpleton* probably.

Last Page of a Notebook Bought in Colorado May 1949

FEB. 18—In twelve days my *Town & City* will be published and the reviews will appear. Will I be rich or poor? Will I be famous or forgotten? Am ready for this with my "philosophy of simplicity" (something which ties in a philosophy of poverty with inward joy, as I was in 1947 & 1948).

The magazines will soon want short stories. List of possibles.
1. Sea-story of old Andy remembering in tempest at sea
2. Ling's Woe fable?
3. Story of freight elevator worker who is present at moment Angel of Death appears on sidewalk to hero. Dream.

4. Sports story of high school track relay team in Boston
5. Preview story of Tony the Imbecile—books incident
6. Preview story of Moon-man & Doctor Sax (sand pits.)
7. Preview story of wild tenorman (*On the Road*).
8. Preview story of Ghost of the Susquehanna
9. Suicide of blind man; (girl) & Reichian giggler; "Palmy-ran" Chicago
10. Story of Tom's "death" & the priest

THE NIGHT IS MY WOMAN

OR,

THE LABORS OF MICHEL BRETAGNE

The Night Is My Woman

On November 17, 1950, after a torrid two-week courtship, Kerouac married Joan Haverty, and in January 1951 they moved into a studio apartment on West 20th Street in Manhattan's Chelsea district. It was there that Kerouac wrote *La nuit est ma femme*, a fifty-seven-page manuscript composed in the patois that Kerouac had grown up speaking in the French Canadian neighborhoods of Lowell, Massachusetts. Kerouac's first-person narrator, the aspiring French Canadian writer Michel Bretagne, ruminates gloomily, but not without humor, on the compromises he has been forced to make in his young life—just as Kerouac himself was attempting to balance his artistic aspirations with the financial pressures of a new marriage.

The events depicted in *La nuit est ma femme*, such as the Bretagne family's move to New Haven, Connecticut, in search of work, are based largely on events that transpired in Kerouac's life during the summer of 1941. (In terms of the chronology of the Duluoz Legend, the action is subsequent to *Maggie Cassidy*, which depicts Kerouac's experiences as a student at Lowell High School.) Shortly after completing *La nuit est ma femme*, Kerouac would in the same Chelsea apartment type out the legendary *On the Road* scroll manuscript, leading Joyce Johnson to conclude that returning to the French of his formative years in Lowell helped him discover the voice of Sal Paradise, the narrator of Kerouac's breakthrough novel.

The translation is by Jean-Christophe Cloutier and incorporates some passages translated by Kerouac, as explained further in the notes to this volume.

I HAVE NOT LIKED MY LIFE. It's nobody's fault, just me. I see only sadness everywhere. Often when a lot of people laugh I don't see anything funny. It's a lot funnier when they're all sad together. I look at their hypocritical faces and I know they don't trouble themselves with sadness. They can't use it. They all know what is said in the Bible: "You do not even know that you are wretched, and miserable, and poor, and blind, and naked." What can they do with that? I use my sadness to spend my time thinking. That's how I understand existing. It's my way. I am tired. I can't even explain myself without lying a little. But I would never write if I did not believe in the idea of living.

My mother told me that the day I was brought into the world at 5 o'clock in the afternoon of the month of March, there was a light like red blood in the air and the snow was melting everywhere. Seems to me I remember that particular day. Every time I see the red sun on a late afternoon it's as if I see my whole life.

I am French Canadian, born in New England. When I am angry I often curse in French. When I dream I often dream in French. When I cry I always cry in French, and I say: "I don't like it, I don't like it!" It's my life in the world that I don't want. But I have it. I am still curious, I am still hungry, my health is excellent, I love my little woman, I am not afraid to walk far, I am not even afraid to work hard as long as I don't need to work 60 hours a week. I can't get up in the morning but when I have to I get up. I can work 40 hours a week if I like the job. If I don't like it, I quit.

My family and my women have always helped me. Without them, I think I may well have died in the snow somewhere— mayhap yes, mayhap no. I never lived alone for long. I dream. One day I will be a man like other men. Today I am a child and I know it and I spend my time thinking. I am supposed to be a *writer*. I published a book, I received $1900.00 for 4 years of work on that book. Before that I spent 10 years writing other things that I was never able to sell. It's possible that one day, once I have gone over to the other side of the darkness to dream eternally, these things, stories, scenes, notes, a dozen impossible novels, half finished, will be published and someone will collect the money that was supposed to come to me. But that's if I am a great writer before I die.

I dreamed for too long that I was a great writer. I picked that up in books. There was a time when I thought that every word I wrote was immortal. I embarked upon this with a big romantic heart. This is possible in the young. At first I used big "fancy" words, big forms, "styles" that had nothing to do with me. When I was a child in New England I ate my supper at the table and wiped my mouth with the dishrag—done, and gone. Why the big words, the grand lyrics, to express life?

Yes, I have slept around apple trees same as Shakespeare.

I never had a language of my own. French patois until 6 years old, and after that the English of the guys on the corner. And after that—the big forms, the lofty expressions, of poets, philosophers, prophets. With all that today I'm all mixed up in my noggin.

I use the word "labors" to express the jobs and the travels that were necessary to undertake whenever I wasn't at home sitting on my behind thinking about the sadness of life.

I begin my work this evening across the street from a Protestant seminary. I open the shutters of my old window and I see the big dark yard. There's ice on the ground. In some windows there are lamps but I don't know if these are the rooms of young students. I'd like to think that while they study theology I study the sad labors of life, and one is just as important as the other.—It's like all things, we don't know everything, only the little we can see with our eyes. There! now I saw two students in two different rooms get up from under the lamps in their shirttails! There, we are all students.

We need but go down the street and we get to New York's waterfront. I am interested in the sea and in boats. Pretty soon when spring comes and we open our windows we'll hear the big boats come and go. To see the water you have to walk in front of the big facades of marine companies as long as eight blocks. After that you go behind a fence and lo, frozen water full of snow, oil, and flotsam. On the other side of the big Hudson are the lights of New Jersey. There's all sorts of debris—wood, barrels, and all sorts of rags in the burlap night. On the other side of the street two old Negroes are burning big boards in front of barrels they arrange to close out the wind. They are shroudy strangers, oldtimers of darkness. They're wearing hats I bet they picked up on the side of the tracks in North Dakota in nineteen-thirty.

I walk all over. I pass by the wholesale meat warehouses. The streets are dark and dirty, the sidewalks are covered in meat juice and filth. In the cold winter wind all alone in the middle of the night some burly boys dressed in bloodied whites bring big sides of beef out of the trucks and hang them with hooks onto contraptions that go down into the basement. The meat goes down, fast. There are men below who unhook it. I can't go in the basement to see what they do after that. I am told that they cut some nice pieces of steak for themselves when they're hungry and then cook them on stoves themselves. I'd like to see those old stoves! It makes me hungry. When they're finished working, that's it, they drink, they play cards, they smoke cigars and one of the guys cooks the steaks. They laugh, they eat well. Morning comes, the buyers come, the street is full of traffic—the men of the night go to bed. This is what life is for me; this isn't so sad. But I am not a wholesale butcher, I am a poor writer with a little piece of steak wrapped in paper on the windowsill.

Later in the night the seminary students sleep, the lamps turn off. I am still up, I am sitting at my desk. My radio is low, it brings me the music of the night; my woman sleeps.

Eh well, there's some peace at least.

I have not liked my life but I have always liked the heart of the world.

So, my first labor.

*   *   *

When I was a child I often worked in my father's printshop folding papers. It was real work; in other words, you could never stop and they gave me a little pay in pennies. But I did it with my sister and my mother, so it was a fun-filled affair, only to help out whenever there was a rush and after that we all ate in the Chinese restaurant. I have always liked Chinese restaurants for this reason. I still see my father happy sitting at the beautiful table filled with covered dishes; he lifts the top, we see the fried rice, the chop suey, the chow mein. He says "Ah! Look how gorgeous!" The owner personally brings us some candied lichi nuts. On my mother's face I see a blush of happiness. Why does a man get married and build his life with his little family, only to die and leave his children sad for eternity?

Yes, the little labors with the ruler to fold the paper, and the gorgeous Chinese dinner and sometimes a show the whole gang, at home in the town of my birth; this wasn't a preparation for the horrible labors that befell me later. Oh life is a dolorous pilgrimage. Where we going? where? Death is nothing; it's the sadness in life that kills me.

When I was a small child, and my father called me Ti-Michel, Ti-Pousse, Tourlipi, Ti-Pette, and my mother called me Ti-Choux, I think I knew what was coming. In my room at night sitting at my little green desk with my little childhood games, I looked out the window with the fear of being alone someday in this abominable universe. I prayed the Good Lord every night, and in church on Sunday I prayed officially in His house. He listened to me: my father died when I was only 25 years old. It would have killed me at 12, 15, 18 years old. It almost killed me at 25. My mother lives, she's an angel of goodness; she's with my married sister. But the abominable universe swallowed me up in any case; I'm a little used to it, that's all. I saw the days of darkness prophetically long ago. Yes, they tell us to get used to life, the psychiatrists have these big words, the words "adjusted" and "mature," and the perverts don't care, the mad laugh. But it's the heart we lose when we win some tricks. Me I can't live without heart.

For all that, we have to work. This is not to say that I have labored like the other men in the world—I've labored rather with my interminable writings in the infantile night—but I have labored enough to be "hung-up" and tired.

My first real job was when I was 18 years old. My father thought it would do me some good. I sold subscriptions to the paper in my town, in the summer of 1940. That very year, also, I began writing with a literary style; before that, from 11 on, I wrote to amuse my private childhood ideas, little stories about the guys, horses, sports. But by now, I had discovered Saroyan and Hemingway. So, I wrote about my job, selling subscriptions door to door, with the tone of a big American writer.

Voilà:—"It was like a stage in the circulation room. I could see the windows of the business establishments across the street and I could see the man who was our boss sitting there with the white shoes. And they came in one after the other, just like in a play. The first one had on a sports shirt under his coat and he walked in with his hat brim turned up and he smiled and said Good Morning to the boss. The boss in his white shoes and the salesman of the smile and then in came the third. He was tall and angular and he walked bent over and I liked him. Blue eyes & a bent walk and this morning he told me that the cops in this town should tie buttons over their holsters because anyone could reach out & kill them with their own gun. A face like a horse trainer or a newspaper man or a Havre de Grace tout or even a trotting horse driver. Mr. Miller, said the fourth man who limped as he walked in. How many did you sell yesterday and Mr. Miller leaned over even more and smoked his cigarette and said, A few."

I had to take a bus at the Square then ride to the other side of the river into the part of town where I was born. It's because I spoke French and it was a Canadian neighborhood, and also most of the Canadians read the other paper in town. Voilà, that first morning I found myself at the end of the street of my birth. I asked myself "Oh come on, what am I doing here, it's the last place in the world I'd have thought to come to on my own."

A man's work is like that. There was a time when a man went hunting wherever he pleased. I saw little spots where I used to play as a child and it angered me, it made me sad & lost. I didn't like knocking on people's doors and bothering them in their homes. I said this to my father that evening. He was an insurance man in his youth; he knocked on doors everywhere. He found it funny my sniveling sadness.

It's at that point that I began to understand that I was not like my father and my relatives in the family. I was lazy, I wanted to be by myself. I didn't like the business that men did. In the morning in my bed, I heard the mill-whistle that sounded everywhere across the sky above town; I looked outside; the men, the women, the young, they were all going to the factory in the cold with their poor lunches. Ah, it made me nauseous to think that some day, one fine morning of the Good Lord, I'd have to go with them into these big dirty places full of din and work that never ends.

All my life I got up after everyone else in the family, once they were all gone to work, and I wrote & wrote so I wouldn't need to work. They left me be: I had scholarships to college and the thing they wanted for me was a career. There are families in Quebec who take one of their sons and put him in a seminary to become a priest, so that the whole family can go to heaven. I wouldn't have hated that. But I would have always climbed the fence at night to go see some girls. I would have been a pretty mixed up priest.

With my first week's pay, $16.83, I went and got myself drunk for the first time in my life. In a saloon on the big street behind the mills they sold jumbo glasses of beer for 10¢. Me and my friends, 2 Canadians Roland and Henri, and one Greek, our famous G.J., we drank us a good dozen glasses each. We thought we had discovered the Good Lord. We took all the old drunkards by the collar and we told them that they were the Good Lord. We sang this in the pissers, in the streets. "All men are the Good Lord!" we hollered at the top of our lungs. Later, in the tree near the river behind a low stonewall, everyone who was going home from the bars watched us wrestle. I puked on my knees and then went backwards on my hands so I wouldn't get dirty. We thought it was funny.

Monday morning I didn't return to the circulation office. I told my parents that I wanted to study in the fall. My father raised his hands in the manner of a Canadian.

We liked it so much getting drunk, the guys, that we prepared to go on a big trip to Vermont. Henri had an old jalopy. I knew some nurses over there. We brought a bottle. Henri had his new tweed suit in green and he'd just had a golden tooth put in. We called him "Kid Faro." It was marvelous. I had taken some trips with my parents to Canada, with a friend to Boston, with another to N.Y. to put my college papers in order, and one time, when I was seven years old, I had walked ten miles in the country with my old childhood chum Jack to go live on a farm. But the trip with the guys to Vermont was more of a real trip than the others. It was funny, it was "Crazy as a

Broom." The morning was cool, the sky blue, the country like on the first day of the world. We yakked, we thought ourselves important.

In Vermont we spoke to the nurses at the hospital, they told us to wait until nine o'clock in the evening when they'll be done working. To pass the time we bought a bottle of whiskey with a name we've never seen again since. It was made in the Green Mountains. We drank that in under 15 minutes. We went to swim in a quarry. I made believe that I was drowned, I stayed under water a long time. G.J. was scared. He almost jumped in the water in his clothes. The others danced. I tried to rip out a small tree from the ground, I twisted it around my back and stood with it and it tore a little at the root. It was beginning to get dark. We were drunk. We got into the car & we returned to the hospital. I was getting out of the back seat to acquaint myself with the young ladies, I missed the runningboard and fell flat on my face in the driveway. I stayed there. I liked it. All the others left to go dancing save for me and G.J. He sat me down in a beach chair and lo, there we were in the beautiful summer night in Vermont, in front of a summer resort near the hospital, me asleep, he awake. Two old ladies were sitting near us. Every time I made to puke G.J. would take off the hat he'd bought for the trip and said, "Yes, it is a fine evening, dear Mr. Bretagne, you are correct."

Well, and where is G.J. tonight? Why live a life which makes us forget so cruelly? I'd be well satisfied to be again in that chair, sleeping, with my funny protector, a poor little greek with hair like a lamb whose father saw the light of day in far-off Crete, than to be here now at this moment that I write in the great dark and dolorous city. The ball of earth is fatal, it hurts us, it does not love us.

In the morning we returned home in the little jaloppy half dead. We ate hamburgers in a lunchcart in the town where my mother and father were born. It was gray and foggy, it was sad. I was beginning to see pieces of death in scenes like that. I wanted to go home to my beautiful bed. Where is that bed today?

*   *   *

At college in the fall I had my second real job. It was in the NYA program for students. I was a secretary for a French professor. At the same time, I had another job in order to eat in the dining hall at Columbia. I washed the dishes. Later I'd bring a pot of coffee to whoever wanted a refill in the John Jay dining hall. I gave a cup of coffee to many famous and distinguished men. Thomas Mann was one. For all that, I went to class, I studied at night, and spent the afternoon at football. I would never have gone to college if it hadn't been for football; my father was too poor. In that sense, I worked well enough to earn a living.

My French professor was a queer and charming man. He didn't have much work for me, routine business, I typed. I went into his office with a smile. He'd holler at me: "Voilà! the Baron Michel de Bretagne has arrived." The poor guy had some paralysis sickness in the spine. He was young, too. He worked like any other man: he got up early in the morning, much earlier than me, and he shaved and he dragged himself to college to work in his office. We'd see him cross campus with his poor tormented crutches. He lived in a beautiful house with his parents near Riverside Drive. I had dinner there one evening. There were candles on the table. When I left I said, in French, "I have to go see my little girl," to make my exit. He said, laughing, "We don't say *little girl*, old boy, we say 'girlfriend.' There's a big difference."

I said to myself, "Because we say 'friend' it takes the girl off the streets? How queer Parisian French is."

One night the Professor sent me to deliver a manuscript to a famous French writer (Louis Verneuil). It was in a big swanky apartment. The famous man came to the door wearing a silk robe. He had a little frou-frou dog. The famous actress Nancy Carroll was there. I could see the tall lights of Manhattan outside the big windows. I saw all this through the door in under a minute. I thought myself far from the saloons and the mills of home. I dreamed of being like Mr. Verneuil. I wasn't far from nothing. The poor young men don't know that the foul darkness is everywhere and always.

What will a young man do with this dream? He will fall. The angels of hell await him. Worse than that, he'll get up one fine morning, he'll look in the mirror, and he'll find that his eyes no longer completely open. The earth awaits him too. You have to bow your head to understand our life.

Around Xmas I worked for extra money for the N.Y.C.R.R. throwing mailbags over the old dirty floor. The bags fell from the big chute, we picked them up, we looked at the name of the city written on them, and we threw them at the part of the floor where the city was written in chalk . . . Buffalo . . . Chicago . . . San Francisco. . . . I was certain of going to all these places some fine day; but I never dreamed of the way I would go. I saw myself going by train with my suitcases in the rack; I wore a nice coat, a hat, I had a watch; I drank in the club car, I slept in the Pullman; I made eyes at the beautiful and interesting women; I disembarked at my destination, I was met by men at the station, and we all went to eat in a nice Rathskeller restaurant. How was I supposed to know that I would go to these places without a hat on my head, with a poor little rag bag, in the behind of a bus, to be met by no one and not eat anywhere because I never had enough money. In my dream I walked with the good men on Main St. after dinner, we smoked cigars. What really happened was I walked all alone, and one time in S.F. I picked cigarette butts in the street to put their tobacco in my pipe.

On the other side of the street from the N.Y.C.R.R. there was an old N.Y. saloon where I ate and drank beers. Time to time I wrote notes on the menu. I wanted to be a great writer all the time. My thoughts were making my stomach excited. I had discovered Tom Wolfe that month before Xmas; since then I have not read anyone so grand, so poetic, so serious in America. He and Melville, Thoreau, Whitman, Twain, we never say that their greatest works were novels proper; with the exception of Huck Finn their best inspirations were in the form of unknown and fathomless *books*—look at *Moby Dick*, *Walden*, *Leaves of Grass, Life on the Miss.*, and *Of Time and the River*. I wanted to write in a large form which was free and magnificent like that, a form which would give me the chance to go out the window and not stay in the room all the time with old ladies like Henry James and his European sisters. I had not yet read Henry James but I had glanced at his manner.

My trip home that Xmas was the most beautiful trip of my life. I write it almost with tears. The bus reached home from the western part of Massachusetts, Springfield, Athol, Fitchburg. There was snow, pines, birches—I had already started calling those "grief stricken birch"—but more than that it was the beautiful starry evenings in winter, the sad little lights in the woods, the old cars of farmers with wood cords in the back seat, and hearing again people speak Canadian and that English where we say "cah in the yahd" instead of "car in the yard." I took out my old earmuff hat and stood outside the lunchcarts when the bus stopped. I smelled the air. My heart was as big as the world. Ah it's glorious to live some times; I do believe it's worth the labor. My father said it; and the Good Lord said it.

At home at Xmas I worked for the Post Office delivering mail with a big bag over my shoulder. They sent me in a part of town where my high school girl lived. It gave me a tiny nostalgia. I didn't see her. There was lots of snow. There were icicles coming down from the roofs of the old wooden houses of New England, something you never see in N.Y. It sounded like bells all around. It was joyous to bring Christmas cards to people's homes. The mothers waved their hands at me. The children helped me deliver, they ran all over the street in front of me with the envelopes. I was the angel that came before Santa Claus. When my feet were cold I went into the saloons to sit near the old wood burning stoves. The old Irishmen spent the whole afternoon with their beers and their pipes and looked at me with their big red eyes.

I always liked sitting in front of the Xmas tree at Christmas with a glass of porto wine, and looking at the little blue and red lights & spend my Xmas with calm thoughts. On the evening of that Christmas, me and G.J. sat ourselves in front of the tree with the wine. At midnight G.J. was drunk. My whole family was in bed. G.J. went to the door of my father's room and he started to make a speech. "Mr. Bretagne," he said, "*vous ne rappele pas mais l'autre matin*—(but he said it in English)—Mr. Bretagne you don't remember but the other morning when I said hello to you while you were walking along the wall of Blazon's store you coughed, and I was walking along the wall of the Social Club and I was caught in the echo between the two walls, and Mr. Bretagne you don't have to believe it but I was knocked down in the snow by the shock. I swear to Christ himself I never heard a man cough so loud." I thought my father was going to be angry, but he laughed. Those were days of grace; the people in my life were laughing. Today they all chase an indefinable health and they're all afraid of communist atoms. I walked G.J. home around the corner, as always. His mother was waiting for him with a little light and her Greek bible. "Thalatta, Thalatta," that means *the sea, the sea*! She was a woman who had lost her husband in her youth and dressed in black for the rest of her life. She worked in the mills. Poor G.J. too had begun working in the mills. He lived on top of a wooden house; you could see the whole town from their window. G.J. would rock himself in the rocker on nasty days, he'd look outside at the town and the river, and he'd say "Why did the Good Lord make us to walk in the mud." His mother read the bible; she didn't understand English. When we got to the house after midnight she lifted her oil lamp in the window and said "Georva? Spiti Georva?" (Lil-George, you are home Lil-George?) "Yes, yes, yes," he said. He walked around the yard with his hands on his head. "Oh God, why does she wait up for me every night? Why didn't my old man live? Why did I have to come into this damned black world?" I never knew a man as sad and as great as G.J. He was like a true descendant of Oedipus the King who took out his eyes; me I'm but a cousin to such things.

I returned to college after the new year. It seemed like the people in N.Y. weren't as strong and profound, they're interested in gay things like some crazy young girls.

I continued with my pot of coffee in the dining hall until the month of May. On Sundays when I didn't work and I wasn't supposed to eat I went into the basement where they kept the food and I would scrape together some pieces of beef and cold roasted potatoes and eat that hidden in a corner like a rat. After that I went into my room, lit up a cigar, and wrote one of my daily plays on the rented typewriter. My plays were drolleries with directions to the stage manager to drive a car around the stage to bring "The sound of time" to the audience. The guys on my floor would read them and found them funny. I took long walks around N.Y. in the night. I stopped studying; I knew what I wanted to know.

I returned to New England in the beautiful month of June hitchhiking with a Saroyan hat on my head. I didn't work until July. I spent the month of June reading Whitman in the fields.

*   *   *

TRAVAIL IN THE MIST

A friend told me there was work in a cookie factory. I decided to try it; it paid over $20. He picked me up one fine morning at 6:15 A.M. I waited for him 5 minutes in the mist sitting on the porch of my tenement with closed eyes. The sun hadn't yet climbed up the hill, on the other side of the river. The big mills sounded everywhere. On the other side of the street I saw a man come out with his lunchpail. He spat out and then hurried to climb the hill to go to work. "Every single morning?" I told myself. The guy showed up and we went to the mill. They put a paper hat on my head, they gave me a shovel, they threw a big cart full of fudge at me, and they said: "Throw that on the belt with your shovel and level it with your hands. It rolls around the rollers over there, it gets flat, automatic blades cut out little circles, it rolls into the oven, comes out cooked the other side, and the girls over there put it in the box. Understand?"

"Yes."

"You can't stop. If you stop one minute the whole factory stops. Understand?"

"Sure." I thought myself strong; I had a whole factory depending on my hands. I started. It was 7 in the morning.

For a half hour I whacked into that thing with all my strength. I'd make big squares of fudge with the shovel and took them out with my hands. After that I'd tear them in two, in fours, I'd break them up with my fingertips, then I'd stamp them level all around.

TRAVAIL IN THE MURK

At 8 I started to think that it was probably 9 o'clock. Not only wasn't it 8 o'clock, it was ten to 8. At five to 8 I started to sweat. I bent down to take out a chunk and my sweat fell into the thing—I just didn't have the time to wipe myself, the boss said that I was going too slow. After 9 o'clock I didn't even try to wipe my forehead. My eyes were too wet to see anything farther than five feet, I only saw my work and my work wasn't clear. Well, I was stuck in a mill. I cursed and I cursed like I've never cursed in my life, I was surprised to see how well I was able to curse. I invented some. I laughed, I cried, no one heard me among the thunder. It was hotter than being out in the July sun. The sweet odor made me sick. I was pretty angry at the other guys in there only because they worked here for years and years that I was sure that each one was crazier than the next. Yet every time a guy passed by and said "How's it going?" I'd always laugh and say "Okay." It wasn't them; it was the people who owned the mill and made it run so fast like this, and the women who were too lazy to make the other *cookies.* That's what I think, and that's what it is. I promised myself to never let myself be eaten up like this again. I started to feel pain in my arm in a manner queer and weak. I stopped for 10 minutes at ten o'clock with all the others to sit in the lockers. My right arm began to stretch on its own; I couldn't bring it down, I had to massage it as fast as possible before a knot could form. I had no strength left.

All of a sudden I thought of the women who make cookies in their little kitchens and I loved them. I thought of their pretty cheeks, their checkered dresses, their little plates, and how in the afternoon the children came from school to try some.

I wanted to leave. My friend told me I'd get used to it. I looked at him and made a face. "How long you been here?"

"Me? Three years November, why?"

"What'd you do before that?"

"I worked in the mills, what you think?"

I returned to my shovel, my fudge that had changed to vanilla, and I started up again. I no longer cursed, I no longer laughed, I no longer cried, I only waited until noon and I went home. It took all day to get to noon, all day and a whole little life in hell. I came out with my hair and my eyes covered in flour melted into my sweat, my pants, my boots, my hands covered with sugary filth, my little white shirt brown like cow shit in the front. I walked home like that, I looked at people in the street with surprise that there were things like this in life and that nobody cared at all.

I saw G.J. in front of a saloon. I told him all about it. G.J. jumped on my back—he was taller than me but I was bigger— and I walked into a bar like that. I put my foot down on the brass rail, leaned on the bar (G.J. clinging to my neck), and we ordered two beers. It was a big fat drollery. The oldtimers it made no difference to them. After that G.J. and I we went into a silk mill; we entered the hiring office; the man was there with his papers and his quills. We entered with our arms stretched out in front of us like the Zombies we'd seen in a picture the other day; we made our feet go slow and automatic like the ghost of death. We asked the man for a job. The poor idiot said: "I don't think you boys will do."

We got out of there running and laughing at the top of our lungs, same as if we'd broken a window.

In the pretty golden afternoon I went to my swimminghole in the woods where we swam bare. I sat on a rock surrounded by water, only my head and my hands stuck out above and I held a book in front of my face, and I read the "Thanatopsis" of Wm. C. Bryant. I wanted to wash myself of the filth in all sorts of ways.

A funny thing happened; an old friar who used to be my teacher at the parochial school passed by on the bucolic bank with his big black robes with some students. I never saw anyone like that there before or since that one time. It's far in the woods, only the young come. I said "Good day, Father." He looked at me; he didn't remember me, it had been nine years.

"Good day. How are you making out?" He said this as if he had prepared me for life long ago. I didn't tell him about the cookie factory, I didn't say anything. He turned around a little farther down to look back at the strange boy who was reading a book in the water. The little students were giggling. I was giggling too. I promised myself to make my own life in my own way; I was certain of everything. I only have to go there this afternoon, go into the water, and sit on the rock with a book, and I will be as certain as I was on that day. But it's ever so far to go play.

*   *   *

One evening that summer I worked for about fifty minutes in the circus. Discouraged, me and G.J. went to see the circus that had arrived that morning at the end of town, at the end of night. It was a circus not so famous as the big ones like Ringling Bros. & Cole Bros., it was poorer, dirtier, more interesting, we thought. The company was from Alabama. We could hear the lions inside. The men who worked were black with dust, they looked mean, they looked like they came from far away. The big tent was old and dirty. It was a circus like the one W. C. Fields ran in one of his latest pictures. We didn't have enough money to go see the show; we watched the girls, we ate popcorn, we walked in the sawdust. There is nothing sadder than bobbyhorses at night with little kids riding, their little faces all serious above the painted horse faces, little hands clutching the bar that doesn't go up or down while the horse goes up & down. Also sad is the ferris wheel, but only when looked at from afar. The greatest sadness is bobbyhorses in the afternoon on the seaside in autumn, like I saw 2 months later . . . G.J. and I spent some time between the ropes behind the tents with gangs of fifteen year old girls and those boys who came to the circus on their motorcycles. We looked at the girls with a desire that is like the desire of senile old men in their second youth, a mortified desire full of death. Their little round flanks wrapped in thin little slacks the color of roses; their cheeks effervescent with beautiful hair, their eyes that glanced sharply like a knife, their ravishing mouths, the scent of the night and the carnival, the pale stars. It seemed as though a big knife in the darkness was tearing out my heart. "She was fourteen and I nineteen, there at the village fair." I wrote that that night.

G.J. and I stopped in front of a wagon all covered in gilt angels, a house on wheels, with windows and curtains, some little portable steps that went up. In the door there was a man with a cigar. It was the boss of the circus. He reminded me of Mr. Miller, he also looked like a tout from Havre de Grace, a man who plays cards in horse stables at night, who leans on the far turn on misty mornings with a clocker's watch. He gave us a big smile.

"You boys want to go to California with the circus or are you staying around here at your mother's apron strings?"

"You going through Kentucky too?" I asked him. I dreamed of going to see the Kentucky Derby with him, I'd meet the trainers and the jockeys with him.

"Kentucky! Boy, I got to see my grandma ever' blessed Fall. We pitch this big tent right outside Lexington, the first thing I do is go and pay my respects, bless her dear heart. You boys come along with us and get three squares a day with pay and you'll see the whole country inside one year. We're pulling out for Kentucky tonight."

Me and G.J. looked at each other with mouths wide open.

"You come on back to this wagon when the show's over and I'll put you to work. Climb up here & sign your John Hancocks."

We climbed up immediately; we wanted to see the inside of the wagon. It was all set up for living; there was a bed, mysterious flags, strongboxes of cash. We signed our names and our social security numbers.

"Ain't no life like circus life, boys," he said with a slap on the back.

We walked around the circus with fat cigars hanging from our lips; all of a sudden we were mysterious & romantic men. "Zagg," G.J. said, "I know I should see my mother before I go but it's too late." He looked sad. We no longer looked at the girls, we were too old for them. All of a sudden I thought about all that great darkness of the America in front of me and G.J. and that filthy circus, and the cold mornings we'd work, and it made me want to go in my trousers. We went to see the cook tent to see the food we'd be eating across America. The two cooks were sitting at a table planted into the ground with a bottle and some cards. A Negro with hair like a Portuguese spoke angrily to them; he was drunk, his eyes were red. He spat on the ground when the two old men didn't listen to him. I watched the Negro, he went to lie down and he started to sleep on a dirty canvas behind the big tent. I'd have to get used to doing things like that.

After eleven the show was over. A big bunch of guys came out of their hay-hideouts all around and they started to bring down the tent even before the people were out. You could see the big tent collapsing like a balloon. They worked fast; they didn't say a word. The merrygorounds, the bumper cars, the ferris wheel, the places where you threw baseballs, everything was taken down. The lights went out, it started to get dark. A big cloud of dust climbed up to the stars. It looked as if the men were hurrying because they'd stolen something. We found the boss and he brought us to an oldtimer who was taking out big canvas bags from a wagon. "Just stand there and hold these bags," he said. That's what we did, one on each side. G.J. sang crazy people songs. We waited for someone to come throw things in the bags. All of a sudden comes a big elephant with a man dressed like a Turk on top. We started to move apart for it to pass. "Stand still!" he yelled; and he started to take off his hat, his rags, big things that were on top of the elephant and throw them in the bag.

"Zagg! Zagg!" G.J. cried. "The elephant's going to step on my foot!"

"No, no" I cried, "don't worry, the elephant's trained."

"That's what you say but look at that damn huge paw near my toes." Then just when I looked the elephant moved a little closer to George. He was standing there wide-eyed looking at the side of the elephant with a fear of death. You saw the large eye of the elephant, the big curved trunk; it looked like it was watching George. George was holding on to the bag but I don't think he even knew. Suddenly he dropped the bag and lit out. "No, no," he was saying, and shook his head, "I'll be a sonofabitch if I'm going to stand for it." He disappeared in the darkness. I was all alone with the bag. The man on top cursed. "Where'd that damn boy go?" He was completely undressed and he looked like a cabdriver, he wasn't a "sultan" anymore. I left to find George. The man yelled after me, I was done too. He was waiting for me behind the ropes, George, pale as a lenten fart.

"Zagg," he said, and grabbed hold of my arms, "I'm telling you that damn elephant wasn't any farther than that from my toe. Not only that, she was lookin' at me. I'm telling you she was lookin' at me. Not only that, she's got skin thick as rock. It's not an animal, it's a mountain. Not only that, these damn things remember everybody everywhere. Me I'm leaving, I'm going home. You can go to the circus if you want. I'm satisfied just going to sit in my chair, I'll never cry about anything for the rest of my life."

"Okay George," I said, "me too I'm going home," and we left. We crossed the great tragic field of the circus. We started to laugh when we were on the bus. It was going to be a great story for the guys. We went home in the beautiful summer night.

Something queer happened. There was a soldier in the bus, he heard us laugh. He looked angry. He started talking with us; he told us he was from Alaska. I had just read about Jack London and the Gold Rush and I knew some Alaska names. I said "Were you stationed up in Juneau?"

"Juneau? What do you mean Juneau?" he said angrily. "You a wise guy or something, Juneau?"

"What's wrong with Juneau?" I said (I was scared, I didn't want to fight, I was too young for a soldier like that).

"So it's Juneau is it? You goddam little wise guy punk," and I thought he was going to hit me, I never understood why.

He didn't let us be until we got to town. I was to meet another soldier from Alaska the following year and it was to be even worse. I guess that Juneau is too far up North and people from Alaska speak of it like Russians speak of Siberia. It's not my fault their damn Juneau. G.J. had been so afraid of the elephant that he wasn't afraid of the soldier. To each his fear in the frightful world. When you're young like that the darkness expands faster than you grow up. Yet you still see a star from your bed at home, and it lasts until you're strong enough and you no longer need stars to strengthen your heart.

*   *   *

My old childhood chum Jack found me that summer. He came to my place one afternoon and we took a walk over to the saloons outside of town and he told me his story. He'd gone into the Army but one night all of a sudden he and the other guys they decided to go take a ride in an Army truck. Jack was at the wheel. There was a sentry at the fence; he went through the fence. They went to New York. On the way Jack stopped at filling stations that didn't run at night, and they broke some cigarettes from out the cigarette machines with a wrench. When they arrived in N.Y. Jack was taken by the police but not the others; because he didn't want to say their names and what they'd done they put him in the Raymond St. jail in Brooklyn. It's an old jail made of blackened rock full of rats. Poor Jack, he was always in a bind, his whole life. He's always been like a brother to me. He was thrown out of the Army. His unit had left for the Philippines; summer of 1941 . . .

But now he knew where there was a good job for us. I told him about the cookie factory and the circus and he laughed his head off. "Yoo-hoo-hoo-hoo! The same old Mike!" The job was digging ditches for a local construction company that had a contract in Portsmouth, New Hampshire, right near Maine, to build a fence around a Navy hospital. A bunch of guys from Lowell were already working; they went in cars at 6 in the morning, every day, and returned at 6 in the evening. Two of the guys were sons of the contractor, the Bergerons. Jack had a car; he was to pick me up at home and charge me $2 a week for gas. It made me feel a little sad, I could see that Jean had grown up and picked up the manners of the world. I've never understood the world anyway, but I had understood Jack once.

Jack picked me up at 6 o'clock Monday morning. I had stayed up practically the whole night reading and writing because I couldn't sleep. It was a grand morning, I could see it through my tired eyes. It made me think of the mornings when Jack and I were kids and we'd get up before the sun to go play far into the woods, when we'd follow the mad cry of the crow into the heart of the forest, and we thought we were Daniel Boone and Davy Crockett. The sky was raw blue with clouds like honeycomb all connected together in little pierced pieces all the way to the end of the horizon. It was as beautiful as the day the Good Lord created the universe. I heard the birds in the cemetery. I looked and I looked and Jack talked. We went up to New Hampshire through shortcuts of old roads I hadn't seen since the times my father had brought me this way to find apples in Autumn. We started to sing.

"Daddy—you want a diamond ring—brand new car—every-thing—Oh Daddy—you're gonna get the best of me."

After that I asked Jean to sing his old childhood songs— "As I was walking in the streets of Laredo one day—I spied a young cowboy—all wrapped in white linen—all wrapped in white linen—and cold as the clay." Jack had always dreamed of the West.

It was about fifty miles to Portsmouth. When we arrived I was sleeping and Jack drove with his eyes half closed. There's always something rotten in a job, if it isn't the pay it's the boss, if it isn't the hours it's the distance, if it isn't the work, it's something else.

We found the other guys; they were all in a big mud field by the water, it was sea water, an inlet. On the other side was Maine, Kittery, Maine. There were shovels and large cement mixers. There was some kind of ironworks in the building at the end of the field with greasy oldtimers sitting out front smoking the pipe. It's always impossible to understand everything we see with our eyes in America. Behind the pines there were Marine barracks. Out came a guy with his bugle and, tara tara, wake up. All of a sudden I wanted to join the Marines. I did the following summer. I saw them come out, strong young men, blackened by the sun, placid in the beautiful military morning with flags and guns racked with handsome black wood. There, in the water comes the finest apparition, a new submarine. The sailors in white were standing on the blue iron deck; the officers in white were in the conning tower. They all talked, they smoked. They had all eaten their nice breakfasts. The cook was there with his cigar in hand. The boat passed through water like a serpent. The length overall of the hull caressed the eyes like when you look at the long legs of a woman. We saw it leave toward the ocean. They were to submerge it that morning. What mystery! Moby Dick was a meditative whale; this is a whale of precision, of modern "know-how," five times worse and ten times more treacherous. I was to learn that the following summer. Oh Ahab!—your poor spear tonight!

We all got on board a truck and we crossed the island. They gave us special shovels to dig deep and narrow; we drove them in with a foot kick then we closed the grip at the top to clamp the sand and lifted it like that. We all worked without shirts. We were in a long line, we passed each other from one hole to another like a game of leap frog. There were some nice fresh breezes from the sea on the other side of the island. I could see a big summer resort by the waterfront far, far away. I thought about all the old geezers that were sitting there in their chairs with tinted glasses that made the waves rosy, their sea thoughts, the little children who dug holes in the sand with tiny colorful shovels, the beautiful girls with bodies of silken white gold waiting for love on the beach. There, we were all in the world together. I wanted to go over there and rip their bathing suits off. I wanted to go in the middle of the green sea on a boat. I wanted everything.

At noon it was hot, me and Jack were already starting to turn red like lobsters. Me I was singing songs from that time, "W.P.A.," about lazy guys who work slow, slow. We worked slow, we all had a cigarette in our mouths. The guys told stories—in English, a curse word at each end, as though they were afraid of being sissies speaking French. In two years they were all going to be on the beaches of the South Pacific.

We ate our lunches at noon sitting around trees, and at one o'clock we started again. In the afternoon the men who work in the earth would surely like to rest their head on the warm sand and sleep. I think the first men they did that, they all caught their meat in the morning.

At five o'clock we all got on board our cars and went to Lowell 50 miles. The Marines asked us for rides; they were dressed in the blue tunics of summer, they were going to Boston to have a good time. In the car they took off their tunics and rode in their shirttails like the rest of us.

Jack and I were so burnt by the sun that we decided not to go to work the next day but to wait for Wednesday. We did that the whole month we were on that job, we worked every other day, it was too far and too exhausting. That night with my red back and no shirt I had 3 hits in a baseball game.

One morning me and Jack were digging alone on the shore of the inlet. After we'd eaten our lunches we laid down around the beautiful trees, near the wooden boards, and Jack told me the story of the girl he was to marry. The boss found us there, sleeping, at 3 o'clock in the afternoon. He was angry as the devil. "What the hell do you think we're paying you for? You guys just don't have any sense of fairness. From now on I'm going to keep an eye on you myself. Come on, start digging those post holes." We didn't say nothing, we hadn't slept on purpose.

"Sense of fairness!" Jack said when the man had left. "You hoo hoo hoo!" he was laughing his head off.

Damn *mautadit* Jack, if he felt like it he'd put all the boards and the shovels in the car and he'd go home with them. When he was a kid one night he broke all the windows of a school with his slingshot, one after the other, a good fifty of them. I can still hear him laughing in the dark near the river—"Yoo hoo hoo hoo! Just wait till they see this tomorrow morning!" It struck him as so funny he had tears in his eyes. After that he put his arm around me and he said, "Wal, let's lope along pardner," and we went to my place.

I started to be afraid of driving to Portsmouth every morning Jack was going so fast. We'd been in a big crackup when we were 17. The guys at work didn't like us because we only came every other day. Sometimes guys are like old ladies. All of a sudden Jack disappeared from Lowell; his mother told me that he went to get married. I didn't see him before the fall.

I was done with the job anyway.

*   *   *

I think my life began to shatter that summer. It's been raining ever since that time. I can say that one evening that summer the night became my woman. Like a Sultan who has 100 paramours in his harem I began to dream of having two hundred, never satisfied—because my life was good in those days, I knew that. My parents were set to move to New Haven to work in new jobs, they were going to be nearby. I was sitting in the hall and thinking about all the accomplishments I was going to have. I was going to be All-American in football; I was going to publish this little story that I had written the other evening about my family moving from Lowell, and it was going to be recognized as a work of genius; so, I was going to be an All-American who was also a literary genius; after that I was going to get offers from Hollywood to act, later I'd become a director and great thinker of modern films; after that, millionaire, married to Lana Turner, I was going to be thrown into politics and be a sort of different Lincoln in a time that particularly needed me; after that, before the funeral (what a queer word!) with the people in tears, there wouldn't be a paramour left.

All of a sudden I realized in the dark parlor that I was a little crazy, nineteen years old catching myself thinking like that on a fat lazy adolescent behind. I looked around me dumbfounded.

As if to punish me the Good Lord took all that apart in 3 weeks.

To start, we moved to New Haven; my father had gone there ahead of time, he was already working, he had found an apartment. I could see that apartment in my dreams, near Yale campus, my beautiful study lamp in a window above the wet and mysterious streets of night, Ah, a son of the gentry. My mother and I packed; my sister helped us, she was set to stay in Lowell. My mother went down to the basement chasing the cat and fell flat on her face; she hurt her leg. That's how it started. En route to Connecticut in the truck the cat got out of the box with his claws and he disappeared into the woods. I loved that poor little cat. The truckdriver told me it was around Wallingford, Conn. Today I bet he's a big fat cat on a farm; he's better off than I am.

My mother and I rode the train to New Haven; it was a miserable & tiring trip in the night; we arrived early in the morning. "Look at New Haven," I said, and there it was, a big dirty town like the side of the tracks, the pink sky above the piles of coal. "Well, well," I told myself, "and the other night I was dreaming of this and that, big pink balloon in golden heavens, Lincoln but different; look how the real world is dull, and dirty, and mingled with vapor and the tired faces of people that make you sick, the discouraging faces of people who eat their own heart in the general pain—everywhere gray shit surrounding their feet. "What are we going to do in this pit of labors?, this troublous dump they call the world," in the filth of all the sadness of eternity. There are men who stick their feet out the window, and warm their toes in the sun and they live like that: for them all things can be bought (legitimate). I looked at my mother: as always she wasn't afraid of anything and saw the dirty world with clear eyes. I don't understand where women take all their strength, they're made so tender, when there's crowds they get crushed. But when the crowd is gone they get up and they're just like they were before, while the men have gone crazy.

Poor little woman, she got up, we took our suitcases, and I helped her go down the big iron steps on the platform full of spit. After that we went to drink ourselves some coffee in a cafeteria. We had to maneuver the suitcases so they wouldn't be in people's way, and go get the coffee, and hang our coats on the chair so that they didn't touch the floor, and wipe the greasy spoons with our napkins. It made me angry because it was my mother that had to do all these things; I always saw her in her little spotless kitchen, and I would have liked it if she had stayed there.

We decided to eat breakfast, spend a little money. The sun came up. We ate our bacon and eggs in the pretty yellow light. All of a sudden I was happy again. It's always like that, it catches the heart, you raise your head to look and all things seem to be trying for the better, a minute ago they were overwhelmingly aggravating or harassing.

We went in the trolley to see the apartment. My poor father had committed to the apartment by phone; it was in an old brick building in the Negro neighborhood where there was swill everywhere on the sidewalks. That morning he was already working in New Haven, he was sitting somewhere at his work with a serious look, and he knew nothing about this latest grotesquerie. My mother looked at the house, the gas tank at the end of the street, the yards full of cans and bricks, completely appalled. There we were with our suitcases in the street; even worse, the movers arrived on time with all our furniture and the paltry things of our lives. We inspected the inside; it was worse than outside, there were broken windows, a nice view of a brick wall, and something on the ceiling that looked like shit. I was young, it scared me. The big movers from Lowell were nice to my mother, we knew their cousins. There we all were in that pig sty trying to figure what to do. My mother absolutely refused to move in there. We decided to bring the furniture in a storage house, and to leave it there until we found something. My little mother had a determined face. We went with the movers. In a big warehouse in the middle of that complex and noising day all the poor furniture that I had seen my whole life with the eyes of a simple child was being dragged out of the truck like the entrails of my family and thrown across a huge dirty platform to be stacked into heaps with the similarly sad furniture of other poor nomadic families. I watched all this with the realization that death was possible. Prior to this I had always thought that death happened only to others. But when I saw my poor little green desk pushed into a corner with the other things in their dust (on the back of this desk there still were the chalkmarks of

my brother dead fifteen years) I understood the great engulf-
ment of the universe—"and I found her bitter." I looked at my
hands, I understood that one fine day, one fine evening to be
precise, they would no longer be hands but some other awful
thing. That one day they'll say, of this here book, the bigotries
of an idiot, "writ by hand a hand no more." I looked at my
mother's desk; in the top drawer she always kept scarves, boxes
of pins, powders; and now there was her drawer in the middle
of the entire world half open, lost, in the ponderous darkness.
It made me want to cry. At nineteen you can't start having
gray hair but you can have your senses lacerated, and your eyes
widened and become more like the stone of the tomb. Thus,
always death in youth, like in the springtime.

My mother and I started our big trek around New Haven. It
was still 10 o'clock in the morning; we walked until 6 o'cl
We had our paper with the ads circled in crayon, th   per
that's always ripped and covered in sweat at the en   he day.
There weren't enough apartments and they wer   expensive.
We walked in the sun as in the desert, fro   e side of town
to the other, we went across dusty par   of Italian children
that splashed in fountains, wide s   hat went for miles with
only trolley tracks and house   ach side with flower pots on
the porch, narrow st   d downtown like alleys through
which traffic w   e some big irritated parade. I no longer
felt like a   te, that and my dreams had all melted in the
brilli   g afternoon, forever.

     , but we saw my father in the evening anyway, and it
seems that I've always seen my father in the evening after the
damned heat of the mad day, I can see him coming down
the street in his straw hat, a solid figure in the sad redness of
the setting sun, and it makes me so happy, a brave man that
has performed labors like my little labor of that day a hundred
times in his life. *And it has not changed him.* I look into his eyes
for counsel about all these things. I only see a kind of united
front between those two eyes, and the kind of pride that is
necessary in a man, the kind that I myself do not have. He was
looking at me with affection; I didn't understand why he loved
me. He was proud of me.

We all sat down in the hotel's tiny room to figure what to
do. My mother made sandwiches with the paltry little things

we'd purchased in a grocery. While they talked I looked at the brick wall outside the window and at the city lights that played upon it. I recalled my dream of the 'son of the gentry' up in his nice fancy window. Then, well, I changed my dream: now, we were a poor vaudeville family in a strange new big city, and I was to save them from their unfortunate circumstances with some heroic feat.

"What're you thinking my little man," my father said in French, tenderly.

"I'd really like to be capable of helping you, *mautadit*, in a manner in which I would be capable." You have to talk like that when you bring out your most cherished dreams honestly, you can't just come out with it cold.

"Poor tourlipi, don't be afraid, we'll manage, don't worry your little head."

"But poor mama she walked all day, she's tired, there's nothing here for nobody. Why didn't we stay at home?"

My father made a face. "Don't ask me," he said in English, "it was her idea."

"Leo," she said. "I didn't want to stay all alone in Lowell while you worked here and Ti-Michel went to school in New York. There!"

"Allright, allright, we overturned it, the pot, now's not the time to talk. We'll manage. Come, we'll go have a glass of beer, we'll have a little fun, if we can't have anything else." We all laughed. We went out, we went to a bar. Like in the old days in the Chinese restaurant back home, my father was happy, my mother had her little blushing joy—but they were a little older, that damned darkness was laboring away.

Yes, the night is my woman, but I was so angry it cracked my teeth when she started making eyes at me in those days. I could see her big legs spread out across the night's sky: I searched for the middle far, far on the other side of the lights. I thought I was going to find some thing there, I had all sorts of names for it; not only did I never reach it; but when I do I'll be too old and it'll be death that I'll find, old bitch bee "*vieille gieppe chiène*." Come, big unhappy woman, I'm embracing you; take care of your boy.

*   *   *

Believe it or not we found a paper house on the sea shore. It's no lie, I climbed into the attic to store some boxes and my foot went right through the cardboard and I got skewered on a beam. I cried like a baby, naturally dammit.

It was a French Canadian who owned the shack. It was on the shore of the Long Island Sound in West Haven. It was a vacation house but the old man said it would be comfortable in the winter. Bradley Point, it was called, with the houses boarded up for the winter (it was September) and the stores a mile up the highway. But the fresh air, the sea, the great vistas of the sun!! It was pouring violently outside when we went to the storage house, my father, my mother and I, to get the furniture with two old mover characters who had an ancient truck. They didn't charge us much; so, my father brought a bottle of whiskey for the gang. It became an adventure. When we arrived we parked the truck in the mud in front of the porch, we put down some boards, and we all carried things through the torrential rain into the house. It was a beautiful little cottage, all the same. I liked it right away. The sea smashed against the rocks in front of the house. My mother said, "I dunno, one of these days this here house is gonna get swept out to sea."

"No, no" I said, "that was only the Sound, they're not big waves here. Rich folks come here. Come on, you're afraid of everything."

The movers were smoking cigars, they were making jokes, they were old characters of life. They said they knew the old character in the shack across the marsh, that he sold clams and didn't give a damn about anything. His name was Popeye. My father was interested. "By God, I'll sell clams myself, the hell with the work. My ancestors were Breton fishermen." We all drank straight from the bottle. My mother was using a tiny paper cup. It really was an awful downpour; we weren't interested in keeping dry anymore, only in having fun. In the middle of the adventure I looked sharply into the gray heavens and I said "Thank you, Good Lord." I thank Him to this day.

I was so drenched that it didn't make any difference, I put on my bathingsuit and I went for a swim. I was half drunk; I was swimming like Tarzan. I went 100 yards and climbed onto a small anchored rowboat that threw itself into the big waves like a cork. What a name—"WE'RE HERE." I sat down.

My mother was in the door of her little cottage and she was waving her hand at me; she was afraid. I hollered over the storm: "Don't be afraid, I'm a Breton! The sea is my sister, she loves me, all is well!" It was impossible to hear me. I went back. I headed to the bottom and turned toward the deep and looked at the great darkness beneath the water with my bewildered eyes: I wasn't afraid, I wanted to see it personally. Toward the beach it was clear, toward the deep it was dark: such is life. I wanted to be a writer, I tried everything.

In the house there was a nice little shower with hot water. What joy! My father had taken his bath, he was already sitting all dried up and clean, he was reading the paper. We had to eat. It stopped raining, the great skies were becoming red and violet. I cheerfully walked the mile to the store, I bought some hamburger, bread, milk, cakes, and came back. My father was sitting on the sea wall with his pipe. The sea gulls screeched on the beach. It was as beautiful as a dream.

"Ti-Michel, I have returned to the sea," my father told me with tears in his eyes. "I've always known that some day I'd live on the edge of the sea of my ancestors from Brittany. It's in my blood, in yours too, that's why you swam like that during a storm. It all turned out well. Sometimes it's worth being alive, *mon ti-Choux*."

We ate a big joyous supper. Night descended upon the sea, little lights stretched out vastly over the water. The stars came out like phosphorescent grains of salt. We sat on the porch with some popcorn, and voilà, we were at home once again.

My big woman slumbered upon the calm waters.

All the way up to those tiny far-away lights, far into the following fall, this "woman" made me pass by on a war ship, and from the deck I looked with binoculars and I saw our little porch from that evening. Because the big woman does not let us remain, she sends us from one side of the earth to the other like the little marbles I used to race in my childhood room.

Some rich young friends came to get me from New York to return to college in their car. My mother made them a lunch. With them I spoke in English and I was a completely different man. They called me "Jackson." We played catch with the football in the sand. After that I packed my stuff, I kissed my mother, and we left. When I saw the little house by the sea from afar my heart ached nevertheless. Ahead of me were all the shiny and interesting things of my college career; behind, my family by the sea and all the sadness of my real life that I had only just begun to understand.

* * *

Three weeks later I got the fuck out of college. I didn't say a word to nobody. I got on a bus and took my first trip in the South. I had my little pencil, pieces of paper, and I was going to be a writer for the rest of my life. It took hold of me just like that. I was entering deeper into my big woman. For me she was America. New England and N.Y. were only her head.

In Maryland when the bus stopped over for a half-hour in the night, one of the Negroes who was riding in the behind of the bus started to sing me his story among the flowers and the weeping willows of evening. "Goin' down to Richmond, boy, my grandfather died. I ain't-a goin' back to no Newark no more, Lord have mercy. Sick *and* tired of that motherlovin' laundry. I'm goin' to stay right where I'm at soon as I get down home and sit down and have me some buttermilk and greens. My mother make it for me in the morning . . ." It was like a song. If that man hadn't talked like that I may well have gone back to school in a couple of days. But no—the great mystery of America "socked me in the belly." I wanted to understand all that. I wanted to go where the train sang "from out" the valley. The stars that melted over the trees, they were the tender angels of my desire for the earth. The moon was making a face at me that I understood. The smell of honeysuckle was only the beginning of my big woman's scent. Yes, now I was ready to come in to find what it was I wanted. I couldn't name it. Like the Negro I wanted to "go down home," I wanted to sit on a little porch in a rocking chair, I wanted to hear the birds of morning in Virginia.

Most of my dreams were of that romantic kind in the black bus.

We arrived in Washington in the morning mist. I found myself a cheap hotel and I started trying to sleep. The hot morning was beginning outside with all the noisings of the big city. There were bedbugs in my bed. I wanted to get away from Washington, cross the Potomac like the men had done in the battle of Bull Run (Manassas?), in the water, take the bedbugs off me, and go get lost into the great green fields off in the direction of the Blue Ridge. Someplace, in the Blue Ridge, was the grave of Stonewall Jackson, and there was a flower in the tree, and the oldtimers talked in the noon sun.

"Goin' down home . . ." and I was only a poor little Canuck who'd read too many books.

That evening it was sad in my room. Outside my window there was a brick wall and a stick-like little tree. I had gone for a walk and there was nothing, only wide streets with mailboxes and trashcans. I wrote my heart out—"*J'écriva mon coeur.*" It made me cry. I had turned my whole life upside down just to write these paltry little things—I was looking at them on the piece of paper. I was thinking that one day someone would read this and cry with me, and it'll do them some good, they'll understand a little better how to live, not hurt anyone as if all men were brothers, and love the little things of our life with respect, not spit on everything, and find a personal peace for themselves made of probity and tenderness. But that's impossible in this here world, and I knew it! Just to earn a crust of bread to eat while you live, you had to go fight and get mixed into the hatred and the shit of others, and into impossibly dirty jobs . . . (yes, there came a day when they assigned me to clean the toilets, 4 years later) . . . idiotic labors like my fudge shovel, the greasy rags of an elephant and the embittering complications of paycheck, timeclock, tax, bill, rent, interest, and a nickel to use the restroom. I already knew that most of the world was populated by morons, America just like the rest. I saw them all spitting in each other's faces from one pole to the other. They called it life, they called it "the economy," worse than everything they called it "necessity" and in the papers they wrote solemn editorials about it. Everything in the damned world was acceptable save for the tears of the heart; those didn't pay, you couldn't sell 'em, you couldn't buy 'em. And they were all I knew, that and the dreams of the beautiful green country stretching itself from one ocean to another around the sun and around the stars of the immortal night.

I was looking at my little paper and I knew all that. I didn't accept it. I was going to suffer, I was going to be a writer, and the Good Lord if no one else was going to thank me. I was already a broke poet. And I wasn't afraid, and I'm not afraid today.

I was just a child and I decided to earn my living in a manner that I found honorable and honest. I was a little lazy, and I depended too much on the help of my parents, but goddam Christ of Baptism I found my own true soul at the expense of a couple of things that won't have much importance on the death bed.

*   *   *

Well, I had to work and try to keep my bones together as tears escaped me from one side of the earth to the other. I returned home to the little house on the seashore. I was going to work, save my money, and cross the country in the spring.

I began once again to walk in the streets of the desert day; my communications with the night were done for the moment. I looked everywhere for a job. I didn't find one before 4, 5 days. It was in a rubber factory 2 miles from my house and not so far from New Haven proper. One morning I got up early and I left with my lunch. The sea was beautiful.

My job was to take a new tire still gummy and hot and pass a little clamp around the ends inside to make it curve in; after that I rolled it to its place and I went and got another one. I did this hundreds of times. I learned a little how to go faster but not too much. There was a noise of hell in the place; the bosses were always right there, the boys looked bored and half dead. Well, I was caught in a factory again, and I had promised myself. I ate my lunch in the beautiful hot sun. I dreamed of my lovely southern fields. A Negro ate an orange sitting on old tires in the shade. My face fell again. I made a fist and I asked myself, "Michel Bretagne, Michel Bretagne!" It was like a voice that called me from far away, like the horns of Wagner in the Magic Fire Music that I listened to at night in my room as I watched the red water. Where? Where? "Where can I go, what will I do?" There was a force in my muscles that made me want to fly like a damned arrow over the road, no matter what direction, and as the soldiers say—Boingg!

I worked until five in the afternoon as sad as Job. I didn't take the bus, I walked home.

I crossed the fields in the direction of the sea, I knew that I would see my house from the hill ahead. There was a pretty little cottage by the side of the road, with flowers, apple trees, a stone wall and a child's swing. If I could only put my parents in there with a little money and myself go take a trip in a boat—to Montevideo, Luanda, Melbourne! "It's beautiful to be rich!" I said to myself—"the damned pigs!" I climbed the hill.

There, the sea, far, far Long Island, and the little shack on the Point my house. What a beautiful September afternoon. I picked flowers, I wasn't ready to go home, I didn't want to tell them yet that I didn't want to work in the damned factory. I went in the direction of the rollercoasters at the amusement park. The sun turned to a color of ancient gold.

I sat an hour in the grass to mourn my follies.

Many of the amusement park buildings were covered with boards for the winter; that's sad, also it makes you cold think-ing of the winter coming; you put your hands in your pocket, you bow your head. The places for cotton candy, popcorn, for ragdolls, rollboards, and all the people who came and went in the general unreward of the ground covered with gray papers. Well, the merrygoround was still open. The last turn; the little children took advantage. They had their little coats, not for summer but for winter, and they rode silently as though they understood the end of the end, the end of the day, the end of the summer, the end of their mortal infancies. Ah the music!— it broke my heart, it came from out of the pines and it went out over the water, way out, way towards the grievous boats in the bloody water, further yet towards the blue form of Long Island and all the damned world in back and the great city too. I ate my leaf of grass, hands in pockets, listening to that calliope in the air that began to be cold, I watched the water, the brown sun, and the children. I died all kinds of little deaths. A fog of dusk descended on everything. I understood nothing, I have never wanted to understand anything else since.

I went home in the dark; the leaves fell, the sea made tender sighs. The star of evening burned in her bed of blue.

I went down the little street of boarded houses towards home. The light of my mother's kitchen shined on the shore alone. What good people, what an unknown and mortified son.

We had a big argument. But there was a letter for me, it came from my old chum Jack, postmarked Hartford. He had a job for me.

Translated by Jean-Christophe Cloutier and Jack Kerouac

JOURNAL 1951

Journal 1951

Typing frantically across three weeks in April 1951, Kerouac wrote the scroll version of *On the Road*, the 120-foot-long manuscript that would serve, after much significant editing, as the basis for Viking Press's 1957 published version. While his journey to the scroll manuscript had been marked by a number of false starts and disappointments, including the lukewarm critical response to *The Town and the City*, by April 1951 Kerouac had moved on decisively from the naturalist grandeur of his early literary idol Thomas Wolfe. He was now exploring new terrains of literary experimentation consistent with what his friend the critic and anthologist Donald Allen later identified as the Cold War period's overriding interests in "instantism," chance, and spontaneity.

Kerouac's relentless and sometimes vexing search for literary forms capable of expressing the energy and breadth of his artistic ambitions finds eloquent expression in his sixty-two-page hand-written journal of August–November 1951. After suffering an attack of thrombophlebitis in August, Kerouac was admitted to the Kingsbridge VA hospital in the Bronx, where he began this journal while bedridden. Still stinging from Robert Giroux's rejection of *On the Road* months earlier, Kerouac struggles to overcome his doubts and enunciate a viable compositional philosophy, finally exclaiming, "I SHALL BE MYSELF."

TUES. AUG. 28, 1951—B (900) I've been in this hospital 2½ weeks filled with growing peace and the most beautiful visions of life and the soul since 1947. I have to stop smoking, I have stopped; result is, sometimes I feel like a little boy and in fact remember whole spates of time from my boyhood; so I could write a Remembrance now ten million words long—how many pages is that?—30,000 pages, about thirty-five huge volumes. Who could read it? Yet the way I feel I'm convinced every bit of it would be good. Foolishness—I'm writing this in bed. The visions, in fact, are the best since 1946 and since childhood. [B (900) above is a count on calory intake, I weigh 166½, too much; 900 c. for breakfast alone, four eggs; ass on bed.] So I worked out second big "labour" of my writing-work-life: the Victor Duchamp *On the Road* epic, which I'll start as soon as I get home, using tried & proven system of *Town & City*—the "daily heap," belief, in fact reverence, humility, much solitude, walking, and now more health measures (less coffee, more tea; alcohol only before dinner, if any). And a world-view backbone to the structure of the fiction. These Tolstoyan feelings . . . I welcome them back, after almost 3 years floundering in "hip-ness" and dissolution and indecision and ambiguity. Though I'm writing this on my back I feel again like my own giant— (and apologies for bad printing). To make a living, though, money for rent, food, money for future need. First, in here, I tried writing a potboiler; I said to myself "Like Faulkner I'll write a goodnatured watered-down monogram of my style, like *Sanctuary*, and make a living"; I'd call it *Hip*; but I don't have the heart for it. It may sound vain, but the act of writing seems holy to me, so much so I can't even be a "hack" in secret; I can't put a beginning and an end onto something which never started and never will end. Holy . . . sacred . . . to use the writ-ten word in honor of life, in defense of life against the forces of death and despair, to make old men lift their hearts a bit and women think (or cry), and young men pause before it's too late for *realizing* to do them any good—why use the word for cheap illiterate vulgar fools who buy books in the mass to titillate their empty beings between vices and hypocrisies. No. But to make

a living. Here's what I've decided: alternatives are as follows:
1. Go home to my mother's, have room of my own, and spend
one year (divided by 3-month visit with Neal in May in Frisco)
writing first publishable half of *Road* trilogy; so getting advance
in September 1952.* 2. Go to sea—save $150 per month, for a
year, or $1800, traveling, note-taking, planning, then going to
Mexico for over 2½ years to compose entire epic *Road* in peace
and quiet, finishing it entirely by Fall 1954, aged 32. 3. Take
$300 I expect on October 25 of this year (or more) and bus to
Florida, living around tracks, four hours afternoon winning an
average of $30, or $180 a week, sending winnings home, to save
either for Long Island house down payment then my mother
pays 40-a-month installments on her own house instead of rent;
or saving for Mexico house & life, probably averaging $9,000 a
year with ORDINARY luck and much more otherwise, always
facing gambler's risk of losing everything—system is this: $10
place on favorite, losing; raise two units of 10, winning graduate
back unit at a time. 4. Going to Frisco in October with my $300
to live in Neal's attic rent-free, working part time job, writing
the epic *Road* in moments of quiet, if any. 5. Signing on with
construction overseas job, like in Alaska or Europe, as typist
or otherwise, for at least $5,000 the year, coming back with at
least 4 G's clear, for Mexico life & composition of *Road* epic in
entirety (which will bring double dividends, being 2 novels, and
lead to other jobs, like Hollywood script, for kicks and study).
These are pure plans and pure alternatives; they inter-cross, and
insomuch as they are allowed to inter-cross, the purity vanishes
and oldtime indecision may creep in. But in any case I shall keep
track of every day left in my life, like this, with the *date* embla-
zoned in my fresh morning thoughts, so no matter what plan I'll
follow, *this* I'll follow. Alternative No. 1 is what I've decided on
at least till I'm certain about that October $300, and then we'll
see about No. 3; meanwhile I'll straighten my seamen's papers.

But now to return to the activities of my writing-soul:—

LUNCH: 800 c. Completed letters to Stella Sampas and
Seymour in England. To keep check, I started yesterday with
$300.00 bankroll, which is now $364.00—(passing up $75
made last Fri. & Sat.) Track is Saratoga.

*Of course meanwhile earning $25 a week on 20th Century Fox synopses.

But how I remember my hometown. I'm going back to it now, thank the Lord, in first half of epic *Road*—(might call trilogy "Fall in America") . . . I remember boyhood dreams that are now, still extant, the most profound thoughts I have . . . that great dreaming hump-hill on Bridge St. that you can see from all over town; the redbrick smokestacks rising like giants into the drowse of afternoon clouds; in fact the yellow wild-flowers dimly powdered on that hill; and—as if Lowell was the world—all this comes back to me here on a bed overlooking all Manhattan north and south, to lend immortal credence to the "phantom isle" on which my life has "faded"—as if this New York of the Eight Million was a phantom isle, or my life faded. This is just talk, fair talk; soon I start the work in earnest, like a Blake. (S: 800 c. sn. 200 c.)

WEDNESDAY AUGUST 29, 1951— 2700 c.; too much. Started today on 900 c. Lost $72.50 at Saratoga yesterday. B-Roll: $288.00 (70). Alternative No. 3 may not be—FALL IN AMERICA is about what happens to a young man in this country in ten years, what on earth it means . . . why, where, when, what for . . . In my past ten years, reaching back to Aug. 29, 1941, what has happened to me? I'm penniless in a charity hospital today; yet in 1941 I thought by now I'd be rich, famous and a father, owner of a house, mature. What happened? If anything, I was at the point of being like in that dream I had down south: a 30-year-old hanger-on (of small pensions?) around Skid Row saloons, going downstreet of an evening with an old mattress under my arm, to sell it for wine, my face beaten but not yet broken, muscular-armed, halfway between football player and hobo. In 1941 I dreamed (I remember it, in the parlor) of such success that when I snapped up everything real seemed dumb—exactly ten years ago was the moment of the beginning of my Fall—Fall in America, the sad Autumns of realization—

Imagine a book starts like this: "What did he say? Did you see him?" "Yes. He had the same strange look on him all the time I was there." "And what'd he say?"

Further betting records in back pages. (L: 850 c.) (Sup: 850 c.) Just right, 2400 for the day. Still don't know what the decision is, by the doctors, on my illness; supposed to walk tomorrow.

Am reading magnificent introduction to *Pierre* by Henry
Murray, *Pierre* itself, and *Under the Volcano*—a superconscious
work that seems valuable to *me* but not to literature in general
(as *Pierre* is)—whatever this means; unless, merely, that I can
see Joyce and Proust to new advantage in Lowry's tremendous
prose, but prose in itself is not enough when you go beyond
my private mulling studious peering, to the larger demands of
literature where you have to be a Melville, provide emotional
dignity, a lifetime of indefinable charm, work of unmeasur-
able sincerity and soul-sorrow, to count: and I agree, what fun
when I learned today that Melville "imitated" Byron!!! *Volcano*
has in it hints of heaven, and that's a lot. Too long I've been
considering myself a literary critic—*Under the Volcano* is part
marvellous, part crap. *Pierre* is a Kraken. Ate another 200 c.
later in day, to go over my quota like a pig (but felt weak). At
8 P.M. nurse told me doctor said I could start walking—which
I'm doing. O Sax!—save me from myself! I want to write *Dr.
Sax, now*—(although, speaking of Murray's *Pierre* intro, I shall
have to ask him to autonomous-inward-operate me no aroused
soul-images or other Jung bunk, the dumb fuck, p. xliv). It's a
sin to know too much, or rather, there's a punishment attached
to knowing too much—I caught myself just now. The snake,
the child—to make deliberate symbols, or just let the legend
of the snake take me over? Prefer the latter—reading Murray's
intro makes me want to write *Sax*, the snake in the pudding
of *T & C* and *The Road*; where I would portray my mother
as she really is (conjuress, mystic, prophet, gravedigger, little
girl, madwoman, pal)—(my father what he really was, sterile,
or that is, impotent, or castrated)—(my brother himself the
Snake)—these mysteries?—but why make such a big fuss over a
spear? (so to speak). In October of 1948, refreshed from *T & C*,
I really had this *Sax*; now all's left is the desire, no more body.
But I'll do it from the bottom of my mind and then all this
means nothing, something else will have to be said.

  Thought and thought till late at night. Where will it get you?
I ask myself—to consume yourself on thoughts of "what you
should do," what is right, "great"—25% or more of your energy
wasted on vanity. EVERYTHING YOU DO IS GREAT, said
Neal, meaning, DON'T WORRY, WRITE! Good and evil as
it haunted Melville concerns me no more—I'm too old now for

problems of duality; my Orpheus emerged some time ago. (I thought of re-writing all my youthful works, including *Orpheus* and *Vanity of Duluoz*, desperate for exploitable themes.) The truth is, now, at 29, I'm only bothered by the spectre of death and as far as I'm concerned that Snake is only age & death coming after me. For while there's life, there's indefinable charm, and ripeness is all.

THURSDAY AUGUST 30, 1951—Started day with big 850 c. breakfast (4 boiled eggs). *On the Road* as I wrote it this last spring is still an existing work of 150,000 words that I ought to do *something* with—cut out, put in, sell. But again . . . that word OUGHT. I'm being consumed by an ecstatic sense of doubt; no greater joy than perfect doubt and all those masks. Ah but these days of joyful reverie on a hospital bed; the pure mornings, the will to do everything (not just "choose"); the air, the vistas, of an America and even a New York City that is young, upgoing, just-beginning. For me, it will be HEALTH, WILL, CURIOSITY, SATISFACTION, THOUGHTS, EXPRESSION forever—functional, not desperate; glad, not dissatisfied—Talk, talk, talk. The immense power of life which is greater than the puny self-problems is the fountain from which I draw my work, my water, my existence; setting an example in spirit. Ah Lucien Carr, you and your little sadisms beneath the evening-star; Ginsberg, your humiliated doubts on the plain of night; Bill Burroughs, don't die!; Neal, verbiage is not your jungle! Phooey. Either I, or Holmes, continually peek(s) over my shoulders at these words. It's all a lie, a lie, a lie, a fucking lie. *J'ai menti.* Last night I dreamed of Mexico—I was with Lucien, suggesting a bar on some haunted deserted San Juan Letran more like the Lowell of my childhood sorrow. What is this writing of lies?—this yakkery?—what for? I'm bound to it by an order that came from heaven *recently* . . . or was it long ago? This is silly. No bold nervous beauty either. If I have to claw it out of myself, literally with a grapple hook bleeding, I'll produce those great books—if I have to rattle on like this till doomsday, till all the rattle is gone and the strike strikes—a venom of lies to heal the body truth, the parent truth, the apparent truth, the truth, the saying, the mouthing, the blah, the belief in happiness. (Future ages will believe in happiness.) Another inch of thought and I'll have it—"what to do," "how to say it." (I lost it at strike strikes.)

Let's solve the problem of my so-called soul today & decide once and for all what to do. I have 10 million dollars in the bank that I might as well spend when I get out of this hospital—(no amount could get me out sooner than the doctor wants). First off, a trip—around the world or straight to Mexico? on ships, freighters, Am. Pres. Lines, or fly, step up tempos?—and why the need for the economy of Mexico now? What's in Mexico that's not in my soul now? Shall I set up a trust fund for my mother, get her out of the shoeshop, get her a house? She'll be afraid alone in a house when I travel. A 2-family house, renters upstairs; or just an apartment in Jamaica somewhere. As for me—a pad in Manhattan, for thinking, writing, wenching, parties, talk, for friends, I sleep there half the time. (It doesn't matter.) Now what else? Give Neal a trust fund—give Joan & baby of course a trust fund, big one, why not?—give Carolyn one—now buy a house in Mexico anyway—Oh, a house over-looking Frisco, on a Sausalito hill—a visit to Paris—but for what? Sooner or later I got to decide whether I'll just spend money (I can't eat more than 3 times a day, can't smoke, can't drink without ruining my health no matter how rich I am) or decide on what to do with my soul. Why,—shall I write, like I used to when I was poor and human? Or shall I just concentrate on beautiful women, romantic voyages, interesting friends? For this I'd have to make rich friends, my poor friends would have to grow rich with me—so I go into business with my poor friends and since money makes money we all get rich together—now my old poor friends are my old rich friends. But they change *their* friends & ways, and no longer interest me after awhile? Meanwhile I lie sideways in a bed with the naked legs of the most beautiful warm women in the world wrapped around my hips, looking them in the eye as I penetrate their soft vaginas. But even this palls after awhile and I see no love on the horizon. The only love is Divine. Adam was a nervous mistaken friendly good intentioned fool; Eve, far from being from one of his ribs, was a cool haughty beautiful dull-souled somewhat vague unfriendly cunt-creature from the other end of the forest who accidentally stumbled on Adam like a little boy is found playing on the riverbank not bothering anybody and told he has sinned. All Adam had to do was ignore her, but he didn't know how and so went along with what he knew were the laws of nature but wasn't much interested. What is nature compared to the desires of the secret mind?—or compared to the idea of God, the abstractions of immortality, beauty and joy. Adam is a fool because he is abstract. Eve is not a fool, only a negative nothing, a hole, a hole of Calcutta containing the universe in suffering, in which Adam will lose himself if he doesn't watch out—The "rib" idea was a trick to make him buy Eve . . . buy a part of himself. It's Eve's mother that you got to watch out for, she plotted it—the wife of Zeus, dammit! (Whoever.) Adam wants to be alone, he needs Eve once a day, for two hours, just like the Mexican peon, that's enough of the drowning nature-bath; time enough for that in the grave; Adam has a MIND to develop, bridges to build, concepts to formulate, sciences to make exact, literatures to elicit from his personality. But what about Adam's mother? She is the earth, the silent stormy gloomy mystic earth. Then Adam's wife is not his mother's sister, but a stranger—a sinister stranger from the other end of the forest. Adam is a multimillionaire. Now he has nothing to do but stand up and assert his right to be Adam the man, in his work, and set his forest in order, or be a goddamn cuckold to that Lesbos goddess primitive Zeus & Haverty got hung with. For this is not only the age of Freud but the age of Lesbos. Adam's got to make up his mind and stick by his decisions. Besides, Adam, by himself, must pray to the morning sun, whether he's surrounded by this & that or whether he's alone—he must pray & praise the universe of God, he must make his sorrows the sorrows of time, the sorrows of—must! must! What do I really mean. And what shall I do now I'm a multimillionaire? (950 c. L.) The bankroll fell to $194.00. Marcus Goodrich, Malcolm Lowry: same. Why should a man undermine himself? If the culture myth cracks, why should the man decay?—(and in the name of "truth" or what we now call facts?). I can't buy the myth, I don't want to die. Are my fondest memories just memories of parts of the myth I can't or won't buy. When I set about writing *The Town & the City* I decided the myth was still vigorous and okay and I'd buy. And I still think, in fact know, that society has good intentions. To accept the world I shall have to reject

the ghost . . . give up the ghost. A good thing to give up. I
hereby accept the world:—This will include everything, everybody, shortcomings and all, including Joan; I accept. (Youz'
all fulla shit.) If I reject the myth I shall have to substitute one
of my own making or decay. *At least I do know I don't want
to decay.* Still, what else is living? "I have decided to consider
annihilation," Melville would have said at this point. But not
me in the morning—dew is fresh on me in the morning, and
it's morning every day. I only succeed in undermining myself.
What is my self made of?—the will not to decay in a universe
of decay ("don't decay, Pyotr Alexandrovich, don't decay!").
What could I make for myself with which not to decay and that
I could believe?—some vaster, sounder universe than *T & C* in
which I can godlike do as I fuckingwell please. And, however,
anyway, what's wrong with the universe I've already got?—just
because I'm not a God in it? But I am, I'm a multimillionaire
in it; of course I'm a god . . . or the trouble is there are no gods
in reality, and the real universe means death for all without
any other God but the Multifarious Mingling at the end of
Eternity. In other words, when you lose your individuality you
lose God; and when you do that, you're on the edge of the
grave of mankind, headed for the Eternal Realms of Immortal
Oblivion? But to live on earth it is necessary to believe in yourself. Therefore reject all possibilities that there are no gods, no
God, no godlikeness—no vast & charming individualities—or
die. Ripeness is all. The study of Character is the study of God
and Man. No other study, whether objective or projective subjective, should occupy the mind of the man who does not want
to decay. Unless you are a member of the new selfless Marxian
generation of the Infinite Mass-Ego Mystery . . . like some of
the doctors around here. (Dostoevsky knew everything.) Ah
this wrangling with myself! I'm too dumb to be a writer and
if I were a millionaire I wouldn't bodder.
    War is the wild excitement of making the earth shudder with
panic and joy—war is the parent of man.
    Then this afternoon I realized that it's not so much that I'm
a multimillionaire but have to stay in this hospital the rest of
my life, couldn't spend it anyway and have nothing to prove
to the world which comes beating a path to my bed-tag I'm so
rich and tragic: so what do I do with this lifetime of solitude

& meditation in a cell? Why, amuse myself; and since it is my amusement to create character (and test it on the rigors of fate), create character it is. But since I am now to be engaged in the production of character I must, I will do it right, find channels for its outflow (bookforms). And since I'm making books, and the nature, or function, of a book, Platonically speaking, is that it be read, then suitable for reading by others they must be, the function not being merely the *writing* of it. And since I produce books, I must market them, or have them consumed, else why else produce them, so I make them consumable, or readable, which is more than you can say for Lowry, Goodrich, Buechner (very good) et al. Since I'm weak and need iron bound discipline, there's none better than that imposed by pure fate—just as the histories of my boyhood marbles were determined by the pure race down the incline (and duly, seriously recorded). They were marbles and their function was to roll, in my case, to roll in races; now the marbles will be characters, their function "becoming the sum of their misfortunes," the sum of which I will have to determine by pure chance, the shuffling of the deck of fate. Just as a marble looks. Just so, and has doom of its own all ingrained even before it races (like old humpbacked Don Pablo, potent Repulsion, impenetrably beautiful silent Ebony Hill), so a character comes laden with a FATE-NATURE even before she, Fate, has a crack at it. All this under the one vast heading of The Chart of Supreme Reality, containing Properties and Categories of Man together with the Irretrievable Types of Happenstance contained in Fate—either a deck, like my baseball deck, or a roulette wheel. No more me, (not too much)—no more friends—just iron-bound hand-downs from God & Fate to my work deck which sits on the lip of destiny, since, incidentally, it is necessary for me to prove that I am a great writer, I want immortal fame. ⌐⌐

Supper was 700 c.—2500 for the day, over again.

FRIDAY AUGUST 31, 1951—Hot, humid day. Started again with big breakfast—800 c. And after all that I wrote yesterday my thoughts are entirely different today—bending to Victor Duchamp again, my self-legend. But really and truly it's time NOW to decide what to do with already-written *On the Road*—Dean Pomeray and Sal Paradise . . . or perhaps Peter

Martin. Yes, yes, yes, Peter—or better, a complete third-person Duchamp type of another order?—or Duchamp himself! Or better—ANYTHING!

A new type—for the study of those who are ignorant of good and evil—Dean Pomeray?—Jack Kerouac: he who knows good and evil and has yet to say a word about it.

Lost some more money at the races. The malleability of "imaginative creation" is finally driving me mad. What I need is to become an immovable fixed saint.

But Dean is an interesting new type. (L: 800 c.) Wrote a crazy letter to Livornese that I probably won't mail, asking to borrow wire recorder. What on earth is ucla, that which made me think of palic yesterday? (I almost understood in a dream.) I'm really crazy now—I talk to myself in public lately.

Slave on one miserable unit in the showering universe of reality that's driving me gorgeously insane—that's what it will have to be like to rewrite Dean *On the Road*!—a paltry, incomplete, unsuggestive pindrop in a circanum of roaring joys. But didn't Shakespeare confine himself to Hamlet for the month?—a drab ragtag at the hem of eternal robes of purple and gold? What's Hamlet to Shakespeare?—an apple he ate one morning.

"High blood pressure, low blood pressure, arthur-itis—no sir, nothin' wrong with him!" (Pic Jackson in here.) (No better humor than that, the American spade's.) (S: 500 c. together with soda 200 c. makes 2500 for day, over again. Weighed myself this afternoon, 169¼ lbs., gained 4¼.) Slob of fat.

There's the reason for being oneself—for the sake of the complete truth. *T & C* is a myth—the language is a camp—Peter is (as Lucien knows) an obfuscation, a lie, and an exculpation. I have a thousand hip reasons for discarding incipient fascisms like the theories of decay, decadence, joy, health—the whole thing a hincty dualism to show off, to blow up, with. No—I'm not going to owe allegiance to those I love (who are a part of me but not my masters, i.e., my brother Tom, Mike, my mother), I'm going to have to tell the complete truth. If this is the decay of a great civilization then I'm part of it; at least I tell the complete truth, and change the horror of trying to lie all the time, for the horror of hell's bright glow. Whatever, in God's name whatever—I SHALL BE MYSELF and write that way, without fear, without shame, in the dignity of my

experience, language and knowledge. (I have it!) To hell with
the lot!—I don't belong to anybody but myself. (SN: 150 c.,
2650 for day, fatso.)

SATURDAY SEPTEMBER 1, 1951—Started with 550 c. breakfast for a change. Show bankroll is $332; place bankroll is 335
dollars in the hole (no good). Show-roll is four days' work, $8 a
day (!) (no good). Yesterday's decision will never be surpassed as
a manifesto of personal belief:—*to be like Duluoz in the morning
again*!! (and as I dug in Liverpool, my Liverpool Testament,
which I've got to find). HERE WE GO, WORLD! (at 29).
Now my show bankroll is $394, or that much in 5 days, about
$19 a day (very good!). [Place bankroll is now only $41 in hole.]
(Ice cream: 100 c.) Yesterday received great letters (2) from Ed
White, whose coming to N.Y. this Fall will enrich my life. Wrote
to him & told him; he's 29, going to be an architect, doing
just the right thing; his kind of nature needs to be occupied
at something solid.—The whole world needs Ed White.—I'm
willing to work at anything to make a living while I pursue my
ideals . . . I'm even ready for the new kind of Spanish Loyalist
Army, whatever it is, as long as I'm fed and given a "gun"—my
ideal is the new type of American democrat who has come to
solve all the social problems of the world. (L: 800 c.) Who
is he?—let me delineate him. He is hip to things.—Because
after all I'm NOT a multimillionaire and NOT doomed to stay
in this hospital for the rest of my life: I am among the striving, the living;—I must do not what "amuses" me but what is
CRUCIAL, at once, continually! (if not eagerly, anxiously). I
AM LIKE DULUOZ IN THE MORNING AGAIN! (800 c.
S—2350 c. for day.) Weighed 168½ today, lost ¾ pound.)

SUNDAY SEPTEMBER 2, 1951—A date that will never come
back. A cold gray Atlantic seaboard day, great for thoughts. 650
c. B. Read paper all morning.
    In notes written earlier in this hospital, for the "legend" type
plan of my lifework, I said: "What happened? (in last 10 years
of my life). Lived & furied & lost." Typical of the "reactionary" plan, the Wolfean-Nietzschean-Aryan structure, to imply
loss; and typical of the other end of the duality, the "Duluoz-
complete-truth-no-legend" plan, the reality structure, or

what-happens-exactly structure (connected with Joyce and yet curiously with Wolfe influences, for to me Wolfe means non-metaphorical, exact, complete description as opposed to sometimes-Proustian metaphor & cover-up)—is anyone willing to understand this?—typical of this second type of plan to rescue the past, not from loss, but from mere desuetude as writing-material, and typical of it to be more involved & interested in reality itself than in theories and legends of philosophic or psychoemotional loss. That's said. I'm in complete agreement with myself to be wary of another wave of "legend" emotion which can cancel out all this and present plans; connected with the possible return of this wave (which is like a dark storm) is my feeling for blood relationship, especially if a non-relative should soon doublecross me, my consequent "pouting, brooding" return to my "own kind" (the legend of that, the *T & C* universe of that). In complete rational accord with the "non-relative world," however (this means everybody except my mother & possibly my sister now), I seem to tend to non-legend plans, the legend of my blood becomes a remote rumour, a romantic abstraction in the real world, understanding of which, after all, I only accomplished in moods far removed from blood-moods, as, for instance, with Neal.

Here's a chart to illustrate:—(the Duality & its properties)

LEGEND PLAN	*COMPLETE-TRUTH PLAN*
CULTURE	CIVILIZATION
(Spenglerian)	(Spenglerian)
My family's *opinions*	My friends' *opinions*
Dark mystery of river night	Bright mystery of Mexican afternoon
Town & City, Peter Martin, American Wolfe, Hal Chase	*Vanity of Duluoz*, Bob Duluoz, Canuck Proust, Neal Cassady
Fame & friendship & joy	Obscurity & knowledge & enjoyment
Dark turrets of Victorian manses of moss	Dreaming parapets of creamy apartment houses
"Best seller lists"—popularity	"—" —mystery
Tender men & harsh women speaking English	Harsh men & tender women speaking French

If I hadn't been split in the cradle I wouldn't know half as much. The only criteria to use for fiction is natural interest . . . how much to talk about gray days in the beginning is how much it interests you, and the intervening events till Frisco likewise and as rememberable. Everything belongs to you because you are poor. (L: 800 c., S: 800, Pop: 100 Total:—1700, 2350 for day.) The strange adventures of—Oh loneliness, it's you will be my auditor—of myself.—To tell a story with all your heart, is that grammar?—to explain yourself completely, in full truth, is that grammar? I should therefore make it a rule to compose willy nilly, swift, ungrammatical, like a dazed man writing down the dream from which he just woke, and as I did with the Ozone Park dream, instead of getting hung up on sentence structure before the baby's even born.

MONDAY SEPTEMBER 3, 1951—Started, wisely, with 450 c. breakfast. Had the vision of Neal in the Hudson—it, the car, the very shape of it, and Neal in it, was the perfect metaphysical representation of our time: it was Neal's way of clarifying all our issues, putting them together and on the road, holding us close, making himself right captain, and on; so that even when we gave Professor Lenrow a ride and chatted about the last time he saw Tom Wolfe as we drove up Fifth Avenue, it must have all been justified at last for Western Neal, all tied-in, and just because he thought of that Hudson All Boat—*started writing today, never to stop again*—(explains wild print here). Neal in the Hudson is even more than this—it was the deliverance of our freedom, the chariot of our meanings, the justification of our rebellions, the boat of sorrows as well as the car of kicks, the expression in shapely steel of our swift thoughts, our traveling sex-room, a "bull session" capable of flying any-old-where and seventy miles an hour, the slave of our eager sometimes meaningless wild irrational needs. The machine-fruition of our nameless yearnings to fly through lyrical space, the reacher of coasts, the hinter of death at any moment, a dashboard-drum, a wild radio, a crosser of the Texases of reality, and with Neal in it suddenly coming around the corner to get us for a trip to the other side of the world it was the climax of youth, freedom, the joy of Western Civilization, spiritual progress, and the triumph of love and friendship over fear and gloom. Wheee!

It's a camp to fake stories—that's what I think about so-called fiction-plots, all that crap.

(Sn: 100 c., Lunch: 650 c. Leaves 1000 c. for ice cream party today.) Thought while dozing, hearing radio: the music between the singer's choruses abstractedly masturbates his accomplishment, like a bemused woman on a cock.—Won about $10 worth of "prizes" at VA carnival in yard here; including dark glasses, lighter, and a cane that I went and lost . . . good wooden cane with a rubber tip. Ate 600 c. of hotdogs etc., to make it 1800 c. for day. Met a girl I wanted to hug and squeeze and then fuck on the spot but couldn't in the crowd in broad day. In photo taken of me this afternoon my skeleton's starting to show. For supper ate 400 c. plus 100 c. miscellaneous, for a 2300 c. total. Weighed myself in the morning at 168 even; have to drop to 165 or 163. (My *skull's* starting to show.) Bankroll is $394.00, broke even yesterday.—The show system; place is in the hole 241 bucks.

TUESDAY SEPTEMBER 4, 1951—Bankroll is $419.00—the 6-day-week average earning is at $102. Place bankroll back in black, at $112, but still a loser. (B: 550 c.) (L: 850 c.) The horses of dawn, the grays racing for the ghost, followed by flaming palominos two by two, have passed the meadows of loss.

P	Ah, favored sailor Give the dying man your peaches Save it up	In ink unknown Print on stone Secret woes of dying does.
O	The worms'll get it: Don't remember your own mind?	
E	Think you're more important than the world?	
M	Though sick men make you sick Your belly's bonanza Won't be ballyhooed below.	

Ice Cream: 100 c.; S: 850 c.—2350 for day.—The Capitalists are offering shiny materialistic slavery, the Communists are offering drab dark slavery: A big ad today said: "The tycoon is dead"—this is so only because he is organized now in an unspoken Union the purpose of which is to promote and "assist in the responsibilities" of the "free world" (the Western Imperialist world). The tycoon was not a philosopher, he was a rugged individualist—the union of tycoon-types adds hypocrisy to selfish evil. But all this is better than the fat Commissar, for everybody, though the battle or even "peace" between two evils won't make a good. Sat in the sunyard writing all afternoon . . . a few miles from a similar rocky-cliff yard at Horace Mann school where I sat out the 1940 graduation exercises in Whitmanesque loll because I had no white pants.

WEDNESDAY SEPTEMBER 5, 1951—And I've finally realized my life is so complicated, full, interesting & rich that I don't have to go anywhere else for all the plots of my writing-lifetime:—Hudson River. . . . Dave haunts it; Baker Field; Warren Hall . . . Sebastian haunts it—and the same all over America. Detroit, Frisco, Denver, No. Carolina—haunted all over. My *first section of confession and storytelling* covers Aug. 12 to Sept. 1, 1949, with Neal across the USA—my first slab of hauntedness, of awesome event, of wonder, of the perpetual but ever-changing agony of life. I also thought: why not write account of circumstances under which fiction is written daily, for a complete record & evocation of American Mood.

At first, during Vets' carnival last Monday, the realization that I *couldn't lose* took away from me a strange feeling of piety that I suddenly realized harsh life had been giving me for 29 or at least 25 years:—and I sheepishly accepted my first prize with the hurt feeling of an angel placed in an evil heaven for the purposes of temptation. The other fellows felt the same—AT FIRST. I wanted Lucien to be there to determine, with his great comprehension of good and evil, how far God had gone, after all, in making life an agony, an uncertainty, a final dark loss for men and women and all the children & monsters of the earth. For if God had made it impossible to lose, everyone, as we became, would have become real robots, dolts, desouled idiots sweating to grab more prizes that already there's no room for and no reason for—as it is, most people are like that anyway, and the only redemption open to the materialist, the greedy opportunist, is that he's going to lose. Hosannahs to

Heaven on High that we've been born to lose! Don't you see
that? After awhile, in fact, I began to get sore when I didn't win
what I wanted, and finally I was brought back to my senses by
losing the cane, going back to the empty carnival in the driz-
zling rain, remembering the dream of the Marin City carnival
and the stale sandwich prize (1947), remembering that loss is
my Shadow . . . remembering . . . & realizing:—he who loses
shall gain Eternal Life. This is the Agony—you can't win, you
can't lose, all is ephemeral, all is hurt. (I had a vision of Tom
Wolfe clutching at his throat!) And now that I understand
agony and loss I shall never write anything but the truth.

B: 600 c. Bankroll: $407.00—batting 12.60, 75-60 weekly
(show). Beginning of *Doctor Sax*: "And now I will tell you
about the snake that lies coiled beneath the dreaming fields of
afternoon." Me, the teller of the strange adventures of myself,
temporarily telling a tale (!). Everything has to obtain from the
bottom of the source, which is my mind. Here I am this afternoon laid out like a Frans Hals in the great dreaming hillside
grasses of the hospital estate, beneath great trees—a hill like
the great hump-meadows of the Merrimack, a grounds like that
of a castle, a haunted house, or the modern castle, the Hospital;
drowsy clouds of immortality fixed upon the slope-top grass,
upon the cornices of Building B, upon the mind forever—this
is the estate of a mysterious multibillionaire, myself, a lonely
eccentric wandering bemused with a twig as red sunset lights
the slopes, sunset from the river, the clean bridge, from that
other dreaming field to the left of the apartment buildings that
can be seen in that 1942 football photo of me (elbows on knees)
taken in Baker Field practice field, in Columbia uniform, field
to the left of this whereon, as in my most spectral dreams of
New York, sit several wooden cottages as in Galloway Lowell,
all of this in full view from this castle grounds of mine &
including Baker Field, even this year's football schedule, and
the El that travels on to Horace Mann & further Manhattan
fields I found in life; sunset with a twig; and by mid-afternoon
golden lulls and lamby sleeps, the multibillionaire, reft of the
desires of the world, knowing only sweet agony & the desire
of time, lies composing with a hillock for a back rest—silent,
dark-glassed, all-microcosmic-and-macrocosmic, doomed,

beautiful, meek, languid, unapproachable, looking, listening, still, sweet, agonized in peace.

The first requisite in this kind of lifetime-writing is to be capable of handling your own personality, in just such a way that it's not concealed, nor distorted, nor apologized away, nor over-stated to the point of madness and boredom.

The alcoholic says: "I need a drink to tell if this is good"— the teahead says: "I'm too high to tell if this is good."

And now, discourse, I'm ready to write about Mike himself, not just pale imitation Joe Martin—Mike, the haunted house, green apples, Rockingham, quarries, he & Robert etc. oh.

I'm going to be a Wolfean Proust, a Whitmanesque Dostoevsky, a Melvillean Céline, a Faulknerian Genêt—in fact, a Kerouassadian Ginsbergian Shakespeare.

Il faut vivre en Anglais, c'est impossible vivre en Français. This is the secret thought of the Canuck in America. *C'est important aux Anglais*—it's important to the English . . . so the Canuck does it. But one thing I must always remember in this Canuck dualism crap is that in 1934 in Montreal I was so homesick to come back home to Lowell and resume my big imaginary world in English—(the Turf)—that I was almost sick, and sat at a desk in Uncle Gil's study and planned a tremendous newspaper for when I got back. The spirit of *pleasure* in solitary occupations is what I've got to recover from boyhood for manhood's work of art . . . The huge gray-day preoccupation with *files*, records, systems, small print, hoary histories in dusty ledgers.

The confession of my entire life will get everybody off my chest.

Another quarter-inch of thought now and I've got it. Shall I just *write my units* every day and file them in proper place?—for whoever told me that I was a *novelist* anyway! Was NIETZSCHE a novelist? "It is late afternoon; the grapes are turning brown!" Who cares that the man who said this was not a novelist? —L: 1000 c. S: 700 c. for day total: 2300 c. and I feel hungry tonight. Spent dusk hours with that girl, on lawn, Blanche, says no, or that is, can't say anything else till dark and has to be gone by then. I talked a blue streak to her, like a mental patient . . . we sat on my afternoon-hallowed spot. Loneliness forever and the earth again.—Shelley Winters is a tragic looking girl.

THURSDAY SEPTEMBER 6, 1951—B: 700 c. Still wrestling
with the dual angels—what'll I write? What'll I do? Dreamed
of losing money and crying. Yesterday the girl, & talk with my
mother over the phone, proves that even though I am a writer
and not just an ordinary writer I will die alone, be buried in a
naked grave, under an unknown tombstone, forgotten:—Why
should I be different than anybody else. From now on I give
no quarter to casual girls—and I'm going to go about my own
affairs in peace & dignity no matter who's around (—like the
beautiful meditations of a bus trip once broken up because a
girl sat near me & smiled). It is my last and only life and I'm
going to do exactly what I please with what's left of it. I'm
going to sea and I'm going to write what I feel like when I
feel like writing. I'm going to Frisco too. Bankroll: $396.00.
Weigh: 167½. That's what you may say about the past—there
was *need*—otherwise it wouldn't have been done—and even
though everybody has died—they were there, there was need.

Today's teenagers are no different than girls of 1937 dancing
to Hal Kemp—different clothes, airs—they all end up married & raising kids . . . the most predictable and dependable
creatures on the globe.

Old songs I'd forgotten—"Barney Google," "There's a
Rainbow on my Shoulder"—

I see there was near-revolution in America in the 30's—New
Deal relief calmed angry poverty-stricken masses—bloody
injustices were perpetrated by police—anti-Semitism was rife—
Harry Hopkins was an idealist—the C.I.O. had bloodbath
beginnings—Walter Reuther was a young martyred idealist—.
The credited producers and writers of the mighty successor to
All Quiet on the Western Front called *The Road Back*, plus the
stars, are all forgotten—and something has gone out of life
that was in the faces of Babe Ruth, the Duke of York, Jimmy
Foxx— You no longer read about the "poor" or the "world's
unfortunates" or the "underprivileged."—

L: 750 c. S: 700 c. Sn: 100 c. 2250 c. for day, feel hungry.
Now I'm exercising running up stairs. Read all day—old *Life*
magazine 37 times, Jelly Roll Morton, Jesse James. Someone
called hospital "to find out how I was"—Joan calling to check
on my whereabouts so she can keep the law up to date; the
empty souled, unloving, unloved blank. To think that Kerouac

got hung up with a blank!—that the model for Peter Martin should have ended up with a dull hearted post, poor gleeful Peter of the night. . . . where is he now?

FRIDAY SEPTEMBER 7, 1951—B: 700 c. Played ping pong, shot pool. Lost $147 at races! Bankroll is $249.00 and in the hole 51 bucks. Lunch: 1150 c., principally ice cream. Weighed 167½ this morning. S: 650 Sn: 200 (egg nog). Total: 2700, still feel hungry. Exercised a lot. Am reading Lomax's "Mister Jelly Roll"—great material by an important writer about an American artist who will live . . . Jelly Roll Morton (without whom maybe Mamie's Blues wouldn't have survived). In the afternoon, in my fields, I discovered once & for all that I need my wire recorder. . . . I recited 5,000 words about the winter night in Buffalo 1944 . . . either that or first "pure" draft to be written in French . . . In any case I need help—after all, the mechanical difficulties of writing by hand are over 50% of the trouble involved in swinging a thought from brain to paper—

SATURDAY SEPTEMBER 8, 1951—A God-given day—and I in the morning, beneath birdy lutings, writing this. The mysteries of the world are all over me today. The pang of life is that the moment you realize you want something it's gone, it's gone, it's gone— This morning the waters of the Hudson are blue and pure as Atlantic waters sparkling in the bay of Halifax in October, fringed by pines—the Palisades, the antique edge of America, are a vast primeval wilderness. The secret voice of America is crying in the wilderness. . . . life is too short, life is too short, bring back my love, bring back my youth. The ungraspable phantom of life will not cease tormenting us. The beauty pure of morning is only a pain of loss— Every man is alone in his pain; every man was made to gawk in graves; with just an hour in the sun meditating upon the tombstones of great men. Oh bring back the original morning!—and stamp it in gold to last forever! Each year I grow more & more horrified of my growing older—thought I'd get used to it, but the moment I'm used to being 29, I'm 30 . . . Life is too short, life is too short, I hear the secret voice of America weeping in the wilderness—I hear among the thrashings of the bush as the morning birds take baths in dew, I hear the secret voice of

America dying, dying . . . Even the crazy men have exploded
and disappeared. These are the thoughts of my sedate and
sepulchral mind this morning.

I think of vast families discovering death one by one—of
sisters who loved brothers, of the brothers who grew old and
foolish; of the sister's cousins that died young—of cousins who
murdered—or the sons of Negroes, who blew Gabriel's horn in
the alley—of the nobel heroic fathers with no brains—of the
mothers who knew a century in one chair—of lost cries still
batting around in the winds of October—of buried infants
remembered by the dying—of charred & ruined houses of
home—of the phantom of what was haunting the ghost of
what is—of the valley in the morning—of the brother who was
the sea, the brother who was mad on the road, and the brother
who only knew dolors and cried.

In the afternoon went to ballgame, Yanks vs. Washington,
with other patients, in a bus; saw Home Run Baker collapse
before he reached first; got drunk on 10 beers; came back and
saw paper and was more surprised to see that Bill had finally
killed somebody with his gun and made headlines to boot,
than that Joan was dead; couldn't sleep at night. (And in the
morning, I didn't mention, I played 3 hours of hard baseball.)
Strange big day. Now I'll believe in life more than ever—I
know Joan didn't care, nor Bill. And to think that I wrote
"Bill, don't die!" only a few days ago. At the ballgame with me
was Slim Jackson (Worthington), yelled, after Mantle's 460-
foot homerun, "He done heard my cry! he done heard my
cry!"—("that mothafucka done heard my cry!")

Even though poor Joan is dead I have to continue this self-
satisfied diary. Had 1200 c. of beer, add that to 550 c. breakfast,
900 c. lunch & 650 c. supper, totals 3300 c. for day of sloppy
self-indulgence. But bankroll skyrocketed to $510.00!!

SUNDAY SEPTEMBER 9, 1951—No breakfast. Bankroll still
rising—is now firm at $508.00—well, almost rising. Average
is 17.30 (gone up), for weekly average earning now at 103.98
(in other words, I'm earning $104 a week & $17.30 daily). I
don't know what's wrong but today I weighed 171½!! This has
got to stop. Last year while living with Sara I thought I was

overweight at 167. Then, as now, I had unending opportunities to eat good things all I wanted. For instance this noon, though I applaud it, I had a dinner like at Aunt Cora's on that seaside farm in Salisbury in the old days—mashed potatoes with lovely Brussels sprouts sauce, two helpings of tender boiled chicken; *four* vanilla ice cream & fresh strawberry desserts. As long as I stay in this hospital I'll grow fatter. But I get out in four days, so . . . Your grave'll just temporarily change plans in the ant's domain. Lunch: 1800 c. Sn: 100 c. Supper: 250 c. Total for the day: 2150 c. That's to make up for yesterday. Wt: 168½.

Sat in the sun all afternoon, with books, paper, harmonica, realizing I've got to decide on my life's work before I leave this hospital, which is several days. I have *visionary tics* (as the time approaches)—epileptic ecstasies of the mind, say like the vision of pines in the morning in Marin County California; comes, vanishes in a second, leaves me wondering how I can fit it into my life's work. In fact today—

MONDAY SEPTEMBER 10, 1951— . . . today I must decide— and to bring this on, I'm going to write the issue. I want to find a way of writing not just suitable for my "next book" but for all books that I will write from now till my dying days—(or my dying dies)—(I don't say "old man" days because I don't want to ever be an *old man* in the heart, or in the will, the mind, anyway)—a form that'll fit me for life, just as if I was going to be a hermit and all I need's one suit: and I really *do* only need one suit. I'm not swayed by the big-business idea of writing which has come into existence in America since bestseller lists and readability surveys—if I'm to be thus swayed anyway, I'm to admit that I'm writing as a business and not "to just make a living," certainly not as the lifework of a man who wants to honor life as long as he breathes because "work saves all" and he doesn't want to occupy himself with anything less absorb-ing, less complete, personal (the unspeakable visions of the individual), and joyous:—like prayer, like oratory, poetry . . . but why defend the indefensible. As if there was any harm whatever in making money. The harm comes from *trying* to make money out of something which in its nature has nothing to do with crass materialism. Never mind the money. It doesn't matter. Make a living as a seaman, as a worker, for now, because money will anyway roll in after 3 books, and supposing it does? The royalty of next month I really don't need. This is not the point. (I get $300 next month.*)

I want to find a *lifetime* form like Balzac, Shakespeare, Dickens, Whitman & others found—because I know I have as much energy, and that I'll rot if there's no "channel" for this energy—(a grand female form for male substances). But I can't think of it. A *Comédie Humaine* is for objective mind—but today I can't "write the issue."

Breakfast: 600 c. Modern times have produced a civilized mankind which is hopelessly and *luxuriantly* subjective—that's why in fact none of us has bothered to read all of the comedy Humaine, which is an objective surface survey of the "chemistries of society." This is why Proust, Joyce, Wolfe & Faulkner & James are the orators of the day—lonely subjective souls (and Céline). Something introspective, secret, censorable & dark has come into man.

So my *lifework*, to keep with the times, & anyway to keep with how I secretly feel, is to be subjective—how everything appears to be *to me*. Now for a vast subjective form—merely the confession of my days.

Breakfast: 600 c. Lunch I: 550 c. Lunch II: (ate lunch twice):—650 c. Leaves 600 for supper.

But not so much "the confession of my days" as to recount the interesting things of my life—and "they," the things, are legion, to me and to anyone interested. To tell all this—*à mon Ange Guardien*. But I won't release the rest of this secret for awhile. Suffice to say, I made an additional beginning in five minutes this morning . . . (as though with me, as with USA Civilization, procurement procedure is more important than material). *Assez!*

Supper: 550 c. Whiskey: 100 c. Sn: 100 c. 2550 c. for day— too much. All day the thoughts, the thoughts—the Visions of America, the Pang; the fights at night, the Neal-like boxers,

*I think—

my realization of what I could write and never will ("I'm Robert Nixon, you'll never hear of me except at Sandy Saddler's camp"—"I'm Jack Kerouac, you'll never hear of me because I gave up fiction"). Spent the afternoon in the dream—wrote a draft of French—This journal using its losefulness. Yet maybe nothing gets done without a great, honest, grave, disciplined journal!

TUESDAY SEPTEMBER 11, 1951—Railroad men by the dewy shacks. . . . an American construction job in the early morning in Arctic Greenland . . . Hot Lips Page singing "Basin Street" like Louis . . . Jelly Roll Morton playing piano in a cathouse in 1907 dreaming of a lion breaking down the door. . . . An old 18th Century redbrick armory overlooking the Bronx morning where Washington's horses once had grazed. . . . Red beans and rice cooked together in a bucket. . . . Rusty old railroad track disappearing round the bend in the pine forest with a couple of shacks just beyond where some of the boys play cards, in Arkansas . . .

B: 600 c. L. (2): 1000 c. Bankroll: $311.00—severe losses today. Sn: 150 c. Supper: 500 c. Total:—2250 c.

WEDNESDAY SEPTEMBER 12, 1951—Getting out today. B: 500 c. Weigh 169½ anyway but feel strong & great. Bankroll upped a little to $357.00—Sat in the morning sun thinking of an American mythology combined with yesterday's American Scenes and Visions of America—a magazine called Big America (for discipline)—taking people I know, putting them everywhere, doing everything, the narrator a tremendous protean figure who finally appears to be a Great Liar. It's GOT to come somehow—I *need* to work—SOON! So this is my last day in the Hospital where I have learned at last to think—and healed—and learned to think on life as a great and beauteous thing, no hassle, *in spite of what happens* or what anybody says. Here's the title for my Lifework Mythologies—*Adventures in Life*.

(. . . the young laborer's father who was a crane operator across the dusts of the Pentagon project, who left for Texas, after a big drunk, for bigger prey.)

Characters of the Mythology (some of them)

OLD BULL BALOON (LEWIS)	JEFFRIES	WILL DENNISON
BIG SLIM	LANDESMAN	SLIM JACKSON
G.J. RIGOPOULOS	TONY	DORIE JORDAN
DEAN POMERAY	HELEN P.	LEON LEVINSKY
JUNKEY	ARTIE SHAW	(PHILLIP TOURIAN)
(CANNASTRA)	SALVEY	BEATTIE G. DAVIES
(FRANK MORLEY)	SCOTTY	JACK BALLOON
(CRU)		(SEYMOUR)
(CHAD KING)		(JERRY NEWMAN)
KINGSLAND		HOT LIPS PAGE
FITZ		MIKE FOURNIER
LITTLE JACK		KELLY
ZAZA		BOB B.

THURSDAY SEPTEMBER 13, 1951—Getting drunk—
Holmes, Liz, Rhoda, Jerry Newman, etc. Feel wonderful, yet
like crying.

SUNDAY SEPTEMBER 16, 1951—Everything set at my
mother's new apartment. I'll have to move my desk in this
week—do a few scripts—pick up seaman's papers—fill out a
Guggenheim Form—above all get going on my work. I finally
solved the 3-year problem, that wondrous *last inch of thought* I
needed, while riding in a bus in the rain past the freightyards at
33rd St. and 11th Ave., en route to Jinny's pad, which is, merely,
tell everything the way it actually happened *PLUS* any other
way you want for a 100% plus universe. In this way, in complete
objectivity, I can write about myself as if I was some other
guy and with as much sympathy AND idealized invention as
I would writing about other people either real or/and/plus
imaginary!!—for example, I can write again about my father,
true or "false" events, even give him *a brother called Old Bull*,
sticking to facts only, such as that he died in 1946 . . . The big
saga of everybody I know everywhere at different stages of
their lives, and this includes Slim Jackson as well as Big Slim
the real . . . the crowded events of men in different places real
or imaginary—and beginning (only because I have the material

ready) with Dean Pomeray (who is 100% real and then more) in that stage of his life when he exploded out of Denver in search of his America & ended up in Frisco (leaving the opportunity open to write about Neal *ad infinitum* throughout his life and also anybody else interesting, real or imaginary) . . . all of it belonging to the same universe of events over which I in my mad laborious imaginings preside, for life. Now the way is at last open for me to write all my life, like Balzac, on one master structure which is my vision of life. All this was decided in a flash, around two in the afternoon, before I went over and balled 24 hours away. Came home today—a letter from Neal, just had his third child, a boy, named, after me, and Allen G., *John Allen Cassady*. With Oct. 25 royalties (?) I may take quick visit to Frisco at last—

But the solution of my lifework I attribute to the month of pure meditation in the hospital and thank God for it—it was getting late, I was rotting away.

Began writing at home . . . several hundred words before supper.

The point of departure must always be the locale, the gang, the *fame* of our character therein.

MONDAY SEPTEMBER 17, 1951—I'm not going to count writing-words until they're relegated officially to the main manuscript, and I'm not certain whether that will be typewritten or written by hand (printed) in a master notebook. Had to go to N.Y. to pick up work at 20th Century Fox and my typewriter in Lucien's loft. Saw Holmes and had long joyous talk with him— (he's typing his novel). Then saw Allen G. and a girl called Nory, a subterranean in somber Bohemian rags with curly elfin head of hair and looking like a pretty boy with a girl's body; we talked till 3 A.M. by candlelight and I was amazed to learn that Adele my old flame is now going with Norman Mailer . . . I thought he lived much more glamorously. They told me how Mailer was attacked by hoodlums in his own house, at a party, and Adele screamed. Talking to Allen (who considers himself hip enough & young enough to belong to these subterranean styles) made me depressed— At 4 A.M. I staggered across the field with my big old typewriter that my father used in Lowell Mass. before I was even born—the typewriter Charley Connors flailed and moaned upon (Jimmy Bannon)—the typewriter

with which I not only wrote *The Town and the City* but my
earliest loomings in 1937. If all my life, in spite of anything that
happens, is connected by that typewriter to the one unswerv-
ing idealistic purpose which was revealed to me in youthful
dreams of pure glory, then I don't care if it weighs a ton as I
carry it across the night. Hello everybody, I'm back—Listen
everybody! (wearing a flannel shirt hanging out, carrying a
briefcase by one finger) I'm Jack Kerouac of New York City,
author of The American Comedy!!

TUESDAY SEPTEMBER 18, 1951—Value this day, Jack, and
thank the Lord. Woke up just after Joan and apparently some
lawyer unsuccessfully tried to get in the house, maybe to hand
me a summons. Alackady, what do I care? Ate a hearty breakfast and settled down to work. What I wanted to say about
today was this:—I feel so happy, so grateful to God for bringing
my soul back to me (it had wandered away and made me mad,
just like Artaud says), that I feel like writing hymns as in 1947
again, and will soon.

Wrote in the afternoon, absorbedly—then took a long glorious
walk which was full of thoughts I think I'll write . . . (perhaps
keep a notebook called "Walks")—thoughts about the unpre-
tentious America to be found in Negro & Italian naborhoods;
things we have now that I love and will vanish . . . B-movie
houses in the afternoon, penny candy stores, children's penny
& nickel toys, real old *cart* diners, even the rubbish in the
weeds near a bus stop,—(America's becoming so pretentious
even flies are disappearing). But this was not an anti-American
tzimis—merely a method of enjoying my consciousness of
America . . . which is everywhere I look on a day like this. A
thousand more thoughts . . . in the evening I realized the close
affinity I have with Sinclair Lewis after all . . . and all day the
burning will to write & write. (Wrote about Dean Pomeray
in the poolroom today.) At night Joan called, got hell from
my mother. Watched television; ate good dinner; enjoyed the
whole day and conclude it with this prayer: "Lord, protect me
from bitterness, from mad disgust, but light my soul with a
portion of your love forever." Because, too, I am an "apprecia-
tor" among men before anything else, narrative, writer & all
that bunk—first and foremost *one who has been called to justify*

the ways of God to man, to praise and explain the hidden riches heaven has bestowed to men on this dark earth, and the hidden infinite unfathomable love within it.

Now it's no longer loneliness I can call it, but the presence of divine love during the shallow hours of personal time; it was never loneliness—; it was the realization of not-aloneness, the roar of peopled darkness all around, the hint of great and comforting love. No, it isn't loneliness that kills men—it's the madness of despair. . . . It's depression, the willingness to be discouraged . . . the ignorance, unreflecting, harried fury of so-called "busy days" . . . loss of childhood pure visions given by angels . . . ordinary misconception of values . . . I haven't the words right now, nor proper inclination, to name the things that kill men. . . . but beautiful loneliness is every man's first, last, and always guardian angel, amen. I wish tonight I could tell in many million words all the things I am going to tell in the next fifty years or so—tell it all in one timeless, roaring, pain-haunted, sweet consciousness of love, not girl-love, life-love, all-of-love, the entire joy and sorrow speaking.

WEDNESDAY SEPTEMBER 19—Went to jail today—for 10 minutes . . .

FRIDAY SEPTEMBER 21, 1951—Hectic events of jail, etc., of Tom & Ed showing up, of Rose, etc., prevented me from keeping diary and also following the bankroll . . . nevertheless I wrote a (1000) beautiful words in yard yesterday afternoon . . . about Dean's birth & his mother . . . "throat-choking hope." Instead of *hope* I wanted a word that means fearful anticipation . . . but hope looks well there. Will write more every day. Soon I'll type first section officially. The Joan-jail-support business almost drives me mad—to me it's like insults rammed down from the sky, I can't do anything to defend myself. The fruit of my labours will not go to her, they will go to me and mine; somehow I've got to fix things to make this certain. She has eyes for my life's sweat-of-the-brow . . . my life's work . . . a thief as much as any other . . . vengeful: all this started because I spoke my mind in a letter—etc. and why bother. This journal is to be about life . . . let the dead bury the dead. Tom & Ed— what a sight!—we drank the Bom as of lovely yore.

> When insults from heaven ramming down
> Crowned the rotund king with ire,
> When Xerxes fleets confused the waves,
> When Agamemnon wailed,
> The light of the sun was the same
> As on that old dry dog turd in them thar—weeds

Mainly life, the gift, is a length of consciousness—it doesn't matter what you do, it's how long you can do it. A great day spent picking up my pay at Fox, paying at support bureau downtown, $5, 3rd Ave. El ride to below Chatham Square (glimpses of Chinamen in groups in crowded doorways below, the thickness of the life-scene), down to Fulton Fish Market on foot, the waterfront, seaman's papers, clam chowder in a 106-year-old sea food restaurant overlooking wharves (Sweet's), back uptown to Jerry Newman's record store, 3-hour conversation with gin & coke in that great backroom (which is greatest in N.Y.) with Bill Fox and for awhile Barry Ulanov (my visions of a Balzacian N.Y. again & how I wish I owned that backroom and could record the era with tape-recorder as it confidentially tells stories behind the hand—and Jerry wants to make *money* with that machine!). Then Tom & Ed & Holmeses at a party at Stanley Radulevich . . . ending with a lyrical ride back to Long Island in Buick 3 A.M. (You see a cundrum in the weeds behind the garage wall and your loins swell, you see thighs, your heart sings with the air of October . . .)

SATURDAY SEPTEMBER 22, 1951—Seriously thinking of resuming this journal on typewriter, loose leaf notebook, to get more details & phrases in that I can also be using for the novels. Sort of hungover today, but elation & joy—ate, saw TV game, sat in yard, read papers, wrote in journal.—Worked out the personal legend, the fictional family, for the whole American Comedy: I'm Jack St. Louis till death do me bury; I have, besides my real father Leo St. Louis (from Rivière du Loup Canadians, who originally were Bretons from the village of St. Louis near Brest, near Daoulas, Brittany), a distant Western uncle whose kin originated from a southern branch of the family before it changed its name from St. Louis to Santlouis (in North Carolina) and whose name is Old Bull Lewis—

(W. C. Fields)—the Western branch having changed the name from St. Louis to Lewis (the same as the Moultries) and to which, by inter-marriage, Dean Pomeray is related, making Neal my Western cousin, which is exactly what he is, & W. C. Fields my lost funny uncle in the night. There are further complications of the clan, including the vast intricacies of the New England St. Louises scattered from Quebec to New Bedford, and in-laws of New York which include the family of Lucien Love or whatever I'll call them. Tom & Ed came at night, we played pool in the Democrats club with Lucien Ouellette of Canada. Took long 3-mile walk in Jamaica colored neighborhood.

SUNDAY SEPTEMBER 23, 1951—Apparently had nothing to write today though I wrote a little & sang a lot by the railroad yards—and did a $5 script.

MONDAY SEPTEMBER 24, 1951—This is the first day that I've had death on my mind since I started this journal. Hooray for me, I always lose what I find. If what I found in the hospital—peace & joy & wisdom & dignity—isn't mine then why should I live. Sometimes I think the whole trouble is economic—otherwise people, when I look back on my family's life, have no destination but the grave through a road of misery & shame. But John Kelly used to wonder if I had a sense of humor.

THURSDAY SEPTEMBER 27, 1951—Big binge—including cocktails at Kingsland's, Walter Adams, recording Maxwell Bodenheim with Jerry, and going to Paterson with Allen. No work—except a few lines in a cafeteria. I wake up drunk in some strange house with my mind reeling—a million images race across my brain and I lay there gasping for breath and twitching . . . getting to be a drunk.

The reason I haven't done much writing in my room is because the light is weak and I've been waiting for my desk & papers to arrive—have to get them myself. Now in these fabulous past 2 days here's what happened:—I went to Fox & picked up a book called *My Turkish Adventure* which is about an American schoolteacher in Turkey, in a brand new green dust jacket. I put it in my briefcase. The next thing, I

despaired . . . went roaring in the streets downcast. It was cool
& gray. I went to a Nedick's for a small 10¢ hotdog—suddenly
in the raw autumnal wind I felt tremendously & miraculously
hungry, so much so that I was almost happy. I was wearing my
only pants, the pearl gray gabardines bought in Spring 1949
when I was a big success to be sharp in, but now only worn in
beat necessity, with the cuff rolled up a peg so I wouldn't have
to hitch my pants high and could let them hang comfortably
around my hip bones, a trick that makes me look like strange
big-hipped Armenian fullback with woebegone trousers (etc.);
wearing them plus my dirty gray flannel shirt, no tie, just this;
sort of light and airy looking garb on cold gray early Fall days,
with the briefcase swinging and dangling from forefinger and
middle finger, with unzipped top, a trick that sometimes lets
beer splash in. I decided to get drunk; already I was a mess.
From then till now 48 hours later I got twice as dirty. Went
to Holmes, started on brews while he typed; had long talk;
for awhile in cafeteria earlier I had written a few lines about
Neal and his old man in the junkyards drinking with Rex (and
other things) and now I dabbled a comma or two. Then Allen
came and he and I migrated to Kingsland's . . . by now I was
drunk on beer. At K's I passed out, woke up next morning
on the floor; Allen also on floor. Got up, showered, tried to
sleep, lay, as I say, in a strange room with my mind reeling and
a million images making me writhe and gasp and marvel and
twitch and feel foolish and great. Then others got up and in
a minute it was "cocktail time" and there's K mixing martinis in the tall glass mixer used in the movie *Adam's Rib* (the
actual one itself) and me just having told myself I'd never drink
again: and meanwhile when was my novel going to get written, my over-the-hurdle piteous second novel which was going
to shoot me into my lifetime work, see? Martinis; Edith Piaf
records; Marlene Dietrich; Billie Holiday; Kingsland dancing,
Allen yelling, a delicious drunken lunch of hotdogs and sauce
and ears of corn; scribbling long inscription in *Town and City*
for John; then we all repair to another cocktail party, Walter
Adams', uptown, whee, in a tenement a long railroad flat done
up chic with thick rugs and there's the two mothers of the two
boys in their cocktail hats and it's five in the afternoon and
cocktails and smart talk while I, ashamed in my dirty filthy

clothes, read Freud's notes on Dosty in library and Walter comes to chat with me about Lowry & Faulkner and Carson McCullers whom he considers greatest American writer; I get drunker and drunker, on Manhattans, eating only chips; off we fly now really stewed in taxi downtown with last dimes and invade store of Jerry Newman and go in backroom and start on gin and Jerry plays me my recording of my chapters on jazz in *On the Road* and it is on street loudspeaker, my own writings, my own lonely voice, saying, "it was a warm mad night in San Francisco in 1949 and me and Neal . . . etc."

Then we all fly, 4 now, to San Remo; enroute I talk to Ann Tabashnik, Normie Schmall, etc., and in San Remo I meet Barbara Hale and Marc Brandel, etc., then Maxwell Bodenheim (and Hugh Bell) and I persuade Kingsland, no I mean Newman to record Bodenheim, so off we fly the 3 of us back to record store where Bodenheim sits in small cubicle saying "I began writing poetry in Chicago in 1902 . . . etc." and me sitting on the floor with beer and Jerry with earphones, then Bodenheim reads his poems, then he passes out awhile, and I call Allen, who comes, Bodenheim wakes up, more talk, more recording, then as I sit on floor looking him straight in the eye Allen Ginsberg recites in a hollow and crazed subterranean river night voice the epic Shroudy Stranger lines. . . . and Newman is bored and wants to call it quits, so I stagger off with Allen and the old poet and we go to his poor cell of a room on MacDougal south of Bleecker but landlady won't have visitors after 10:30 and we have to file out of pitiful room and talk about poetry in the street. And then Allen and I stagger off to Paterson N.J., where I wake up next morning in his father's house with a wondering fear and persuasions of my imminent death but as if the bats of whiskey consciousness & not so much an honest presagement. And Allen the Great and I, after hour of records and big breakfast, walk five miles around Paterson N.J. . . . . visiting East Side Park, talking about Mexico, going down River St., gazing at the Passaic from little bridge, talking about the Stranger, down to river, mills, the Stranger's arboreal broken-down brick piss house home by the weeds and tincans of the river slime, the Stranger's private hiding place and beach, the horrid grim cliffs and chasm of the Falls, talking about Joan, and Bill, and Lucien, and Neal, and all, and circling around

the city and looking at Garrett Mountain for the castle of Dr.
Sax and going up and down until we were so exhausted Allen
couldn't talk and I took first bus back to N.Y. after snack and
desultory sad communications with his father the famous poet
Louis Ginsberg whom I like and who asked us how was old
Bodenheim. . . . said B. drank too much and wasted his talents
thereby and I'll be goddamned if that's not what I'm doing.
But enough of this too, too weary doggerel and dread drear
dream. . . . back on Times Square I saw a foolish fight on the
sidewalk, 20 men stood by without moving a muscle to stop it,
and I threw my briefcase on the sidewalk and moved up to stop
it but the big guy looked strong and none of the watchers made
a move to help me, in fact no one probably saw me, and I said
fuckit, if they want the world this way, let them stew in their
own evil, and I picked up the briefcase and went home. When
I opened it here in my little cell and took out the book (*My
Turkish Adventure*) which I have to do for tomorrow afternoon,
it was completely torn and abrased and stained from the beating
it took *inside* my briefcase in these past 48 hours. And so I write
this as my testament of faith. . . . for I believe in life not so much
in men, or women   I believe in life   I have nothing left to live
for but life. . . . Oh God up in heaven save me and help me!

All this written Thur. morn at 1 A.M.

During Thur. daytime moved in my furniture with Lucien
& Cessa Von Hartz his fiancée. We made a beer party of it.

~

FRIDAY SEPTEMBER 28, 1951—So now I finally have my
desk, radio, papers & innumerable tiny mementos (including
old clothes harkening back to Fall of 1948 and the New School
& early excitements of wild bop which have since subsided, for
there's no more Royal Roost and I no longer wear my Western-
hip shirt). I couldn't resist yesterday springing to the typewriter
to tell my tale. . . . Think I'll make the journal on type, then.
Now I must write. Breakfast: 650 c. (And write to Neal . . . and
lots of things to do, but mainly *write like mad*.) [Till Oct. 25.]
Supper:—950 c. Wrote all afternoon—the drunkness of old
Dean Pomeray . . . "the poor chagrin of bums."

Good Lord, spent all day breaking my head over 3 sentences.
At this rate I'll die under a rock. Got to make it—I'm sure to

go crazy if I don't. *It's just a matter of deciding to take things over!!* Coffee: 100 c. Snack: 750 c. Total for the day:—2450 or more, too much. (Note: Later discarded 3 sentences.)

Ah, I can't even write any more. And then again, it's not that—it's forgetting that *I have no time for poetry*, only time to tell, tell, tell . . . exactly what it is. Spent the weekend at one thing or another—Carolyn & Paul arrived from South, little apartment in gladdened turmoil. I spent time with Jinny. I decided never to drink again at last . . . now I'm really on my way to something. More anon. On Saturday I ate 800 c. in food and the rest all beer—also some dexedrine, tea. It was my last foolish damn binge. On Sunday I had no more than 2000 c. all day. Decided I'm a man of 30 now, no more foolishness. More anon.

MONDAY OCTOBER 1, 1951—Did 2 scripts, went in town with Nin—handed them in—at night, after wandering around B-Way and writing in cafeterias, attended jazz session at Birdland, saw Rudy Williams, Eddie Lockjaw Davis, Terry Gibbs, Don Elliott—nothing much doing, except that Williams combines Sonny Stitt and Charlie Parker and may become great (not enough melodiousness in his tone & ideas, unlike Parker). Was with Rose—later in shroudy stranger weeds of night with her—& she be great. No drinking whatever. I've made up my mind. Be high on life. Ate 1500 c.

TUESDAY OCTOBER 2, 1951—Woke up feeling fine—joined little Paul, my mother & Rose in sunny yard. Watched Giants-Dodgers playoff II. Talked to Nin & Paul. Rain in afternoon broke up Indian Summer day. Last 2 days literally (for me) fasted. Wrote in late afternoon. Oh and incidentally I finally typed first pages of official manuscript of *On the Road*. So here it is, Oct. 2, **1500-words**. Wrote considerably more this evening but haven't typed it yet. This journal grows dull?—I figure to compose 75,000 new words and incorporate 75,000 others from *Road* ms. before Xmas—end of book or bust:— this depends on sobriety, staying put, stamina, purpose and general soul health.

WEDNESDAY OCTOBER 3, 1951—A day in baseball history, with that homerun by Thomson . . . Nin, watching on TV

with Paul and me, predicted it. Fretted all day . . . my thoughts
wandering from great regimen of writing to fears of physical
stagnation. But more & more my plans tend to finishing *On
the Road* by New Year's—*then* I can *move* . . . no carousing till
then. Did a script in afternoon & night. No time, no room to
write in this disordered house. The peace & quiet of hours of
the days for production of art works which come handed to
rich writers on a golden platter, I waste my youth trying to
get—Oh fuck, Gorki said it better and he was right. All the bull
Giroux had about my being "free"—how can you be free when
you haven't got a moment to yourself, no security, no release
from money worries, not even solitude to work in, debts, con-
finement (he's in England as I write this—the editor with the
money bled from the souls of writers via the company check)—
nothing but shit falling from heaven even if you're working on
gold. There'll come a day when society will provide security,
basic honest security, not only for every earnest artist & writer
but every child born James Joyce & T. S. Eliot, Giroux's big
heroes, would have written much more if all their youth hadn't
been consumed in banks & schoolrooms fretting at the shitty
britches of others.

The playoff: in the dark of the afternoon, tragic Maglie ran
off across a littered field—all was lost, the great effort to catch
the Dodgers a cruel joke now, a thing in the iron breast of
laughing time; the field littered with paper because the Giant
fans were disconsolate & disgusted enough to throw it all over.
The Dodgers win the pennant!—but they only win a ghost; for
not only baseball, but victory is an illusion, a flame, illusion in
man's soul beneath the bleak skies, so who cares? The field is
dark, the sky is dimming, October again and another year and
anyway the players are going home to rest . . . and Maglie ran
for his shower, disappeared in the gloom in a storm of confetti
thrown with painful tenderness & hatred of life. Suddenly
Thomson hit a miraculous homerun—and wild drunkenness
possessed the Giant fans—more anon. (Illusion!—but sweet
joy of life!)—etc. There was the sudden realization that winning is possible on earth.

THURSDAY OCTOBER 4, 1951—Wrote all day—all about
Old Bull Lewis, Dean & Tom Watson. So imaginatively tired

that I couldn't continue my baseball description in yesterday's slot, as I wanted, to do it justice. At night came to N.Y. and got oldfashioned high . . . meaning the wild smoke. A wild smoke, but dulls the sympathy and then dulls the mind . . . a wild smoke, but leaves no man. Leaves the echo in the well, Saturday morning Lowell Massachusetts hurrying downtown to see *Snow White & the 7 Dwarfs* in the holy dark of the Keith theater Lord bless us all. Holmes & I had biggest talk of all—we dealt with American things exactly as we'd seen them.

FRIDAY OCTOBER 5, 1951—Got up at Holmes'—went for scripts and down to waterfront for my seaman's papers. Now I can ship out any time I want and I'm mightily tempted:—the thought of having friends, great voyages, food, money, girls in ports . . . and if I could only get a job as yeoman typist I'd have a desk, a gimmick for solitary writing at sea. (Reading this journal last night, high, I was struck by its tone of pompousness and selfishness—the mere fact of recording calories, losses, gains of all kinds, a business yet.) But I'm going to write the poem of things. . . . The drowsy gulls, on midafternoon piers . . . But this is pompous. Then I be pompous. My seaman photo reveals a tragic almost Frank Sinatra-like face of a desperate fugitive manner . . . but unlike all other seaman pictures before, old Keroach looks like he might be part of the crew. Came home stoned—rested—in the evening after supper, began again the reverie & the writing. Loneliness forever and the earth again, and I know that I'll never love or be loved again—on this pompous globe—this gnashing balloon—this what-have-you—my soul is now like a streetcorner in Chicago in January, north side— If there's a girl left who could absorb my bull—but there isn't . . . I'm not sad about being alone or loveless, only about growing older to die: I never dreamed it would happen to me, and it did while I wasn't thinking, and now I face eternity with bleak eyes and nobody knows it. I mean, imagine, Maman starting to be disgusted with my presence in the house. I grow evil, malign, suspicious, gloomy, indescribably annoyed, envious of the joys of others— *Goal is finish* On the Road *by Xmas.* Here's another typed-up spate: **2500-words** tonight. And Lord, Lord I have such a time not being literary—I don't want to be literary, I want to say exactly

what I fuckingwell mean. Keroach! Keroach! The salt shroud
of the sea is after you—

SATURDAY OCTOBER 6, 1951—One of those days when
it almost tears my head off to write . . . It's so hard and I'm
so dense and want so much. Tried writing in the park, everywhere—but I think I did well with those "hints of heartbreaking loss filtering into the dark poolhall with chinks of October
light" or maybe I didn't. Of course I did—(doubts, thinking of
Giroux saying. "But your best writing is when you don't know
it, your *narrative* . . .). I'm going to do what I *want* whether
it's good or not. At night did a $5 script . . . took several walks.
Isn't it funny for a guy like me to know that there's nothing
in the world to want and only loneliness & death to expect
out of all want, endeavor, or non-want, whatever your illusion
is—and yet be glad! and yet be glad! Tonight: **800-words** . . .
good ones.

SUNDAY OCTOBER 7, 1951—Good old October . . . this
morning cold rain, wet leaves, hissing radiators. I took a
pre-breakfast walk. What about the little girls you always see
in America on a gray Sunday morning—coming back from
church—the 12-year-old in a pink coat with white shoes, the
8-year-old one in a robin's egg blue coat and white shoes—
holding hands; and after noon you always see them going to
the poor corner B-movie with their pesty little brother between
them; and they sit in the brawling seats waiting for the lights to
go out, (angels painted on the ceiling dome of the Royal Theater, Lowell, Mass. 1928) for the show to start; the serial, the
cartoon, the short subject, the coming attractions, the news,
the ads, another cartoon, and finally two horrible B movies,
the first one cowboy, the second horror "Monster Meets Wolf
Man"; with melodramas roaring on the gray screen, the kids
chattering, fidgeting, changing seats, screaming, wrestling, the
smell of peanuts and chocolate, the presence of lonely Sunday
afternoon adults somewhere in the gloom ("I'll never come
here again on Sunday goddamit!"); the gray screen, the sadness of the heroics, of the mounting music, the scratch of the
soundtrack,—hell I don't know—and here come our little girls
in late Sunday afternoon, the sun's come out, throws their

shadows hugely on the sidewalk, they've had their big Sunday, they go home, they hate to take off their little pink coats & white shoes, they hate to think that Sunday's now behind them instead of in front of them (as it has been ever since Friday afternoon), they don't *dare* think that as a particular Sunday. This Sunday will never return to the face of the earth—and I think they know they will die. Oh Lord protect these little ones and love them.

And I accomplished nothing today except these words. Wrote in vain.

MONDAY OCTOBER 8, 1951—Did scripts—thought of going to sea—fiddled—faddled—Yanks beating Giants— it started off as a beat day but ended up with a great discovery of my life . . . (for now they're coming left and right in an Autumn of crisis). The discovery occurred to me while listening to a fellow who's doing exactly what I am . . . but on alto, *Lee Konitz* . . . how can I even begin to describe it. It was at Birdland. Lee was playing "I Remember April" as I've never heard it *conceived* and as he never played again last night: he stood with the alto on his gut, leaning to it slightly like Charlie Parker the Master but more tense and his ideas more *white* . . . more metaphysical . . . in fact he looks exactly like a 12th century monk, some Buxtehudian scholar of the dank gloomy cathedrals practising and practising endlessly in the bosom of the great formal school in which he is not only an apprentice but a startling innovator in the first flush of his wild, undisciplined, crazily creative artistic youth (with admiring old organ monks watching from the background)—but specifically:—like you take "I Remember April," and as big beefy intelligent Negro Cecil Payne watched in amazement (the baritone sax), he foresaw the tune straight through, took complete command of it, let measures of it carry it along on its own impetus while he busied himself *within it* with his own conception of it—a conception so profoundly interior that only the keenest ear could tell what he was doing and this didn't mean David Diamond, it meant Cecil Payne (*and* me) (*and* others in the club)—beautiful, sad, long phrases, in fact long sentences that leave you hanging in wonder what's going on and suddenly he reveals the solution and when he does, with the same vast foresight that he brings to a tune.

You now understand it with vast *hindsight*—a hindsight you wouldn't have gotten without his foresight, and a hindsight that at last gives you the complete university education in the harmonic structure of "I Remember April," a beautiful and American structure to boot. And at a moment of his saddest, seemingly lost note which became found in the conclusion of the "sentence" I suddenly realized "he is doing exactly what I'm doing with a sentence like 'hints of heartbreaking loss that filtered in with chinks of October daylight from the street' and here I've been worried all along that people wouldn't understand this new work of mine because next to Daphne du Maurier it is almost completely unintelligible (for instance)!—*does LEE KONITZ worry about VAUGHAN MONROE*? Let the dead and the dumb bury the dead and the dumb!

Do musicians and hip people and intelligent people run to hear Vaughan Monroe when they want to find out what's the latest development in American jazz or American music?—No, they run to hear Lee Konitz. Does Lee Konitz make a living playing these loomings of the monastic school for his peers and confrères?—no, he makes his living some other way (I believe as a teacher in the Tristano music school on 34th St.). Would Vaughan Monroe know who Lee Konitz is?—he would probably have heard of him from one of his sidemen, just as probably some pompous 16th century Peer who wrote poetry might have heard from one of his clerks about another poem-writer in government . . . Edmund Spenser; but would have no interest in knowing him or meeting him because his interest is *social* (Vaughan or the Peer, Vaughan in terms of MCA money, the Peer writes poetry to impress the ladies in his circle) and Konitz' (or Spenser's) interest is artistic or shall we say *laborious*, workaday, *genuinely hung-up* in the art, the craft, the agony of the thing, and probably would pay no attention to the imposing figure of Vaughan (or the Peer). Does Konitz try to tone down his imagination to make his music more understandable to the masses?—he's not playing for the masses, he's playing for musicians and listeners in the great up-going formal school, and he knows, as much as Bach or Beethoven knew, that the masses or at least masses of listeners would catch up and listen in the future and find their souls transformed, as his is, thereby; just as James Joyce knew that his *Ulysses* was but a prophetic image of styles of the soul to come, not a puzzle or any of that nonsense. Does Lee Konitz listen to the advice of well-meaning friends who say "It's all in the heart, play with your heart, when you do that you can even play with—well not Vaughan Monroe but say Woody Herman—and it'll be great, great!"—No, Lee Konitz prefers to play alone, which is the same thing as playing with Tristano, that is, *interior music*, the unspeakable visions of the individual (again) rather than tone down his mad vision in the name of "heart" or "great" or whatever shibboleths his well-meaning friends have; or like John Holmes & Giroux telling me where my greatest power lies, whether they say "heart" or "simple" (dig that?—a simple heart!) when all the time I have an unspeakable, mad & beauteous vision for which I need mind more than heart (but not much more) to bring it out and nothing "simple" about it at all; like people in Ireland telling James Joyce to concentrate on Irish Naturalism, or in America telling Wolfe to concentrate on the "really fine & worthwhile stories like you see in *Good Housekeeping*," or so on endlessly and now, talking about myself, the point half disappears— In any case my great decision I noted down in pencil in the gloom of Birdland at 2 A.M.—"Now—BLOW AS DEEP AS YOU WANT TO BLOW." Because I saw then, watching Konitz, master of all the musicians except Charlie Parker & mad Miles Davis, the interior laws of art . . . that it develops constantly and anybody who holds himself back, tones himself down, for reasons of success or even just popularity or *love of his circle* (my reason?) is simply backing away from the forefront of what everybody will be doing years from now and will thereby lose his power as prophet and saviour of an art, or, simply, as great unprecedented genius in his field setting the example for the others; in any case, toning down is, in the end, proof of mediocrity & insincerity—but worst of all, toning down, *backing down from what you know*, is waste, shame, stagnation & death. Therefore I've decided to make *On the Road* and all my other forthcoming books *exactly* what I want without regard for commercial or even *LITERARY* or personal or whatever consequences; my only human aim left, to gain the admiration of those who know the present day problems of consciousness as expressed in writing and not only those who practice it but those who (like myself and jazz) observe it from their own field.

Naturally, no more than Lee Konitz, I mustn't expect to get rich off prophetic arts, deep & beautiful as they are and as they will be recognized when masses of observers catch up; not even expect to make a living; so must find some other way which dovetails into my work. And this way is going to sea!! (And further, I saw that it would be December 1st before I could even begin on the "underwriting" of parts of *Road* from last Spring's ms., in other words, I couldn't possibly finish my *On the Road* by Xmas as I try to delude myself; no, my lifework is found; I must make a living like a man now; the sea is healthy, solitary, it moves; I can save money (!) (which I never do)—and so on. It ought to be clear now (?) to reader.

TUESDAY OCTOBER 9, 1951—Wrote all that Lee Konitz stuff today. Today, at home, took walks and wrote; the decisions arrived yesterday or as I say, written up today, made me lyrically happy just around sundown: October fires filled the westward huge sky as I walked in the wind and wondered where all the ghosts are who've flown the coop . . . and black locomotives upchugging smoke . . . and my sense of smell so sharp (no smoking) that by it alone my whole boyhood and life reeled through my brain . . . like in the bakery, like by the gas station (October 1941, Atlantic White Flash, Hartford), like Jamaica Avenue traffic, like cheeses in old dark Italian groceries, and that wondrous dry weedy pollinated dust of empty lots and city fields in October.—Those wonderful guys, five Italians of about 40, in Luigino's on 48th St. last night:—they were so hungry that when the preliminary pizza came and the head bozo began cutting it they looked at it with real *mouthwatering* furtive looks; once they had taken several succulent bites and got the gnaw-hole out of their stomachs they immediately began arguing, politics or gossip, with heated gestures; then the waiter brought glass mugs of the richest beer I've tasted in years, and they drank this to lubricate the forum; and in the five the types of men were discernable (just as in Mexico I used to dig groups of men in all night marimba cafeterias as gangs just like my old G.J.-Salvey-Scotty-Freddy-Sammy-Dasloff gang, the dour one, the calm one, the noisy one, the braggart one, the hero-punk one, the beloved one & leader, with always *a tremendous face as evidence of his typehood* [Lord,

yes!])—in the five Italians, obviously recent immigrants with
good jobs (it takes *Latin* faces incidentally for the study of man
and "gangs of chums") were as follows:—an argumentative
one, with gestures, quite mystifying me in the midst of what
seem'd a tirade by pulling out a picture of a baby, then subsiding when the others paid no real attention; then a quiet one,
who began speaking and drew the respect of all except Loudy
who was jealous or just plain miffed anyhow, the quiet one
smiling & explaining; an even quieter, graver one listening &
nodding (and all the time I knew they had families and dense
histories and throat-clutching lifetime agonies just like me and
you, and they were FAMOUS among themselves, like you and
me, O rich and unbelievable life!) (Think of it!—a poor Negro
entertainer who just died was called *ADONAIS* BERRY); and
others in the gang afraid to speak, not commanding enough
to nod gravely, younger, waiting for seniorities, satisfied. And
then I ate my riti and my home-made apple pie and just-roasted
coffee which was superb and went to Birdland and waited (for
the show to start) an hour with my million images.

WEDNESDAY OCTOBER 10, 1951—Well, and I keep changing—all I did was get drunk in local bar (Clancy's), for no
reason, and late at night cried . . . *apparently* for something
I've abandoned—I don't know what. The loneliness of my
mother—my foolishness—

SATURDAY OCTOBER 13, 1951—Got drunk, I guess—and
with Jerry Newman in the San Remo Thursday night yelling . . .
next day driving all over (to College Point for instance) getting
out his new record release (Schoenberg & Satie album) . . . visiting little dark Balzacian businesses on 10th Avenue (distribu-
tors) . . . Every conceivable kick; in fact I saw Allen & only yell'd
at him . . . a binge all out of proportion. Jerry Newman said I
would be great if I wrote like I talked—now what am I going
to do about that Lee Konitz business! (not only Jerry but Carl
Sandburg said that to me—in effect, that is, for Sandburg said
"Sometimes you get literary, otherwise you're all right, just
don't be literary, there's no need for it, don't worry about it, ha
ha ha hee hee hee! and he laughed and put his arm around me,
real eccentrically (!))—s'fact. . . . So now, today, a beautiful day,

I took a 4-mile walk round by the colored section of Jamaica
(Jelly Roll Morton used to drive there in one of his two Cadillacs on Sundays with his wife to visit friends, I can just picture
some bleak Sunday afternoon in the winter and him in his gray
fedora standing by his car getting photographed by a big fat
cousin)—walked around there thinking: "I must finish *On the
Road*—I must concentrate on my career—no farting around
and going to sea—this is a waste, a waste—a guy with a successful first novel practically REFUSING to write a second one
& make himself an honest dollar & establish his name in the
field & stop being a bum"—and the way to do it, I thought &
thought . . . start in 1935 with Jack St. Louis and his father Emil
St. Louis driving from (1934 Plymouth) Narragansett (letting
Emil's partner Dastou go back to Lowell by train) on a whim
to see N.Y. but also to meet Old Bull Lewis a distant cousin
of Emil's who'd written he was in N.Y. and gave his address
(in the Bowery Chinatown), and they go there & find old Bull
with old Dean Pomeray—the 9-year-old Dean, the three of
them having just driven all the way from Colorado selling flyswatters door to door. . . . so that *On the Road* is divided into
2 main adventures, 1935 and then the contemporary one with
the boys grown up & together on the road understanding the
mystery of change, death (Emil having died), time, whatnot,
everything. See?

Nevertheless—**600-words**: It's recording and explaining the
visions and memories that rush across my brain, in narrative
or otherwise logically connected sections—such as disserta-
tive— . . . what I had during a long happy walk. If I had a
portable tape-recorder everything would be okay . . . just walk
& talk. Tonight I came upon a crowd in a field, with a cop in
the middle, and a bloody hunk of human flesh in the weeds,
apparently a miscarried baby dumped there, with a redleaf tree
nearby framing a blue dark moon. How strange— And wild
little pickaninnies screaming with glee, uncontrollably happy,
outside a hardware store on Sutphin Blvd.— The things I know
don't last long anymore, they jump out of my head, I drink
too much now . . . For the life and death of me I can't write
On the Road . . . and I have to, I have to, or I'll just die off for

God's sake. To hell with it—I'm going to write something else. 40,000 words in this diary and nothing on *Road* . . . I used up all my excitement fooling around—the excitement that would have gone into another book—either I have a good time or I write a book. I don't know anything about it—I resign—I'm not going to write another goddamn word.

The worst mistake I made (and am now making) was ignoring my friendship with Tom Simonetti in the hospital just so I could doodle like the above in my "writing position"—& ignoring, for instance, my mother today, just for above doodlings. No—I must write only when I definitely have something to contribute to the body of the ms.—but enough rules & childish talk. I am going to go on with what I started Sept. 16—God help me—the objective Dean *Road*—

It's killing me!—Good Christ and the trouble is there's nobody can help me or give advice!—how much longer.

No I won't do the objective Dean *Road*.

SUNDAY OCTOBER 14, 1951—Another beautiful heartbreaking day. Took a walk, as usual; sat in the park thinking about a huge picaresque Johnny Dreamer *Road*; and then ONE WEEK IN AMERICA. Talking with my mother . . . she said the reason I've been fiddling for 3 years on *Road* is because Neal isn't a big enough subject for a real novel and yet I've been trying to write about him—in fact I remember when I abandoned Ray Smith because Neal & Hinkle & Allen didn't seem to be impressed (Dec. 1948). It was at that time that I became interested in the "myth of the rainy night" . . . The beginning of 3-yeared fumblings through Red Moultrie, Chad Gavin, the Walking Saint, the Cook, Pie, Sal Paradise and now Jack St. Louis (also of course Ben Boncoeur & earlier Freddy Boncoeur, the Mexican ideas); and even others; remember American Times? All a loss, a big sad loss . . . a waste of my poor sad soul . . . a nonsense . . . a foolish refusal to make an honest living (or buck anyway) and stop chiseling off people in the name of *T & C* (a juvenile work comparatively to what I could do now). Bah!—And some men have *real* troubles, like Bill.

"Zadok the Priest" by Handel—Ah God

Mozart Violin concerto No. 3 in G.—Where's my work??

My trouble is the horrible feeling that everything has happened before in a more interesting way and now nothing's really happening—the feelings of a senile soul. I feel most like Ginsberg than anybody else in the world today—that horror of being guilty and yet no longer desiring salvation in the least . . . not caring whether you're in hell or not because everything anyway is so vague—and strange—and to Ginsberg increasingly more malign—less innocent . . . "Out of the murderous innocence of that dolphin-torn, that gong-tormented sea" is what he wrote in my notebook in the San Remo (to me a serious place, no girlish "Remo") . . . and are they his own words? If so he's greater than ever. (Hart Crane, I believe.) YEATS

NEW YEAR'S RESOLUTION
1. Start studying again . . . at least 1 hour a day in tomes, with notes, preferably in the library, to whet the appetite for knowledge and to stock up on learning for phrases, allusions, depth of imagination
2. Listen to more classical music & especially modern (Bartók, etc)

Looking at map of Denver, it gives me amazed sorrow to realize that we lived there in 1949 . . . actually lived there, the same home lights at night that now shine in my tragic little bedroom. Oh God I love life, I beg forgiveness, I want—TO BE SAVED but so saved as to burn, burn, burn—saved to be a burning nerve, for maybe my days on earth aren't long (phlebitis already's come back). I want to be like Balzac—and burn, burn—make a lot of money—burn it too—and in my love and respect for other people and for the world, burn! burn! I can't stand it the way it is now—it's got to be saved—etc. etc.—I wish there was a God to hear me and understand me. I abhor nature—and does that make me a vacuum?—nature's the vacuum. And in poor Denver when I was a young man of 27 I used to waste my time with *Private Philologies* yet! Let me write some dialogue.

(It wasn't any good.) Weary of fiction, weary of time.

TUESDAY OCTOBER 16, 1951—Drink your beer, eat your food, and do your writing—this is the sum of what I learned yesterday when I went to light the darkness of my mind at Ed White's lamp. Also a dose of his good humor helped . . . He made me realize that the saga of all of us—not only Neal in Frisco, but Bill, Hal, Jeffries, Tomson in Mexico (and Helen Parker), Burford, Temko in Paris, Seymour, Morley etc. in England, Lucien, Allen, everybody in N.Y., Brierly in Denver, and so forth endlessly—this saga is inclusive of anything & everything I ever want to write and he told me not to worry about nonsense. "*You've* got so many things to do," he said . . . He showed me a letter from Hal Chase, who's half mad with hypochondria but has a love affair with "a black orchid . . . an Indian maid . . . Nilotic figure" . . . and worries someday she'll find "an *amante* more blond" and forget him. Meanwhile Ginger, old Dark Eyes, is playing a guitar & singing folk songs in a Greenwich Village club! "Write!" says Ed White. And Burford in Paris told a girl that I was her best reference for a job on a small magazine out there . . . The saga of all of us—and even the ones among us who don't really exist, yet do—like Old Bull Lewis . . . "Make sketches, like painters," says White; and this afternoon I did, of old diner and old B movie on Sutphin Blvd. (But I need my sense of humor—a glass of beer!) I want to work, turn out novels, create the American Comedy, the master structure, my vision of life; and live, eat, drink, love, travel, & laugh . . . (but too tense about it). Well by God I resumed writing today!

The things that men do when they're sober make men drunker when they're drunk—the greatness of sobriety is only appreciated by drunkenness and also high-ness of drug takers. Now you take George Arliss—in all his pictures he used to walk through affairs of state holding his two lapels . . . Had 10 brews after I wrote the above paragraph. I'm now writing this high on beer, from "the things that men do" to this . . . Spent half my precious day composing my "plans" for Guggenheim Fellowship. Ten beers were had in Clancy's bar with Romeo Nadeau my new French Canadian friend, & his wife, & fellow-Canadian Gerard Paillard of Waterbury, Conn.—Romeo was bartender, beers on house—great! *Who else can write the American Comedy? Hey?*

A little comfort won't kill the suffering monster . . . Also, tonite reading the paper I felt that things were happening

again. It's like Joan Adams said . . . 1951 was a beat year . . .
poor girl.*

~

WEDNESDAY OCTOBER 17, 1951—This day (it's now 2
A.M.) will never, never, never return, so therefore I salute it
now. . . . You see my pitch? Did a $5 script—went in—wrote
sketches of Hector's cafeteria—visited Bill Fox at store—Allen
came—we ate pizza—drank at store and in bars—Bill threw
us out—visited Allen's room in the Mills Hotel (now called
Greenwich) where we discussed the "cosmic Italian dormitory"—same place I stayed seven years ago in Fall of 1944
after I jumped ship in Norfolk to come back to Céline and
Joan Adams was young & pretty & later told me I should have
come back for her instead, or that is, what she really said, "That
was the time when you should have tried (making love to me)."
The sad bums' hotel—Allen said Old Pomeray would regard it
with awe because it is after all an enormous big-city flophouse,
a universal, a cosmic vast dreamlike flophouse in the great city
of New York—We decided the shroudy stranger came there
years ago—We decided some of the bums are not really bums
but worse . . . they're men who could live at the Y and eat at
Stewart's but want to save money! (groan, moan). We decided
to ball Dusty next out . . . I shall describe Dusty soon . . . why
keep a diary chaste? The Mills, or Greenwich, has at least a
thousand cell-like rooms half of which face two 8-story inside
courts; on the bottom there are chairs for bums; during the
day great conversations go on, the ceaseless murmurous voice
of men rises a hundred or more feet to the sad Italian ceiling
which is webbed & strange. Allen said recently two strange
beat Negroes painted an enormous mural in the great echoey
hall depicting an "Egyptian-Cape Cod port, a city on orange
blocks" (you've got to hear his descriptions to realize the precision of his madness). We also talked about the recent events in
Mexico—Lucien's drunkenness, Joan's death, Bill out on bail
& speculated on Hal. So the circle swirls. While we were drunkenly examining bookstand I realized (watching a browser) that

*[(It was actually the great year of my enlightenment, & Gary Snyder's, too,
(1960 I say this)]

men come here to dream . . . We discussed the Pope's vision of Virgin Mary in the sun (last year at this time) . . . the setting sun. Allen said: "With all the Church beneath him & millions of believers including the barefoot ones of Mexico & the world and T. S. Eliot & everybody this Pope Pius, like a mad Father Ferrapont, has a completely Dostoevskyan vision of the flaming sun and everybody (including me) believes him! and this is the greatest miracle since the atom bomb in 1945, in fact much greater." [Allen had visions in 1948 but he didn't have the world to report it to.] Whoo! Bed at 5 A.M.

THURSDAY OCTOBER 18, 1951—Wrote the great initial Dean Pomeray speech to Tom Watson & the football passing scene in the Denver dusk & "great riot of October joy"—a tremendous afternoon of writing. My new method is ACTING OUT what I write . . . SPEAKING OUT—(alone in the house)—and now of course don't need wire recorder no more!!—thank God—*I tell you, today, Oct. 18, 1951,* On the Road* *took off from the ground.* At night did a $10 script— wrote important letters, my first in a long time—I'm really rolling now—here we go. I want to write a good novel each & every year . . . publishing the first one Fall of '52 and then '53, '54 etc.—someday have $. If I had $ right now I'd fly to Paris this weekend.

"Love the art in yourselves," says Stanislavski, "don't love yourselves in art."

(Wrote no such letters.)

FRIDAY OCTOBER 19, 1951—Handed in $10 script—spent $4—Ah Lord, Ah Lord, my heart is at a mad and feverish pitch tonight—Tonight I know the greatness of the suffering of man—and the beautiful *noblesse oblige* of his complex, subtle loneliness in this oldfashioned dark, sad earth— Poor Fitz! poor Bill! poor Neal! and ah dear, poor me— Today, like some days in my past or any man's past, I received rebuffs—or more importantly I THOUGHT I did,—till I made rebuffs—but no mind; I'll remember everything from this personal (Ah mighty Proust!) itinerary:—Went to Fox, then to Support Bureau, talked with Irish clerk; then stood on corner of 23rd & 3rd Ave.

*[(*Visions of Cody* . . . later title)]

for an hour thinking—then to Jerry's store where Bill Fox laid hints down on me about my being a chiseller I guess—& as soon as I'm positive what he means I'll ask him to be more implicit indeed—then I tried to find Johnny Holmes, fumbled on Lex (and here's the scene of the play: couple necking in livingroom, fellow comes through with towel around waist, says "Flaming youth" and exits, next fellow looks harried: "How about a saw? how about a saw? I want to borrow a saw"; then another enters, says "What about that salami in the cellar?"—a play composed during this miserable day); then I bought knockwurst, sauerkraut, came home, beer, ate; then Tom & Ed came but were sleepy and wouldn't get in the bag with me; and only guy I should have seen tonight is Fitz. As I write this, though, live show from Birdland—new beautiful bop, I love it, nobody knows how great it is—right now 1951!!!—when else for Christ's sake were drums so subtle, altos so heartbreaking, trombones so vocal?

To hell with all the doubters & bastards that lurk inside my soul. I want to dig the subterranean mysteries & the eyrieal mysteries & the jazz mysteries (as I certainly told the Guggenheim people in my new plans for artistic creation)—& the mysteries of the great bop piano—and mysteries unheard-of—& not only the mysteries of Dean Pomeray but of tremendous soaring wobbly passes in October empty lots. . . . Wheeeeeeeee! And all this goes on at my desk in the middle of the night, a poor lonely hand scribbling. . . . I no longer ask what for, it's the only solid thing left in my life aside from the stout personality of my mother . . . who never changes an iota while I leap every day from one extreme clutching my neck to another sleeping till the sad red sun goes falling down as children scream. But today, today, today (and Terry Gibbs as I write this, sad young Jew kid from Bronx, chews gum, attacks vibes, what else? but an artist of great & heartbreaking sensibility & knows it but can't say it though maybe in one of his notes he will cry it out & everybody knows & the man's got to concentrate mainly like all great musicians on the architecture of the tune and get it by the balls or go back to Egypt & the Greeks and Swing)—Terry Gibbs, take a bow in my hollow roaring pages. . . . today, today, today—what indefinable charm each day in our lives has!—and even more amazing, its ineffable *accomplishments*—O ragged sailing heart! Ah me Sebastian! Mischa Aver! all the mad sensitive Russian screaming ones! They're for me! Oh for an oldfashioned tea party!—with Vicki appreciating every mad twist!—to be a Normie Schnall for a Vicki Russell Armiger!—I haven't lived, I mean it!—Mad laugh of Symphony Sid in the night! Now Terry Gibbs & Don Elliot dueling at the vibes . . . "Flying Home"—2:30 A.M. Oct. 20 '51 and no NEW Jerry Newman to record it (but just wait till I get my tape recorder!)—

How say it?—I wonder what my poor feet are up to, as my poor mind wanders . . . On Union Square today, dreaming (as I did 3 full years ago with my copy of Whitman's *Calamus*).

Say!—this new bop is apocalyptic!—even Jimmy Ford— New bop has a continual noisy going restless leap of drums— accents & also Chinese cymbals—driving everything ahead of it undyingly, restlessly—nobody can help but lean to the issue—go! go!—the mysteries of swing allied to the mysteries of the future—AND NOBODY KNOWS IT!—Do we have to wait for Marshall Stearns Jr. & Barry Ulanov Jr. to tell us this in 1962, that the Bop of the Fifties is GREAT??? BAH! I say.

SATURDAY OCTOBER 20, 1951—"I'm getting more and more to feel like a haggard ghoul"—(what happens when men have those "spiritual & physical lapses" Proust attributes to women's leaving for other lovers). Sat in Richmond Hill park for an hour in the beautiful crisp, windless, pale blue afternoon of October with dusty green leaves turning an early orange; kids playing in the field before the great black montage of a city of old locomotives gathered for Saturday afternoon in the L.I.R.R. yards. . . . I realized too much of my life is a struggle to rid myself of guilt . . . the hell with it . . . this is what is consuming poor Ginsberg . . . NO—it's the Past and the general joy of Time that is now going to be my central mental absorption; guilt distorts the Past (the pure past of merely exactly what happened) and cripples the Present. I had 3 other big thoughts that I've since forgotten . . . but I'm deciding to drink less & spend more of my time now in N.Y. sketching from the Bowery to the Bronx . . . a Leonardo doesn't faddle . . . Oiled my typewriter in the afternoon; put in new bed in my now cosy tiny room; & wrote a bit. . . . I'll soon have a total of words. Blah blah.

MONDAY OCTOBER 22, 1951—Didn't want to go out Saturday night but did and just got drunk again. Somebody said I'd last 2 more years—as if I was a Cannastra. Miserable, I feel miserable . . . I'm trying to avoid the things that killed my father plus I suppose new ones. All that matters is pure gold!! Did $13 scripts Sunday—I'm not worth the paper this silly diary's written on—thank God I'll read it someday. [Sat. night was Dusty's party with R. & Jerry Newman & everybody there & me too drunk to know it & passing out for at least the 25th time in 1951.] IT'S ALL MY FAULT AND I KNOW WHAT TO DO NOW.

Liszt's Legend No. 2 "St. Francis," so much like Beethoven I thought until a giveaway lapse in judgment and taste near the end . . . the trills . . . Anyhow. —When was it . . . before I learned the tremendous adult fact that in Mexico you can get all the emotion of Spanish nights, fiestas, roses and unimaginable cantinas from listening to the music on the jukebox while watching some sullen strawhatted bastard eating at a tortilla counter—

Bop musicians don't play what they want; not four bars later, overcome by genuine guilt because of this, they try technical show-off tricks. The reason: what they want is *obvious* to them (they think); they don't know that just a step beyond is something they *don't* want because they've never known it before. But bop has freed jazz and made way for "crazy" phrasing; at its greatest, soon, after Charlie Parker's greatest pupil grows up, or maybe Tristano's, it will be music like Mozart's.*

It's all my fault and I know what to do now.

Oct. 1942 in Nova Scotia Canadian Navy guardhouse; Aug. 1933 in old magazine store Merrimack St. across from St. Jean Baptiste, the shadow; Oct. 1927 in crib at midnight, Hildreth St., woke up by mother & visiting actress in Opera House play—My women never understand—I want them to wear a housedress all the time . . . fashion, that makes me sick, works its vanity on them. Why don't they understand that I know what I'm talking about . . . instead they'll go and get their masculine instruction from—fags, what-all.

In actual writing moments you get bored & chickenshit.

*[(Q. V. Chet Baker 1953) (John Griffin 1958) (Ornette Coleman 1960)]

TUESDAY OCTOBER 23, 1951—October, don't run out!—but he has to. At 2 A.M. wrote about Tom Watson's grandmother; at 3 A.M. about Tom Watson's grandmother's lace curtains. Wrote all day further into Tom Watson's closet, from 11 A.M. on, with trip to N.Y., no script, thinking for an hour on front steps on 45th St. at B-way, back home to write, not much success but now I have a big spate ready to type tomorrow. Deciding once for all on the next six, crucial months—O dark thing . . . Reading old mad Proust; eating good food, taking long walks, getting hung up on sentences . . . This I've got to do for 6 months . . . then I'll be 30, and *twice an author*. Worth it?—

1. TO DEFINITELY ESTABLISH MY CAREER BY SUR-MOUNTING THE 2ND NOVEL PROBLEM (Mailer didn't, Merle Miller didn't; those who don't, don't *rise* or make it.)

2. TO IMPROVE, CULTIVATE, UTILIZE MY SENSES & HEALTH IN GENERAL BY NOT DRINKING ALCOHOLIC BEVERAGES EXCEPT STRICTLY IN MODERATION WITH FRIENDS (Every time I get stewed I notice the next day a paralysis of my ordinary working senses & the introduction of fits of guilt, horror, sorrow, wild despair that take up another 48 hours until the return of the previous sober absorptions)

3. AS A REWARD FOR THE ASCETIC DISCIPLINE OF WRITING A WILD TRIP WHEN BOOK'S DONE (There's been no deliberate adventure in my plans since Spring 1950—tea made me seek security not adventure— so I married Joan—If I can't go off hitch hiking at the conclusion of *On the Road* when I'm 30 in March then I shall have to give up to middle age & grow fat

4. TO MAKE A LIVING AND SAVE MONEY FOR NECESSITIES EVENTUALLY GO TO SHIPS (The time for this should be *after* I've proven I can write that 2nd novel better than the first, & *after* I've had a land-crossing fling in the Spring of '52)

5. MAKE A DOWN PAYMENT ON A HOUSE IN LONG ISLAND FOR HOME AND HEADQUARTERS (Head-quarters in N.Y., there'd be no peace; and of course it's my mother who will need this house when she retires on Social

Security & whatever else I can arrange for her; I can't say
my house isn't well kept etc. The place that'll say I'm not
broke; my room, my records; eventually my kids' house?)

6. WRITE "PROUSTIAN-WOLFEAN-FAULKNERIAN-
GENETIAN-MELVILLEAN-CÉLINEAN-WHIT-
MANESQUE-DOSTOEVSKYAN-KEROUASSA-
DIAN" NOVELS IN BALZAC SYSTEM TO AVOID
GETTING HUNG UP ON TWO OR THREE GREAT
WORKS LIKE JOYCE FOR LIFE WHEN THE SAME
MATERIAL CAN BE POURED INTO INSTAL-
MENTS (This is the big subject:—a book about Neal, a
book about jazz *Pictorial Review Jackson and Jazz*, a book
about Jack St. Louis *The Vanity of Doctor Sax* (decided to
meld *Sax* & *Duluoz* together today), etc., each in its own
good time, with *Old Bull Lewis** to come. In this way I
stand a decent chance of making a living as a writer instead
of martyrizing myself until it's too late, like T. S. Eliot,
Joyce, Proust

WEDNESDAY OCTOBER 24, 1951—Went into N.Y. for
work; wasn't any, went to Holmes for chat & 3 beers; at 2 A.M. I
roared through the 53rd St. subway station kicking over a huge
trash barrel as Ginsberg, trying to guide me after our 20 beers
with Holmes & Harrington, hustled to pick it off the ground.
3 A.M. Harold Goldfinger is lechering at me in San Remo john
& telling me about Huncke in 1933; 6 A.M. I am staggering 2½
miles after sleeping to end of F train line, at 179 St., walking
through gastank dark of Jamaica, splashing in puddles, weeping for my lost youth in Lowell when similarly I used to come
home near dawn but never had to walk more than a mile and it
was the tenements of Moody St., then the panoramic wild joy
of the bridge, then the sleep of home neighborhoods in Pawtucketville—nothing like the sprawling terrifying dark hells of
Long Island that reach in every direction endlessly as millions
upon millions of human beings sleep in places they would like
to call home but can't because the place they're in and I'm in
is too enormous and incomprehensible and frightening. God,

---

*Old Bull Baloon

how I thought of my father; & when I got home my mother was just getting up (it was 5:30 rather)—and I thought of the darkness of my youth in Lowell.

LITTLE PAUL BLAKE: "Well I shore like these red popsicles."
HIS PAL: "Sometimes I do and sometimes I don't."
LITTLE PAUL BLAKE: "Well, sometimes I do—sometimes I don't—and sometimes I do."
ME: "Do you like fudgicles?"
LITTLE PAUL: "I shore do, I say yum yum."
ME: "Is that what you say, yum yum?"
LITTLE PAUL: "I say yum yum ALL the time."

THURSDAY OCTOBER 25, 1951—Again went in to N.Y., no work; again lured, but this time productively, sketching in 3rd El and on 9th Street near Bowery then long meditative walk down to Chinatown to look at difference between Chinese movies & B movies; and en route trailed Victor, the strange Jesus Christ who'd traveled to Provincetown with little Jeanne Nield in 1950 on a beat motorcycle and they'd slept in a pup tent in Helen Parker's backyard the first night, in Truro woods, trailed this bearded mystery to his musty doorway at 41 First Avenue next door to a wine factory where ten husky gangsters were busy packing wino apple wine in cases so that old Pomerays (thousands of whom I subsequently saw all milling around in front of the Salvation Army trying to sell old pants, old razors, and one guy wanted to sell an old cloth khaki belt for 10¢) so these could get stoned in all sidestreet alleys. Roaming there, I noted that the bum's got an *adventurous* spirit—not only like Rex wanting to sleep on the sidewalk but wanting to wear overalls, baseball hats, jackets and adventure in the open with the other boys, raise the bottle with a yell, and in fact some of them have these marvelously adventurous slouched hats and the look in their eyes is wild, daring; even tho most of them just sit on steps muttering as their brains no longer register legitimate complaints or satisfactions, just twitches of something still alive. On Lower East Side Henry St. I saw a little mother cat and kitten playing in shadows of the doorway of a busy grocery store full of women and children. It was a mighty good day.

FRIDAY OCTOBER 26, 1951—My royalties due today. Jack Fitzgerald driving down from Poughkeepsie to get me tonight. October meanings in this greatest of my Octobers since 1941 are now reaching climax as Halloween pumpkins appear on fruitstands, as I don my red woodsman's shirt, as trees turn fiery brown and dull red, and as I consider a trip to Lowell for Halloween. . . . and tonight, by moonlight, Fitz and I reel off the Hudson Valley of our mad dreams (Mad Murphy and Doctor Sax).—Typed up **1800-words**—but wrote much more than that and much better in my scribbled secret notebooks that had better become my real work or I'm a failure—I am *not* satisfied with those 1800 words—the notebook sketches are greatest I've ever done . . . tonight I dashed off a sketch about the Bowery which is completely without sentence form and is better than the greatest of my sentences except the "heart-breaking loss" one but only because IT was something special. My main ms. doesn't live up to my sketches; it's like a painter, his canvas oil job doesn't equal his street sketches in pencil . . . to make everyone realize that *he has not taken Mr. Stanislavski's advice* . . . love the art in yourself—. Wrote at least 4500 of them golden secret words worth a dollar each . . . heh heh heh! So today altogether I had to do with 6,500 words & that's Oct. 25 '51. The great hungup parts of *T & C* were nevertheless siphoned through sentence structure *and* groove (if anybody can still know what old high priest means)—(through restricting sentence forms and unnecessary statements of mood).

THURSDAY NOVEMBER 1, 1951—I don't know how I'm going to be able to catch up with everything that's happened but this time unlike December 1948 I'm not going to let it all go to pot . . . tonight I have to do two scripts, write letters and already today I've written (in sketch books) well over 5,000 words:—it's been fourteen years I took to reach writing maturity:—now all that remains is work, life plans, etc. Sometime in next few days I've got to record my trip to Poughkeepsie with Dusty & the 5-day binge in its entirety & the offer A. A. Wynn made, thru Carl Solomon his nephew, to advance me money to finish *On the Road** and my mad discovery as to how to do it

*[*Visions of Cody*]

into a book so revolutionary & fantastic that on that basis alone it would certainly make me famous and I hope wealthy, and soon, and launch me off on an unprecedented writing career unknown in the "literary" world before.

SUNDAY NOVEMBER 4, 1951—(Another binge, with Dusty, Tom, Ed)—My big mad revolutionary idea was to hitch hike to Frisco with mad Dusty and write it in my secret sketch-scribble notebooks as we go along—. Nobody's ever reached fresh from life with scenes, faces, conversation, panoramas—*painful as life itself & rich* . . . Not gainsaying this is a great idea but I was doing *On the Road* with Dean Pomeray and Carl Solomon thinks it's really great writing "the best of your generation that I know of" and he's an Artaud-Genet-Michaux type which is hard to please. So I'm stuck with whether I should stay home advance or no advance and finish *Road* as I had it (& remember it *took off* recently)—OR—go to the next step in my "development" & hit the humble road with pencil in hand (submissive to everything, open listening, Whitman like). I think it isn't as good as it sounds (will ask Ed)—because the *imagination* of Dean's *Road* is what stones Solomon, the brevities too, and Dusty's road may only be a glorified diary??? (& drunken?)

(Poughkeepsie is recorded elsewhere.) Here it is Sunday morn Nov. 4, 1951, and I'm alive & thinking & scribbling at my desk. I had no coat for the Winter—I got no royalties from Harcourt, still in debt—and Mrs. Whitebook and her son Jack Enoch gave me his gone Camel's hair top-coat, brown, dark, rich, the best coat I've had in all my life and it was given to me. (They didn't know I had no coat of my own.) So thank the Lord and my neighbors for my new coat. It makes absolutely no difference to Joan that I have no coat—"The only thing I care about is my baby" and probably only wants to choke it to death. She told the judge I would collect $500 semi-annual royalties, and earned $30 a week on scripts.* No wonder I have to send her that fin every week. But now, now I may get that advance. Ah balls this is absolutely the last time I think or write about her. I have to struggle on under the weight of her own shame

*It's actually $20 average—$18 this week.

& horror and yet try to fashion books out of my own belief & joy. VERY WELL THEN I WILL. (She used to beat her head against the wall of our 20th Street room and it was a stone wall, just because she was infuriated about something; this was supposed to be my doing, who was only trying to mind his own business in the midst of slowly realizing the mental illness of his spouse; (dumbly put but true); and that, plus the hours & hours spent at a mirror with makeup just to go out in the street to a part time waitress job or the like, that's some of her shame and horror.)

In Poughkeepsie I learned from Dusty that a woman can be fun again. O dear me October's gone again . . . Paris! Paris next!

MONDAY NOVEMBER 5, 1951—Decided yesterday to stay home till Wednesday and write at least 3,000 more words to show Solomon & Wynn in an effort not only to secure the advance but prove to them and myself too that I can "turn out" professionally:—in which interest I let the scripts go hang till then. Wrote 700 wds. yesterday afternoon, to be typed (Dean & the propitious traffic light). I can finish this *Road* by March 12 if I get an advance—then I can start another novel immediately & get another advance! This is really what I want to do, Balzac the thing, not moon along. Go, go, go!

The seaman on the porch looking into the lace curtains or the oval livingroom was as much out of place as an old shawled lady on a flying bridge. Took long walk doing mental sketches (of old house) for *Road* chapter . . . where Neal & boys go . . . found the house under great black L.I.R.R. watertank. And also got Jack St. Louis, his sniffling nose & the long red sun in Queens.

Pretended I was sick so Maw wouldn't have to go out with "friends" (her idea) . . .

How good *is* my writing?—Working today on thousands of words of mad material . . . Dean throwing the passes, driving to Wyoming girls, etc. "—The moon in the red tree . . ." I go on and on in relative ignorance . . .

Ah the cafeterias of the Mexican night . . . the sad voices, the poor guitars . . . I want to go to Frisco, to Mexico, to Ecuador, and then Paris and Rome . . . yes.

TUESDAY NOVEMBER 6, 1951—Still writing those 3000 words in a bid for that thousand bucks. At times I weaken, even get bored—but I'm doing it for my own fun anyhow so I go on, quickly recovering . . . blah blah . . . But I haven't worked as absorbedly as this (and without benzedrine) since I was a kid drawing cartoons, & that's what I prayed for in the hospital.

Because all I have to do now is work on visions of Dean Pomeray, eventually visions of character itself . . . visions, visions,—to hell with "narrative." Such as, for instance, "Oh tenormen of the American bop night, Oh four brothers, that ineffable grace that came into your pale hands, your thin sweet faces, your bent studious neck we see here under these rosy lights of jazz—where did it come from?"—It's all I care about, the things that haunt *me* not someone else—& getting down to the bottom of it even if it takes till five o'clock in the morning. Working like that gives me such muscles that tonight for instance I did two full scripts from 11 to 3 A.M. and went right on, after a 2-mile walk and chinning 15 times, with this. (It's Wednesday now.) *Dostoevsky me no Dostoevskies!!*—I'm finally interested in exactly what I'm doing and there's no reason for me to do it—as, for instance, *Under the Volcano* is now out of print. Like a child again I'm absorbed in my own imagination—and speaking of cartoons Solomon (whether or not but he did) said my work, to him, was mainly & completely visual. It's now Thursday, 4 A.M., I have **3500 new-words** to show and I will now write a few more. Why did Blake address his rose the way he did?—So he'd be noticed by the Poetry Society, or get a job on *Puck*, or make five farthings?—No, because he told the rose and he recorded the fact that he told the rose and he really told that rose. (It's about 11,000 words written now on *Road* since Sept. 16—pretty "slow.")

THURSDAY NOVEMBER 8, 1951—(That Dusty, or similar, *Road* is going to be merely an added thing that I'm going to do, not the shit end of a dualism—

And now, today, I took in those new words to Carl Solomon's pad on Prince St.—(digging the Bowery again en route, looking for soup, one joint full of afterwork Puerto Ricans drinking beer and singing in chorus with the jukebox unfortunately didn't have soup [I had 25¢], finally I found some barley soup in a little tiny lunchroom on a cold dark howling corner run by a Greek . . . With steam in the windows, sawdust on floor, I'm going to sketch it, digging the Bowery and Italian teamsters on Thompson St. again as I did in Spring of '46). Carl said I must write a synopsis or prospectus of *Road* so that his uncle will know where it's headed before he considers parting with moneymoolah . . . and I tried to write a synopsis in Carl's (after lovely supper of succotash hotdogs Olive called *Frankfurt pederaste*) but couldn't. What is the synopsis of *Road*? What, in fact, is *Road*? *On the Road* is the first in a series of novels about members of my generation who interest and haunt me because they—but I'll try it on foolscap—or should I tell it here? The point is, be a Roman with a Roman; I'll "talk Turkey"? ("Road" is "Cody.")

MONDAY NOVEMBER 12, 1951—I'm beginning to see my own tragedy. All I have to do is look in the mirror. The moment is coming when I really and truly must decide to go cold-turkey on all alcohol . . . I just can't restrain myself after 3 brews. This last weekend was too much for me—I'm so depressed tonight (Sunday) that I don't know what to do. The hospital month of great self-discovering joy is already being blurred and that's the story of my last ten years . . . too much drunkenness, it finally eats at the sources of your strength & belief, especially if you're insanely sensitive. Poor Wolfe, that's what it was killed him.

TUESDAY NOVEMBER 13, 1951—Further confirmation today about advance. Alright, I'll spend the winter in honest work. And last night ah me I read *The Vanity of Duluoz* and cried—there's my 3rd book already . . . (*Vanity of Sax*). Solomon and I had a tremendous talk too—he saw Artaud in 1947 screaming in the Rue Jacob at 7 o'clock in the evening and doesn't know whether he was the old man on the couch or the poet who trembled. We also picked up John H's book for A. A. Wyn. I walked around Rockefeller Center today wondering if I could write a N.Y. *Vanity of Duluoz* with a portable tape recorder . . . it's almost impossible to capture this ocean in a thimble but I think I could but again I might write (or tell) too much with a machine—Oh phooey. *Scratching his chest, showing his teeth to no mirror*—Shakespeare's soul is now waiting for release from the inanimate object called the moon. Solomon says he won't go traveling till the atom bomb is captured . . . otherwise traveling is fleeing. We talked about mad Legman—who makes exposés of new images like Solomon & Harrington the joking symbolist. Ginsberg knows. (About my "tragedy" yesterday, it's taking care of my responsibilities that counts, not stop-drinking or such—it's being a man, taking care of things. Now I go to work for the winter. And now that I'm getting money I don't know what to write any more.)

Well, and so, I've just, now, 5 A.M. Tuesday morning, read most of this diary and I do find that the mental condition in the hospital was far superior to the mental condition after the first five or six drunks (not before, though). Drinking is OK, I just overdo it. Agreed . . . I'll try to take it easy. Another curious thing, the *smallprint pages* from 46 to 50 are curiously devoid of any humor . . . some reason connected with the print mayhap; a crabbedness . . . as if, for me, it's be wild, not cautious. What anxieties. Tonight was the first night that I can remember that I couldn't think of what to write, as if it was *upstairs again* (used to live upstairs in big flat, big literary position, weed couldn't *ride*, Giroux first, that is, the baneful influence of success (on a fool like me) (check in black CASH 1949 notebook) then the baneful weed). How much happier it is down here where my mother and I don't even have enough room to turn at the same time in the kitchen. That's because of what I learned in the hospital. Now that I've got Dusty out of my mind because of her deal the other night I can return to the strengths the secrets of which I learned and didn't and won't forget. There are some beautiful lines in this book on the subject. Last night, as I say, I read *Duluoz*—something is coming, a wonderful joy. I won't lose it. I think heaven punished me this past weekend when just before I danced so crazily to Stravinski that I tore my own shirt off in Dusty's living-room I had told Allen I wasn't interested in God any more, just people, in dumb unmemoried contradiction of that "infinite unfathomable love heaven bestowed to men"—words I wrote a matter of hours before jail and which reminds me that it was also in jail I wrote "Ever moreso gentle am I than death." Also, reading *Duluoz* makes me realize that where once I was like two men now I'm like five and it's curious to figure whether this means I'm crazy or just some kind of Great Shaman Fool of New York, from the provinces, some crazy dumbsaint of the mind, or maybe just New Man or something. I don't *feel* crazy, it seems if I want to I can be perfectly normal, stop the machine, go to sleep, say something quiet & sensible. But the way I forget one thing after another—and this is principally because I live by every 24 hours—and I wish this was a 24 hours like the ones I discovered Konitz in, so I could write—I often wonder if I'm clinically crazy, as for instance, my mother once asked me about that Vermont car crash, its effect on my head. Or maybe I'm just simply "maniacally self centered," as Allen says of John Hohnsbein now; this is a diary; it has a millions I's. Since *Duluoz*, for one thing, I've become more boyish & silly but there's no doubt that I've become more intelligent too (& boyishness is a trap to make people teach me?). What anxieties. Dear Lord, I give you my soul.

Goodnight gentle readers, sleep; sweet music to your dreams.

(And now I remember a dream . . . a river, the Concord River, night, Mary Carney's house . . . and I tell you, I swear, all I have to do is look at "sweet music to your dreams" to rouse the image of that dream of the Mary Carney river night* . . . as Proust says, or might have said, inanimate objects and even words in themselves contain the imprisoned spirit of something we once lost).

The reason why I didn't write tonight, I think, is really because I wanted to describe a second story corner office that's closed for the night but you can see through it from one window to another around the corner because a red neon is shining around that corner . . . (as you can see, nothing could be harder to describe & mainly I had no room for fitting it with Neal & the gang bound for Wyoming in the car). This scene haunted me tonight and because of my "advance" I foolishly looked for myself in art instead of the art in myself. That window might have been Chin Lee's on Kearney Square. Anyway I know now, advance or no advance, the unspeakable visions of the individual, dealing with the *source* of the mind; no time for poetry but telling exactly what it is, and other such discoveries scattered in this book (and this being the reason

*Maggie Cassidy

why I re-read it tonight) are the thing for me to do . . . how intelligently put . . . and tomorrow, therefore, I'll go on writing. (Or that is, today.)

Did a $6 script after fried clam supper. That shivering-in-the-chest feeling of joy only just now returning, 48 hours after the drunk ended. And this afternoon, seeing a dark part of 5th Avenue near St. Patrick's I had a lovely visionary tic . . . of a dark shoe repair or similar repair shop on some gloomy afternoon on Aiken Street in my observant infancy, yair. (The best journal entries are those that know when to stop.) —A full November moon, and mild.

WEDNESDAY NOVEMBER 14, 1951—I'm on the verge of some kind of crazy discovery that'll tear my head off for good— or make me great. The system of writing I use when sketching is tranced fixation upon an object before me, "dreaming on it" expresses it exactly; now I'm about to try the most dangerous experiment of my life, the same tranced unconscious fixation upon the object which will now be the successive chronological "visions" of Neal, in other words, I'll decide ahead of time generally where he's at, with who, what doing, and dream on it. As in the sketches, as in all portraitures, present tense. So that the second draft may be the only conscious and of course the only grammatical and what's most important maybe—the only legible. *It's 4 A.M. in the morning and I am about to try the experiment and I'm scared.*

IT WORKED—but I would have written it in huge letters if I was positive it would work when the time comes for dialog, for voices of others. Generally speaking, it works, and I can report here, as if I was an inventor at his peak, that I've gone still another greater step beyond the fruits of the hospital discoveries . . . and I knew this was so, because I couldn't sleep the night I first realized it, Oct. 25, the day I wrote the Bowery sketch from memory, realizing that I was in myself revolutionizing writing by removing literary & that curious "literary grammatical" inhibition from its moment of inception, removing most of all of course, the obstacles that came from my own personal stupidity which is still with me but temporarily under control. (And someday must tell the strangest tale of tonight's discovery which is actually going to influence my entire life and

yet I'm not excited and why should I be—the scatological block
I had, the fear of "soiling" bound notebooks no matter how
small.) Incidentally, I sketched a bakery window and a bleak
rectory across the street today, at Parsons Blvd., and spent an
hour in the Jamaica library & read photographs.

THURSDAY NOVEMBER 15, 1951—Because I go to bed at
5 I'm all screwed about days, but at 1 A.M. this morning I did
an $8 script, walked 2½ miles. During day, in N.Y., I sketched
people going by Stewart's cafeteria in the rain—another mad
discovery, to sketch visions of people who in flashing by clutch
at the heart for unspeakably individual reasons. Oh Proust's
Combray cathedral and that aunt who eats "creamed eggs on
one of the flat plates with writing"!—my God that old teahead
of time! Realized tonight that I read a lot of Proust last July in
No. Carolina when I thought *Faulkner* was influencing me to
write of "facebones" Pomeray. I love Proust so much now that
in the history of my affections he ranks with Wolfe & the man
of the Karamazov darkness. . . . (nothing but gloom, turrets,
dark wood and one white hurdle fence, that's Karamazov-town
to me). And now to Dean Pomeray and the Wyoming girls.
(Failed miserably) (Because girls didn't exist.)
    The secret of "what happened next" is not a narrative secret
but merely what the teller genuinely hung-uply wants to explain
& unfold next about the subject he's on, whether it's action or
a turd.

THURSDAY NOVEMBER 15, 1951—A miserable, one of the
worst days I can remember—all indecisive, pepsic, stupid, lost,
dull, irritable, terribly empty . . . and I lost a 20th Century Fox
play script in the subway . . . and got no joy out of anything
I saw or did all day, in fact suspected the worst . . . and even
stared glumly at my Proust. Lack of sleep . . . a touch of phlebitis . . . constipation, making my belly swell . . . long hair, no
money to spare for haircut . . . can't write, failed last night . . .
can't even look anybody in the eyes . . . baggy pants, sweaty
shirt that should have been in the laundry 2 weeks ago . . .
remembering things about my past life that I never remembered before and which are unutterably dreary (I used to like
James Melton & identify him with the hero of *Serenade* when

he sang, all this while my father dozed in a chair so that now I can't even begin to estimate how many hours I wasted in my youth, which is now gone, doing fruitless, asinine & futureless dull-assed things like that instead of hitch hiking on the wild, wild road or throwing flowers into the rooms of pretty dancers, Goddamit to hell I'm getting sick & tired of it & I'm leaving *I'm going to French Morocco*.) Sketched in the 42nd St. White Rose Bar tonight . . . "Following Lee Konitz" was the subject, I saw the lucky bastard in the street. Ah shit, I say . . . it's a terrible enough world without having to be *divided* in yr. own fucking soul. Divided—divided—divided—divided. (Now I'm using a better lead in my pencil.)

Oh what turmoils!—I'm about to become an unspeakable reporter! It's taken me all this time since Oct. 25th to really realize why I couldn't sleep that night and why my "IT WORKED" of 2 days ago wasn't enthusiastic at all; to realize that 3 things prevented me from seeing clearly what had happened, which was so gigantic that it cancelled out *even what I decided in the hospital*. The 3 things were the brief real falling-in-love with Dusty; the deadening effects of the 5-day binge (on the 5th day I lost complete control & defecated a runny lost liquid in my shorts while Dusty & Allen were so out that when they woke up they both asked, like fighters, "What happened?"); and thirdly the offer from A. A. Wyn to give me money on a book in progress which was already subconsciously rejected by my development psyche. So since that time I've been "sketching" [which is in effect the discovery itself] *and* "writing" as of yore, both at the same time, lamenting and realizing now & then that the writing isn't as pure and really truly as good prose as the sketching. And because money was about to be paid to me. . . .

No, my road is clearly & undeniably now this:—

1. So-called sketching is merely writing about living things, either in front of you or foremost haunting yr. memory (latter is Proust), & the result is not "literature" and certainly not fiction but definitely something living (all this applies to *me* at least, for I know that Dostoevsky *imagined* a living thing almost every time, & so Balzac, but my idea is, these were 19th century absorptions & hangups

no longer genuinely possible, the thing now, as Céline, Proust, Wolfe, Genet & Joyce have shown, being no longer fictions, imaginings of reality, but the great interior monologue of the modern tongue written either in exile, jail or sickbed . . . what I'd call THE TRUE STORY OF THE WORLD—IN AN UNDERTONE—FROM UNDERGROUND—"behind the hand," as in Jerry Newman's great Lips Page record, "shh!") and generally speaking I'm to be forgiven for saying that it is not "fiction" or even "literature" in the literary & publishing sense. Add Henry Miller to the list—an imitator of Céline but a man who in my estimation is more important than Henry James.

2. This "sketching" is the actual writing that I will have to do from now on because I don't believe in the rest any more—so-called "objectivity," so-called "story," the *pretense* of it, the *smirk*.

3. A new concept beyond the one I figured in the hospital of how to "divide" my work into books, sections, parts. My Balzac-idea was one character at a time—Neal, then Bill, then Seymour, then Henri, then Lucien, then Vicki, then Dusty, then Ma and so on. Now what should it be?—(as, for instance, "sketching" a trip to Ecuador; to Frisco to resurrect Neal; to Europe to cry; to sea to this and that (to Ecuador to find Bill)—a month in N.Y. looking up everybody, sort of underground interviews, that's what I meant by unspeakable reporter . . . In effect, *mon vieux*, this might mean a *permanent complete daily journal*!!) Some new division, a legitimate one, for this living mass of visions of people, places, confessions, sounds etc.—in other words, some way of *forming* the sketchings in major units. O talk.

Now I'm thinking out loud & wasting diary space. More anon.

I haven't really said why I want to sketch & tell the true story of the world as my appointed part of it flows through my soul—it's because I am in love with my life and I don't want to sell it or fluff it or betray it, and that's what I mean.

Soon now, this journal will end ⌒

And I believe that there is a general movement at this very moment among the great hidden honest writers living in the world today, some of them bearded saints, one of them that old Spanish Reichian eccentric who lived in the California woods and wrote the legends of the Pomos and other Indians in his own hip crazy way, but he only one of many, a movement of men who in the 19th century would have been great novelists but are now so bared down to the bony truth that fiction can only be fiction to them from this moment onward, who know that the modern world can only be expressed in great straight statements made on the spot almost like Christ speaking from the Cross as the winds rise and just as crucial & fatal as that, men who have come to learn that there is nothing more amazing, instructive, filled with soul-saving love or apocalyptic and world-making than what actually happens anywhere at any moment, and soon, (as Whitman knew).

I say this movement is growing the more so as cheap novels increase on bookstands and quite naturally.

But I'm not concerned with reforms, only my love life.

From now on when I say "write" I therefore mean "sketch"— Another great discovery, to sketch, or write, to music—to any sound.

Find the center of the long tirade and add another eye within the eye ☞— Wrote till 5—sketches of "Voyeurs" & "Jamaica Night."

Now I'm REALLY a "writer"—no more stultifying artifice. . .

The Saturday nights of my boyhood are haunted by the Hit Parade and the funnies . . . the HP, always big harps unfolding new tunes, it's been going on since I can remember, back to 1930. In a minute—

FRIDAY NOVEMBER 16, 1951—Talked with A. A. Wyn in his office; verbal agreement about money after Farrar Straus sees my ms.—If they offer, Wyn will up them, if they don't he might try to keep it down to next to nothing. Anyway I really ought to go to sea immediately—black gang, S.I.U., at once, then I'll be a *writer*. Then got gloriously drunk in Glennon's—It's becoming such a universal bar I knew everybody there—Allen,

Dusty, mad Paul Fopatitch, Harrington came in, Raduleviches, suddenly Tom & Ed came in and I was stoned; ended up going to Dusty's with a young kid called Dick Davalos who lifted me drunk off the table and said he didn't like to see me "abandoned" by my friends, which I was by then. Allen, meanwhile, had a joybangful from a doctor for kidney stones and at dawn I remember him telling me the greatest stories I ever heard about Africa . . . the *real* Africa. Came home the next day, a little sick, bringing food. Incidentally on Thursday I lost a script in subway, which was luckily returned. Also I got orders from VA hospital to report for re-check Friday . . . I shall go and dig it in the November now. Feel okay. Made important decision about the Neal book—*no false action*, just visions of what I know he did, NO TIME, NO CHRONOLOGY, composing willy-nilly, as Holmes says, a book surpassing the problem of time by itself being full of the roar of Time (not his words).— Now, if I go to sea—what difference does it make to us today that, or that is, *if* Dostoevsky had gone to sea on unutterably dreary 19th century Russian merchantman, or Proust, or even Genet . . . but maybe my soul is interested in the quality of the red light on the Buenos Aires waterfront roofs . . . eh? I feel that my nature, which now's reached violent maturities, that express themselves in super-sobrieties of enormously absorbed writing-work or complete money-flinging happy drunkenness, can best find itself what it needs if I were a seaman with money on land, solitude at sea, hell on earth, write on water, gabble in cities, scribble in ships, etc. *I'm about to be 30. I've finally solved the lifework. What remains is intensities only.* Intense writing, intense drunks, intense travels, intense responsibilities, intense laughter—Duluoz abroad in the international world! Duluoz taking care of himself, money in his wallet, awed, scribbling around the world, a great friend of many, a lover of beautiful women in distant rooms, a man recording the secret consciousness of the times around the world—.

SATURDAY NOVEMBER 17, 1951—Wedding anniversary. The one with Edie is Aug. 22 which was a date that had mystic significance in my childhood because it was yearly the traditional opening day of the big meets in my marble-racing *Turf* . . . great races went down in history on that date, say

Repulsion winning (beating Kransleet a length) the Sarah Downs Handicap. Nov. 17 had no significance whatever & neither did marriage. There's no sense talking about death unless you really know something about it, which is only when you're dying or someone dying around you like Polonius. The sadomasochism of modernity is its blind spot, its Achilles' heel, its ambiguity, its failure—I'm thinking of Cocteau, Ginsberg, Genet, the painter Fopatitch, maybe Peter Van Meter. I had a dream this afternoon, woke up at noon, deliberately dozed back, and I was taking a young hipster to the Yale Club for a big alumni party to which I was invited, I was wearing a leather jacket & didn't care, I was going to set a new chic style thereby, & I told the kid "We can even smoke weed in here it's so cool, that is to say, so chic & unknowing of things like weed," but lo and behold it was a wild party, almost everybody was in leather jackets, hundreds of hipsters, smoke, wild girls, confusion, queers & one guy who waved me over and I thought it was Peter Van Meter but it wasn't & I said across the room "Peter?" and he shook his head, his buddy also smiling at me, their wild girls sitting on the floor with inscrutable faces.* I *know* now that an anarchy will come in America in this decade or the next . . . a rockbottom strange virility like the one in the dream and yet tremendously opposed to the virility-idea of the 1900's, some kind of Dostoevskyan change is due—and it will be sado-masochistic, bisexual, futuristic. *My position, when it comes, will be inconceivably oldfashioned though I'm sharp enough now to be able to predict it & as I say, to be able to reject it with one hand while accepting it with the other, because, really, I'm too busy for politics, for modes, say, having to do things that span the old and the new, for a reason which will be unknown to them but will teach.* And my teachings, as Proust's teachings through Neal, earlier Wolfe's teachings through Sammy, and Joyce's teachings thru the young man who called himself Duluoz & was myself, will reach somebody through somebody and something else strange and living will happen, the purpose of which will always be a mystery but the existence of which will be accepted as permanently valuable & contributing to some great wave of understanding and acceptance through the

*A dream prophecy of the "Beat Generation" in 1960!

world . . . the world that ever proceeds towards a light, a thing, won't be able to talk about it till it happens and it always happens, that is to say, it's already happened, is happening in fact now and every single moment, and the name of it is Life. O wiggling life! HOW ELSE CAN YOU KNOW HAPPINESS EXCEPT IN LIFE?

So this is my last "prophecy"—I prophesy life. (The trouble, after that dream, is I should have dealt in facts to support my prophecy but later . . . I want to save this page to include the closing factor of the entire diary, my re-visit to the Hospital . . .) Did a $6 script, walked a few miles, dug sunset clouds, sketched midnight lunchroom; pondering "Go to sea now or finish Dean *Road* first?" Maw's all for sea in long run.—Hot tapioca pudding with cold vanilla sauce . . . This is like Proust's cake soaked in tea, it rouses a million sensations of Lowell. Goddamit I want to use the Proustian method of recollection and amazement but *as I go along* in life, not after, so therefore why don't I allow myself to write about Neal and using his real name in my own private scribble book for my own joy!— Doesn't my own work & joy belong to me any more? *IF I DON'T DO THIS, I LIE.*—Tonite's "work" consisted of nothing but expositions about "Dean" for the "reader"—*ASSEZ, maudit Christ de Batême—Si tu va être un écrivain commence à ce soir ou commence jamais!!* [Here's what I wrote—"Of course Dean immediately conned the whole gang, Bill Johnson who was the central golden boy before him, Al Buckle the real pillar . . ." —what mincing camping crap]— and I have a real tragic actual Neal in my thoughts all the time that I repress for this kind of coal, here I am with a real mind & won't use it. If I can't begin tonight I simply never really will—that's all. The real, the real, afraid of the rest— Oh Jesus forgive me—

Teach me to write "for your own future reference"—if I were in Istanbul tonight wouldn't it be best to fill an entire notebook with the things that I see in front of me & with my visions of what I see plus whatever haunted hangup was underway (say my relation to ship or whatnot) instead of . . . some dumb story or other. The story is the echo chamber of my own brain maybe . . . let me tell the story of right now for instance . . . but not now . . . but if I do, completely, I might get to Neal via the honest way. Oh help me!—And supposing Allen had kept *complete track* of all that Africa adventure; who is it always says fiction is more interesting than truth? *There's only one story and that's completely what happened in actual life somewhere, sometime*; and there's no way of knowing it unless you were there and scribbled it down as it took place. Another possibility is the complete memory of someone, or something, which can only be, as Proust said, the memory that haunts, not the necessity memory, the one that says . . . "What belongs here now is—"; rather, the memory that begins "Oh God that time that he—"

TUESDAY NOVEMBER 20, 1951—Why does the mere sight of the French word, future-tense verb *BOULEVERSERA* in a review from *La Voix du Nord* fill me with a premonition not only of the great joy I will get from Paris next year, next Spring, but the joy and purpose of all my life? These past days I sketched in St. Patrick's Cathedral, Garden cafeteria, & was standing in front of 42nd St. Grant's picking my teeth when old Dark Eyes Ginger stopped in the flowing crowd & stared at me with amazement—We talked & sang all night; I showed her "Home in Wounded Knee" for her folk repertory—Poor Ginger!—lost, eager, idealistic, mad . . . Poor Hal!—sick, broken, crazy, confused, blind. *I Accept lostness Forever*

Tonight I know everything. It's also the night I discovered that I can write down the entire universe of my dreams, my subconscious dreams, as well as the rest . . . And how to REALLY do Neal or anybody, bless my soul, bless and protect my bursting, my breakable, my unlosable soul. (I'll win.) It's like Bobby Thomson's homerun, my soul tonight—Oh fancy name for childlike place. —Happiness is like a baby olive; you can't take big bites out of it, or hurry it along; despair is like the pit, the closer you are to it the sweeter is happiness. So it's this (baby olive or no baby olive):—everything is really lost, don't ever be fooled. My own destruction is nevertheless the only thing that will ever prevent me from believing in the holy contour of life.

FRIDAY NOVEMBER 23, 1951—What to say? Went to the hospital this morning at 10, rising from Dusty's couch after a big Thanksgiving party with Ginger, Mardean, Alan Ansen, Lucien, Jerry Newman, Cessa, Allen, and others. Ansen is amazing . . . and reminds me of the fact that my communication on every level of the mind is only possible with people like Ansen with the sole exception of Neal . . . how sad my life will be even later than this. At the hospital nothing really happened, maybe because of hangover, or maybe I forsaw all of it anyhow. Tonight I'm writing a big letter to Neal. Wrote 3300 words of it at midnite—I think my next journal should be in "scribble" instead of print.— (I think I drink because I want to make people respond wildly, be happy, enthusiastic.)

SATURDAY NOVEMBER 24, 1951—Walked 2 miles in Jamaica, sketched a little; typed up Neal's letter; ate beans & ham, bought cider & bread; walked again at night, thought "Now, and *now*, the time is coming to '*sketch*' *your own mind*, and what is more specific, sketch the flow of the universe of Neal or anyone else that already exists intact in yr. mind." Is this the answer? Maybe the only answer is work—ragged work no; the answer is absorbed & profound work, profoundly hungup struggles with the pencil to go fast enough to delineate what I really know. This really *dear* diary now comes to a close . . . I may have decided the great work-factors of my life in its pages, I may not—but anyway it's dear, and Duluoz went on. —The truth is hilarious, that's what. . . and garrulous . . . and ridiculous. The value is in the dream; life is a dream. Feeling is the key for me. Admit it, putting together a ms. for publication form is hack work . . . composing itself must be wild, undisciplined, pure, eager, coming in deep from under, the crazier the better. Thought all, all night—I decided to write till Xmas, then put papers together & see what I've got.

SUNDAY NOVEMBER 25, 1951—Something that you feel will find its own form. That's all there is to it. So, after a 1½ mile walk, I started on *the redbrick wall behind the neons* to prove this & begin my-life-alone-in-America: I'm lost, but my work is found. Last night there was a face in my window, saying "Write what you want." I thought it was Faulkner, I think it was really Dr. Sax. I'm going to write over 3000 words a day like this and see what I have at Xmas.

So the growing peace, and the most beautiful visions of life, that began three months ago & which were great enough for a Remembrance 10,000,000 words long, the peace has led to a mind filled with work and a soul fortified with the knowledge of the inevitability of loss—and so goodbye sweet journal, adieu calm book, may the best hearts find you.

Epilogue

I think a change has come in my life
and though that'll mean so very little
a few years, 10 years, 50 years, 100 years
from now, maybe the work that I'll do
because of it will mean a lot and
I hope it does—whether my children,
historians, or that ancient-history worm
reads this, I say it anyway, I hope
it is true that a man can die and
yet not only live in others but give
them life, and not only life but
that great consciousness of life that
made cathedrals rise from the smoke
& rickets of the poor, mantles fall
from illuminated kings, gospels spread
from twisted tortured mouths or living
saints that sit in dust, crying, crying
crying, till all eyes see.

⁓

OLD BULL IN THE BOWERY

(1952, MEXICO CITY)

[WRITTEN IN FRENCH PATOIS]

Old Bull in the Bowery

Between the completion of the 1951 scroll manuscript and the publication of the 1957 Viking Press edition of *On the Road*, Kerouac continued to tinker with and reimagine the parameters of his narrative. In a January 10, 1953, letter to Neal Cassady, composed in Richmond Hill, Kerouac proclaimed: "In Mexico, after you left, I in 5 days wrote, in French, a novel about me and you when we was kids in 1935 meeting in Chinatown with Uncle Bill Balloon, your father and my father and some sexy blondes in a bedroom with a French Canadian rake and an old Model T. You'll read it in print someday and laugh. It's the solution to the 'On the Road' plots all of em and I will hand it in soon as I finish translating and typing."

Kerouac composed this French text primarily in two separate notebooks from December 1952, in which he had given it two working titles: *Sur le chemin* and *French Old Bull in the Bowery*. Despite his claim to have found the solution to *On the Road*—which involved creating an imaginary narrative of Kerouac and Neal meeting as children during the Great Depression—he was not yet finished with this particular draft. In 1954, he set about translating *Sur le chemin* into English, embellishing as he went, an effort resulting in a forty-three-page typescript, *Old Bull in the Bowery*.

Kerouac never completed that translation, however, and *Sur le chemin* exists in Kerouac's archive as a bilingual text scattered across several 1952 patois manuscripts, his partial 1954 translation, and English-language inserts, two of which he also inserted into *Visions of Cody*.

The text included here, edited by Jean-Christophe Cloutier, represents a conflation of Kerouac's unfinished translation and Cloutier's translation of the remainder, along with some passages originally in English that have been interpolated according to Kerouac's indications.

IN THE MONTH OF OCTOBER, 1935, in the night of our real restless lives, a car came from the West, from Denver, on the road for New York. In the car were Dean Pomeray, a wino; Dean Pomeray Jr. his little son of nine; and Rolfe Glendiver, his step son, 24. It was an old Model T Ford. All three had their eyes tied on the road in the night through the windshield; when they closed their eyes they saw the road roll, white line in black floor; but it was Rolfe driving all the way. The others didn't know they had the right to sleep in back on the blankets and the old cans and the old suitcases deboxed with their ropes tied around, if they wanted.

Rolfe wore cowboy boots, he was a cowboy on the Robeson Bar O Bar Ranch at Gunnison, Colorado, the other side of the Great Divide from Denver; a real cowboy, he broke boncs, he'd have a broken back in ten years; he castrated bulls and rode the long fences with shears and pliers, eyes half closed in the wind. He had a handsome face, a fine nose, blue eyes, and laughed with white teeth. He was very nice but lost himself in his thoughts; they didn't understand him at home. He was the tragic son of broken marriage and death of both parents, he was all alone among the aunts of eternity in a big house full of incomprehensible bustle with doors that opened on the mountains of snow and rock, the Rockies, and the great dun bleak land of Denver plain. The house was on the foot of the mountain, near Morrison Road.

Old Pomeray had his wine, a bottle of port wine, California Four Star brand; he was a Larimer Street wino in Denver; his little son panhandled for him; had spoken for him in the night courts with great teeth of district juvenile courts going in his face; at present they lived in a flophouse together, the "Skylark" near the Windsor Hotel at Larimer and 19th. Rolfe was the son of Pomeray's wife from another marriage, his poor wife tragic and dead who'd had the big jaw draped and fallen like the drapes of life . . . all kinds of death we had not so long ago. Rolfe was the only one of the Glendivers who took pains with the old widowed alcoholic and his little son with the dirty ears the family'd occasionally let stay in the field house. There had been nights when you saw the light of the big house and the brown light of the shack at the same time in the same wind. . . .

Okay, he was going to drive them to New York to meet Uncle Bull Baloon who had found them a place to live in the "Bowery," in New York—near Chatham Square and China-town. Baloon was the brother of the mother. They believed that, they were going to live in New York in a real place with sinks and a stove and the father was going to work his trade as a barber in the exciting blue morning of the Bowery, with rags whipping in the wind, "We'll cook our steaks ourselves," he'd say, the old man, explaining to his little son beside the cold radiators of poor Western hotels during the Depression, "we'll be able to save our money to eat." It was not a practical idea, but there was no one in the car who knew that.

The car crossed the great gray studies of Indiana in the fall when the sun isn't lighting the harvest stacks. It was vast, beautiful; the boys didn't see anything, they talked about their plans; in the nights the harvest moon came out and they saw the harvest stacks with their melancholy frowse making little hairs in the somberness, clear like that. It was the great land around where Pomeray's parents came from. "Near Dakota, Rolfe? We all come from here, we all had pitchforks. I had a Aunt Mandy that lived in Keota Ioway, one in Poplar Bluffs had cans of pork and beans by the cases." They talked full of lies all night.

The little boy never let his head fall, he looked directly ahead of him with his eyes fallen, understanding what was going to happen, once in a while he'd look at his foot and fix a tape bandage inside his shoe, no socks and the foot all black and dirty; a shirt under a little black sweater full of holes; a tennis ball in his hand. It was little Dean Pomeray, they called him "Dopey" now in the gangs of little Negroes and Indians who played in the street at Welton and 27th near the gas tank of Denver, "Dopey" because he thought his thoughts way behind their fires, they could see his eyes brillianting in the darkness, a little boy frightening and frightened by the Phantom of the Opera of our childhood, the big ghosts of wind that hid near the redbrick warehouses of Market Street back of Wazee and stole with black rags for gloves the little winds that came out of the boxcars so lonely. "Damn it was dirty!"—you'd think the

foreman of the first floor would show up in a minute with his
pocketbook broken in a can if you should ever ask him to stay
for the night. Little Dean and his father had found the key to
the joy of innocence, they thought, in this trip. The poor blah
blahs of cold corners . . . It had been decided; the little son let
the old man be, he wasn't going to say anything; but he had
his own ideas—but the thing that ran his father was God. He
was a Catholic, from his mother, he sang little altar boy songs,
little heart-boy songs, in the haystacks dirtied by the horses of
Nebraska; he waited in the wind praying for the toot toot of
the engineer of the chain gang freight before rising from the
barrels of the tracks to climb a gondola. He saw the mountain
stars in the sky; trees yelled at him and his father near creeks;
malignantly crashing from every leaf; the great wheels rolled
underneath them like gigantic beasts haggard with fright walking arm-to-mouth pushing in the whitenesses of the fog the
empowdering monstrous weights of steel that screamed on the
track with a "squee squee"—it was the dog of their try-sleep in
coats in the night, heads on iron.

In New York they were met by Uncle Bull. In the letter,
the second letter, explaining, he had said to come on to an 18
Pott Street address. When they entered New York the cowboy
and Pomeray and little Dean began to ask for 18 Pott Street.
It was gray and dirty, little Dean was scared. He—for a little
reason like the boy who's too small for the bed and the bed
doesn't belong to him—got scared when they passed dirty garbage cans leaning one against the other in front of a theater
show, and Negroes with big hats passed who spat early in the
morning. It wasn't glad like he'd imagined. Dean thought to
see big black buildings undersupported by golden light, like
windows cut in cardboard, with the little smoke that comes
out of hidden pots and the big marble floor with potted plants
inside the windows, women in gold printed on the windows
like plaques of golden banks, like on restaurant menus of old
newspapers found on the ground. Rolfe and Pomeray were
impossibly lost in the city. Fifth Avenue. "Eighteen Pott Street.
You got *me*, mister!" said the New Yorkers hearing it.

"Go down this way," said Pomeray. Rolfe looked the other.
They turned the car in the middle of traffic, Lord and Taylor's
at high noon, to think, to turn. Sixth Avenue. They found

their way to Pott Street only by the grace of God . . . There were policemen who tried to explain to them how to get just to Chinatown, and they didn't understand. Aw mystery.

They found the way only when an old bum in Lafayette Street told them with motions and actions, how—an old clown in rags, a sick devil agitating himself in the dirty winds of the street late in the afternoon his big sunken teeth enduring life hard in the redness of seven o'clock autumn and the other boys all lined up behind him like murders with hands in their pockets. "Not when you get to the corner of the two hockshops," the bum was yelling earnestly, "the corner of the *three*!" It was red and sad to see him disappear around a platform of old wood and iron. Like that, the instructions anxious and direct showing them exactly how to find the corner he meant, they didn't have to read the signs, just look, but they asked themselves if the bum wanted to play the fool and yakked about it, and they found 18 Pott Street. Old Bull was there on the sidewalk, cigar in mouth, with a gray fedora hat and a dark gray overcoat that flapped in the wind; he was yakking with his big toothless mouth, with a Chinaman. The boys in the car gaped; it was something new.

The Chinese was dressed in an old gray sweater, and old pants, no hat, gray hair—he owned the queer loft upstairs, second story, with big curtains in the show windows. It was a place for cards, on old boxes from his store, where he lit an old bulb once in a while and played cards. There were bags of rice, boxes of dried fish and noodles in the black corners. On the floor he had put old blankets on cardboard, and that was for the convenience of Uncle Bull when he got drunk and couldn't make it to his room at the Roxy Hotel on 42nd Street while waiting for his relatives from Denver. It had been a wild week between these two but there was no more time to talk about it, the others had arrived.

Pomeray was Bull's brother-in-law; he had married the sad and sick woman, the dead one, the sister of Old Bull. She had left Canada to marry a man from the Middlewest, a minister of a man with a big hat, Smiley Glendiver; after his death married the bum. There had been sad voyages in the old cars in the West in the 1920s under the telephone wires that make the children fall asleep, mirages, fights, warnings.

"Pain isn't dead," said the mother Henrieta in her bed. They swallowed her in her box, they lost her in the earth; they wanted to put a stone on her ground but they forgot, like she.

Bull's real name was Guillaume Bernier-Gaos, he came from Quebec. His brother-in-law was the father of Leo Duluoz who was coming from Boston now with his little son of thirteen, Jean, to meet the parents in Chinatown, and had with him the key to the apartment Pomeray was going to occupy. It was a mixup of black old men, a dotty tenderness.

The old Chinese was called Ching Boy, his brother Sam Boy of Boston was a friend of Bull's; Old Bull knew everybody, lived here and there from New York and Boston and Butte Montana and everywhere, a real worker; he was a gambler, operated hand printing presses when he wanted; for his living was a conductor on the railroad, an oldtime boomer, went from one railroad to another following the important seasons; it had been a long time since he worked. He found himself every year a little worse than the year past, he felt sad.

Rolfe Glendiver was the only man there who wasn't all bowled over and scared for advantage, the winnings, the losings—the pain of death—except the Chinese gentleman. "At the carnival where you can't lose you'll learn losing was your only hope, you bunch of beasts!" Rolfe more or less thought.

It was night when they arrived at 18 Pott Street. It had taken them all day looking, in the Bronx, Greenwich Village, they'd eaten lunches in the car. Night on Chatham Square. The October wind was starting to rise like a phantom in the streets. There were some streets cobblestoned—some black like the dog. The elevated was overhead, dirty, crashing, dropping sparks. They were around the corner from Bowery Street, not directly under the El. *Bouge, Saloon* was written on the little stick-legs of old women who passed, their mouths bite-bottle broken. Workers came out of nearby shops, pessimistic because of facts. Over the old roof of the loft could be seen high office buildings with white and blue profound lights; below, the red neons of bars made red creams on the sidewalks of dust and spit. It seemed there were phantoms climbing the sides of the buildings that were like Italian palaces. There was a big brown sick light quivering and eating in the sky in little pieces like rats in the wind of God; that was high over the city, it told a story funnier than dramatic; New York wasn't as bad as the angel of its rainbow that jumped out of all the sad lights and arranged itself in the Profundity as if to see what it had lit; a cloud a bitch to understand when you look. Little Pott Street was illuminated a queer rose, half Chinatown and half the Bowery of warehouses.

"Listen, Bill," said Pomeray, "I know you think I'm just a damn bum—after the last time we got out of the car in Butte when you was working your Blackjack table and I told you the boys was waiting for me in Cheyenne—that's another story—I'm gonna hit all the barbershops in New York *tomorrow*, we'll see if I'm just a drunk without no hands—mm?"

"Think nothing like that," Bull told him. "My sister told me to help you when I could—you and little Dean—"

"Okay, alright!" the old man cried, almost in tears, leaning to hear, little Dean watching his father full face in wanting to understand.

"—and so I don't think no bad thoughts about you"—Bull said not listening—"but I believe you try like you can, even though it don't work a hell of a lot—Come, my friend Ching Boy has a bed for you upstairs, on the floor but you can sleep there tonight if we don't find Leo and the key to the rooms."

"Where are the rooms?" demanded Pomeray, finger stiff so's not to forget.

Bull looked at him with his calm air, "On Henry Street, not far to here."

Pomeray wobbled his head; you could see he was thinking something else; that he'd already begun to forget, to tell himself not to forget, to see strange dreams that rose like walls in front of his mélange of images of what was going to happen. He had thought it out in dreams, head-on-hand, in big rooms.

They took their stuff out of the car, brought it upstairs. Rolfe was smoking a cigarette in the street, hands in pockets; a woman passed on the other side of the street, Chinese, Rolfe said "Fweet fweet angel, you goin home?" and watched her hurry home, his eyes pure and laughing, his mouth turned under as if hidden. He laughed. "Hyoo hyoo hyoo!—she shore ran off when I said that, *damn*!" He was laughing.

"What you gonna do Rolfe?" Uncle Bull was saying descending the high stairs of the loft that were big enough for ten men

shoulder to shoulder, big enough to sit a surly class of taxidriv-
ers, with little iron rails up and down the sides for summer
sitters. Bull was interested in Rolfe, he had seen him once, in
1929, in Denver, in a winter when he worked for the Burlington
Railroad there, the year Omer Leclerc worked the railroad with
him. He had known Rolfe's grandfather with the white hair,
old Wade Glendiver, who was killed in the crackup with his
grandson after a long life in the West since the 1880s when he'd
raise his big black peak-crowned hat politely to Baby Doe as
she came out on muddy Larimer Street to her waiting carriage
and some oldtimer'd whoopee to see her, and it. For a time
Old Bull himself had stayed in the white cottage under the
cottonwood in the yard, the house his brother-in-law Smiley
Glendiver, his sister's first husband, kept on the property, a few
feet from the old field shack so that some times you'd have seen
three lights casting relative glows in the Western night. Smiley
had been mayor of a small town in his time . . .

"No," said Rolfe, who had grown up in the big house, always
had one car after another, hot rods, before he'd left to work on
ranches, sick to return home, "no, I'm goin for a walk, see the
city," and was leaving.

"There's a hotel down the street, rooms, if you want a
room," said Uncle Bull. "You got a little money of your own?
We'll make out here—I bought eggs and some coffee, bread,
potatoes, I'm gonna make a big supper for the boys—We're
going to wait for Leo, my nephew from Massachusetts. You
never knew him, your mother was his aunt." Rolfe couldn't
hear what he was saying in the wind, from the hole in the side
of his mouth—in the impossibleness.

Rolfe pushed his hat over his eyes and went down the street
in his cowboy boots. "Yay, I'll be back."

How dark it was in the windows of the loft—little Dean
from behind the drapes was watching the wind that had eaten
Rolfe. On the other side of the street he could see a room,
with a bulb, an old bed, a box on the window, a little Chinese
boy who cried on a chair near a glass of water, a great shadow
that walked one side of the light to the other. In Bowery Street
he saw bums pass; there was one in a white shirt, no coat in
the cold night, and big red nose impossibly bloated, walking
lost, eight cents in hand, and his hand clenched—in back of

him gangs of drunks in black clothes, one had a baseball hat, another an Army greatcoat, the generals of the dust were throwing themselves down the street to the hole.

Dean's father was dressed in an old impossibly eaten coat, and an old black hat that looked like he'd picked it up on the side of the railroad track—a floppy hat willynilly rolled by rain, shroudy, like a cowboy with one eye and a little pointed head—He too his nose was red—his whole face, red and sad— He spoke in a little voice you could hardly hear. He had blue Irish eyes. In Denver sometimes, when little Dean stayed at the Glendivers to assuage the conscience of the grandmother, the father lived in an abandoned house under a viaduct; he read old pocketbooks there that he found among shitpiles of bums, shoes, bottles, pieces of house plaster. He was a real impossible bum. You could see him from the viaduct walking sadly among the immense six foot weeds of his yard, his piles of boards he never used, the cover of a magazine in his hand, rolling like a sad old ball in disaster. "If I can find another paper bag to re-inforce my bag—it won't make no difference if it's already been wet—If I could find three!" He wasn't forty-three years old but he looked sixty. He drank wine with hair-heavy-greasy maned Indians in the livingrooms of the abandoned houses— sometimes in the cellars when they got afraid.

Little Dean was dressed in big jeans, torn in one knee a lot, and sneakers and a little Navy pea coat for children given to him by the Glendivers. He almost looked like his father but only in the eyes. He had passed his boyhood between his father and the Glendivers. It was only eight years before, in 1927, that Dean was born, in Salt Lake City; at a time when for some Godforsaken reason, some forgotten pitiably American restless reason his father and mother were driving in a jalopy from Iowa to L.A. in search of something, maybe they figured to start an orange grove or find a rich uncle, Dean himself never found out, a reason long buried in the sad heap of the night, a reason that nevertheless in 1927 caused them to fix their eyes anxiously and with throat-choking hope over the sad swath of brokendown headlamps shining brown on the road . . . the road that sorrowed into the darkness and huge unbelievable American nightland like an arrow. Dean was born in a charity hospital. A few weeks later the jalopy clanked right on; so that now there were three pairs of eyes watching the unspeakable road roll in on Paw's radiator cap as it steadfastly penetrated the night like the poor shield of themselves, the little Pomeray family, lost, the gaunt crazy father with the floppy slouched hat that made him look like a brokendown Okie Shadow, the dreaming mother in a cotton dress purchased on a happier afternoon in some excited Saturday five-and-ten, the frightened infant. Poor mother of Dean Pomeray what were your thoughts in 1927? Somehow or other, they soon came back to Denver over the same raw road; somehow or other nothing worked out right the way they wanted; without a doubt they had a thousand unspecified troubles and knotted their fists in despair somewhere outside a house and under a tree where something went wrong, grievously and eternally wrong, enough to kill people; all the loneliness, remorse and chagrin in the world piled on their heads like indignities from heaven. Oh mother of Dean Pomeray, but was there secretly in you a lovely memory of a jovial Sunday afternoon back home when you were famous and beloved among friends and family, and young?—when maybe you saw your father standing among the men, laughing, and you crossed the celebrated human floor of the then-particular beloved stage to him (to put a rose on his coat). Was it from lack of life, lack of haunted pain and memories, lack of sons and trouble and speechless desire that you died, or was it from excess of death? She died in Denver before Dean was old enough to talk to her. Dean grew up with a childhood vision of her standing in the strange antique light of 1930—which is no different than the light of today or the light when Xerxes' fleets confused the waves, or Agamemnon wailed—in some kind of living room with beads hanging from the door, apparently at a period in the life of old Pomeray when he was making good money at his barber trade and they had a good home. But after she died he became one of the most tottering bums of Larimer Street, making futile attempts at first to work as a fieldhand for his wife's farming family outside Denver (the Glendivers) to make a home for Baby Dean but leaving him there in good hands to hop a freight for Texas to escape the Colorado winters, beginning a lifetime swirl of hoboing into which little Dean himself was sometimes sucked later on, when at intervals, childlike, he preferred leaving the security of his

Ma's relatives, which included sharing a bedroom with his step-brother, going to school, and altar-boying at a local Catholic church, to live with his father in flophouses. Nights long ago on the brawling sidewalks of Larimer Street when the Depression hobo was there by the thousands, sometimes in great sad lines black with soot in the rainy dark of Thirties newsreels, men with sober downturned mouths huddled in old coats waiting in line for misery. Dean used to stand in front of alleys begging for nickels while his father, red-eyed, in baggy pants, hid in the back with some old bum crony called Rex who was no king but just an American who had never outgrown the boyish desire to lie down on the sidewalk which he did year round from coast to coast; the two of them hiding and sometimes having long excited conversations until the kid had enough nickels to make up a bottle of wine, when it was time to hit the liquor store and go down under ramps and railroad embankments and light a small fire with cardboard boxes and naily boards and sit on overturned buckets or oily old treestumps, the boy on the outer edges of the fire, the men in its momentous and legendary glow, and drink the wine. "Wheeoo! Hand me that damn bottle 'fore I knock somebody's head in!"

This was the chagrin of bums suddenly becoming wild joy, the switchover from all the poor lonely woe of one like Pomeray having to count pennies on streetcorners with the wind blowing his dirty hair over his snarling, puffy, disgruntled face, his revulsion burping and scratching a lonely crotch at flophouse sinks, his agony waking up on a strange floor (if a floor at all) with his mad mind reeling in a million disorderly images of damnation and strangulation in a world too horrible to stand and yet so full of sweet nameless moments worth living for that he couldn't say no to it completely without committing some terrified sin, attacked repeatedly by images of horrible joy making him twitch and marvel and gasp as before visions of heart-wrenching hell penetrating up through life from unnumberable hullabalooing voices screaming in insanity below, with piteous memories, the sweet and nameless ones, that reached back to fleecy cradle days to make him sob, finally sinking to the floor of some brokendown pisshouse to wrap around the bowl and maybe die as he certainly would some day—this misery with a bottle of wine was twisted around in his brain like a nerve and the tremendous joy of the really powerful drunk filled the night with shouts and who knows what huge illumination from out his bulging power-mad eyes like floodlights. On Larimer Street old Pomeray was known as The Barber, occasionally working near the Greeley Hotel in a really terrible barbershop with a great unswept floor of bums' hair, and a shelf sagging under so many bottles of bay rum that you'd think the shop was on an ocean going vessel and it had been stocked for a six months' siege. In this drunken tonsorial pissery called a barbershop because hair was cut off your head from the top of the ears down old Pomeray, with the same tender befuddlement with which he sometimes lifted garbage barrels to city disposal trucks during blizzards and emergencies or passed wrenches in the most tragic, becluttered, greasedark auto body shop west of the Mississippi (Arapahoe Garage by name where they even hired him), tiptoed around a barber chair with scissor and comb, razor and mug to make sure not to stumble, and cut the hairs of blacknecked hoboes who had such vast lugubrious personalities that they sometimes sat stiffly at attention for the big event for a whole hour.

"Well now say, Dean, how've been things in the hotel this summer; anybody I know kick the bucket or which. Dan was up at Chilian Jack's when I passed through, said he forgot if you remembered that fifty cents he owed you."

"Can't talk right now Jim till I get the side of Bob's head done—hold on just a second whilst I raise up that shade."

And a great huge clock tocked these dim old hours away while young Dean sat in the stove corner (in cold weather) reading the comic pages, not only reading but examining for hours the face and paunch of Major Hoople, his fez, the poor funny chairs in his house, the sad sickening faces of his hecklers who always seemed to be eating at the table, the whole pitiful world in back of it including maybe a faint cloud in the distance, or a bird dreamed in a single wavery line over the boardfence, and the eternal mystery of the dialog balloon hiding parts of the visible universe just for speech; that and *Out Our Way*, the ragdoll rueful cowboys and factory workers who always seemed to be chewing wads of food and wrapping themselves miserably around fenceposts in the great sorrowful burden of a joke and of time; yet most amazing of all the clouds, the clouds that in the cartoon sky had all the nostalgia of sweet and haunted distance that pictures give them and yet were the same lost clouds that always called Dean's attention to his immortal destiny when suddenly seen from a window or through houses on a June afternoon, lamby clouds of babyhood and eternity, making him think, "Poor world that has to have clouds for afternoons and the meadows I lost"; sometimes doing this, or looking at the sad brown or green tint pictures of troubled lovers in sensual livingrooms of *True Confessions* magazine, his foretaste of wild pornographical joys to come; sometimes, though, only fixing his eyes on the mosaic of the tiles on the barbershop floor where each little square could be peeled back ad infinitum, tiny leaf by tiny leaf, revealing in wee encyclopedia the complete history of every person in existence as far back as the beginning, the whole thing a dazzling sight when he raised his eyes from one tile and absorbed all the others and saw the crazy huge infinity of the world swimming. In warm weather he sat out on the sidewalk on a box between the barbershop and a movie that was so beat that it could only be called a C or a D movie; the Capricio, with motes of dusty sunshine swimming down past the slats of the box office in drowsical midafternoon, the lady of the tickets dreaming with nothing to do as from the dank maw of the movie, cool, dark, and perfumed with seats, and as bums slept, roared the gunshots and hoofbeats of the world, baggy-eyed riders who drank too much in bars around Hollywood galloping in the moonlight photographed from the back of a truck in dusty California roads, with a pathetic human plot worked in to make everybody overlook that the riders really are themselves. What disappointment came then into little Dean's eyes who didn't have a dime to see the show; not even a penny sometimes to take ten minutes selecting a candy from a lovely becluttered counter in a poor dark candy store where also there were celluloid toys gathering dust as those same immortal clouds passed over the street outside; the look of disappointment he had on those nights when he sat amidst the haha-ing harsh yellings of the bums under the bridge with the bottle, when he knew that the men who were rich tonight were his brothers but they were brothers who had forgotten him; when he knew that all the doings and excited negotiatings of life which included even the pitiful acquisition of the night's wine by his father and Rex led to the grave, in the end, in the unconscious end; and when suddenly beyond the freightyards in the mountain dark illuminated by great stars, where nevertheless and wondrously in a last hung dusk, a single red flame of the sun now making long shadows in the Pacific lingered on Berthoud's mighty wall as the world turned silently, he could hear the Denver and Rio Grande locomotive double-chugging at the base of a raw mountain gap to begin the big climb to dews, jackpines and windy heights of the mountain night, bearing the sad brown boxcars of the world to distant junctions where lonely men in mackinaws waited, to new towns of smoke and lunchcarts, for all he knew as he sat there with his ragged sneakers stuck in the oily yard and among the sooty irons of his fate, to the glittering Alhambras of San Francisco and fogs and ships. Oh little Dean Pomeray if there had been some way to send a cry to you even when you were too little to know what utterances and cries are for in this dark earth, with your terrors in the malign and inhospitable world your every unnamable tiny pain presaging huge death, and all the insults from heaven ramming down to crown your head with rage, pain, disgrace, worst of all the snotted poverty in and out of every splintered door of days, if someone could have said to you then, and made you perceive, "Fear life but don't die; you're alone but everybody's alone. Don't you know the winner wins a ghost, the loser gains a sadness? Oh Dean Pomeray, you can't win, you can't lose, all is ephemeral, all is hurt."

Old Bull Baloon (speaking of loneliness and the diaphanous ghost of days) a singularly lonely man, and most ephemeral, along about one of these years went broke and became so beat that he went into temporary partnership with Pomeray. Old Bull Baloon who usually went around clad in a poker-wrinkled respectable suit with a watch chain, straw hat, Racing Form, cigar and suppurated red nose (and of course the pint flask) and was now fallen so low, for you could never say that he could prosper while other men fell, that his usually suppositious half-clown appearance with the bulbous puff of beaten flesh for a face, and the twisted mouth, his utter lovelessness in the world alone among foolish people who didn't see his soul in other words the hounded old reprobate clown and drunkard of eternity, was now deteriorated down to tragic realities and shabbiness in a bread line, all the rich history of his soul crunching underfoot among the forlorn pebbles. But his and old Pomeray's scheme was well nigh absurd; little Dean was taken along. They got together a handful of greasy quarters, bought wire, screen, cloth and sewing needles and made hundreds of flyswatters; then in Old Bull's 1927 Graham-Paige they headed for Nebraska to sell door to door. Huge prairie clouds massed and marched above the indescribable anxiety of the earth's surface where men lived as their car belittled itself in immensity, crawled eastward like a potato bug over roads that led to nothing. One bottle of whiskey, just one bottle of whiskey was all they needed; whereas little Dean who sat in the rattly back seat counting the lonely pole-by-pole throb of telegraph lines spanning sad America only wanted bread that you buy in a grocery store all fresh in a happy red wrapper that reminded him speechlessly of happy Saturday mornings with his mother long dead—bread like that and butter, that's all. They sold their pathetic flyswatters at the backdoors of farms where farmers' wives with lone Nebraska writ in the wrinkles around their dull bleak eyes accepted fate and paid a nickel. Out on the road outside Ogallala a great argument developed between Pomeray and Old Bull as to whether they were going to buy a little whiskey or a lot of wine, one being a wino, the other an alcoholic. Not having eaten for a long time, feverish, they leaped out of the car and started making brawling gestures at each other which was supposed to represent a fistfight between two men—so absurd that little Dean gaped and didn't cry. And of course the next moment they were embracing each other, old Pomeray tearfully, Old Bull raising his eyes with lonely sarcasm at the huge and indefatigable heavens of life with the remark "Yass, wrangling around on the bottom of the hole." Because everybody was in a hole during then, and felt it. They returned clonking up Larimer Street with about $28 which was promptly that night hurled downward flaming in the drain like Milton's fallen angel—a vast drunk that lasted five days and was almost humorous as it described crazy circles around town from the car, which was parked on Larimer at 22nd, little Dean sleeping in it, to the old office over a garage in a leafy side street that Old Bull had once used as headquarters for a spot remover venture and where pinochle at a busted dusty rolltop desk consumed thirty-six hours of their fevered reprieve, to the Glendiver farm outside town (now abandoned by the family and left to Old Bull) and where drinking was done in barns and ruined livingrooms and out in cold alfalfa rows, finally teetering back downtown, Pomeray migrating back to the railyards like the meek-eyed pigeons owned by sadistic trainers to collapse beneath Rex in a pool of urine beneath dripping ramps while Old Bull Baloon's huge pukey tortured bulk was finally reposed on the plank in the county jail, strawhat over his nose. So little Dean woke up in the car on a cold clear October morning and didn't know what to do, Gaga, the beggar without legs who clattered tragically on his rollerboard on Wazee Street, took him in, fed him, made him a bed on the floor like a bed of straw and spent the night thundering around in bulge-eyed excitement trying to catch him in a foul hairy embrace that would have succeeded if he'd had legs or Dean didn't.

There came a time much later, after years of hopping around with his father like this and on freight trains all over the West and so many futilities everywhere that he'd never remember them all, when Dean had a dream that changed his life entirely. He dreamed he lived in an immense cosmic flophouse dormitory located in the Denver High School auditorium; that one night he was walking across the street in an exhilarated state, carrying a mattress under his arm; all up and down the street with its October night lights glittering clear swarmed the bums, with his father off somewhere doing something busy, excited, feverish. Then Dean realized he was fifteen years older; he wore a T-shirt in the brisk weather; but his beer belly bulged slightly over the belt. His arms were the muscular arms of an ex-boxer growing flabbier. His hair was combed slick but it was thinning back from bony frowns and Mephistophelean hairlines. His face was his own but it was strangely puffed, beaten, the nose in fact was almost broken, a tooth was missing. When he coughed it sounded harsh and hoarse and maniacally excited like his father. He was going somewhere to sell the mattress for wine money: his exhilaration was due to the fact that he was going to succeed and get the money. And suddenly his father wearing an old black baseball cap with a witless peak came stumbling

fumbling up the street with a convulsive erection in his baggy
pants, howling, "Hey Dean, Dean, did ya sell the mattress
yet? Huh Dean? Did ya get thirty cents for it yet?"—and ran
clutching after him with imploration and fear. This was the
dream from which young Dean woke with a repugnance only
he could understand; it was dawn; he was eight.

It was dreams; reality was more tender. His father let him
put his hands in the pockets of his own coat, to keep warm,
the same coat; they laughed and shivered together. "Paw don't
do that in *his* dreams," little Dean told himself, understanding
himself.

Some gamblers arrived to play cards with Ching Boy and
Bull, young Chinese, one with a sharp blue suit and black
shiney shoes; from time to time he raised his head from the
game to ask questions in Chinese from Ching Boy, about the
man and the boy sitting on the blanket in the corner. Every
time Ching Boy told him something swiftly—because he
didn't want to talk about it—Bull looked at both of them with
an expression of curiosity as if he understood Chinese. He did
not understand it but was trying to understand what was going
on and saw clearly.

They all waited for Leo Duluoz.

Leo was driving from Boston in his 1934 Plymouth, with
his son Ti Jean, 13.

"We'll go eat in a good restaurant, we'll do our business,
we'll see a coupla shows, maybe the rodeo and then we'll come
back, after a little sleep in a hotel. Eh? Your mother won't even
almost know. We've got to help those poor devils, Bill told me
and Omer told me, they're as poor as Job. Maybe we'll be able
to go and see a coupla races at Belmont, ah?—But coming back
we can always go by way of Narragansett. In any case," coughing, choking on his cigar smoke, "in any case we're gonna try
to have a good time if we can."

The father Leo Duluoz was talking like that, driving the car
across the night of Connecticut. He was dressed in a brown
suit, brown hat, he was a big fat man; the little boy was dressed
in corduroy pants, long ones, with a sweater and a jacket of
black cloth. Death was falling into their ears, in the angels, the
future of their mortality; in the fog of the night you could smell
the *miguelle* universe of St. Michael honey of the Guardian

Angel. But both of them thought of the great city burning on the shelf of America ahead in the big darkness. And after the city, all the long United States, the big woman sleeping on the earth beneath the moon, one white leg in the North, one rose leg in the South, and all the great railroads that crossed her grand belly.

"Imagine driving all that way from Denver to New York," Leo was saying to his son, "those are great distances, across profound spaces of earth, it's not like our little trips to Vermont in New England, you know, it's not buying clams like at Cape Cod."

It was Leo and Jean, a man and his sad son, they didn't seem to make themselves happy in the action of their lives in the New England town, they wanted to take a big trip but they bit the nail doing it. It had started with Jean sent by the mother to meet the father at Revere Beach where he was fishing for a week, by car with Omer Leclerc, the guy the family knew who drove for the father, worked in the shop. But at Revere Beach everything broke, Old Bull hadn't waited long enough on the fisherman's porch, he had left in a rowboat to get clams, drunk, with two thin men who looked exactly alike who wore old hats with buttons who worked for the fisherman, and he disappeared in the bars on the other side of the rollercoasters. Omer couldn't find Bull, had lost Leo; Ti Jean took a long walk on the beach with his hands in back of him and was completely lost from the others; Omer got mad and took the bus for New York, he wasn't going to spend his big weekend looking every-where for everybody on Revere Beach—if they were going to New York get going! He too was drunk. Once he'd almost swallowed his tongue and turned blue and everybody thought he was dead. Baloon, in the abominable destruction of their plans, took the train, not finding Leo; Leo was at the wrong pier anyway; in the train Old Bull played cards, with the boys, his big necktie hanging low, making statements to his partners like "I see the mystery of your trouble!" looking at the man seriously and willing to tell him if he wanted to know but the man not asking being charmed by the suave audacity of that idea, and not wanting to start a big talk in the little current of the game. Leo and Jean all alone on Revere Beach found their way and came out for New York; "They were taking themselves a trip anyway. Tell your mother we lost the others; that's what happened."

And they put their faces to the darkness of the road and came, through Hartford after much trouble, and came down to New York. It was a big night in their lives, it was their first trip together to New York in a car; the father had already come on the Boston–New York boat, and once by train; but now it was the big road, the actual black carpet of the city.

"Ah Ti Jean, and what you thinkin now, all wrapped inside your head? Ah," stretching, "your old man ain't able to drive all night like he used to—My rheumatism bothers me this week." He made a little face, looking for himself in the legs for pain. Ti Jean had a constant fear of crashing, the mother'd told them to be very careful, warned them; the old man wasn't such a good driver; but he had done a lot of driving, on many occasions panicked by something, the whole family crying out, but nothing happened; the old man watched what he was doing. The danger was supposed to come from his fatal tragedy, some accident. Everybody believed it—especially Omer, he always drove when he got in that sad car. The old man now sent the car headlong to the bottom of a hill of great distance with a white line in the darkness more frightening than a ghost. All the bumps of the road picked up the car and placed it like a boat: after many hours it seemed safe. "Oh it'll pass. We started our lives in cemeteries, eh?" looking at Ti Jean the kid to see if he understood, licking himself. "Oh I shoulda played that damn Prevaricate the other afternoon, you weren't with me, you remember"—seeing his little movement—"I started with a show bet of ten dollars on a 6-to-1 shot in the first. Came in, paid $3.20, I picked up a nice six bucks. I put six dollars across the board to place my damn black bum, the ten on the nose of the poor goat who missed Prevaricate by a nose. The black bum was third."

"Third? It was close!"—looking at each other surprised that they understood each other's interests.

"You don't think I was sore Ti Jean!—your mother'd cry if she knew, I played my last twenty bucks on the top of the card in the third, didn't come in, I left, I drove in the damn traffic of Lawrence, it was her twenty dollars for the stove—I'll have to take some out of the shop again, I don't like that taking out of the shop." You could see the black brooding expression that Omer Leclerc was imitating in Leo.

"Ain't it just the lil life! When I think about my father's family—":

His father Jacques Duluoz was a carpenter from St-Hubert, Quebec, who built his own house in Nashua; his grandfather was from the mouth of the St Lawrence River, bay of entry for the Bretons of the net from Armorica, the wanderers and fishermen from the last *plâge* of Europe, Ti Jean's ancestors.

The L'Heureux were Norman, with an English name in their forest of humanity tree, but the Duluozes were Bretons as far back as anybody could remember, one hundred percent through, to the village of Duluoz itself at the cape of the Gaulic Celt, from Father Duluoz to Mother Bernier-Gaos who was a relative of Bernier the Atlantic explorer though god help her in her own dispositions among the floors and kitchens of our everyday cookpots and Fellaheen pans.

Jacques Duluoz was father to a fantastic, intemperate clan. His potato farmer parents from the Gaspé Peninsula in the North, by Rivière du Loup, which is up above Maine and New Brunswick near the mile-wide St Lawrence maw in those awful Baffin sweeps, a plain Mongol and bleak and harsh like Abraham, with all of them descendants of a Breton captain of Montcalm's-versus-Wolfe armies of the City of Quebec; descendants of him, a Breton of land, and of the original New World American mother of their new soul, an Indian squaw. Her Old World Fellaheen heart was lodged in the Iroquois Nation, the Tribe of the Caughnawaga, whose fires were never warm enough, and whose blankets, pots, and horses were sorrowful like March when it drizzles in the morning ground. Crystals of the ice mesh on the mud in the stone, the gray blanket moves, vapors rise from the pitiful village of the original life.

There had been seven or eight Duluoz brothers, only four survived; that many sisters, most of them dead in childhood; one maniac, several cripples; figures fantastic and impossible to believe. The stamp of the wild Duluozes was the snub nose, and a batted mouth with the lower lip, curled, moist and pathetic, like great crybabies tormented, people for weeping and speechifying, with big throatbroken sobs, at the lips of cold graves, for sighs and wonderment, choking for too much, for rage, black sadness, baggy dumbfoundment in the face of the ever alien, the mortal truth; all gabbling with broken mouths in eternity rooms of life. "A-bwa, a-bwa!" Ti Jean used to say, at the age of four, on the porch steps of littlekid afternoon, imitating the sound of the Duluozes when they got together, when Uncle Joe drove in from Nashua in his old flap top Reo for a session in the parlor. "Oh *mon pauvre Leo*, my poor Leo, you're looking worse every year, your rheumatism'll kill you, we'll bury you in the rain like all the others. Me, I cant sleep nights any more, I have to sit up in the dark—O death, death, *la mort, la mort!*"

Most known stamp of the crazy Duluozes, least appreciated, was the inclination to "talk too much," *bavassée*, jabber all the time, a-bwa a-bwa, to which the incrustation of a few years' midnight death-understanding and loss of a thousand autumns of sorrow would tend to bring tears, tears, tears—that inclination, dumb to prove sorry—The poor Duluozes well known for their excess soul. People in French Canadian patois said "The damn Duluozes, all they can do is jabber and eatin and chewin life to death, and it's cry, and it's cry—they're all afraid to die." And people said "They're all a-scared to die but they all want to swallow everything in sight, round *tous rond, ils veul envalées la vache tous rond*, the whole cow"—the whole hog, pigs of life, with great pink tears in their eyes, if you hated them.

The original descendant of 1760 had been Baron Louis Alexandre le Brice de Duluoz and was presumably a baron's son from a baronetcy in stormbrow-y Brittany sent back to honor the squaw of his barracks days, and to occupy a land grant on the Wolf River, his from the British because he was an officer. And if he was a Paris fop when his father yelled at him to go back and make a man of himself in the cold new world (that was the story) he nevertheless fathered a horny handed human beast of toil made fit for these howling New World winter voids by hot dull blood and pocky skin—Amadeus Duluoz. And Amadeus begat Guillaume, and Guillaume begat Joseph, and Joseph begat Ovila, and Ovila begat Henri, and Henri begat Jacques. And Jacques begat Ti Jean's father, the dark moody Leo, and all those contemporary Duluozes. A string of tough farmers five feet tall with necks bent back in gales and eyes blue snow.

And Jacques begat Leo's brother; Ernest. Ernest Duluoz had thin lips and an icy face, he had no particular feeling for his brothers; he walked away from their funerals talking about his house. In fact he smiled at their funerals. He was a railroad brakeman and then a carpenter; there never was an American white garage putterer with tools and hobbies like the original Canuck with his miserly cold dead calm; no Yankee to out freeze him, to make a better fire on a cold day, use less wood, save more words. He outlived them all.

Jacques begat Joseph, who was sick all his life, cried, gasped all the time; from asthma, sadness; a grocer built like a pickle barrel, 230 pounds, bilious sufferings made his face gray like doom, tragic as an undertaker's curtains on a dark afternoon, the furious summing pathetic caricature of all the Duluozes in him was packed inpent unkeepable explosions of sorrow, mournful huge man, he had the soul of a harassed saint, he was a big, good man trying to endure life and so much of it enlivening his great gut, throbbing there, lamentationing, sometimes he couldn't stand it and flew into enthusiasms and coughs that shook the ceiling, he and Leo his favorite brother began yelling contests of joy—"Do you remember the time you were—and I—*Ah pauvre Leo*, poor Leo, they're all gone the days of boyhood—You were so pitiful with yr little leg, I wanted to help you—Argh, what's the use." They'd begin fighting about something and go home and not see each other for years, these tortured brothers. Under the black skies of mortal woe, there never was a more hung woeful face than Joseph Duluoz's—

And Jacques begat Jean Duluoz, hardlegged, short, powerful, a lumberjack; he ate 12 12-inch pancakes with 144 waves of the fork at winter's breakfast dawn, because of his appetite the worn out Duluoz mother Clementine, sister of Pomeray's wife, had to rise before the rooster hallooed the snow, and whip the eggs, about a dozen, and batter real French Canadian *crêpes*—an uneatable amount, this was all in the old days—for this noncommittal woodcutter who only curled his lower lip as if to cry, when he said his commonplace good morning at the door. By noon he was back, rubbing his hands for more. Absolutely no love in the crafty strength of his eyes, and in his horny hand not too much sympathy.

Four baneful brothers, they never looked when they passed in the hall, in the sad dream; they yelled at each other in the

yard, then Ah—they passed the ground to the grave swirling for dust, expressions of pain on their mouths. Several,
magnificent sisters, could have lambified and made their lives
gentle:—Caroline, who became a nun; Justine, schoolteacher
who had learned a lot from her aunt of the same name; and
Marie Louise, woman of warm understanding. As little girls
they had to pout and play house and make way for the boys.
All except Clara, who was mad as a lark in the lattice trapped,
she threw knives with *furioso* sneers at her brothers and sisters,
they ducked under the kitchen table. She had to be rolled in a
rug, screaming. Insanity in the family, they put her away, she
kept coming back. She brooded like a wild hawk over a family
of crazy fools and yellers. Magnificent street fights, with Leo's
fists in the air in suspenders on lavender Sunday afternoon,
offering his opponent to cross the line; shouters and cheerers
from wooden swings, popcorn stands, barbershop quartets.
Bam! Leo pops him one in the eye, gets a swipe of knuckles
on the burning bleeding cheek. Tears, gasps, they rassle in the
gutter. Leo wins, the fight is over, Lil Armand Duval goes
home to cry bitter love's dream in his mother's dress. "Look,
Lil Armand Duval," says Leo to Ti Jean driving through
Nashua on a red afternoon, years afterward, in the Sunday lost
streets there's the little man alone on long spindly shadows,
"to think we fought with fists and hate—Armand! Armand!
Dammit he went in that street he can't hear me, he's almost
down the bottom of that street—"

The crazy family of Duluoz . . . the grimfaced look-up
Duluozes. Rumors that an uncle So and So had removed his
trousers in the presence of a lady on a Sunday morning, not far
from church, in a quiet street about nine, or ten in Canada; later
threw a flaming mattress down on his keepers, and pisspots in
his long underwear down that Dark Corridor.

Stoutlegged brusque Father Jacques for his part was coming
home sober by the dark railyards one night when a whore gave
him a "sst" near the team, crooking a finger to herself. "Ah?"
he yelled enraged. "*Putain! Cochonne!* Whore! Pig! Slut and
bitch! Go home! Go home! God oughta burn your ass for
approaching a man like that! *Salope! Peau!*" He strode with a
plane in his hand, over every rail he jammed his shoe on with
a side down step, hard chested and neck and ribs conjoined in

one hammered mass, sore. "Crapitating around in the dirty holes of the night to piss with drunkards! Harlot! Argh!" and he raised his plane at her. Vein popping with Breton rage he often sat behind the stove muttering day and night. Suddenly he'd burst into tears about his own father, "Oh my poor father Henri; he worked so hard and never had a day off or anything to own in his life. Even if you beat the animal to death the skin'll never be yours.—Poor old man I see his hands, his big sad face—aïee, aïee, *les Duluoz* will always be poor and lost in the darkness—Argh! *ma mère, ma mère, ma pauvre mère*— with her baptism of potatos, I see her in the cold wind with that Christ of a river all iced *solid* for 6 months—Her hat, she wore a special hat to go to mass Sunday mornings—the pathet- icness of that rag—*ces rubans egarouillez lui tombais dans guêle, pauvre bon femme!*—Her ribbons'd fall all haggardly in her mouth, poor old woman—I'd see her stop at a road shrine and pray with her face blue from the cold, there she was with her knees knocking before the little cabin—I saw her in a dream not two weeks ago sitting on the ground, the blanket's over her head, she's selling potatos—The golden bonnet's rolling in the wind—the cold wind, she's got a candle—she doesn't look at me—My little dead sister's sleeping with her head on the potato box—Jeannette Ange!—Ah me Christ of the Baptism they can take this finished-up goddam life and throw it right to the Devil!" he'd start shouting, getting up from his chair to rage on solid feet.

"Jacques! Jacques! The children!"

He'd grab the oil lamp and start swinging it around and around his head. "The children the children we'll burn em your goddam children! Argh! Get out of my way! I defy God to burn this house down!"

Mother and children ran shrieking to hide in corners—"He's going to blow up the house!" The old man roared, his rage was only forming.

"Strike! Strike this house down and strike me dead! *Varge!* Go ahead, damn you, strike! *Frappe! Claque!* Why the hell wait!" If he had a good thunderstorm during one of these moods, old Jacques Duluoz went out on the porch with his wild oil lamp and swung at the lightning with screams. "Hit the house! Hit me! Go ahead! Bang! Let loose! Goddam it, come on! *Coigne! Un coup!* Slam! Bang! Clack me one, go ahead I dare you! Boom! Boom!" The thunder answered in kind from its huge heaven; the old man raved, tiny and yelling in speechless macrocosmic cracking black world night.

"Jacques, have pity for the children," the mother wailed from the kitchen corner. "Oh *Dieu*, I'm afraid—The Devil makes him mad—I cried to you God from my suffering—I was a young girl, I didn't understand that I was going to have thirteen children and work and scrub with my hands all the hours of my life—A little sleep in the night of innocence—Oh pity! have pity! Jacques you frighten us!"

Some of the brothers came home and waited on the porch till the old man quieted down, till darkfaced and spent he turned his back on them, silent; the depthless paternal sea; and went back to his stove corner; where one Sunday morning, after many quiet curses, he suddenly merely sat still, raw hands on his lap folded in grim resignation, and was dead. By the time she was dead too, the weary mother, Clementine, thin in her sickly grave, her call for deliverance darkly and forever satisfied. World, the happy endings on this crashing screen.

Clara was put in a madhouse. Baby twins died; were buried in an almost anonymous dual grave, face up, unaccomplished, unexplained in the pit of night. From the depths of earth's evil sorrow wailed the Duluozes.

At seven little Leo was run over by an ice wagon, Marie Louise cradled her little brother in her arms, he was to be crippled for life. But a white haired 70-year-old hobo passing thru town, learning of the accident, came to the Duluoz house and offered his assistance in exchange for a meal and a lunch for the road. As everyone watched he kneaded the boy's leg and made a few pulls and left him able to walk, no longer a cripple. "What is your name?"

Tall and white-maned he flowed into eternity out of sight, across town and over the grass to the railroads, the hills; little Leo never forgot him.

"Is it a saint?"

"There's an old savant for you—He came out of the mountains."

"He healed Ti Leo—"

"Say what you want, me I'm going to say a little prayer—"

Gray heavens lowering all around, standing in shirtsleeves by the old wood house, the Canadians nodded dumb heads in unison of sad mystery.

"It's worth going to the *presbytère* to change my holy water—"

"Bring the crucifix. You might as well bring the crucifix too. *On est aussi bien.*"

"Did you see him walk as straight as a savage?"

It was 1896, a carriage went by on the dirt street, suspendered brothers convened to talk with the passing baker, they rolled smokes and jawed in the bleakness, a woodpile stood high in the raw mist. The women, satisfied, taking one last look over immensity and pain, the iron racked skies wrung over with the legibility, that Yah of defeat, went back in their kitchens to the cookpots, where on the vast iron range with its Quebecois scrolls and rose-paintings, boiled the pork scraps for the festive New Year pie. They did the sign of the cross at the crucifix, then looked at Little Leo in his bed and nodded with their dark, greedy faces of faith. The older ones began to leave home. "*Bon*, it makes one less," was said in the kitchen.

All is ephemeral, all is hurt. The wind in back of the barn at night sings poor *adieu*s that a family almost misses hearing, and only in the narrow rear of heads. Even bare, rugged souls look blearily from their cellars of superstition and doggedness, which is their one, their only workshop, and weep for what is gone. A family starts, they're all together, they fight—they don't understand the morning, the truth, the pureness of the morning, the meaning of the frost in their bedroom windows, the big breakfasts of their communal winter—and after that— we don't see them any more. In the case of the Duluozes, they snuck out one by one, over the doorstep and down to Time, a rueful ghost on each of their heels, and death on his. Leo looking eagerly, Ernest immaculate, John calculating his old advantages, Joe puffing for life, Marie Louise sad, Caroline prophetic, Justine the last to leave and lay the pans aside in honor of their mother; shamefaced clan, piteous, still talking about it, leaving the loony Clara and some remnant cousins and all their dusts of furyation to fall in a house that no longer had the ring of entirety in its beams, as happens to all houses.

"It's one hell of a thing, Ti Jean, to come from a family like that; we agitate ourselves in life all to pieces to think of the things that are done gone. God doesn't seem to love us; he seems to be mad about something. Ah Charley was alright for example, we didn't like him but he was alright, I understand guys like Charley, they want their good times, they want to get excited. Shore." He was talking about a business friend he'd worked for once. "Nothing we can do, Ti Jean, with avarice and the—We'll find ourselves a little trip here, we'll see if we can help the old bum with his kid, we never saw them, their relatives, we'll chew the rag a little, maybe we'll eat a little feed, and me and you'll go to Times Square see some shows. The burlesques and the vaudeville shows and the new pictures and they say they got French pictures—it would be beautiful, ah, see a picture in French? It would make your eyes cry to see a little scene with the lovers on the bed. Marie Louise told me that, she saw one in Boston—Good. Put your little blanket round your knees there and sleep if you can—I'm going to drive straight to New York and I'm not talking any more."

And the little boy slept in the black machine of eternity guided by his father across the night.

The old man saw all kinds of wings of black angels in the sides of his window; once, at four o'clock, he saw the moon come out from behind a cloud that was illuminated by it, giving it a big face of God of a woman lying on a big black bed with a face of a devil all around and through it.

"Damn, *mautadit*," he said to himself low, "it's making black faces in the sky, I've got to watch the road." He was going fast at six o'clock in the gray morning, hands gripped cold on the wheel, hat slumped over for the eyes that looked joyously everywhere. "Ha ha!" he said, and coughed, "Look at that Walter Winchell guy with the flowers, a character like in a movie but look at his face all gray from his night work—a florist I guess?" And Ti Jean woke up, to the new day, the great voyage.

Leo and Ti Jean arrived at Eighteen Pott Street at seven o'clock in the morning eyes brilliant and buried in their sockets as if they didn't see any more. Uncle Bull had won $280, lost the same, and re-won $80. When Leo came in, his great unmistakable shadow of coat and paper-in-pocket appearing in the door, Bull yelled "Damn I missed $200 just like that!" It filled him with joy that Leo had arrived—now they were going to straighten out. They'd have a little fun, some talk in the smoke. Things would develop; they'd talk now with anxious eyes about what to do. "Come on, boy!—you took your little trip to New York after all!"

The same Chinese were there; tired, the bottle on the floor was low. Old Dean Pomeray and little Dean were sleeping on the floor.

"You got the key to the place?" demanded Bull clapping Leo on the arm.

"Yes—but Omer didn't tell me the address yet, of the place— That's another problem the place. He was drunk when he left Revere Beach. He forgot to leave a note, anything—He sent a telegram to you the fisherman told me?"

"He was drunk."

"I figured, hell I'll take a little trip to New York anyway—I figured what was ahead of me or dead in a corner. Where is he Omer?"

"Omer? We have Rolfe with us—Rolfe has the address, he's gone to take a walk, he wanted to see the city, he'll come back to eat, we have a little food here. Ha?" Bull asked himself in his head. "Aw yes. It's Omer who wrote him the address."

"So Omer knew all these people when he was in Denver with you?" Leo asked—they talked like that in the middle of the floor, all the others watched, they were talking loud as if everybody had to listen with them.

"Oh yes. Well there, that's them, sleeping, see em? They got in last night, they tried to sleep all night; we've had a little game. We won't disturb them—bring your things in—Gonna continue the game and wait for Rolfe this morning."

"But where's Omer?"

"Don't worry yourself—"

The little boy Ti Jean was already in, standing in a corner. He was watching everything. The Chinese men at the table made him think of his magazines he read, the cartoons in the newspapers, the cartoons he drew himself with his paper and pencil at home in his littered bedroom. He looked at the little boy sleeping with his father on the floor. His father Leo was already engaged in the poker game. It was too late to ask questions.

Old Bull Baloon, beneath the light, had a big round face, cracked teeth, a red nose, and eyes almost buried in the enormity of breakage around there—the face broken like a plate—the most crazy funny face you ever saw—His eyes gleamed—he had cheeks red from booze—But he was aging. He was around 65. In the corner was his old cane, it bowed its head beneath his hopeless coat, he didn't use it often but his feet were starting to give out, he didn't work often on the railroad, if at all, he had to fall from the caboose like a poor old tired woman at the end of the track, a poor old man in pain. He went down the main line with his white lamp and his red lamp, like a shadow with broken shoulders, talking to the brakeman when the brakeman wasn't there; he no longer saw the disaster on the track, he looked for it in other places, always mistaken. He'd been brought before the board of three, four railroads; for putting an engine on the ground, shoving a boxcar off a spur burying the trucks in the mud of a swamp, forgetting cold that a hotshot passenger train was ten minutes late and meeting it in the plains and had to go backward into a siding to let him go a half hour late. He sat in front of his stove in the caboose, the bottle in a drawer, and waited out the rainy nights and the big black work of the glistening track. The fire pleased him when it was deep and November night red.

These days he was keeping the money he had saved through the years, won through years playing cards, lost, re-won. Sometimes you saw his face fallen, hat on the bottom of his head, whistling a little tune. In his eyes little green interested slits danced. He spat in the spittoon. He hid his destruction.

The other boys, the Chinese, could see his face in the light and tell his story from that. He was a funny and frank Occidental. He said all kinds of impossible things looking at his hand.

"The corners of the king have upsidedown ass holes," he'd say, studying his cards. "We'll have to find him a piece of sonofabitch to enlarge his figure—poor dog, we'll travel his fifty cents. Did I ever tell you that ghost story about the laughing nightgown?" But he showed his teeth and didn't tell it.

"I have all the ghosts in hand," he'd say.

"Crack on my head," said another player.

"Fish em out a five, deck."

"What? Old canvas grips soft out exploded with the handles ready to run. Burlack saps." In Bull's eye you could see two red skeletons against an eyeball.

The others acted bored, once in a while someone said something strange like "I had you, yes," the Chinese addressing one another you'd think from afar with little voices very serious and alarmed. The sons of Ching Boy, named Ching Bok and Sammy Boy, were in Bronx Jail for the murder of a girl in a hotel room with a broken bottle, they and another Chinese boy; they were ironing their socks on ironingboards among steel bars when the sun went down red in May New York. Seven years gone, they wouldn't tell who it was had killed the little woman, they were headed for life terms with their secret. The old man was very sad, "They were good boys, it was the other, Poy, who did the damage . . ."—so thought he sitting in his rice darkness. He'd had a store with them, frogs in tanks, doves; they'd made a lot of money; chickens, eels. The other boys playing cards were all sons of his friends and the friends themselves in the village. They looked out the windows of Chinatown in the days of blue air, the afternoons of the golden bars of thought beside the washtubs; Ching Boy was a respected and well known man.

He looked at everybody fatigued with tenderness.

He played cards from love of the red and the black in the night.

The game continued chip-chip. Ti Jean sat on an upsidedown pail in the corner. Old man Leo gave him one look across the smoke and said hat-on-head "Find yourself a little place there and sleep, we've been driving all night." And Ti Jean sat in the brown sadness of his corner and watched life. He was a strange little boy. He always had heavy thoughts. He never wanted to talk with anyone. He wanted to see New York but had to wait in the loft with the bunch. While waiting, he passed his time among them dreaming imaginary pictures of life that came out from the things they said and the faces they made in the game; he saw their windows.

All of a sudden a Negro came in with a beard in his chin, Slim Jackson, a tall skin-and-bones with a big yellow eyeball red threaded behind each great brown eye, a well formed nose and a drop of beard flowing from his chin; very sad, very fast, with a saxophone case in his hands, and a long necktie that seemed to fall from his coat halfway to his feet. With him was a little Negro boy of eleven. "This is my little brother Pictorial Review Jackson. I'm gonna leave him here for twenty hours and I'm coming back to get him."

"Okay Slim," said Ching Boy.

It was said that he and Slim smoked opium together in his rooms; *hasheesh*, *kief*, *dagga*, *gangee*; once in a while they put a sniff of heroin on a razorblade, or else they shot them some cocaine five, six times in an hour; a gang of friends. "We're going to have a shipment from my great uncle in Peking tomorrow. Come and join us."

"Yes, if I have time," said Slim with his eyebrows going up and down fast like a comedian. "Ziggity zow," he said, jiggling himself a little, "I gotta go play in a record session with my girl, she's gonna sing six or seven songs—I Want a Little Girl *I'm* gonna play without words—Ha!—You Can Depend on Me—Smoke Gets in Your Eyes—I want to be in my best shape. Louis's gonna be there—I got cigarettes—Shot of Vodka! Here I go!"

"Bring money for the game tonight," said Ching Boy, and the young Chinese laughed.

"Yay. I'll be seeing you, Dad. Hey, Dad!"—sincerely searching in his eyes—"See ya later! Pic, take care of yourself."—falling on his knees to the child—"You got a dollar to eat, there's places all around, it's early in the morning, take it easy. Play with that lil boy there."

"It's a lil white boy," little Pic told him in the ear.

"Well, it's alright, he'll let you play with him."

"I don't wanta play with him."

"Well sit here."

"I'm gonna wait for you."

"Naturally, angel. Until tomorrow." He squeezed his fist with the dollar in it; he adjusted the little hole-hat on his head. And Slim Jackson left, swift, his case swung, his hands; he had to go to work. At night he stood in front of nightclubs with his horn, stamping his feet, the fog came out of his mouth; he talked with Roy Eldridge in the dark street. "What ya say, man?" "Hey Little Jazz!" And they endured in the winter that's around their music. Ti Pic looked at the men and the children with averted eyes.

"I'm gonna blow my brains out this morning!" Slim shouted at the top of his lungs, hitting the stairs hard, whaling the doors.

As usual Leo was beginning to lose; he was starting to get mad. "Goddamit I had the king and I forgot I saw his damn brother and the deuce on the other side of the table. I play cards like a numbskull." All the others regarded him curiously at this confession. The play continued.

"Why don't you try to get up and come play cards," said Leo seeing old Pomeray's eyes open on the floor. "You don't know me, I was your wife's nephew; Leo Duluoz."

"Aw yeah—well—I'll have ta—" the man said from the floor and didn't move.

"If you get up we'll fry some eggs!" yelled Bull Baloon. "And I bought a little bit of hamburger if you want to make a tomato sauce to mix with them pork and beans."

All you could see was a cracked grin in the shadows of the floor. The little boy Dean was frozen tight at his father's side. His eyes'd been open for a long time. Old Pomeray said nothing; he had forgotten; he lay down again with his eyes open. He took his bottle of wine and took a long drink leaving just a drop; up on an elbow. You could see the moon in his wet kisser; a Bowery moon. He smiled. Little Dean was asking him a question in a little voice; it seemed you could hear the old man reply in the tiniest gentle voice. Dean threw the tennis ball in his hands, in the gloom.

Old Pomeray's old shoes, cracked from the West, were on the floor, split. You couldn't find father & son for the black robe that fell from them.

After awhile little Dean got up to the window and began to play a fantastic game; he sent the ball from one wall to another, catching it after the fourth change of direction to bounce it up and down; for this sometimes fell flat on his face. The other two boys watched him interested. Ti Jean came up to play. Little Dean looked at him with blue curious eyes, like an old man's; he kept his mouth firm-closed and studied him to see. Ti Jean struck out his hand for the ball, smiling at the ball; took it, did the same thing almost without jumping. The little Negro was afraid to jump, move. Little Dean and Ti Jean jumped together to whang at the ball against the wall, punching with fists, hard and furious, until the men yelled at them in big voices to stop. They stopped. Old man Pomeray was watching them very gravely from up on his elbows, studying them. Dean held out his hand for his ball: Ti Jean gave it back with a little plop and a laugh of pleasure. They looked at each other; Dean had shown that he knew how to play, Ti Jean'd had his fun. He left to place himself among the men at the game; Dean's father was telling little Dean to come back where he was. Little Dean was saying no, seriously, biting his lip, pushing his chin down on his fist; the old man was saying yes. Dean had to lie down, fix himself to wait to get up to leave. Ti Jean had already forgotten their new acquaintance, was watching the men; little Dean had already lost everything from his side. You could see him, eyes in the ball, mouth in the darkness, feet buried in the floor, in the hay, in the great foundation of darkness and rags that sat in the base of their corner like a drape, a battleship deck of pain all split in the thoughts of the poor Hag who saw in the light of the room immense black profundities of the contract of life, the well-known shadows, telling himself Yes, believing himself and counting himself in his head, pressing his mouth on his teeth wishing it.

And he turned to little Dean. There were tears in his eyes, "Just like we've always done in Denver Dean—you and me!! That's what it's gonna be! Didja have so much to complain with, batchin with me?—think your mother's folks woulda done so much better for the way they talk?—The Skylark is called a flophouse by some people—but you went to school didn't ya? And in the winter we was warm, Dean. In the Saturday mornings we was warm we was happy—"

"I ain't sayin nothing daddy," scared the others would hear.

"—wasn't we? We went to the barber shop together and I worked, and you roamed around town picking up scrap and Saturday night we always *did* have a good meal at Jiggs' buffet of chickenfried steaks usually and always *did* see a movie— *didn't we Dean*? That's 'cause I'm your father and wanted to do well by ya—*didn't I Dean*! And so there's some folks won't name no names, call me a bum, a wino, came and said because I drink and get drunk don't take much to get me drunk they say—So you sometimes talked to the judge to help me out—and sometimes you even panhandled dimes for me because—*Dean*—but didn't I love ya? *Didn't I?* Ain't I offerin you everything I got right now? Be workin, working again—I ain't gonna drink much—look, all I got's this little poorboy bottle tokay left, that's all, *Dean—Dean*—" His voice didn't even rise.

The little boy said nothing, waited, to grow up.

A Chinese came in the loft with an ironingboard, went out by the back door, Ching Boy said something to him in Chinese, business. Leo Duluoz shook his be-hatted head. Ti Jean watched his pop's face, blackened with rage; reddened, from sadness; lowered, to look at the floor; lips pinched, saying to himself "What a damn world—what a poor world," in French. Around him all the brownness of great dreams of life, the phantoms with him, the smoke, the darknesses on the floor near the spittoon of spit and cigarettes; Uncle Bull Baloon's great knees in fat pants, dropping ashes on his pants, brushing them off with big coughs and looks at the clock on the box, ruined like a great corpse in a coffin, not yet cut by the embalmer, teeth rotten, a great cracked smile on his Christ of a clown's face.

Rolfe had taken himself to Times Square via the El with a little walk on 42nd Street from Third Avenue till the Times Building. You saw him in front of the overall store with the long sideburns—it seemed you could see gray rocks over his head, drizzle, mountains of used tires, as if he was thinking it. Have you ever seen anyone like Rolfe Glendiver?—say on a street-corner on a winter night in Chicago, Fargo, cold towns, a young guy with a bony face that looks like it's been pressed against iron bars to get that dogged rocky look of suffering, perseverance, finally when you look closest, happy prim self-belief, with Western sideburns and big blue flirtatious eyes of an old maid and fluttering lashes; the thin muscular kind of fellow wearing usually a leather jacket and if it's a suit it's with a vest so he can prop his thick busy thumbs in place and smile the smile of his poor grandfathers; who walks as fast as he can go on the balls of his feet, talking excitedly and gesticulating; poor pitiful kid sometimes just out of reform school with no money, no mother, and if you saw him dead on the sidewalk with a cop

standing over him you'd walk on in a hurry, in silence. Oh life,
who is that? There are some youngsters who seem completely
safe, maybe just because of a Scandinavian ski sweater, angelic,
schoolboyish, saved; on a Rolfe Glendiver it immediately
becomes a tragic dirty sweater worn in wild sweats. Something
about his tigrish out-jutted raw facebone could be given a woe-
down melancholy if only he wore a drooping mustache. It is
a face that's so suspicious, because so normal, so energetically
upward-looking like people in passport or police lineup photos,
so rigidly itself, looking like it's about to do anything unspeakably enthusiastic, maybe criminally affectionate, and so much
the opposite of the rosy coke-drinking boy in the Scandinavian
ski sweater ad that in front of a brick wall where it says "Post No
Bills" and it's too dirty for a rosy boy ad you can imagine Rolfe
standing there in the raw gray flesh manacled between sheriffs
and Assistant D.A.'s and you wouldn't have to ask yourself
who is the culprit and who is the law . . . who "wired Dad"
who had tennis rackets in the back of the car; and who did
not. He looked like that and God bless him he looked like that
Hollywood stunt man who is fist fighting in place of the hero
and has such a remote, furious, anonymous wildhaired vicious-
ness—one of the loneliest things in the world and we've all seen
it a thousand times in a thousand B movies—that everybody
begins to be suspicious because they know the hero wouldn't
act like that in real unreality. If you've been a boy and played
on dumps you've seen Rolfe, all giggling excited and blushing
with the pimply girls in back of fenders and weeds till some
vocational school swallows his ragged blisses and that strange
American iron which later is used to mold the suffering man-
face is now employed to straighten and quell the long waving
spermy disorderliness of the boy. Nevertheless the face of a
great hero—a face to remind you that the infant springs from
the great Assyrian bush of a man, not from an eye, an ear or a
forehead;—the face of a Simón Bolívar, Robert E. Lee, young
Whitman, young Melville, a statue in the park, rough and free.

Rolfe had asked a few questions; he was walking slow.
"Nothin's gonna bother me," he told himself. Only girls. He
saw thousands passing. He lost words to address them; only
looked at them. He spent his time leaning, laughing, and
watched them. He walked.

He went in two shows, sitting in front alone, boots crossed, laughing "Hyoo hyoo!" at every little feeble joke yuckled by old man Windy Smith Whiskers in the cowboy B movies. Laughed all alone in an empty aisle. From time to time in the audience of the theater, upstairs or downstairs, you could hear other idiots laugh. Others seemed to catch the little gay looks on the faces of women in the insipid stories; most of the audience said nothing, laughed for nothing, waited for the show to end, to get out in the newsreel streets.

Rolfe wandered downtown again, without knowing, as it destinied, and got to the North end of the Bowery, around East Fourth Street. He scratched his head in the shadow of the Cooper Union. He ate in a big cafeteria lit all brown in the sad night of the city. Rolfe hurried from there, it was too sad. He wore his hat, his cigarette dangled from his mouth, his boots moved slowly. There were no more girls in the streets. Twenty-four hours he'd been gone in these occupations of walking and watching. He wasn't tired. He hardly knew he passed a night and a day without sleep; didn't bother him. In the vast regions of himself, bored. He looked at the city. Laughed. Inside he was dead. He'd dreamed himself before. He saw everything with eyes blue and dead. Poor Rolfe, his life in Colorado had cracked him—he'd had the big smashup in his car that killed his grandfather, broken his ribs; broke his heart with his first girl (Jean Darling of Golden), put in a year in reform school for abducting her and bringing her in his car across the state line to his brother's cabin, wouldn't let her free for three days; *abducted*, wept at her belly for love; and when the father arrived took him on in a big fist fight, a prominent man of Denver; drank in roadhouses in the night and one time saw a Texas guy stomp on a man's face in the driveway cutting off his tongue between his teeth. He'd been sick to see life when he was little but it took his present age to stop him with a knife stuck in his craw. The big knife of life that comes out of the night, when you're at a carnival, and penetrates your heart. The sadness of love in the smell of the night. The mystery of the moon. Haggard eyes at five o'clock in the morning. The fog that falls on the bread of our life. Rolfe walked. Suddenly it seemed to him that his dead mother walked in front of him, shimmering, an apparition; she was Catholic, she was doing her sign of the cross; the street was Second Avenue. Beside him walked his phantom. His phantom left to walk on in front of him. He saw it in front of a store on the other square. He stopped in front of a jewelry store and looked at rings. He pointed his finger at the glass. Nobody around. He hurried to walk deeper. His face swallowed itself. He passed a bar, went in.

A lot of men were singing, there was beer in mugs, onions, crackers, the odor of vinegar, night; an old saloon with sawdust floor. He went in the toilet; a well dressed man followed him in. When Rolfe tried to do his business the man tried to watch. Rolfe stared at his face, his understanding too wide eyes—Rolfe could hear his heart beat; he sensed himself with a maniac. He fixed up to leave. The man said nothing, looked away. The man also hurried to leave. Rolfe followed him. The man sat down with some other men at a round table in a corner where they were singing in a gang; a young man with a turtleneck sweater had hair curled like a Portuguese. Rolfe left the bar.

He stood in the doorways looking at people. He hadn't slept for five days, drove from Gunnison to Denver before starting the big trip. You could see his strange eyes beneath the hatbrim, his ranch suit beneath the topcoat as though he had come out of an alfalfa field and put on coat and hat to visit the moon of New York.

He hurried in an old street.

Suddenly he saw the time in an old delicatessen window with Hebrew writing; seven o'clock. He had been gone from Pomeray and Dean and Bull for 24 hours. He'd found no girls, had not seen the burlesque of gold like he wanted to do—poor tourist!—He looked at the name of the street, Henry Street. He remembered it, the address Omer had written him. "I'll see the place; after, go get the gang."

He went up the street counting numbers. It was dismal, the wind was black, full of stinking smokes of fires, sad. Cats scurried like rats. Rolfe went through a hole in the fence, an empty lot inside, cans, swill. There was an old fire, an old spectre of a ragman, rags on a wagon. The city above, the kitchens of light. The mad dream of life. Rolfe did his business against the fence, waiting, in a dream. The ragman had seen his dream; eye to eye in the dark had seen. It was suffering—you have to firm your lips in the cold. The two men had fallen from the stars of the East and the West but they knew the same face of life. The ragman left on the other side; you couldn't see him any more. Rolfe left the lot, his hat straight and unnecessary on his head; walked in a store and bought a quart of milk.

His mouth was white. He found his address and climbed the tenement steps in the dark street. He went up in the somberness, cold smell, odor of the harbor; the great black ships were disengaging themselves from big buildings, the Els were going up and down in the dream; there were little white houses in the darkness (beneath) the rivers, streets and parks long lost. He looked at the long gray stairs between the bars of the middle well, a sad roof on top somewhere. He stopped, remembered a beautiful morning in Colorado when he'd slept near some red rocks in his sleeping bag, the blue sky, the smoke of his fire, singing "Ramona" and cooking eggs in his fryingpan.

He reached the top floor, looked around. He rubbed his eyes in the sadness, looked on his paper, the right number, 10. A little wire ran along the ceiling and then buried itself in plaster. He tried the door softly; locked. The light in the hall was green like fish. He climbed another flight, came to the roof door. Locked. He didn't know what to do. He looked through the big hole of an old lock in the wood. The latch. He took out his knife, opened it softly, and lifted the little latch. He shrugged. He came out on the roof. The city was all around him, black; red lights, brown, and blue; he could see great fogs of light further. He shrugged in immensity. "If the guys back home could only see me," he said. "Drove all the way to stand on this roof, to scatter on the ground . . ." he told himself. "Drove all that road and now here I am on the roof of the city. From here you could see all the way to Colorado, everywhere, all the way to California, it seems, thinking about it—it's nothing but a huge black and dirty trap, I'm buried, lost, drowned—I thought there were blondes in the street, men with guns, waterfronts—there's nothing, only the dream. I'm heading back. Pomeray can have this place here. I was gonna stay a little but not any more." He went down the fire escape and looked in the window, careful not to fall, wiping his hands from the sooty black bars, his big coat hanging.

There was no light in the first room, nor the second with its little bathtub and sink, but in the third room a light, golden, and a naked girl on the foot of the bed.

"Wow! Wow!" he said.

The walls were cracked; somebody's painted Baudelaire's face with the crack—his name written underneath, an artist had lived there.

The young girl was talking with someone in the room; it seemed she'd forgotten she was naked; her eyelashes were heavy from black cream. She waved her arms, licked her lips—she was telling a dramatic and absurd story, about her work—How pretty she was!—shoulders of gold and of white! All the time Rolfe watched her flesh. He was kneeling, nailed, at his post.

The girl's thighs were divided white and brown from the sun of the summer of 1935, she'd stayed with her aunt at Asbury Park, stretched herself in the sand to await the blond boys of intelligent tenderness who never came, the women of good sense who would teach her to want the road of life. She bought little pitiful rocks of paint and string; she prayed at her altar in her room at the mirror, she did pirouettes on the little place of floor between mirror and bed, sink and door. Hot summer mornings she slept naked shoulders with the flimsy window curtain moving in the breeze, showing her to the fire escape, the flower pots. For fun she'd bleached her hair for autumn. She bit her lips suddenly ashamed of her present adventure. She lowered her head watching others in the room, as if she had no shame. "Do you find me pretty?" she seemed to say, heavy-eyed.

Suddenly a shadow moved, and a tall girl six feet tall with red hair passed, in a black slip, to go in the kitchen. Rolfe jumped. She took off her slip, she got in the bathtub from which vapors of hot water rose. She was so tall she had to sit knees-at-chin in the little tub; her hair was tied high, you could see her long fine neck with the freckles. The water rose just almost to her shoulder, there was foam. Rolfe hung himself tighter in his corner. He listened for talk. He was making faces, eyes.

"He thinks he's in St. Petersburg," the girl on the bed was laughing. "What a place to think of!"

"Just old people in the winter, pensions, *I* know," said the redhead in her tub.

"No!" cried a man with a funny voice. "St. Petersburg *Russia*."

"Ha? Well goodness, that's even worse!" cried the little blonde laughing. The big woman waited, her face like a hospital attendant in the tub. Suddenly the brown arm of a man came out and pulled the blonde across the bed yelling and you couldn't see her any more, just the other one. Rolfe could see her wiping her nose. He wanted her to stand so he could see her; he didn't believe he had already seen her. He was all mixed up in the visions of legs of both. He was stoned. He was scared, he looked around, wanted nobody to catch him, disturb him.

"That's how it goes," cried the woman in the tub, washing her back, "they start wrestling, playing, pinching, torturing each other, all of a sudden they're deep in a long kiss and they dont move any more, just a little—the woman—just enough to move the tassles of her dress—if she has one—ha ha."

"What you saying, baby?" cried the man from the other room. "Hurry up with your bath, we're gonna tell stories."

"They're those damn people pose for dirty pictures on cards!—They're havin a party!" thought Rolfe.

"Aw! Again I'm seeing a skeleton in the corner! What are we doing in Chicago?"

"Now it's Chicago!" laughed the blonde buried somewhere—

"Well, I'm so high on this damn stuff I thot you had a big steel brace here—What would a woman be doing with a steel wire?"

"Yes, I'm coming little ones," said the Amazon in the tub, and she got up, grand and foamy, to reach for the towel on a pipe overhead. Rolfe shot like a jack-in-the-box when she got up, he was on the roof in an instant eating his lips. He came down again, slow. She was gone in. He listened. Heard nothing. "I might as well go home," he told himself sadly. He asked the sky, "How?" "This is the house Pomeray's supposed to live in? But yeah!—Well now what in hell are we doing? Yay, if I could have them naked girls with me in my room! Omer played us a wood!—damn Kentuck! All the good times we had in Denver in hotel rooms and look what he does! Man, the girls! I'll have to go tell em, have to go back to Denver, that's all, *damn*—I gotta go chew crap." And he went downstairs.

Inside the apartment, on the bed, it was Omer Leclerc him-self, a "hepcat" he called himself, came from near Boston, was the pressman for Leo Duluoz in his shop in New England; he was having himself a big weekend in New York. Omer lived with his mother in a tenement on a canal. He made good pay; had good times and girls in his town; went to New York from time to time on binges; talked with everybody; some thought him crazy but he was a hard worker, a good son to his mother. He had curly hair parted in the middle; small, bowlegged, strong, looked everywhere quickly. It was the apartment intended for old Pomeray. It belonged to a certain Dick Clancy who never came there; Omer used it when he wanted, he'd been caught funny this time but he had what he always wanted: two girls; no courage yet to take out his dirty pictures. He had a deck of playcards with men and women all swallowed up naked in love.

All the great city emerged from this place with its old plaster on the floor and the old architect board and chairs and a big magnificent bed put there by someone probably Clancy. Omer Leclerc knew everybody, Clancy for a long time, was having one of the biggest nights of his life, two beautiful girls with him for two days and two nights, one day in bed, this one the last; the two magnificent to play, laugh but so strange and they had been tapped on the head by a big dose of Benzedrine the whole gang, enough to kill, Leclerc was really out of his head and believed himself in Chicago, St. Petersburg Russia. "Beelzabur, Balabur, Bloobloom, what we gonna do in this big *grisette de bebette*" he babbled. "Isn't it cloudy out?"

"All day. But now it's night," Nicki said, the big one.

"Already night. It was morning, night, morning, night—My angels, how can I ever thank you! My heart's all broken in little pieces to love one more than the other, the two of you so beautiful, hell I talk like a Spaniard when I talk the truth."

"Oh, he's cute!" laughed the little blonde Peaches. She had dark hair bleached blonde. It made a fantastic combination. The light was now out. It was dark in the room, except for the kitchen that was now like brown in the heavy reflections from the city outside. Everybody on their backs you could tell from the way of their talk, like mummys, like telling ghost stories in the dark.

"For hours and hours I've been thinking profoundly of the little dimple in your shoulder, Monda."

"Monda. Oui, Soupçon, Soupçon—I hear all your pretty words, why do you have to go back to Boston tomorrow?"

"For work for krissakes!" said Omer looking at her, making a face in the dark.

"It's not every week of the year Peaches," said Nicki, "that we can be honored by the presence of Mister Leclerc."

"Ah but sometimes I believe you're playing me a wood!" yelled Omer sick.

The women laughed.

"Grow a little mustache and I'll tell ya!" laughed Peaches; and suddenly Omer looked in the corner of the room and saw the skeleton of a man.

"There! There it is, the phantom—the skeleton—it follows me everywhere. One corner, another corner—"

"Omer—drink some milk. Boy I can tell how hard it would be to take care of you."

"He ate all my brothers—he scared all my kids—"

"Ah you're raving, poetry—"

"Blow, Omer," said Nicki low.

"I'm afraid of St. Petersburg Russia!" Omer held his head, pressed hard, he was really frightened.

"Aw that again!" cried the little blonde disappointed.— "Finish your story Nicki, about the guys that used to give you a hundred dollars a night to play the tiger with—"

"We'd put on tiger suits, we got down on our knees, growl-grow—" and Nicki did this at Omer, who returned it. All three cigarettes in mouth. "It's nothing. There were two men once who bought a big barrel of oysters and broke them and cut them and threw them in the bathtub, and they made me sit in there for a hundred dollars."

"Ah let me kiss you!"

"Did they get in with you?" asked Peaches eyes in the dark.

The wind of October made a big lament between the tenements; in the night Omer sensed but didn't know the presence nearby of Rolfe, Pomeray, little Dean, Bull, Leo, Ti Jean waiting for him. "Another drink!" he yelled.

"There isn't any."

"We should have wine—the skeletons would leave—"

Later———

"Nicki!"

"Yes?"

"Let me play my fingers down your spine again, this time we'll make the chills rise—"

"Ooh yes," said Nicki, burying her mouth in her own shoulder, wrinkling her nose, "aren't bodies wonderful?"

"Wow," said Peaches; and at midnight the little model had to go. Omer was in his bathrobe, sitting on the edge of the bed, head fallen in her lap. Peaches was saying: "But yes, I have to get up early tomorrow morning, gotta go to work."

"Everybody has to work," said Omer.

"Of course idiot!—How long you gonna stay there in my lap?"

"Okay, go on then. Go walk alone in the street, in the barrels—"

"We won't be here tomorrow night," said Nicki, to Peaches, and they understood each other's plans.

"And me," yelled Omer, "I'm waiting for—"

"For what?"

Omer didn't know. He fell headfirst in the pillow. "Did you get her address Nicki?" He saw bats on the wall. Peaches left, with a little vivacious face full of the promise of the great Fifth Avenue and the great success of fashions there. You'd see her tomorrow, hatbox in hand, running through traffic. In the lobbies of big offices of the Millionaire Thirties . . . 1935, sad and gray year. Omer endured.

"Omer don't bang your head on the wall," said Nicki, because Omer suddenly in the agony of his desire had thrown his head against the wall, bang, arms falling tired.

"But it's not possible to pass two three days like we were and not make love." *What does she want to charge me?* he thought in his steeltrap head of Canuck workingman, mentally figuring his little figures he always kept in a wallet book, *a hundred dollars?*

"I told you, I'm in love with Vincent," said the woman.

"Well, Vincent ain't here."

"I have to keep my word cool."

"Aw, but I'm sick from it—from *you*—!! You're beautiful! If we started to make love maybe you'd forget Vincent."

"No."

"You're big as I am, bigger, you could beat the hell out of me. He he!"

"No, my love."

"You're playing with my hair, I like that."

"I love one man at a time."

"Aw but I had too much of this Benzedrine, I've lost 20 pounds I bet."

"You look it—Did you see your face, it's like a skeleton."

Omer lit his wood matches, looked in a little mirror from her pocketbook. "My God, my eyes are big! My cheeks high! Play the radio!"

"No radio. You look like a baby."

"Why'd you give me all that? You know I never had dope before."

"It's not dope—it's a medicine—You been high, huh? Come on let's dress and go hear Lester at the Savoy before it's too late. I'll bet you anything he swings tonight!"

"I bet—But I wanta make love to you."

"Oh no."

"We're all alone in the night, in the tenements of the Lower East Side—it's cold—we've *gotta* make love!"

"For what reason?"

"So we'll know each other better—so we can start our . . . be together, close—our *love*—come on let's love each other."

"No!"

"Come on let's love each other."

"I told you. But you don't dig that I love you too; I know you after these two days! You remember we met only 2 days ago, and here we're talking love—"

"In bed, hey what?"

"—I never saw you before, never been involved with you before—I got lotsa problems, I live a dangerous life. They got guns in the house those guys I live with, they steal."

"You been with them—You know what I mean—I never can talk right, ah?"

"Sure—Oh, one way or the other. We had gang affairs—on the roof, in the summer when it's *hot* in your 'cold' Lower East Side, man!"

"Yah, I know those guys are robbers. It doesn't make me happy—I mean, they can do what they want s'long as they let *me* alone—" Omer spoke with authority in his words. ". . . the thoughts we hide about criminals."

"If you wanta call it *criminal*—" It hadn't made a hit with Nicki.

"It *isn't* criminal?"

"I say," yelled Nicki showing her teeth "do what you want, you only live once."

Suddenly Omer had a paranoiac dream: he had a vision that Nicki really wanted to make love with him to get a chance to fill him full of Benzedrine, and after that, half dead her gang of robbers would come in and carry him away, take his body, put it in a car, fill the car with alcohol, crash it, burn it, to say that their ringleader Zaza was really dead. Omer sweated great drops. He thought of the porches of Cheever Street in summer moonlight.

"Honey, you're all wet—; let me wash your brow with cold water."

"Nicki—I know why you don't want to go all out with me—"

"Why?"

"Because you wanta wait for the guys to get here—I'll confess you my thoughts—Wanta? Really truth?"

"Yes, yes."

"You wont have to if the guys get here—Ah Nicki I'm afraid—I'm afraid—You're gonna be sore at me."

"Well tell me!"

"Nicki, I'm afraid you want to steal my body for yr gang."

She listened, eyes slitted. "Yes? Why?"

"To put in a car, burn—to use my body—to hide the boss of yr gang of guys—You unnerstand, I see skeletons . . . I think I'm in Russia—It's all been an impossible hallucination everything we been doing for the last 2 days, it makes me realize the mad foolishness of my life—I gotta go back to work—"

"Poor Omer!" Nicki kissed him, but he didn't feel he deserved it.

"You're not mad? It's crazy dreams! of a nut! Of a smalltown lout! You cant unwind crazy ideas out of your head once they're there—we come to the city of NY, we want to have a good time, not spend too much—You'd think I wanted you to help me tie myself up—I dont understand those insulting ideas to you—"

"Oh no it's not insulting—it's a funny little dream, a fairy tale."

"Ah it's a nightmare."

"But you've already told me," she laughed in his ears.

Now she accepts me because the guys are coming any minute! thought Omer.

"You accept me because—"

"What?"

He looked at her in that half dark. "I was going to confess you another idea. But you're too beautiful." He kissed her hard on the mouth; he caught her lips open. He'd done this a hundred times both nights, the kiss always lasted a half hour, this time it was wilder, they went into each other's bodies to seek like angry people. She sank. The man had won, the woman made her little act of loss, their two bodies shivered as if they were cold, crazy and violent, the teeth chewing in the poor mouth, the legs, crazy, the arms everywhere, the importance of life. Omer with every beat of his heart faster and faster thought "She's going to give herself to me now because those guys are coming . . ."

It wasn't the guys who were coming; it was him, that simpleton.

Immediately Omer wanted to cry in her arms for the folly of it all, and made believe he was.

"But what is it?" she asked when he gnawed her arm.

"I thought—the whole time we were having our love—that those guys were coming, that you were gonna sell me out for money—The whole time! Up till the end!—Just now!"

"Naw! Yes truly? Poor Omer! Gawd, pull yourself together. Since you're able to tell me these things you'll be all right. Come let's get dressed go see some jazz!"

"You understood me?!" cried Omer, happy.

"These ideas were developing for 2 days—you have to explode them—just like the rest of you—it's a big scientific study—There's a doctor, from Vienna, some boxes for cancer because there isn't enough love, dig—Man, if I could tell you all the stories I know! I went through a whole high school, the girls just like the boys. I developed them one after the other—they'd come to me, I'd tell em 'You still don't know what to think of love?' I lived nearby, in an apartment; it was in

San Francisco, not far from Van Ness & Lombard—Know that corner?—The little Chinese guys with the well-combed hair, in sweaters, I showed em little tricks in my bed—Like the best of springtime—open your happiness bed early—parturience—I was out of my head on Mexican marijuana. Max had fetched me some, a shopping bag full—cured. I had those little blondes high for the first time in their lives—You shoulda seen their faces!—"

"*Holy Batchism*" cried Omer.

"—Sitting in bed, flipping out, looking up for whatever they'd lost—'What's happening, ba-by?' I always asked—"

"What'd you do with those babes?"

"Went, daddy, went," she said. Suddenly she jumped and grabbed her drummer's iron brushes that she kept with her wallet, and played sharply on the table, in her slip, sitting at the end of the bed. "Lose me, you *mother*, lose me!" she cried. She played seriously, neck melted, like a hepcat, up to three minutes, four minutes, Omer was lying back.

"I'm just another one of your 'Johns'."

"No you're not a John!" she cried angry and snappy.

They got dressed. The clothes were falling off Omer. He was standing in the kitchen with one hand on the wall, all haggard, a blue suit, nothing else. He raised his collar. Nicki was even taller in her high heels. She played with the keys.

"Come on."

She supported him on her arm; he was really weak. "We've got to get you some fresh air—some food—some jazz, baby, jazz. Ooh, look at the beautiful pumpkin in the candy store! Oh how I understand these naborhoods here, they swing, I lived in quite a—Walk faster—" She was taking great leaping strides and he was going fast twinkling his little paws like he had sneakers on; Omer was as sincere as crossed eyes.

Going down the cold subway staircase, "So how d'you like that little Peaches?"

"Boy, there are some wild girls in New York. How come she wanted to be with us for 2 days—It's sad to live in Boston."

"There's some wild ones there too, come on. The world is waking up. Some day we'll see paradise on earth, kid."

"Eh, boy, Nicki—you're one beautiful woman."

"Aw, you're as pale as powder,"—in the street, around a restaurant light in Times Square—"We have to put some pancake
makeup on you to add some color."

Omer swallowed, looking everywhere; his face was all wet;
he was trying real hard to keep upright. The Benzedrine had
eaten 15 pounds off him, and he was just a little bowlegged
country boy. The big redhead applied the pancake; his face
was coffee red. He looked like a ghost who'd played a part in
a Broadway play, he played the part, and then died before they
could remove the powder. In the back ways of Times Square
the ghosts were raising their arms with thoughts on the whole
of life. "Here we'll go on the uptown train." She was taller than
he was; she supported him. People saw this phantom and that
shiny-eyed Amazon, and marveled.

At Times Square station suddenly Omer stopped and said
"No, I can't make it to the Savoy. I'm really too sick and tired,
I've gotta go sleep for 2 days. At my friend's place in Jamaica."

"No, come with me. We'll pass the time together in hotel
rooms, we'll talk—come, love."

"But I've got no more strength. We'll do it some other time!"

"No, right now!" said Nicki stomping her foot like a little
girl. "I still haven't seen Red—he's gonna give me money if
he found any—the sleeping pills—my coat that I told you—"

"Can't do it," said Omer head in hand—*I am going to die* he
thought. "Gotta go."

"But why, when we were loving each other—"

"It's not personal, I'm just dying—"

"Dying of what?"

"I'm gonna fall to the ground!"

They argued—they decided to disengage—Nicki was on
one side of the subway—Omer the other, inside the turnstile.
He had his package of vellum paper around his arm that he'd
purchased in New York for his work at the print shop in Massachusetts; the package was all torn up. "Oh come with," said
Nicki.

"Aw—aw—" It had been three nights since Omer had slept,
really slept, alone in his bed.

"Alright!" She got mad, she left, walking fast: she stopped,
looked on sadly, walked slow; and started up again, fast, to get

away, and Omer watched her leave in disbelief. She ran back. "*Come with me.*"

"Can't ya see I'm in need," cried Omer seeing her; he leaned his head between the bars, on his hand.

"*Come with me.*"

"Okay."

"There!"

"Coming in or out? But where we going! But what're we gonna do! But I'm gonna die! My heart's going too fast, my eyes are slammin and clackin some big hits, I dunno what I'm seein, Nicki! I can't do it.—"

"Alright first off you can do it. Alright if you don't wanna. I gotta go—Look, I'm gonna go—"

"I would, I would, I would but it's been two days!"

Omer looked at her, big girl of a little sister, a tiny corner in his heart for all of her torments and her big luminous loathsome face. "Are you gonna leave?"

"You see that I'm gonna leave."

"Aw yes we must leave, aw yes we must leave," said Omer sadly, watching her go, letting her take her leave, not stopping her, waiting to stop, waiting to think, letting her leave herself, slowly, looking back at him, from herself, over her shoulder, mournful, wanting to go play, Omer too dumb to accept it, too sick to talk about it, to think about it. Never to see her again— without an address—Only her name, Nicki. Her second name wasn't her real one.

Omer walked, hands in pockets, small, angry with himself, flayed, debauched; it was all a mad dream; there were teeth seizing him in the dark corners. Love was all tangled up with spikes. The Benzedrine was teaching him the dream of death, he saw the earth of the grave over his eyes; and now that Nicki was gone, his body was seized by pure sensations at the thought of Nicki. It was too much to grasp, he was afraid to waste time, had to go to work, he looked for clocks, in the subway. In Massachusetts, in the brown printshop of night, he'd stand upright on the platform of the big press, and they'd start the pages of the *Billerica News*. Boom, it was Omer who understood that big beast of a black greasy machine, so tender in its middles, so vast, interesting like a rule book perfectly written by a succession of industrial savants; the parts perfect. It made Omer's head split in half. The people of New York didn't know that this little Canadian from Massachusetts had sneaked into town for a weekend and had hooked himself a coupla dolls, they'd see him clack up his heels, tap on the sidewalk, disappear into the great rednesses of the piers at 5 in the afternoon; they'd see him asleep in the subway like a heap.

When he arrived at his uncle's house in Jamaica, he'd wanted to save some money but he'd spent it anyway buying spare ribs for the girls. The uncle and the aunt were in the middle of arranging the floorboards around his bed; working with hammers, it was a tender disaster in the tiny apartment. It was an old couple—hardworking, the old man happily busied himself in the yard with his sidewalk and his tree, the old woman listened to her radio in the hall; went to bed at 10 o'clock. Before he could ask him if he wanted to help them Omer said, "I have to lie down" and laid down on the bed in the extra room, without ceremony, fleeing so fast pulling the rags over his head that he didn't defrock himself.

He was about to feel worse the next morning. But before he'd slept two hours he was woken up by Uncle Bull Baloon. There he was, cigar in mouth, the bulb behind his head up high; the damn Bank Dick.

"W d is it?"

"Old Pomeray's arrived from Denver, where's that damn place o' yours at?"

"I told Rolfe—in the letter—Rolfe here yet?"

"Well Rolfe says that there's naked ladies staying in the place and that you made a mistake—"

"Rolfe—made a mistake? Look, I have the other key myself! Somewhere in those pants there!"—fed up with his pants— "It's Leo who has the key?" Omer wasn't exactly quick.

"Yes. But now they're afraid to try it. They're already talking about going back to Colorado. Been spending the whole day with em, poor Pomeray's got no head left, he's all eaten up by wine—much faster than I thought."

"Whadda we gotta do?"

"Get dressed! We gotta bring em there, make em feel at home, before they leave. You and me gotta get back to Boston with Leo and the Kid in the Plymouth—gotta work—"

"Ah," Omer saw his uncle in the door, "I'm sorry about all this."

"Aw, you gotta get goin already?"

"Yes, Arthur. Thanks. I'll tell my mother the good news. They ordered a beautiful 36 Pontiac." Dark trees made little scratches in the glass, it was the Long Island wind, at the window.

The old man and his wife had put away the dope from the bucket on the street, the doors, the double windows; it was time to leave. She was an old friend of his mother's; they'd given little pies to Omer for dessert on the first evening; the guy was a factory guard far into Long Island, the woman sewed in a dress factory. They were sitting, both of them, in big chairs, faces fallen; the design of the living room linoleum was painful to look at, it strayed, in blue and in brown, from the floor's natural vanishing lines. The other rooms of the house were dark and scary. The hospitality of these good people was lost in the ruin of the dream they'd once had in their eyes—the *quest* was dull. Suddenly, it was over.

Omer and Bull were returning to the city, to Manhattan, in Leo's Plymouth that Bull had borrowed. Bull drove. Halfway across Brooklyn, on Atlantic Avenue, he said "Wait a minute, I gotta buy some coffee." Omer waited outside. Bull was all alone in the store, there was nobody, it was a little neighborhood market. He saw his coffee at the top, he took the pole and started to bring it down. Just when the proprietress came out, some old lady, all the cans fell on the floor. Bull, his big behind moving fast, grabbed the chair and put it around the spot and with a handful of cans got up onto the chair to put them back. He'd put up three, when two others fell. He went down to chase them, and another one fell. He made a face. He climbed back onto the chair and stood up to put the cans back when all of a sudden the chair broke. He fell flat on his feet, but he fell against the Cornflakes counter, and all the Cornflakes and the Wheaties and the Grape Nut Flakes fell into a big heap in the aisle. Plack, another coffee can and some Rice Krispies. There was nothing more he could do. He took out his wallet and gave the old lady $2 for his coffee can.

"Good god, I had to give her a tip!" he said in the car. "Let's get outa here!"

Crossing the Brooklyn Bridge they saw the whole city, dark, illuminated, the sad ships surrounding it. "What in the hell we all doing in New York?" cried Bull, driving, nose hovering over the windshield, leaning forward, giving himself little slaps to the face with each thing he saw in traffic.

"Poor Rolfe—What's Rolfe doing in New York."

"Hey, it's a hell of a mixup. Pomeray—his kid—Leo—his kid—It was quite an escapade of mistakes."

They looked around the Brooklyn Bridge; there in the dark roofs was the gang, holed-up and hangjawed, waiting for fortune; Bull and Omer anxiously looking to see down there. "We'll turn right at the bottom of the bridge here."

One time Bull had, in his youth, started off with a bunch of book salesmen that he knew and they'd all left from New York in the car to see a girl in Fall River, and they reached the Cumberland Mountains in the valley where they got them old wooden shacks all lit up at 9 in the evening in the rain showing washtubs and tragic mothers at their labors and above the riverside trees that don't climb 15 feet over the other a wall of black mountains and rock-lifts with their mangled and chewed-up pines peeking through the impossibly lost tops in the fog. A terrible place, Bull and the salesmen standing crack-knee for so long in an old station while one of the guys was sick for a half hour in the shitter. They bought some moonshine; it hit Bull an hour after he drank it, he was laughing his head off, somebody had told them they were on the road to Louisville, Louisville okay, it was gonna be some goddam Mint Juleps "and ceytenly th'old Carstairs," cried one of the salesmen; they arrived at the Ohio River at 2 in the morning, it was sad lights in the spring darkness. Old Bull had always remembered this beautiful moment in the episode; it was the night he'd made love to the Mrs. Blood woman, who was up in her beauty parlor at 5 in the evening and Bull had gone in to convince her to join him on the beach by the river all night, with the car and some hotdogs. Voyages do not scare men of gold.

Big New York loomed over their faces like a black wall.

"Who was it that put this whole damn thing together?" Omer waking up.

"No one! McGee what's-his-name Pomeray had asked me to help him out, find him a place to live—in New York, okay, in

New York, he'd have Rolfe to drive him. I told Leo; he said he wanted to take a trip to New York anyway. I told you to give me the key to your damn place, in Lowell. No, you forgot and you left it for Leo."

"The damn apartment yes, it's the key to the damn apartment."

"I know it's the key."

"There's somethin that ain't right somewhere."

"Somebody's a total numbskull."

"Somebody'd fall right into a hole on the sidewalk," said Omer not knowing what he was saying.

He should have given the keys to Bull, then everything would have been set. But suddenly you couldn't see how it was gonna work any more.

They arrived at 18 Pott Street. It was midnight. Rolfe's car was gone. "Oh come on, they didn't leave!" cried Bull, exiting the Plymouth; he looked up into the windows of the loft. Leo was in there, shrugging his shoulders to say gone, with his hands, *from* him, just like that, *over*, stone faced. "Ah? He means they're gone!" cried Bull in his teeth. He and Omer jumped up the stairs, Bull with big leaping steps like a football guard of 60; Omer like a mad gazelle with a small swiveling head. It was gray.

"Yes," Leo said in the hall, "they left."

"Where for?"

"For Denver."

"For Denver again?" cried Omer. "Rolfe this? Rolfe Glendiver yr sure?"

"Yeah Rolfe, your Rolfe —he was here just a minute ago— well, a half hour, they left, yes, a half hour. Rolfe had been gone for 24 hours, he came back and told us that there were nude women in the apartment and we couldn't move Pomeray in there. We all thought he was mad!" Leo cried, throwing out his arms. "And your Pomeray. An old louse of a bum if I ever saw one—all day long he was sleeping on his cardboards and blankets, and after that he started to drink his wine, lit a fire, with the electric hot plate, made coffee, some eggs that Bull had left him"—Leo was talking to Omer—"Oh it was a day! I'm telling you, was that poor damn wretch a real bum, or what? Ain't it just a lil life, though?"

Bull and Omer realized the tragedy of these excited words of Leo's. In the corner Ching Boy was sitting, on a crate, legs spread open, throwing dice on a little tablecloth; the others close by, men of all kinds, Chinese, Irish, Greek, there was one who was a Greek from 23rd Street and 8th Avenue and he'd grown close to the Chinatown gang because he had a little lunchcart the other side of Chatham Square. On many evenings there, enshrouded, river ghosts pass by, guys who drink Bay Rum in clinker excavations. All those men, playing, weren't thinking about what had just happened . . . The little Negro was still there, in the corner; and the quilts still on the floor, near some grocery bags. Nothing had changed, except that Pomeray and little Dean and Rolfe had left. Old Bull, scratching his jaw, was bothering himself raw in his old damp heart, inside of which only a small warm fire was left in the vastness, he himself also lost, gone.

"Aw, it's too late to go find em?" and looking at the others with his big blue eyes wanted to see everyone else's expressions.

"Look," said Leo, "Rolfe left a pack of cigarettes." Omer looked; they were Raleighs, cork tipped, next to an unimaginably chewed and mangled book of matches—nothing doing—

The little Negro boy was still waiting for his brother Slim Jackson.

Ti Jean, all of a sudden, saw everything from his dice game corner; there he stood, arms held backwards, looking at the athletes of life in their game—looking at the players and the yakkers too. The poor Little Boy hadn't eaten all day, his father had had a couple of drinks and didn't think of eating, as usual, and Ti Jean followed him in this, in their adventure. Now he was hungry but the day continued—He too had seen the Pomerays depart. In his hand was the tennis ball; Dean had given it to him.

"Why'd they do that!" exploded Bull.

"I never seen such sad people—They figured they couldn't get inside the house with the naked women, and got it into their heads that it was over and they decided to go back to Denver. They talked about it, he and Rolfe, for a half hour."

"They're Oklahomans," said Bull, "they're a one of a kind race."

"Rolfe was certain that he couldn't—He told us the story of the girl at the edge of the bed, no clothes on, and of a tall redhead in a black slip who was going out, and a man—it certainly wasn't Omer's place: Ah Omer?"

"Sure it was my place Leo! That was me in there! I've been using that place for girls from time to time; I knew the farmer and his kid were coming, but I didn't know when—Boy, Leo, I'm tellin ya I had myself a time this go around!" Leo looked at him cigar in mouth like a straight popsicle.

"It's Rolfe's fault," said Bull.

"Why Rolfe?"

"He decided—But the old man wanted to leave too. He was scared of New York, he just never went outside of this loft—He stayed in bed all day—the little boy he played a bit—" He paused, to listen, "Ti Jean—. . . . Rolfe he looked angry—And that's how it happened. It rained a bit, you remember, and he sat down, hearing Rolfe—I figure that Rolfe's as crazy as a broom—"

Omer: "Rolfe isn't crazy—It sounds like he didn't know what was happening—He's a damned bastat, I remember; dammit, I didn't see him! Ah, he shoulda—He looked in the windows?— It just didn't come into his head to think that it could have been my place—Ah well, what a frizzy of blah blah blah this is."

"But they all wanted to leave!" cried Leo. "I was trying to tell him the poor guy, wait, Bull went to see if he can find Omer, and he's gonna bring you to the place himself. But I don't think they even believed in Omer's existence. I kept telling em, Omer Leclerc! Omer Leclerc!"

"Well don't yell my name!"—all the men in the loft, the players too, had started to shout at the top of their lungs—

"What'd the little boy do?"

"I dunno, I didn't see him. Well—I told myself, this poor man, this poor child, like feathers in the wind—Sure—" looking on, making a face. "The poor father, we didn't hear him talk, he didn't say two words."

"Oh he can talk!" cried Bull. "I've known him!"

"Gone? But they could've had the place!" cried Omer. "Dammit! Oh how hard life is! Well, we gotta find our road, time to go. Gimme the keys to the car, Leo."

The little Negro had spent the day alone, looking at the others; the other two little boys had too, Ti Jean and Dean. The children hadn't talked.

The wind ran in the street. Rolfe's car was lost, gone, Bull saw this beyond the drapes. The drapes had the hollow scent of the surroundings. All the men buttoned up their coats more tightly as did the children seeing this. A wind came into the loft. Bull joined the dice game. "Canada," he said, "it's where the poppy dopple goose blows s-s-s-s—bring me home seven!" The dice hit seven; Bull picked them up to click them, stooping down to do so, puffing, almost exploding. You heard him talk, but you weren't sure that he'd said what you thought he said. Leo his nephew watched him, he too was putting hands to knees and stooping down for the game. They were all tired, hair on their foreheads. The Chinese had lost all their teeth, did whatever they did; some were coming in to tell the others that supper was ready at home. You could see families sitting, indoors, eating with chopsticks, sitting in their chambers of eternity.

"We're in Chinatown!" said Leo, he shouted at the top of his lungs. "Dammit we're gonna have ourselves a feast in Chinatown before we go to Boston."

"Me I'm going North," said Bull.

"You're coming to Boston with us."

"No—I'm going to Butte Montana—to work—the Boston and Albany, the Boston & Maine—phooey—Am gonna try the Great Northern this winter, if they want an old rail like me—still—after all the years I spent my time sleeping in bottle beds of red neon hotels like those whore houses where you suddenly find yourself all jammed up with your pants halfway down so you can't run—The law will get us, hand in pocket. Think about the three sets of eyes that watch the road tonight—" Bull was saying this over his hat, that he'd extended, from his forehead, straight out, a little curl of his messy hair climbing up his pate. Old Bull went over to the other side of the floor, picked up the old bum's blanket and put it over his shoulders. "S'cold as a bastat!" he cried to himself, making a face, and walked on the floorboards thinking.

"We're gonna go eat a good feed!—eh Omer, a good feed?" Omer was lost in the trunks of the car, gone.

All of a sudden the little Negro spoke to Ti Jean across the great room, and in such a normal way that the men, except for

Bull, weren't listening, "Hey Lil Boy, who was he that Lil boy with the sick old father? What was he doin lying there?"

"He was my blood brother."

"Your blood brother? What was it he'd done?"

"He'd been poor, they came here in an old car and were waiting for Rolfe and Rolfe had left and when he came back he said, 'No they're not there the naked women' and so they all kept their heads down, and decided to leave. My father was telling them to wait. Uncle Bull went over to see. They loaded their stuff in the car and Dean gave me the tennis ball, said 'Okay'—and Rolfe looked at the engine one time, angry faced, and they went into the street and left for autumns at the tracks—from here to Arlington and Santa Anita and Fair Grounds Louisiana."

Ti Jean saw everywhere in America great race tracks lost in the rain; there were crowds of men in gray raincoats, wet horses, jockeys bleak and bewildered in their colors with their little white legs spotted with mud and little drops in the face, piles of hay near the barn with gray boards where the Kentucky trainer sat talking to the young jockeys of Arkansas and Texas and New York who listened to learn—and you could see old Pomeray walking behind the barn looking for a job, little Dean looking everywhere.

"Ah'm from Nawth Ca lina my self," said the little Pic with his funny voice, his speech seemingly coming from afar, as if from the other side of the valley. "We came, me and my brother, we—he came to get me in the middle of the night, from my aunt's house—in Rocky Mount, yes—we had a house with windows, the grandfather hated me. My father was dead, 'Pic,' he'd say, 'go live with your howling aunt.' There were watermelons on the porch. The old man was blind. He tried to grab me. I wanted to go from grandfather into our little house in the middle of the log field—There were owls in the trees, on the edge of the Tar. We ran me and Slim in the night from Big Easonburg woods, near the white church, to turn onto the tar road and there was a big black snake squashed in the street, we could see by the moon, a little white dog was following us, the frogs were crying out like madmen with dumb little faces, some were—it made me wanna cry. He took me out through the window in the middle of the night, yes, and when we left, through the woods me on his shoulders; there was a white line in the street."

And it was true. And then they had hitchhiked to New York, the little boy sitting on the suitcase so that Slim could play his music in New York. His wife had just died, Slim, of a baby; he kept his little brother for a son in their apartment in Harlem, he'd moved everything from her mother's, he left only a little sock of Pic's in the middle of the floor—Slim and Pic lived alone, in the spare room, the musicians' room. He'd once stayed in the room of a friend of Count Basie's, Hot Lips they called him, Count was there and they'd talk about life back when they'd played in Nebraska in the house of love and ran from the bar downstairs to the rooms upstairs, the bass player too; stories of the jazz life, their big round faces of a generation behind the bottle, "There's always gotta be some women singin, man." And one of the youngest and tallest in the gang asked a question, and the guy hears him but doesn't answer, just looks at his match with a proud smile happy to be with the old friends all talking. "Look at this old picture of Slim here, looka that face!—That man is *twisted*!" showing the picture with stiff fingers; laughing in the staggered room. "Hey, I bet them Roman soldiers got high, sittin in a room all alone at noon with his helmet by his side, all *down* with his thoughts,"—suddenly, staggering away—"sittin not movin a muscle, listening for the sound of the Roman bell to see what time it is and listenin to the girls all laughin in the tenement court downstairs—man, he's *high*!"

Slim didn't want to stay at his mother's, he had no home in Rocky Mount because his father had left and his mother was dead. There was a feud between his family and the family of the dead man, who was an uncle. He had no place to go, Slim lived one day to the next as a musician, running all over town to play, to eat, to drink, to smoke, the whole gang together throwing each other wheelbarrows of wild jazz. It was almost enough to make you forget your poor dead little wife. He had a picture of her, beautiful as a princess of the Nile, gone.

The little Negro had a low voice around his little brown and red woolcap. They slept together now, in a vacant apartment, only floorboards, in the building of a friend in Harlem—But they now looked for a home of their own, and for money.

They'd suffered through a lot of hunger pangs, and embalmed comforts in the fog, on the road; New York didn't bother them much, though. Slim's old father was hiding out in Harlem; he had murdered a man in the South, had bounced the high-way camp by throwing himself into a ravine, they didn't find him, was an old ragman with a broken hat in the dump lots of Harlem—early in the morning in winter—he slept in an impossible flop that had no working toilets, nor any warmth of spirit or Heart; an old dormitory with broken windows, shoes and ashes in a corner. An old man singing: Song of the Old Negro Hobo "Crossed the Niobrara." You didn't know from where he'd found the songs, whether you heard what you thought, whether it was coming out of his mouth! or out of some rusted up black iron lodged in his throat, a weary heart broken all the way down to his socks, an impossibility fallen into the eyes of all the yards dirty with snow.

"They're gone," said little Pic, "They didn't wanta wait no mo," and "humph" he said, "un-huh," and shrugged a little, "just wouldn a want no more, no? s'm . . . You done lost the man's hole, axlebrain, you done lost the man's hole," he mocked, recalling one from home, he didn't take his eyes off Ti Jean's ball.

Old Bull took out his bottle and took a little drink, you saw his hat flashing in the light, his face red, his enormous nose immaculate, his teeth missing. He looked over his shoulders to see if someone had seen him.

Slim Jackson came back at one in the morning: he looked happy; he'd made his money, played his music. "Come on Pic, we got a beautiful little warm room to sleep in tonight, at the Cecil Hotel—You'll sleep tonight."

"Slim, stay with us!" cried Ching Boy. "We'll have a big dinner in my store—in the light—no?—it's too late?—"

"I gotta go to Chicago, I'm gonna play with a big band— the drummer's an old friend from North Carolina, we went to grammar school together—Suddenly I find him in a big band, today, at the session; Jimmy—was there!—I go talk to the leader—I played, I swung—like Lester Young! It went! Wow! Man, we rolled; he kicked that drum in when we rolled. He beat it to death his next chorus, the alto saxophone. I was doin a riff. You shoulda been there. I came in low, real low, like from underneath it s'prised everybody with a wild idea! They dug! I came on strong with my best efforts—I wrestled the horn up & down—That's all I could do. Yessir daddy, I stretched myself *out*."

They'd had it, their session. They started off tipsy in the morning, strap on neck, a piano, a bass, a guitar that struck the rhythm, a trumpet and a kid who came from the South; and Slim, with his tenor. They crashed the first train from the first tune and they started. "The guitar was Charley St Christian or somebody like that," said Slim's chum, the drummer. "Meet me in Georgia Avenue, and we'll drive on to Chicago. Got that straight, George Washing-tone?" he said, the drummer, Jimmy, hat placed on the ground in the sidewalk after the session, to drive up to reach their plans.

And the Kid with the alto, "A lil Negro from Chicago?" asked Slim. Wham, Slim blasts big notes in the baths of bars, "I Got Rhythm," behind him the lil kid didn't give a damn he was playing his alto saxophone with fantastical notes, Slim heard him and he heard himself, it was a new medley of music, it was going everywhere, seeking all funny spots and everything, but the kid found them up high. He emerged from the ideas of others like a dinosaur, then rose, neck extended, to the top of the mountain; played like that, bopping horn in the kisser, his knees shaking a little making his pants fall a tiny bit each time. Slim was astounded; around all this the trumpet kid from the South played the same way, with impossible whinnies from the trumpet, he got angry and he grabbed him and gave him a big hit filled with bucketfuls of ideas. They blasted together like that at ten in the morning; a young Jew was sitting there, by the record player, leaning on his arms like some movie idol, looking, big blue eyes, red cheeks, as if he wanted something, 17 years old, an expensive watch on his soft arm's wrist.

"Blow," he said.

Had it, the session, the inventors of music in the morning, in the hangover school of America, rising up to their art like local thieves, and all of a sudden on the side of the building, from the toilet, "Hey!" a tramp in the wall like in the war. They all of them gassed with the noise that we all wanted to hear.

"Go!" cried the kids, shivering through a big wave, yet all standing on the same floor arm in arm looking at each other in line, bouncing with the whiplashes of the fantastic drummer that you wouldn't believe; he was kicking the bottom of the bottom floor of the world with his foot, he dropped bombs on the cities of joy, he looked directly in front of him with neck locked, his hands working the noise of time's arrival, while Slim pulled out in front with buttock strikes. The lil kid throws himself into the sky to knock his idea!—in the middle of a chorus that no one was playing! Slim purred one out of the big engine with both hands held forward to tear the doors doawns! The alto, circling in place, to think, spurted out a string of broken wings all written in gold and afterwards gave out an impossible tweet-tweet from his tone, at the same time putting a stop to the idea Slim had started, picking up a piece from the edge of the trumpet's idea, and threw a little yell to say that this was it, that's it we said when we said it in our spot at (at five years old) four o'clock at five years in the morning of the cities of the past.

"That man is *bent*!" cried Slim pointing to the young lil bird at the alto who came from the far West, and for his reward, a grave and surprised smile from the young man, an artist.

"Come on lil Pic," he said, leading him by the hand, "we're gonna go find the room to sleep in, and tomorrow we'll take our suitcases out onto the roads an' find the damn station. Ey? Boys? Find peace when you're dead. It aint no fairytale joke to be in need & to try to live from one day to the next."

"And to stay in the same place," said Bull.

"Chicago, I'm gonna blow my brains out, Chicago. I hope we don't have a crackup in Cleveland," cried Slim at the top of his lungs in the staircase.

"He's tired, give him some peace," said Ching Boy, seriously, everyone looking at his white face and he not knowing he'd said anything special, other than a little sentiment.

Ti Jean watched Pictorial Review Jackson pass in the street with Slim—who was to die a year from now in a crackup in the South—around the corner, toward the night of the city, of America, walking fast in the wind, hurrying, looking at the big circus into which you saw them disappear. They too were going to Chicago, to the immense winter snow, golden banjo.

He thought about the faces of bums in newsreels, all their mugs white like in minstrel shows, like Negroes, all buried in a sad rain, all black. Ti Jean wanted to go home.

"Alright," said Leo, "we might as well Omer. You're coming, William?"

"No."

"But why?—"

"I changed my plans, I'm not going to Massachusetts."

"Eh well—"

"I have to continue my circle in the world—Gotta take off again. Say goodbye to Gaby."

In the street Leo said, from the car, "We're gonna eat in Chinatown—at that open restaurant over there—We can smell it, smell! Eh? Come with us. We'll eat us a good little perfect dinner and after that am gonna have a good cigar. After that I'll be ready to leave."

"You could eat at Ching Boy's in the morning."

"No, it's too late, time to go, Bull. Poor damn Bull, what're we gonna do, uncle?"

"Ah yes—okay—" Bull didn't know what to say.

"We'll see you—"

"Well yeah—well known—"

The Plymouth started, Omer was driving, tongue wagging, he'd combed his hair; they were awake, they had to drive and spend the night on the road and arrive in the morning. That was life, dammit. No Nicki, no more St Petersburg Russia. "Ah beautiful Nicki. The gas tank's almost empty! Dammit!"

They left. You saw the little boy with the big eyes surrounded by his baseball cap, watching. Bull was all alone in the street when they turned the corner with a little sad puff of gasoline. The other men didn't play long; all of a sudden they all went to bed in the darkness. "Might as well not have supper," said Bull—Sitting, at the end of evening, hands on knees, the last two old friends.

"No," said Ching Boy.

"We'll go to bed—"

"You gonna sleep here—?"

"Well, no, not that, I'm leaving, you go to bed, at your place, Ching Boy, and thanks for your kindness. We didn't talk between the bars of a jail for nothing, ah? We understood each other, ah, when we spent white afternoons telling each other the stories of our lives? Old Frisco!"

"It didn't bother me, the business with your brothers."

"Your ancestors were proud and smart men like you, Ching."

"Yes, and yours big hearted, thin headed," laughed Ching Boy, looking at Bull over eyelids thick as a shelf, to rest his hardworking eyes.

"That a compliment or no?" laughed Bull, but Ching Boy went out, with the lamp, turned it off, the two men went out into the street. They looked, both hands in their pockets, it was goodbye.

"Goodnight, gotta go, I'll see you tomorrow before leaving."

And Bull went down, another snap of the hat, sharp, and went around the corner, on Bowery Street, where a dark wind made powdery dust clouds in the aura of the lamp; turned back one last instant, to tie his boot, quickly, on a hydrant, and left, a boat between his legs was floating there behind his strides in Chatham Square only to disappear from one of the spokes, Pott, Mott, East Broadway, Bowery Street or the alley of the red eyed black cat.

The old Chinese was already on his own way. The old buildings were dark. There was only an ash can on the sidewalk.

It was the bridge that you could see in the night from on high, and even higher the eyes of man could see the whole city from an airplane, the island, the people; the rivers, the smoke from various places; the little holes where all the rats of life ran into, lost in darkness, impatient maladies of all kinds; unknowingness of joy, innocence in love, of Rabbits. The belief is caught in their throats. A rabbit sits majestic in the sun.

Far down the road the poor guys were returning to Denver, for another winter there, around the tracks and the poor lunch-carts of Larimer Street, and Rolfe for the great fields of snow cracking and shimmering in the gray winds of the North—he watched the old face of light that was being projected and caught on the road. Rolfe was going fast, every moment deadly dangerous. There were curve signs, ↱   ↰. But Rolfe watched his wheel, his road; the ditches shone from within their brownishness, you could see the dry grass. All their eyes were searching beyond the hubcap for whatever was happening in the jaws of mortal hunger.

A big broken hole. The giant clouds glowed white in the night, the Plains grass was yellow, it roundifilated, it wrote huge windy words, softly, outside, across the fine crish-cracking of the struggling car in which the men kept their tongues stiff in their sorrow.

THE END

Brigash, cass mi gass

December 17, 1952
3 A.M.
Rooster
Fellaheen Rooster

Text reconstituted and edited by Jean-Christophe Cloutier
Translated by Jack Kerouac and Jean-Christophe Cloutier

TICS

Tics

From 1952 through 1953, Kerouac was working across a number of notebooks on what would become *Book of Sketches* (published posthumously in 2006). The mode of automatic writing and deep description characterizing that book are quite similar in tone and content to *Tics*, a short open-ended typescript that he wrote casually between 1953 and 1956. It is clear from the opening passage that Kerouac originally intended to develop *Tics* into a full-length book, though his imaginative and thematic aspirations for that book seem to have gotten rechanneled into *Memory Babe* (begun in 1957; see page 249 in this volume) and *Old Angel Midnight* (composed between 1956 and 1959).

Tics is an exercise reminiscent of Proust's exploration in *Remembrance of Things Past* and the concept of involuntary memory—the sudden welling up of vivid and powerful reminiscences. Just as the flavor of the madeleine in *Swann's Way* transports Proust's narrator back into detailed memories of his childhood home, Kerouac opens up channels of memory by recalling the experience of eating bread and butter dusted with sugar in his mother's kitchen in Lowell. Each entry in *Tics* serves as a verbal snapshot taking its place in a literary photo album.

(Note:—Tics are involuntary shivers of memory) (these from 1953)

* * *

A BUNCH OF PEOPLE sitting on a screened porch in Rosemont on some cool golden afternoon & there's a garden hose—children—I have a little girl friend—There is joy unrememberable, a dream of some kind of lost whatnot—What tic recalls it? I must find out what tics recall what visions, how, how many, where—This is the beginning of the book of Tics

* * *

INK DARK NIGHT in Sunnyvale, sitting on the ground waiting for the others to finish beans—Under pure profound California keen night stars—The lunchcart, the masht potatoes with gravy, the soup, meat, coffee—The smell of steam, water, coalsmoke—The smash-by of the Dark Zipper or the Lark—The emptiness of the track after the fleet—Dull brown light in the crummy where the conductor's reading SF Call Bulletin & swigging by his oil lamp—

* * *

THE THRILL of the yellow pink NY Daily News on the back page on a summernight when you see the flash photo of the 2 boxers—Zulueta & Persley—the baldheaded white sportshirt photographer who took it at ringside, you see on the almond smelling subway of dust & city night sorrow the 2 black sad wet bodies, the leather gloves, the strain of hard jawbones, the teeth, the mouthpiece bulging lips, the African gloomy broken grick & grit of it in the great Rome Metropolitan night of it—the smell of cigar smoke, the TV of it in sour sud bars—the darting hook, the bobbed cottonhair head—the wrinkled worried boxer brow—Guys in hospitals watching it on TV in dark sweet ward all the city bejewelled Babylonian Outside—the voice of the TV announcer, the crash clang of

241

the subway, great black hot winds of the tunnel blowing on the pink News fluttering the page as you look—Manny New York of handpainted ties, sports shirts, Broadway, Madison Square Garden & later the perfect littleprint serious boxscores—The poor invalid shivering with joy in the hospital bed for this is all he has—The tired weary face of the handler is like the face of Vaudeville, poolrooms, Times Square pineapple & papaya stands, Greenwich Village gangster bars, the compositor room of the gray great Morning Telegraph

*   *   *

BEFORE TELEVISION when the poor sick guy'd listen to the radio—I was at home, winter, the voice of the announcer so dear & human in the morning it made my chest shiver—The arrangements of their programs, leftover childhood dreams over the *passage* from one song to another the little sad subsidiary static ticking *history* of it in the tiny radio hole void,—the thought of the men of the radio shaving in the morning, the bowl of lather, the razor, the big gruff ignorance of it, a little dotter of the house weeping over *this* after they die—the clear blue bell trumpet of morning shivering in my chest all of it— The hundred thousand details of life once ungraspable now too-graspable & overwhelming in the Macrocosm, learned from T—

*   *   *

THAT GRAY WALL on the gray out-of-Lawrence Street thru which we always went Sundays driving to Salisbury beach, my first vision of city bleakness, inexplicable unexpected granite wall round & rolling with the outgoing road, you went thru the heart of a suburban area before the highway to Haverhill that followed the Merrimac—O, even, the spectral late afternoon gold on the low rocky Merrimac near Haverhill, lost Sundays

*   *   *

THE MONTREALISH REDMORNING ALLEY back of St Joseph's parochial school when gritwinds blew on dirty snow dung of dump wagon horses, fences leaned, Brothers of the Order in black ravened cloaks florped in the keen—Come to order at

8 A.M. for lineup in the gravel, the kids—the rednose snuffle-
bums high on rackety drivers' seats with reins as old & gray
& sad as Time—the barrels by the fence, the other alleys,—

                              *   *   *

WE'D BE SWIMMING up the track in dark Templeton, old Hog-
head Charley HawHaw the loudmouth, he was the funniest
old brushballoper in the world with red face, seegar, great
thunderous vocal chords, Sammy White or Sammy Something,
a maniac of excitement & he loved to push his Diesel thru
the curves of the night out beyond Margarita towards Salinas
& Watsonville, westbound now, this is all in the South 250
miles down of Frisco, the San Luis subdivision, pure stars &
sorrow—

                              *   *   *

THE SMILE OF MY BROTHER GERARD is like the smile I saw in
the helicopter in the sky when it flew with the mail which had
been written by the smiling faces of the world bending with
pens over desks—

                              *   *   *

TI NIN—she had a boyfriend on the corner in a house all
somehow made of glass & davenports & sun streaming in hot
choky—Brunelle, he played a saxophone, took lessons, his hair
had a marcelle wave, he was pretty, his farts were interesting,
they played tennis in the ground real gannahook cosh turm
with stripe & pit pock wire net, smashing the little coo-cherd
up & down the smoss & here I am 25 years later with Nin married & mother in the South & me & Mardou, my Negress, lie
face down on the bed in the dark holding hands

                    walking down to
                       infinity
                      down a different
                    road no asphalt
                     no plot just
                     death just
                       tenderness & death
                      of death

*   *   *

OF THE JOY that I see whenever in reading my prose so blackly neatly typed on onionskin whitepaper & bound in my black-binder book looks up at me in the bright little nightlamp down bending it within it I see my whole life has been preserved & been made into something more important than I myself, in other words an angel has made a record of it & in original language of the angels for the angels, pure, monophylactic private murmuring intonated long song of life I have here created—my shelf of prose—it looks up at me not only as I say sometimes with Gerard's eyes popping up thru great images he made me see (as I said elsewhere) but I see in it another being than myself whirling with life in the anxious reality of himself & it's like watching a great ballet of myself a drama of myself—with the background drapes not a stagehand's work but the color of time & rain itself—Poetry

That's what I was intended to be, a Poet

Poet on Earth

. . . in eternity there's Great Neal being wild & silly in a parlor, high, with Golden Davenport colors in the air—he's the Holy Goof on Earth—also a Poet, he has said: "Mind, Rise, Mind"

A GREAT MAD DRIVER IN THE NIGHT

*   *   *

A TALL MAN has come to me & advised me to write an elegy (on my own death) at once—Hee hou hea haaha

Doctor Sax

O ------------ O

We stare into each other's eyes
in the gray light of
Paradise Alley
Me'n Mardou

We stare into each other's eyes
in the gray light of

Paradise Alley at
5 o'clock in the
kid screaming
afternoon
cymbals
in
Egypt
I do see there
and castanets of eyes
Ovals of the Goddess Snake

* * *

EXECRABLE SPANISH AMERICA

AFTERNOON IN A WELL TO DO MIDDLECLASS HOUSE on the outskirts of a Mexican jungle town, with awnings even over the graveled drive, a tree, some pale shade, vista of long hot bare field to outside-of-town Indian dobes—The radio plays slow lazy mambos, there is static of an afternoon thundershower—The hero sits in his chair eyes closed in a dismality 100 times worse than that dismality of Julien Green Villages of Provincial France—he is an excited Spaniard part Indian businessman with little mustache, large worldwide ego, all the egomania of a French Canadian hero à la Charley Bissonette rushing eagerly to parties in Lil Canada & out at Long Pond—but this griffa Indian Cocksman taxi executive rushes on eager white shoes in the oppressive broiling humid heat of a jungle village, over stinking sidewalks to the heart the Europeanized heart of town where the radio station is & the announcer his buddy who goes cocking with him at night in their 52 Chevrolet neat & whitewall tired, the sad roadhouse outside town in the Linares Road or the Navajoa or Tampico Road—The clouds of southern America hang huge in the heat, it's late afternoon turning red but no breeze, no coolness, José the hero is dozing in his father's redbrick & glassbrick house at the outskirts of town among the few well to do Spanish families (their contempt of the sad stinky tortilla Indian, the long dust of filth afternoons, the coyote dogs snapping at flies in rotten meat noon drowse at the mercado, José's whole being is pointed to disentangling himself from every possible contact with the Indian life which

was the basis of his life white Spanish blood or no, glassbrick
house or not, 52 Chevvy or not, privilege of hearing his own
buddy's voice announcing afternoon boleros on the station or
not)—It's in fact close to suppertime and so José's mother will
soon serve supper, porkchop, while Indian women in the wailing yards pound the mournful tortilla on the humble stone he
will eat fancy at lace tablecloths no Carrie McNally of Peoria
or Blackfoot North Dakota or St. Paul would be caught dead
with even if you could get a sale at Russek's, but tablecloth to
the Manzanillos a sign of great privilege & advancement in the
Cosmos of Mantes, of Navajoa, of Matamoros, of Guaymas—
late, hot, red afternoon, the breeze ruffles up the driveway tree,
the sun flashes white hot off the front porch stucco, the static
cracks & crashes on the radio as a storm rumbles down the
earth of the valley of the world, a fly jumps from the vase to
the French blinds to the black mahogany chair—José is bored,
but half asleep in his chair, waiting for tonight, for Carmenita's
kisses—O how he hates her guitarplaying Indian brother from
the machete swamps down the Rio Road—how could one
forget the brown meek humble sweaty background & think
only of the—how could one get rid of tortilla yards, stone
steps, beaten dirt of huts, fish heads outside stickhuts, grass
roofs, stinking smokes, bawling dirtymouth brown babies, the
shawls of jungle mothers, the cake of hard black footsole, the
fine white dust on dark brown feet, the pain, smell, misery &
Indianness of the New World Real—& think only of cars with
whitewall tires & new horns that go TRA PA TA PA?—Suits of
Palm Beach, dancing the rhumba, rum & coke at Chiquinilla's,
books in the library shelf, gravel driveways, frosty glassware,
blinds in windows, potted flowers of white stucco porches,
loneliness & dignity of long white walls of bighome gardens,
dresses from Lima or Mexico City or even Panama City—mustaches, pomades, barbers, gloves in the jungle winter (yellow
kid)—radio announcers, the South American time gong bell of
radios, b-l-o-i-l, *que hora es señor a la cuatro de la noche—Hoy!
Solamente Hoy! Mas Grande Baile del Mundo!—*"—
     The little mustache, the impossible dismal bleakness and
nowhere to go, really, even for rich, almost rich José, nothing
to do—nothing to do & all that bare southern America, all
that land, that jungle shooting out four sides under eternal

afternoon world clouds motionless in the haze—all North &
South America of the New World suspended for a minute in
the hot afternoon's most torpid moment in one inexpressibly
dull gaspink yawk void gloom, in Lowell they're frying hamburg as kitchen doors slam, it's under the same clouds, on the
same world shelf, nobody knows what to do there either, Irish
of New England or Mestizo Middleclass of southern America
it's all one long hot waiting in the afternoon of boredom & the
burden of time all colored by the same hopeless New World
bleakbrush forever & for the poor ten times worse & ingrained
in dust itself forever—wrangly sad Fellah mutts sprawled in
yards, one covered with sores & flies—one shithouse in the
entire village for visiting people who have to go and it's a stone
crap caked mess in a ruined courtyard of a poolhall with torn
greens on rained on tabletops & the sodapop is warm—Radio
crackles boleros, excited eager announcer yurbles—good God
there is no hope at the end of the hot dry street & no hope
beyond & no hope here & no hope anywhere! And especially
no hope in those homes on the edge of town where hope is
supposed to be, hope & middleclass solidity, quality, & kind—
Bleak as an eye in heaven, as a formal mind struggling to free
itself from these bonds of language to a pure sea of images—

*   *   *

THE WALLS OF THE LOWELL REDBRICK THEATER in the hot
afternoon, the back of B. F. Keith's, the fire escape, the puff
clouds hanging in the blue day bowl & the way they march
majestically past the high stump tower chimneys of the Silk
& Cotton Mills—the reflection of Sad Lowell in the rolling
river—the old rubber tires on drowsy afternoons drying off
mud by the river bank, the slick on the rocks—Strange eternity
in the Polish tenements of Lakeview & the corner of Bridge
& Lakeview where old men were famed for cloudgazing in
old Lowell histories unwritten—who'd seen bridge traffic
change—from carriages to automobiles—Sad Sunday afternoon in Lowell when we'd been visiting relatives, very distant
stranger like relatives—The sad 2nd story flats they live in, have
white ceiling light casting a dimmer shadowy potted plant light
into the Piano room—The alcove, the piano is gloomy as a
casket, huge black unused—They sit blearing, saying "Well you

know I havent seen him for two years now—he was working in Haverhill last time I heard of—" & I a little kid have to sit there & outside it's bleak Sunday, people pass drowned in streets of purple red ray sun, cars black as coffins pass—Everything is unspeakably *visiting* in nature, as tho not alive in the world anymore (& not home in soft overalls & free in fields to roam & ragged wood of yard, personal dust)—now it's the Visiting in the World so trapped & cant move & swallow the doom of Sunday whole—

> *Au typewriter*
> *toujours!*

*   *   *

MEMORY BABE

Memory Babe

Begun in November 1957, *Memory Babe* was one of the first major projects undertaken by Kerouac after the publication of *On the Road*. It took shape in a series of notebooks and diaries, its compositional history overlapping with that of *The Dharma Bums*. Kerouac initially hoped to place both manuscripts with Viking, but increasingly turned his attention to *The Dharma Bums*. While he became intermittently reinvested in *Memory Babe* at several points during 1958, he eventually let it drop once more to focus on a different project, *Lonesome Traveler*, published in 1960.

A letter Kerouac wrote in May 1961 to his agent Sterling Lord reasserts his commitment to completing *Memory Babe*, describing it as a bridge between *Visions of Gerard* and *Doctor Sax* in the overarching structure of *The Duluoz Legend*—though chronologically the events portrayed in *Memory Babe* occur closer to *Doctor Sax* than they do *Visions of Gerard*. Like those works, *Memory Babe* provides an intimate account of Lowell and its Franco-Canadian community through the lens of Kerouac's childhood. Those books remain the most comprehensive literary ethnography of French Canadian life in 1920s and 1930s New England, mapping and preserving a lost world in a way consistent with Kerouac's aesthetic of memory.

The text presented here is derived from two typescripts: a twenty-foot-long scroll dated June 1958, and a twenty-two-page typescript in which Kerouac revised the first third of that scroll for Sterling Lord. A note on the first page of the revised typescript identifies *Memory Babe* as "A Nostalgic Review of the Good Old Days meant to be read simply for the pleasure of reading."

O N THE LAST NOONDAY BEFORE CHRISTMAS VACATION
I was coming home from Bartlett Junior High School
in Lowell Massachusetts, not yet 14 years old, in the 1930's,
running ahead of all the other school children (having left
my home room on the fly) so that I could have an extra five
minutes to try to get home via my favorite shortcut, over the
rocks of the Merrimac River just downriver from the White
Bridge on School Street. It was surprisingly warm and drowsy
for December 23, almost like an Indian summer lull in the air.
Wannalancit Street is the steep hill street that leads down from
the school, in the mornings it was always a great scene of slowly
straggling children mounting to their classes, some of them on
bikes, which they ambled from side to side, slowly, pumping
hell out of their legs only because they were too proud to get
off and push the bike, which would have been easier. Coming
down the hill was always very easy, especially after the afternoon classes and you knew you were done with school for the
night. But now we had another (shortened) afternoon to go to
school, for silly (I thought) Christmas celebrations and paper-
pastings in windows, I wished it was the end and we could
start our Christmas vacation. I was wearing my usual baseball
hat cocked slightly to the right, and a dumpy sweater over my
shirt, with the collar opened wide, and the usual corduroy
pants. I was gawky, beginning to grow, but still a child, still
with a child's blue liquid stare and a child's chagrined look
and smile. Wannalancit Street was a quiet old street with nice
old New England homes where I always imagined little boys
with glasses lived, who wore white sneakers and white duck
trousers and never had to worry about enough money to buy
a bike. It was always brown screened porches way at the back
concealed by old trees, the actual New England everybody
imagines, as apart from the New England of my own French
Canadian experience, the New England of tenements (later)
and of Canadian neighborhoods with closely huddled white
cottages on cobbled streets or dirt roads like Sarah Avenue
where I was living at this time. At the foot of Wannalancit
I turned and looked back and saw the kids starting down

after me. I hurried right, on Pawtucket Boulevard, then left
on School Street and across the street to the iron pickets of
the orphanage with its silvery windows behind pines where
I always imagined a man knitting in the window seeing all.
Then down further where the board fence began, hiding the
orphanage where little boys in short black pants and little girls
in black dresses trimmed in white lace played with balls or see-
sawed and there was one square little hole in the fence where
you could stop and peek in at them or where they themselves
could look out at free homecoming schoolchildren. Beyond
them you always saw the supervisory nuns with their huge
crucifixes hanging by their sensual Winged Victory black hip
shrouds, like the forward motion world hips of the great Venus
de Milos of antiquity. I hurried past there, taking one quick
look at the sad children, and on the bridge. The White Bridge
was made of white concrete and already had many cracks in it
from swollen spring Merrimacs when the river, instead of as
now, would come slurring over the Falls in a hungry slurge of
brown dirty waters from New Hampshire in the North and
would pound against the concrete bottoms of the bridge and
boil brownly and lunge on, huge and snaky, over the rocks
and down towards the Moody Street Bridge in so monstrous
a watery mess that you never could quite believe your eyes
when it got like that in March. Now, in December, with no
recent heavy snows and no rain, the river was quiescent and
only the day before I had managed to cross the river over
the rocks. There were little wooden stairs near the railing of
the bridge where the canal was (the canal ran parallel to the
river behind its own higher protective granite wall) that you
could use to go down to the concrete canal walk which in
earlier days, before I was born, when my father was wooing
my mother with his spindly pants and funny hat, used to be
the loverslane walk of lovers. Now the police had put a stop to
that, because of several suicides, so when I jumped over the
rail and went down the steps I was always going against the
law but I always did it so fast nobody in authority ever saw
me. I went down the steps, hurried along the concrete walk,
which had iron rails, and down to the part where it was not
very high above the sands of the river shore and there I jumped
down into the sand and hurried to the gurglings of the river

where it wound and slithered among slatey antique rocks that were as sharp as razors sometimes altho some of them were just simply round and smooth like sea pebbles. Sometimes the river formed pools among slate castles, or sometimes it broke loose and flung itself (five feet wide at points) in a deep and dangerous run. Usually I could find convenient ways to jump the dangerous places but today I realized there must have been some snow melting in New Hampshire the day before, the river was a little bit higher. I hurried over the rocks following my usual route. I sat for awhile contemplating the dangerous looking midstream which had widened from five feet to about six overnight. It was hot and drowsy almost on the rocks, it brought back memories of the summers when we'd go down there with sticks and string and worms and fish for dirty old suckers that we never used. Actually I had never fished myself but watched the other boys. Further down, under the Moody Street Bridge, the rocks had formed pools that were so perfect they were used all summer as swimming holes by the boys of Gershon Avenue and of Little Canada across the river. I watched the children crossing the White Bridge now and felt strong and self sufficient to be a rock crosser. But I saw after awhile it wouldnt do, I'd drown, and had to turn back. I considered going further down the granite walks but realized the steps had been torn down at the Moody Street Bridge so there was no other alternative but to go back the way I came and get home later than anybody else. I went up the steps, vaulted back on the bridge with my famous two handed leap (hands on rail, feet over without touching) and suddenly decided to go home via Pawtucket Boulevard and not go to school that afternoon. But I knew my mother would make me go to school anyway. I was too young at this time to play voluntary hookie. "I'll say I'm sick," I thought, "and then I'll stay in my room all afternoon and play races, and baseball too." I had all my games in my room. I went by the orphanage again and went down Pawtucket Boulevard, past the orphanage grotto where on summer nights my mother and her cousin Bea would go do the Stations of the Cross, then suddenly I was passing my Uncle Joe's gloomy brown house on Mt. Washington Street (Bea's father) and I was very thirsty and decided to go in and ask him for a glass of water. Opening the kitchen door I

realized there was no one awake or about. It was dead silent.
The sun slanted into the old Canadian kitchen with its brown
woodworks and religious calendars on doors and as always
there was the faint aroma of Cu-Bab cigarettes which Uncle
Joe had to smoke for his asthma. *"Mon oncle Joe?"* I went to
the tap and poured a glass of water in a huge strange Uncle
Joe glass and then walked into the livingroom where Bea's
piano was, and suddenly I heard a stirring in the bedroom and
Aunt Leontine came out through the bead curtains with her
glinting spectacles and thin New England righteous face and
said in a voice as familiar as the voice of my dreams:

"Ti Jean?"

(AUTHOR'S NOTE:—American writers who write and
speak only one language are lucky. I write in English but I
speak French to my family. My French family on my mother's
side arrived in Quebec Canada a few miles north of Maine a
long time ago. My father's side 1756. So dont say we're not
North Americans. What I have to do here is transpose the
French talk into understandable modern American English,
and then add the exact sound-spelling of the old French behind
it [the French of the Seigneurie], in italics parenthesized, in
case any French people or French students are interested. The
reader can skip over anything he likes, he being the Prince in
this case here. Besides I want the reader to see what I had to go
through and what fun it was to know 2 languages.)

"Ti Jean? What's the matter Ti Jean?" (*Cosse qui à Ti Jean?*)

"Nothin, I was thirsty, I wanted a glass of water." (*Rien, java
soueffe, j'voula un verre d'eau.*)

"Joe—Ti Jean came here to drink a glass of water." (Okay,
okay, Etc. Etc., I'll now shut off the French and leave that to
Heaven, we'll get on with an English story, and why crowd a
page?)—Uncle Joe came out, huge and fat and bald, with his
great sorrowful Breton eyes, coughing as always, breathing
desperately in his asthma, with his crooked pathetic grin. "I
was taking a little nap, Ti Jean. How is your papa?"

"Okay."

"Why dont you ask Leo why he doesnt come to see his poor
old brother who's sick?"

"He's only the other side of the river," said Aunt Leontine.

"I know."

Uncle Joe began to wipe a tear from his eyes. "All the struggles that poor kid and I been through in our boyhoods in Nashua and we buried our father and our mother and our sisters and brothers and he lives only less than a mile away the river and doesnt even come to see his old brother." I didnt want to explain that my Pop was really afraid of seeing Aunt Leontine and yet I wondered too why indeed Pop didnt come see poor old sick Uncle Joe, I realized it was because he was all involved in his business and his gambling and his new friends now and didnt want to be reminded of the mournful Duluoz (let's say Irish pioneer invaders of French Brittany) (and Scottish too) past of funerals, wood cracking in the sea when sailors and princes drowned, tears, nets, Iroquois squaws in America etc. "Tell your Papa to come see me real soon, Ti Jean."

"I'll do that, Uncle Joe."

"I'm so happy you came to see your poor old Uncle" and Uncle Joe gave me a big sick sweet kiss and I loved him but I was afraid of him and he lighted one of his asthma cigarettes and I was terrified because I had been smelling them since birth and they always reminded me of funerals since the few times the family got together t'was for funerals. I hurried out into the bright warm December sunshine and crossed Salem Avenue, thinking for a moment:—

"Will I go right down here and see Joe? No he said he was coming tonight" so I went on, took a left on the wooden planks of the Moody Street Bridge, and walked home across the great sad river of eternity which is that mad beautiful Merrimac in New England.

II

WHEN I WAS REAL LITTLE and we lived in Centreville across the basin of the river where it swung seaward my sister Nin used to take me by the hand and lead me a mile and a half to the Royal Theater to see the old Tom Mix movies and then, when we'd cross the Aiken Street Bridge, I always did see the Moody Street Bridge and to me it seemed it led off to the ends of the world even beyond the final farthest gray mist Indian-face trees and pines I'd first seen from my crib on Lupine Road. But now I was all grown up and going right across this bridge to my new home, and not only that but I could see clear over the rail, as in my early days (later than the sister-walking days) I'd started one bright red sun morning to go to my first day of school at Saint Joseph's Parochial and Desjardins was walking with me and said, "Ha, you cant even see over the rail of this bridge can you?" I was shorter than the rail, tho I could see thru the bars, "Well," he'd said, "dont worry, come a day suddenly you'll be tall yourself and you'll be able to see over the rail of this bridge and by that time I'll even be taller myself and it all leads to nothing" or words to that effect. I'll never forget the philosophy of that boy's statement that morning. And now, lo, I could indeed see over the rail of the Moody Street Bridge and indeed it did mean nothing. Too, I remember the times when I'd come home from that parochial school a few months later imagining myself a movie all in myself a movie, or being filmed by drooling rabid happy angels in Heaven with their Chaplin handcrank cameras, "The Day of Little Jean Duluoz," how he gets up in the morning, eats his oatmeal and toast, goes to school over the Moody Street Bridge, almost beginning to be able to see over the rail, and how he comes home from classes at noon, pondering sad thoughts, jumping against the winter wood wall of the bridge with the back heel touching (a trick, of kids) and now I no longer considered myself a heavenly movie but I was sufficiently nostalgic to remember those days and too, look with special sorrow on the little boy that I had been. That Moody Street Bridge—many's the time I've since dreamed of it as having holes in its planks, planks missing, you have to crawl carefully over its battered skeletal structure and beneath you the March waters rage and foam over rocks like armies of falconry horses piling on, it's terrifying, and the dream is always by spectral dreamlight, OON, and indeed there were some planks loosening and years later when I did return to Lowell (at age 32) and took nostalgic walks over the same bridge, there they were, as prophesied in the dream, actual planks missing and a wooden sawhorse put up by the city to warn you to walk around them . . .

On the other side of the bridge, in my own homecountry of Pawtucketville now, was the huge orange brick Textile School with its great dreamy fields all around, and the dump along the river, down to which its dreamy mowed lawns swayed and

dropped, and the eternity orange brick smokestack that rose
from the little powerhouse in back, and its thousands of sling-
shottable windows, and the whole thing in my day dreams
like a vast castle full of courtiers and I cant find my way from
room to room and all the rooms have high ceilings and high
sunny windows and the floors are hardwood floors, a Versailles
of the child mind . . . But it was on the baseball and football
grounds of this school that my gang and I played all our mad
aftersupper pepper games and doubleplay infield games and in
the fall football, as sister screamed to watch, it was the great
center of our imaginations in Pawtucketville, or at least perhaps
like the Wall of Avignon must seem to the children of the
slums of back Avignon where winds blow dry dust on Sunday
afternoons and gutters run with dirty water.

I passed the immense school, crossed Riverside Street, and
there I was in the little French Canadian shopping center of
Pawtucketville with its candy stores, hardware, drugstore,
groceries, little thread shops and the particular candy store of
our hangout days, Destouches', where wheezy old mournful
Destouches was always sitting panting (asthma too, I think)
and when we asked for candy he'd say "*Go behind the counter
and get it yourself, bring me the penny after.*" I always, as now,
stopped there to look to see for the latest sensational display
toys Destouches might have roused himself to get up and lay
about, but no, if he ever did put up a new display in his dreary
window it was a miracle annually. But the *Shadow* magazines,
the latest, were there, of course I never had enough money
to buy the newest, latest, freshest, most mysterious *Shadow*
magazines, and Destouches wouldnt even let us look at them,
but we could stare at the cover:—and *Phantom Detective* too,
and *Star Western* and all the great magazines, pulp, that we
devoured in our little lamplights of home learning the English
Language as it's always learned: by reading, no matter what
the reading matter is. I went up Moody Street a little further,
past the thread shop, a few tenements, and then left right
into the little hole in the fence that gave egress to the famous
"park" which was a kind of empty lot connecting Moody
Street across three blocks of sand and grass, past cornfields
and one long low concrete block garage, to my little dirt road
Sarah Avenue of home where huge trees stood high and bare

in the December sun waving gently in a growing wind and
gave promise of steaming dinners at home where my mother
had her usual New England boiled dinner and bread and milk
waiting for me and Ti Nin (Ti Nin my sister was a sophomore
at Lowell High School way downtown, she walked home too,
but often got rides from boys in rumbleseats). This was the
park that could scare you to death at night but in the daytime
it was (now in December) nice drowsy walking, with the old
grass brown beneath a few patches of old dirty snow, and our
hoop up on the tree where we played our ferocious basketball
games, and then the other fence, also with a hole, then the
dirt of Sarah Avenue, where I took a left and walked along past
Phebe Avenue which fed into Sarah (Phebe where I'd lived 3
years in my littler days when I couldnt see over the bridge
rail) and down past a few cottages to my own, saddest of all,
white cottage, 34 Sarah Avenue, with its neat little porch out
front with white rails, the two front parlor windows, the two
front bedroom windows (where Ma and Nin slept) and the
little scraggle of brown grass out front separated and elevated
from the sidewalk (with a little concrete wall) and the iron pole
that stuck up which I always grabbed, jumping up on the wall,
and swung around three times from the top portion sinking
and slipping down to the bottom before my three gyrations
were done, then up the little steps of the side porch and into
the kitchen where the boiled dinner was steaming in a huge
pot on the stove, and my mother, plump and pretty in her
apron, with rouge and happy face, having listened to "Portia
Faces Life" and all the other soap operas and the news on the
radio all morning and washing clothes and mopping floors and
singing and chatting with Irene Callahan in the little cottage
next door, said to me, as a thousand times before, "You'll
have to go right back to the store and get a loaf of bread and
some butter and you might as well get a quart of milk, here's
the money."

"But I'm tired I just walked all the way from school."

"You gotta go, Ti Jean, we've got to have the bread. You can
buy yourself a Boston." And so every day I had to turn back
and go back across the same park, to buy these things, but
every day I had my extra penny for a Boston candy bar.

AND SO BEGAN THE ALMOST DAILY RITUAL of my Boston
candy bar. I'd always get the groceries at the same store, near
the hole in the park fence, and come back with the bags and the
candy bar, just a little penny chocolate covered peanutbutter
bar but before opening it, and walking slowly, I'd start: "Ti
Jean, we're going to give you a candy bar and we want you to
guess from the letters in its name what bar it is."

"Okay."

"The first letter is B."

"O boy it's going to be a Boston."

"The second letter is O."

"O boy I cant miss now, it's going to be a Boston? What's
the third letter?"

"The third letter is L."

"What the hell? L? Why? You mean to tell me it's going to
be an old Bolster?"

"The fourth letter is S."

"O durn it I dont want it."

"Alright, we'll give you another candy bar, the first letter is
B, the second letter is O."

"A *Bol*ster!"

"And the third letter is S."

"Well then it cant be anything else but a Boston, it's the only
candy bar in the world with the first three letters are B O S."

"That's right, and here's your Boston, son, eat it."

"O boy," so, strolling slowly with the groceries across the
park, I'd slowly open the paper and start in sucking on some
of the chocolate at the end of the bar and then bite down into
the rich peanutbutter material and chew slowly and savor and
it was always drowsy noon and the taste of milk chocolate and
peanutbutter in my mouth, how crazy children are, and it was
always the dream of the Saviours sending me the letters spelling my bar, just like the old cartoon I'd seen in the Boston
American funnies long ago about the little prince of the far
away island who refused all the desserts that the worried court
advisors brought to him: puddings, sweets, even ice creams,
and ices, fruits, taffies, then finally pheasants under glass and

still he wasnt hungry and wouldnt eat anything then finally you see the funny little Jello airplane landing in the outside dream Gretchen fields and out comes the Jello Boy with an inverted Jello rilled all red on a platter and rushes to the palace (cherry Jello!) and the little prince pitches right into it and saves the Kingdom with his announcement of the celebration of the Jello Kingdom or some such fantastic story I never forgot. By the time I'd reach the other hole in the other fence on Sarah Avenue the Boston bar was gone down the way of the princie's jello and I'd walk home happy.

That day my sister was late coming from school and my mother said we'd have to eat and couldnt wait. As usual first I went to the ice box where our four Kremel puddings were poured out to chill in four little separate little kittymilk saucers and I'd take my own two Kremels (my sister had the other two) and suck a little bit off the edge of the saucer and put them back. Then I sat down to my boiled stringbeans tied together like faggot sticks with string, boiled potatoes, turnips and carrots, with huge gobs of butter on my thick crusty French bread (from a Franco American bakery) and two huge glasses of cold milk, a healthy dinner and what I ate practically every day of the week.

"Where'd that durn Ti Nin go" said my mother looking at the green electric clock which kept turning and turning and was so high in the wall it could hardly be reached so that sometimes you'd see it turning through dusts of time and cobwebs of clocks and you'd see the little cobwebs follow the second-hand awhile then fall off. "That little flimflam it's already twelve thirty." Twelve thirty was the awfulest time for me because it signified I only had 25 more minutes at home and had to start the hot disgustingly drowsy (bellyful) walk back across the park and down Riverside Street and over across the White Bridge again and then up that steep horrible Wannalancit hill to silly classes again where we all sat around chewing the erasers on our pencils till the whole room smelt of chewed soft wet erasers, a sickening memory, and of bananas in desks where kids who didnt go home for lunch left their lunches together with (afterlunch) balled up greasy wax papers and apple cores and pieces of stale bread with stale butter left over from an October lunch by some kid long left his desk empty to move to

Lawrence or Fall River. But twelve thirty had its compensations in the fact that it was usually the time I'd mopped up all my gravy with the bread and butter, drank all the milk, and the great moment of going to the ice box and removing my two nibblesucked Kremels out and putting them before me on the table and taking several preliminary sucks all around the edges until the middle part of the pudding sagged all alone and then carefully working with the spoon edge to peel back the harder layer of the top and eating it (pure caramel cover) and then sinking down into the main pudding, which was paler than the cover, but creamier, tho less caramelly and eating that. And still Nin hadnt come and I had licked both my saucers dry. My mother went out to look up Sarah Avenue so like a rat, like on many other occasions, and mindless of the reprimand I'd get, I sneaked to the ice box and took both of Ti Nin's Kremels and sucked the little suck on the edge and put them back slyly and went to the bathroom and swooshed water all over the place like my father did after meals and I was done.

Now I began to figure out how to act sick so as not to go to school that afternoon and suddenly the clouds passed over the sun, the whole kitchen darkened, the green clock looked different, a cool breeze came in the window, and I realized it was going to rain or snow or something and then here came Ti Nin in her boyish bob with her big healthy fullgirl 16 year old face bouncing into the kitchen and sitting down to her boiled dinner and my mother saying: "How come you're always late now."

"We got a ride but the fellows went all over town and took their time."

"You poopsie, eat your dinner and forget the fellers. Who was it, Tommy Cudworth again?"

"No, Michel Lemaire."

"You'll have to step on it, it's already quarter of one."

"Yeh—hey Ma bring my Kremel." At this I ran upstairs and went to my room and lay down to look sick. Suddenly I heard my sister yell "*Eh twé, voleur!* (O you, you crook!) Ma, Ti Jean took bites outa my Kremel again!"

"Yes yes I know."

"Why does he do that all the time?"

"Well he doesnt take much."

"Yeah, look at the big bites he took this time, the little crook! *Crook*!" she yelled upstairs and would have done better or more accurately calling me "mouse," the mouse that nibbleth, or better, rat, but I hid and trembled and was beginning to work myself up to the woesome look of the sick boy. And suddenly the rain began to shatter on the shed roof right outside my window and I got up and looked out, the bare apple trees were soaking with that clean rain-on-the-treetrunk look, dark and fragrant, and maybe there wouldnt be any school after all. I wanted to go downstairs and listen to the radio to see but I had to play it safe and be sick. Ti Nin dashed upstairs to change and took one quick look in my room to say "*Tannant d'voleur*, if I catch you again in my Kremel I'll fix you good." I answered nothing. We went on fighting over Kremels for years. We were always fighting, it's amazing how a younger boy feels that he is being devoured by his older sister and always wants to fight back by nibbling away at her rights. In my dreams I see us pulling each other by the hair over Kremels and later over money.

Ti Nin's girlfriend around the corner, Millicent Devlin, had a return ride from the same boys, I could hear the horn blowing in the rain outside, she ran out and went to school and now I lay there sad and my mother called from the foot of the stairs, "Time to get going, Ti Jean."

"I'm sick."

"You're sick, what you got?"

"*J'ai mal au coeur* (I got a stomach ache)." She came up and touched me on the brow:

"How come you've got a stomach ache."

"I ate candy this morning in school . . . Joe had candy. Him too he's sick I think."

"Well you aint gonna have any more of your durn Bostons from now on! You're alright go to school."

"No I feel like throwing up." She sighed and heard the rain drum harder and said:

"Aw well, the vacation's beginning anyway and it's raining" (and here, and the reason I was so fortunate in this life) she suddenly became tender, she put her hand on my brow, not caring whether I was putting on sickness or not, knowing I simply wanted to stay home and play in my room, "stay home then . . . stay in bed Little Angel and after that I'll make some nice hot chocolate, Little Bug, Little Kootie, maybe you'll be okay tonight."

"*Oui.*"

"Awright, well Mama's been up now since seven in the morning and I did a big wash and my ironing and now I'm tired and I'm gonna sleep in my room, I'm gonna take a little nap."

"*Oui.*"

"Sleep my angel" and with that inexpressible tenderness, or rather that tenderness which is incommunicable to anyone who never had a commiserating and compassionate mother, she kissed me and went out of the room like a tiptoeing Archangel and closed my lovely door against the harshnesses of the world and I heard her tiptoeing around her bedroom and I knew that I was saved.

All I had to do was lie there about a half hour, watching the gray rain in my windowpane, and then when I'd hear her snore in the quiet delightful rained-on house, get up and play my great gray games of childhood. And so lying there I fell into a trance and stared at the ceiling, and saw Heaven in the ceiling, or stared at my little green desk, which had been my dead brother Gerard's desk, green as an earlysummer apple and remember his sweet compassionate face and the way he and I would spend whole rainy days together playing in the house with his Erector set, or I'd stare at the little dusts in the linoleum of my bedroom floor or listen to the eaves dropping down waterdrops, the little klookloo talks of the rain (that conceptionless rain that doesnt think while all we do is think) and then I fell asleep a little and woke up refreshed and ready for my games. It's paradise to be a boy, to be home on a rainy day and not have to go to school, and have long hours of solitude and childly thought.

IV

THERE WAS SOMETHING ATLANTEAN IN MY PREOCCUPATION WITH GRAYNESS, with gray skies whipping over things, being blown from the Northeast Atlantic, and with my preoccupation with dusty records something surely Faustian, or Gothic, or knightly. It all had to be gray, dim pale blues, distant hills in the Mohawk country, something strange and still westward surging. Yet it all came rising out of nothing but a boxful of odd assorted sized marbles, which were my horses. In these poor sometimes-chipped marbles I saw the lonely forlorn heads of great Ladysman racehorse champions, I saw the mud of the tracks on rainy days in the Western Massachusetts (Mohican Springs) racetrack of my imagination where they ran . . . and in the names of the jockeys, names I've since forgotten except for a few like Art Cooper or better, C. W. Swain, I saw the rain blurred mists materialize, that I wanted. My mother snoring in her afternoon nap I got up and took out my marbles and took out my ledgers with all the records of each marble (horse) and the records of their owners and jockeys and began to set up a day of racing. First I'd assemble the horses for the first race according to the proximity of their talents: smaller marbles had lower talents and sometimes larger but chipped marbles would race with them and lose, or else win by fantastic margins if they didnt happen to roll on their chips . . .

But to explain: at the head of the race, on the far side of the room, was the runway, an old Parcheesi board held up by two thick old books (the family medical book) (and some old bible I guess) and I'd just line the marbles up on the incline, even to even, nose to nose, with a ruler, simply lift the ruler and out they raced beneath the uplifted ruler, down the incline, across the smooth linoleum (which I always mopped carefully with a dry mop for specks of dust and stuff) and come thundering down the "stretch" which was where the linoleum left off and the bare floor made the marbles rumble deeply and they'd bash into the wall. And I had a terrific photographic eye and could tell how they finished 1-2-3-4-5 but not up to 7 and more. I'd quickly out of photography eye memory write down the finish in pencil. *Boocap first by a nose* (that being where the marble called Boocap happened to hit the finish line wall just a split of an inch ahead of the next marble) then *Caw Caw second by 3 lengths*, 3 lengths being simply the length of three marbles, and so on down to fifth place, then I'd run the also-rans a little unimportant record-necessity race of their own and get the final form chart finished and laboriously hand type it in pencil in my beautiful gray strips of paper I'd gotten from my father's printing plant, everything had to be gray and it had to be raining. If on a day when I planned to race my marbles it should happen to be sunny, I would transfer the scene from gray misty Mohican Springs to Postmon Park, a sunny racetrack closer to Lowell, full of well dressed dudes and rich women and flags waving in the sun, and resume the Postmon meet, with attendant special handicaps and Derbies (of a higher order, with bigger purses, than my favorite beat Mohican Springs where everybody was gaunt and sad and poor but kept running their meager string of horses in the hopes of making the big time someday at sunny Postmon Park). Mohican Springs however was the scene of the great sad gray Derby of all our imaginations, you cant sometimes think of the Kentucky Derby at Churchill Downs without thinking of rain, and roses in the rain, the hoop of roses around the winner's neck (Cavalcade, Omaha), the old names and old rainy records there. Now I sat there writing out the list of entries for the great anticipated Derby, & Derby plotted at school desk when I was supposed to be pondering over Sir Walter Scott altho at times in the jousts of Scott's knights I thought I detected the hint of distant gray hills and the scent of rain, with far away, further away echoes of Robin Hood which led my imagination back to the hills behind my own house and brought me by Vicoan circumlocution to my Derby at Mohican Springs.

But also it all had to be written on gray paper, or sometimes pale green paper (the green to go with my dead brother Gerard's desk) and the general gray green of rain. How noble was the name of Ladysman, and the name of Don Pablo, and the great sad names, Amber Hill, Gunwale, Arctic Post, Head Play, Time Supply, names I'd gotten out of the official race charts of the world but only recently I'd begun to make names of my own which would supply me with the proper raininess: Sweepogan, Chippewa, Zarney Green, Sarada, Smoker, Chopdown, Repulsion the champ, Retaliate his lesser brother, Elenac, all the names, I hoped against hope to come up someday with a rainy gray name as great as Jack Westrope all by myself. Jack Lewis almost made it but not quite.

After writing out the list of entries I'd then rig up a little newspaper, all by hand, with a headline, announcing the day's card, and a few cartoons showing bettors discussing the race (I could draw) and then a few news items discussing breeding or money matters. All my marbles had names, sexes, ages, ratings,

owners, money-earning records, dams and sires, and about all
of them I always wrote a little item showing their improvement
or downhill decay and semi annually I held a great marble
smashing bacchanal where the idea was to knock chips off the
marbles and render some of the horses crippled, incapable,
some had to be destroyed, time had to go on beneath this
rain, this dust of records, so that for instance the great Don
Pablo was practically smashed in half that year and descended
from Turf greatness to a minor position as plater racer in opening races or perhaps the last sad race when the sun is sinking
behind the rainy hills

[The text from this point on is from Kerouac's scroll version.]

and it's so dark you can hardly see the horses (in imagination) racing across the back stretch and the last horse is likely
to be led in by lamplight by an old bowlegged barn hand who
coos endearments nevertheless to old Boocap and says "Alright
so they're gonna make glue out of you but I love you still" and
in the middle of the night he carries off the crippled horses in a
makeshift van and brings it back to Wyoming to pasture forever
in the meadows of God. Without the smashing of the marbles
the racing seasons would have gone on year after year with
no change, unlike real life, sometimes marbles were utterly
demolished in half (smack against one another I'd ram hordes
of marbles, chips would fly) and that horse would have to be
"destroyed," or retired to stud, and then I'd go out and scour
all Lowell for greater newer marbles. Color had a lot to do with
it, since the white and orange Time Supply mustnt look too
much like a similar sized new white and orange marble, I had to
look for new color combinations and finally (a little later) I did
discover the greatest horse of them all in a large sized ballbearing, pure silver, no other horses like it, which I promptly sold
to the Jack Kerouac stable and made Jack Lewis (me the jockey)
and named him Repulsion because I knew he would repulse all
other horses forever . . . which he did. But also I did find some
vast marbles as big as a golf ball who were tremendous rolling
off that incline and across the smooth linoleum and booming
down the woodfloor stretch with a noise that thrilled my heart
and smashing into the wall 12 lengths ahead of everybody's
Derby entry, great champions, Y Z Z, who sometimes beat

the smaller but heavier but smoothrolling Repulsion. Then I'd
have my phantasies, and lean on the rail with my father, or with
my said cousins Ned Gavin and Tod Gavin from Arkansas,
we didnt have much money and we hoped to win the purse
or have to head out . . . We saw Postmon Park in the sun the
flags whipping as the great goal of our lives. But when I bent
my serious little head over the gray records of past Derbies,
and sighed to see so much time had slipped by since the early
almost disappeared-into-mist days of my "Turf," and when I
filled the gray sheets with minute informations, sometimes I'd
cry, or a tear would come into my eye, or remember an old
favorite that had to be destroyed, it was sometimes too much
for me. Too, I had the old Victrola in my room and cranked it
and played the same record prior to every race, "Dardanella,"
or sadder records sometimes, like Al Jolson and Rudy Vallee
(just as, at Rockingham Park where my father took me they
always played records over the public address system between
races). But Dardanella, the sound of the old saxophone sections
and of the banjo strumming the beat and the trumpets, etc.
the savor of my grain race tracks became indissolubly mixed
with the sound of the record, and to the point too where there
is no describing the amalgam of emotions with rainy day, no
school, marbles, dusty old papers, my pencil, Dardanella, even
the dusty hole inside the Victrola, the dust on the floor, the
rain sounds outside, the cool gray Atlantic feeling in the room
that seemed to open out westward to the Mohican lands, the
whole, in any event, mad assorted details of a complete childhood madness and sublimity that kept me happy and absorbed
that afternoon (as on many others) while my mother slept,
my father worked, my sister went to school, and that old river
rushed on, swelling now, over rocks, the whole swirling imaginary memory babe mind and dreams of Kings and Horses and
later heavenly visions.

When I looked up from my games at around 4 o'clock suddenly
it was clearing and it had gotten colder and there was a phantom
smell of snow in the windowpane. My mother was still sleeping.
I looked up from my dusty records and I wanted to go outdoors
now to where the brass & iron clouds were splitting to admit
the look of the now pale winter sun, winds were blowing from
somewhere, it would soon be rockety old winter in the yards

and fields of Pawtucketville where I knew by now G.J. and
Salvey and Rondeau and the others must be home from school
already (eating their bread and butter sandwiches quick gulp in
the kitchen before rushing out screaming letting the backdoor
slam, aow, and out like arrows into the scre fields)—but I had
to keep up my pretense of being sick. I heard my mother get
up and go downstairs yawning and heard other noises down
there where probably old landlord Mr. Froufrou was coming
around to see about the broken door. I put away all my gray
and blue papers in the closet box, the marbles back in their box
barn, the jockeys and owners and handicappers and winners
and losers all disappeared in the mist of the brain, and I tiptoed
downstairs to see what was going on. My mother was so sleepy
she seemed to have forgotten I hadnt gone to school that day.
J peu tu allez jouer dehors? Si tu veu ti loup. Whoopee I rushed
upstairs and put on my overalls and older sweater and got my
things ready for the big baseball game I played by myself in the
yard with a long new nail and a few ballbearings I mean the
very ballbearing that was that great racehorse Repulsion. Here
too my records and dusts of histories were so vast there was no
keeping it all on paper. The days of the great teams, of course,
were gone, nothing in contemporariness can ever match the
great past, just as when oldtimers get together and discuss Cy
Young or Honus Wagner they wont take comparison of any
Warren Spahns or any of your latter day Mazeroskis. My great
hallowed old names had been Henry Currier, Ches Queen, Bill
Seifer (he was still pitching), Cy Locke the greatest shortstop
of all time, all names I'd actually culled from the Lowell telephone directory but now in this new phase of mine I wanted
to make up my own great names that would fit better that
particular sorrowful flair I wanted. I had been looking for a
long time for the perfect name for the perfect all time centerfielder and got it one day when I went to the Rialto Theater
to see a double feature and it was an English movie with an
English butler called Tibbs, a picture full of fog, redbricks of
Chelsea, tuxedoed gentlemen, gray food being served on gray
trays, weeping women with long vampire hair but I came out
of that theater and stepped into the momentous snow of time
with Tibbs burning in my mind. "Frank Tibbs, Frank 'Pie'
Tibbs" the greatest centerfielder of all time and he'll be short,

with a dark complexion, strange, wont say much, will wear his
pants real long almost down to his ankles (in prep school years
later as leadoff man for my prep school ballclub I wore my pants
the same way) and he will swing lefty with a long mean black
bat like's never been seen in baseball. So I'd rushed home and
installed Pie Tibbs in centerfielder for the great hallowed old
Pittsburgh Plymouths of my imagination and immediately he'd
created a sensation especially as it was all up to me as I'd kneel
there snuff nosed in cold dusks pitching the little ballbearing
towards myself and over the little plate and smacking it with
the nail, the "ball" would go lining over shortstop (which was
a rock) and drop "safe" outside the three huge outfield circles
I'd drawn out there at the ends of the yard to indicate the areas
of putout effectiveness by the outfielders and sometimes real
long whacks that would carry the ball clean over the fence into
the next yard for a homerun. When the ball was simply rapped
against the shortstop rock or any other infield rock including
the pitcher's, I'd rush over, kneel, put the ballbearing between
thumb and forefinger and flick it or hit the firstbase rock. Thus
for years, and with my recordsbooks beside me in the mud
under our 2 apple trees in the backyard (which faced another
brown house that had grapevines and pretty young dotters I
never paid attention to) I carried on enormous pennants and
world series and piled up a nostalgic mass of names and great
players some of whom have long since died I'd say. Then I'd
rush to my room again and write down the great names of
the Hall of Fame of my own baseball history, the names of
the great winning managers, Chase, Adams, Devine, Sloane,
Ma affey, James and Simon. The names of the great sluggers,
Henry Currier, Tibbs, Ches Queen, (feet tall), and especially
the thunderous booming hitters Kirk Bancroft and Buck
Barabara and in the very nose of my imagination these names
smelled up thoughts of mud, nails and ballbearings whenever
I saw them even if they belonged to someone else in a movie
or in a book. . . . It's too much to describe in every detail and
now as on many other occasions my mother came out and said
Ti Jean pourquoi tu jou tuseul, why dont you go down the street
and play with the other kids, I cant understand why youre
all alone, what are you doing there? I'm playing my baseball
league. "But I dont see no baseball league" and I had no way in

my childishness to explain to her that it was all in my mind and that upstairs I had every record of it. . . . "*Rente dans maison bpi vien mańgez des ritz cracker pi t peanutbutter pi tu la.*" "Okay." "It looks like its going to snow. Tomorrow night we'll put I mean tonight we'll put up the Xmas tree." So sitting at the round wooden table in the middle of our kitchen, chomping on my crackers and peanutbutter and pouring more and more milk into my huge childly glass (a sight, for me, if I were an angel looking down on earth, and saw a little boy drinking his milk, enuf to break my heart, dont ask me why) I seriously pondered the latest developments concerning Frank Pie Tibbs and then back to Mate and Ladysman my great horses who had just won Derbies that very afternoon and nothing indeed couldnt induce me those days to go out and play with the other boys till I'd finished the gray legends of my brain.

Just as I was returning indoors with my nail and ball and recordbook I saw the Kewpie my old cat merging through the fence, he was coming home for his food, we went in together and my mother saw him and yelled "*Allo Kewpie, ta tu faim la?*" and she immediately opened the ice box and mixed up his dinner in a nice clean plate and poured fresh milk in a saucer and laid it all down on his poor pitiful little spot in the corner of the kitchenette (off the main kitchen) where, as I lay flat bellydown watching him from underneath, he lowered his little nose and whiskers and began chomping away a big hungry happy meal. *Cest tu bon? cest tu bon?* I always said when I did this and he never did pay attention but just went on, with those quick movements of the head the way a cat dives into his next bite, eyes closed (like a drunkard eating) and chewing with quick satisfied jerks of his jaws and then how pitiful it was in my heart to see him finish that and move slightly on his fixed paws and turn attentions to the milk, the poor kittymilk, which he lapped sending little bubbles of milk flying around on the newspaper and sometimes on my close nose. This sight, on the floor, of a cat lapping his milk, is something a boy should never miss and always when I did this I'd slowly caress Kewpie's back and repeat "*Ah ca cest bon, ah?*" and he'd agree by his silent lapping and one occasional green look of his eyes as if to say "The big nut is at it again, why doesnt he mind his own business." But Kewpie was my old pal, about 8 years old now, the greatest cat we ever had for longevity and for general loyalty, whenever I went to bed at night he always took three turns against my chest as I held the covers up for this and then plumped himself, back to my chest, and slept till dawn with me, purring at first then subsiding with a few knocks of his purr motor into a deep easy sleep. But poor Kewpie was getting old by now and was beginning to scratch furiously at mangy ears. He was a gray cat, with white tiger stripes, and his face, with the pink nose, the white snout, I cant forget . . . After Kewpie had done eating he wandered off to the kitchen floor, stopped, bent to lick himself quickly along the back of the tail, and then a few quick scratches at his ears, balancing himself all the while with that graceful balance I think Da Vinci tried to capture in his pencilled notebook sketches, and then he wandered off to the parlor couch and turned around a few times and lay down to sleep, didnt like that (I was still watching) so sat up again and eased himself down in the cat buddhaposition, which is on all four paws looking sternly ahead eyes slitted, and thus he meditated in the gray parlor as cold winds began to blow against the window and it was time for me to go out and find G.J. and the gang. By this time my mother'd turned on the light in the kitchen and was preparing supper including a big pot of New England baked beans in the oven for tonight's party and for my Pa's hearty breakfast Saturday morning . . . *Ma allez were mes chums, ma.*" "*Okay pi retrouned a 6 heurs pour ton supers, mue pit tue pit Ti Nin on va allez a Lambert cherchez les groceries pi apra cas on t va achetez laubre.*" O boy. I ran out, slamming the kitchen door, aow, off I shot like an arrow leaping all three porch steps, over to my pole on the little sere lawn, where I did the usual 2 sinking gyrations, and up Sarah Avenue on the run, slamming my fingertips rat-tat-tat along passing wood pickets and left up the little dirt road called Phebe to Georgie's house which stood there with a backyard that dropped a sheer 15 feet after the wood picket fence into a dreamy meadow owned by the rich man in the big mansion behind the trees, all fenced in and never used for anything except our big Big-Parade war battles or summer dreamings or rat-tat-tat machinegunnings. And from this parapet in G.J.'s yard you could see all of Lowell across the back Textile field and far the dump and over the river, Little Canada far away and behind that the smokestacks of the mills leading to downtown Kearney Square where now, as I stood in the dusk thinking about it, I imagined all the bright lights coming on then in the 5 and 10's) and department stores and the people lined up for the yellow buses that revved there waiting for the scheduled time to pull out discharging Lowellians in every 10 directions of the city with big happy Xmas packages. But it was also a gloomy yard, something about the big pines that rose from the lower meadow and the general heaviness of trees to the left, something about the brown paint on G.J.'s house and especially the atmosphere and savor of G.J. himself (and his mother) made it one of the gloomy yet gleeful headquarters of my soul. I went in the little tar alley and yelled up to George's second story window "Georg eeeeee" and his mother came out to the porch and said (as on many other occasions) "Yorva not here." She wore long black widow's mourning weeds, she had been in mourning for 10 years now for her Greek husband who had had a long black handlebar mustache that was the only thing G.J. could remember about his father as long ago he'd leaned over the crib and looked at him, like that . . . Downstairs lived the Goslins, with little Goose Goslin the head boy of the children but a little too young and too small to play with me and my gang tho he was a happy little ballplayer and even now in late December emerged from the hall with a baseball hat and baseball glove and wanted to know if I wanted to play catch. "No Goose, it's the basketball season." How strange it was, too, that little Goose bore the name of one of the great ballplayers of all time . . . I ran down Phebe again, heard cries in the park, and there he was, G.J., involved in a hot game of basketball with Rondeau and Scotty and Salvey and the Houde brothers, using a practically air-empty sodden little ball to throw against a simple barrel hoop that had been nailed to the big tree-trunk. What furious, ferocious, insane games they played at that hoop and with that pathetic ball! The Houde brothers, Mike and Pete, never spoke to each other much but when they got into these games with the kids (they were both well along as teenagers) their language came out in furious sneaky hip-whacks they gave each other while dribbling around, and they always got on opposite teams so as to deliver these messages more and more. Rondeau was a mad hellnecked screaming kid we called Whattaguy because he was always boasting, I could hear him screaming above the rest as the game furyated now in a dusk gloom almost impossible to see what was going on. But you could tell the game would go on till well after dark. They didnt care. Meanwhile what massive clouds were gathering over the sandbank at the end of Phebe, what oranges of sudden low sun showing, what bloody sawdust in the air of heaven, what snows impending from the grim secret hills to the north. How exciting it was to be in a keen dusk, to hear the cries of my gang, to rush up and join the game, to plow and shuffle with the crazy kids in the dark. Typically, however, old G.J. was all tired out laid out panting in the grass saying "Phew, I'm through, I have a cold." Poor G.J. always thought he was going to die from a cold. He was the favorite of the gang, the funny guy of the gang, whenever Mike or Pete Houde shot sensational baskets now he lay there grinning saying "Ah good old Joe Joe Dee Joe Joe sinks another one" . . . "the real high de jo jo speed not seen since the happy days of Old Kid Shine, how are you Memory Babe" he says to me as he sees me come to sit beside him to dig him and laugh with him. G.J. called me Memory Babe because I could remember things in our distant childly pasts everybody had forgotten, like sometimes I'd say "whatever happened to that kid Ernie Noval used to know walked with us to the Dracut field and used to have snot coming out his nose, Henri de Bourgerac," "Henri de Bourgerac! O you Memory Babe you!" and he'd grab a fistful of my hair and drag me around to all the members of the gang "I want you to meet high speed jo de jo jo Memory Babe the only and only memory king of the world. No kidding Jackie, how did you ever remember that kid's name, when you said that name just now my brain stuck out a mile to realize I had lost the name in bottoms of my closet but here is shining Memory Babe remembering all all all." And he'd keep that fistful of hair and chuckle. G.J. had curly hair and a big nose and big yellow eyes and was tall and skinny and funny. He had completely mastered the gang simply by being funny. He couldnt fight, couldnt play, all he could do was talk but with his talk he had completely subdued, me, Salvey (a great athlete), Scotty (a great quiet athlete) and even Rondeau who screamed so much you'd have thought it was

impossible to master him. Rondeau was insane: one afternoon
we'd gone into his kitchen to have a bread and butter contest,
I saw him eat about 16 slices of fresh bread with lots of butter
and with this he rushed out eagering for a game of
basketball. . . .

Now the corner light, sending its yellow halo down on the
dirt of Phebe and Sarah, was on and the game had a little
light to send it on but the Houde brothers suddenly quit and
decided to go home, still not speaking to each other but headed
for the same supper table. Only Pete spoke once in a while and
he was a funny one too, he said "Alright ye lads, go on with
the game, old Pitou Houde is now going home to eat his beans
and hamburg and will rejoin you shortly in the outcome of the
season." "Say Pete where's Rubber Hoyle tonight?" "Rubber
Hoyle is in his cellar turning baseball bats over his lathe and
plotting next spring's sneaky sacrifices and double steals and
writing out his list of hitters." "Where's Zagg?" "Zagg is sopping up the brew in ye old club and is about to come staggering
down Gershom Avenue piffed to the gills singing to the ladies
in the windows and does he care?" "Where's Mike going?"
"Mike is going to his house to eat hamburgs and beans, as I
am, only he eats more bread than I do and after that he will
drag his weary bones down to the club which is operated by Ti
Jean's father the estimated Leo A. Kerouac and there he will
bend to his pool with that famous break that sometimes sends
billiard balls flying as far as Lawrence Massachusetts." "Where
will you be tonight Pete?" "Tonight if all goes well Old Peetoo
Houde is going to be suqriting in the weeds with a local lass
whose name shall remain unknown." He was really a kind of
a strange little bowlegged French Canadian W. C. Fields and
we always followed him half a block to ask him such questions
altho he never paused but walking right on home, Mike silent
and scowling at his side, and our final question had to be yelled
half a block "Where's the moon man tonight Pete?" "The
moon man," he said, turning the corner and disappearing up
Gershom, "is having secret conclaves with the great shadow
inside the tomb of Dracula whose bats are about to be let loose
from the belfry of Ste Jean dark church so that all you little
piffles will have to close yr windows for seventeen summers to
come because once they get in your hair you cant get em loose

unless you call on old Petto Houde who knows all the secrets of happiness. . . ." And still making these strange speeches probably, disappearing, and Mike not even listening. We went back to our game but all sat down sweating in the December evening grass for just a second and sighed and Salvey said "I think I'll make elastics tonight." "Elastics, what are you talking about." "I think I'll put elastics in my ice cream tonight." G.J. grabbed a fistful of Salvey's hair and stared at him with loving amazement. "What else Salvas old boy?" Salvas was a slight, pale, nervous, funny little kid with big ears who was really my best friend in Pawtucketville but such an insane explosive type you never knew what he'd do next and it was his typical routine to come on with strange meaningless statements like this that always amazed *George*. Rondeau, a dark, wiry, proud-of-his-common-sense Canuck, "Ah pay no attention to Salvey, he's nuts." Scotty always sat, dark, paying little attention, always counting his advantages and if he'd had barrels of money in the cellar he'd been down there during the game re-counting and checking it with red ink. That was why we called him Scotty. His advantages he pondered were not always concerning pennies but, as now, saying suddenly in the midst of hilarity "Tonight I'll spot about ten strings at the club and that will leave me approximately 40 minutes time to go down and see my cousin Joel and see if he can lend me his ice skates for vacation and if he doesnt lend me them ice skates I'm going to crush his head with a baseball bat." "Why dont you ask him to bring Sir Walter Raleigh" asked Salvey, and again G.J. grabbed a fistful of Salvey's hair and stared into his eyes with loving amazement. "Repeat that will you please, sir, will you please repeat that sir de jo jo." "Why doesnt he ask Sir Walter Raleigh to go screw his sister?" "O you rat! O did you hear what Salvey said. O that slave Salvey I'm going to tie him in chains and break his arm in my hall! O that strange terrible Salvey." "O that immemorial Salvey" I said. "That's it that's it . . . did you hear it men? IMMEMORIAM! the great Zagg has spoken: Immemoriam, a word I can never remember. When I grow up to be sixty nine years old and have 48 million dollars I'm going to tie Zagg in chains, me and Billy Chandler planned it, and every day we'll come to him and hold a beautiful cup of cocoa, a girl, hot milk, cold milk, peanut butter, Bostons, Bolsters,

Clarks, Old Nicks, Baby Ruths and a thousand immemoriam antiquities and we're going to say right Zagg, say it, say that WORD. And Zagg will have to say IMMEMORIAM or he starves to death or we whip im to death using the long whip of the Zorro." "It's not immemoriam, it's immemorial?" "Zagg where did you FIND that word?" "In the dictionary." "Dont lie to me, I know you made up that word so that you could fool the city fathers and make your way across that river . . . Jesus it's cold, I'm dying of the cold, boys I'm going home." "What you got for supper tonight G.J.?" "Same as usual, porkchops and bread." "Well," says Rondeau, "I think I'll sashay home myself and pile into them good old beans and hamburg and bread and butter and then see what I can do tonight with a little game of pool at the club." "Me," says Scotty, "I'm going to spot ten strings which will give me approximately 40 minutes to go see my cousin Joel and see if I can borrow his ice skates for vacation." "And me," says Salvey, "I'm going home and see if Joe Joe De Joe Joe got into Sir Walter Raleigh's ice cream can." And thus they all wandered off into the evening, it was getting cold, they all huddled in their jackets, I could see them parting at the corner with casual handwaves, great blear trees of December bent over their heads, shook over their heads, they all went off to home and supper lights and I went home myself laughing and thinking and came to my house and slid around the pole twice and there was my father's Plymouth parked in front of the house so he was home so I went into the bright warmth of the kitchen to see what was going on but not without one final parting look at the huge silver clouds could be seen massing in the evening darkness over my apple trees and suddenly one snowflake fell and swept across my nose. This is a nice kind of thing to close the kitchen door on, when you're 13, and when you have a father to pay the heat bills and supper bills . . . and especially when your father weighs 230 pounds and looks like he'll never die.

The oil stove was pouring out great heatwaves, it was warm in the kitchen, and there was my Pa sitting at the table in his white shirt with the sleeves rolled up but his necktie tied at the neck, his great frowning serious Breton face bent over the prelimi-naries to an immense supper of hamburg and boiled potatoes (my mother peeled them for him in his plate) and bread and butter and milk and for dessert he still had half a cold date pie in the ice box. His fingers were ink stained, as always, from a long day's work at the printing shop he owned, where he put out his two little weekly newspapers (the *Billerica News* and the *Lowell Optic*) and a whole mess of job printing that included such complicated jobs as a bound volume of our family doctor's family tree, with photographs. "*Ten, l Ti Pousse*" he said as I came in and whipped off my jacket and went in the bathroom to wash my hands. "*Cosse qui fat d bon aujourdhui?*" "*On va achetez le Xmas tree assoir pi ont va l'arrangez.*" "Well Gabe," he says to my mother, "I'll have to go to the club and look over the books and then be back around 9 to meet Mike and the gang. What you gonna have good for midnight snack tonight?" and there he was already pitching into his supper with huge serious bites, head down, his chair pushed back from the table to allow room for his great paunch bent forward tensely, eagerly, to his huge meal, usually 2 orders in all. "I thought I'd have some nice cold cuts like boiled ham and stuff . . . Bea and Shabby like boiled ham." "I'll bring back some beer at 9. Come on Boozie!" he yelled to my sister upstairs. "Time for supper." Suddenly Kewpie jumped up on Pa's lap and instead of saying Scat yak! he just fondly caressed it and said "*Ah ti Kewpie, i veu du hamburg?*" and he took a little bite of hamburg off his fork and gave it to Kewpie who dropped it temporarily on his huge cigar-ashed thighs and then gobbled it up, leaving a little grease spot and my mother said "*Eh twe, j'ai faite cleanez Ste culotte la ainc hier. Fwai tut changé encore asoir.*" My Pa put Kewpie on the floor and gave him another bigger bite of hamburg and chuckled his chuckle I never forget: rich, compassionate, affectionate, the chuckle that to me held up the world more firmly, by far, far more firmly than any of your Herculean and Hesperidal arms, shoulders and pillars. . . . For in that chuckle I had seen that the world was a fitting place to live in because it meant that man was kind, man was attentive to the wants of others, man was alive, and man had a sense of humor (so to say), man had glee in his heart and not just sour wronks. Kewpie circled around his chair looking up at him with the same belief I had. Now my father leaned back a little, chewing bread and hamburg and potatoes, and eased a few notches in his huge belt, wiped his brow with his handkerchief, and resumed his well earned supper. Everything flew when he ate,—"*Ya tu encore d la date pie?*" "*Ben oui.*" "Bring it on, MacDuff, bring it on!" He kept making his own crazy jokes at the table but not like expecting appreciation or laughter, but like W. C. Fields not caring, like I saw favorite friends of mine in future life when they sat at kitchen table and went on talking, chewing, laughing, paying no attention to the effect they were making. . . . Meanwhile now the wind beat about the golden windows of our kitchen, winds from dark hell battling at the sills of gold heaven, some of the wind sneaked in but the old stove sent out those heatwaves and all was warm and suppery in the old home, the cat in the middle of the linoleum, satisfied, washed himself with that particular savory long lick of his *fur* meaning he was through eating for a few hours and was ready to take a nap in the lap of comfort home. Our apple trees knocked dry limbs over the roof, a few licks of snow were seen whirling across the kitchen light that fanned out to the side porch. "*I neige!*" said my mother with amazement, always it was amazement she announced either snow or rain. And as always she went and took a look out the window and shook her head. My father reared back, finished, and opened the evening paper, waiting for his date pie without a word, and scowled furiously at various front page reports by the local big paper. "Bwah," he said, and "*Fe!*" and "*La marde!*" and "That old reprobate!" or "That old clapped-up sonofabitch." "*Leo, parle pa comme ca en avant de les enfants!*" and he looked up, stunned, as tho he had forgotten where he was, and remembering where he was it didn't seem to make much difference, only stared at my mother a moment with packed stupefaction, and went back to his front page with a deepening scowl that now became so dark it was on the verge of becoming the famous burper rage G.J. kept talking about: "Zagg, when your old man is sore at something the look that comes over his face would be enough to scare everybody on Wall Street if he was a big financier there, I'm telling you that scowl of his would cause a stock market crash . . . And his cough! If those guys ever heard him cough OOOOO gooo gla bla blall b pow the way I've heard him on certain winter mornings Zagg, especially on Gershom where the wall of the club and the wall of Blazon store captures all the echoes, Zagg the very walls of Wall Street would topple down in sheer terror, Zagg, take it from me. Zagg you're very lucky to have an old buck, as you know I only saw my own old buck once, I was in the crib, I looked up, I saw this huge dark man with huge handlebar mustaches looking down at me. Zagg behind him was the angels of Greece!" "I know G.J. . . . I appreciate having my old buck around." "You dam right better too, Zagg, or I'll sic Kid Salvey on you to bite your balls off." So I feasted my eyes on my father when he read the papers because then he didnt see me because whenever he did see me looking his way he always liked to talk to me and embarrass me in that special way fathers do to their boys, kidding them a little too much. When it was my opportunity to feast on his scowl at the newspaper I always remembered what G.J. said and also my earlier childhood man fear that my father would die someday suddenly, there'd be a smell of flowers in the house, he'd be gone forever, I would cry my eyes out in the dark forever . . . the Oedipal dark. Especially since my mother and her cousin Bea I could hear all the time in their long silly talks discussing how sick Uncle Joe was, how soon he going to die, how all the Kerouacs were all sick and ready to die, and my father Leo would go very soon and the way they carried on it seemed they wanted these men to die. "Pa," I said, "I saw Uncle Joe this noon, *j men a d lecole, pour un verre d'eau.*" "*Pauve Joe. Cosse qui ava a dire?*" "*Rien . . . I voula tu vienne le voire.*" *I dit que tu rest lautre bord de la rivière pit to vien jama le voir. "Ah ben, un bon jeour la . . ."* "*Estamac flasse*" said my mother, referring to Aunt Leontine, knowing my father never wanted to see her and since Uncle Joe was bedridden that is, chair ridden with asthma, he never could go out so the only way to see Joe would be to see *estamac flasses* too . . . *O Gabrielle*," mimicked my father now ferociously, "*j'ai lestmac flasse . . . ya tu un tu peu de manger que je peu avoire . . ?*" With this he plunged into his date pie with huge incomprehensible bites, swallowing without chewing, pushed the chair back, practically pushed the table away, went to the bathroom, swooshed huge waters around his mouth, spit out the water, wiped his hands, and was done. And now, fresh cigar smoke spuming behind him, he walked fast across the kitchen with the paper to his easy chair by the radio for a moment of reading, his 230 pound bulk making the whole

kitchen shake. We saw the light come on in the parlor, heard
him flop into the poor chair, heard him cough hugely, and we
sat there at the kitchen table inadvertently grinning because of
this good, strange yet simple man who was the man of our lives
alright. "*Ah l bonhomme*," said my mother shaking her head
fondly, eating, "*s pa que'l ti bon homme ca*." My mother peeled
another potato for me and I put butter on it and mashed it all
down with a fork and ate. Be mindful of the present vision
before your eyes counseled Saint Edgar Cayce, and now I realize I wish I had been more mindful of that present vision in
those winter nights in the home kitchen when my father was
still alive and was scowling over his newspaper in the den. . . .
Suddenly, even, he let out a huge burp that made the cat jump.
And then "Ham!" as he cleared his throat to read the
editorial.

"Those were the good old days" said Zagg the town drunk
after whom G.J. had named me for no particular reason (at that
time) as he leaned against the fence of the club, the fence that
was sagged in considerably from the dozens of times me and
the gang had thrown ourselves against it, backs first, to get the
thrill of it sending us bouncing back into snowbanks. It was
after supper, dark now, the lights were all on in Pawtucketville,
the snow was flying prettily across the arcs of streetlamps, my
mother and Nin and I were all bundled up going to Lambert
grocery for meat and the Xmas tree, Zagg the drunk was leaning against the fence drunk talking to himself and as we passed
by he said it "These were the good old days" and threw up
his hands and said "Woo woo!" because he looked exactly
like Hugh Herbert and he knew he looked like Hugh Hubert,
everybody had told him so anyway. In fact it was amazing,
he had the same elastic? face that looked like it was about to
squeeze around and disappear, he had the same voice, the
same funny walk, so he kept throwing up his hands saying
"Woo Woo." I never had found out what his last name was
but he was known as Zagg, (my gang-given nickname), and
he was the town drunk of the area. You'd see him all the time
staggering around, or slopping over hamburgs and coffee late
at night in the Textile lunch, or waiting outside the door of
the club saloon where he wasnt always allowed, or going home

late at night weaving and saying "Woo woo" to his house which was apparently at the end of Gershom Avenue. "*Ten,*" said my mother, "*l bohomme Zagg ye toujours sou. Mended mue donc pourquo qu'on homme boeu comme ca.*" We got off the sidewalk to walk around Zagg, who leaned against the bent fence looking up at the sky, mouth open saying "Woo woo" to the snow. "*I pourra seulement pas s tirez chez eux.*" But in my own vision of Zagg was something else: the way he prowled the night, always gay, at that time I didnt know what it really meant to be drunk, all I saw was the gayety and the fact that he talked to everybody and said anything he wanted on the streets and nobody bothered him, I thought he was a great strange mysterious being with the secret of joy in his hand. Saying Woo woo to the snow, all around in the street, was to me so funny, so great, I looked over my shoulder as the women dragged me off. And something awesome about the drunk anyway, since we'd been told as children that when a drunk falls on you he crushes you to death, we always walked around drunks a great distance to avoid that . . . But therefore what awesome power and weight, what awesome glee, freedom, to go around the streets like that. And yet in my child's heart I knew he was just a pitiful bum too, but there seemed to be something else attractive about being a pitiful outcast in a world where everybody strived to be acceptable and everybody boasted about going to church and confession and about the fact they were working . . . "*Vien t en Ti Jean, cosse tu guard a se maudit foulla?*" We arrived on Moody Street, the snow was only dusting and fanning along the sidewalks, it was a dry snow and had no chance to cling and start piling yet, in fact all the stars were showing over the telegraph wires of tenemented Moody so we knew it wasnt going to snow much more. "*Ont lara teutben pas d neige pour Nole, Ti Nin.*" Lambert's market across the street was one golden light, inside there was Mr. Lambert himself standing in the back at the butcher log with huge meat hackers cutting up golden meats for the ladies of Pawtucketville. Out front, in the snow, beautiful evergreens stood leaning against the paned glass windows with boys standing around in muffcaps selling them. The street was crowded and joyous. Blazon's candy store had a larger than usual gang standing in front laughing

and smoking and talking: they were all there: Vic Sawyer, Vic
Albert, Mike Houde, Pete Houde, the lot, pretty soon they'd
amble into the club across the street (where now my father was
scowling over the ledgers) and get in a little bowling. "What
ye say Madame Kerouac!" called Pete Houde gayly from the
corner. "Allo Pete!" "How's the old Xmas tree?" "O we're just
going over to Lambert's now to buy one!" "I reckon Ti Jean
is gonna help you put it up, hey what?" "O sure!" And my
sister grinned quietly, all the drugstore cowboys were looking
at her as usual. We waited at the corner as a big yellow bus
with Moody St written on it swirled up growling in the snow
stopped, discharged local people, and went on up the hill of
Moody to the end of the line where sad white birch leaned
together on the fields that led to Dracut and the dense woods
beyond. I thought of all that snow and white birch out there
tonight and wished I was taking one of my usual long walks
in blizzards. Rubber Hoyle came prowling by, through with
his baseball bat work in the cellar, head bowed, as the boys
yelled at him from the corner "Hey Rubber, I bet I hit 400
next spring!" "You hit 400 and I'll sign you up, Vic!" "I hit
more homeruns than Hank Greenberg this year!" "You'd have
to play 154 games to do that boy!" "Where you goin now
Rubber?" And Rubber, thin smile, answered not, and bent on
to his goal, which was probably a hot stove league discussion
somewhere downtown . . . We went inside the grocery store
and my mother bought groceries and then went in back for the
meat, for ham and chops and various cuts. Mr. Lambert's huge
rosy face exuded joy over the dead hanks of beef. Great sau-
sages were twirled around behind the glass case. His assistant
went in and out of the great ice box with the wooden door:
inside were hanging beefs like Rembrandt's gory and splashed
with blood. Sawdust on the floor. And in the back room the
smell of pickle barrels and of deeper herrings and sorrows back
there where I always imagined Mr. Lambert's old father must
be sitting counting gold coins in a little corner by a candle . . .

Ti Jean Kerouac that strange little boy standing in the golden
butcher shop with his mother and sister, staring at meats. Wondering about the cat in the backroom, the butcher shop cat,
that mangy scrounger, seen leaping up on a bag of potatoes
to lick his tail, all gray and ragged and I wonder what Kewpie

would say. Looking up at the ads for hams in cans, at the decorations for Xmas hanging over the counters, all the laughing people in the store with their snow rosy cheeks, the big fat mothers, the boxes everywhere with the familiar names of families scrawled on the sides . . . "Morrissette . . . Noval . . . Rondeau . . . Beaulieu . . . Salvas . . . Blazon . . . Demarchais." Mr. Lambert wrapt up our goods in nice thick sleek paper with little grains of brown in them and my mother dumped that in her shopping bag, we got apples, Lemon and Lime in quart bottles ("That's for our ward eights tonight," she said, meaning the drinks Pa mixed with gin) and we went back to the cold corner where the fresh trees gave off that wintergreen gum smell and we examined the trees. "*S lui la ye trop skinny*" said my mother. She wanted a nice full fat tree, like anybody else sensible. We picked it out and I took it by the wood bottom and Nin grabbed a hold of the top part where we'd stick the star, and off we marched home and down Gershom, past the club where we could hear all the alleys roaring as the bowlers got going for another night of smoke and roaring. We ducked slightly at the little sidewalk level window just to see Pa through the iron grates sitting there in his little office with the candy for sale in glass cases, talking to a bunch of the boys, counting the till, frowning, smoking. My mother knocked but he didnt hear in all the racket. I could see beyond in the gloom the great bent bodies of poolsharks tensely ready for the break. We went on home with the tree. "*Leve les un peu, tu l drag dans rue.*" We got home and carried it proudly into the parlor, turned on all the lights, the cat came out to smell the tree, and Ma and Nin went upstairs to unpack the annual box of tree decorations. My mother came down also with the portrait of dead brother Gerard she had hung on her wall and said "*T S tanne mon faire un beau ti coin pour Gerard dans salle, drette contre laube, avec des fleurs pi un tite chandelle.*" On a wall shelf deep in the parlor too was the statue of Ste Terese I had seen a thousand times in my dreams turning her head to look at me, with her huge crucifix and flowers across her arms, the inexpressibly sad face. "*On peu mettre ca contre son potra. Ben aright, mes c'est ta right la.*" We already had the green tree holder ready and as I held it by the middle Ma and Nin got down on the floor and eased it in and tightened the screws from the side and pretty soon after a little maneuvering it was straight up, a great bare green tree in the room. Suddenly I realized what glee it was to be in the house decorating the tree as the cat watched, to be alone with Ma and Nin occupied in such a tender and innocent concern, I felt that strange shiver in my chest I always felt when I became completely happy. They were happy and smiling and delighted, they'd bought a new set of balls to hang and all kinds of new tinsels and they were taking them out of their boxes with oohs and aaahs. They started to lay the long streamers of red and blue paper snake around the tree and then they began carefully tying on the colored balls and then my mother got on a chair and put up the star, my favorite star, right at the top. Then came the business of the colored bulbs and their wires and plugging it in in the unattainable plug behind the piano. Finally it was looking very pretty. *Un beau arbre fattez pis rond.* Then the misty business of hanging the tinsels, till finally the tree looked like it was hanging with icicles. Then my mother arranged the ikon of Gerard with flower and an ikon candle and to see the whole effect we put out the parlor light and looked at it and all said "Ahhhhh." It was so beautiful, reddy-blue, dim, pretty with all kinds of little dancing lights and colors, and the shrine of Gerard was the most beautiful thing we'd ever done for Ma. *Ma Ste Terese contre lui la,* I said. *Mais pourquoi Ste Terese, you pas d place anyway la.* Ti Nin seriously went behind the tree to hang more tinsel, she was all bemused in her work. I loved her sometimes because she was so simple and piously so. Nothing fancy. *"Ten garde ta tite soeur Ti Nin, la, tu we comme quay fin?"* *"Oui."* *"Al larrange sa toute beau la, pour tue ca. Fausshe toi peu pu avec yelle asteur."* *"Oui pi volle pu mon cremel."* *"Ouit ti bi di!"* I cried sweeping up Kewpie and holding him up to see the tree and letting him put his little moist nose against the biggest reddest shiniest ball. He stared at himself in it with his huge nose and pearshaped profile. He wanted to reach out and grab a tinsel. In fact when I put him down on the rug he did grab a few tinsels and slapped off a ball and chased it in the hall. *I neige tu encore?* We looked outside, still snowing, it swept in a wordless shroud across the arc of the lamp. Already many of the windows of the homes on Gershom and Sarah were red and blue and green with Xmas tree lights. It was a great night. Now Ti Nin and Ma went in the kitchen yakking happily over their accomplishment and cooked up some cocoa as I sat on the couch, lights out, staring at my tree and my shrine. That day Ti Nin had gone to the library to get books and they were piled there on the couch. I took the first one, *Roll River* by James Boyd and decided (tho I'd never read an adult book yet in my life) to read it in its entirety in the easy chair right under Gerard's picture. I moved the chair a little closer, sat down, and began to read by the flickering candle and the tree lights. Immediately I was lost in a great new world I never dreamed existed, up until then I'd always read just fairy tales and cowboy and detective magazines. Here all of a sudden was a serious sunshiny morning in the South and the man was driving a spanking pair of bays with little flicks of his whip, he owned a mansion, there were tragedies in the air, there was a great river rolling, I knew I would finish it all. Ma was standing in the door looking at me fondly. "*Ten, gard Ti Nin, Ti Jean, ya ime assez son potra de Gerard qui sassi entour pi i lit.*" By and by Bea, Cousin Bea, came in and they all sat around the kitchen table and yakked and I went on reading and suddenly I looked up from my book, stared at Terese to see if she would move her head, which she slightly did, with that slight sighing turn of statues, and then I looked at Gerard and he nodded slowly at me with his saintly, pale face and blue eyes, and then I looked at the star above the tree and it sat there majestically swelling and I knew this would be the happiest Xmas of my life. After Bea Shabby came. Shabby was a great quiet truckdriving French Canadian who lived down the street and was divorced but a little stuck on Bea (who was a widow), they always met at our house, the house began to fill up, a couple of Ti Nin's chums came in stomping from the snow and whooping in the kitchen so I decided my quiet meditation was over and put on my jacket and went down to the club to bowl a string or see who was there and maybe come home with Pa.

Now I had on my good old muffcap and pulled it down over my ears and bent my way down the shroud of Gershom, glad. O all the strange sad songs of the Thirties, "Wait for Me Darling," "Ah Sweet Mystery of Life," I could see it all swirling there in the snow like the faces of my mother and father and sister and Bea and Shabby and all the rest, what lone sorrows hid behind the fences like angels kneeling with both hands to their faces. There, even Ernie Noval's home had Xmas lights in them, Ernie Noval the evil sex fiend who always had girls, even

he believed in Xmas. And Bobby Morrisette's house had a huge
tree in the window and in the kitchen I could see the brown
light where almost the whole boisterous family was sitting now
by the hot stove, Melaye and his brothers wailing away at their
pishnut game, smack of the finger and the little wood disc
scooted across the board and knocked another one in. And up
that strange little street of sorrows, X street, the huddled cottages, like in my dreams the narrow hill cottages, the lights,
the telephone wires, up to the top of the hill behind which my
birches and forest began and all the way up to New Hampshire
the sad snow was swirling and it was quiet in Lowell now. Even
tho in later life you find out that nothing exists but what is
thought to exist, what good can it do anyway . . . ? The very
picket bespeaks something other than that, when I grabbed a
picket and tried to pull it off it was cold and hard and wouldnt
move. Up high Harry Charity's house, the 4th floor of the
Gershom tenement, I could see even there the skinny lights of
a cheap skinny tree and could imagine all his little dirty brothers and sisters staring with shining eyes at it. On Blazon's
corner now no more standers, they'd all gone into the club,
only the yellow light of the store falling out there, showing the
marks where they'd stood against the wall. I went in the club
to join them, by the side door. What a roar and a blast of smoke
met me as I opened that door, always, especially on winter
nights when all the windows are closed and everybody feels
warm and secure inside. What faces, personalities, hundreds of
well known friends and enemies all milling around, smoking,
spitting in spittoons, bowling, shooting pool, yakking on waiting benches, drinking cokes. All four alleys were going to town
with big gay bowling parties. In New England in those days
(probably still) we used small balls about the size of a can-
nonball and duck pins, fat low squat pins, with the small ball
it was possible for great strong men like St. Jean or kid de jo
djo to send that ball rolling down the aisle like a shot out of a
rifle, crack, sometimes they'd hit pins square on and make
them bounce up in the air to come down and clobber poor
Scotty Beaulieu the pinboy who was trying to make his decent
living. There in fact was poor Scotty, bent to his work, gathering up pins and setting them up, holding three pins in each
hand, going as fast as he could. Great superior pinboys like Pete

Houde could set up pins twice as fast but Scotcho was learning. The pool table was taken over by the greats: St. Jean, Mike Houde, Carrouspel, they were playing rotation and at this moment little Pee Too Houde was bent seriously to a difficult long shot that he accomplished beautifully with a straight whack right in, the great gunshot of the ball placking into its pocket's back wood, a sound I would have liked to imitate without playing pool sometimes. Seated around the table on benches were the regular gangs and there was G.J., younger than anybody, staring wide eyed at everything hoping without hope to get in a game or get to bowl but this was a big night. Inside the little office my father sat reading a magazine and puffing on his cigar. Whenever the game was over he had to come out and rack up the next game and collect the money. He never played pool himself unless it was for money, on bets, a big game, but of course he never took on the champs. He bowled more than he shot pool. He had taken this job managing the alley for the Centreville Social Club as a kind of civic activity, there was no money in it to speak of, it was a good hangout for him and only 5 houses from home. Sometimes he threw out a wise guy and wasnt too popular, he wasnt afraid to throw out anybody, he was one of those fat men who probably cant fight at all but can scare anybody and if it came time to fight would probably be unbeatable from sheer rage. So he wasnt popular and some of the wise guys referred to me as "the little Christ Kerouac." They called me that during huge battering autumnal football games out back in Dracut Tigers and piled on me sometimes and one guy even punched me one time in the pileup, to get even with my father, so on the next play I sneaked up on him as he was sweeping left end and hid behind a would be tackler and there he was smiling thinking himself in the clear when I, 13, came up on him low and hit him head on with arms around his knees and he was out like a light and had to leave the game. He was six feet tall, too, and 17. My father was glad about that. But as a rule my father never taught me to hit anybody or revenge for anything, it was just the spur of the moment rages that made him so formidable. Right now he wasnt interested in anything but the arrival of his best friend Old Mike Fournier, getting the night's business over with by turning it over to his assistant, and going home for the big

party. I sat down by G.J. "Zagg, de jay de jo jo has just left me
an ancient message from Kid Shine, which was brought to me
by snow pigeon that came sailing across the river and into the
open window of my shit house, saying that Kid Slavey cannot
come to the club tonight due to previous commitments. He
said . . . you know what Salvey said after you left and he walked
me up Phebe? He said he was going home to see if King Kong
was in his kitchen." "Did you eat your porkchops?" "Zagg I
did but I blew up at my mother again. God will punish me for
screaming at that old lady someday, I'm telling you Zagg I just
cant help it, sometimes she makes me so mad and I start yelling
at her and she just sits in the corner with her bible and answers
me not, Zagg what do you think God will do to me for being
like that?" "He'll break your arm in the hall." "Do you realize
that Scotty is down there in that pit right now counting every
penny he's going to earn tonight, that he's already added it up
and he even showed me a little slip of paper a minute ago all
written out in red ink with his new red ink pen, he's got it
figured out that by 1938 he can buy a used car and we can all
go to Vermont and swim. Zagg, I'm telling you it's a crazy
world . . ." And he leaned over and spit into the spittoon to
show he was just as big a guy like the rest. He even borrowed
a butt from Pete Houde and lit it awkwardly and held it in his
mouth, hat over eyes, and leaned back and crossed his long legs
and said "Ah shit." New parties of bowlers kept pouring in, it
looked like we would never bowl but I asked my father for just
one string, he said to use Scotty's alley and G.J. and I rushed
out and suddenly we were standing in the bright lights of the
bowling stage, as angry guys stared at us thinking "Little
pricks get an alley because his old man runs the alley" and G.J.
said "Zagg we better get this string over with fast, we're going
to be murdered." "Okay I go first" and as Scotty waved at us
with a sad smile down-alley, I started with my famous style
(imitating Pete Houde's beautiful easy soundless style where
the ball never plumps on the floor but is just eased gently with
sweeping arm, down the line, with a hook) and baff, I had only
2 pins to hit, and hit them for a spare and G.J. wrote down the
score. "Hurry up Zagg I'm telling you we're goners, they're
going to throw poolballs at us." We hurried through our
string. It was a great night for me, I hit 121 which is amazing

for a kid, and G.J. as usual hit about 78 or 68 throwing balls down the gutter and laughing and swearing and sometimes running after the ball after he'd thrown it. We were too scared to start another string and quit. Big gay parties of drinkers were taking over. Upstairs the club saloon floor was roaring with the stomp of a thousand drinkers and poker players and up there they had 3 more pool tables. "Zagg how swiftly we die," said G.J. suddenly, back on the bench, and "How poor we are." Sometimes he'd say things like that, with his dark Greek face fixed in utter despair, and I always knew then that G.J. would be a great man somehow. "Empty baseball fields is all that's waiting for us," he added, incomprehensibly, throwing his butt away. "Think I'll go home Zagg." What a sad bed G.J. slept in, on that high house on the parapet receiving all the blizzardy winds of the whole river, the great trees clanking outside. "I'll go wrap myself up in the angel's hair and perceive the cool breeze of heaven, Zagg," and he went out the side door, bent, to his home. I followed him and walked him home in the cold. "What say, Memory Babe," he said, turning and seeing me. "Heaven will respect us, Zagg, Heaven will respect us." "What's Heaven, George, I mean what you see?" "I dunno, Zagg, I aint read any philosophical books lately and I dont care. Wanta come in my house awhile." "I dunno." "My mother likes you, Zagg, she appreciates it sometimes when you come in say hello to her." "Okay . . . look, G.J. our new Xmas tree, see it in the window." "It's nice, Zagg, naturally we dont put up no Xmas tree in my house . . . it's too gloomy." "Why?" "I dunno Zagg, my mother doesnt care and my sister doesnt care. I guess my house is too marked by death for celebrations." We went up Sarah in the snow, side by side, heads bowed, in the sudden sadness. "There," he said pointing up at the windows of his house, "gloomy lights . . . my mother is sitting in the corner waiting for me. My sister's already in bed. The wind blows through the windows. It's cold. Zaggo, old G.J. aint long for this world." We went upstairs and into the kitchen. A low lamp was burning on the table, his mother sat in the corner as he said with an old bible in her hand, a Greek bible. She smiled at me. Around her head was a dark shawl, like the ladies of Mexico, and her dress was all black and her shoes and stockings were black. G.J. fell disconsolately on the kitchen couch and stared up at the ceiling. "There you have it Zagg." I could never talk to Mrs. Aposotolos because she couldnt speak English nevertheless she always kept talking to me about something and G.J. would translate it with a sad smile. "Do you realize what she's saying Zagg? She's saying she's so glad I have a nice chum like you, now what do you think of an old lady like that. I'll tell you one thing Zagg," getting up and pacing up and down in the kitchen, working himself up to a fury, "though my old lady is all in black and cant speak English and don't have nothing to do with any of the ladies around here she's the best goddamed old lady in this town, I dont mean your mother, Zagg but all the rest of them. She works in a shoe factory to support me and Ruby, she never complains, Zagg every morning at 6 I can hear her coughing in the bathroom and I come out and look at her cooking her pitiful breakfast on the stove and no matter how cold it is or hot it is or whatever the mailman's bastard can try to get to, this woman goes to work, just for me, for worthless me . . . but I promised on the bible and on my mother's name, Zagg, comes the day when I'll be a big burper on Wall Street and buy her everything she needs and for once in my life I will have done something decent, just for once . . ." Poor George, and how he got himself worked up to raging and pacing back and forth in that gloomy kitchen, finally he'd start cursing and waving his fist and making such speeches his mother would become perturbed tho she couldnt understand what he was talking about to me, and would yell "*Ra la ma ana a fat tap apta*" in a big Greek outpouring and G.J. would become quiet, sigh, throw himself back on the couch and stare again at the ceiling. "That's the story of my life, Zagg. Old kid de jo jo is lying on the couch in his kitchen wondering whatever will happen to all his *robbons* some day. Zagg I know I dont make sense but can you see what I mean?" sitting up to ask me earnestly. "Sure George." "That's why I like Salvey so much, he comes into this house and says 'G.J. what happened to your coffeemaker?' and I'll say 'What coffeemaker?' and he will say 'the one that we threw ice cream at Sunday.' or some such silly thing like that and Zagg, it makes me laugh! I see him coming to visit me on stormy days, I see him plowing up ye olde Riverside Drive out there, head down, collar up, he's coming here just to make me glad, Zagg. He knows how miserable I am. He comes right in here and tells my mother all kinds of nutty stuff she cant understand. I'm telling you Zagg, that Salvey has opened my eyes. He's good. He has a good heart. That's something. O when I think of all the dirty pricks in this world and how much they think of themselves . . . Let it be, let it ride, old de jo jo is now ready to hit the sack and forget it for another day. Give my regards to your ma and your pa, wish them a happy Xmas and all that, Zagg, and see ya later." He let me down the hall with the hall light. "Good old Memory Babe," he chuckled, "if your knees was as ancient as mine the phantom detective could never catch up to you." Then as I went down the alleyway between the houses he was speaking to me from the porch. "It's all up there, Zagg," pointing up at the snowing sky, "it's all up there. Adios Zagg. Give my regards to Kid Shine and the gang." I went on home thinking about George. Then I saw my house, the lights in the window, heard the faint whoop of the big party in the kitchen, and I forgot poor George.

I peeked in from the front porch, through the window with the little Xmas lights, and could see the heads and shoulders of partiers in the kitchen, hear their cries, get that orphaned feeling I always used to get when I'd stop on winter nights to peek into my home windows before going in and always making a phantasy that I am actually an orphan and am hungry and just returned from freezing China and want some food and to be adopted by 2 nice parents like Leo and Gabrielle Kerouac? Will they accept me? There was old Mike, I could see him hugging Alice Gallagher in the kitchen and yelling loud laughter, behind him sitting politely laughing on a chair was his son Mike, my buddy, my second brother, who was along to help his old man in case he got too drunk and also to see me about our plans for what to play all day tomorrow Saturday Xmas Eve. Alice Gallagher lived in the house next door, she also had her Xmas tree up by now, I could see it in her window and her husband Charlie who was about to join our party in a minute was standing in front of the tree putting up the last tinsels as the little kids watched. Their home had always seemed to me in my childishness the typical perfect beautiful "English" American Home (they were Irish, of course) where you had nice new furniture and thick rugs and fancy kitchens and people who talked English instead of French brought glittery presents on Xmas

Eve all wrapped in the fanciest wrappers from downtown and
they drank egg nog. Actually they were very simple people but
to me they were mysterious "Americans" whose lives were ever
so much more joyous and bright than the life of the "Franco-
Americaines" and indeed brighter than the life of the Greeks
like G.J.'s bereaved home. I went down from the front porch,
around the back, and again peeked into the kitchen door to
watch them before going in. Poor Mike, I mean my Mike, the
young one, one year older than me, he was a little bored now
because I was late getting home, he wanted to say to me:
"Podner, tomorrow we lopes out the back wood section and
go see how Jack Holt's makin out with his traps, or if not that
we can head for the hill country and see if Buck Jones is still in
his shack." I went in, greeted by whoops, "*Ten, Ti Jean yest
arrivez!*" "Where ya been, ya little tyke!" yelled my father, and
old Mike ruggled the top of my head with his big rough hand
and chuckled, his face was all rosy with liquor and his eyes
shiny. My mother was in the kitchen mixing Lemon and Lime
soda with big shots of gin, chipping ice out of the box with the
ice pick, setting up ham sandwiches in a big platter, all rosy and
cute in her party apron, with lipstick on her lips, all gurgling
with joy yakking with Alice and Nin and her friends. Meanwhile broody Bea our cousin (Uncle Joe's daughter), a blonde
with a flair for the tragic, was sitting in a corner of the kitchen
brooding at the floor. Shabby was a big handsome truckdriver,
extremely polite, who merely puffed on his pipe and smiled at
all the jokes. He was a good simple old soul. Nothing bothered
him. He came to see Bea but he never seemed to look at her,
till sometimes she'd speak to him, unexpectedly, and he would
answer very little, so that in the solitude of my mother's chambers Bea would often complain "But he's a nice man I know,
but so unromantic!" Alice Gallagher was a cute blonde woman,
very sexy, who caused a great deal of talk among my gangs.
"Zagg one of these days I'm going to sneak up to that Gallagher house and watch that Alice undress in her bathroom, and
if that Charlie ever catches me I'll run I'll fly." . . . Charlie
himself, who came in now, was a handsome darkhaired Irishman full of laughs and white teeth, he came in waving a new
bottle of gin, the house was in such an uproar Kewpie was
hiding upstairs on my bed. They all drank and began

reminiscing. My father was in his element, white shirt with the sleeves rolled up, necktie off now, sitting shiningly at the table saying "Remember that time we decided on the spur of the moment to go to Canada, Charlie?" "How can I ever forget forget it Leo! 'HOOO HOO'." "There we were, midnight, drunk as hoot owls, the whole gang, me, Gabe, Alice, Charlie and Mary Nestor and her boyfriend Taft, we didnt know what to do next so I just said, hell let's get in my Plymouth and drive to Canada, we'll be back Monday, it was just a joke but Mike they took me up on it!" "I remember that one." "So we all piled into the car, no suitcases nothin, the women had on their house aprons, we left Ti Nin Boozie here to babysit for Alice and feed Ti Jean and off we went, it's only a 9 hour drive nowadays. O boy what a time we had. Remember the donuts Charlie?" "Hoo hoo the donut shop, where was that up around Vermont someplace." "Well we went in there for donuts but they were hard as rocks so we started pitchin em at the bottles of pop on the back shelf, I hooked three bottlenecks by God and won 50 cents from Charlie." "Taft didnt get a one!" "We paid for all the donuts! He almost called the cops the poor devil who ran the joint!"—"Oh it was a mad trick." And my mother yelled "And all the ladies had was a few boxes of Kotex and the customs man look at me and said 'Is that all you gals bring with you on trips?' That's just what he said then we drove into Canada and all started to sing 'Au Canada' o boy what a time we had and we come to Aunt Alice's house on St. Hubert Street at 7 in the morning and got them all up and old Doc didn't give a damn, he come right downstairs in his bathrobe and cooked up the biggest breakfast you ever saw, Canadian bacon, about 2 dozen eggs and bang, he goes down the cellar and gets out that white liquor of his that they make out on the farm and he poured a big can of cherries in there and we were off." "Yes," my mother yelled in, "and then he took the whole diningroom table and pushed it in the door and made a bar, we was all sittin around on the rug all day, no chairs." "Boy did we get piffed!" "And that night," said Alice, "we went to that nightclub there and had a heck of a time dancing . . ." "That was the night that little Romeo with the mustache didnt know Gabe was my wife and started serenadin her, you know, and O boy but she was in love that night. . . . ha ha ha ha."

"Thats not true I wasnt makin eyes at him at all . . . Bea that's the godshonest truth!" "O my," said Bea interrupting all the hilarity with her usual philosophical sadness, "wouldnt life be grand if we could all have a good time like that every day." "Bea why dont you get on that piano and play Rachmaninoff." "O I dont feel like it tonight." Shabby puffed on his pipe. Old Mike got up and began to sing "By the light . . . of the silvery moo-oon" and everybody immediately joined in and a big songfest was on and Mike and I went in the parlor and sat on the couch before the tree. "Well old Podner," said Mike, who looked like a young Errol Flynn with his chiseled features and blue eyes and serious lip-wettings and deliberate gravity, "how's about you and me takin off tomorrow for Pine Brook and go see the lay of the land out thar?" "Will you come get me." "Shore, pod, I'll be over around 8 or so and we can saddle up our old grays and go canterin out across Dracut Tiger fields and mosey on down the backtrail country and say, we can come around through Rosemont and Centreville and come back by downtown and go up to my house for a little bit of beans, you know." "Okay," (but I didnt intend to eat none of his mother's beans, she never put enouf molasses in them and my mother said they were *bleme comme un vesse de careme*; white as a Lenten fart). However we agreed on a big day of cowboying around the backwoods and then "Say, after that we can go down the Merrimack Square Theater and see the new Marx brothers." "Now you're talkin Brother! I'll ask Pa for a quarter and you get a quarter too. Hyoo hyoo hyoo!" he laughed, slapping his thigh in anticipation of the Marx Brothers "you remember that time the doctors asked Groucho what his medical education was and he steps up and says 'Dodge Brothers, late 29' and the way he rolls his eyes, hyoo hyoo hyoo!" and Mike got up and imitated it and glided around the parlor, stopping to look up at the tree from his crouched position with rolling eyes, puffing on the imaginary cigar. "Who's that a picture of?" he asked suddenly. "That's Gerard." "Is that him? Say, pod, you sure looked just like him, you know?" In the kitchen they were all getting up and going next door to Alice's house, we all went outdoors in the swirling snow, whooping, and Mike and I had to walk on both sides of his father to see he didnt slip in the snow, he was really piffed by now. For that matter so was Charlie, and my father Leo too, but old Mike when he got piffed he didnt step too easy. "Got a nice present for me, Podner?" said Mike smiling and I realized I hadnt even bought a present for Mike yet. "I got a nice one for you. Give it ya tomorrow night, amigo." What an enormous difference there was between Mike and G.J., my range of friends ran from normal French Canadian podners who went playing cowboy with me, to strange sad philosophical Greek boys who preferred sitting and talking about life. Mike wasnt interested in such things at all, his idea of a day was to go out and explore the woods and jump up on rocks and dig around and follow creeks and go down by the river. He was always Buck Jones, he was always leading me the way down the trail, cantering, turning around to shout instructions. Actually we were kind of big by now to be still playing cowboys but Mike didn't care and insisted. In a short while that would all be over with. In no time at all Mike suddenly grew to almost six feet and began going out with girls, sometimes big fat screaming harlots of Little Canada, and seemed to enjoy that as much as anything else he'd ever done. As for my private games and racing horses and baseball records in my room, he had no interest in all that, once in a while he'd look over my shoulder and marvel at the precision of my handwritten print.

Now they were getting really drunk in the Gallagher kitchen and my father held the floor. "Charlie if you think we're crazy you aint heard nothin yet. I've just got to tell you about Rosaire." "Hoo hoo hoo" howled old Mike almost falling off the floor. "Dont ever tell him that story he'll never go to church again!" all choking on his cigar with happiness. "Rosaire was a priest Charlie, and you know up in French Canada—" "Up in Canada," my mother interrupted, "when you're the oldest boy in the family the family doesnt feel that it will go to heaven unless the oldest boy goes into the priesthood." "Yeah, but this guy Rosaire was not cut out to be a priest, O he was a wild one with the women and with the bottle too, O my God, but he went in the priesthood so . . . he's a nephew of Mike's here . . . so he comes down to Lowell one Xmas and we have a big party for him and he's supposed to say 11 o'clock mass next morning so we're all having a big time, there he is with his collar around his neck, backwards, you know, but getting PIFFED? My God how that guy could put it away. He was a good boy, dont get me wrong, he just admitted it to all of us 'I didnt wanta be a priest, I had to follow my father's wishes, so here I am' and Mike here before the night was half out had to lock up his daughters Lorette and Jeanette because Rosaire kept sitting them on his lap and even when they were locked up he tried to get in anyhow. O he was a devil that one! So come midnight he takes his last drink so he can go to communion, and boy he fills up a waterglass like this fulla gin and puts it down and bang he's out, so we put him to bed and in the morning Mike picks him up and dumps him in the shower and pours hot coffee down his throat . . ." "This is a priest?" cried Alice in shiny eyed amazement. . . . "That's right, so here he is just about a little unsteady on his feet and a big headache but they drive him to the 11 o'clock mass, so you know us, the dirty dozen, the old gang back there in Centreville we used to have, Ti Jean will tell you, remember kid those wild parties we used to have and that time Vendette playing a ghost behind the piano with that white flour all over his face and puts his face in an empty frame, with a candle underneath, and Blanche Taft's playing the funeral march on the piano, o we had the times . . ." "I used to make pot after pot of coffee!" yells my mother. "Big drip pots with 15 cops in each one." "15 cops is right, tried to come to our door and break up our parties, I used to know some of the boys . . . talk about your wild generations and Twenties and all that junk—so you know, we were a crazy gang, we all got together and went to the 11 o'clock mass to pull Rosaire's leg, we all sat in the front row and there he comes out, wobbly, and tries to kneel and almost falls over and the altar boy knew what was going on and caught on to his dress there, and helped him get up, then poor Rosaire turns around to bless the people and first thing he sees is us waving at him surreptitiously from under our straw hats." "What's surreptitiously mean there Leo? Dont pull those big words on me!" yelled Mike pop eyed. "It means," and my father wiggled his hand snakily "it means a snake in the grass . . . So we're all waving at him, and I'm making cross eyes at him, you know, o he was furious, he didnt know whether to laugh or cry or run away or have another drink or what, and the ladies there they were doing all kindsa things, poor dog he never got over it but by God I did see him smile just a little bit when he turned around . . . That night, God is on my bible, here he comes again and we all get piffed again. O boy! In those days we were young and we had good times and werent afraid of hangovers like today, by gosh we've had our good times. Aint that right Mike?" putting his arm around Old Mike. "Like those times we go on those big fishing trips in Fall River, hey Mike?" "Yup," sighed Mike, and the party became sad and quiet, the angel of silence flew over the house, it was Xmas eve now, all the souls sighed in the little sad kitchen, the kiddies were sleeping upstairs under rosy eaves, all was well, and my sister Nin sighed and put forward her favorite gambit: "Ah, what is life?" "If anybody could answer that, Ti Nin," replied Cousin Bea, trailing off, her attractive blonde head looking down, as Shabby puffed manfully and said nothing. I looked at Young Mike and he was rolling his eyes like Groucho Marx as tho to say "Groucho doesnt care about such things, hyoo hyoo." When the party was over Mike and I had to hold on to old Mike's arms now, to help him across the snow, which was falling less and less now, even some stars were appearing over Boof Paquetee's house. "Guess the snow'll stop." My father drove old Mike and the boy home and my mother cleaned up the kitchen, everybody went home, and it was time to go to bed. But first I went into the parlor and sat under my shrine of Gerard and went on reading my book *Roll River* getting deeper into the tragic story now where somebody drowns ice skating in the winter then I looked up at Gerard's picture and wondered indeed what life was all about and felt like imitating Nin and say "Ah, what is life?" "*Va t couchez la Ti Jean, yest tard.*" So I washed my teeth and went upstairs to my room, turned on the light, took out my diary and painstakingly scribbled the day's entry: "School." Then because it was a diary I figured I had to have something "official" in it, that is, something that had really nothing to do with my actual life, so wrote in "Saw about coming Santa Anita Handicap in American in which Discover is picked. Nice sports coming along." Then I contemplated the rest of the day's events and put them down in my usual laconic childly fashion. "Made some races. Rained then it snew." I thought "snew" was a clever past tense for

"snowed." Concluding: Put up tree. Boy O Boy. Read. Bowled
121. Ha ha. Hit hay at 11:45. Oh hum. S'all." S'all, and I rolled
into bed as the midnight window rattled in December's grasp,
my mother turned out the light, and Kewpie jumped up on the
bed as a thousand times before, I raised the covers, he turned
exactly three times purring and then plumped himself against
my chest and I lowered the cover, put my arm lightly over him
and we slept together like that the long sweet night. . . . Trees
knocked in the old Lowell wind. Someday I'd know despair,
probably not much worse than the despair I knew even now
and everybody knew even now, but I was sleeping under my
father's roof and under the further roof of my real Father and
my dreams were pure. And Kewpie's dreams were pure. Soon
I could hear my father's thundering snores from his own dark
room. So all Lowell slept waiting for Saturday Christmas Eve
the big day preceding the biggest day.

Saturday morning was all blue and gold with that early sun
creaming the 3 inches of snow or so that had fallen. Black were
the boughs and twigs of the trees in all that pure whiteness.
Rosy early 7 A.M. sun was coming up over the hill of Lupine
in Centreville across the river where I'd been born, it was so
beautiful I pushed open the double window and crept out on
the roof and made tracks down to the edge and looked down
on the yard and jumped (about 8 feet) and opened the cellar
door and went in the cellar to see the darkness and to get the
strange feeling of coming out of there back to the world of
snow and crystal icicles hanging from lonesome familiar eaves.
It was just like the childhood dream I'd had on West Street,
never will forget it, of icy crystals and joy and sleds going by
and people laughing and singing in the street and somehow
I'm the handsome Hansel & Gretel prince opening wide his
French gable windows to the glory world to sing out hullaballoos of Christmas song. That was a childhood dream, now
I was older, more tragic, but I remembered it, sensed it as I
stared at the pristine morning. I marveled at the wiseness of my
cat to be out there too licking his paws in the snow and looking
around and the blue and orange sky. The sun was warm, it was
clear that the snow would melt by late afternoon, unless colder
winds came. It was Saturday, I was in my overalls, and I had all

day to play and do anything I wanted. I went in the house and
my mother said *"Ti Jean? Comment s as cfa? T e pas encore de
boute?" "Jai sorti par le chaussie en hau." "Mechant . . . tut va t
cossez les pates." "Est pa peur, she comment sautez." "Jai faite tdu
bon grio pour tond edejeunez. Veu tu test toast la pi commencez?"
"Oui." "O boy ja I mal a tete aprea toute ca hier a soir, O boy
moi je bu plus."* . . .

By and by here comes poor old Mike to come play with me,
I saw him from the parlor window coming up Sarah Avenue in
his little knickers with the long cloth stockings tied at the legs
with elastic, and his little jacket of black leather and his mittens.
Always a lonely sort of little boy in the huge family he belonged
to, the second from the youngest, with two brothers and five
sisters . . . five grownup sisters the whole slue of them sitting
around their mother in the sewing room, pulling him by the
ear when he misbehaved, sending him constantly to the store,
a huge guffawing family, they called "Alexander Cash Market"
"Alexander Cash mon Cul" and roared with laughter. Summer
nights I'd sleep there in their big house and hear laughter and
noise everywhere, as sometimes the sisters would stay up late
telling stories and shrieking. Then at dawn Mike and I would
sneak out to go on one of our long hikes. Sometimes we had
to bring Snorro along (his kid brother) (real name Robert)
because he was the baby of the family. One time we dragged
Snorro and the dog Beauty clear to Pelham on a 5 mile hike
that took all day to and from. Mike was the kind of lonely man
who would grow up to be a truckdriver, jut-jawed, serious, sad,
I see him driving big rigs across the night with no complaint,
laughing at jokes in truck diners, sleeping in cheap hotels. Now
as a child he was all intent on being a cowpoke and didnt feel
right till we had gone up beyond Gershom and hit the edges of
the sandbank where the long Dracut Tigers fields began with
little knolls, rocks, trees, dense little forests, snowy meadows
and beyond all that the beginning of pine forests that led to
New Hampshire. Mike slapped his thigh and said "Giddap"
and off we went galloping across the field. Suddenly he ran up
a knoll and scanned the horizons with his hand over his eye,
slapping his thigh saying "Whoa there, take it easy Red." He
had a red bay horse, I had a white one. I pulled up behind him
and said "Whoa there. What's up pard?" "I think I see dust

out there in the desert, I think the posse's found our tracks."
"Well let's go then." Off we galloped, faster, urging our horses
full on, till we reached the pine forest and both jumped off and
hid behind rocks to peek further. All we could see were the
distant redbrick smokestacks of Lowell, and curling smoke in
the gray iron air of New England December. "See that smoke
yonder. I think the Indians got wind of the posse. Mebbe we
wont have any trouble at all. In any case, Buck, let's amble on
down the valley to our camp." So we went galloping down the
dirt road into the hollow, where was a pond surrounded by
little New England homes, and skirted that, whooping, and
dove into the Pine Brook woods where nobody would ever see
us. A crow cawed in the crazy gray air, leading us further in to
the woods. Mike jumped up on a big rock under a pine tree
and sat down to rest. "Well pard," sez he, "it looks like we done
hornswallered that posse." "I'll rustle up some grub, Buck,"
I said and began making fiddling moves with sticks. "Wait,"
said Mike, "no time to eat just now. I think I hear a horse
comin." We ducked down and Mike said "Here he comes, Buck
Jones. I guess he's got a message for us. Nope, I reckon not,
he's ridin right on by. Say did you get your quarter to go see
the Marx Brothers this afternoon?" "I'll get it." "We have to
bring Robert goldurng it but he has his own quarter too. Well
I reckon I'll pitch right into these beans and wrap my stomach
around some sourdough and coffee whiles I'm at it. Hyah hyah
hyah!" he suddenly laughed. "I'd like to see the expression
on that posse's face by now. Hoo hoo!" He slapped his thigh
and laughed and bent over. He really played. Suddenly he was
running like mad in the other direction and I galloped after
him thinking the posse was coming but when I caught up to
him he was as pale as a sheet. "What's the matter?" "Dint you
see it?" "See what?" "That snake . . . I just saw a black snake
about six feet long under that rock." "Well I didn't see it."
"But I'm not playin, it's true. I aint going back to that rock."
We hurried down to the brook edge and sat down on rocks.
The banks were almost overflowing with winter thaw waters. It
was a quiet brook with just farmland across the way and woods
this side. It was our summer swimminghole, even the Oblate
brothers of the parochial school came swimming here with
the kids, casting off their raven garments and jumping in the
water with big white bodies, whooping. We also called it Bare

Ass Brook but now so many girls were coming to swim there the practice was dying out. In the winter it was a lovely spot to just sit and eat beans and discuss Buck Jones. The pines, the rushing gurgling water, the patches of snow, the reflection of the gray clouds in the silver gray water, the crows cawing back yonder . . . "Yessir," said Mike, "aint nothin I like bettern the wide open spaces out in these parts. I reckon I'll get on old Red now and head back to Dodge City and see if Lil's in the gamblin hall. I gotta go to confession this afternoon too. You want to go with me Jackie?" "Nah . . ." I had gotten into the habit of not going to church any more because I didnt believe any more than the man in the moon was real. But Mike said it was so and that he was carrying a bundle of twigs. Mike and I had received our first confirmation together and swapped names and knelt side by side with new rosaries in the candle-flickering little basement—like Church of Ste Jeanne D'Arc. "How come you dont go to church no more?" "Aw I reckon I will soon . . ." I was too busy with my room games. I adjusted my baseball hat to a jaunty angle and tried to look handsome. We got on our horses and headed up the brook towards Beaver Brook and on down through the farming fields to where the brook emptied into the Merrimac River near the Rosemont dump. Now we could see all Lowell across the basin of the river in its Saturday morning brightness. The sun was coming out making what was left of the snow melt. It was going to be a sunny afternoon with a red sunset by the time we'd come out of the Marx Brothers movie.

So as we started down Lakeview Avenue towards the heart of Centreville (the part of Lowell where we'd both been born) we left behind us our fields, our gray woods, the vision of which had been instilled in our hearts by so many old movies, cowboy serials that used to run at the Royal Theater for 15 weeks in a row with all the kids screaming for the conclusion. Continued Next Week and you'd see great soft gray wagons tumbling down dusty gorges, the heroine in calico dress gasping, great spiders of film-defect across the general snowy mystery & electricity of the old films in the texture of which Mike and I had discovered the sense of rain in the woods out by Dracut. The old dream . . . And when you saw the hero cowboy riding away at the end, waving his white hat, you went with him into the

old American dream of space and plains and deserts, which
to Mike was embodied by playing Buck Jones and to me too
but also my games, my gray rainy games in my room. Now
we were back in town heading down Lakeview Avenue along
by the street where I was born, Lupine Road, I never even
knew which house it was, every time I passed there I'd look
and wonder and remember the pine trees on the hill above the
house as my first memory. At the heart of Centreville were all
the stores and old gray wood tenements around where our
fathers had played cards and had clubs before we were born
and so there was always a mysterious soft sadness somewhere
around there. Now our fathers were centering their activities in
Pawtucketville across the river. To the French Canadian kids of
Lowell Centreville must seem almost as ancient as its namesake
in the Medieval pope capital of France. The church there was
St Louis de France where I'd been baptized (Mike too) and
where my brother'd had his funeral. I was always afraid to go
in there . . . Our pride and delight this Saturday morning was
in revisiting our old farmer field in back of the parochial school
where we'd played our first games as little chums of seven and
eight years old. There we had a tree we'd named The Fresh
Air Taxicab, we used to climb it, sit in it and play that we were
Amos and Andy. There were little thickets and hills all around
too, great for all kinds of games including sliding in the winter.
But as we revisited our tree now we saw that it was dead, there
was a gaping hole in it and the limbs looked done. "Well, I
reckon our old fresh air taxicab aint gonna last much longer,
Jackie. Boy did we sure have fun here. Remember that morning
you stept right in a cowflap. Hyoohyoo hyoo! I chipped off a
little piece of the tree and put it my pocket as a keepsake. A
few years later the tree disappeared, too. We ambled on down
to Bunker Hill St. where Mike was born and where he lived
when I first met him, in those first days when he'd come to my
house Sunday mornings in his white knickers, to come and get
me for church, and for my mother he'd dutifully go down the
cellar and haul up a bucket of coal. We also passed my own old
house on West St., a little white cottage with creeping roses
and a big lawn and a back shed where we'd put on plays and
hammered at the organ. Mike with his loyal arm around me
pointed out the holes in the fence: "Things keep a creeping

along dont they?" We went up West Sixth Street, past the old waterworks the sight of which, in its redbrick and huge windows with inside huge pumps, is as sad as time. We hit Bridge Street and remembered the time we'd gone up to the reservoir on top of Christian Hill up there on a long afternoon of eternal sun and shadow, the windy light. "Yessir, we shore did have our times, Jackie." We went down Bridge Street with its stores and tenements and came to the bridge, which crossed the river where it foamed again over scummy rocks and then went up to Lawrence and out. Across the bridge immediately you saw the narrow walls of factories and warehouses and pinpointing down the middle to the Square at the end where the stores and multitudes were. As a little child I had always been taken across this bridge to come to Lowell center and at night, with those red neons shining among the factory redbricks, the gay lights, the drear wind, the spindle footed men with derbies hurrying nowhere it had always represented to me the heart of Cityness. Especially and saddest of all because my father's printing shop was right in back there, behind the canal, a great dreary plant with dusty windows and huge presses roaring and my father always in his printer's apron walking around scowling. The Merrimack Square Theater was just opening as we arrived, the last of the line of waiting kids was being fed in. We got in just in time for the beginning of *Monkey Business* and suddenly when we saw Harpo peeking up out of a stowaway barrel and taking the barrel cover as though it was a boudoir mirror and pretending to powder himself we laughed and laughed. Then in the later parts of the movie when all the children were entranced by Harpo with his angel face plucking beautifully, sometimes showering fingertips over the harp's chords, we all felt like crying and we all knew Harpo was an angel from heaven come to make little children laugh and cry. It was only years later I discovered there is a famous harpist in India who has also taken a vow of silence and plays the harp to multitudes of children as he roams across from Bombay to Calcutta and up the Ganges to Benares. Of course our great madhatter Groucho was gliding around importuning widows with warts on their chins, and finally we saw Harpo again on a bicycle chasing a blonde but he has a fishingpole with bait at the end of it and he's chasing that too, as tho giving himself motive power. Then there's Chico looking and fishing around a haystack and when Groucho says what're you looking for? he says "A needle." O Harpo Marx! playing his gray harp of gold for all the quiet children in the balcony as adults yawn in the orchestra! Stealing silverware, bug spraying the guests, powderpuffing his white fair face with fishbarrel cover. Harpo! who was that Lion I saw you with? Always chiding with his horn in the cane of his golden belt. Always emerging from his pockets another Harpo hand for the harp, screwing it on to his wrists! Was his vow of silence an Indian Harp? All those other movies we didnt care about, the 1930's southern accents of Una Merkel, evil old slick crooks with gray lapels never winning out they had big hands and ghosts in the diary room. All of us eager eyed watching for the black spots in white snow, insects in heaven. The rainy first Rintintin movies of our hearts! Lon Chaney leaving a puff of smoke and a spot of blood on the gray brain rug. And always late in the afternoon when the show was almost over and we saw the heroes eating off trays in beds we all grew hungry and wanted to go home and eat. Feeling dopey we were always herded out in toto by the ushers, so other lines of kids could come in, and outside the street was real and we didnt know it any more. We went home with our Harpo in our hearts.

DOING LITERARY WORK:
AN INTERVIEW WITH
JACK KEROUAC

Doing Literary Work: An Interview with Jack Kerouac

This conversation between Kerouac and his longtime friend, the writer John Clellon Holmes, was forwarded to Stella Kerouac via the Sterling Lord Agency in February 1985. Holmes explains in his accompanying letter to Kerouac's widow that he had conducted this interview by mail in June 1963, as part of his research for his book *Nothing More to Declare* (1967). In 1985, Holmes was moved to revisit the exchange as a result of what he considered to be continuing and damaging public misperceptions "about Jack's dedicated and responsible life as an artist," which most of Kerouac's biographers had done little to quell or correct. Holmes hoped to publish the interview but was unable to do so prior to his death in 1988.

Holmes was one of Kerouac's most loyal friends and ardent supporters, and their ease and familiarity with each other is evident throughout the exchange. Holmes presents Kerouac with a deft series of questions regarding his life, his process, and the evolution of his stylistic and conceptual concerns in a fashion rarely matched in other interviews.

IN the early summer of 1963, I was writing a series of essays on the Beat Years to be called *Nothing More to Declare*, and I asked Jack Kerouac if he would help me with the one on his work. We had known one another for fifteen years, and had talked life & literature & truth for a hundred nights or so (as young novelists tend to do), and he readily agreed to my request. His public notoriety as a sort of literary Marlon Brando was at low ebb that year, and scholarly attention to the scope of his work had yet to begin. He was feeling peevish and neglected by the world, and I (being four years younger) was still laboring under the illusion that critics could be educated, and that my book would do it. Though he was living in Northport, Long Island, and I was just across the Sound in Old Saybrook, Connecticut, he had been so grossly misquoted in the press by then that I suggested that we do our interview through the mails so that his answers to my questions would be absolutely accurate to his special way with language. He thought that was a good idea, and only stipulated that his replies be used in "their entirety" so as to reflect the way his mind went on as well.

The exchange took place in mid-June, and it consisted of two letters—my questions in the first (June 12, 1963), his answers in the second (dated only June). I have intermixed the letters here to join each query with its reply, but I have amended or excised nothing, except for a closing paragraph in my letter that would have confused the sequence. The exchange proved to be too long to work into the narrative essay that I eventually wrote, and it has remained in my files until now—an oddly formal, earnest, sometimes evasive Alphonse & Gaston routine between two friends, doing literary work, aware they are speaking for the record, but occasionally lapsing into the impatient shorthand of long acquaintance anyway.

When my book was published, with nothing of the interview included, he wrote to say that he felt "redeemed" by what I had written about him, and the two letters were never mentioned between us again. After he died in 1969, the tide of books about him began to rise, but good or bad (it seemed to me) few of them did proper justice to Kerouac's essential gravity and dedication as a writer. In any case it is the novelist rather than the "King of the Beats" who is reflected here. We were writing to each other as craftsmen in the same vocation, brothers in a common endeavor, and I offer this exchange now as evidence of the stubborn fidelity to his own purchase on the truth that motivates any writer serious enough to be taken seriously. I have retained Kerouac's original spelling and punctuation as well as my own. —JOHN CLELLON HOLMES

HOLMES: Nagging needle-nose notions first: Do you still see yourself as a shambler after people who interest you? Was it a mystery in those people that interested you? Something you couldn't immediately understand?

KEROUAC: When you're young and enthusiastic, and you're a writer, you should follow what it pleases your heart to follow and not what writing-coaches or even parents tell you to follow. My young friends were charming and charm is a mystery. Nowadays I wouldnt even shamble after the Aga Khan and his entire *hareem*.

HOLMES: *On the Road*— "He had fallen on the beat and evil days that come to young guys in their middle twenties." Did this happen to you? Why? For instance, I knew you then: what moulting occurs at that period? A last weaning? What? What in your case?

KEROUAC: Death of my father, hardship of my mother, myself ill, poor, working without hope of help or being published, meanwhile grubby jobs and the essential shame of hitch hiking.

HOLMES: In *On the Road*, you still see things in terms of superlatives, exuberance, "the most beautiful girl," "the greatest smile in all the world" etc.: after this book this kind of superlative begins to fade, you become more precise and yet sadder too. Was this simply a stylistic honing? A surer grip on your mind and meanings? Or a disapointment, a reconciliation?

KEROUAC: A disappointment. I was an imbecilically joyous healthy lad bent on thinking only "glad" thoughts but for deliberate philosophical reasons, in fact as a deliberate counter argument to Oswald Spengler and all his Late Civilization

Skepsis. Finally the world creeped up on me (especially after the publication of my books) and drove in the lesson. I get the message. I have a message I'll send back.

HOLMES: What does October mean to you? Time of work? Return to toil? End of seasons and irresponsibilities? October: a sobering time, the twilight of the year; metaphysical, waning, serious reds invest the world.

KEROUAC: October is when cold winds rattle your windowpane and you can wrap up in blankets and sleep again like a man of the North. October sweeps away the cobwebs of summer's essential cancerous fungoid diseasedness. I love the cold. My ancestors are from the North. Nietzsche said: "It is late October, the grapes are turning brown."

HOLMES: *On the Road*— "I want to marry a girl, so I can rest my soul with her till we both get old. This can't go on all the time—all this franticness and jumping around. We've got to go someplace, find something." I remember the country-family-farm end of *Town and City*, and it was your aim then, and re-echoed here: what happened? Why is Duluoz caught in the franticness? What immured him in franticness? What deluge of reality drowned his mind and its dream? There's a loss here somewhere, and it starts with the uprooting from Lowell, plunge into the ugliness of the World City, attraction to that against the will, though still hankering, and then (sometime in the early 50's—why do I feel it was Mexico-time 1952?) there is a subtle, somehow final shift. You attain yourself, your finest work is done during that time, but you are changed afterwards, and that particular hope (girl-home-god) wanes.

KEROUAC: "Girl-home-God" waned when a girl doubly betrayed me in the most horribly dishonest way imaginable. I hit the road and discovered I'd never really known how to "rest my soul" anyway, which is, by cultivating my own heart in solitude. "Be ye lamps unto thyselves," were Buddha's last reported words. Millions of silent hermits know this and need no "help" from anyone, thank you.

HOLMES: In *On the Road*, page 124— ". . . longing for death, the womb, the lost bliss . . ." Tell me about this longing, coming at the bottom of reality. And was it this, foreshadowed in you so long, that opened you to Buddhism when the time came?

KEROUAC: Everybody longs to have not been born at all whether they admit it or not. They remember the bliss of before they were born. S'why infants cry when they come outa the womb. You have to drag em screaming into our miserably "swell" party.

HOLMES: What does Dean-Neal-Cody's recurrent WE KNOW TIME signify? (I think I know, but tell me?)

KEROUAC: "We know time" applies to the beat of the clock, a jazz beat drumming the tune along to its end, the beat of the tires on the road getting us there, the beat of the heart, of the hammer, of events, appointments, getting things done, going on to new things, seasons, bing, bang, the beat in fact of an ordinary housewife's day or of a crazy crosscountry hipster's day, who cares? To question "WE KNOW TIME" is non-sequitur, everybody's running around like a bunch of chickens with their heads cut off anyway and *enjoying* it. When the freeway is wide open and everybody's rolling playing different radio stations and the announcers themselves are beating out commercials and tunes in a beat of their own, it's like a scene in Hell, which is what Time is.

HOLMES: *Visions of Cody*— ". . . as if Cody and I were construction workers not dissipates who dissipate so much it becomes a principle and finally a philosophy and finally a revelation." Do you see dissipation as an attaining-to-something, or as a relaxation-from-it? And even though of course BOTH, how do you view all our vast dissipations in light of our intentions and our basic seriousness? Are we irrevocably of two minds? I feel this break in you, this unceasing sense of division, even down to the fact that finally Duluoz is *not* Kerouac. Kerouac includes Duluoz but is very much more, Duluoz often does not understand but Kerouac, at the very moment of speaking in Duluoz' voice, does always see around him, and beyond. Can we, in our widest consciousness, only remain *in* life via the bridges and abysses of dissipation? Or what?

KEROUAC: "The pathway to wisdom lies through excess" (Blake? Goethe?) This, I say, applies to all artists in their youth who shall be worth their salt. *The derangement of the senses* has to be undergone at least once in a lifetime or the artist has not seen the other side of his consciousness, nay his conscience, really. Neal and I were both young devotees of Rimbaud as well as the barefooted Christ, fans of *On the Road* should know. The mature and quiet Raphael of later years in a Vatican apartment, do we know what secret dissipations and exesses occurred in his youth at some wayside inn in Bologna? Because "Dean" and I were *not* construction workers but wanted to be artists, therefore we dissipated on principle. Any ethic or esthetic which forbids this bids fair to turn art into government propaganda and artists into pencilchewing bureaucrats.

HOLMES: What happened in 1949? The "false understanding": was this New York, literary life, intellectualism, all seen by you as a verging from your real road? Was it the failures and exasperations of all that (681 Lex, Giroux, partying and pooping) that pivoted you "back into America," and thus towards Neal, Mexico, Sax, and your true self? In other words, I see pivots in your life: uprooting from Lowell and entrance into World City with its fevers, interests, ambitions, involvements, but you are basically still the youth after first weaning. Then in 1949, the choice between Fame & Cocktail parties and all that, and the "trucks on the road." Which, however, led to end-of-the-road Mexicos where everything became clear and blank: the last pivot turning you back, your brood has been on consciousness ever since, because the road ended after all, and the outer world has only distracted and momentarily interested you since; when you went down into yourself in *Sax* you came back forever different; no major pivot really since then; only losses and exasperations and Melville's unfolding of the onion day after day, but the onion is yourself at last. What of these pivots?

KEROUAC: In 1949 I saw that a writer can become a sort of society figure as long as he observes the rules more or less, can, in fact, become a criminal among the rich, that is, a criminal bullshiter. When I say "rich" (and I left "rich" in there because I like the poetic sound of "a criminal among the rich") I mean those people who actually collect priceless *objects d'art* to place around their homes and would fain do so with celebrated humanbeings also. I can just see Thomas Wolfe or even Gregory Corso dipped in bronze and placed smack in the foyer of a wealthy lady's home. Even the "poor" collect things, of course, but anyway I got scared, got a sensation of dullness hovering about, I was bored and eager to get back to my earlier studies, so I went back to what I romantically and naively called "The American Road Night" (a pose) but which I realize now was just my own goofy ideas. *My own goofy ideas*, Sir! Otherwise what? O shit, I just wasnt having any fun (in the lionized scene). Essentially I'm a narrative reporter and had to go resume the coverage of my story which at the time was Dean and the western gang, that's all.

HOLMES: *Visions of Cody*— ". . . this lifelong monolog which is begun in my mind": and it WAS begun then in 1951, seems to me. You cast off home, Joan, literary hopes, etc., went down into yourself, "who is the dark youth going there, sketching, sketching." Because you HAD given up something, and your work truly begins then, your best work, your own acceptance of your own particular consciousness. What happened to cause it? No abstraction please: Vet Hosp.? end of marriage? some crisis of emotions (Joan vs. Memere?) stands behind *V.O.C.*, triggering it. You've made a choice which made you yourself. The next works you did (*V.O.C.* and *Sax*) are maybe the best of all. Some interior balance was at its most certain and most precarious, and even when you write some about that year later in *Traveler* a little of the astonishing verbal depth (you never went deeper, soared higher) touches the account. Am I nuts?

KEROUAC: Yes in the Vet hospital. I had time to think at last *without interruptión* and unfolded my secret desire in writing at last:—to tell exactly what happened and not worry about style but only worry about completeness of detail and the hell with what anybody thinks. In fact I didnt dream any of it would ever be published except in the madhouse. I stood in front of a bakery window in the cold winter one night scribbling furiously everything I saw, down to the last coconut cake cherry. People thought I was . . . what?

(No order salesman would ever scribble so much and so fast and look like I did.) Then I rushed into my Ma's house and went on scribbling from memory the visions of other things I'd seen on the street that night. I knew I had it but I was ashamed that I was not going to help my mother in this mad new way of writing, which I called "sketching." That was the beginning of spontaneous prose, October 1951.

HOLMES: *Visions of Cody*— ". . . back to the sense of life I had as a child uncomplainingly getting up at seven in the morn to go to school and on Saturdays joyously to go play, etc." ("Back to the open air of the world"): where was that joy misplaced, lost, or is it just growing of which you speak here? The rainy days of boyhood unreachable from the bleak bored afternoons of manhood? Or was it certainty, warmth, immediacy, the uncorrupted eye, and finally no-split-between-the-hope-and-the-eye? The consciousness orphans us from the simple terrors and richnesses of the unconscious, and we are of two minds after that.

KEROUAC: The moments of joy in childhood? Sounds like a question in *Readers Digest*. I've felt joy since, on whiskey, off whiskey, who cares? The universe pours moments of joy all around:—exaltation comes and goes like *tics*, among sorrows, O among sorrows.

HOLMES: Were you reading Joyce before or during *Dr Sax*? Dumb questions of influence are a drag, but seem unavoidable in this book. Here all the levels of consciousness mix and mell and fuse; here the child's sense of place, the surreality of imaginings and the absolute reality of the wrinkly tar, all wash together, with elaborate verbal funning, horrors of your own out of pulp mags and Draculas, the precise far-off voices of family talks, the weird satires of Count Condu etc., all exist similtaneously, and I must ask about Joyce's shadow on this book. (On re-reading, by the by, this seems one of the surest, deepest books you've done: the keys are here, and do you realize the reliance on one-syllable adjectives that gives the prose itself a hard, graphic ba-ba-ba-doom beat that is incredible?) Was this the beginning of spontaneous-prose (and I want no esthetic explanations of that, you know what I mean)?

KEROUAC: I was not influenced by Joyce in *Doctor Sax* but actually by Proust, whom I'd just been avidly studying with Neal in Frisco. The detailed recollections etc. but I was prepared to swing them out fast. I wrote the entire book in Bill Burroughs' bathroom, no other place was private, therefore all the references to urine, by the way, which Malcolm Cowley wondered about. The vision of the Snake and the Flood occurred one mysterious October night when my windows were rattling in Ozone Park 1948:—I saw the Snake's big mountainhead in the deeps leering up at me, Jesus you shoulda seen my eyes wide open as I sat on the edge of the bed. Sax, of course, is The Shadow who is also myself because I used to play the shadow, and Dracula and all come from old movies. Old Bull Baloon is W. C. Fields who used to actually play poker with my father backstage on the B. F. Keith's circuit. The mixing and melling really comes from Melville's *Confidence Man* mysterious mellings, and from general education in melling, from Spenser, *Walpurgisnacht*, Kafka and all the rest, and yes, from the levels in *Finnegans Wake* and levels everywhere, my dear. Specifically, though, the last mad parts that jump and dance and make faces were influenced (the very afternoon before) by my seeing the movie of *Alice in Wonderland*, the color one of about 1950.

HOLMES: *Dr Sax*— "I understood mysticism at once": how old were you then? Tell me more about this understanding? Care to give me a line or two to add to this, that you might have put in then, except you had other things to do?

KEROUAC: When the nuns told me the thunder was a ball, I was eight. They said a *white* ball appeared in their window as they sat knitting in the convent. (It was probably what mountain fire lookouts call "St. Elmo's Dance," a peculiarity of lightning.) This simple, almost sorrowful mysticism is very common among the matter-of-fact Medieval French Canadians who preserved such things for centuries in Quebec while France went "encyclopedic" and "rational" and "enlightened" and "pragmatic" and finally "existentialist," hor hor hor. (Incidentally the Quebecois also preserved Medieval French pronunciation.)

HOLMES: Did your Catholicism loosen to secret doubts with Gerard's death, or thoughts about it afterwards? You seem to imply something like this in *Sax*. Tell me about your dealings with faith? (mwee he he he he ha ha!)

KEROUAC: My Catholicism *began* with Gerard's death, after all I was only four. All this past winter I've been praying to the Virgin Mary but lately the Supreme Court has begun to scare me. Nevertheless I still "wink" at Her when I pass. I think she nodded at me last October. I know there are all kinds of explanations about superstition and clinging to early training, but what is there so un-superstitious about the explanations of psychologists who dont even know that what they're saying is only a new kind of superstition? "Smith did not face the realities of life." Smith did not face the realities of *what*? And the "*realities*"? Not even Einstein, Lucretius, Gotama, Molière, Shakespeare or who you'll have . . . the *realities*? In their own superstitious way they never heard of the word used like that. Did you ever see how completely "irrational" people sometimes live lives of sweet gentleness and peace somehow? It's because of grace. "The people of Denver," complained a mining engineer around 1850 or so, "are too happy to know what they've got here." They were in a state of grace. My faith is this:—grace is when you're as you were, like in the Army, "As you were!", and not as you might be. The pragmatic Pavlovian dialectical materialist psychologists of this world are all standing at attention while a lot of the people of the world are at ease, because of grace, which is free, see. Free from Heaven. Thus my faith.

HOLMES: Why is the color BROWN the color of your boyhood? It reoccurs throughout *Sax*, and is the color of the 30's too, and books, and shadows, and your mother's bathrobe, and a dozen other things. Does it hold loss, twilight, severance from warmth, and all that the river swept away? And the mysterious and heavy weight of books?

KEROUAC: Yes. Chairs were brown, many houses and tenements were painted brown, and my mother's bathrobe was brown when I was an infant in her arms, the river was brown in spring, even our kitchen table was brown mahogany, the

radio too with its big brown paper speaker, all, all brown—
The 1930's were brown because also not yet all that antiseptic
white of today—also streetlamps were brown compared to
some of the eerie blue white ones of today which obscure
the stars of night. But dark laughter will come again, O
Sherwood Anderson of the brown Ohia. . . . Whiteness
and antiseptic light of today is also as tho we were all being
grilled by brainwash police.

HOLMES: What was the Castle in actuality? Was there a Castle,
or just an old shit-littered house? Or is it all an imagining? How was it metamorphosed in your mind? And SAX
HIMSELF? God, Fields, Pa, the first muttering, interesting,
enigmatic person you shambled after?

KEROUAC: There was a big spooky stone mansion next door to
where I was born on Lupine Road on the Centreville Hill.
The idea of Sax is that the Great World Snake of Evil, or,
Satan, shall be released by the dark forces of the Great World
Castle which is located on the hill of my birth. This meant
that I considered my birth and all birth as evil. The Arabs
say "Rejoice at a funeral, weep at a birth of a newborn" or
to that effect. Also notice where I say near the end of *Doctor
Sax* "The neck of the world was free." This was because I had
a boil on my neck once, at 16, my mother finally squeezed
it out after three days of packs and compresses, she gave a
yell as it leaped out at her like a snake. Small wonder I'm
convinced that flesh is corrupt as well as corruptible, awful
disgusting in fact, and that at 24 after my father's death I
kept singing the Gershwins' "Why Was I Born?" (to which
my poor mother objected, you see). Maybe I shoulda been
a doctor.

HOLMES: Hateful query now: *Sax can* be read as a masturba-
tory guilt fantasy (World Snake: penis. Seminal doves. The
horror of WHITE (sperm) which runs through the book.
Sax himself: midnight, skulking, muttering Sex. And the
universe disposes of its own Evil when Aztec-Lawrence Bird
of Heaven castrates the threatening Snake, the worm in the
Apple of the World, wrenching Jackie out of innocence into
puberty's dark, double reality, sin became real (though at the

end the rose is entwined in the hair—By God). What is this fantastic wrestle with Evil, Knowledge, etc. to you NOW? Certainly, it's no mere spoof, despite its trappings, but rather as if you fought through fear and guilt of Catholicism to acceptance of the befuddled, complex loneliness of pre-adult life. Is this all errant, PR crap on my part?

KEROUAC: The sperm is *it*, Satan. We always think of Snakes Spitting Venom. The Bird of Paradise takes care of all this by carrying it away, as will happen. As will happen in the Golden Eternity. And Catholicism has every good reason in the world to look upon life with guilt and even fear, as *you* would if you were watching Nero's games or just a bullfight or an ordinary Congolese or even Zurich street riot. Now *I've* got a migraine.

HOLMES: *Now relax a while; put on Pontificating Hat*: Your statement, "I don't know, and I don't care, and it doesn't make any difference" has been more misunderstood than anything you've said, always interpreted as a social-anti-credo, a disavowment, a know-nothingism. Though I think it says exactly what it means, can you add to it, comment on it, put it in its proper context?

KEROUAC: It's just what you say to yourself when you cant figure it out any more, nothing, anything, and you have to give it up and make breakfast and carry on somehow, like everybody else in the world. *It's the despairing cry of a philosopher giving up*, dont you all see that? Because . . . so what difference would it make if I, J. K., *did* know and *did care to know* and it *did* make a difference. —Alan Watts was jealous of this line, it enraged him at first. It's pure Zen. It means "Well zen I dont know." And I don't know. I dont know why I killed that roaring mouse. —"Know-nothingism" is an expression which is used among specialists at Harvard and Princeton: if you dont know what *Leuconostoc mesenterioides* means, maybe you're a big smart knower who knows what C to the sixth power and H to the fifth power, cubed, plus C-COOH, comes to, but I know something too:—Cooh you too. Thoreau went to Harvard.

HOLMES: You've said that each book is a "piece of the whole," but how does each book come to you? Does a segment of The Experience coalesce in your imagination, seem to have "poetic" form or shape? Or does a single image come to you, perhaps an event at the center of the action, around which you group everything else that happened and seems to be germane? More or less as Faulkner once described the germination of *Sound and Fury* as the single image of a girl, shimmied up a tree, peeking in an upstairs window, her muddy drawers being observed by her little brother lower on the tree. He went on to discover what led up to, and away from, this single image. Comment on that in terms of your arbitrary cutting of the Legend into suitable *lengths*.

KEROUAC: Yes, the urge to write, the very *tic* that sprung pencil out for *Doctor Sax* germinated right smack from that "wrinkly tar" dream, just as Faulkner's tree-girl image gave him a thrill to write his way into *The Sound and the Fury*, but I'd already pre-written and mediated the "plot" long before so I just rolled it right off in three weeks. However, I have to cut the "Duluoz Legend" into suitable chronological lengths—I just couldnt pour the whole thing into one mould, if I did it would be a big round ball instead of figures. I suppose Lipschitz thought of this, one final big round ball sitting on a pedestal. But no, he divided his ball. Would Mozart blam all the 86 keys of the piano at once with his 86 fingers? or divide his ball into suitable symphonies, concerti, sonatas, serenatas, masses, dances, oratorios . . .

HOLMES: What about spontaneous prose, "the book-movie" etc.? Tell me the whys of it, and when it came to you. I don't need a JUSTIFICATION of it as a method; but Í'd like an EXPLANATION of why and how you arrived at it as *your* way; and when; I remember the anal, Giroux, one-sentence-an-hour, Melville-of-the-Pierres, FIRST attempt at *On the Road*, that so boggled you (nights in Glennon's reading enormous, complex, exfoliating sentences of pot-perception), and that finally led to you sitting down (in Chelsea with a roll of paper) to just BLOW the book; it seems the breakthru happens (as it does in Zen) out of that strive, anxiety, concentration on the koan, until finally a what-the-hell, not-for-me exasperation pushed you over the top into satori-prose, and simply putting-down-what-was-there in continual, unbroken onrush. Is true? Tell me the moody history of your style. (And rooftops of Mexico at the bottom of your self and the world, that turned you to poetry. Plus the goad of bop, words commensurate to the onrush of your mind; syllables to fit the elisions & veers of consciousness; how you found the bone—indeed, what the hell happened in Mexico, or was it there? I'm confused.)

KEROUAC: Bookmovies . . . I kept staring at the screen in movies but staring at the white electrical particles instead of the story, then I'd wake up and see there were actual events and noise going on with everybody in the audience avidly interested like children in a madhouse, in what was "going on." Out of this profound insight into the art of the cinema, I decided to invent movies that would be complete movies but in words on a page, not just a scenario. They would be complete movies about the completeness of everything, with parentheses even. People would be able to look at my page and become the camera themselves and even see *unphotographable* moviettes within the movie. This is my most ambitious invention and is only the first step to the complete movie of the future when people will actually be able to see the movie going on in another man's mind, with headsets connected to encephalographic equipments, and instead of saying "Think I'll read some Faulkner" you'll say "Oh hum, think I'll tune in some Faulkner" and adjust the Faulkner Telepath Tape and adjust your headphone nodules and just lie back and see and feel substantially what you see and feel in your own dreams, with variations. Tuning in on cretins will be especialy tasty at this time. There will be no more geniuses. Only Telepath Set repairmen. —Spontaneous prose explanation is in "Essentials of Spontaneous Prose," all there, except the courage to really go ahead and *do* it came to me while I was listening to Lee Konitz take on "I Remember April" from the middle of it somehow, the "pithy middle eye," and ripple and swim right out of it carrying it shining on his horn (all, all a long story) triumphant, the tune in his pocket, October night 1951. I swore in my notebook right there in the dim blue lights of Birdland "Blow As Deep As You Want To Blow." . . . American writers would shrivel up and never write an honest word again if they listened to the critics who call everything silly no matter what it is—John, if critics say your work stinks it's because they want it to stink and they can make it stink by scaring you into conformity with their comfortable little standards, standards so low that they can no longer be considered "dangerous" but set in place in their compartmental understanding—*Do* what they say, i.e., either die and get out of sight, or write their way—This leaves you no nub of heart—So the only way to continue is the way you've discovered—If you dont like what you write, start all over again, go back to the beginning—I say this with respect to narrative writing, not to research writing, of course—The mind *is* spontaneity and no doubt about that whatever and this is the only possible ethic for the future of man and his thinking and story writing—The rest is dishonesty, unintelligence, dullness, cant, repetitiousness, imitation of ignorance—How fast is spontaneity? Just as fast as God sends the statement, is all—No faster. And remember that a story is a poem and a poem is a story.

HOLMES: Baldwin, and most other negroes, have complained about your "wishing to be a negro, etc." Denver night in O.T.R. They accuse you of being Crow-Jim, romantic, ado-lescent, and dare you to read that paragraph in the Savoy. Answer them through me. Indeed, tell me about what negroes have meant to you, expatiate, and I don't mean on any foolish social-cum-liberal level. Why are we all such unhappy white-men, and, searching something, enamored of the joy-without-cause we feel in negroes and others? Tell me off, Merlin.

KEROUAC: I *was* romantic when I wrote that line and I meant it when I wrote it. I was a kid and I wanted to have more fun in Denver that night in 1949. James Baldwin wants to stir up as much interest in his Civil Rights fight as he can, get everybody involved, all the writers probably, but I have no time for politics, just Art.

HOLMES: And now, Buddhism. (No snap-judgements here,

please.) Where are you now? What lies ahead for us? (I often feel that some sort of Buddhism lies ahead for the West like a fatality.) What drives us to it? What moulting of the consciousness has carried us all beyond the either/or of the Faustian intelligence? What sustains you, now, through your day—you've always carried on a dialogue with the Unseen. What in God's name orphaned you so from the silly involvements you describe some of your boyhood friends as growing into? It happened back there in the dark.

KEROUAC: No Buddhism at all lies ahead for the "West," but, just as you call it: the either-or of Faustianism. Space-exploration is pure Faust, the Gothic Spire has taken off from the gantry and is going where it was meant to go, into the heavens. The essential Faustian person is of course German—von Braun is Faust at work, his colleagues in Russia too. Buddhism (Chan, Zen) is of no concern whatever to anybody in the "West" but powerless scholars and solitaries. However, Buddhism will thus be carried to other planets eventually. Buddhism, is, in fact, all *about* endless chiliocosms. So maybe the Faustian West is the Vehicle itself in disguise. The Space Vehicle with the Bodhisattva inside etc. It's just too huge a subject to fit into your book as an "answer," Jesus God!

HOLMES: Personal one-sentence (or more if you care to) takes on your mind: object—to triangulate you in the world:

what do you think of:

Lenny Bruce	Mailer	Baldwin
Genet	Burroughs	Gelber
Thelonious	Algren	Rauschenberg
Salinger	J. Jones	Kennedy
Ornette	Rechy	Evtuschenko
Ray Charles	Styron	Snyder
Mort Sahl	Sartre	John Cage
Existentialism	Zen	Reich
Cunnilingus	Castro	Sade
Spengler	Lawrence	LSD
etc.	etc.	etc.

KEROUAC: I prefer not to. Beethoven, deaf, listened to the light.

HOLMES: How do you place yourself (without secret pride *or* humility) in American literature? Whose son are you? What is your word to the world, in connection with such things as Cold War, Communism, Atom Bomb, twilight of Gods, human dilemmas of 20th century? You get the idea: what are we to *do*, Kerouac?

KEROUAC: I cant rank myself till I see what more I write, if any.—What is the world to *do*? Individuals should sleep more, really, and be alone more.

HOLMES: Place Neal, for once and all (and not just NOW, but what he meant to you once, how it changed), in YOUR vision. Neal, it seems, to me at least, was at once himself to you, but also he represented something, he embodied something, and it changed and deepened as you went along, but always it was essentially the SAME thing. What was it, as you look back? Was it Neal's way with reality? The hope in that way? I'm not reducing you or your work to ONE thing, but Neal is the secret after which you ran so long, or he embodied it. What was it?

KEROUAC: Neal hasnt changed, for me, any more than Dr. Samuel Johnson ever changed for James Boswell. We had a few tiffs over money just as Johnson and Boswell had a few tiffs over protocol but they never lasted as tiffs. The fact that Neal no longer writes letters or cards to *anybody* is perfectly alright with me and could've been foretold. I'm essentially his biographer for life. He reminds me of my lost brother who died when I was 4 and at the same time he reminds me of my father very much. Both Neal and I are Kelts. If Kelts was spelled with a "C" our names would be Serouac and Sassady. My name Kerouac is Cornish in origin, means "House in the Moor" in Brythonic Keltic. His name is Goidelic Keltic. He *leaves me alone*, like no one else does, by that I mean, when I'm with him there's no need to talk or cater or pester. We just sorta suffer together in silence. Of course, when we talk there'll be torrents. Another Kelt I know leaves me alone like that, I mean Lou. Neal has the biggest brain of us all, at least as high-perfect as Lou. And Neal's "way with reality" is straight, busy, hilariously complicated, Chaplinesque, innocent, exasperated, hopeful, comically sneaky

sometimes . . . like a caricature of mankind but without a
trace of pride, fatuous "reserve" or any of the hypocritical
snips of mankind I never could stand. He sees in me a dopey
brother, almost like Laurel to his Hardy, but you'll notice
Hardy really loved Laurel above all men. So all's always well
in the end with "Dean and Sal."

HOLMES: Is Ginsberg the Wizard that *cast* a spell or *dissolved*
it? Evil AND knowledge? Worldliness? What? Disentangling
who influenced who most is all but impossible, but I see his
figure in Columbia Halls, I see him throwing ponderous
dark books at your head, pelting you with complexities and
sniggering all the while, only to become grave (himself),
sobered perhaps by you, until now you two run in separate
grooves, but ominously side by side, though a world away.
And yet it was YOU broke him out of the strangulations that
followed his hospitalization. Or am I again over-simplifying?
Women; tell me about women? Do you idealize them?
Exclude them? Are you *seasonal*, for Christ's sake? I remember in letters your celibacy of Mexico-Buddhism: did you
see sex as distraction, evil, betrayal? Pardon the intimacies.

KEROUAC: When I met Ginsberg I'd already "read everything,"
but from the point of view of the heterosexual poet, say. He
taught me the nether, or other side, anyway, of poetry (he
and Burroughs and Herbert Huncke). One of the few "dark
books" thrown at me by Allen was Genet. I could never
have understod Genet without some kind of insight into
the classical homosexual mentality, nor Gide and the others
for that matter, nor Rimbaud above all. For instance I was
now able to compare the relationship of Uncle Edouard and
Bernard in *The Counterfeiters*, to the relationship of Prince
Myshkin and Ippolit in *The Idiot*, and see something about
the difference between lechery and compassion among men,
or facsimiles thereof. It's ridiculous of Colin Wilson to think
that I ever had anything to do actively with a homosexual
"camp." I was an observer. Ginsberg did indeed "pelt" me
with complexities not the least of which was the surrealistic
liberation from literary armor, for which I am most grateful.
So, and but, here he came with Rimbaud and Verlaine under
one arm, Hart Crane and Genet under the other, and at

his sublimest moments Blake and Dante, and he taught me the Metropolitan New York Poetry Underworld *Crise*: while with Whitman and Wolfe under one arm, and Joyce and Shakespeare under the other, I taught him the countryside glance.

HOLMES: Finally, a superceded confession, me to you: for years I honestly (and with real pain) felt you could not live much beyond forty. It seemed to me that your brain and spirit would be pulverized with all they had to carry; that even your physical toughness would have to shrivel; and, frankly, I had years of premonition of your death. You'd just die one day, too soon, having simply USED everything up: it didn't seem to me you could go on (because we all DO go on by the degree of consciousness-grip we have on hopes and possibilities) and you seemed to be exhausting them one by one, burning yourself up in your own mind; and I had actual moment-to-moment depression to think that you could not be saved (not FROM anything, but FOR yourself, some peace of achievement and satisfaction that you'd earned), and that (just privately) you'd vanish out of MY world—goad that you were, inconstant that you seemed, exemplar and buddy, the brother I'd never had whose role you filled for me to rage against, and brood on, and elevate and put down; all *that*, the honest picture of you I've carried in my head these years. But that you'd vanish, just die out of it all: I've had that clear certainty, hateful to me, for years; and yet, reading the books these past days, that TOO has fluttered away into a husk of black-birds, and I see it as only the dire, Germanic, Dostoyevskian, exacerbated drama of my OWN mind, and that you carry what you carry in your own gait, and I don't (finally) know what you'll do, or how you'll end, and that what prevented me from ever really *understanding* you was the very lust to understand which proved to be nothing but MY image of you, and not you at all. Now I don't think you'll die, or maybe you will but it won't be any inky tragic collapse of any doomed hero-of-art, from which the world will recoil with tardy understanding. But you've been dead in my imagination, even in some dreams, and I thought I'd tell you . . . Something more may come of this.

BEAT SPOTLIGHT

Beat Spotlight

Beat Spotlight (circa 1968) is the last of Kerouac's scroll compositions, running to approximately three feet in length. An incomplete but fascinating fragment, *Beat Spotlight* juxtaposes the humble printing business of Kerouac's father in Lowell, Massachusetts, with the media scrutiny experienced by Kerouac following the publication of *On the Road*, the glare of the "Beat spotlight." It's also a final statement of Kerouac's aesthetic aims, as he compares his lifework as a literary artist to the aspirations embodied in the printer's scrapbook of his father, described as a "a vast and memorable legend of early 20th century America." Something quite similar can of course be said of the impressive and voluminous achievement of Kerouac's own memory project. As he nears the end of his life, Kerouac counterpoises the ambitious scope of that achievement against persistent misrepresentations of his work, as instanced in a visit by "two flippant middleclass American journalists."

W HEN I WASNT EVEN BORN and no one knew what my face
looked like, around 1921, my father Leo Kerouac used to
publish and edit a weekly newspaper called *The Spotlight* in
Lowell Massachusetts featuring ads of the latest movies (William S. Hart, Conway Tearle, Theda Bara) which he himself
designed and sometimes he'd come home late at night riding
on the side car of his linotypist's motorcycle and show his four-
year-old son Gerard how to draw the boxes and draw in the
names of the actors and the movie titles, I know because he
used to do that for me only a few years later. *The Spotlight* also
included local business news, theatrical news, a funny column
he himself composed in which he and "Tillie the Wife" would
go out to movies every Friday night and what they said as they
walked out at eleven under the darkening marquee. "Tillie"
was supposed to be my mother in a sense but actually "Tillie"
had a Brooklyn accent but the kind of Brooklyn accent only a
French Canadian 1920 smalltown businessman could imagine.
Around 1921 *The Spotlight* was doing so good my father was
able to afford to put up a big poster sign over the Chinese
Restaurant in the center of town, right on the roof, showing
the shadow of a big fat man in a swivel chair smoking a cigar,
and the words *The Spotlight*. The Chinese Restaurant was Chin
Lee's and Chin Lee himself was a good friend of my father's
who used to play cards with him till dawn and on every Christmas sent us either a Ming Vase, or boxes of strange lichee nuts
and Chinese candy imported from Canton. I remember vaguely
now, seeing that giant fat man shadow with the cigar in the
swivel chair overlooking Kearney Square in Lowell in the old
lights of that time's city night. For many years as I moved from
New England to New York to the South to the West and back
again I kept possession of old editions of *The Spotlight* which
my father'd pasted into a huge scrapbook 4 foot by 4 foot but
it finally got lost somewhere in Carolina tho by that time the
paper had turned crinkly brown. Somewhere in that vast and
memorable legend of early 20th Century America was a small
brown crinkly notice of my birth written like in the following
terms by my father: "Had a new kid this weekend, called him

Jean-Louis, gave Charley Connors a cigar." The reason why I say no one knew what my face looked like before I was born is in reference to the famous Zen question "What did your face look like before you were born?" Recently in San Francisco I had a very interesting meeting with some Chinese gentlemen of the same family, father and son, and I can't help thinking that there's a connection between big Shadowy Leo the Spotlight with his Chinese friends, and myself with mine. But I shudder to think what Big Shadowy Leo My Pop would have said to see what the newspapers of America said about me when my books were published and I came into the glare of the "Beat Spotlight." And that if I myself were publishing a weekly newspaper nowadays (and he could have left me all his printing presses but lost them all on the horses) I would only be able to call it the "Beat Spotlight." It all started when I came to New York City on Sept. 3 1957 to see what had happened with the publication of one of my early books, *Road*, books I had written in poverty and some of them in self-imposed exile with no hope of ever seeing them published but only writing them because I thought it was my duty on earth to tell the story of what happened to some of the people I knew. Because of my early training in the Catholic Church, the extremely mystical experience of First Communion and First Confirmation, there was imbedded in my believing tho confused head a belief that life was holy, that I should write about it pointing out the holiness throughout the squalor and commonplaceness, that the very streets of life were holy, that somehow the eager faces and tortured mouths of my compatriots in the American Night of my experience meant much more than the "facts" adduced, that like Dostoevsky I was doomed to suffer out all my life to "draw breath in pain" and tell their stories, that in the idealism of this endeavor somehow I would be rewarded someday, that I would be justified and my people be justified (my heroes in the various stories, the road characters, the dharma bums, the subterraneans, the desolation angels, all the rest), that my father might gladly look back from his grave at what I had decided to do with his legacy, that my brother Gerard also would bless me, that there was nothing nobler in the world for me to do with my lifetime than to dedicate it to telling true stories about life as I had seen and lived it. And that anyway there was nothing else to do to believe in because I was so bloody bored in the oldest French sense meant by Baudelaire and called in French "ennui," or "ennuyez." Nothing in college had taught me any of this. After years of trying to invent a system of making up stories about American life I suddenly in 1951 in despair gripped my head, stared at the floor, ran to the typewriter, slipped a long roll of paper through and started to type out the true story of what actually happened, all fiction forgotten and all tricks of afterthought and revision forgotten so that when I told my true story it would be like telling it through an ordeal of fire, either get out of it right away for once and for all, or get burned. So I fought through the ordeal of fire to tell the *Road* story and simply presented it that way, as it was, to the publishers. For six years they shook their heads over the manuscript. Finally they went ahead and published it but first behind my back and without my knowledge they made a few "changes." They took out some scenes they thought were irrelevant, such as love scenes between actual lovers, or "dirty words" here and there, and generally applied what they call their "house style" over the narrative rush of my story. But nevertheless the crazy true story shone through. But I didnt think it would make any difference anyway. At the time I was living in poverty with my mother on a back porch apartment in Orlando Florida which was blessed by a huge ancient tree that cast some shade but cursed by a tin roof that let all the late afternoon western sun heat sink into our kitchen and so when we ran our broken fan it only blew hot heat. But in those days we somehow enjoyed our pre-dinner cheap port wine and our hamburger suppers and our after-dinner pecan sandy cookies and the few blips of cool night air that came. It was Sept. 3rd when I was invaded by some reporters who said they were from *Time* magazine saying that my book was being published in New York and they wanted to take my picture. But I had just gotten back from a useless bus trip to Mexico City (more about that later in harkening back) and had somehow got sick down there on some kind of mumps, or dehydration, or something, so that I could hardly stand up my parts were so swollen. It was awful. In all the utter seriousness of my life suddenly walked in these two flippant middleclass American journalists wondering if the reason I looked so sick wasn't because I was drunk, or a

dope addict, or just naturally depraved. They took my picture
sitting there weakly in a rocking chair. They went off and
mailed the pictures to *Time* magazine in New York. The literary editor on that end, not knowing that I am the son of a huge
black shadow called *The Spotlight*, simply threw in his precon-
ceived angry opinions about me, comparing me to a noncha-
lant gumchewing hood with a switchblade and a black leather
motorcycle or a black leather road or something, and let it go
at that. But at the time I still did not understand the significance of this journalistic nonchalance of theirs because I was
still involved in the questions of my own work and its mainly
"holy" impact on my own belief in myself. The night of Sept.
3 1957 before I was to take the train to New York, and after the
photographers had left my mother's little backporch flat, I was
reading Dante's *Divine Comedy* trying to figure out what he
meant by the Leopard being the Incontinence of worldly pleasure, the Lion the violence of Ambition, the wolf the fraud of
avarice, and Lucia being the patroness for the blind (she the
illuminating grace). Or that Rachel was the "contemplative
life," or that St. Paul was the "chosen vessel," or that Beatrice
(whom I'd read about before in *Vita Nuova*) was Divine
Wisdom itself saying with luminous eyes "I come from a place
where I desire to return." I thought that with the writing of
my half dozen books, the acceptance of the first one now, to
be published in the morrow, I had come to the highest point
of mature human understanding of the world as it is. So I
blithely continued with my studies and planned further books.
Something disquieting about the questions of the newspaper
people slipped back to my forgetful half of brain. I thought that
my redeeming wit could measure against all the Ciacco hogs
of Hell. A good wolf is better than a bad lamb. I'd come sooty
off freight trains in California and run into jazz joints yelling
for more music and nobody'd ever noticed. The only spotlight
ever trained on me so far was by cops in the Arizona desert
wondering where I was going with my full pack at 2 A.M. in the
red moon, only a year ago. But these newspaper people had
seemed strange, like members from the United Nations or
something, with their elegant tones coupled irrationally with
vulgar questions like "Do you believe in people being hurt?"
"Did I ever say I wanted people to be hurt? in that book?" "Just

asking" and down goes the note. Or: "What have you got against America?" "What have I got against America my God it's the only thing I write about? What do you mean?" "Are you Slavic?" "I certainly am not, I'm a Celt." "Doesnt sound like a Celtic name?" "It's an old Breton name older than Ireland." "Are you sure?" Then they'd ask: "What have you got against responsibility?" and so on until I really became confused wondering what they really meant. But I was about to find out as I came to New York and fell into the Beat Spotlight for three years.

It wasnt until I got to New York I realized what was really going on with all this alien business of asking me questions about things I'd never thought about, as tho I should have presumed to understand America from just a few hitch hiking and railroad adventures in the night (or old college and high school and football adventures, or even early drunken seaman adventures). There was something going on in America I was about to learn. But meanwhile it seems to me today rather ironic that on the night of my departure to all this in New York I should have been studying Dante's leopard of incontinence because with the publication of *Road* I became drunk for almost 3 months (and the papers mentioned it and omitted it not). And Dante's lion of ambition because the money suddenly started to pour in and I answered the requests of everyone to write for money. And Dante's wolf of avarice, goes with it. But let's look at me now as I arrive in New York, still rolling my own cigarettes with Bull Durham paper to save money, scratching through a Sept. 4 New York trash can looking for a newspaper to see what kind of reviews *Road* got from the literary critics. Not a thing in sight. Old papers covered with spit. So I trudge to the publishers office.

It was also something that was about to be understood by my poet friend Allen Ginsberg who received a *Life* reporter several years later in his apartment on the Lower East Side of New York (just a kitchen with a kitchen bathtub and two back rooms) and the reporter said "I've come here to write your story and the story of the Beats but I'm not going to be sympathetic." "Then why have you come here?" asks Allen.

"And in fact," he adds, "you look evil to me. Why dont you just leave?"—But the writer stayed and smiled that "chatty" commuters' chatty smile, I mean that smile you see among welldressed men in suits and neckties carrying hard leather briefcases but their eyes are slitted and they're all pouring into Grand Central station from their jobs on Madison Avenue and Fifth and elsewhere, something in America that's almost as archaic now as I think of it as the extended beak of the Cro Magnon horse on a cave—"I've come to write some nasty news about you whether you like it or not and I'm staying"—"But why dont you leave?" insisted Allen—

APPENDIX

I WISH I WERE YOU

I Wish I Were You

While living in New York in 1944, Kerouac was introduced to William Burroughs, Allen Ginsberg, and David Kammerer by a Columbia University undergraduate, Lucien Carr. Carr was the impious sun around which the nascent Beat Movement had revolved. In August of 1944, however, Carr stabbed Kammerer to death in Riverside Park, claiming that he was acting in self-defense against the elder Kammerer's decade-long sexual stalking. In the days following Kammerer's death, both Kerouac and Burroughs were arrested as accessories after the fact, as neither had reported his knowledge of the killing to the police. Those charges were nullified when Carr was charged with manslaughter rather than murder.

Kammerer's death provided the material for *And the Hippos Were Boiled in Their Tanks*, a hardboiled novel collaboratively composed by Kerouac and Burroughs in 1945 (and published by Grove Press in 2008). Writing the book in alternating chapters—under the pseudonyms Mike Ryko and Will Dennison—Kerouac and Burroughs created the first major literary work of the New York Beat Movement. It records an impression of 1940s New York bohemia in blunt, streetwise American prose reminiscent of Raymond Chandler and Dashiell Hammett. In a March 1945 letter to his sister Caroline, Kerouac identified the work as "a portrait of the 'lost' segment of our generation, hardboiled, honest, and sensationally real." Publishers, including Simon and Schuster, did not share this glowing assessment, and after a round of rejections Kerouac set about transforming *Hippos* into *I Wish I Were You*, on which he worked until August 1945.

CHAPTER ONE

W E ARE ALL THE POSSESSORS of a certain courage, that's
it. Provide for the fact that we insist on using that flimsy
word, and here's a truth; not a truth to open eyes, certainly,
but a dismal human fact for all it's worth. Courage!—that's the
word as we use it. At that time, as now, we were all possessed
of our certain eccentric little courage. Will Dennison knew
when it was time to go to bed, and did. Ramsey Allen preferred
death to life as long as life didn't respond to a certain whim.
Phillip Tourian . . . he had the maddest courage of them all: he
searched the four corners of New York City in a quest which
he called an "investigation of our culture," and never slept!
Michael Ryko liked to sleep and face his nightmares, with a
kind of lazy curiosity: the rest of the time, he was either drunk
or just dozing. (I think his courage was the least rigorous,
though certainly not uninteresting, if one may put it that way.)
Then there was Praline LaJeune: anyone could see that she was
just ripe for a disease of some sort, any kind, providing it was
horrible enough and bound to eat out her beautiful, ineffable,
self-corroding flesh. Praline LaJeune and Phillip Tourian were
in love. Their love took a form of insanity that was simultaneously charming and destructive. Then there was Feinstein,
the intellectual: he had something more than courage, he had
impertinence: but to do him justice one must add that he was
sad, always sad. What a group! There were others too. Like
Janie Thomson. Everybody in the group came from the four
corners of America, drifted there to New York City, to form a
little group, as dismal and futile a little group as all the other
little groups in the place.

That's what Manhattan is, a place full of little groups. No
more monstrous a city has ever been put together. You'd expect
to draw a sense of warmth and comfort, as the saying goes,
from all these buildings and streets and restaurants and bars.
But no . . . Take everybody in Manhattan and have them pitch
seven million or so tents in the plains, and very likely some

335

semblance of humanity may emerge. Other than that, Manhattan will continue as it is, a place that kills everything that comes to it, one way or the other. Manhattan will do it more quickly than any other human encampment on this earth of life. Manhattan is a death trap, built right over hell: have you not seen smoke coming out of holes in its streets? What more proof does one need?

All this has to be properly elaborated, like a theme. Don't be fooled by the strains of some Mozart symphony stealing out of well-lit rooms, where the window is opened, it's summertime, voices inside are full of loving perception: someone saying "See? See?", triumphantly. Don't be fooled by that. Around the corner of the window lurks that which kills; around the corner, barely visible, is the aura of death wearing a shadowy cape gliding back and forth or up and down, smelling of dead cats wrapped in packages. What a monster! . . . and how it thrives in this town!

But after all, even death gets lonesome in the country.

So we all came to New York because we were lonesome. All of us with our special little satchel of courage. We were all heroes. One has to be a hero to just live, that's a fact. That's what baptism must mean: baptism must be some sort of decoration for having come into life and death. No questions asked! The heroic infant is a strong and silent type.

Our own particular little group had something happen to it, something that reached out and touched everybody in it. Therefore, unlike many other little groups, ours became an expression of something, and gained, it must be admitted, a certain amount of notoriety. Responsible for this elevation from the murk of nothing-happens, was Phillip Tourian. But then without Ramsay Allen, nothing would have happened anyway. Then there was Will Dennison, the fellow who had that strange courage of knowing when it was time to go to bed and doing so: perhaps he was a key, too. It's hard to say.

One thing certain, is that the events that led up to everything began on a Saturday night in August.

A night when Will Dennison exhibited that special courage of his. He was standing on Sheridan Square, down in Greenwich Village, with a toothpick in his mouth. He had just eaten an early breakfast in Riker's. It was some time after three o'clock in the morning. He just stood there, in a slouched, stooping attitude, perhaps wearily watching what was going on. Everybody knows what Sheridan Square is like on Saturday nights, after the bars have closed: the whole place is lit up like a carnival, there's music coming from juke boxes in Mexican and Italian restaurants, traffic wheels about, people are all over the sidewalks. This is a time when you see drunken scenes that are unforgettable. Here, Will Dennison had once seen a big blonde flatten a sailor in a furious fist fight. That sort of thing attracted his attention: he would linger for that. But on this Saturday night, there was only the usual carnival scene; and the drunks were not original. They milled about, growling. Someone was having a bitter argument with himself: in a moment, now, he would start swinging, that was certain. Someone else yelled "I've got a cab!" and six others rushed across the street to spill into the cab, men, women. A jolly party. God only knew where they were going. Everybody was going somewhere. The streets led away from the Square in all directions, streets of light, some of them ending dimly way yonder at the waterfront, but most of them leading to more light.

In this feverish cluster of lights, moth-like men lingered to see what was going on. They stood on corners, in doorways, watching. There was time enough to return to the gloom of their rooms; time enough before putting out the light to sleep. Manhattan is the greatest artificial enemy of darkness and death in the world. Manhattan and death have signed a sardonic contract. Yet, you see, one can hardly suspect that: look at all the light! That's what these men on corners and doorways were thinking. But Will Dennison, he knew that on top of every streetlamp, in the murk just above the shade, sat the shadow . . . waiting and watching and scratching itself. Smelling of cats wrapped in packages, dead ones; smelling of closets where such packages are kept over the years. All you need do is open the closet door, and a hurricane of stench will rush out to you. But no one knew where that particular door was, until they blundered into it; meanwhile, they stood around or wandered about looking for other doors. Yet, ironically enough, there was only one door to open.

So Dennison put his courage to use. While everybody else was waiting around in feverish and eternal anticipation, he yawned and went home, with the *News* and *Mirror* under his arm, and the toothpick dangling from his mouth.

He went home along a narrow street that spoked out from Sheridan Square, leaving all that light behind him, advancing into the shadows, himself a tall shadow stooping slightly.

Dennison was an expert in little things. He went through all the little motions wearily. He took out his key ring, unlocked the street door, closed the door, went up the steps, unlocked the door of his apartment, went in, closed the door, and turned on the light. He dropped the *News* and *Mirror* on the couch, peeled off his seersucker coat and dropped it on top of them.

He went into the bathroom, turned on the light in there, and sneered at the mirror. This reminded him of his teeth. He picked up toothbrush and toothpaste, and washed his teeth.

That's all you could hear in his apartment, some swooshing in the bathroom sink, water running, the little sounds of daily toiletry. Outside of that, no other sound. The curtains moved slightly in the open window, as though the night were only occasionally sighing. Loud voices in the street below. No matter! . . . some drunks who do not know when it's time to go to bed, so carry on like madmen throughout the night.

Dennison went into his bedroom and sat on the bed. He was staring into space, automatically undoing his tie, the way men sometimes do before pensively going off to sleep . . . when the buzzer rang. This then would put a crimp in his musings, in his plans, in his yawning abstractions.

He jumped up and went over to push the button that released the street door. Then he picked up his coat off the couch and hung it over a chair, so no one would sit on it . . . this is what he was thinking. He put the papers in a drawer. He wanted them to be there when morning came. What else? He was going through all the little motions of self preservation. There were steps in the hall outside, so he went to the door, stooping slightly, wearily, to handle the door knob. He opened the door with a flourish. He had timed it just right so that they didn't get a chance to knock. He didn't know who they were, but he strongly suspected it was a contingent of our little group. Other contingents were scrabbling around somewhere else. This contingent was dropping in on Dennison at four o'clock in the morning.

Dennison showed his teeth before he even saw who it was. That was a trick of his: he had learned to smile pleasantly everywhere except at his mouth. It was a private joke of his that we all immensely enjoyed . . .

Seemingly out of nowhere, with startling abruptness, Phillip Tourian was in and through the door, clicking his heels noisily, head erect, cigarette smoke trailing after him, eyebrows arched. He was sitting in the most comfortable chair in the room with a leg over the arm before the others were all in. This was certainly Phillip, to be sure. He had thrown himself in the chair with a slam. He was grinning at Dennison . . . with amusement.

"We have come, Uncle Edouard."

"So I see."

The others were Ramsay Allen, Mike Ryko, and Agnes O'Rourke. Agnes was the most important person at the moment. She had a bottle of Canadian Club in her hands, holding it up for Dennison to see. "Look what I've got!"

"Canadian Club! Come in, come right in and sit down." By now they were all sitting down anyway, except Agnes, who stood holding up the bottle in an effort to prolong the surprise. Dennison stood there shaking his head.

"Well, well." And then, "Do sit down, Agnes."

She sat down, Dennison closed the door; then he went to the cupboard, reaching in two long white hands. He had some cocktail glasses. That's the way we were, very hospitable . . .

Ramsay Allen was an impressive looking big man with prematurely gray hair, around his late thirties. He was looking at Dennison, with his head cocked to one side: "Well, Will, I hope you don't mind our dropping in at this late hour?" All by way of a parody on people who say such things at such times. Dennison was alert to everything. He cocked his head to one side also, and said, "Why no, not at all. Make yourselves to home." He rubbed his hands zestfully, like a host.

"Guess how and where I got it?" Agnes wanted to be asked. Dennison picked up the bottle and started to pour around. Yes, he wanted to know. Agnes waved the story over to Ramsay

Allen, who was sitting on the floor at Phillip's feet. "Tell him, Al."

"We were in the Pied Piper, just before closing time, standing at the end of the bar drinking beer . . ." Allen's voice trailed away; vaguely. He then wound up another turn of effort. "Suddenly Agnes says to me, pick up your change and follow me. I've got a bottle of Canadian Club under my coat. We walked out. I was more scared than she was. I hadn't even seen her take it . . ." Allen turned his face up to Phillip to grin. "That was just before we bumped into you at George's . . ."

"I must say," Dennison commented, "that shows commendable enterprise."

"It was easy," Agnes said. "I'm going to do it again."

"Not when you're with me."

Agnes smiled at Will when he said that. Phillip picked up his glass and said, "Dennison has civic pride . . . doesn't want to go to jail for anything less than grand larceny." That's what he said. We were always saying something or other like that. Then again, there was no point in not saying anything at all.

"I need some water. I can't drink this stuff straight." This was Agnes, the only woman in the room. She was a sturdy Irish girl with close-cropped black hair and a vigorous, manly look about her. She always wore pants, as tonight. Dennison went to the bathroom and brought her a glass of water. Agnes thanked him.

"It's a pleasure," is what he said.

Everybody began to drink. Phillip coughed on his and reached for Agnes' water . . . he drained the glass fitfully. "Get her some more water, Will."

"Not a broken leg, I trust?"

Phillip was going to get up when Ramsay Allen took the empty water glass and went to refill it himself.

"Just the weight of the world," Phillip told Dennison.

"Yes?" hissed the other. "You must tell me about it sometime."

They were good friends, these two, but one was wary of the other. Now as to Ramsay Allen, he just sat on the floor at Phillip's feet, and there was never any question of circumspection there . . . Goofy is the word for the smile he had on his face as he looked up at the young prince in the easy chair.

Phillip was eighteen years old at the time, or perhaps even seventeen. He looked like a beautiful Oriental woman, with his white skin and green, serpentine eyes hemmed in by high cheek bones, and black hair tumbling in clots over his brow. When he walked, he looked like any other young American, however. He swung along, clicking his heels, head erect, scowling a bit. He was slender and wiry, with hard muscular forearms always showing beneath perpetually rolled up sleeves. It was hard to say what people on the street thought of him when they saw him. From a distance, he looked like a hoodlum, for that's the way he dressed, like Mike Ryko—the nearer you got to him, the more exotic he was, and surely he was resented on the streets for that.

He called himself Phillip Tourian, although he had a choice of names. His father went under the name of Rogers. Mr. Rogers, at the moment, was in Atlanta on narcotics charges . . . Mr. Rogers had had several names in the past. Phillip liked Tourian best of all. No one could be sure what nationality he was . . . true, his father came from somewhere in the Near East, Phillip himself had been born in Istanbul, his mother was American, he had Greek and Syrian and Armenian uncles, and one Magyar aunt. Still, as you can very well see, it was hard to say *what* he was. Surely there must have been some Oriental blood there somewhere . . . or was it just Ural-Altaic?

As to Phillip's companion, Mike Ryko, he was a plain Finn with reddish hair and bony features. It was habit to sit and say nothing for hours, which is just what he was doing that night.

Phillip and Mike had had a talk that night, before meeting Al and Agnes. They had stood at the bar in a Greenwich Village tavern, talking . . . one of their favorite occupations. They liked to look upon themselves as artists, both of them. Young intellectuals, that's what they were. Out of the welter of their lives, they were trying to fit things into a pattern, God knows why . . . For if ever they were offered a patterned world, of course they would die of boredom. Young intellectuals! Phillip was now going to spring his latest theory on Will Dennison. He, for his part, cared not a jot for anything of the sort. Still they came to him—we came to him, all of us, to have our theories smashed. There was your Dennison!

"I've been figuring out a philosophy," Phillip told him now, "of creation as good and waste as evil. So long as you're creating, that's good. All waste is evil. It's dichotomized like this: there's creative waste, such as talking to you now, such as all of us sitting here drinking and talking . . . and then there's wasteful creation, such as the *Saturday Evening Post.*"

"Well of course," replied Dennison, pouring himself another drink, "I'm just a befuddled bartender, but where are your criteria to tell waste from creation? Anybody can say that what he's doing is creation whereas what everybody else is doing is waste. The thing is so general it doesn't mean a thing."

Phillip immediately changed the subject. Now he wanted to know if Dennison had any hasheesh. Dennison said he had some, but not much. Phillip insisted he wanted to smoke some. So Dennison fished out a marijuana cigarette from a drawer and lit it up and passed it around. Everybody inhaled deeply. Nothing happened.

"This is very poor stuff." Dennison took another drag, and looked at the cigarette. "Marijuana is very hard to get now, and I don't know where I'll get any more after this is gone." Phillip took the cigarette and smoked some more. Dennison poured himself another drink of Canadian Club.

"I had some very good stuff in New Orleans," Ryko put in. "Two or three drags and I was floating down the street."

A lull fell over the room. Someone blanked the cigarette in the ashtray. The smell of burnt hay lingered . . . Gradually, the smoke from the cigarette was stealing out through the open window, curling over the sill and down into the night. Everyone was silent.

There's a picture for you! People exhaust one another so quickly. It seemed as though there were nothing to talk about any more. It was five o'clock in the morning. Ryko had begun to doze on the couch.

Something had to happen, someone had to do something. Al sat on the floor at Phillip's feet, a large flabby gray-haired man venerating an adolescent—as he had been doing for three years, ever since first meeting him in Paris. Phillip sat ignoring his admirer: eyes slitted like an Oriental, continually gesturing, he kept on talking: he had to. To him, silence was death. There was no end to his curiosity. Now he wanted to know this from Dennison, now that from Agnes. What was he trying to decide? All this insane thirst! He did not work: his father's uncle paid for his keep, he lived alone in a hotel off Washington Square, where he knew a hundred people. He spent his days and nights drinking, wandering around the city, talking to people he met in bars . . . with Ramsay Allen at his heels, like a faithful pooch. Allen did not work either, except when he had to: usually, in such cases, he cleaned out garbage for his landlady or did odd jobs. His life was Phillip . . . and he was old enough to be his father. A strange pair!

And there Ryko slept on the couch. Like the Finn in *Nigger of the Narcissus*, he seemed to be dreaming all the time. His presence there was some sort of mystery to Ramsay Allen. He saw nothing there to interest Phillip—but Phillip had met Ryko in a bar, several months ago, talked: presto! they were friends. Now they were three, routing out the mysteries of the city together, wandering around in a perpetual alcoholic fever. To look at them! . . . Fagin and two young and dirty Oliver Twists!

There was a brief silence in the room during which there was heard music coming from a car parked down on the street. Voices argued. Then the car roared off in first gear clear up to the end of the street. It was going off to join the rest of the noise around Seventh Avenue.

Three perfectly useless citizens, that's what they were. But no one was complaining. An Irish cop might say to himself, "Now there's three that'll bear watching, or me name ain't O'Toole." But that was all.

We could understand Phillip with Ramsay Allen, because Allen was a faithful dog; we could understand Phillip with Ryko, because they were more or less alike on the surface; but we could not understand the three of them together. It was mad. Like everything else.

So Phillip picked up his cocktail glass and bit a large piece of glass and started to chew it. You could hear the noise across the room. Ryko woke up, and Agnes O'Rourke made a face, as though someone were scratching fingernails on a blackboard, on a cold dry day. Ramsay Allen watched for awhile . . . "What are you doing?"

Through a mouthful of glass, Phillip said, "Eating glass, what the hell do you think?"

Like that! Allen picked up his own glass and took a bite. He too began to chew glass. The crunch of teeth against broken bits of glass filled the room. Ryko sat on the couch in full amazement.

"They're going to die!" cried Agnes. "Like Cellini, or someone . . ."

Dennison watched for awhile and then said, "No, all this talk about people dying from ground glass is hooey. There's no danger if you chew it up fine . . . it's like eating a little sand." Satisfied with his thesis, he watched some more. Ryko went and sat on the window sill.

Ryko said, "I'll be damned."

Dennison got up and said, "I am neglecting my duties as a host. Is anyone hungry? I have something very special I just got today."

Phillip and Al were now picking stray pieces of glass out from between their teeth. Al had gone into the bathroom to look at his gums in the mirror, and they were bleeding. "Yes," he said. "Let's have some eats." Phillip said he'd worked up an appetite on the glass. Al wanted to know if it was another package of food from Dennison's mother.

"As a matter of fact, yes, something real good." Dennison went into the closet and rummaged around for awhile, and came out with a lot of old razor blades on a plate with a jar of mustard. He set this down on the table.

"You bastard!" said Phillip. "I'm really hungry."

"Some gag, hey?" said Dennison. He felt pretty good about it, his whole body shaking with silent mirthless laughter.

Ryko came up and poured himself a drink. "I saw a guy eat razor blades in Chicago. Razor blades, glass, and light globes. He finally ate a porcelain plate."

And after awhile, even that was over . . . eating glass, and talking about things like that. The marijuana was no good, the whiskey was almost all gone. Poor defenses against the phantom lurking outside the window! We always knew it was there, we still know it now. But we contrived, sometimes, to erect little defenses, little divertissements. Not that we wanted to forget death and darkness. No. But after all, we were alive, and there was time on our hands. That's what Phillip thought . . . so he ate glass. He had punctured a hole in his ear lobe a few days earlier, and passed a safety pin through it, and let it hang there like an earring. Allen, of course, was also in the latest fashion, and wore his safety pin proudly at the swollen ear lobe.

We understood, I suppose. Ryko least of all understood. He dreamed. Dennison, of course, knew everything . . . He lacked the end of his little finger. One day, in his youth, he had told someone, "I'd cut off the end of my little finger for you." Invitation! So home went Dennison to sit at table and cut off the end of his little finger with a razor blade. Was that a gesture? . . . one worthy of a Greek hero!? Yes . . . but only half of it: he then never told the object of his affections about the mutilation, and went away, and never came back.

Now everyone was drunk except Dennison and Agnes. Phillip was talking to Al. They were fidgeting around the room nervously. Phillip smashed his fist down on the marble mantelpiece: he was talking about William Blake.

Dennison wanted less noise. "The landlady's just above, on the next floor." Phillip went over and opened the window wider.

Agnes sat in a stupor of boredom; she had already begun to yawn. She liked Ramsay Allen very much as a person, but she couldn't bear him when Phillip was around. Separately, they were remarkable people; together, they were unbearable, noisy and dangerous. With that Ryko, they were even worse, for he was on the verge of madness, and sometimes got so drunk that he lost his psychic balance altogether.

Dennison finished the last of the Canadian Club.

"Let's go up on the roof!" cried Phillip, aflame with his idea.

Al said, "All right," jumping up as though he'd never heard such a wonderful suggestion.

Dennison said "No don't. You'll wake up the landlady. There's nothing up there anyway."

"To hell with you, Dennison," Al said, sore that he should try to block an idea coming from Phillip. Phillip and Al lurched out the door and started up the stairs, talking in loud voices.

Dennison closed the door and sighed.

"I'm going home," Agnes said. Ryko was asleep on the couch. He had been dozing with his head against the wall, now he occupied the whole couch and snored, his feet on top of the pillows. Dennison went over and removed the pillows.

There was a loud commotion on the roof and then the sound of glass breaking in the street. Agnes and Dennison went to the window. Agnes said, "They must have thrown a glass down on the street." This seemed logical to Dennison; he stuck his head out cautiously, looked up, and looked down. There was a woman down in the street looking up and yelling.

"You crazy bastards, what you wanta do, kill somebody?"

It was getting gray in the street.

"Shut up," said Dennison. "You're waking everybody up. Beat it or I'll call a cop." He was a firm believer in the counter-attack. He had his little plan. He rushed back to the light switch and turned the light out in the room, to make it seem as though he'd gotten out of bed and gone back again. After a few minutes the woman walked away, still yelling and swearing. Dennison and Agnes waited in the darkness awhile, a darkness milky with dirty gray light from the murderous, hot August dawn . . . Then he turned on the light again.

Dennison was swearing. "All the trouble those two have caused me in the past! They piled up my car in Washington, the bastards, and got me thrown out of a hotel in Boston when Phillip pissed out the window. Plenty more of the same Joe College stuff . . . 1910 style. This happens whenever they get together."

"Isn't that so?" Agnes said. "I like Al but not when he's with Phillip. They act so silly together . . . By God, something's bound to break soon. They'll get arrested sometime."

"The sooner the better, I'll be rid of them." Dennison was fuming in his gentle way.

"I'm going to bed, Will." Agnes opened the door. "Say goodnight to them for me."

"I'm going to bed myself."

Agnes left.

Will Dennison went back to the window and looked up . . . there was the sound of muffled voices up on the roof. He sneered with his teeth and pulled his head in again. Ryko was snoring on the couch . . . he didn't care. He was as good as dead, all the time.

"I hope they don't get the idea to jump off," Will announced to Ryko. Ryko didn't hear him. "Well," said Will, "they can roost up there all night if they want to. I'm going to bed . . ."

He paused, listening to his own voice; and for any further noise from the roof: there was silence up there now. They were probably sitting on the edge of the roof with legs dangling over, six flights up, smoking and thinking . . . A perfect pair of idiots!

The gray light outside was growing, fanning out . . . and as it did so, hotter and more breathless became the dawn. A terrible August dawn . . . like anything breaking out over Africa, it would seem. Dennison went to the window and looked up. He saw nothing. They were probably gone. Scrabbling about in dirty dawn streets, two beggars in tatters, drunk and disorderly and dangerous. Rimbaud and his Verlaine! They probably were overturning garbage pails, insulting old newsdealers, throwing rotten oranges at passing trucks on Seventh Avenue . . . anything!

Will turned out the light and undressed. Ryko was not snoring any more. Now he might be awake, wondering where he was . . . a stupid dreamy Finn . . .

Dennison stretched to his full length beneath the sheet and was almost simultaneously asleep.

It was six o'clock.

Ryko was awake. He heard Phillip and Al returning from the roof, whispering . . . It would be well to feign sleep, or they would lead him outside to all kinds of stupid acts . . . madness in the sane Sunday morning streets.

The door opened furtively. "He's asleep," whispered Al. "Let's go."

"Wait a minute, I want to leave him a note."

There was more whispering in the hall. Phillip was scribbling a note.

"He's a good boy, I guess," Al said. "Mike is a good boy, allright."

"Yeah," said Phillip. He came over and dropped a piece of paper on Ryko's chest. "Now let's go." They went away, closing the door carefully, whispering in the hall, scuffling down the stairs . . .

Ryko opened his eyes and picked up the note. By the gray light he could very clearly see that Phillip had written an eternally indecipherable note in French. Not a word, not a letter, was legible. It was a mad scrabble of pencil-tip, nothing more. He stuck it in his pocket and got up. Dennison was asleep, that was plain: there he lay stretched out on his bed, sharp features upthrust, like a corpse on a morgue slab . . .

Ryko waited breathlessly until he could no longer hear the voices going away in the street below . . . Phillip and Al chattering away as usual. Then he opened the door, closed it, and went down the stairs. A clean bed and sleep, that's what he wanted.

He was weighed down with an insufferable weariness and fatigue. He stumbled along the sidewalk. It was hot and breathless: Sunday morning: bells would start ringing somewhere soon, that was certain. Ryko would curse at the first old woman he met if she intended to go to church. "Vieille vache!" That would tie the knot! Then he could sleep . . .

We all marvelled at this young man's sense of decency: he was always as polite as he could possibly be. It was hard to believe that he could curse at old women, but he claimed he had, many times.

There he went, that morning, stumbling home in the hot dawn. The phantom of darkness and death hid in dim doorways, and watched him pass. It lingered in a dark corner of the room back there and watched Will Dennison as he slept . . . It sped through the dirty air alongside the subway train, in the musty tunnels beneath the city: Phillip leaned on the subway door watching the darkness reel by, and saw there, the phantom . . . The phantom looked over his shoulder with interest at Ramsay Allen, who stood eagerly behind his beloved . . . The phantom was everywhere in the city . . . Long avenues of early morning stretched towards misty rendezvous: trolleys grated and clanged in the sleepy air; trucks growled; people walked, some stumbling, like Ryko, to home. The night was over. Day had come. The phantom was only forced to hide, that's all. What courage was necessary to live that day, that morning! How red-blooded and lusty a race the phantom had for his nourishment! The same as always . . .

CHAPTER TWO

DENNISON WOKE UP WITH A START at two o'clock the following Sunday afternoon. He squinted at the wrist watch
on the chair beside the bed. It was two o'clock of a Sunday
afternoon in August, of that he could be sure. Sleepy or not,
only the facts interested him. He got up, a tall spindly man in
his underwear, and began the day by pulling on his trousers,
seersucker trousers they were, and scratching his head.

Then the buzzer rang again. That's what had awakened him
so abruptly. He went with a businesslike air to the button and
pushed it . . . That was Dennison's life for you, a continual
ringing of the buzzer. People flocked to him like lost sheep.
Insecure Americans they were, coming up to this man of dis-
turbing security at all hours of the day and night . . . They
wanted to make sure that they were still there, for Dennison
proved it by speaking to them and paying attention to their
complaints . . .

Dennison had his shirt on when his visitor walked in. This
visitor was Danny Borman. A husky, rather tall, Italian of inde-
terminate age. He glided into the room with a charming smile
on his face and said, "Oh I'm sorry if I got you up . . ."

"Nothing at all, Danny, I would have slept all day if you
hadn't come . . ."

They went on like that for a whole minute while Dennison
dressed and combed his hair . . .

Well, now, it seemed things were not going well with Danny
Borman the past two weeks. He was a shipyard worker; he
couldn't get on a contracting job where all the overtime pay
was, and didn't want to tie himself down somewhere else. He
told all this to Dennison, who listened, as always, with that
gratifying intelligence that made you certain of the purpose of
your visit—whatever it was.

Of course, Danny Borman was not exactly the type who
needed Dennison—at least, not in a vague way. He had come
for a definite purpose. Dennison suspected a touch, a loan,
was in the offing. Danny sat still for a moment, saying nothing . . . There was always that cruel furtive look in his eyes. A
gleam in his eye, too, suggesting unspeakable notions, such as

bayonetting dogs when no one was watching, at night somewhere . . . That was Danny. But a very polite person, altogether.

Finally he said, "Will, I'd like to ask a favor of you."

"Yeh, what?"

"I'd like to borrow your sap."

Dennison had been expecting something far worse. He
shrugged and said, "Sure, Danny, glad to oblige." He went
over to the bureau and fished out a black-jack from under a pile
of shirts. Dennison was thinking what a contrast this Danny
was to Phillip and Al, who would never lift a finger to get
money for themselves so long as they could mooch off someone
else. Danny, in a way, now, was a lot like Agnes O'Rourke—he
had enterprise. Altogether a charming Sunday afternoon call.
Dennison wiped off the black-jack carefully with a silk handkerchief and handed it to Danny.

"Watch yourself," he said.

"You know me. I'm always careful."

Danny got up. Dennison asked him which way he was going;
he was going uptown; Dennison was planning to visit Al this
afternoon, in which case he would ride uptown with Danny.
At the door, Danny said, "After you."

Dennison placed a hand on Danny's shoulder. "Please, I
am at home here." That was pretty high tone and Danny just
had to walk out first, he being a stickler for etiquette, having
read Emily Post from cover to cover . . . he realized Dennison's
consummate finesse, there. The next time, perhaps when he
brought back the black-jack, there might be vouchsafed him
an opportunity to dart home an equally refined touché. Danny
had that on his mind the remainder of the day.

They walked along the street, in the hot afternoon sun.
On Seventh Avenue scores of young women strolled this way
and that, looking for security, for a man, that is . . . In the
subway, there they were by the scores. Many of them found
Danny Borman attractive: he and his pin stripe double breasted
suit, the light blue shirt, the blue polkadot bow tie, the well
groomed hair. Well, if they wanted security, a man, there he
was! Dennison, now, with his musty stoop and dreary factual
expression . . . not so alluring a catch! Danny Borman mopped
his brow with a perfumed handkerchief.

"I'm mighty grateful, Will," he was shouting over the roar of the subway train. "I'm in a kind of a fix, and this will come in handy."

"Not at all," Will returned kindly.

Danny got off at Times Square, waving goodbye. There he went, through the crowd of Sunday strollers, off to Times Square. From the center of the city he could pick any direction he chose, any person to follow . . .

It was a beautiful day for strolling, in spite of the heat . . . Now we none of us knew what the relation was between Dennison and Danny Borman. Any cop on the street corner can tell us as much about it as anyone . . . Danny was just one of those countless unidentifiable individuals that roam New York City, year in and year out. They'll never give you their address, or if they do, they've already moved: that's a fact. You're never sure what their names are: anyway, they might not have given their actual names away. People like this, when they died, when they by some hook or crook got to Bellevue Morgue, were always being described in the newspapers all the more vaguely than ever. The police records are full of such things . . . No ant in a dark cave under the root of a tree in winter, can boast of such anonymity.

We only knew that Dennison had met Danny Borman somewhere, somehow—as bartenders do meet people, all kinds of them. Only Dennison was not a bartender all the time . . . Come to think of it, Dennison himself we hardly knew . . . He was all the more anonymous because you couldn't recognize him in a crowd: he looked like a bank clerk, like Heinrich Himmler. At least Danny Borman could be recognized in a crowd!

Yet they had met, two perfect strangers to everyone, and had known each other for awhile, as now, in Manhattan. There it was. They parted at Times Square and Dennison rode on up to 50th Street, where he got out and had himself a bit of breakfast in a restaurant.

Then he walked to 52nd Street, between Fifth and Sixth Avenues, to where Ramsay Allen lived. It was a second floor walk-up apartment, with a French window at one end looking over a leafy and dirty backyard. On the wall, over a huge filthy fireplace full of cigarette butts, was a watercolor of a young man in bathing trunks, sitting underwater, with a finger against his cheek looking hammy and pensive, all done in mauve and light blue and pink. One of Allen's artist friends. There was a long easy chair in the room . . . the only comfortable chair in the whole of Mrs. Frascati's rooming house. Half of Mrs. Frascati's tenants were in Allen's room at the moment, plus some people from the East Side. Dennison walked into a den of smoke and talk . . .

Hugh Maddox stood by the French window looking at the dirty backyard and scowling over his latest problem. Jane Bole and Tom Sullivan, the East Side people, sat on the couch with Ramsay Allen and a girl by the name of Bunny. Bunny was in love with Ramsay Allen. A Boston girl, from a Good Family, who claimed to be a kleptomaniac and was therefore absolved of all past or future thefts. In the long easy chair sat Agnes O'Rourke; on the arm of the chair was Della Packard. Della was an experienced Lesbian at twenty, with two or three soul-searing affairs behind her, and four suicide attempts. . . . We knew all this because she talked about it constantly, with an insane egocentricity.

Sitting in a chair by himself in the corner was Chris Rivers. This fellow never took a bath nor cleaned out his room nor brushed his teeth, and there he sat grinning, showing his teeth covered with green scum, a silly sort of a person smiling and grinning idiotically in periodical turns around the room, like a lighthouse beam . . .

Seven people altogether . . . nine with Ramsay Allen and Dennison. Three of them lived in Mrs. Frascati's . . . Hugh Maddox on the top floor, next to Chris Rivers' astoundingly dirty room; and Agnes O'Rourke, on the floor below that, in a large room completely unfurnished except for a couch in the middle of the room and an enormous bookshelf with one book in it.

Dennison had no place to sit down. He waved to everybody and went to the French window to talk to Hugh Maddox.

Hugh Maddox was a longshoreman, an Irishman about thirty years old, who came from a rich family, it was said, but who was no longer in contact with them.

"What's new?" Dennison asked him.

He said the F.B.I. was looking for him. Dennison was surprised.

"It must be about the draft . . . that's the only thing I can think of. They were asking about me down at Pier 32. Nobody knows my address down there."

"Well what is your draft status?"

"I don't know exactly. You see, I gave them an address care of somebody else and this girl moved after that, and when they came to my new address the janitor thought they were from the finance company and told them he never heard of me. Then I moved out of that place without leaving a forwarding address because I owed a month's rent."

"What was your original classification?"

"It was 3A but my wife and I are divorced since then. That's two years ago."

"Well what are you going to do?"

"I'm going down and see them. No use trying to get away from those guys. I may get three years out of this."

"Oh just explain to them it's all a mistake."

"It's not so simple as that. Jesus I don't know what the fuck's going to happen."

Dennison sighed. "What you need is a lawyer," he said.

"Yeah, and pay him with what."

The conversation was taking a turn Dennison didn't quite like.

Hugh Maddox scowled down on the yard. He was a slightly built man with dark hair, blue eyes . . . perpetually swearing, too. Another indecipherable individual of Manhattan. No cop on the street corner could place him either—perhaps only the F.B.I.

All these people in back of them were putting up a continual wall of talk and smoke . . . Someone, Agnes O'Rourke to be exact, got up and said, "Well I have to go now."

At this Ramsay Allen jumped up and said, "Well if you must." Everybody laughed, Dennison included. Jane Bole dragged Tom Sullivan to his feet and said "Come along dear." These two lived somewhere in the East Forties and spent each Sunday afternoon making a round of visits throughout the city . . . They had quite an itinerary . . . Ramsay Allen knew of no

way to get off their route . . . They kept coming: a pair of perfectly dull people, trying to achieve a vague synthesis between
respectability and criminal sophistication: they both had police
records and you heard about that all the time.

Everybody started to leave, grudgingly. Ramsay Allen went
to the sink and busied himself with what he hoped might
seem an intimate toiletry. Chris Rivers finally emerged from
his corner and approached Dennison.

"Hi Will, how is it?"

"Fine, Chris."

"Say by the way, could you see your way clear to lend me a
quarter."

"Why certainly." Dennison fished in his pocket for a quarter.
Chris sidled away throwing back a fishy grin. He could never
work himself up to ask anyone for more than fifty cents: he
didn't work at all either. No one knew anything about him.
He left alone, going off to spend his twenty five cents, out
on the sunny afternoon street. You'd see him stroll this afternoon, too. Perhaps he liked to stare at those Sunday afternoon
women who roamed around looking for prince charming.
There he was!

Jane Bole and Tom Sullivan left; they were going to visit
someone else, next on their route. Bunny sulked because Allen
hadn't asked her to stay . . . She stood in the doorway awhile, as
Allen went on with his business at the sink: then she was gone
. . . Everybody left but Hugh Maddox.

He stayed about ten minutes rehashing his problem and
looking gloomy, and swearing up and down.

Al said, "Well I guess it will turn out allright."

Hugh said he didn't know what was going to happen. "And
don't say anything about this to Mrs. Frascati. I owe her a
month's rent."

"Don't worry."

Hugh left after awhile.

Allen closed the door with a flourish. "Thank God," he said,
"a little peace at last. Why, those people woke me up at twelve
o'clock and they've been here ever since."

A very popular person, was Ramsay Allen. Everybody wanted
him to pay attention to them, this charming Virginian. To add
to his charm was the fact that he paid no attention to anyone

but Phillip Tourian. As to Dennison . . . Allen regarded him like a brother. They'd met years ago in a bar where Dennison was bartender: they kept in touch. You saw them together sitting around and talking like two old men, tired and full of fine, almost imperceptible humor. They had a habit of cocking their heads to one side. It had all begun in a bar years ago . . . They regarded each other with that weary yet considerate way, like someone's uncles. One would leave town, say Allen, to follow the wild Phillip . . . A year or so later, they'd get together again. "Well," Dennison would say, "what's been going on in your life?" They regarded each other's lives with dignity.

"Now I want to tell you about the amazing thing that happened last night," Allen was now saying.

Dennison rubbed his hands together and said "Yes?"

"Well, when we got up on the roof Phillip rushed over to the edge like he was going to jump off, and I got worried and yelled at him, but he suddenly stopped and dropped a glass. You heard it?"

"Yes, and I heard the woman . . ."

"I went over and stood on the edge with him and said 'What's the matter?' and started to put my arm around him. Then Phil turned around and hugged me, very passionately I must say, and dragged me down with him on the roof . . ."

Allen paused. He watched Dennison in suspense.

"I must say," the latter said, "it looks like you're getting there after four years. Well go on—what happened then?"

"He hugged me several times, and for awhile I thought he was going to kiss me, then suddenly he pushed me away and got up."

"Yeah, well what happened then?"

"Well, then Phil said 'Let's jump off the roof together shall we?' And I said 'What's the point in that?' and he said 'Don't you understand? After this we have to . . . it's the only thing to do. Either that or go away' . . ."

"What did he mean by that? Go away where?"

"I don't know. Anywhere I guess."

"Why didn't you say okay dearie, let's fly to Newark tonight."

Allen was very serious about all this. Dennison, for his part, had been hearing this sort of thing ever since he'd met Al. He was accustomed to it . . . He could jest about it and Allen could understand . . . They were men of dissimilar tastes, of course.

Allen was considering the latest remark. "Well I didn't have money for one thing . . ."

Dennison jumped up from the long easy chair. "Oh you didn't have any money hey?" He started pacing around the room: he was now jesting for fair: there was something pathetically urgent about Al's story: his only proper response, then, was to circumscribe the trembling nerve Allen was holding out to be touched, and laugh at it from a rear position. "Do you expect to have money sitting on your ass? Go to work in a shipyard. Hold up a store . . . Here you've been waiting for three years for this opening and now—"

"Well I'm not sure I want to."

"You're not sure you want to what?"

"Go somewhere with him now. I'm afraid there would be a reaction and I wouldn't accomplish anything . . ."

Dennison went over to the fireplace and banged his hand down on the mantelpiece. Now he was turning his back on the trembling nerve. With dignity. He turned, as he had to. "So you want to wait. Tomorrow and tomorrow and tomorrow—waiting till you're dead. Do you know what I think?" He squinted at Allen, showing his teeth, like a policeman grilling a suspect . . . "I think this whole Phillip complex is like the Christian heaven, an illusion born of a need—" he spread his arms eloquently—"floating around in some nebulous misty Platonic nowhere, always just around the corner like Prosperity but never *here* and *now*. You're afraid to go away with him, you're afraid to put it to a test because you know it won't work . . ."

Allen flinched and shut his eyes, and drew back in his chair, crying "No! No!"

Dennison had managed to return the trembling nerve to its proper place inside Allen. So now he sat down and said "But seriously Al, if you did go somewhere you might succeed in making him, after all that's what you've been after all these three years."

"No, you don't understand at all. That isn't what I really want."

Dennison jumped up again . . . the nerve kept coming out tremulously. He sneered magnificently: "Oh so this is a case of Platonic love, hey? Nothing so coarse as physical contact, hey?"

"No, I do want to sleep with him. But I want his affection more than anything. And I want it to be permanent . . ."

"God give me patience! Patience I need!" This is what Dennison said, tearing at his hair. Perhaps now he wasn't jesting anymore, though it was hard to tell. "Now listen, I'm going to say it again and I'm going to say it slow. Phillip isn't queer . . . Anything permanent is impossible. Unless of course it's just friendship you want." He walked over to the French window and stood with his hands clasped behind him like a captain on the bridge of a battleship.

Al said "I want him to love me."

Dennison turned around and took a toothpick out of his shirt pocket and started digging at a cavity. "You're nuts," he said.

"I know he'll come around to my way of thinking in time." Allen sat on the couch saying this, abject and pensive.

Dennison came over and pointed the toothpick at Al's chest. "Get yourself some scratch and he'll come around tonight."

"No that isn't the way I want it."

"What you want is impossible."

"I don't see why it should be . . ."

Dennison said "Well of course he isn't influenced by money at all, you've noticed that haven't you?"

"Well, he is, but he shouldn't be . . . I don't want to admit that he is."

Dennison said, "Facts, man, facts!" Now he took on a bourgeois *père de famille* tone and looked full at Allen, the black sheep son. "Why don't you make something of yourself, something he'd be proud of and look up to. Look at you! You look like a bum!"

Ramsay Allen had on an English tweed suit looking like it had been slept in for years, a cheap Sixth Avenue shirt and a frayed Sulka tie. That's what he wore all the time, the only clothes he had . . . He looked like a bum.

Dennison drove home his point, his plan. "Now I have it from reliable sources that there is at the present time a tremendous shortage of drugs in this country owing to the war. Marijuana is selling for fifty cents a stick whereas before the war it was ten cents a stick. Why don't we cash in on this situation, get some seed, and start a marijuana farm? . . ."

"Well," said Allen, cocking his head to one side, "now, that sounds good to me . . ."

"You can buy the seed in bird stores . . . We can sow it out in the country somewhere and come back in a couple of months and harvest our crop. Later on when we build up a bankroll, we can buy our own farm." Dennison stood up to his full height and swelled out his chest. "Think of it, man, a field of marijuana as far as the eye can see. . . ."

Ramsay Allen smiled.

"You can't get anywhere with Phillip or anything just sitting around," Dennison continued. "Hop to it! Be aggressive. Why, some day you'll have enough money to keep a whole harem of Phillips."

This annoyed Al. Dennison made him promise to go and buy some bird seed the first thing in the morning . . .

That was settled. Now they were hungry. Al went on inquiring about the marijuana business . . . Now, there was an idea, perhaps . . . Then he wanted to know what did it mean when Phillip said this last night, and should he call him up tonight or just go down to the Village without calling, or was Phillip really in love with Praline LaJeune and if so should he do anything to break it up . . . They were sitting in Hamburger Mary's eating dinner . . . Dennison ate his food and said yes, why not, no, go ahead, and stopped listening to him. He'd heard all this for years. The more this thing dragged on, the more Al seemed to obliterate his own character in an acid bath of anxiety.

"Hop to it!" Dennison thought to himself. He could see Al, and himself, rushing around town, stimulated on cocaine, making money, cancelling appointments, telephoning long distance, pausing only to take Turkish baths and more cocaine, rushing out again, aggressive and magnificent, clad in Panama suits, wearing cameo rings perhaps, flying out to the marijuana farm in a cub plane and dropping empty whiskey bottles on the countryside below . . . That's what he saw in his mind's eye. Amusing thoughts! . . . What he liked best about it was the sight of feverish human activity. His mind expanded: poppy fields in Mexico! in Persia! He saw himself sitting in a compound with a Persian woman on his lap, a gun on his hip, natives to shoot at outside the window . . . That's what he liked by God! Feverish and perpetual human activity, always one step ahead of death, unthinking and insane, while death made a detour and came around to pull you over to the curb at the other end of the night road . . . By God, give death a merry chase, that's the ticket.

After dinner Al went off . . . he didn't know whether he'd visit Phillip or not. He bounded off in his long nervous stride, a lost sheep in the middle of a moiling herd of sheep he didn't like. Dennison, for his part, had his work. He started off for the bar on 46th Street where he worked.

There they all were, the monstrous drunken Americans, in the Continental Cafe, as it was called. The place was open all the way across the front in summer with doors that folded back. There were tables where you could sit and look at the sidewalk if you wanted to. There were several waitress-hostesses who would let you buy drinks for them, if you wanted to. Inside the bar was the usual chromium, red leather, and fluorescent lights. The regular sprinkle of soldiers and sailors, a couple of whores with two Broadway Sams, one fag . . . all standing at the bar. Three plain clothes detectives at the far end of the bar, drinking scotch. Dennison took off his coat and transferred everything to his pants pockets. He found an apron with a long string so he could loop it around and tie it in front. Then he stepped behind the bar and said hello to Jimmy, the other bartender, who was already there . . .

There they all were, gesticulating and shouting and drinking, with the soft August night coming on outside. Madmen! The music bleating in the juke box, playing the refrain of themselves to which they not even listened. Dennison had long ago decided not to bother with them.

The three detectives said "Hello kid" when they saw Dennison. They had Jimmy waiting on them hand and foot asking for scotch and cigars and lemon peel in their drinks, and more soda and more ice. These three were always in the place sopping up free drinks because the boss thought they would help him out in case of trouble. No one could possibly cotton up to these three, least of all Jimmy, whose work was trebled. He was winking at Dennison. Then he brought the lemon peel to the three dicks. Now they were telling him a lot of horse shit about how he was a swell guy and so was the boss a swell guy and he ought to treat the boss right, Jimmy ought . . . They had that burly unconcern of the plain clothes man, always swaggering around noisily and scratching their crotches, or winking at each other in conspiratory stupidity. They all carried guns, which of course gave them the finishing touch. The sentimental fools were likely as not prepared to shoot anyone who annoyed them, or at best, arrest them if necessary.

The juke box was playing a song called "You Always Hurt the One You Love." It was a big hit that summer. People sat in bars all over America nodding sagely as they heard it: they knew! . . . from experience! . . . you always hurt the one you love. Three sailors at the other end of the bar, Dennison's end, called out to him. "Hey Jack, how come that machine never plays what we want?"

"I don't know," Dennison said. "People are always complaining about it." One of the sailors asked him where all the women were in this town, and he said they were in Brooklyn, hundreds of them on every corner. He told them how to get there, but they couldn't understand the directions . . . notwithstanding which fact they started out for Brooklyn anyway. Dennison took their glasses off the bar and sloshed them through dirty water and they were washed.

He stood behind the bar watching, feeling like the only sane man in a nut house. It wasn't so annoying as it was frightening, because there was no one to contact . . . not a soul in the place, in anyplace like this. He expected any moment would erupt with unspeakable brutalities . . .

The fag was being obnoxious with two sailors. It might break out there, Dennison decided.

There was a sudden commotion at the other end of the bar and all eyes turned there. A man about fifty years old dressed in slacks and a light gray coat and hat was having words with the three plain clothes dicks. He was saying, "You mind your own business." He looked like a man of some intelligence and wealth; his eyes were bloodshot and he had been drinking quite a bit, but he had himself under good control. It seems that he had been kidding the waitress and the three detectives hadn't cottoned up to that. He stood glaring at them. One of the dicks came up and said, "Get the hell out of this bar, you prick."

"Who are you?" the man wanted to know. "It's none of your business, as I said before."

One of the dicks gave the man a shove and a second gave him another shove—just like a relay team—until they had him behind the phone booth. Then they pinned him against the wall and began slugging him methodically. From Dennison's end of the bar you could hear the pounding against the phone booth, as on a muffled drum, as the man's head beat back from the punches . . . They hit him for quite a while, about thirty times or so, in a monotonous kind of ritual, and the man didn't even raise his hands. His knees buckled after awhile, so they took him and threw him on a chair. After a few seconds, the man started to come to, and raised his hand like a man pushing covers off his face. At that one of the cops scented danger and hit him again, knocking him off the chair onto the floor . . .

Then the other two helped him up and dusted off his clothes and found his hat. One of them said "Jesus, who hit you, Mac?"

The man's eyes were glazed . . . he looked like a case of light concussion. He stood around awhile and then focused his attention on one of the cops, the one who had helped him up. "Thank you," he said. The cop said "Any time Mac." The cop with the man's hat put it on his head, and then grabbed him by the collar at the back and by the belt. He shoved him along to the front of the bar and gave him a push which sent him across the sidewalk into a parked car. He bounced off the car and looked around with that glazed expression, then staggered off in the direction of Sixth Avenue. People stared back at him and laughed.

The cop who had thrown the man out came back from the door laughing like a schoolboy and scratching his crotch. The other two cops were leaning against the end of the bar . . . one had a match in his mouth, and was shaking all over with laughter.

"Let's have another scotch Jimmy!" said the cop who had thrown the man out. Everybody in the bar was laughing. You expected the cops to turn around and offer a toast, they were beaming with such excitement, and before such an appreciative audience.

Jimmy, for his part, took his time about getting the scotch. You could see by his face he felt more like serving them a Mickey.

"I been around a lot," Jimmy told Dennison out of the corner of his mouth . . . he had a way of speaking so that his lips didn't move; still he left open a corner of his mouth to let the sound out. "I done a lot of things too, but I never got so callous I could stand around and enjoy seeing something like that. These morons in the bar laugh and think it's funny until it happens to them. Now if it was *my* joint I'd tell those cops, now listen fellows you made a mistake. There's plenty alleys around here, you don't have to beat somebody up in the joint." He rushed off to serve someone a beer; he came back and opened the hole in the corner of his mouth. "And then, on top of everything else, they'll walk out of here and won't even leave a dime on the bar. If they were any sort of characters at all, they'd say here Jimmy here's a dollar for you . . ."

Dennison nodded wearily. Jimmy went back to the end of the bar, in some sort of moral indignation . . . There he was, telling the waitress about it.

The man in the gray suit came back with a uniformed cop. The three dicks were still there at the end of the bar but he couldn't identify them; he just insisted to the cop that he had been beaten up in the bar. One of the plain clothes men gave the cop the high sign, and the cop turned to the man and said, "Well what do you want me to do about it, Mister? You say yourself the guy ain't here. Are you sure you've got the right place?"

"Yes I'm perfectly sure. And if you won't do anything, I'll find someone who will." He was calm and dignified in spite of the beating he'd taken . . . he was smoking a cigarette and did not touch his swollen jaw and lips, nor call attention to his injuries.

The cop said, "Well what do you want me to do? You've had too much to drink, Mister . . . why don't you go home and forget about it?"

The man turned around and walked out. Now the owner of the Continental Cafe had come down from his apartment upstairs and the cops were telling him what had happened. The owner listened to all this with a haggard and harried look. He was silent awhile, staring at the plain clothes men yet not seeing them, just worrying about everything in general that happened to him all the time. "You guys better not be here," he finally said. "That prick looks like he will cause some trouble."

The three detectives looked at each other and put down their drinks. One of them finished his drink quickly and started out. They walked out together looking worried. The owner of the bar leaned on the counter and rubbed his scalp . . .

In a few minutes the man in the gray suit was back with five plain clothes men from the nearby precinct station. They took the license number of the place, talked to the owner a while, and left.

Dennison put both hands on the counter in front of him. The juke box was still playing "You Always Hurt the One you Love." Dennison watched the owner go back upstairs to his apartment, shaking his head.

There were no further disturbances that night . . . On the average there was one disturbance a night. After that, possibilities seemed to be exhausted . . .

Later on, it is true, just about closing time, four sailors came by and said, "Let's go in here and start a fight."

"No you don't!" the owner cried. "We're closing up," and with that he closed the door in their faces. After that the owner went behind the bar and counted up the proceeds for the night while his bartenders got dressed and ready to go home . . . The chairs were upended all over the place, ready for the floor-cleaner's nightly labors. The floorcleaner was a little Negro with a big bottle of whiskey in his pants pocket.

"I done laid down a hipe," he kept moaning. "I done laid down a hipe."

Whatever it meant, it sounded awfully discouraging. Dennison went home. He read the *News* and *Mirror* on the subway downtown . . .

When he got to his room he assembled on top of the bureau a glass of water, an alcohol lamp, a table spoon, a bottle of rubbing alcohol and some absorbant cotton. He reached in the bureau drawer and took out a hypodermic needle and some morphine tablets in a vial labeled Benzedrine. He split one tablet in half with a knife blade, measured out water from the hypodermic into the spoon, and dropped one tablet and a half tablet into the water in the spoon. He held the spoon over the alcohol lamp until the tablets were completely dissolved. He let the solution cool. He dropped a pinch of absorbent cotton in the spoon and gently insinuated the tip of the hypodermic into the cotton: then he sucked up the fluid into the hypodermic, through the cotton, leaving the spoon as dry as a bone. He fitted on the needle and started looking around for a soft spot on his arm. He wasn't at the intravenous stage yet. After awhile he slid the needle into his arm and slowly pushed the plunger down to the base of the needle. Almost immediately, complete relaxation spread over him.

He sighed happily and went to bed, putting out the light. He saw first an Oriental palace with dancing girls dressed in all manner of fabulous costumes, and heard the tinkle of their anklets. This absorbed his attention for awhile. It was an amazing setting, worthy of a Hollywood production. The longer he looked at it the more incredible it grew.

CHAPTER THREE

LIFE IS THE MOST MONSTROUS thing possible. The natural condition of the universe is darkness and no-life . . . It is space dotted with things to which life is some sort of unheard of perversion. The moon is sane, not mad. It is the earth that is mad. What happened on the earth that it should have grown life? Against the tremendous odds of natural conditions, life pops up eagerly, foolishly. The head of a foetus, a human foetus, is bright crimson with bizarre networks of blue blood vessels and veins . . . ready to explode from the very force of its own hot stupid blood. You could squash such a thing with a sledge hammer and there's your pulp of red and blue nonsense.

The point is, however, that there is no why. It just happened. Not even an accident, with that touch of destiny that accidents do have . . . just a happenstance. What a word! . . . happenstance! There it stands.

One of the only things you can be sure of, if you are yourself life, and particularly a human being, is jealousy of death. While this is going on, there's pain at every breath you draw, the knowledge of end in the charming offing, idiocy all around, and self-made brutality and distances . . .

Still there are people who sit around and think about all this, whilst there are others rushing around five or six thousand miles away, eighteen or nineteen years ago, introducing themselves as Persian princes to American women. That's how Phillip Tourian's father approached Phillip's mother-to-be, in Istanbul in 1926 . . .

In the same way that life just came along, like a mushroom or a cancer, and spread all over the face of the earth, for no reason at all, some time ago—in this same way, did Phillip Tourian come along. He shortly became a foetus. Grotesquely, like all the others. He never knew why, did Phillip: that's the reason he spent all his energies running around from bar to bar talking to people: searching outside himself he wanted to know what little plan went into his making. There was none, of course. No plan in anything. You walked down to the end of the street, past that last streetlamp there, and disappeared in the dark. You were always passing, never stopping . . . If you tried to stop, someone was behind you pushing you, some little eager foetus interested in the brightness of the last streetlamp.

It seems that the only thing life has to its credit is that it never learns. That's the great cry of the Socialists: "The masses never learn, no one ever learns!" Of course not . . . there's nothing to learn. They cry: "Why? Why?" And there's no why. Just jealousy of death . . . or perhaps that's simplifying matters.

Phillip's father was named Abul Tourian Esses Sampatacus Jahan, and there was a Mohammed somewhere in it. Of uncertain parentage, he was. There he moiled, in the swarm of the Near East, starting off as a gamin, growing up without question, selling rugs for awhile, looking around and deciding to overlook whatever long dark corridor of mystery stretched away from his wiry existence. What did it matter to Tourian? . . . Just once, he had given the matter some thought, in a moment of awe and puzzlement, and then—full of exploding red blood and surging blue veins—he had dashed after the first woman that passed and had never since troubled himself with what was obviously of no point . . . No one in the Near East, or anywhere for that matter, ever really looks at the stars. At one time down there, Babylonian priests had looked at the stars. But they were dead now. Who cares about all that anyway? . . . or all this? There seems to be just about as much sense in living as there is in dying.

Phillip's father was a slender man with very handsome features. There was something hard and dead and glassy about the eyes and upper part of his face, but he had a charming smile, and certain quick gestures that won the admiration of the females. He had a way of turning his body sideways when he walked through a crowd in a movement that was aggressive and graceful at the same time. He never jostled, or was jostled, in any way.

Outgrowing the crudities of his early youth, as they say, he gradually established himself as a sort of underworld broker dealing in dope, women, and stolen goods on a wholesale basis. If someone had something to sell he found a buyer and collected a commission from both ends . . . he let others take the risks, he let others jostle around. Life is packed close in Istanbul and places like that. Tourian, turning sideways here and there, was always able to establish himself a path through which to pass in fine fin-like grace. As Phillip put it, "The old man isn't a crock, he's a financier." As an American, Tourian would have been one of those who pass through congested Times Square when the light is green, in sleek fast cars, with a destination gleaming in their eyes. His life was a network of complex transactions through which he moved, serene and purposeful . . .

Phillip's mother was an American of a Good Boston Family. After graduating from Smith she was travelling in Europe when her Lesbian tendencies temporarily gained the ascendance over her inhibitions, and she had an affair with an older woman in Paris. This affair plunged her into anxiety and conviction of sin. A typical modern Puritan, she was able to believe in sin without believing in God. In fact, she felt there was something soft and sinful about believing in God. She rejected such indulgence like an indecent proposal . . .

After a few months the affair broke up. She left Paris resolved never again to fall into such practices. She moved on to Vienna, Budapest, and came finally to Istanbul.

Mr. Tourian picked her up in a cafe introducing himself as a Persian prince. He saw at once the advantage of an alliance with a woman of good family and unimpeachable respectability. She saw in him an escape from her sinful tendencies and breathed for a moment vicariously the clear air in which there are only facts, and anxiety, inhibitions and neurosis dissolve. All the subtle intuitive power that in her was directed towards self destruction and self torture was here harnessed to self advancement. She made an attempt to incorporate this vision of harmony evoked by Mr. Tourian.

But Mr. Tourian was serenely self sufficient. He did not need her, and she turned away from him and descended on little Phillip with all the weight of her twisted affections . . . She dragged him all over Europe with her on continual obsessive tours, she kept telling him that he must not be like his father who was selfish and inconsiderate of her feelings. Mr. Tourian accepted this state of things indifferently.

He built a large house and started a legitimate business which prospered side by side with his other enterprises, which absorbed more and more of his time. Drugs, which he had used periodically for years to sharpen his senses and to provide the stimulation necessary for long and irregular hours, were becoming a necessity . . . he was beginning to break up, but without the conflicts and disharmony that accompany a Western breakdown, as it were. His calm was becoming apathy. He began to forget appointments and spend whole days in Turkish baths stimulating himself with hashish. Sexuality slowly faded away in the regressive calm of morphine . . .

Ramsay Allen met Mrs. Tourian in Rumplemeyer's in Paris, in 1939. The next day he had tea with her at the Ritz and met Phillip. Al was 34 at the time, Phillip was 13.

Allen came from a good Southern family . . . he was unusually popular in certain Richmond circles. He had been engaged to at least four debutantes, and each time had dashed off to reconsider the matter. After his graduation from the University of Virginia he had gone to New York for a summer and discovered that it offered wider scope to his sexual tendencies.

On each of his four escapes from the possible ordeal of being anchored firmly in Southern society, he had gone to New York to think things over. After awhile, his visits there became protracted stays. He worked as an advertising copywriter, a publisher's reader, and often he didn't work at all.

He had an older brother who was ambitious and a steady worker. This man, a few years older and more sure of himself than Al, was about to go to town with a paper mill of which he was part owner. He offered Al a job in the mill: Al decided to go back home, for a while at least. He had excellent prospects of being a rich man in a few years. He got back in the swing of things and was about to be engaged to another flower of Richmond womanhood. Still he was not sure of what he really wanted to do about that, about marriage. He went to Europe that summer . . .

Little Phillip was very much flattered that an older man should take the trouble to see him constantly and take him to cinemas, amusement parks, and museums all over Paris. Phillip's mother would no doubt have been suspicious except that nothing concerned her any more but her illnesses now, which were gradually taking organic form under the compulsion of her strong will to die. She had heart trouble and essential hyper-tension.

Al had tea with her almost daily and kept suggesting that after all she should return to America now that she was so ill. There she could get the best medical care and if the worst should come, at least she would be in her own country. Here he looked piously at the ceiling. When she confided in him that her husband was a dealer in dope and women, he said "Great Heavens!" and pressed her hand. "You are the bravest woman I have ever known!"

At this time, it so happened that Mr. Tourian himself was also looking towards the New World. His deals were so extensive that the number of people with real or imaginary grudges against him was growing to unmanageable proportions. So he began dickering with an employee of the American consulate. Needless to say, he had no intention of going through the tedious steps proscribed by law for immigration to America. The negotiations took longer than he had planned . . . While they were still in progress, Mrs. Tourian died in Istanbul.

For seven days she lay in bed looking sullenly at the ceiling as though resenting the death she cultivated for so many years. Like some people who cannot vomit despite horrible nausea, she lay there unable to die, resisting death as she had resisted life, frozen with resentment of process and change . . .

There was no one around her sufficiently keen, in a certain way, to understand her predicament. She was not sure of herself . . . she spent the last seven days balancing life, which she hated, against death, which she feared . . . She became so absorbed in this introspection that her body, weary of neglect and waiting for the word from above, died of its own accord. In some respects, hers was a complete death: her paralyzed soul, rid of all function by this neurasthenic indecision, went down the drain with everything else . . . rather absent-mindedly. As Phillip put it, "She sort of petrified."

After that, Phillip arrived in New York with his father. Al was back on the job in Virginia, in the paper plant, and wrote long letters to Phillip. Finally he grew bolder and began to spend weekends in New York. Mr. Tourian was busy with his new enterprises . . . things were harder in America . . . he paid no attention to his son's visitor. It got to the point where Al called Phillip the first thing on arriving at La Guardia Field: when Mr. Tourian answered the phone, Al would say, "Oh hello Mr. Tourian, is Phillip in?" Mr. Tourian was too preoccupied to know whether the boy was in or not. "Tell him I'll be over right away."

Al and Phillip would sometimes be gone for whole weekends, on mad trips to Boston or Baltimore or Washington . . . Young Phillip was obsessed with all kinds of desires . . . he wanted to drink, hike in the mountains and woods, meet as many people as he could, ride in a car at ninety miles per hour. Al, for his part, was too genuinely ravished by all this to make any attempts on Phillip's person . . . That could come later. In a way—considering Al's other affairs with older men in town— Phillip represented some kind of angelic and virginal symbol of homosexuality. Al began to write long lyrical poems to the boy.

They toured New England, Pennsylvania, New Jersey and Maryland, upper New York state. One long weekend found them in Montreal, in the whore houses on St. Catherine Street. And finally one summer they went to New Orleans in a car Al had bought for the occasion. It goes without saying that he was neglecting his job back home . . . and finally he did altogether quit. His irate brother wrote him a letter denouncing him as a "worthless tramp and a degrading pervert," and as far as he was concerned, he could stay that way. So Al cut off all contact with his past life and dedicated himself to Phillip. He moved to New York permanently and got a job as a longshoreman, then as a tutor. He finally found the ideal position, as tutor for a rich old woman who really didn't want to learn French but only wished to have someone to tell her troubles to. This old monied bitch had one complaint in life: that her daughter had gotten married without her consent.

"I'd given her all I had in my power . . . education, security, the comfort of a home . . . I took on the responsibility of a father, for her. Don't you think that's true? And then she went off and married that horrible man. I do think that she should have given *me* some consideration . . ."

"Yes," Al would say, reaching for another cheese soufflé, "you're perfectly right, Margaret you're perfectly right there."

The old woman had Al in for three hours every day, at five dollars an hour. Al spent the remaining twenty one hours with Phillip or worrying about where Phillip was when he couldn't find him, and gnawing his heart out wondering whether Phillip might not love him some day.

Phillip was a most precocious boy. He had long ago learned that to get what you wanted, you must be relaxed . . . this he inherited from his father. He attended a few private schools but promptly threw that up in favor of the wild free life of self-education through experience and extensive reading. By the time he was sixteen he was more than a match for Al in matters dealing with culture and anything else they found worthy of busying themselves with.

The love poems did not faze him. He knew what Al was after, but he also knew how to hold him off. In a way he liked Al a great deal, as most people did, and he didn't want to lose him as a friend. Besides, when Phillip began to get around among the young intellectual sets in New York and Boston, it added greatly to his decadent glamour to have this gray-haired Oscar Wilde tagging after him . . .

Phillip began to involve himself in love affairs, to Al's extreme consternation. It was characteristic of Phillip that he should have chosen as his one true love a young sculptress from Boston who looked like a younger Madame de Castaing with however much more sex appeal . . . They copulated to excess and oftentimes mutilated each other . . . They had orgies in baths of wine . . . Helen would sometimes tire of Phillip and run frantically outside, and there pick up a handful of mud and cry: "I'm sick of you! I want to create something with my hands." They had met at a Communist rally in Boston Common, in the rain. Al was somewhere around during all this, waiting with abject patience . . . Helen herself began to spend weekends in Manhattan.

It was at this time that Phillip's father was caught negotiating the sale of 20,000 grains of heroin.

He drew five years in the Atlanta penitentiary and the fines left him flat broke . . . Mr. Tourian had been losing his grip in America. When he got to Atlanta they had to ease him off the morphine habit in an interminable series of ephedrine injections . . .

A relative of Tourian, a New York Greek who was also a very influential politician, took over the guardianship of the boy. The idea was for Phillip to drop in on his uncle once a week in case he needed any extra money or wanted help of any kind. Phillip lived alone: his rent was paid, he had a limited allowance, and he was as free as a bird. This would have elated Al except that now Phillip and Helen were thicker than ever. Helen's weekend visits from Boston increased.

Al stayed on. Instead of abating, his passion for Phillip was growing stronger by the day. And it was now increasingly evident that Phillip resented Al's attentions. When his antagonism began to express itself in an open way, Al only retreated deeper into his masochistic position and hung on . . .

The fact that Al was a homosexual did not bother the sophisticated Phillip: it rather amused him. But what he now began to resent was Al's abject and melancholy demand to be loved. Al felt that it was coming to him; he had a ruined life to prove it; in so many ways, he made Phillip conscious of a most reprehensible and loathsome responsibility. Phillip did not see it as a responsibility, as anything of the sort. He clearly saw that it was Al's own error. And Phillip felt he had nothing in his power to retract the situation. He began to tell Al off . . .

And yet their friendship had been so strong, there was something so intimately tied up with his mother there, Phillip could not quite call it off altogether. When Al, in desperation, began to make advances, Phillip rejected him wearily. Things were beginning to drag horribly. The essential sado-masochistic nature of their relationship was at last coming to surface.

Meanwhile Phillip's fantastic education continued. Dennison, the bartender he and Al had met in a Baltimore bar, became a kind of successor to Al as a teacher. "The best thing for you to do, my boy, at any time, is to drop every book in your hand, burn all your paper and pencils and poems, and concentrate on living. Didn't you ever hear that song 'Life is Nothing but Living'? You are now living in a civilization, not a culture . . . in a late life of facts." Needless to say, Dennison at the time had been buried in a book himself, Spengler's book. Phillip absorbed all of Dennison's sober commonsense and clear vision; he had already absorbed Al's wit and charming intelligence.

Equipped with this formidable business, Phillip proceeded to rout out all the intellectuals he could find anywhere—the "little oases in the wasteland," he called them—and annihilate them. He eventually got a room in a family hotel off Washington Square and got to meet some of us, Feinstein, Ryko, Quincy, Alexander, and several score others. He also met Praline LaJeune, a beautiful blonde, a veritable capacious sea of womanhood, who, in her own sweet and innocent way, could attract any man in the world. She attracted Phillip. She of course didn't try to resist him.

Phillip and Helen were just breaking up at that time anyway. Their relationship was impossible . . . Tempers like theirs could not counterpoise. She was of course annoyed, nay whipped into annoyance, by Phillip's hesitating refusal to send Al off packing. At this time anyway it would have been impossible to send Al off packing . . . he just would not go. His life had left his body and gone into Phillip's. Those few times that Phillip was in accord with him, were enough to make him deliriously happy. He never doubted his emotions . . . He told Dennison to go to hell whenever it came to a question of giving up the Phillip idea . . .

Dennison, in his weary way, had developed an interest in these two. He was curious to see what would happen. And he thought Al a most interesting psychological phenomenon. That's what he said . . . The fact, however, is that Dennison genuinely liked Al. He was attracted by his fantastic courage, his color, his charm, and his twisted life. There was something ugly about Al's life that seemed beautiful to Dennison. He became Al's only living father-confessor. Dennison was excellent and superb even, in this role: he himself, like Phillip's father, had left sexuality by the wayside some way back there on the opium road . . . Dennison was something tied on to a brain. Occasionally he had a woman in his rooms—but there never was any question of dedicating his energies to luring a woman up there. They came, he received them . . . Sometimes he went and had himself a Turkish bath. Once a year. The rest of the time he worked, earned money, ate, slept, had his junk, and examined the people he knew under his shabby microscope.

Phillip and Praline LaJeune developed in accord a flaming romance. They fled each other in order to be more fascinating, and bounded back into each other's arms. They sat around for whole days at a time in a wreckage of books and talked and kissed.

Phillip had met Ryko in a bar. Ryko, the moody Finn with the mysterious air of the confirmed introvert, fascinated Phillip . . . Phillip and Feinstein went up to Ryko's apartment the next day. Ryko lived there with his woman, Janie Thomson. When they got there Ryko was asleep. Janie woke him up and he growled at her; then, getting up from his couch, he announced that he was hungry. The girl went into the kitchen to fix his dinner. Ryko scowled at Feinstein and said nothing. Feinstein was terrified.

After that, Phillip and Ryko became close friends, and Apartment 32 became the meeting place of the whole bunch. Phillip and Praline rendezvoused there perpetually . . . The others, mostly students, were there at all hours of the day with their tons of books. The whole thing was beginning to find its focus in one apartment . . .

It finally did. Ramsay Allen became an incurable caller. He told Phillip that he thought his little chums were charming . . . Eventually Dennison himself came, once, twice. He came, looking like something from an African compound, and squinted at all this young silly life . . .

Life *is* monstrous, but the young don't believe so. It was therefore amusing to gather it all in its mad unconcern under one roof and look at it. . . . No one bothered about death and darkness—even if they did read Rilke and discuss him. No one even bothered to ask why. Things just were. . . .

The last streetlamp down at the end of the street, the darkness beyond it . . . the mad twistings of destiny, beginning in Istanbul in 1926 . . . or for that matter whatever destiny went into the bringing-about of all the others, Dennison, Allen, Feinstein, Praline, Alexander, Quincy, Janie, Ryko, all of them . . . was not under consideration. These then were the little foeti crowding the race while a man lay in apathy in a Georgia penitentiary and a woman's bones rotted in the Turkish dirt . . .

Off they rushed, these kids, to see Tchelitchev's *Cache-Cache* at the Museum of Modern Art, to see themselves . . . They talked about it endlessly over their Pernod. None of them had looked at that painting long enough to learn not to talk about it.

Phillip was still trying to find out what plan was in his making. He wondered if he shouldn't become an artist, another Rimbaud. This became the big issue. Art! All over the Village the ghosts of 1912 lay sleeping on dusty bookshelves . . . and these little pip-squeaks were going to decide about art. And they did, by God.

Meanwhile Ramsay Allen employed all the artistry in his power and made great contributions to everything. It was, as the French say, *très formidable*! We had, at least,—(this is essential)—a little collective womb of our own . . . in which to play hide and seek, cache-cache.

CHAPTER FOUR

A LL THE LIVING DETAILS that go into the making of a climax are perhaps absurd, for maybe it is the people alone who matter—what they look like, what they wear, what they say, how they act—and not what they do. Fixed shadows, they may be, surrounded by a swirl of details, details like making phone calls and appointments, eating and sleeping, smoking and drinking and talking, standing, walking, or running, or sitting down, and rushing around in a perpetual human activity that is so mortal that no memory of it exists the next day.

For when we remember people there is only one picture . . . we see them as in a mental portrait, alone, doing nothing but sitting for the portrait. We see their faces and the clothes they wear, we see their eyes and the way they comb their hair, and they just sit there staring at us out of the frame of the mental portrait, alone and quite noble!

Perhaps absurd! . . . the fevered activity of their doings!

And yet again, maybe it is the goings-on of people that attest to their true personalities. Without that which they are doing, they may only be shadows without meaning, and one surrenders himself to a serious error believing that the inert remembered portrait is enough.

Personality and action! There is a way of reconciling these two, by seeing that the sum total of both produce eventually the portraiture that a person will bequeath to the minds of the earth. The portrait becomes a picture now . . . there is the person himself, and then there is a background, his background, cluttered with the ruins of his life's action . . . Pillars of ruined purpose scattered over a moor, as in a surrealist painting, and the face of the remembered person staring out over the wreckage of his activity.

At any rate, there was much activity, a mad flurry of it, springing from the events on the roof of Dennison's apartment house. These activities began on Sunday . . . they tumbled over one another and began definitely to point towards a climax, as the saying goes. Then and there, in the hot August dawn, on a rooftop, Phillip and Al were swept up in their destinies like wraiths in the updraft of sighing life . . . It was Phillip's moment of frozen realization. It was Al's moment of consummation and premonition.

Phillip decided that he would go away. And the moment he had decided that, it was made suddenly clear to him that he had wanted to go away for a long time.

He had seaman's papers. He was going to ship out with his new friend Ryko.

"Right away! And Al mustn't know a thing about it!"

"Why?" demanded the naive Ryko.

"Oh Christ you don't know him like I do. If he ever finds out he'll do something . . . I don't know what."

Ryko showed the palms of his hands and quietly said, "Why all the fuss?"

"The whole point of shipping out is to get away from Al. Don't you see?"

"Yes but you sound afraid of him."

Here Phillip looked askance at his new friend. "I have the gravest fear of Al. I have a feeling . . . that even if we sailed to a foreign land without his knowing about it, he'd be there sitting on the beach when we got there, smiling and waving at us, with five or six little Arab boys at his feet. Wearing a beret and cracking clam shells."

Ryko slapped his knee in appreciative amazement.

"There's something bizarre about Al's power." Phillip closed his eyes and shook his head. "Honestly there is."

Ramsay Allen, for his part, had like a child spent all day and night Sunday brooding ecstatically and turning over in his mind the marvellous events of the roof. Trembling from a most acutely sweet yet ineffable pain, he had nursed the aching and delicate events of a Saturday night, spending a whole Sunday at it . . . The most religious moments of American life are undergone on Saturday nights. Al had sat in his dark room smoking cigarette after cigarette, while the curtains spread and puffed in, bringing in faint rumors of 52nd Street, the jazz music and street traffic . . . He had sat like that interminably, full of soft and fearful joy. He hadn't dared go out and find Phillip. There was something he wanted to preserve, some perfection he wanted to absorb before jumping back into the continuity of living.

It was the most innocent day of his life.

On Sunday afternoon, Phillip began to pack his things in Washington Hall for transfer to his uncle's apartment on Central Park South. He threw clothing and books into an old suitcase while Ryko sprawled on the bed watching.

For money, Phillip had to go to dinner at his uncle's Long Island house in Queens. Ryko was persuaded to spruce up a bit, and the two of them went off to Long Island, into the wilds of the Bourgeois cottage.

Uncle Pete's mistress sat at the head of the table, gorgeous and formidable in the candle light.

"Uncle Pete," said Phillip after everyone had had dessert, "you'll have to give me some money to get things I need . . ."

"Sure, sure, kiddy." Uncle Pete flashed a broad Greek smile with a lot of gold teeth. "Now you're going to be a war hero, a merchant marine, I shouldn't finance a war hero? I'm patriotic yet." He handed his nephew a crisp twenty dollar bill, avoiding the look he was getting from the tall dark woman at the head of the table. "For my brother's boy I do anything." He turned around and flashed the gold teeth at his mistress. "The Tourians they got hearts of gold, and guts yet . . ."

Uncle Pete had a bullet proof car in the garage, and spent a lot of time watering the lawn and yelling hello at the neighbors, dressed exactly like them, in shirtsleeves with dangling suspenders. It wasn't that he was trying his best to be respectable . . . he was only making the best of a good thing. The neighbors liked him, but they grumbled when swarthy men drove up to Uncle Pete's in black Cadillacs and spilled out silently, like so many footpads. The neighbors said, "I don't know about that Pete Rogers!"

After dinner, Phillip and Ryko wandered around the neighborhood, giving it the once over. They had been living in Manhattan for so long that now they were bemused by all this suburban shrubbery and lawn, with soft lights falling out of windows. The quiet streets were dark. The stars were near and dazzling, practically touching the slanted rooftops of the half-timbered English style houses. A million treeleaves rustled a vast soughing orchestration . . .

"It gives you a tremendous feeling of isolation," said Phillip.

There were some small boys yelling and running around in the dark. They'd be calling each other from all kinds of dark places, and calling back . . . They flitted under streetlamps and disappeared again. They were playing some sort of game in which the darkness figured as their wild and joyous partner.

Meanwhile, the Bourgeois sat in their well lighted homes, not deigning to notice the darkness.

On Monday morning Phillip was up early to finish his packing, and after that went uptown and bought himself a membership book in the National Maritime Union. He cleaned up odds and ends, of which there were many with regard to shipping out in wartime . . . Then he came hurrying back to Apartment 32, to his friends, to Praline LaJeune, and was full of wild jubilance.

Apartment 32 was on the third floor of a rather shabby apartment house just off Washington Square. You went up to the door and pushed in: it was never locked.

Praline was sitting on the couch with her legs curled up underneath her, having a cup of coffee with Janie Thomson. Ryko was still in bed, having his customary morning coffee and cigarette, daily served up to him by his woman . . . He yelled "Well?"

"All set."

"Oh Phillip are you really serious about all this?!" This was Praline singing out. Out of a vague negative silence, she would sometimes cry out like that in a quavering sing-song voice that sounded like a denial of everything. She had long black hair, an exquisitely pale complexion—like Phillip's—and a habit of reacting perpetually, as though she couldn't assimilate a blessed thing that was ever said or happened.

"Poor petite," snickered Phillip dropping down on the couch beside her, "who's going to drink Pernod with her after I'm gone? . . ."

They started to neck. Ryko was mumbling out the details of their program for getting a job on a ship, from the bedroom, and a moment later he emerged in his shorts, with a cup of coffee in his hand. "Flaming youth," he said, and sat down in the easy chair.

"You guys think we're going to wait for you to come back?" demanded Janie, curling up her lip at Ryko. "We can get other men better than you."

"Oh well you've got to be faithful to us boys out there, you know."

Janie said "Humph!" with astounding significance.

Ryko grabbed Janie and pulled her into the chair, saying, "We can be flaming youth too."

Janie slugged Ryko over the head with a copy of Rimbaud's *Season in Hell*, and at that point the door in the hallway blew open and in sailed Erwin Feinstein, all eager and beaming.

"Well if it isn't the parasite," Janie greeted. "Have some coffee."

"Thank you," beamed Feinstein, "I will. How are you Praline? How are you Phillip? How are you Mike? And how are you Janie? How are all the little oases in the wasteland this dreary morning? . . ."

That was Feinstein all over . . . a ridiculous little monkey at the time, about sixteen years old, one with big ears, a huge vocabulary, and no brains at all. He dropped his seven books on the floor and flopped on the couch amid the human wreckage . . .

"What's this I hear," Feinstein now said, "about you deciding to go to sea?"

Phillip groaned. "Eee," he said, "no! How did you find out?"

"From Alexander."

"It's all over the damned N.Y.U. campus," Ryko said. "Now if Al doesn't find out about it, it'll be a miracle . . ."

Feinstein jiggled his knee up and down from sheer excitement and said, "Why all the secrecy?" He looked around at everybody, playing the wide-eyed little boy.

Phillip told him.

"But why do you want to sneak out on Al?" cried Feinstein. "He's so convenient!"

"He's getting inconvenient," Phillip replied swiftly.

And in reply to this, the little monkey said, leering at Phillip and grinning from ear to ear, "But how can Faust escape his Mephistopheles?"

That's the way things were in Apartment 32 . . . To add to the confusion there was a dog and a cat in the place. The little black cat, full of feline hell, prowled among the wreckage and disorder like a panther in a jungle of scattered books, bottles, pillows and what-not. The dog went on occasional tantrums, overturning tea tables and chairs, as though some of the silliness had gotten into her too. Phillip was her lover; he stimulated her constantly. You only had to yell "Phillip!" and the dog would take a fit and race around barking.

The place was always a shambles. Janie could not keep up with it . . . You couldn't keep a place clean that had become the clubroom of a dozen or so twentieth-century young intellectuals, so called. Either people came there with a half dozen books or they came with a bottle. And they all smoked, which added to the confusion. At any hour of the day, you could find kids in that place, in the daytime sitting around bawling in loud voices about Nietzsche and Rouault and T. S. Eliot and drinking coffee; or in the night time, scattered around sleeping in chairs and on couches.

No one in the place—that is, Janie and Ryko, who lived there; and Phillip, who practically and unofficially lived there—made any claims to being Bohemian. Bohemianism was a lost word. But no place in Manhattan could boast a purer Bohemianism . . . It stirred like something alive, this apartment. Cockroaches raced around in delirious freedom . . . The dog and cat were always one step ahead of the mistress . . . a situation which in turn later introduced a little colony of maggots. No one acutely minded. The Board of Health has a hell of a time keeping track of all the real hygienic menaces in town . . . like the law, whose long arm can't always reach everybody, into all the obscure little doorways where lurk the Danny Bormans.

Besides, the whole point was that no one could ever be lonesome in this open house asylum . . . People were always pushing in the door and and shouting cheery "Hellos." Young people don't have as yet that stodgy pride, that sour fussiness which created the "God Bless Our Home" placard that hangs in millions of American homes. Whoever conceived that monstrous slogan must surely have wasted away a few months later in his cozy nook; and it is certain that he was no young man.

Considering, though . . . there were some really comfortable easy chairs in Apartment 32 but they had rents in them, with the melancholy cotton bulging out. The walls were hung with bright watercolor paintings, about ten of them . . . They had been done by some unknown southerner: splashed with sunlight and green trees, they were. When the sun shone the apartment rippled like the inside of an aquarium from the moted reflection of these bright things.

At the moment, now, a new arrival was barging in. It was John Alexander, swishing in from outside, full of news about what had happened on the Fifth Avenue bus. "A woman!" he bellowed. "I can't say exactly *what* she was, Russian *or* something . . . God! She had a fur piece, mind you in the dead of summer, and a terrible black hat that hung over her ears . . . and a *huge* necklace and bracelets and *four*—four rings on *each* hand . . . *eight* altogether!" Alexander heaved a large happy sigh. He was a big aristocratic looking adolescent hulk . . . In the winter he always wore a white scarf, and gloves, and attended ballets and the theater with rich old ladies who had taken a liking to him. "And the lipstick! And rouge all over her face practically down to the chin, and flaming red fingernails, and this *immense* purse with sequins and enormous initials embroidered on it! Oh God!" he roared. Whereupon he rolled on for some time with his story. These were the things he was interested in . . . Old dowagers gleamed in his eye. If they sat behind drawn blinds in old brownstone East Side houses, in those grotesque black velvet dresses they all seem to take to, weighed down with jewelry and gloom and spite, John Alexander would like to sit with them, would like to be charming and while away the hours . . . Anything they needed, he would get it for them: he had the perfect chairside manner.

He himself came from a wealthy tribe of New York insurance brokers. He was at N.Y.U., however, only to learn the business side of things. A few previous years at Yale had tuned him to the right pitch. Now he haunted fashionable shops on Fifth Avenue, and the better cocktail lounges. This had proved to be fortuitous: one old dowager had picked him up . . . She wasn't heavy enough with ice to suit Alexander, but he did deign to escort her to the opera, and to private recitals here and there.

His interest in Apartment 32 was purely academic . . . he had had Ryko do several term papers for him. His interest was getting less and less academic, however, since he had subsequently taken a liking for both Janie and Praline . . . Praline, from force of reacting, was always bounding up against someone or other, ricocheting, as it were . . . and it was plain to John that she would ricochet against him some time.

"Everybody's got to help me move my stuff!" Phillip announced. "There's drinks in it, my uncle's going to give me some more money."

"I still don't believe that you'll actually get a ship." Praline announced this, blushing and looking at Phillip, in a kind of underemphasized complaint against the world.

"Your ego'll be severely jolted!" he warned jokingly.

She uttered a piercing "Oh!" and punched him in the arm, blushingly . . . Her nerves were all shot from reacting in all directions from everything. She lived, indeed, in the smack middle of a bloody self-made war . . . She wanted Phillip, anyone could see that, but she hated what she wanted because she wasn't sure she wanted anything. He was a great positive force upsetting her negative security . . . So that, refusing to admit to her life that she wanted Phillip, since that would be treason, she nevertheless being a very versatile creature, found some way by God to just as well deny her denial of Phillip.

And now evidently he was going to be forcibly denied her altogether.

They started to wrestle . . . They knocked over the portable radio which had been playing Brahms. The dog nervously joined the fray. Feinstein jumped up so he wouldn't get kicked on the shins by the flying feet . . .

"Oh God!" groaned John Alexander, who disapproved of spectacles such as these. He removed himself to the other room in a kind of a huff. "Really Janie," he whispered savagely to her, "how *can* you bear those two when they start wrestling . . ."

"For krissakes!" yelled Janie at the combatants. "You're so silly!"

There was a flash of Praline's thighs, and a lot of silly giggling and shrieking on her part. She answered Janie, in the midst of her exertions, as follows: "Oh nuts! I always wrestle with my brother!"

Praline lived in Manhasset with her mother and brother, and attended the New School of Social Research in Greenwich Village. She spent more time wrestling and necking with Phillip Tourian in Apartment 32 than she did in school. Which was just as well.

"Come on Phil," Ryko was saying, "get a headlock on her."

"Oh yeah!" yelled Praline. She proceeded to tumble Phillip flat on his back. A very athletic girl.

It became very festive when Walter Quincy . . . he had come in search of a certain book . . . arrived a little drunk. He was looking for Lucretius; he had to study for an examination.

"Best line in that," Phillip told him, "is 'Aye, men have died from terror of the mind!' Here's your Lucretius." He had fished it out from a heap of books in a disorderly corner of the apartment. "The rest of that is just an extension of terror."

"Well," said Walter, "anyway, does anyone want a drink." It developed he had a pint of apple brandy with him . . . Why he was drinking in the middle of the day nobody knew. It wasn't really a vital point. Everybody tried some of the brandy, and the pint disappeared without Walter's showing any sign of sadness.

So there they were, the seven of them, and the two animals, and all the cockroaches, having a great time in Apartment 32. It was always like that . . .

Eventually, Phillip put his foot down and demanded once and for all that someone help him move his stuff. Ryko went into his den, a little room at the other end of the place, to put on a shirt. Janie followed him in there.

"Mickey," she said, "don't go."

Ryko said "Huh?"

The girl forced him to sit down in the easy chair—this was the chair he sat in to read, or to stare out the window at dirty rooftops—and dropped herself on his lap. She was now launched off on a campaign to dissuade him from going to sea. All so futile, of course, because Ryko had been thinking of going to sea for six months without any visible signs of movement . . . He sat in the chair now, looking out at the rooftops, burdened down with the weight of his woman. A depressing scene . . . There were heaps of dust in the corners of this little room, as though the room itself were rotting dreamily, like its inhabitant.

He said, "Oh take it easy, we'll be back in a few months with loads of money."

"Mickey don't go."

"Oh boloney."

As he said that he realized what he had done . . . She had an opening now: she was going to cry. He took her hand and bit the knuckles gently. "When I get back we'll go to Florida or someplace for the winter."

"I don't want you to leave me."

"I'm *not* leaving you . . . I'm going on a trip to make some money."

She sniffled. "You *are* leaving me."

Ryko lapsed into a general silence of desperation. "Even Phillip doesn't really want to go," she went on insidiously. "He only wants to shake off that old queer bastard Allen . . . *He* doesn't want to leave Praline."

Ryko shrugged helplessly.

"He loves her," she said, going through the tear drying motions with the back of her hand. "He loves her like you'll never love me, because you're so stupid and dumb . . . I wish you had as much sense as Phillip. *He's* an Indian."

This was one of Janie's characteristic remarks. She would come out with something that was entirely meaningless to anyone but her . . . She was an extraordinarily natural girl, it was clear.

"Well," said Ryko, stabbing in the dark, as it were, "if Phillip is your Indian why don't you go and bother him." This was of course another blunder . . . Now Janie had the final and glorious opening.

"Oh you're so cute!" she cried, and kissed him. "My little Mickey is jealous . . ."

Here, he had to grin sheepishly. But finally—displaying what was for him a remarkable sense of assertion—he pulled himself together and said: "I have to go on this trip. Good Christ do you realize that I haven't had a cent of my own for months? I can't go on spending your money like this."

"You can always get that little job back!" she snapped angrily.

Now everything was taking on the proportions of a real domestic squabble.

"Aah!" There was your Ryko for you: if he couldn't think of anything else to say, he said "Aah!" in great disgust.

"Oh why don't we ever get married!" Janie said.

Rather placidly, he replied, "Oh we will some day."

"You bastard, you know you'll never get around to it."

"Hell! Who am I to marry? And who are you thinking you want to marry, Rockefeller?"

Janie had a trust fund in her name, providing her with some thirty odd dollars a week . . . On top of this, her father in Denver kept sending her money every time he wrote a letter. Her father was a happy old widower who liked to spend his weekends at ranch parties out there, and write and tell his daughter about it. His name was George Thomson and he could drink anybody in Colorado under the table.

Janie, a slender blonde with a flamboyant almost masculine air about her, had deserted a rather insane life out in Colorado with her father—the steak fries, the drunken hunting trips, the wild automobile rides—for this decidedly more insane life in Manhattan . . . She had originally come east under the pretext of wanting to learn to paint. Her father believed in her implicitly, that is, he didn't care what she did.

Janie had met Ryko in a bar. Bars are where Americans seem always to meet, especially if they're New Yorkers . . . She had thought that this bony red-haired Finn was the most wonderful guy in the world. He was a writer, she told her friends, and he was a genius . . . Besides, she added, he was so cute. No one in the world had exactly that same shape of neck and back: you could recognize him immediately from a distance if you saw him with his back turned. They had begun by getting drunk in bars and rushing off to cheap hotels. Ryko could drink whiskey for breakfast . . . that was another recommendation.

Finally, after Janie had gotten herself an apartment—the ill-fated Apartment 32—Ryko had casually moved in. He was, technically speaking, a merchant seaman . . . After a few trips overseas he settled down in Apartment 32 to write. He was writing, they said, a huge prose poem called "The American Night." This went on for quite some time . . . Ryko's parents lived in Pennsylvania and every now and then, on the impulse of a pang of some kind, he hitch-hiked out there on nostalgic returns. A gloomy brooding drunken hoodlum . . .

Poor fellow! He was in the clutches of a woman far too shrewd for him, the dreaming Finn . . . Still, if it wasn't a matter of being in someone's clutches, he was otherwise lost. It was hard to say what Janie wanted of him. She supported him, she ministered to his every need . . . He never worked any more. He never even helped with the dishes . . . There was just enough of the dance-hall romeo in him to save his life, that's it.

"I don't want you to go to sea," Janie now said firmly.

"I'm going."

"Then you can go to hell."

There was a lot of noise in the front room. Everybody was getting ready to go and move Phillip's junk . . . Janie went into the bedroom to pout. There were all kinds of convenient rooms in the place for the kids to brood and pout in.

"Janie doesn't want to come," Ryko confessed guiltily.

"Come on Janie!" they yelled. There was no answer.

"There'll be drinks in it," Phillip said at the door of her bedroom. "Come on, we'll have fun."

Janie said nothing and hid her face in the pillows. Ryko went over to pacify her. He said a few words and got no reply either.

"Well let's go," he said, and everybody started out. "Sure you don't want to come?" he threw back. There was no answer . . . The dog glared at him.

They went around the corner to Phillip's place, Feinstein and Quincy disengaging themselves from the party because they had something else to do. It was arresting, in Phillip's room, to see a picture of his father on the wall, with the penitentiary numbers underneath. Beside this display, there hung a masochist whip from a nail. Phillip tenderly laid away the poster of his father and the masochist whip in a box. He had reproductions of paintings, chiefly of the Impressionist and Paris school period; books, record albums, easels, an amazing assortment of medicine bottles, a saber of some sort, pornographic pictures, whole boxes of assorted junk he had picked up during his three years in America . . . It was all eventually carted down to the lobby of the family hotel. John Alexander, who loved to hail cabs, went out to hail one . . .

"Well," said Mr. Gross the proprietor of Washington Hall, "we hate to see you go, Mr. Tourian." He was checking Phillip out in the guest book. "Allow me to wish you bon voyage." Mr. Gross was a fatuous old man who smoked Egyptian cigarettes. "I must say we've never had quite so cooperative and charming a young guest." He smiled as Phillip paid him the back rent. "And so now you're going to sea," he added, folding the money in his hands in a very courtly manner.

"Yes . . . you've heard the old saying haven't you? The sea instead of the paint brush. Better I could not do."

"Oh yes," said Mr. Gross, "oh yes indeed." He was going to say something else but the lobby phone rang. The taxicab had come, and Ryko and Alexander were hauling the boxes of junk into it.

"Mr. Tourian," said Gross, "it's for you. Take the call in the phone booth."

Phillip dashed into the phone booth and called out, "Hello hello," rather merrily.

"Phil?"

"Oh. Yes."

"You sound surly," said Ramsay Allen. After a pause he said, "I didn't come yesterday." This was Al's way of justifying the present call. He had spent all day Sunday holding himself back. "I'll come down today."

"No don't."

"No? I've got something to show you, Phil . . . it's about Neoptolemus and Philoctetes, an essay by Edmund Wilson called 'The Wound and the Bow.' It's amazing how it fits in . . . with us. Really! Philoctetes you see is exiled on an island because of a terrible sore but he has a magic bow that the Greeks want, so they send Neoptolemus to steal it from him and—"

"Yeah!"

"Well, I guess you don't want to hear it over the phone. Now shall I come over?"

"No."

The silence which followed at Al's end of the wire bore an odd similarity to all the desperate talking he had done a moment before. It was a kind of baffled pain, with confusion in it where Al seemed not to want to be pained.

"God, Phil, what's wrong?"

"I think it would be better if you stayed away."

"Better for who, Phil?"

"Better for me."

"But why? What's wrong? Is it . . . is it on account of Saturday night?" Al said this with such a soft undertone of assurance that Phillip saw red.

He clenched his teeth and said, "That was my way of saying goodbye."

"Goodbye?" bleated Al, out of his mind now. "Where are you going?"

"Nowhere. I just don't want you down here any more, that's all."

Phillip slammed the receiver down on the hook and barged out of the phone booth. At the other end of the wire, which he had just shut off, a great new despair was begun . . . He could feel it all the way across the city.

The others were waiting in the cab.

Phillip jumped in and gave the driver his uncle's address. "I hope the old bastard gives me enough money for us to get drunk on," he said, putting his arm around Praline. That was the way he put it.

CHAPTER FIVE

YOU STAND UNDER A STREETLAMP in the night rain and mourn whatever in this rotting life on earth could have consumed you and made you hate death. Now, instead of that, it's gone, whatever it is you might have fiercely loved during your torturous stay, it's gone and you've nothing else really to bother your little head about . . . You retch at the thought of the absurdity and the insipid folly of yourself. Or if what you want is not altogether yet out of your grasp, you can nevertheless feel it slip away in the slow death rattle all around you. Again, you begin to envy death, an invalid beggar jealous of the healthy young factory worker, to put it one way. . . .

The rain falls on you and you don't at all care. You also realize that you have never really cared. Whatever it is that you wanted in life, that alone has made you care . . . Yet you realize that you didn't really care, for how explain how placidly you accepted that which you wanted, when you had it, before this night rain, this time marking the point at which your desire has become an impossibility. All authentic desire is unreasonable: it comes when the object of its yearning is out of reach. Before that, all desire is willy-nilly and a bit drunk and silly, unthinking and vain. Now that this particular night rain is falling your desire has come to birth. Whatever you wanted is slipping away, and with the consequent slipping-away comes the first authentic desire . . .

Ramsay Allen therefore became desperate. He was now armed with desire, with it as he had never known it . . . He was now consumed with failure—which seems to be the only thing that can eat one up into eternity.

He hurried back towards his room on 52nd Street. He was mad with a new bravado . . .

Unfortunately Dennison happened to be entering Mrs. Frascati's rooming house just as he bounded up the steps.

"Well, Al, where have you been in this rain?"

Al couldn't tell him that he had been wandering along the East River. He couldn't tell him anything except the facts, which would lead to confusion. That's the way it is: the quintessence of what you are is going to be misunderstood perpetually by well-meaning bores.

"Why, I was just over to Tom Sullivan's . . ."

"What on earth for?"

"Oh just cadging a few drinks . . ."

They went down the dim hallway into Al's room . . . Al picked up a slim volume and tucked it under his arm.

"I was just going down to the Village, Will. We can ride down together."

"Well, let's wait till some of the rain stops, shall we?"

Al sat down on the couch desperately. Dennison made himself comfortable in the long easy chair. He said, "This morning I got a letter from a detective agency to report to work. I applied for this job about a month ago and had almost forgotten about it. Evidently they haven't checked on the fingerprints . . . and the fake references I gave them. I went down and accepted the job, Al. They handed me a batch of summonses to get rid of . . ."

"Swell, Will."

"I spent all day running around town to serve a summons on someone named Leo Levy, who is, I must say, a very elusive Jew. Give a New York Jew a few partners and he'll get himself so incorporated you'll always end up serving papers on the wrong party."

"Yes, I suppose that's the way they are . . ."

Dennison was pleased with his new job. It goes without saying that he was all through with the Continental Cafe. "Do you know," he said, "that bartending can be the worst kind of work . . . I remember one time in Newark, I had a cold and felt lousy, and one of the regular customers said what's the matter Will, you're so quiet tonight . . . Americans always think there's something wrong if you're not continually blowing off your mouth. I went on that way all night saying nothing . . . Finally this regular customer began to take it as a personal affront and got very sour about it . . . Americans instinctively mistrust silent people, you know, as though they were spies or F.B.I. men or worse. . . ."

"Especially in bars," put in Al wearily. "Say, I think it's stopped raining now. Let's go, shall we?"

Someone was knocking on the door. "Who's there?" cried Al, jumping up. The door opened and Agnes O'Rourke stuck her head in . . .

"Hullo there." She came in and sat down on the couch next to Al. "I think Hugh is being held by the F.B.I. . . ."

Dennison sat up. "Yeah? He told me Sunday they were looking for him. He planned to go down there this morning and see them . . ."

"Well he did, and he hasn't been back. I called there . . . it's the House of Detention . . . I called there this afternoon and they wouldn't admit that they were holding him. I'm sure he must be there because we had arranged for him to contact me if he could."

"Did you ask if they were holding a Hugh Maddox?" Dennison asked.

"They wouldn't admit that they were holding anybody by that name."

"Come to think of it," Dennison mused, "I never did know whether his name was Madix, Maddocks, Madox, or Maddox, or how many d's are in it . . ."

"Well," said Agnes, getting up, "I'm going to look into this tomorrow the first thing. I'm not going to work."

"Well then, good luck Agnes. Let me know how things turn out."

Agnes swaggered to the door and stopped there to turn her head. She always held her head a little to the side, in a kind of virile defiance and challenge . . . "I'll find out all right. So long now."

When she had left, Al went to the window and stuck his nose against the pane. "It's stopped raining, Will, let's go . . ."

"If you like."

It was around midnight. The subways were crowded with people reading the *Daily News and Mirror* . . . Dennison asked Al what was wrong. They were leaning against the subway door staring dejectedly at each other.

"I called up Phillip today and he told me he thought it would be better if I stayed away from there. I asked him what he meant, and he said 'better for me' and hung up . . ."

"Did he seem serious about it?"

"Yes . . . it was all said in a very sulky tone."

Dennison leaned over and said, "Well let it ride for awhile, why don't you."

Al compressed his lips together. "I'm going down there now," he said after awhile. "I'm going to climb into his room . . ."

Dennison squinted at him. "Well, that's taking the bull by the horns."

"No, you don't understand. . . . I'm just going into his room while he's asleep and watch him for awhile. After that, I'll leave. . . . I'm bringing along this Edmund Wilson essay to leave on his bed."

"And suppose he should wake up? He'll think it's some vampire hovering over him . . ."

"Oh no," Al said in resigned dejection, "he'll just tell me to get out. This has happened before . . ."

"What? . . . What do you do, just stand there?"

"Yes. I just get as close to him as I can without waking him up and stand there till dawn."

"You'll probably be arrested for attempted burglary, or shot, more likely."

"Well," said Al, "I'll just have to take the chance. I've looked the place over . . . You know the place, Washington Hall. I can take the elevator to the top floor, then climb up on the roof by the fire escape and wait there until three or four o'clock. Then I climb down into his room. His room is on the top floor, the fifth . . ."

Dennison shook his head. They had arrived at Sheridan Square . . . They got out and went up on the street. It had stopped raining altogether.

"Don't get into the wrong room and start hovering over some perfect stranger."

Al said, "Well, I know which is his room."

They were standing near a newsstand. Across the street, in a bar, a lot of noise and music was going on . . . It didn't really matter what night it was, Saturday or Monday, the bars in Manhattan were always the same.

"Well," Dennison said, "I wish you luck." He tucked the newspapers under his arm and looked at Al. Al walked away. Dennison went home down the narrow silent street leading off the Square . . . All the time he knew when to go to bed—it was getting to be awful.

Al hurried along up Christopher Street. When he got to Washington Hall the street door was locked and the elevator man on duty wouldn't let him in. Al wandered over to Washington Square and sat on a bench.

He knew in advance that nothing would stop him . . . but he just wanted to sit there and think about his determination. After awhile, his plan began to formulate itself, without any effort, as though his determination rather than his mind were functioning for him. Finally he got up and went back to Washington Hall . . .

This time he went down an alley and jumped over a wooden fence. Two cats scattered away . . . In the dark, he was in the cat world, the surreptitious night world denied to normal men and angels . . . The cats growled at each other the other side of the darkness. Al was one of them . . . He knew that his eyes were gleaming. A unique madness was in him, one granted to very few men, he thought. He tiptoed along until he came to the fire escape. He would have emitted a loud cry if the circumstances of his plan had permitted. The cats snarled in the darkness. . . .

Al jumped up and grabbed the fire escape. The loud creaking noise silenced the cats . . . Al held his breath. Then slowly, amid great creaking and squealing of rusty iron, he started up the fire escape.

Someone was looking at him from an open window. "What are you doing there?"

Al recognized this person as the elevator man who had refused to let him in. "Oh, the elevators aren't running so I thought I'd climb up here instead of bothering anybody. I just want to see a friend of mine . . . How about taking me up in the elevator?"

These mad remarks were absurd . . . Al was reaching the end of his mortal tether . . .

"All right," said the elevator man, "come in here." He extended a hand to Al and helped him in to the hallway. As soon as Al was on his feet the little Negro produced a length of steel pipe stuck in rubber hose and said, "You wait right here till I get Mr. Gross." Saying this, he waved the pipe in Al's face . . .

"I'll wait," said Al, smiling . . .

He was thinking that if he ran out of the place at this point, he wouldn't be able to come back. He decided to wait and talk his way out of the situation when Gross got there. There was no doubt about the fact that he would eventually be led to Phillip . . .

Mr. Gross arrived a few minutes later in a dirty blue and white bathrobe with egg and coffee stains all over the front of it, followed by Pat the elevator man. Al walked forward and said, "You see, Mr. Gross—"

"We'll do the talking around here!" shouted Mr. Gross, stopping Al with outstretched hands. His voice was full of authority. "Watch him, Pat!" Pat stood there rocking back and forth on his heels, slapping the steel pipe into the palm of his left hand, with a crafty gleam in his eye . . .

Al said: "I just wanted to see someone I know in the house."

Gross said, "Come along." They led Al down to the lobby desk. Gross went over and picked up the telephone. He held it in a lordly manner. "Who do you know in the house?" he asked.

"I know Walter Quincy."

"Well, we'll check on that right now." Gross stepped over and rang Quincy's buzzer . . . After a considerable interval, Gross was talking over the phone in unctuous tones. "Mr. Quincy, there's someone down here who says he knows you. We want you to come down and identify him. Sorry to disturb you but it's quite important."

After awhile, Quincy came down from the third floor wearing a silk bathrobe. Al started to get up.

"Just sit right there," said Gross, and turned to Quincy. "Mr. Quincy," he said, "do you know this man?"

"Yes," said Quincy casually. "What's all the trouble?"

"We found him climbing up the fire escape, and he claims he was on his way to see you . . ."

"Certainly," said Quincy calmly, "I'd been expecting to see Al tonight but I didn't feel quite well and went to bed early. It's quite all right, Mr. Gross."

"Well," said Gross, "if you say so, Mr. Quincy."

Al grinned. He said to Walter Quincy: "Well I'll come back tomorrow, Walt. Sorry I got you out of bed."

"It's okay," said Quincy. "See you tomorrow then. I guess I'll go back to bed now, I've got an exam on Lucretius tomorrow . . ."

"Well, sleep tight," said Al. "See you at Vanzetti's."

"Right."

Quincy started back up the stairs and Al got up as if to leave.

"Just a minute!" said Gross, holding out his hands to Al. "You don't seem to realize that this is a very serious matter . . . If it wasn't for Mr. Quincy you'd be on your way to the police station right now. In fact, it's really my duty to call the police."

"Well," said Al softly, "I'm sorry—"

"Oh you're *sorry*! Well, your being sorry doesn't make a particle of difference. I happen to be responsible for the lives and property of everyone in this building. Do you know that it's against the law even for people that live in the building to climb on the fire escape?"

"No," said Al, cocking his head to one side, "I didn't know that."

"So you didn't know that, and you pretend to be a man of intelligence!" Al hadn't had a chance to pretend anything . . .

"Of course, now that you mention it," Al went on in placating tones, "it does seem reasonable. I guess I just didn't think."

"It's about time you did some thinking, isn't it?" said Gross. "Here you've gotten Mr. Quincy out of bed and myself out of bed—"

"I'm sorry to have disturbed your sleep," said Al quickly.

"Well! . . . that's not the point! This is a criminal offence. Why, if I did the right thing, I'd call the police this very minute . . . Do you realize that?"

"Yes," said Al, "I appreciate it."

"Well! You appreciate it, do you? The only reason I *don't* call them is because of Mr. Quincy, one of my finest guests." Here Gross shook his head and sort of laughed. "Why, I don't understand this thing at all. If you were a college boy it would be different, but you're a man of practically my age . . . Now isn't that true?"

"I promise you," Al said, "that nothing of the sort will ever happen again."

"Well I can promise you that if it does, you'll certainly go to jail!" Gross shook his head again in acute puzzlement. "Now, since Mr. Quincy says you're allright, I guess we'll let it go. But you know don't you, Pat, that I really should call the police?"

"Yes, Mr. Gross," said Pat.

Gross stared at Al in a bit of a prissy huff and said nothing. There seemed to be some kind of a vague dismissal in all this, with the result that Al made a move to leave.

"Just a minute," said Gross, holding up one hand. "You don't seem to realize that Patrick, here, my elevator man, risked his life tonight . . . It seems to me he ought to have some say in this matter." Gross turned to the elevator man. "Well Patrick, what do you think we ought to do?"

"Well," said Pat shaking his head, "I don't like to see anybody go to jail . . ."

"I think you owe Patrick an apology," said Gross severely.

Al turned to Pat. "I'm sorry about this thing—"

"It's pretty easy to say you're sorry," interrupted Gross, "and I'm not going to stand here all night talking to you . . . After all I've lost enough sleep as it is, though I guess that doesn't mean anything to *you*. Last summer wasn't it, Patrick, that a thief climbed up the fire escape and stole twenty dollars from someone's room? I think it was Mr. Cucci's room, am I right or wrong?"

"Yes sir, Mr. Gross," said Pat, "I think it was . . ."

"We'll forget about this," Gross went on, turning to Al, "I'm willing to let it go just this one time."

Al said, "You're being very lenient and I thank you. Sorry for all the trouble I caused you . . ."

"I think a lot of Mr. Quincy and I'm only doing this for him, you understand?"

"Yes, I understand," Al said. He began to edge around the desk shyly.

"I know I'm not doing the right thing but I'm going to let you go. I hope you realize what I'm doing for you, because after all this is no laughing matter."

Al nodded, edging away all the time.

"All right Pat," said Gross, "let him go!" Pat stood aside warily and Al slipped by. He went down the hall, and paused to turn around and say goodnight, as graciously as he dared. Gross stood and stared at Al, and did not deign to answer.

The little elevator man went to the street door with Al and opened it.

"I should have told Mr. Gross that I also know Mr. Tourian in this house," Al told the elevator man in a low confidential voice. "Don't you think so Pat?"

Pat maintained his silence, opening the door wider in a righteous flourish and waiting.

"Well," said Al, "say hello to Mr. Tourian for me when you see him. Goodnight, Pat . . . Thanks for everything."

Pat looked at Al craftily . . . Al was standing outside the door cravenly and Pat was closing it. Suddenly, something occurred to Pat . . . he held the door open a few inches and said, "Mr. Tourian? That Phillip boy? He's gone, he moved out today . . . he's gone to join the merchant marine."

"Oh is that so?" said Al conversationally . . . he was smiling broadly. But Pat wasn't to be lured into any more of this. He closed the door in Al's face, shook the knob a few times to make sure it was securely locked, and waited for Al to go away from there . . . Al waved feebly and slinked off . . .

He stopped in the nearest doorway to consider what he had heard. It all sounded like a fantastic conspiracy to bluff him . . . It was all silly, of course. No such thing had happened.

He hurried off towards Washington Square . . . Benches and walks were bright from the washed glitter of the earlier rain. Everything looked dark and clean, with earthy odors. Here was Al, walking around in circles. He went down the street a ways and peered up at the windows of Apartment 32 . . . they were dark, no one was there right now. Where was Phillip? Where was everybody? Where were the kids? . . . He wanted to play, too. But they were always hiding from him, as though they didn't like him, and besides he didn't live in this

neighborhood . . . Phillip didn't want him to live around here.
So he had to live in the other neighborhood uptown and he
didn't belong down here at all . . .

Al walked around the Square a couple of times to think.
Each time he passed the little side street, he would look up to
see if there was any light in the windows of Apartment 32 . . .
They were still dark. The kids were off somewhere, playing.
In Manhattan, you can never find anybody: the place is so
big . . . anybody you might want to find, might be miles and
miles away, yet still be in Manhattan—among the ten thousand
bars and hundred thousand streets. It's hopeless: you can't find
them even if you search all night, all day, all night again . . .
all your life.

Dennison was sleeping. No, he mustn't bother Dennison . . .
Al decided, in fact, that there was no point in seeing Dennison. There was no point in seeing anybody or doing anything
except Phillip . . . And Phillip couldn't be found. Phillip was
one who found you himself.

Al went down the subway steps three times, on Sixth
Avenue, and three times he came back up on the street to
stand around staring at everybody. Each time he went down
the steps, he knew he would come up again. There was no
point in that either . . . that was clear. Finally Al went down
the subway steps a fourth time, and with great effort, pushed
himself through the turnstile. He was on the uptown platform
and so he couldn't possibly go anywhere but uptown . . .

There was nothing downtown anyway . . . Just Brooklyn,
the Far Rockaway ends of night. Phillip wasn't out there, certainly . . . Phillip wasn't in the subway station either. And he
wouldn't be uptown, certainly. If you rode all the way uptown
on this subway train, it took you to the far ends of the Bronx.
You could ride on the subway all night long from Rockaway
to the Bronx, traversing the earth back and forth for a nickel,
until the conductor threw you off for loitering. That's the way
it was, if you couldn't find the kids, and Phillip, who was with
the kids, playing . . .

If you couldn't find Phillip, you were going to get thrown
off for loitering, right smack off the earth. That's what it was.

A wretched little man came up to Al and said, "You need
faith just like everyone else . . . Take this home with you and
read it, and find your faith in God." The little man handed Al

a pamphlet that had a picture of Jesus on it . . . Al automatically took the pamphlet; and the little man wandered off . . . automatically also. The train was coming, making a lot of noise, making the platform tremble. The "D" train, it was.

Al stared at the pamphlet and threw it away. The subway doors were opening and he would have to decide for good whether or not to get inside and be taken uptown. Well, he stepped in, and the subway doors closed behind him. Once they're closed, you can't get out, because the train starts, and it's impossible to open those doors anyway. They're operated on a single control. The man who closes the doors won't open them again for love or money. Everybody in New York knows that by now.

So the train started uptown.

The little man had seen Al throw the pamphlet away . . . The little man was annoyed . . . he concealed his pique, however. He just couldn't understand people who didn't need faith . . . everyone needed faith, by God. That much was certain. How else does one stay alive, if not with faith? Hey? Is there anything else that keeps one going? The little man was certain there wasn't anything else, he was absolutely certain by all that's holy.

CHAPTER SIX

WITH RAMSAY ALLEN'S DISCOVERY of Phillip's intention to ship out, there now began a final kind of relationship between them which could only lead to a ferocious settlement.

You had that exact feeling when you saw them walking down the street together—(for Al had decided to make a tremendous effort to seem reconciled to Phillip's proposed departure, and was accompanying both boys to and fro from the union hall as they went about the business of getting their ship). Phillip, who had always walked like a man possessed, with his heels scuffling and clicking, head erect and eyes brooding downwards, was now transformed into daemonic man himself, a mad young swashbuckling seafarer, as it were, and he walked as though he were now on his way to hell and the ends of the earth. There walked Phillip, with the perennial cigarette in his mouth, eyes cast down in painful concentration . . . and over him, practically, hovering and bounding along with head cocked to one side, lunged Ramsay Allen solicitously.

It was something to behold. They were both ragged and mad-seeming, and behind them scuffled the lazy Ryko.

In the three days that followed, that time which was not spent in the union hall waiting in line, signing papers, arguing with officials and conspiring against the bureaucratic system, was spent in one long dissipation that assumed proportions of grandeur as it heroically progressed.

The days were spent in the union hall in an irritating series of conspiracies to circumvent red tape. All the new guile that was in their modern power was employed.

The nights were spent in Greenwich Village, in the Bowery, on Times Square, on waterfront streets, in one blazing zig-zagging trail that left in its wake perhaps one hundred new acquaintances and one hundred forgotten conversations.

It was a welter, and it is very difficult to ascertain where it began and where it ended, this three-day orgy of unconstrained living.

It may have really begun on Tuesday morning, when Phillip and Ryko barged into Walter Quincy's room in Washington Hall. Rather hysterically these two wandered restlessly around Walter's room opening books and slamming them shut, demanding whiskey, and announcing that they were on their way to France. Walter stared glumly at them: he had an exam on Lucretius that morning: he was too sleepy and preoccupied to be impressed. He did, however, in his own good time inform Phillip of Al's abortive attempt the night before to get up to his room; all of which didn't faze Phillip. "I could have wired my condolences from France if he had been arrested," is what Phillip said. "Now how about that whiskey?"

Down on the gray morning street, Walter watched them swagger away towards Seventh Avenue with his bottle. They scuffled their feet and spat and talked in loud voices. "*Plonger au fond du gouffre*," Phillip was saying, "*ciel ou enfer, qu'importe?* Around here it's like being a fish in a pond. It's drying up and you've got to mutate into an amphibian or perish, but someone like Al keeps hanging on to you and telling you to stay in the pond, everything's going to be allright . . ."

"That's the way it is," Ryko averred, spitting on the sidewalk. "You got to get on your drunken boat, your *bateau ivre*, and sail off into the Goddamned unknown." They shot through a slow-moving, sleepy, coughing and grouchy crowd of office workers and rushed on. That was the last Walter Quincy saw of them for quite some time. Perhaps he was watching the first steps of the insane three-day trail they were about to blaze. It began innocently enough, or perhaps not so innocently, going west from Washington Square, from where Walter Quincy stood, going west in the gray morning street towards Seventh Avenue, and before it was to come to an end, and if one should trace their meanderings on a map of Manhattan, it would cover miles, innumerable bars and restaurants, streets streets streets, and indescribable distances with regard to penetration of human areas . . .

It is impossible to view the thing chronologically. There was no time and there was no logic. After the alcohol they drank sufficiently enervated part of their systems, the three days became, as may well be suspected, either eternity or a flashing moment—they couldn't say.

They talked to people, they heard people talk to them, they saw faces and eyes, they walked and rode on subways and sat on benches, they drank beer and rum and whiskey and Pernod, they staggered down dark streets, they slept where they could, they saw the sun and the moon, they even saw movies—and they would not tire.

But the essential picture to be drawn, once more, is the picture of the three of them walking down a street: Phillip scuffling along, fiery and preoccupied; Ramsay Allen lunging beside him faithfully, busily, attentively, with his perpetual anxious search into Phillip's face, which was always averted from him; and Ryko, a little apart from both of them, eager yet languid, walking with eyes to the pavement, amazed by everything that happened.

Phillip and Ryko made a great drunken decision. They were going to desert their ship in France in spite of the war and go to Paris, and there live in the Latin Quarter. "At night," Phillip said, gesticulating with his hand as by an inner unbearable agitation, "we'll slip off the ship with all our clothes on, layers of it, and hide out in the port until the next night, then start

off, traveling in hay carts and such until we get to Paris . . .
I'll be a deaf and dumb French farmboy and you do all the
talking." He worked himself up into a blank-eyed frenzy.
"We'll live from hand to mouth in Montmartre, we'll beg . . .
there'll be a whole lot of incunabular little Rimbauds to help
us out."

Suddenly they were certain that this is what they were going
to do, come hell or high water, *ciel ou enfer*! Running across the
cobblestones of some Seine quayside in the dawn, after a scrap
of bread or meaning . . . Why, they were both so thoroughly
American, these two kids, they were absolutely convinced of
Paris as the place, the one place where every chip of rubble in
the gutter could but be thoroughly saturated with symbol. A
veritable sponge of a city, was Paris, that could be squeezed to
produce elixirs of atrocious sweetness. "It is a violent Paradise
of mad grimaces. I alone hold the key to this savage parade!"
You could go there, and after awhile words like that would
come natural to you . . .

All the sad humility of the American landscape left behind
you. No more dreary Brooklyns and weary Chicagos, places
like Boston and Los Angeles where trolleys clanged in the
morning air and people were on their way to work, coughing
wretchedly in the damp grayness, and names on buses like
Pico and Boylston Square . . . You could lose the words spoken
in American railroad stations and cafeterias and find yourself
a new set of bitterly agitated cries. "*Ça me navre!*" "*Merde!*"
"*J'men fiche!*" All this would no doubt shorten your life, but it
would also make you absolutely drunk with it.

Fortified with this decision, and with alcohol, undaunted
by the delay in the union hall—where officials regarded these
two prospective seamen with some mistrust—and drunk from
sheer energy and elation of change and wild departure, Phillip
and Ryko, with Al happily along, scattered themselves all over
New York, their emotions strewn in the street like pieces of a
puzzle . . .

Somewhere on the East Side, on one of the nights, in the
apartment of a charmed, and charming, person who had picked
up these three marvellous people—so he considered them—
Phillip and Ryko went into fits of ecstasy over Bach, which
was being played on a phonograph . . . There they lay on the

floor beside the phonograph, with Ramsay Allen facing them in the Indian-sitting posture, while scotch and soda was plied to them as from a machine. Ryko could only yell some incoherent words . . . "Cathedrals in the snow! Monks! Monks! . . ." There was a woman in the room who was positively disgusted with them. They scattered their way back outside, to the bars again, where there were more faces, more conversations, more drinks.

Will Dennison was evident at intervals during the three days. He worked all day and came home to rest, only to be set upon by these three drunkards who were eager to spend his hard-earned money. Dennison didn't mind. His knowledge was by way of being a state of consciousness under the glare of floodlights . . . Everywhere he saw established fact and ruinous retreat from fact. These three friends of his, in their exalted, almost epileptic state, provided him with enormous amusement. They diverted him. He came home and found them waiting on his doorstep, like three street gamins . . .

They were spontaneous and foolish, and somehow all three of them had a certain amount of character which rendered unto their actions an absurd dignity.

It is also highly probable that Dennison was well aware of the fact that these people would never again be valuable to him. People are only important as their circumstance—in heaven, without their circumstance, the appurtenances of their running lives, people would be boring, ghostly and of no use in anything. Any way you look at it. And no matter how ineffable and fleeting may be the circumstances of people who flash across our lives, only to disappear after a certain time, it is this ineffableness of them that leads the way to eternity. We shall remember them, we shall remember them . . . but God help us if we meet them in heaven, sitting around doing nothing, with their lives finished, and staring us in the face.

So swirled these three gin-smelling hurricanes in and out of Dennison's life for three crazy days.

Tuesday evening Dennison took them to dinner in Chumley's . . . He had Helen Varowski, a waitress from the Continental Cafe where he used to work, along with him. There was a kind of pre-arranged seduction involved, but that was quickly squashed by the three drunkards.

It was the night of Phillip's *acte gratuite*. He had had numerous daiquiris and didn't like the taste of the cutlets he was eating, whereupon he picked up his plate and flung it over his shoulder. It crashed on the floor, making people jump from the sound and bringing waiters scurrying.

"That's all right sir, we'll take care of it," said the waiter stooping down to pick up the mess. No one had seen Phillip throw the plate except those at table with him.

"I was reaching for the salt," explained Phillip.

"That's all right sir, I'll bring you another meal."

"Make it lamb this time."

And oh how Helen Varowski hated Phillip Tourian anyway. "You won't get away with it next time." She was always in a huff in Phillip's company, like a cat in the presence of a dog. "You're lucky they didn't see you."

"Oh it doesn't take much intelligence to talk your way out of these things." Phillip was always alluding to Helen's intelligence. "The customer's always right, you know."

"Some customers maybe."

"That's what I mean."

Here Ramsay Allen leaned over and whispered in Dennison's ear, "Isn't he wonderful?"

Needless to say, after everybody had had their dessert, Helen said she was going home to Queens and said good night. She didn't want to be seen leaving the restaurant with these people. She liked Dennison, but not when he was with those people . . . She swished off. That girl had fine legs, she had.

What did Dennison think of the two boys' plan to jump ship in France and go to Paris? Al nudged Dennison when the question was put to the man by the boys, trying to communicate a significant look . . . he didn't dare shake his head. With weary perspicacity Dennison understood.

"What are you going to do for food in France?" began Dennison loyally. "Everything is rationed, you need books for everything. After all there's a war on over there and Paris isn't even taken. And anyway why didn't you guys get your ship today? It all sounds premature to me."

Phillip waved his hand casually, dismissing all difficulties. "Ryko's in trouble with the union because he's behind in dues but tomorrow he's going to talk his way into getting a ship.

As for Paris, it will be taken by the time we get there. They're going to break through Caen and St. Lo any day now. As for the ration books we'll just say we lost our books, we'll say we're refugees just back from a concentration camp."

"Who's going to say all this?"

"Ryko, of course. He's half French, I'm going to be deaf and dumb."

Dennison turned in his chair and peered dubiously at Ryko. Ryko returned an insolent look: he was full of martinis. "That's right, my mother taught me French and I can speak Finnish too."

"Finnish, hey? Oh well, do what you like. It's no skin off me."

"I don't think it's a good idea at all," Al put in gravely.

"Caution is no virtue in the young." Dennison turned his head away, ignoring the furious look he was now getting from Al. "In fact, come to think of it it's not a bad idea at all." He gazed calmly at the wall, dreamily, in fact . . . "France—well, give my regards to the place when you gets there . . . if you gets there."

All the wheels now seemed to be turning against Al at last. Time had become a speeded-up treadmill and Al, limping, couldn't keep up with it. He kept losing ground, and there was nothing at the wrong end of the treadmill but a nice deep pit, dark and final.

During these three drunken days, Al tried to prove that he was as energetic and as creative as Phillip. He was going to show him a thing or two . . . One night they slept in Central Park, on the grass, the three of them. They had been in the Bowery the night before and were about to retire in a grimy doorway when Ryko said, "Let's not sleep here, it's too dirty . . . let's go to Central Park." Like three perverted Bourgeois comfort-seekers they had then rushed up to Central Park to sleep . . . In the damp dawn air, Al produced a small notebook and began scribbling a sonnet.

It was as though he were saying, "See? I can write poetry too. I can do all the things you can, just as well as you. I'm really not old . . ."

In desperation, Al had taken Ryko aside and put it to him this way:

"Why don't you try persuading Phillip to let me ship out with you?"

"It's perfectly allright with me, you know."

"Do you think he might relent?"

"Maybe."

"You two guys wouldn't know how to get food or money in France. I think the three of us would make a better go of it, don't you?"

"You may have something there. The more the merrier's what I say."

"Yes," said Al nodding his head, "that's what I think too."

"Alone I imagine we'd starve."

"Very likely. Both of you are young and impractical. So why don't you ask Phillip . . . ? Give him all the arguments about food and money."

"Okay."

"Do that, Mike."

"I will."

Here, Al put his arm around Ryko and ordered him another hiball.

Al was also very busy demonstrating how right he was about "getting food and money." Phillip and Ryko didn't have a cent in their pockets during the entire three days. It was Al's duty to see to the expenses of the binge. He borrowed money from countless sources, all of which was never to be paid back; he stole money; he worked for money; he made dates with union hall women who could help the two boys get their ship. He did everything in his really amazing power to show that they couldn't get along without him. But Phillip refused to be impressed by any of Al's great *coups*.

When Ryko put Al's proposition up to him, Phillip was adamant.

"I told you the whole purpose of shipping out is to get away from Al."

"But why? He's not a bad guy and he's very useful."

"Eee, you don't understand!"

Al made a date with an employee of the union, a bow-legged girl wearing horn rimmed glasses, a luncheon date. She could help Ryko straighten out his difficulties with the union if she so desired. But first she must be impressed, that was it. She had met Al once at a party. He was always distributing his great charm everywhere . . . now it was going to bear fruit.

To pay for the luncheon, Al had run down to the Village to borrow money while Phillip and Ryko waited for him at the union hall. When Al got back he went upstairs and came down again with the union girl. They all went to lunch around the corner.

Al launched things off telling funny stories and being very attentive. This girl, who looked like a frustrated ballet dancer, and who was obviously paranoiac, full of diffuse, sprayish suspicions like a sprinkler on a windy day, had probably decided to cancel her suspicions for just this once. It was too much fun sitting at lunch with these three perfectly mad people. Whatever they wanted of her, she didn't care, just for now. And they were so charming and attentive . . . except, it must be admitted, for Phillip, who sulked in his own corner and snickered when she spoke of the common man. She was a Communist and things got very merry indeed when Ryko and Ramsay Allen began to recount the radical experiences of their past. Ryko had been arrested on Boston Common as an agitator, Al had been in trouble in England once. No one was overplaying his part.

All existing forms of sincerity had evidently been exhausted, for here sat these people in full consciousness juggling the forms of sincerity handed down by their forbears like so many red and blue rubber balls. This is what annoyed Phillip, made him sulk: he was trying to divine a new kind of sincerity. The new vision, he called it.

Finally the girl said, "Well I think I can do something about that trouble of Mike's. After all it's no sin to be so eager to ship out in spite of failure to pay dues . . ." That was the way she put it. Sin worked its way in any which way you looked in that great political world of hers.

True to her word, this pathetic little creature did indeed speak in behalf of Mike Ryko that afternoon, with the result that the union system relented for a moment and handed him the little document he needed. Now it was only a matter of waiting until the next day to get their ship.

Working like a beaver to prove his indispensability, Al thereupon hurried off to get some money with which to celebrate their success with the union girl. He returned a few hours later with ten dollars and a pawn receipt ticket.

"Look," he said, holding out the pawn ticket. "It's for two small brilliants."

"Where did you steal them?"

"I had tea with Mrs. Burdett."

Mrs. Burdett was an old Virginian and a friend of Al's family who considered it his duty to have tea with her at least once a month. She saw herself as an exile, and Al as a kinsman. She was the typical old maid who lived alone behind drawn blinds, and with cats, two or three of them. She wrote to Al's mother.

"While she was out of the room in the john I helped myself to these. I found them behind some old lace in a drawer."

"Good work," said Ryko.

"Now let's go out and spend it," was Phillip's comment.

Al stole, connived, bounded around the city borrowing money, wrote sonnets in Central Park, did everything he could think of to move Phillip's heart . . . Sometimes his zeal took on hilarious proportions.

Phillip had hit a bus stop sign on Seventh Avenue out of sheer tension and impatience. The sign wobbled back and forth on its heavy base in a repetitious mocking curtsey. It was an effective demonstration, an exteriorizing of symbol which Al felt compelled to emulate, nay exceed. He rushed up to a candy store nearby and jumped up on a wooden shelf for newspapers. The shelf promptly collapsed beneath his not inconsiderable weight, making a great noise like a disaster. Al fell flat on his back. The Greek ran out of the store and grabbed Al by the arm. He was going to make him pay a dollar for the damage, or he would call a cop . . . Al paid the Greek while Phillip giggled.

This was where Dennison suddenly broke out into laughter. His perpetually wry amusement had collapsed, like the wooden shelf for newspapers, and in its place came this mad laugh the likes of which was rarely heard in anyone. He was laughing just like people ought to laugh, hysterically, with a pained expression, "Ha ha ha ha!" Embarrassed and frightened, Ryko wanted to know what he was laughing about. He watched Dennison with frozen apprehension, and then began to giggle. Dennison continued to laugh. It was getting worse and worse; it was an irresistable laughter; it would soon choke Dennison to death. He would die before their very eyes of a horrible new kind of hemorrhage, the self-destructive nature of which somehow only he could perish by.

Things were carrying on in a most impossible way . . . like a horse race, the saddest thing in the world, where there can only be one winner and all the rest are losers.

Al hadn't as yet dared ask Phillip outright to let him come along on the voyage. But in many ways, Al expressed his cumulative tension without saying a word, as in the incident of the wooden shelf.

One night—it is impossible to say which night it was—the three madmen barged into the Beggar's Bar. The Beggar's Bar was the perfect place for them. In it was contained the bizarre nourishment they craved, for now all three of them had become so feverish from dissipation that nothing would suit their demands. In the Beggar's Bar talented and effeminate young men played the Appassionata Sonata for them. The proprietess was a temperamental German pantomimist who had as weird an appearance as could be provoked on any canvas: her face was pasty white, almost green, her hair was jet black and hung over her brow in a grotesque set of bangs designed to make her look young. She wore a red slack suit perpetually. Her eyes flashed green. She had that horrid kind of mouth that is painted on a mask, wide and leering and crimson.

She would come swishing up to the boys as they entered and lead them ceremoniously to a filthy little table in a corner. Candles were stuck directly on the table tops. It was a cellar bar, you went down some evil-smelling steps to get there. It was gloomy inside, and damp and smoky.

"Dis iss de most continental bar in de United States," she would hiss to them confidentially. "You vill find nozzing like dis anywhere else."

Then she would serve them a horrible drink called the Beggar's Sip which was a mixture of cognac and cold coffee.

Phillip wandered around the place restlessly, going into the back room where were hung satirical paintings. The flickering light of the candles from the main room illuminated these decadent paintings gloomily.

There was an Italian tenor who sang there. He sang "*L'Amour Toujours L'Amour*" looking directly at Phillip . . . A little while later, Al very affably got to know the tenor and cadged a few sticks of marijuana from him. In a moment, the three drugged maniacs were all over the bar talking with everyone . . . The talented and effeminate young men played for them on the piano. Someone sang a dirty song. A morphine addict came in and began to perform on the platform; he collapsed a while later.

Phillip was insanely happy that they had found this place. "It's for this kind of thing that I want to go to Paris," he said, and saying that, he hurried off and began to talk with one of the performers, a tall sophisticated-looking German woman who sang naughty French songs, with her long legs crossed as she leaned against the piano. She was a very haughty woman. There were rumors that she was a Duchess, or some such nonsense. She screamed hysterically when the homosexual waiter walked across the floor while she was performing.

The dishwasher was a Martinique Negro jungle dancer who dressed exactly like a Liverpool waterfront Negro and who had immensely long hands. It was his lot to wash dishes while inferior artists performed out front. He told this to Ryko, who was helping him with the dishes. "You must see my dance sometime," he said, and without warning, he stuck out his incredible hands and began to dance a jungle dance in the filthy kitchen . . .

Our three friends lolled in this place until closing time, until they were thrown out, exhausted and broke. At least six men were willing to put them up for the night, in deference for which they preferred to carry on in the Bowery . . .

"We haven't seen our women for ages!" suddenly complained Ryko. "Boy are we going to get hell!"

"We'll see them tomorrow," Phillip said.

"Oh boy is Janie going to be sore, and Praline too for that matter."

In the Bowery they met a drunken middle-aged poet who offered to buy them drinks. They got drunk again while the man recited sonnets he had written. Phillip was very much impressed by them, with the result that at dawn, in Central Park, Ramsay Allen himself composed a presentable sonnet.

They lay on the grass, on newspapers. The skyline of Manhattan around the park was barely visible in the grayish gloom. Al leaned back against a tree and watched Phillip, who was sleeping. Pencil in hand, Al watched. Then he began to scribble on a piece of paper. Ryko, pretending to be asleep, was watching out of the corner of his eye . . . There was the whining grate of a trolley from Columbus Circle.

Ryko presently said, "What are you writing, Al?"

Al smiled and shook his head; he wouldn't say. In the damp light that was growing, Ryko could see Al's disheveled gray hair, his crumpled coat, the stringy once-expensive tie that hung from the dirty collar of his shirt. Beside him the brooding black-haired Phillip slept, curled up rather pathetically on a spread-out newspaper black with war headlines . . . And Al was composing a sonnet.

Ryko turned over on his back and stared up at the gray impenetrable heavens. Again there was the screech and grate of trolley wheels from Columbus Circle.

He looked again at Al. He seemed old now, face contorted in thought and pain and defeat . . . Somehow he looked like a respectable Virginia business man figuring out the fiscal budget, in an odd moment in the park, as it were. And he was composing a sonnet . . .

A policeman sent them off packing at eleven o'clock and they went back to sleep in another part of the park. Now the city was full of noise and it was difficult to sleep . . . The hot sun flooded down upon them mercilessly. Again a policeman told them to move on. Merciful night was what they yearned for, these three.

In the afternoon it was once more necessary to connive against an obdurate system. The union wouldn't let Phillip and Ryko ship out because they hadn't attended a union meeting the night before, of which they had been of course uninformed. True, they could get jobs at the "open job" window, as it was called, but here were to be had the residue of jobs left over by the members in good standing for the use of the reprehensible element. (Phillip and Ryko, reprehensible as they were, refused to be placed in that unfavorable position.)

It was Ryko's day. He was inspired. Their shipping cards would be completely valid once more if only they could get them stamped by a union official. He put his marvellous plan into action.

He and Phillip walked into an office in the back of the hall. The union official was talking over a phone, with his hat on the back of his head. Ryko leaned casually on the desk, waiting for the man's attention. When he had that, he said, "My friend and I were not able to attend last night's meeting because we were in Washington. We were just refused a couple of jobs because we hadn't attended . . ."

"What were you doing in Washington?"

"Oh well, it was an idea we got last Sunday or thereabouts. As you know the Congressional debates down there are going on . . . about the Pillsbury post-war bill, you know?"

"Of course."

"And we wanted to see it for ourselves. You know how it is, we had a little money, we got drunk and decided to go down there to listen to the reactionary poll-tax Southern Democrat bastards, who're always griping whenever any legislation on the side of the common man is introduced . . ."

"Yes, I know."

"As it developed, we didn't get back to town till late last night, long after the meeting was over. I was wondering if you could fix our cards so we can get a ship today. We've no money left, you see."

"Let me see the cards."

The man took the cards and stamped them properly. Ryko and Phillip walked out righteously, like two brothers who have just been bailed out of jail by a union after a strike. They had identified themselves as liberals . . . for this, they could be excused for the sin of failing to attend the union meeting. The beggars!

To add injury to insult, they went to the back of the union hall where a desk was covered with petitions to be signed. The petitions were all about the Pillsbury post-war bill, which had inadvertently just saved their necks. Over the desk was a sign reading, "C.I.O. Political Action Committee."

The two boys, who unfortunately professed no political affiliations, nevertheless signed the petitions gratefully. Phillip

signed "Jean-Arthur Rimbaud" and Ryko signed "Paul Verlaine." It was their contribution to the union's drive for the
common man.

Al was now progressively growing more desperate as the
boys' success at the union hall, odd though it was, began to
point to actually getting a job on a ship. He had devised a new
plan of action: the more money he could get, the drunker they
would be, the longer, then, it would take them to get their ship.
So while they were busy that afternoon lying to union officials
and signing false names on petitions, he had gone out and borrowed some more money. He came back at closing time and said
blithely, "Well, I've got some more money here. No ship, boys?"

"Tomorrow's another day," said Phillip sternly.

And off they were again. They went and waited on Dennison's doorstep until he came home. They all had dinner and
then went to a party at a girl's house.

This girl was named Betty-Lou East. She lived in a cellar
apartment not far from Dennison's, a cozy little place with
white-washed stone walls, plenty of books and records, furniture scattered tastefully about, and lamps here and there to
light up the place. She greeted them effusively; she was very
fond of Al, who was a fellow Virginian.

Betty-Lou was a Southern girl and a Christian Scientist. She
had very definite opinions about Christian Science, and also
about the future role of radio in education. She told them how,
after the war, recorded university lectures on all subjects were
to be played twenty-four hours a day on the radio.

"That sounds Goddamned awful to me," Dennison drawled.

"Why Mr. Dennison, you *are* terrible cynical!"

This girl wasn't however bad looking, with that sullen slant-
eyed look of the American Southern girl. Still you could tell that
she would become a stodgy busybody of a matron in no time
at all. She had a clumsy walk, which wasn't a good sign, and
a mind weighed down with new-fangled yet everlasting pruri-
ence. Right at this moment, she was as attractive and useful to
men as she would ever be. After that there was no telling what
manner of incredible enemy to men she might become.

And she certainly wasn't going to be of much use to women
either.

There were a lot of dull people there, some Russian friends of hers who came to the party with a lot of rum. Everybody was supposed to sit around breathlessly while she played Josh White recordings . . . they were *so* full of social significance. Ryko was ingratiating himself with Betty-Lou; he had taken a liking to her bosom, evidently. He looked more like a hooligan than ever before, that night, as he hadn't shaved since the dissipation began some days ago, but Betty-Lou seemed to accept him as he was. Ryko put his arm around her and listened amazedly to her favorite records, listened, as it were, religiously. Meanwhile, Dennison was bored. To avoid conversation with the people of the party, he repeatedly took himself off to the bathroom, where he enjoyed a regal solitude.

Phillip and Al were in Betty-Lou's kitchen helping themselves to slices of cold roast beef and greeting her guests in an offhand way. Finally, in a supreme fit of impatience, they left the party in search for new guests, and returned fifteen minutes later with two French sailors.

Things became very confusing when the French sailors arrived. Phillip and Al had managed to create the misconception in their minds that they were being invited to join in at a whore house party. The Frenchmen just couldn't begin to understand that Americans were in the habit of rushing around bars picking up people to join them in a drink and a lot of talk, in private homes, on a respectable plane. Still, one of the French sailors proved to be obtuse enough *not* to believe that such goings-on actually did exist in America. He began obstinately to woo Betty-Lou. He was going to make himself believe that she was for sale, *parbleu!*, like she should be.

At one point in the party a large brown rat ran out of the kitchen into the middle of the room. He stood there indecisively for a moment, crouching and confused, then emitted a squeak and ran into the bathroom. Betty-Lou cried "Land sakes! There's that old rat again!" She hurried into the kitchen and buttered a Graham cracker with phosphorus paste. She broke the cracker up into small pieces and Ryko helped her scatter them around the kitchen and in the bathroom. Dennison was standing around, skeptical.

"That won't do any good," he said. He had once been an exterminator in Chicago. "Rats get wise to phosphorus paste," he said.

"Well Mr. Dennison, what else can I do?"

"And besides there're so many holes in your apartment that all the rats in New York can come in." He wandered back to the party, satisfied with his thesis.

The party became wilder. Ryko maneuvered himself on the couch with Betty-Lou and put his arm around her . . . they were promptly steeped in an earnest conversation.

"I don't like, I never liked that Phillip," she said in a low voice.

"I don't either."

"There's something about him, you know, that I can't, can't stand."

"What is it?" inquired Ryko eagerly.

"Oh I don't know." She sighed. Just for the space of a moment she had leaned her head on his arm. "I'll tell you what it is . . . there's the smell of death about Phillip. That's the only way I can put it."

"How interesting!"

Not long after Betty-Lou had said that, Phillip Tourian surreptitiously looked through her handbag in the kitchen and found himself a dollar bill. There were so many holes in her apartment, indeed.

The party finally broke up amid crumblings of self-respect. There were effusive drunken farewells. Everybody straggled off towards his own hole, like the rat after he'd got the squeak out of his system. The phantom was laying out the phosphorus paste at the proper places, for the propitious moments. The Russians went one way, the French sailors another, our friends still another . . .

Dennison went to bed again and the three drunkards carried on. It was almost as though these three were loath ever to part . . . Or as if they were sentenced to die, and were trying to crowd as much life as possible into their last days. They barged into Village bars and began conversations with all kinds of people. People bought them drinks . . .

In the morning, while Phillip and Ryko slept on his floor, Al went out and washed windows. He came back laden with money. He got them drunk again, so that they were too late at the union hall to get a ship. He got them so drunk they didn't care whether or not they did get a ship, at least, this was so with Ryko. Ryko was lured from all sides by any manifestation of life . . . Still, Phillip was charged with that kind of purpose that showed in his walk, in his actions, in his speech. He had become so tense and impatient it bordered on hysteria.

He kept knotting his fist and saying "Eee!"

"What's the matter Phil?" Ryko would ask drunkenly.

"Goddamnit this isn't getting us to sea, all this drinking and running around. Do you by any chance remember that we were supposed to get a ship?"

"Sure . . . we'll get one tomorrow, don't worry."

"Tomorrow! Tomorrow!"

Al hovered nearby, leering from perverse success.

Off they went again, to scatter themselves all over the city. In a bar on the Brooklyn waterfront they sat around discussing James Joyce, Philoctetes and Neoptolemus, the portrait of Jean Cocteau in the Museum of Modern Art, Rimbaud and Dostoevsky. And jazz . . . the new jazz, on which Ryko was an authority, the drunken hoodlum. They had gotten to Brooklyn on the subway somehow, perhaps by mistake. On the way Phillip had leaned against the subway door watching the small lights flash by in the tunnel darkness, with Al standing over him anxiously, like a poor worried mother, and Ryko sprawled on a seat dozing.

They found slatternly Spanish and Mexican neighborhoods full of muttering and moaning in the hot night, and small restaurants and bars . . . From the bay came the deep-voiced call of the big ships. In the bars the juke boxes were loud, and swarthy men milled at the counters drinking beer and straight whiskey. Some of them were tattooed like savages and spoke of Peleliu and Guantánamo Bay and Oran in harsh casual voices . . .

Every time Phillip heard the moan of a ship from outside, he winced.

"At sea," he rushed to say, "I want to re-examine myself completely. Goddamnit I want to find out if art is more important than life, or if it is at least life . . ."

"You're perhaps too young for art," Al said, cocking his head. "It's only when you're discouraged with life as is that art becomes appealing. Don't you think so, Mike?"

Ryko was in a fit of ecstasy over a jazz record being played. He shook his head from side to side, he made faces and gritted his teeth, and didn't hear anything else.

Phillip said, "I want to find the new vision. There's something new in the air and I've got to find out what it is . . . We can't go on this way."

"What's wrong? What's wrong?" cried Ryko, coming out of his reverie.

"It's allright with you, you're an aesthete . . . the aesthetic of things as they are satisfy you because you're a pure poet."

"Isn't the artist amoral?" yelled Ryko. He slopped down the rest of his straight whiskey. Anything he had said that night was meaningless; he had been drunk for days, and he couldn't exactly take it that much.

"The artist I'm afraid is at base moral indeed . . ."

This is the way they had been talking for quite some time. They were like wandering ghosts in a city predominately busy with the realities, so-called, of daily living—and what they had to talk about was very thin indeed in inverse proportion to its enormous volume.

"Rimbaud's prose is what I'd like to achieve . . ."

"Thomas Mann or Goethe or somebody said art was suffering seeking form, and there's your Dostoevsky in a nutshell . . ."

"How about another drink boys?"

"You'll find the face of the sea shaggy and familiar, as though you'd known it all along . . . You'll be bored."

"I want solitude, solitude, when the minutes don't go ping-ping-ping."

"What Joyce did was dig down deep in himself and venerate that sufficiently to transform it into art. We're too irreligious . . . we don't venerate any more. Christ, what's left to venerate!"

"Drink up, boys . . ."

They ate Mexican food in a blueish little restaurant full of flies.

Then they returned to Manhattan like lost souls, going straight to the Village bars, to where middle-aged pompous intellectuals bought drinks for Phillip and said, "You speak of James Joyce but I doubt if you know anything about him." Establishing themselves thereby in a position of dominance, they were qualified to buy him and his two friends drinks.

Ryko wandered around insinuating himself drunkenly into conversations while Al stood behind Phillip and his patron and grinned. There was something desperate and foolish coming into Al's smile . . . it had begun to lose its old affable quality, and to take on more of the idiotic. Sometimes, when Phillip snapped at him, Al's crazy smile broke out meaninglessly. He looked then like a village idiot, say, who is being burned at the stake by a sadistic assemblage, and who grins and says "Wow! This sure hurts!" as the flames lick up to consume him.

And then they were on the streets again, as by arrangement with a crazy fate. Once a small boy, about twelve years old, with black hair tumbling over his brow, came by, and Al greeted him, "Hiya Harry."

The boy waved his baseball glove: "Hiya Al."

"Who's the little Arab boy?" snapped Phillip, grinning slyly.

"What's this? What's this?" cried the drunken Ryko, who understood nothing.

Rather irrelevantly, they were suddenly passing through Washington Square, from where they could see the windows of Apartment 32.

"Look! Do you remember that place?"

"That's where we're going to be drawn and quartered when we return."

"Well boys," said Al, "women are inconvenient anyway."

"Yeah," said Phillip, "let's do away with them altogether."

They hurried on towards some sort of terminal of the night they felt was coming rightfully to them . . . But always they ended up in a bar, or in someone's apartment drinking, or on park benches. There was an exquisite sensitivity had come to their limbs now, after all the drinking and fatigue, which made mere contact with a park bench or with a chair some sort of sensual thrill. Every kind of thing that happened grated on their sensibilities like a great rasping abrasive.

They were walking underneath the roaring Third Avenue elevated train, which made them shudder. Or they stood in the front train of the subway and watched themselves hurtle forward into the tunnel-ends . . . which made them swoon. Or they heard music, and were mad with it . . . Or a scrap of conversation, while wearying them, came clear and cold like ice water on their drowsy senses.

Finally they found themselves in a theater watching a French movie. It was the Apollo theater, on 42nd Street, and they were sitting in the first row of the upper balcony watching *The Port of Shadows.* They puffed on their cigarettes and paid rapt attention to the film . . . Its quality of shadowy street-ends, the carnival in it, the fog over the bay, the old man who played Bach and spoke in a whining voice and was lecherous with his niece, the fatigued little Frenchmen who worked on the waterfront—all this marvellous welter of human activity and weariness and slow sweet delight had been filmed for them. No one in the theater that night understood the film so well as they . . . and none could project himself into it, but Ramsay Allen.

The Port of Shadows was principally the story of a French army deserter, played by Jean Gabin, who comes to Le Havre to get a ship and leave the country; and while he is going about his business, he meets a girl who falls in love with him. There are scenes in the fog, on docks, in rainy streets, or in gloomy houses with rain beating on the window pane, and in taverns. The people are painfully real. Sadly, but with determination, the soldier decides to leave France in spite of his love for the girl . . . Their love is a kind of tragic binding in the darkness, they kiss in alleys, they are oppressed and weary from life, they are absurdly beautiful and full of agonizing dignity. The soldier gets his ship . . . But just before sailing time, he decides to see his girl for the last time, just for a moment . . . Can it be that he does not want to leave her? It turns out that such is the case, according to fate, for when he visits her, for the last time, a gangster shoots him in the back. The last scene shows the ship sailing out of Le Havre harbor in the gray dawn, without the soldier . . .

When the picture faded from the screen, Ryko turned to Al and asked him what he had thought of it. Al had been watching the film part of the time, and part of the time he had been watching Phillip, who sat beside him broodingly absorbed. "It was the best picture I ever saw," Al said, and he turned and looked at Ryko for the first time with any semblance of compassion. It was as though he wanted Ryko to see the tears that were in his eyes, and to see everything.

So Ryko wrote this.

CHRONOLOGY
NOTE ON THE TEXTS
PERSONS MENTIONED
NOTES

Chronology

1922   Born Jean-Louis Kérouac on March 12 at the family home at
        9 Lupine Road in Lowell, Massachusetts, the third child of
        Joseph Alcide Leon (Leo) Kerouac and Gabrielle Lévesque
        Kerouac, and is baptized at St. Louis-de-France Church
        on March 19. (Father, born 1889 in St. Hubert, Québec,
        immigrated with his family to Nashua, New Hampshire,
        where he learned printing. He later moved to Lowell,
        where he became the manager and printer of *L'Étoile*, a
        weekly French newspaper, and sold insurance. Mother,
        born 1895 in St. Pacôme, Québec, also immigrated as a
        child to Nashua. Orphaned at age 16, she was working in a
        shoe factory when she married Leo Kerouac on October 25,
        1915. Their first son, Gerard, was born on August 23, 1916,
        and their daughter Caroline was born on October 25, 1918.)
        Family speaks French-Canadian at home.

1923   Father opens his own print shop in Lowell.

1925   Family moves to 35 Burnaby Street. Gerard becomes seri-
        ously ill with rheumatic fever.

1926   Family moves to 34 Beaulieu Street. Gerard dies on June 2,
        buried in Nashua, New Hampshire.

1927   Family moves to 320 Hildreth Street.

1928   Kerouac enters St. Louis-de-France parochial school, where
        classes are taught in both English and French. Family
        moves to 240 Hildreth Street.

1930   Family moves to 66 West Street.

1932   Family leaves Centralville section of Lowell and moves to
        Phebe Avenue in the Pawtucketville section, where father
        becomes the manager of a social club. Kerouac attends St.
        Joseph's parochial school.

1933–35 Enters Bartlett Junior High School in 1933, where all classes
        are conducted in English. Begins keeping his first journals
        and records his achievements in sports. Develops a baseball
        game played with cards, marbles, and dice, and invents an
        imaginary league and fictitious players. Writes short stories,
        draws cartoons, and invents mysterious character "Dr. Sax."
        Reads extensively in school and at the public library.

1936   Merrimack River floods in March, causing extensive damage
           to father's print shop. Family moves to 35 Sarah Avenue.
           Kerouac enters Lowell High School in the tenth grade.

1937–39   Excels in sports, especially as a sprinter in track and a run-
           ning back in football. Reads Thomas Wolfe, William Sa-
           royan, Henry David Thoreau, Mark Twain, and others.
           Father sells his shop in 1937 and becomes a printer for hire
           while mother begins working in a shoe factory; financial
           strain is increased by father's gambling and drinking. Family
           moves to tenement at 736 Moody Street. Kerouac becomes
           close friends with Sebastian Sampas and discusses litera-
           ture, philosophy, and politics with him and a small group
           of friends (who for a time call themselves the Young Pro-
           metheans). On Thanksgiving 1938, scores winning touch-
           down for Lowell High School against local rival Lawrence.

1939–40   Graduates from Lowell High School on June 28, 1939.
           Receives football scholarship from Columbia University
           on condition that he attend Horace Mann, a preparatory
           school in the Bronx, for a year. Lives with his mother's step-
           mother in Brooklyn and commutes to school by subway.
           Publishes his first fiction in the *Horace Mann Quarterly* and
           is introduced to live jazz in Harlem by classmate Seymour
           Wyse. Writes about jazz and sports for the school newspa-
           per.

1940   Enters Columbia in September. Fractures tibia in his right
           leg during his second game with the freshman squad and
           spends months recuperating.

1941   Receives high grades in French and literature courses but
           fails chemistry. Spends summer in Lowell and in New
           Haven, Connecticut, where his parents move in August.
           Returns to Columbia in September. Quarrels with the
           coaching staff, quits the football team, and leaves school.
           Moves to Hartford, where he works as a gas station atten-
           dant and writes a short story collection, "Atop an Under-
           wood" (some of the stories are posthumously published
           in *Atop an Underwood: Early Stories and Other Writing*
           in 1999). Returns to Lowell when his parents move back
           to that city. Registers for naval aviation training after the
           Japanese bomb Pearl Harbor. Becomes a sports reporter for
           the *Lowell Sun* while waiting to be called up.

1942   Quits the *Sun* in March and goes to Washington, D.C.,
            where he works on the construction of the Pentagon and
            as a short-order cook. Returns to Lowell, then joins the
            Merchant Marine and sails from Boston in July as a scul-
            lion on the army transport ship *Dorchester*. Sails along the
            Greenland coast before returning to Boston in October.
            (The *Dorchester* is sunk by a German submarine on Febru-
            ary 3, 1943, with the loss of 675 lives.) Accepts invitation
            to rejoin the Columbia football squad, but quits after he is
            benched during the Army game. Stays in New York during
            the fall and begins affair with Edie Parker (b. 1922), an art
            student from Grosse Pointe, Michigan. Works on novel *The
            Sea Is My Brother* (published in 2011). Returns to Lowell in
            December.

1943   Fails examination for flight training and is sent in March
            to naval boot camp in Newport, Rhode Island, where he
            is committed to the base hospital for psychiatric observa-
            tion after repeated acts of insubordination. Transferred
            to Bethesda, Maryland, where he is diagnosed as having
            "schizoid tendencies" and given a psychiatric discharge
            from military service. Joins his parents, who are now liv-
            ing at 94-10 Cross Bay Boulevard in Ozone Park, Queens,
            New York. Rejoins the Merchant Marine and sails from
            New York in September on the *George Weems*, a Liberty
            ship carrying bombs to Liverpool. Returns to New York in
            October. Divides his time between Ozone Park and apart-
            ment on West 118th Street that Edie Parker shares with Joan
            Vollmer Adams. Meets Columbia undergraduate Lucien
            Carr (b. 1925).

1944   Introduced by Carr to William S. Burroughs (b. 1917),
            Columbia undergraduate Allen Ginsberg (b. 1926), and
            David Kammerer (b. 1911), Carr's former scoutmaster who
            had followed him to New York from St. Louis. Sebastian
            Sampas dies on March 2 after being wounded while serving
            as an army medic on the Anzio beachhead in Italy. Works
            on *Galloway*, novel that eventually becomes *The Town and
            the City*. Carr fatally stabs Kammerer in Riverside Park on
            August 14, then visits Kerouac, who helps Carr dispose of
            his knife and Kammerer's glasses. Kerouac is arrested as
            a material witness after Carr turns himself in and is jailed
            when his father refuses to post bail. Marries Edie Parker

in a civil ceremony on August 22 and is released after she obtains bail money from her family. They move to Grosse Pointe, Michigan, where Kerouac works in a ball-bearing factory. (Carr pleads guilty to manslaughter and serves two years in prison.) Sails from New York in October on the Liberty ship *Robert Treat Paine*, but jumps ship in Norfolk, Virginia, and returns to New York. On November 16 Kerouac estimates that he has written 500,000 words since 1939, including "nine unfinished novels." (One of these is published as *The Haunted Life* in 2014.) Edie returns to New York at Christmas and they move in with Joan Vollmer Adams in apartment on West 115th Street.

1945   Kerouac and Burroughs collaborate on *And the Hippos Were Boiled in Their Tanks*, a novel based on the Kammerer-Carr case (published 2008). Explores the Times Square underworld with Burroughs and Herbert Huncke, a drug addict, petty thief, and street hustler. Completes novella *Orpheus Emerged* (published in 2002). Separates from Edie during the summer. Helps care for his father, who has stomach cancer. Hospitalized in December with thrombophlebitis, a debilitating circulatory condition in the legs possibly related to his 1940 football injury; Kerouac also attributes his illness to his heavy use of Benzedrine and marijuana.

1946   Kerouac, Burroughs, and Ginsberg are interviewed for the Alfred Kinsey study *Sexual Behavior in the Human Male* (published in 1948). Father dies on May 17 and is buried with Gerard in Nashua. Kerouac continues work on *The Town and the City*. Agrees to Edie Parker's request that their marriage be annulled. In December Kerouac is introduced by his friend Hal Chase to Neal Cassady (b. 1926), a self-educated car thief and hustler from Denver who is visiting New York with his wife, Luanne.

1947   Travels to North Carolina in June to visit his sister, Caroline, and her second husband, Paul Blake. Leaves New York in July to visit Cassady and Ginsberg in Denver, traveling by bus to Chicago and then hitchhiking the rest of the way. Meets Carolyn Robinson, a graduate student at the University of Denver (she and Cassady marry in April 1948). Travels by bus in August to San Francisco, where Henri Cru (a friend from Horace Mann) gets him a job as a security guard in Marin City. Travels through California before returning to New York in October.

1948   Completes first draft of *The Town and the City* in May. Be-
        gins writing an early version of *On the Road*. Visits sister in
        Rocky Mount, North Carolina, in June after the birth of his
        nephew Paul Blake Jr. Meets writer John Clellon Holmes
        in July. Takes literature courses taught by Elbert Lenrow
        and Alfred Kazin at the New School for Social Research in
        New York. Cassady arrives in Rocky Mount while Kerouac
        is visiting his sister at Christmas and drives with him back
        to New York.

1949   Leaves New York in January with Cassady, Luanne, and Al
        Hinkle and drives to Algiers, Louisiana, where they visit
        Burroughs and Joan Vollmer Adams, who have been living
        together for several years. Continues on to San Francisco
        with Cassady and Luanne, then returns to New York by bus
        in February. Columbia professor Mark Van Doren recom-
        mends *The Town and the City* to Robert Giroux at Har-
        court, Brace, who offers Kerouac a $1,000 advance in late
        March. Kerouac and Giroux work on cutting and revising
        the manuscript. Moves to Denver in May and rents house
        at 61 West Center Street in Westwood. Continues work-
        ing on *On the Road*. Travels to San Francisco in August,
        then drives back to New York with Cassady, visiting Edie
        in Grosse Pointe along the way. Moves in with his mother
        at 94-21 134th Street in Richmond Hill, Queens.

1950   *The Town and the City* is published on March 2; it receives
        mixed reviews and sells poorly. Travels to Denver in May,
        then drives with Cassady to Mexico City, where he visits
        Burroughs. Returns to New York in August. Meets Joan
        Haverty (b. 1931) on November 3 and marries her in a civil
        ceremony on November 17. They live in a loft on West 21st
        Street; then move in with Kerouac's mother in Queens. Re-
        ceives a long letter from Neal Cassady in December. (Ker-
        ouac will later say that Cassady's "fast, mad, confessional"
        letters inspired "the spontaneous style of *On the Road*.")

1951   Moves to a studio apartment at 454 West 20th Street in
        Manhattan with Joan, who is working in a department
        store. Writes story *La nuit est ma femme* (The Night Is My
        Woman) in French in February and March. Begins new
        version of *On the Road* on April 2 and types it in three
        weeks on a 120-foot-long paper scroll. Separates from Joan
        and moves in with Lucien Carr and Allen Ginsberg. De-
        nies paternity when Joan tells him she is pregnant with

his child. Robert Giroux rejects the scroll version of *On the Road*. Hires Rae Everitt of MCA as his literary agent. Suffers severe attack of thrombophlebitis while visiting his sister in North Carolina. Enters Kingsbridge VA Hospital in the Bronx in August. Burroughs accidentally kills Joan Vollmer Adams in Mexico City on September 7 after she drunkenly challenges him to shoot a glass off her head. Kerouac leaves the hospital in September and returns to Richmond Hill. Begins rewriting *On the Road* in an even more spontaneous form (reworked version is posthumously published as *Visions of Cody* in 1972). Moves to San Francisco in December to live with Neal and Carolyn Cassady and their children at 29 Russell Street.

1952   Works as baggage handler for the Southern Pacific Railroad. Receives $250 advance for *On the Road* from Ace Books. Daughter Janet Michelle Kerouac is born in Albany, New York, on February 16. Kerouac begins affair with Carolyn Cassady. Drives with the Cassadys to the Arizona-Mexico border, then takes bus to Mexico City, where he stays with Burroughs. Writes *Doctor Sax*, May–June. Joins his mother and sister in North Carolina in July, then moves in with the Cassadys in San Jose in September. Works as a brakeman for the Southern Pacific. Begins keeping dream journals later published as *Book of Dreams*. Lives in a skid row hotel in San Francisco for a month because of the tension caused by his affair with Carolyn Cassady, then returns to San Jose in November. John Clellon Holmes publishes novel *Go*, in which Kerouac is fictionalized as Gene Pasternak, and "This Is the Beat Generation," an essay in the November 16 *New York Times Magazine*. Kerouac travels to Mexico City with Neal Cassady; writes novella *Sur le chemin* (*Old Bull in the Bowery*) in French; then returns to his mother in Queens.

1953   Writes *Maggie Cassidy*. Meets with Malcolm Cowley of Viking Press to discuss the possible publication of his work. Travels in April to San Luis Obispo, California, where he again works for the Southern Pacific. Leaves job in May and sails from San Francisco to New Orleans as a kitchen worker on the S.S. *William Carruthers*. Returns to Queens in June. Writes *The Subterraneans*, October 21–24. In response to questions about his composition methods from Ginsberg and Burroughs, writes "Essentials of Spontaneous Prose."

1954   Leaves New York in late January to live with the Cassadys
        in San Jose. Works as a parking-lot attendant and studies
        Buddhist texts. Returns to his mother in Queens in April.
        Hires Sterling Lord as his literary agent (Lord will repre-
        sent him for the rest of Kerouac's life). Works on *Some of
        the Dharma* (posthumously published in 1997). Malcolm
        Cowley publishes essay in *The Saturday Review* in August
        in which he credits Kerouac with inventing the phrase "beat
        generation" and writes: "his long unpublished narrative, *On
        the Road*, is the best record of their lives." Kerouac visits
        Lowell in October.

1955   In January Alfred A. Knopf becomes the sixth publisher to
        reject *On the Road*. Joan Haverty takes Kerouac to court
        seeking child support, but his lawyer, Eugene Brooks (Allen
        Ginsberg's brother), succeeds in having the case postponed
        because of Kerouac's recurring phlebitis. Kerouac and his
        mother move to North Carolina, where he writes *Wake
        Up: A Life of the Buddha* (published 2008). "Jazz of the
        Beat Generation," excerpted from *On the Road* and *Visions
        of Cody*, appears in *New World Writing* in April. Travels
        to Mexico City in July. Begins *Tristessa* and *Mexico City
        Blues* before going to San Francisco in September. Meets
        the poets Kenneth Rexroth, Lawrence Ferlinghetti, Michael
        McClure, Philip Lamantia, Philip Whalen, and Gary Snyder.
        Attends poetry reading at the Six Gallery in San Francisco
        on October 7 where Allen Ginsberg reads from *Howl* for
        the first time. Visits the Sawtooth Mountains of Idaho with
        Gary Snyder in October. Rides freight cars through Cali-
        fornia. *The Paris Review* publishes "The Mexican Girl," an-
        other excerpt from *On the Road*. Kerouac returns to North
        Carolina and begins *Visions of Gerard* on December 27.

1956   Completes *Visions of Gerard* on January 16. Hitchhikes to
        California in March. Lives with Gary Snyder in a cabin in
        Mill Valley, where he writes *Old Angel Midnight* (posthu-
        mously published in 1993) and *The Scripture of the Golden
        Eternity*. Hitchhikes in June to Mount Baker National For-
        est in northern Washington. Works for two months as a
        firewatcher in the Cascade Mountains, staying in a look-
        out cabin on Desolation Peak. Returns to San Francisco in
        September before going to Mexico City, where he begins
        Desolation Angels. Ginsberg's *Howl and Other Poems* is

published by City Lights Books. Kerouac returns to New York in November. Viking Press accepts *On the Road* for publication.

1957   Makes his final revisions to *On the Road* in January. (Viking had insisted that names and locations in the book be changed to avoid possible libel suits.) Begins affair with writer Joyce Glassman (b. 1935, later Joyce Johnson). Sails in February for Tangier, where he visits Burroughs and helps type his novel *Naked Lunch* (a title originally suggested by Kerouac for a different manuscript). Visits Paris and London in April before returning to New York. Moves with his mother to Berkeley, California, in May, but in July they move to Orlando, Florida, where his sister is now living. Visits Mexico City, then goes back to New York. *On the Road* is published on September 5, becomes a bestseller, and makes Kerouac a national celebrity. (In *The New York Times*, critic Gilbert Millstein calls it "the most beautifully executed, the clearest, and the most important utterance yet made by the generation Kerouac himself named years ago as 'beat,' and whose principal avatar he is.") Despite the success of *On the Road*, Viking rejects all of Kerouac's unpublished manuscripts, including *Doctor Sax*, *Tristessa*, and *Desolation Angels*. Writes play *Beat Generation* (published in 2005), childhood memoir *Memory Babe*, and novel *The Dharma Bums* in Orlando during the fall. Returns to New York in late December to give a series of readings with live jazz backing.

1958   Gives series of interviews, including one with Mike Wallace for the *New York Post*. *The Subterraneans* is published by Grove Press in February and receives almost entirely bad reviews. Buys house at 34 Gilbert Avenue in Northport, Long Island. Suffers broken arm, broken nose, and possible concussion when he is beaten outside a bar in Greenwich Village. *San Francisco Chronicle* columnist Herb Caen uses the term "beatnik" in print for the first time on April 2. Kerouac drives from New York to Florida and back with photographer Robert Frank. Moves into Northport home with his mother in April. Begins sketches later published as *Lonesome Traveler*. Neal Cassady begins serving sentence for marijuana trafficking in July (he is released from San Quentin in the summer of 1960). *The Dharma Bums* is published by Viking on October 2. Affair with Joyce

Glassman ends. Kerouac's health worsens as the result of
years of heavy drinking and Benzedrine use.

1959   Records narration for partially improvised Beat film *Pull My
        Daisy*, directed by Robert Frank and painter Alfred Leslie.
        Writes introduction for the U.S. edition of Frank's photo-
        graphic collection *The Americans*. Grove Press publishes
        Doctor Sax as a trade paperback in April, and *Maggie Cassidy*
        is published as a mass-market paperback by Avon in July.
        Kerouac begins writing column for *Escapade* magazine.
        Moves to 49 Earl Avenue in Northport with his mother.
        Travels to Los Angeles in November and reads from *Visions
        of Cody* on the Steve Allen television show. *Mexico City Blues*
        is published by Grove Press. On November 30 *Life* maga-
        zine publishes "Beats: Sad But Noisy Rebels," article by staff
        writer Paul O'Neil attacking Kerouac and Neal Cassady.

1960   Works on *Lonesome Traveler* and *Book of Dreams*. Totem
        Press publishes *The Scripture of the Golden Eternity*. Avon
        publishes *Tristessa* as a mass-market paperback in June. Film
        version of *The Subterraneans*, directed by Ranald MacDou-
        gall, is a critical and commercial failure (Kerouac received
        $15,000 for the film rights). Spends summer at Lawrence
        Ferlinghetti's cabin in Bixby Canyon in Big Sur, where he
        suffers mental breakdown while trying to deal with his
        worsening alcoholism. Sees Carolyn Cassady for the last
        time before returning to Long Island in September. *Lone-
        some Traveler*, a collection of travel pieces, is published by
        McGraw-Hill on September 27.

1961   Meets Timothy Leary in January with Ginsberg and takes
        LSD. *Book of Dreams* is published by City Lights Books.
        Leaves Northport and moves with his mother in April to
        1309 Alfred Drive in Orlando. Spends a month in Mexico
        City during the summer and completes the second part of
        Desolation Angels. In August *Confidential* magazine pub-
        lishes "My Ex-Husband Jack Kerouac Is an Ingrate," article
        detailing Joan Haverty Aly's ongoing attempts to collect
        child support from Kerouac. Writes *Big Sur* in Orlando,
        September 30–October 9. Goes on an extended drinking
        spree in New York in the fall.

1962   Meets his daughter Jan, now 10, for the first time when
        they undergo blood tests in February, and is ordered to pay
        $12 a week in child support. Grove Press publishes the first

American edition of Burroughs's *Naked Lunch* in March.
Big Sur is published by Farrar, Straus and Cudahy on September 11. Buys house at 7 Judy Ann Court in Northport
and moves there with his mother in December.

1963   Works on novel *Vanity of Duluoz* (a different work from
unpublished manuscript of 1942). *Visions of Gerard* is published by Farrar, Straus and Cudahy in September and receives poor reviews.

1964   Gives drunken reading at Harvard University in March.
Sees Neal Cassady for the last time when he comes to New
York City with Ken Kesey and the Merry Pranksters dur-
ing the summer. Sells Northport house and moves with
his mother to 5155 Tenth Avenue North in St. Petersburg,
Florida. Caroline Kerouac Blake dies of a heart attack in
Orlando on September 19; she is buried in an unmarked
grave because Kerouac is unable to pay for a headstone.

1965   Suffers two broken ribs when he is attacked in a St. Petersburg bar in March. *Desolation Angels* is published by
Coward-McCann on May 3. Visits Paris and Brittany in
June in an attempt to research his ancestry. Writes *Satori
in Paris* soon after his return to Florida.

1966   Moves with his mother in the spring to 20 Bristol Avenue
in the Cape Cod town of Hyannis, Massachusetts. *Satori
in Paris* is published by Grove Press. Visited in August by
Ann Charters, who is compiling his bibliography. (Charters
will publish the first biography of Kerouac in 1973.) Mother
suffers massive stroke on September 9 that leaves her paralyzed. Kerouac briefly visits Milan and Rome to promote
the Italian publication of *Big Sur*. Marries Stella Sampas (b.
1918), the sister of his Lowell friend Sebastian Sampas, in
Hyannis on November 18.

1967   Moves in January with Stella and his mother to house at
271 Sanders Avenue in Lowell. Completes *Vanity of Duluoz*.
Gives lengthy interview to the poets Ted Berrigan, Aram
Saroyan, and Duncan McNaughton for publication in *The
Paris Review*. Sees his daughter Jan for the second and last
time in November.

1968   Neal Cassady collapses and dies on February 4 in San
Miguel de Allende, Mexico. *Vanity of Duluoz* is published
by Coward-McCann on February 6. Visits Portugal, Spain,

Switzerland, and Germany in March. Sees Burroughs and Ginsberg for the last time in early September when he goes to New York for the taping of William F. Buckley's television program *Firing Line*. Returns to St. Petersburg, moving to 5169 Tenth Avenue North with Stella and his mother.

1969   Completes *Pic* (published in 1971). Suffers cracked ribs when he is beaten outside a bar in early September. "After Me, the Deluge," article in which Kerouac disassociates himself from the New Left, appears in the *Chicago Tribune* on September 28. Collapses at home on the morning of October 20 and dies at St. Anthony's Hospital in St. Petersburg on October 21 from massive internal bleeding caused by cirrhosis of the liver. A Requiem Mass is held at St. Jean Baptiste Church in Lowell on October 24, after which Kerouac is buried in Edson Catholic Cemetery.

Note on the Texts

This volume contains a selection of previously unpublished writings by Jack Kerouac. They appear here under the following titles: *On Frank Sinatra*; *America in World History*; *A Couple of Facts Concerning Laws of Decadence*; *On Contemporary Jazz—"Bebop"*; *Private Philologies, Riddles, and a Ten-Day Writing Log*; *The Night Is My Woman*; *Journal 1951*; *Old Bull in the Bowery*; *Tics*; *Memory Babe*; *Doing Literary Work: An Interview with Jack Kerouac*; and *Beat Spotlight*. *I Wish I Were You*, which was written in collaboration with William S. Burroughs, is included in an appendix. (Portions of *Private Philologies, Riddles, and a Ten-Day Writing Log* appeared previously in Douglas Brinkley, ed., *Windblown World: The Journals of Jack Kerouac 1947–1954*, Viking: 2004.) *The Night Is My Woman* and *Old Bull in the Bowery* were originally written in French, and are presented here in translations by Jean-Christophe Cloutier that incorporate translations that Kerouac made of some portions of both works. Unless otherwise indicated, all other translations from the French present in this volume were also made by Jean-Christophe Cloutier. The source for all the writings included is the Jack Kerouac archive of the Berg Collection of the New York Public Library.

On Frank Sinatra appears in a handwritten journal dated May 6, 1946–July 21, 1946.

America in World History and *A Couple of Facts Concerning Laws of Decadence* are both taken from a handwritten journal dated September 3–October 9, 1946. The first was begun on September 23; the second was written in May following the death of Kerouac's father.

On Contemporary Jazz—"Bebop" is from a handwritten journal dated February 24–May 5, 1947. The manuscript contains the following explanatory note: "A Paper for Tom Livornese." Livornese was a jazz enthusiast and pianist who studied at Columbia University in the mid-1940s, during which time Kerouac helped him write two essays for one of his music courses. (Those collaborative efforts, "Jazz and the Modern Symphony" and "The New Music," were published in the Spring 1985 edition of the Kerouac fanzine, *Moody Street Irregulars*.)

When he moved to Westwood, Colorado, in May 1949, Kerouac began the notebook to which he gave the title *Private Philologies, Riddles, and a Ten-Day Writing Log*. The residence in Colorado proved to be brief and the notebook was completed in Richmond

Hills, Queens, in March of 1950. As the title indicates, it is very much
a catchall containing a number of distinct sections, including (in
addition to the three segments indicated by the title) an unfinished
play, a draft of a poem written with Allen Ginsberg and ultimately
published in a number of different versions as "Pull My Daisy" (see
Jack Kerouac, *Collected Poems*, The Library of America: 2012), and
other assorted notes and fragments.

The Night Is My Woman is a translation by Jean-Christophe
Cloutier of the fifty-seven-page manuscript *La nuit est ma femme*,
which was composed by Kerouac in February and March 1951 in the
French patois that Kerouac had grown up speaking in the French
Canadian neighborhoods of Lowell, Massachusetts. The archive
contains two typescript pages of excerpts translated by Kerouac;
these passages have been inserted into the present translation to
complete the text, and are indicated in the notes. Further information on *The Night Is My Woman* may be found in the Translator's
Note included in this volume.

Journal 1951 is a sixty-two-page journal, written August–November,
that Kerouac began while a patient in the Kingsbridge VA Hospital in
the Bronx; his original heading for the journal was simply *More Notes.*

Old Bull in the Bowery is a translation of the French manuscript
Sur le chemin, which Kerouac composed in December 1952. In
1954 he began an English translation, titled *Old Bull in the Bowery*,
which was not completed. The translator, Jean-Christophe Cloutier,
describes his preparation of the text in the Translator's Note included
in this volume.

Tics comes from a typescript containing a series of short prose
pieces apparently written from 1953 to 1956, similar in genre to the
work published in *Book of Sketches* (Penguin, 2006).

Kerouac began *Memory Babe* in November 1957, not long after the
publication of *On the Road*, making preliminary outlines and sketches
for it in a series of notebooks and diaries. He continued to work on it
in 1958, in tandem with the composition of *The Dharma Bums*, and
in June of that year completed a twenty-foot scroll of the work, which
remained unfinished. In a May 5, 1961 letter to his agent Sterling
Lord, Kerouac included a list of all the titles intended as part of his
literary cycle the Duluoz Legend. Among these was *Memory Babe*
(immediately following *Visions of Gerard* and preceding *Doctor Sax*),
which he described as "to be written," also noting its chronological scope as 1926–1932. Around the same time Kerouac sent Lord a
twenty-two-page typescript constituting a revision (notably providing
English translation for some of the Québécois dialogue of the scroll)
of roughly the first third of *Memory Babe*, describing it on the first
page as "a nostalgic review of the good old days meant to be read

simply for the pleasure of reading." The first part of the present text of *Memory Babe* is taken from the 1961 revision, and the remainder from the point where that version breaks off in mid-sentence (see page 266), from the 1958 scroll.

Doing Literary Work, as explained in its opening paragraphs, is an interview conducted by mail in June 1963 by Kerouac's friend the novelist John Clellon Holmes, undertaken as part of Holmes's research for his book *Nothing More to Declare* (1967). The text included here is taken from Holmes's typescript.

Beat Spotlight, probably written in 1968, the year before his death, was the last of Kerouac's scroll compositions. The title is mentioned in a list of future projects in a letter to Sterling Lord (April 20, 1968), with no further description of Kerouac's intentions.

In 1945, following the August 1944 murder of David Kammerer by their mutual friend Lucien Carr, Kerouac and William S. Burroughs collaborated on a fictional version of the event. Written in alternating chapters, it did not find a publisher at the time, eventually appearing in 2008 as *And the Hippos Were Boiled in Their Tanks* (Grove Press). *I Wish I Were You* represents Kerouac's unfinished attempt to revise the unpublished novel in a radically different style, while retaining much of the original dialogue. (Although Burroughs is listed on the front page of the 53-page typescript as coauthor, he does not seem to have been actively involved in the revision.)

The texts in the present volume, taken from Kerouac's manuscripts and typescripts as specified above, are newly prepared clear texts. Slips of the pen, missed keystrokes, omitted punctuation (where the omission does not appear to be deliberate), and misspelled proper names have been silently corrected. Letter cases have been regularized to capitals at the beginning of sentences and for proper names. Titles of works and passages in French have been printed in italic type. In *Journal 1951*, several footnotes were added by Kerouac at later dates. These are indicated by brackets in the present volume. With regard to *Memory Babe*, it should be noted that Kerouac, who had used real names in the original draft, in his unfinished revised version substituted fictional names for a number of characters. The text presented here maintains the names used in the first draft throughout.

Persons Mentioned

Many of the works collected in this volume are autobiographical in nature and as such feature many of Jack Kerouac's family members, friends, and acquaintances. This reference list provides brief biographical information on those figures.

Joan Vollmer Adams (1924–1951), common-law wife of William Burroughs, who shot her to death under obscure circumstances in Mexico City in September 1951.

Alan Ansen (1922–2006), Brooklyn-born poet.

George "G.J." Apostolos (1922–2010), childhood friend of Kerouac who appears in a number of his Lowell-based works.

Vickie Russell Armiger (b. 1924), close friend of Herbert Huncke and other New York Beat writers.

Virginia "Ginny" or "Jinny" Bailey (1928–2006), Greenwich Village folksinger who briefly dated Kerouac.

Joseph Henry "Henri" "Scotty" Beaulieu (1922–1975), childhood friend of Kerouac who appears in a number of his Lowell-based works.

Freddy Bertrand (1922–1990), Lowell-born childhood friend of Kerouac.

Paul Blake (1922–1972), Kerouac's brother-in-law, husband of Caroline "Nin" Kerouac.

Paul Blake, Jr. (b. 1948), son of Caroline Kerouac with Paul Blake.

Rhoda Block (1923–2002), Bronx-born friend of Kerouac who appears as Mona in *On the Road*.

Justin Brierly (1905–1985), Denver attorney and benefactor of the teenage Neal Cassady.

Beverly Burford (1924–1994), friend of Kerouac's from Denver. Beverly was the sister of Bob Burford, and appears in *On the Road* as Babe Rawlins.

Bob "Burf" Burford (1924–2004), Denver-born writer.

Dan Burmeister, Denver acquaintance of Neal Cassady, who introduced him to Kerouac. In 1950, Burmeister and Kerouac maintained a brief correspondence.

William "Bill" Burroughs (1914–1997), American novelist and leading figure of the Beat Generation.

Mardean Butler (1928–2000), Indiana-born writer and poet who moved to Greenwich Village in 1950 to pursue her artistic aspirations.

William Cannastra (1921–1950), aspiring writer in the New York Beat orbit who died in a subway accident.

Mary Carney (1921–1993), high school girlfriend of Kerouac who served as the muse for *Maggie Cassidy*.

Lucien Carr (1925–2005), friend of Kerouac whose "New Vision" aesthetic philosophy was influential over the New York Beats during the 1940s. Carr worked for many years as an editor at United Press International.

Carolyn Cassady (1923–2013), painter and theatrical designer who became Neal Cassady's second wife in 1948.

Neal Cassady (1926–1968), Kerouac's close friend and muse.

Billy Chandler (1920–1942), childhood friend of Kerouac who died at Bataan during World War II. Like Kerouac and Sebastian Sampas, Chandler aspired to be an artist.

Haldon "Hal" Chase (1923–2006), Denver-born anthropologist who befriended Kerouac at Columbia University.

Charles "Charley" Connors, Lowell-born editor and friend to Leo Kerouac. Connors was fictionalized as Jimmy Bannon in *The Town and the City*.

Bruce Crabtree (1918–1933), mathematician who was friendly with the New York Beats during the 1940s and 1950s.

Henri Cru (1921–1992) befriended Kerouac at Horace Mann in New York, and they remained lifelong friends. Cru appears in *On the Road* as Remi Boncoeur.

John L. "Jack" Fitzgerald (1922–1998), jazz writer and actor whom Kerouac befriended in New York in 1943.

Mike Fournier, Jr. (1921–1991), Lowell-born friend of Kerouac who served as the basis for Joe Martin in *The Town and the City*.

Bill Fox, business partner of Jerry Newman at Greenwich Music Shop and Esoteric Records.

Bea Franco (1920–2013), born in Selma, California. Franco was romantically involved with Kerouac in autumn 1947. She appears in *On the Road* as Terry.

Allen Ginsberg (1929–1997), American poet and a leading figure of the Beat Generation.

Louis Ginsberg (1896–1976), father of Allen Ginsberg; also a poet.

Robert Giroux (1914–2008), renowned American book editor and publisher; Giroux edited Kerouac's *The Town and the City* for Harcourt Brace & Company.

Alan Harrington (1918–1997), Massachusetts-born novelist who introduced Kerouac to John Clellon Holmes in 1948.

Joan Haverty (1930–1990), Kerouac's second wife, who appears in *On the Road* as Laura. Haverty was the mother of Kerouac's only child, Janet "Jan" Kerouac (1952–1996).

Luanne Henderson (1930–2009), Neal Cassady's first wife who appears in *On the Road* as Marylou.

Al Hinkle (b. 1926), Denver friend of Kerouac who appears in *On the Road* as Ed Dunkel.

John Hohnsbeen (1926–1970) befriended Kerouac at Columbia University and later became Peggy Guggenheim's personal assistant.

John Clellon Holmes (1926–1988), American novelist and poet. One of Kerouac's most trusted friends and interlocutors.

Marian Holmes (b. 1923), first wife of John Clellon Holmes. They divorced in 1952.

Pete Houde (1918–1993), Lowell-born childhood friend of Kerouac. Houde appears in several of Kerouac's works as Gene Plouffe.

Herbert Huncke (1915–1996), New York street hustler and poet who served as a mentor to Kerouac, Burroughs, Ginsberg, and others.

Frank Jeffries (1923–1996), Denver-born friend of Kerouac. He accompanied Kerouac and Cassady to Mexico in 1950 and subsequently appeared in *On the Road* as Stan Shephard.

David Kammerer (1911–1944), friend of William Burroughs who became acquainted with Kerouac in 1944. Kammerer was stabbed to death by Lucien Carr in August 1944. Carr, who was sent to a reformatory for manslaughter, claimed he was resisting Kammerer's sexual advances.

John Kelly (1913–1966), author of *All Soul's Night* (1947). Kerouac met Kelly through Robert Giroux in 1949.

Beatrice "Bea" Kerouac, cousin of Jack Kerouac, daughter of Joseph and Leontine Kerouac. Beatrice often appears in Kerouac's works as Blanche Duluoz, including the edited typescript of *Memory Babe*.

Caroline Kerouac (1872–1944), Kerouac's aunt, Leo Kerouac's sister, born in Rivière-du-Loup, Québec. She became Sister Antoine de Jésus after joining the Daughters of Charity in 1893.

Caroline "Nin" Kerouac (1918–1964), Jack Kerouac's sister.

Gabrielle-Ange Kerouac, née Lévesque (1895–1973), Kerouac's mother, born in Saint-Pacôme, Québec, and raised in Nashua, New Hampshire.

Gerard Kerouac (1916–1926), Kerouac's older brother who died of rheumatic fever at the age of nine.

Jean-Baptiste Kerouac (1849–1906), Kerouac's grandfather.

Joseph Kerouac (1881–1944), Kerouac's uncle on his father's side; he appears in a number of Kerouac's works (including the edited typescript of *Memory Babe*) as Uncle Mike.

Leo Kerouac (1889–1946), Jack Kerouac's father, born Joseph Alcide Leon Kerouac in Saint-Hubert, Québec, and raised in Nashua, New Hampshire.

Leontine Kerouac, née Roleau (1882–1975), Kerouac's aunt through her marriage to Joseph Kerouac. She sometimes appears in Kerouac's work as Aunt Clementine.

John Kingsland (1927–1997), met Kerouac while Kerouac was dating Edie Parker; Kingsland was dating Joan Vollmer, Parker's roommate at the time.

Jay Landesman (1919–2011), founding editor of *Neurotica*, a literary journal featuring Beat writing.

Liz Lehrman (1928–2014), New York–born painter who dated Lucien Carr in the early 1950s.

Elbert Lenrow (1903–1993), professor of American literature at The New School.

Tom Livornese (1924–1990), a jazz pianist who studied at Columbia University; Kerouac befriended him in 1946.

Roger Lyndon (1917–1988), Harvard-trained Princeton mathematician.

Varnum Lewis Marker (1926–1993), New York acquaintance of Kerouac.

Marie Louise Michaud, née Kerouac (1878–1962), Kerouac's aunt, Leo Kerouac's sister, born in Saint-Hubert, Québec.

Adele Morales (1925–2015), New York–born painter who dated Kerouac briefly. Morales later married novelist and journalist Norman Mailer.

Dorothy "Dusty" Moreland, Wyoming-born painter who was romantically involved with both Allen Ginsberg and Kerouac.

Charles Morrisette (1909–1987), first husband of Jack's sister Caroline; Morrisette appears in *Visions of Cody* and *Tics* as Charley Bissonette.

Jerry Newman (1918–1970), recording engineer and founder of Esoteric and Counterpoint records. Newman befriended Kerouac through their mutual friend, Seymour Wyse.

Edith "Edie" Parker (1922–1993), Kerouac's first wife.

Helen Parker (1920–1993), born in South Dakota, was romantically involved with Kerouac and Allen Ginsberg; she was also briefly engaged to John Dos Passos.

Robert Rondeau (1921–2007), childhood friend of Kerouac from Lowell; he appears in several of the author's works as Billy Artaud.

Roland "Salvey" Salvas (1922–2004), childhood friend of Kerouac. Salvas appears in a number of Kerouac's Lowell-based works.

Sebastian "Sammy" Sampas (1922–1944), close friend and early literary confidant of Kerouac from Lowell.

Stella Sampas (1918–1990), sister of Sebastian Sampas. Kerouac maintained a correspondence with Stella over many years, and she became his third and final wife in 1966.

Norman Schnall (b. 1924), Bronx-born friend of the New York Beat writers.

Carl Solomon (1928–1993), Bronx-born poet and editor. Allen Ginsberg's "Howl" is dedicated to Solomon.

Allan Temko (1924–1990), New York–born architecture critic whom Kerouac befriended during the 1940s.

Bill Tomson (1929–1982), Denver-born friend of Neal and Carolyn Cassady.

Barry Ulanov (1918–2000), New York–born jazz critic.

Emma Vaillancourt, née Kerouac (1871–1967), Kerouac's aunt, Leo Kerouac's sister, born in Rivière-du-Loup, Quebec.

Mark Van Doren (1894–1972), poet, critic, and university professor. Kerouac studied under Van Doren at Columbia.

Lucia "Vern" Vernarelli (1920–1995), Brooklyn-born painter affiliated with the New York Beats.

Francesca "Cessa" Von Hartz (b. 1929), Barnard graduate who married Lucien Carr in 1952. They met while working for United Press International.

Ed White (b. 1925), Denver-born architect who befriended Kerouac during their time at Columbia University.

A. A. Wyn (1898–1967), publisher and editor who founded Ace Books.

Seymour Wyse (b. 1923), born in London, befriended Kerouac during their time as students at Horace Mann in New York.

Celine Young (1924–1972), Barnard student with whom both Kerouac and Carr were romantically involved during the mid-1940s.

Notes

In the notes below, the reference numbers denote page and line of this volume (the line count includes headings). No note is made for material included in standard desk-reference books. Quotations from Shakespeare are keyed to *The Riverside Shakespeare* (Boston: Houghton Mifflin, 1974), edited by G. Blakemore Evans. For references to other studies and further biographical background than is contained in the Chronology, see Ann Charters, *Kerouac* (San Francisco: Straight Arrow Books, 1973); Ann Charters, ed., *Jack Kerouac: Selected Letters, 1940–1956* (New York: Viking Penguin, 1995); Ann Charters, ed., *Jack Kerouac: Selected Letters, 1957–1969* (New York: Viking Penguin, 1995); Ann Charters, *A Bibliography of Works by Jack Kerouac, 1939–1975* (New York: The Phoenix Bookshop, revised edition, 1975); Barry Gifford and Lawrence Lee, *Jack's Book: An Oral Biography of Jack Kerouac* (New York: St. Martin's, 1978); Tim Hunt, *The Textuality of Soulwork: Jack Kerouac's Quest for Spontaneous Prose* (Ann Arbor: University of Michigan Press, 2014); Joyce Johnson, *The Voice Is All: The Lonely Victory of Jack Kerouac* (New York: Viking, 2012); Paul Maher Jr., *Kerouac: His Life and Work* (Lanham, Md.: Taylor Trade, 2004); Dennis McNally, *Desolate Angel* (New York: Random House, 1979); Hassan Melehy, *Kerouac: Language, Poetics, and Territory* (New York: Bloomsbury, 2016); Gerald Nicosia, *Memory Babe: A Critical Biography of Jack Kerouac* (New York: Grove Press, 1983).

ON FRANK SINATRA

3.1 Sorelian] Georges Sorel (1847–1922), French philosopher and radical political theorist, best known for *Reflections on Violence* (1908).

AMERICA IN WORLD HISTORY

8.15–16 Céline of France . . . Ford's assembly lines] In Céline's *Journey to the End of Night* (1932), the protagonist Bardamu travels to the United States where he works for the Ford Motor Company.

10.5 Sessions, Harris] American composers Roger Sessions (1896–1985) and Roy Harris (1898–1979).

A COUPLE OF FACTS CONCERNING LAWS OF DECADENCE

13.1 Henry Morgan] Radio and television comedian (1915–1994).

14.31 Orgone "Institute"] Under the aegis of his Orgone Institute, the Austrian psychoanalyst Wilhelm Reich (1897–1957), author of *The Function*

of the Orgasm (1927) and *Character Analysis* (1933), propagated his theory
of orgone, a supposed form of cosmic energy that could be accumulated for
healing purposes in boxes of Reich's design. Reich was subsequently convicted
of fraud and died while serving a two-year sentence.

ON CONTEMPORARY JAZZ—"BEBOP"

19.10   Ellington idea . . . Lester Young idea] Edward Kennedy "Duke"
Ellington (1899–1974), composer and bandleader; Lester Young (1909–1959),
jazz instrumentalist on saxophone and clarinet.

19.26–27   Basie, Lunceford, Goodman, Shaw, Benny Carter, Don Redman]
Bandleaders Count Basie (1904–1984), Jimmy Lunceford (1902–1947), Benny
Goodman (1909–1986), Artie Shaw (1910–2004), Benny Carter (1907–2003),
and Don Redman (1900–1964).

20.5   Dizzy Gillespie] John Birks "Dizzy" Gillespie (1917–1993), jazz trumpeter and bandleader, one of the architects of bebop.

20.18   Shelly Manne . . . Stan Kenton] Manne (1920–1984), jazz drummer
associated with Woody Herman and Stan Kenton before becoming a central figure on the West Coast jazz scene in the 1950s; Kenton (1911–1979),
bandleader and composer.

20.31   Pete Rugolo] Composer and arranger (1915–2011) long associated with
Stan Kenton.

20.32   Boyd Raeburn] Jazz musician and bandleader (1913–1966) noted for
the novelty and complexity of his band's arrangements.

20.33   Ray Brown] Jazz bassist and cellist (1926–2002).

20.33   Mercer Ellington] Jazz trumpeter, composer, and bandleader (1919–
1996), son of Duke Ellington and eventual leader of the Duke Ellington
Orchestra following his father's death.

20.34   1946 Herman band] Woody Herman (1913–1987) disbanded his band,
subsequently known as the First Herd, in 1946; in 1947 he organized a new
band known as the Second Herd.

PRIVATE PHILOLOGIES—RIDDLES—AND A TEN-DAY
WRITING LOG

25.11   "On the Road"] Kerouac is here referring to "Shades of the Pris-
oner House," an early attempt at *On the Road* featuring Red Moultrie as
protagonist.

25.12   T & C.] *The Town and the City* (1950), Kerouac's first published novel.

27.3   "Ling's Woe"] "The Fable of Ling's Woe," 1949 typescript by Kerouac,
held in the Berg Collection.

27.13–14   Kafka's penal machine] See Franz Kafka's "In the Penal Colony" (1914).

27.15   shmoo] Cartoon creature created by Al Capp in the comic strip *Li'l Abner* in 1948, in a sequence published in book form as *The Life and Times of the Shmoo*. Shmoos were benevolent creatures who offered themselves as food for humans but were exterminated because of their deleterious effect on the economy.

27.31   Charley Ventura] Jazz saxophonist and bandleader (1916–1992).

29.12   Joe Christmas] Doomed protagonist of William Faulkner's *Light in August* (1932).

31.1–2   Francis Martin] Character in *The Town and the City*, depicted as having a morose sense of humor.

31.27   *La Kermesse* de Rubens] Painting (1635–38) by Peter Paul Rubens, also known as *The Village Fête* or *Village Wedding*.

32.9   "rain-&-rivers"] Kerouac composed a road journal titled *Rain and Rivers* beginning in January 1949. *Rain and Rivers* provided source material for *On the Road* (1957), and some of its dates overlap with the dates covered in *Private Philologies—Riddles—And a Ten-Day Writing Log*. *Rain and Rivers* is included in David Brinkley, ed., *Windblown World* (Viking, 2004).

32.15   "Junkey" of *T & C*] Fictional name for Herbert Huncke (1914–1986) in *The Town and the City*.

32.33   Peter Martin] Protagonist of *The Town and the City*.

36.22   Spenser] The poet Edmund Spenser (1551–1599).

37.12–17   Bran the Blessed . . . Rhiannon] Mythological figures in the medieval Welsh compilation the *Mabinogion*.

38.6–7   "You can do anything to my flesh . . . *but leave my bones alone.*"] See Allen Ginsberg's "Complaint of the Skeleton to Time," written in 1949.

38.22–23   Hopkins . . . *horn*] The poet Gerard Manley Hopkins (1844–1889) wrote in his diary in 1863: "The various lights under which the horn may be looked at have given rise to a vast number of words in language. It may be regarded as a projection, a climax, a badge of strength, power or vigor, a tapering body, a spiral, a wavy object, a bow, a vessel to hold withal or drink from, a smooth hard material not brittle, stony, metallic or wooden, something sprouting up, something to thrust or push with, a sign of honour or pride, an instrument of music, etc."

38.25   "And in a Dongeon deep him threw without remorse."] See Spenser's *The Faerie Queene*, book I, canto 7, stanza 15, line 9.

38.27–28   "O that I were there . . . their Maybush beare!"] See Spenser's *The Shepheardes Calender* (1579), "Maye."

448 NOTES

40.1–4 "Before Nelson's pillar . . . Green and Ringsend."] James Joyce, *Ulysses* (1922), chapter 7.

40.14 Alain-Fournier] Pseudonym of Henri-Alban Fournier (1886–1914), author of *Le Grand Meaulnes* (1913), translated into English as *The Wanderer*.

40.25 Chauntecleer Chaucer] See Chaucer's "The Nun's Priest's Tale."

40.28 Spike Jones] American bandleader (1911–1965) who specialized in musical parodies including "Cocktails for Two" (1944) and "Hawaiian War Chant" (1946).

41.4–5 Whitman's sudden use of KELSON] See "A Song of Myself," section 5: "And that a kelson of the creation is love."

41.13–14 Melville's great passage on Dutch whaling-vessels] See *Moby-Dick*, chapter 101, "The Decanter," in which there is a reference to "2,800 firkins of butter."

41.36–37 Herman Charles Bosman . . . *Cold Stone Jug*.] The South African writer Bosman (1905–1951) killed his stepbrother in an argument in 1926 and was sentenced to death; the sentence was commuted, and he was released after serving five years. *Cold Stone Jug* (1949) is a fictionalized memoir of his experience of incarceration.

42.18 James Joyce Yearbook, 1949] *A James Joyce Yearbook* was edited by Maria Jolas.

44.8 Chad Gavin] In early 1950 Kerouac began another iteration of *On the Road* featuring Chad Gavin as protagonist. See the typescript "Cast of Characters in *On the Road* as reconceived Feb. 15, 1950."

45.31 "Crazy Sunday"] Short story (1932) by F. Scott Fitzgerald, originally published in *The American Mercury*.

52.24 *Aumónes!*] Alms! [Tr. note]

52.29 *Âme!*] Soul! [Tr. note]

57.1 *Plays I've seen*] *My Heart's in the Highlands* by William Saroyan; *The Beautiful People* by Saroyan; *Native Son* by Paul Green and Richard Wright based on Wright's novel; *Flight to the West* by Elmer Rice; *Crime and Punishment* by Rodney Ackland based on the novel by Dostoevsky; *Red Gloves*, adapted by Daniel Taradash from Sartre's *Les Mains Sales*; *Hamlet*, directed by and starring Maurice Evans.

58.31 *arrangeur*] Arranger. [Tr. note]

58.32 *manger*] Eating; to eat. [Tr. note]

58.35 Gene Tunney] American boxer (1897–1978), world heavyweight champion, 1926–28.

60.36 Joe Martin] Older brother of Peter and Francis Martin in *The Town and the City*.

61.18   Warren Beauchamp] Warren Beauchamp appears as Ray Smith's road companion in "Ray Smith Novel of Fall 1948," an early attempt at *On the Road*.

62.5   Ghost of the Susquehanna] See part 1, chapter 14, of *On the Road*.

62.6   Reichian] See note 14.31.

THE NIGHT IS MY WOMAN

65.2–12   I have not liked . . . the idea of living.] The first paragraph was translated by Kerouac. [Tr. note]

65.7   what is said in the Bible] See Revelation 3:17: "Because thou sayest, I am rich, and increased with goods, and have need of nothing; and knowest not that thou art wretched, and miserable, and poor, and blind, and naked."

65.9–10   I use . . . thinking.] In translating this sentence, Kerouac excised a clause in the original in the middle of the sentence. Translated into English, the original reads "I use my sadness—it's the sadness of an old dog with big watery eyes—to spend my time thinking." [Tr. note]

65.31   mayhap yes, mayhap no] I translate the French patois *teudbien* (*peut-être bien* in standard French) with "mayhap," a hybrid of "maybe" and "perhaps" that Kerouac uses in many of his works, such as *Visions of Gerard*, *Big Sur*, *Pomes All Sizes*, and others. [Tr. note]

66.32   shirttails!] "Shirttails" here translates the French patois *kitchimise*, meaning *queue de chemise* in standard French—literally, tail of a shirt. In *Visions of Gerard*, Kerouac uses *kitchimise* without translating it. [Tr. note]

68.14–16   Ti-Michel . . . Ti-Choux] These terms of endearment have been left untranslated, as Kerouac often did in his published works, but in English this passage would be "Lil-Michael, Lil-Thumb, Tourlipi, Lil Fart, and my mother called me Lil-Cabbage." [Tr. note]

68.40   Saroyan] Fiction writer and playwright William Saroyan (1908–1981).

69.3–19   Voilà: —"It was like a stage . . . and said, A few."] This passage appears in English in the original manuscript. [Tr. note]

70.40–71.1   Crazy as a Broom] This is a literal translation of the common French Canadian expression *fou comme des balais*, or, in Kerouac's sound-spelling, *balas*. Kerouac translated it literally—"crazy as brooms"—but in singular form, on the bottom of the manuscript page as a footnote. [Tr. note]

71.25–37   Well, and where is G.J. . . . Where is that bed today?] This passage was translated by Kerouac. [Tr. note]

72.2   NYA program] National Youth Administration, a New Deal agency focusing on securing employment and educational opportunities for young Americans.

72.29   Louis Verneuil] French playwright, screenwriter, and actor (1893–1952) who had many of his works adapted for the Broadway stage from the

450

NOTES

1920s to the 1950s. Kerouac likely wanted to change the name for publication and so wrote *Son Nom* (His Name) rather than Louis Verneuil; for lack of an alternative the real name has been retained here. [Tr. note]

72.31–32   Nancy Carroll] Movie star (1904–1965) whose films included *Abie's Irish Rose* (1928), *Devil's Holiday* (1930), and *Laughter* (1930).

73.7–22   "Buffalo . . . in my pipe.] This passage was translated by Kerouac. [Tr. note]

73.27–38   I had discovered . . . at his manner.] This passage was translated by Kerouac. [Tr. note]

76.5   TRAVAIL IN THE MIST] This phrase appears in English at the bottom of the corresponding page of the original manuscript, underneath a squiggly line that horizontally crosses the page. [Tr. note]

76.31   TRAVAIL IN THE MURK] See note 76.5.

78.18–19   "Thanatopsis" . . . Bryant] "Thanatopsis," a poetic meditation on death, was written in his teens by William Cullen Bryant (1794–1878); it was published in *The North American Review* in 1817.

79.7–8   a circus like the one W. C. Fields ran] In *You Can't Cheat an Honest Man* (1939), directed by George Marshall.

79.26–27   "She was fourteen . . . at the village fair."] In English in the original. [Tr. note]

79.36–80.15   "You boys want . . . circus life, boys,"] All dialogue spoken by the circus boss is in English in the original. [Tr. note]

81.8–24   "Stand still!" . . . damn boy go?"] The elephant rider's lines are in English in the original. [Tr. note]

81.27–28   pale as a lenten fart] I follow Kerouac's translation, in *Visions of Gerard*, of the French Canadian expression *blême comme une vesse de carême*. The colloquial English equivalent would be "white as a sheet." [Tr. note]

82.7–12   "Were you stationed . . . wise guy punk,"] The dialogue between the narrator and the soldier is in English in the original. [Tr. note]

82.25   My old childhood chum Jack] In this section of the original manuscript, the narrator is often erroneously referred to as "Jack" rather than Michel by his friend "Mike." In his final translated excerpt, Kerouac confirms that he intended to name the "Mike" character "Jack" (in effect flipping their two nicknames). In order to avoid confusion, the names have been adjusted accordingly in the translation; thus, Jack here is the narrator's friend, and Mike/Michel is the narrator. [Tr. note]

83.31–32   "Daddy . . . the best of me."] In English in the original. The lyrics are from "Daddy" (1941), composed by Bobby Troup, a number one hit for Sammy Kaye. [Tr. note]

83.34–36 "As I was walking . . . cold as the clay."] In English in the original. The lyrics are from the traditional cowboy ballad known as "Streets of Laredo" or "The Cowboy's Lament." [Tr. note]

85.6 "W.P.A.,"] Song (1940) composed by Jesse Stone, recorded by Louis Armstrong and the Mills Brothers. W.P.A. is the New Deal employment program the Works Progress Administration.

85.31–34 "What the hell . . . those post holes."] In English in the original. [Tr. note]

85.38 *mautadit*] A milder version of *maudit*, similar to saying *darnit* in place of *dammit*. [Tr. note]

86.30 Lana Turner] Movie star (1921–1995) known for such films as *They Won't Forget* (1937) and *The Postman Always Rings Twice* (1946).

87.1 we moved to New Haven] The episode of the move to New Haven is also recounted, in a radically different tone, in *Vanity of Duluoz* (1968). [Tr. note]

88.6–11 We decided to eat . . . or harassing.] This passage was translated by Kerouac. [Tr. note]

88.31 noising day] Kerouac wrote this phrase in parentheses next to the French *plein d'train* (full of noise). [Tr. note]

89.2 "and I found her bitter."] See Arthur Rimbaud, *A Season in Hell* (1893): "One evening I seated Beauty on my knees. And I found her bitter. And I cursed her."

89.26 brillianting] The French original here is *brillante* (glittering); I have adopted Kerouac's translation of the word in *Old Bull in the Bowery*. [Tr. note]

90.36–37 "vieille gieppe chiène."] In Kerouac's manuscript, "old bitch bee" is followed by the French phrase; I have duplicated this in reverse here. The standard French form would be *vieille guêpe chienne*. [Tr. note]

92.3 The sea is my sister] In the French original, "the sea is my sister"— a gendered switch from his 1944 novella *The Sea Is My Brother* (published 2011)—is written *La mère est ma soeur*. In standard French this means "The mother is my sister"; since *mère* and *mer* are homonyms, and since Kerouac wrote French phonetically, this is an example of the kinds of resonances that are lost in translation. [Tr. note]

93.16–21 "Goin' down . . . in the morning . . ."] In English in the original. [Tr. note]

94.3 Bull Run (Manassas?)] The Battle of Bull Run, fought on July 21, 1861, near Manassas, Virginia, was the first major battle of the Civil War and was a major Confederate victory.

95.20–97.5 One morning I got up . . . He had a job for me.] Translated by Kerouac. [Tr. note]

95.34   Magic Fire Music] Instrumental passage in Act 3 of Richard Wagner's *Die Walküre* (1870).

JOURNAL 1951

101.14   Victor Duchamp] There are multiple holograph fragments and notes in the Berg Collection for a version of *On the Road* featuring a protagonist named Victor Duchamp, such as "Home and the Road" (1950), featuring a chronology of Duchamp's life.

101.25–27   Faulkner . . . *Sanctuary*] When Faulkner's novel *Sanctuary* (1931) was reissued in The Modern Library in 1935, he stated in an introduction: "To me it is a cheap idea because it was deliberately conceived to make money."

104.1–2   *Pierre* . . . Henry Murray] The ninety-page introduction by psychologist Murray (1893–1988) appeared in the 1949 Hendricks House edition of Melville's *Pierre, or The Ambiguities*.

104.2   *Under the Volcano*] Novel (1947) by Malcolm Lowry (1909–1957).

105.2–3   my youthful works, including Orpheus and Vanity of Duluoz] *Orpheus Emerged* is Kerouac's 1945 novella (published in 2002). *Vanity of Duluoz* here refers to the work of 1942, not to be confused with the 1968 novel of the same title.

105.28   *J'ai menti.*] I lied. [Tr. note]

107.32   Marcus Goodrich] American writer (1897–1991) best known for the novel *Delilah* (1941), based on his experiences on a destroyer during World War I.

108.6–7   "I have decided to consider annihilation,"] While serving as American Consul in Liverpool, Nathaniel Hawthorne was briefly visited by Herman Melville in 1856. Hawthorne recorded some of the conversation in his journal: "Melville, as he always does, began to reason of Providence and futurity, and of everything that lies beyond human ken, and informed me that he had 'pretty much made up his mind to be annihilated'; but still he does not seem to rest in that anticipation; and, I think, will never rest until he gets hold of a definite belief. . . . He can neither believe, nor be comfortable in his unbelief; and he is too honest and courageous not to try to do one or the other."

108.11   Pyotr Alexandrovich] Pyotr Alexandrovich Miusov, wealthy liberal in Dostoevsky's *The Brothers Karamazov*.

108.26   Ripeness is all] *King Lear*, V.ii.11; spoken by Edgar.

109.11   Buechner] Frederick Buechner (b. 1926), American novelist whose early novels are *A Long Day's Dying* (1950) and *The Seasons' Difference* (1952).

110.23   Pic Jackson] Pictorial Review Jackson, the protagonist of Kerouac's posthumously published novella *Pic* (1971). He also appears in *Old Bull in the Bowery*, included in this volume.

116.18   Frans Hals] Dutch portrait painter (c. 1582–1666).

117.15   *Il faut vivre . . . en Francais.*] You have to live in English, it's impossible to live in French. [Tr. note]

117.32–33   "It is late afternoon; the grapes are turning brown!"] From Friedrich Nietzsche's *Ecce Homo* (1888, published 1908): "On this perfect day, when everything is ripening and not only the grapes are turning brown, a shaft of sunlight has just fallen on my life: I looked backwards, I looked ahead, I never saw so much and such good things all at once."

117.39   Shelley Winters] Actress (1920–2006) who appeared in *A Place in the Sun* (1951) and many other films.

118.19   Hal Kemp] Instrumentalist and bandleader (1904–1940) whose hits included "The Music Goes 'Round and 'Round" (1936) and "Got a Date with an Angel" (1937).

118.22–23   "Barney Google," "There's a Rainbow on my Shoulder"] "Barney Google (With the Goo-Goo-Googly Eyes)" (1923), song by Billy Rose and Con Conrad, popularized by Billy Jones and Ernest Hare (duo also known as the Happiness Boys); "There's a Rainbow 'Round My Shoulder" (1928), song by Al Jolson, Billy Rose, and Dave Dreyer, performed by Jolson in the film *The Singing Fool.*

118.27–28   Harry Hopkins . . . C.I.O. . . . . Walter Reuther] Hopkins (1890–1946), close advisor of Franklin D. Roosevelt who helped design New Deal programs; Congress of Industrial Organizations, trade union federation created in 1935; Reuther (1907–1970), labor union organizer who became president of United Auto Workers in 1936.

118.30   *All Quiet on the Western Front . . . The Road Back*] Novels by the German writer Erich Maria Remarque (1898–1970), published in 1929 and 1931. American film versions were made in 1930 and 1937 respectively.

118.32–33   Jimmy Foxx] Or Jimmie Foxx (1907–1967), baseball player who played first base for the Philadelphia Athletics and the Boston Red Sox.

118.37   Jelly Roll Morton] Professional name of early jazz pianist and composer Ferdinand Joseph LaMothe (1890–1941).

119.8–9   Lomax's "Mister Jelly Roll"] *Mister Jelly Roll: The Fortunes of Jelly Roll Morton, New Orleans Creole and "Inventor of Jazz"* (1950), biography by Alan Lomax.

119.11   Mamie's Blues] Recorded by Jelly Roll Morton in 1939.

120.17   Home Run Baker] Baseball player (1886–1963) for the Philadelphia Athletics and the New York Yankees.

122.9   *Comédie Humaine*] *La Comédie Humaine*, general title for the interconnected multivolume fictional work by Honoré de Balzac (1799–1850).

122.27–28   *à mon Ange Guardien*] To my Guardian Angel. [Tr. note]

123.10   Hot Lips Page] Oran Thaddeus Page (1908–1954), jazz trumpeter.

126.39–127.1   *to justify the ways of God to man*] See Milton, *Paradise Lost*, book 1, line 26.

128.15   Jerry Newman's record store] Newman (1918–1970), a Columbia student who was a close friend of Kerouac, used a portable recorder to record many early bebop sessions, operated the Greenwich Music Shop, and founded the recording labels Counterpoint and Esoteric.

129.25–26   Maxwell Bodenheim] Writer (1892–1954), poet and author of novels, including *Replenishing Jessica* (1925); he lived an increasingly derelict life and was murdered along with his wife Ruth in a Bowery flophouse by a resident in whose room they were staying.

129.35   *My Turkish Adventure*] Memoir (1951) by Pamela Burr, an American teacher in Istanbul.

130.28   *Adam's Rib*] Film (1949) directed by George Cukor, starring Katharine Hepburn and Spencer Tracy.

130.32–33   Edith Piaf . . . Marlene Dietrich; Billy Holiday] Piaf (1915–1963), French chanteuse; Dietrich (1901–1992), German film actress and singer; Holiday (1915–1959), American jazz singer.

131.1   Freud's notes on Dosty] Sigmund Freud published his essay "Dostoevsky and Parricide" in 1928.

131.2–3   Carson McCullers] American novelist (1917–1967) whose works include *The Heart Is a Lonely Hunter* (1940) and *Reflections in a Golden Eye* (1941).

132.31   Royal Roost] New York jazz club that in the late 1940s presented Charlie Parker, Dizzy Gillespie, Tadd Dameron, Dexter Gordon, and other innovative musicians.

133.18–20   Rudy Williams, Eddy Lockjaw Davis, Terry Gibbs, Don Elliott . . . Sonny Stitt] Williams (1909–1954), alto saxophonist; Davis (1922–1986), tenor saxophonist; Gibbs (b. 1924), vibraphonist; Elliott (1926–1984), trumpeter, vibraphonist, and vocalist; Stitt (1924–1982), saxophonist.

133.37   A day in baseball history] On October 3, 1951, the New York Giants won the National League pennant when Bobby Thomson hit a ninth-inning home run off of Ralph Branca of the Brooklyn Dodgers. As it was the first ever nationally televised baseball game, and was also broadcast by radio to American troops in Korea, Thomson's home run became known as "The Shot Heard 'Round the World."

134.22   Maglie] Sal Maglie (1917–1992), major league baseball pitcher who started for the Giants on October 3, 1951.

NOTES

455

135.7 *Snow White & the 7 Dwarfs*] Walt Disney's animated feature was released in 1937.

137.16–18 *Lee Konitz*... "I Remember April"] Konitz (b. 1927), alto saxophonist and composer, associated with the cool jazz of the 1940s and 1950s; "I'll Remember April" (1942), song by Gene de Paul with lyrics by Patricia Johnston and Don Raye, from the movie *Ride 'Em Cowboy.*

137.22–23 Buxtehudian] Dieterich Buxtehude (1637–1707), German composer and organist.

137.29 Cecil Payne] Bass saxophonist (1922–2007).

137.35 David Diamond] American classical composer (1915–2005).

138.11–12 Daphne du Maurier] English novelist (1907–1989), author of *Jamaica Inn* (1936) and *Rebecca* (1938).

138.13 *VAUGHAN MONROE*] Popular singer and bandleader (1911–1973) whose hit recordings included "Tangerine" (1942) and "Let It Snow! Let It Snow! Let It Snow!" (1945).

138.21 Tristano] Lennie Tristano (1919–1978), jazz pianist and composer; he had wide influence as a teacher of improvisation beginning in the 1940s.

139.5 Woody Herman] Bandleader, clarinetist, and vocalist (1913–1987).

141.33–34 Carl Sandburg] American poet and writer (1878–1967).

143.37 "Zadok the Priest" by Handel] Anthem composed in 1727 by Georg Frideric Handel for the coronation of George II, and sung subsequently at every royal coronation.

144.8–9 "Out of the murderous innocence] See W. B. Yeats, "A Prayer for My Daughter" (1919), line 16: "Out of the murderous innocence of the sea."

144.9 that dolphin-torn, that gong-tormented sea] Final line of W. B. Yeats's "Byzantium" (1930).

145.13 *amante*] Lover. [Tr. note]

145.29 George Arliss] English actor and playwright (1868–1946), noted for his portrayals of Disraeli, Voltaire, Cardinal Richelieu, and other historical figures.

147.9 Allen had visions in 1948] Ginsberg's experience of hearing the voice of William Blake reading poems was described by him as a turning point in his identity as a poet.

147.24–25 "Love the art . . . yourselves in art."] See Konstantin Stanislavski's *My Life in Art* (1924).

148.31 Terry Gibbs] Jazz vibraphonist and bandleader (b. 1924).

149.6 Don Elliott] Jazz trumpeter and vocalist (1926–1984).

149.7   "Flying Home"] Jazz composition (1939) by Benny Goodman and Lionel Hampton, with lyrics by Sid Robin.

149.12   Whitman's *Calamus*] Group of poems published for the first time in the 1860 edition of *Leaves of Grass.*

149.19   Marshall Stearns Jr.] Jazz critic (1908–1966), frequent contributor to *Down Beat, Record Changer*, and other periodicals; founder of the Institute of Jazz Studies in 1952 and author of *The Story of Jazz* (1956).

151.14   Merle Miller] Novelist (1919–1986) whose books include *Island 49* (1945) and *That Winter* (1948).

162.38   *Serenade*] Novel (1937) by James M. Cain.

165.3–4   that old Spanish Reichian eccentric] Jaime de Angulo (1887–1950), born in France of Spanish parents, settled in California in the early twentieth century and studied native tribes of California as a linguist and ethnomusicologist.

168.22–24   *ASSEZ, maudit Christ . . . ou commence jamais!!*] Enough, dammit Christ of the Baptism—If you're gonna be a writer start tonight or never start!! [Tr. note]

169.14   *La Voix du Nord*] The Voice of the North. [Tr. note]

OLD BULL IN THE BOWERY

175.26–27   California Four Star] In the original French, the brand is "Mission Bell." In one of Kerouac's earlier translations, he gives the brand as "Italian Swiss Colony." [Tr. note]

176.22   Dakota] In the original text Pomeray asks if they are near Iowa. [Tr. note]

176.36–37   the Phantom of the Opera] Lon Chaney portrayed the title character of Gaston Leroux's 1910 in his 1925 film (directed by Rupert Julian).

180.37–38   "Hyoo hyoo . . . I said that, *damn!*"] In English in the original. [Tr. note]

181.9   Baby Doe] Elizabeth Tabor (1854–1935), known as "Baby Doe," whose marriage in 1883 to the Colorado copper magnate Horace Tabor after he divorced his first wife created a scandal. She lived lavishly until her husband lost his fortune in the Panic of 1893.

182.36   with throat-choking hope over] Following this phrase, the pagination of Kerouac's typescript skips pages 11–19 and resumes with the following: "for wine money: his exhilaration was due to the fact that he was going to succeed and get the money." This section corresponds to the first of four English inserts, which Kerouac had labeled in the original manuscript "ON

THE ROAD Lil Neal Material, page 4 to 12." A revised version of this insert appears in *Visions of Cody*. [Tr. note]

185.30   Major Hoople] Principal character in long-running syndicated comic strip *Our Boarding House*, created in 1921 by Gene Ahern (1895–1960).

185.37   *Out Our Way*] Syndicated single-panel American comic strip first drawn in 1922 by J. R. Williams (1888–1957), known for its portrayal of rural life.

190.40   *miguelle*] *Miguelle* is French patois for *miel* (honey). In Kerouac's pronunciation the "g" was silent. [Tr. note]

193.1   black brooding expression] At this juncture the typescript jumps from page 23 to 33. The following section tracing the history of the Duluoz clan, from "His father Jacques Duluoz" to "the ring of entirety in its beams," is the second major English insertion Kerouac mixed into *Sur le chemin*. It is absent from Kerouac's translation typescript yet is taken into account by the latter's pagination. Typescript page 33 begins with the tail-end of the insertion with the words "shamefaced, clan, piteous . . . in its beams." The version of the insertion text as it appears here is largely taken from the notebook in which it was first composed as an integral part of *Sur le chemin*; however, since Kerouac revised some of the text on pages of the second notebook to *Sur le chemin*, the revision has been used whenever possible. [Tr. note]

193.10   L'Heureux] L'Heureux is the fictional surname Kerouac gives to his mother's side of the family, the Lévesques. In the scheme of the *Duluoz Legend*, Ti Jean's grandfather, Jacques Duluoz, married Clementine Bernier-Gaos, his paternal grandmother. Clementine's siblings include Guillaume (Old Bull Baloon) and Henrieta, mother to both Rolfe Glendiver by her first marriage to Smiley Glendiver, and to Little Dean Pomeray by her second marriage to old Dean Pomeray (now widowed). Since Clementine was also mother to Leo Duluoz, Henrieta was the latter's aunt, as he reveals to Old Dean Pomeray when they first meet. Old Bull is thus uncle to Leo Duluoz, Rolfe Glendiver, and Little Dean Pomeray—and is Ti Jean's grand-uncle. [Tr. note]

193.15   Bernier the Atlantic explorer] Joseph-Elzéar Bernier (1852–1934), Canadian explorer, born in Quebec, who led expeditions into the Canadian Arctic, 1904–11.

198.3   the old man raved] Kerouac describes a similar scene in his short 1941 piece "The Father of My Father," published in Paul Marion, ed., *Atop an Underwood: Early Stories and Other Writings* (1999). [Tr. note]

199.7   *On est aussi bien.*] *We might as well*: the phrase is left in French in Kerouac's English manuscript insert. [Tr. note]

200.31–32   Walter Winchell] Gossip columnist and radio journalist (1897–1972).

200.34   to the new day, the great voyage.] These phrases, which do not appear in the French text, were added by Kerouac in his typescript translation. [Tr. note]

204.39   Roy Eldridge] Jazz trumpeter (1911–1989), nicknamed "Little Jazz."

206.24–207.6   And he turned to little Dean . . . that's all, *Dean—Dean—*"] This passage corresponds to the third English insert, labeled "MATERIAL OF 'HA? NEAL?'" [Tr. note]

207.28–208.35   Have you ever seen . . . rough and free.] This, the fourth and last of the English inserts for *Sur le chemin*, was labeled "ON THE ROAD 1–3." Readers of *Visions of Cody* will recognize it as a description of Cody Pomeray, the "Neal" character of that novel, rather than Rolfe. The archive shows that Kerouac rewrote and revised this text several times; the version used here is from Kerouac's 1954 typescript translation. [Tr. note]

211.16   "Ramona"] Song (1928) by Mabel Wayne and L. Wolfe Gilbert, performed by Dolores Del Rio in the 1928 film of the same name.

211.27–37   "If the guys back home . . . but not any more."] In his typescript translation Kerouac excises this passage. [Tr. note]

214.11   Dick Clancy] The character who appears here as Dick Clancy was named, in another draft translation, Bill Kelly. Both are offshoots of Bill Clancy, the name of a "football-hero-hobo" character that Kerouac had invented in his early writings. (See 60.34 in this volume.) [Tr note]

217.16   Lester at the Savoy] Lester Young (1909–1959), jazz saxophonist and longtime member of Count Basie's band; the Savoy Ballroom opened in Harlem in 1926 and for thirty-three years featured big bands, including Chick Webb's Orchestra and Al Cooper's Savoy Sultans.

219.19   "She's going] At this point Kerouac's 1954 translation breaks off. It is not known if Kerouac did not complete the translation or if the remaining pages were lost. The rest of the translation is by Jean-Christophe Cloutier. [Tr. note]

219.25   "But what is it?"] The original French patois reads: *Mais cosse quy ya?* rather than the standard French *Mais qu'est-ce qu'il y a?* On a separate sheet in his archive Kerouac toys with translating "cosse" simply as two letters ("W d"): *Cosse tu fa dans la vie?* "W d y do for a living?" However, since Kerouac usually translates *cosse qu* and its variants into fairly standard American English I have translated it as "what is it." At other points where it seemed appropriate, I have opted for the more experimental "W d" to approximate the speed of French Canadian speech. (Kerouac also used "Whatzit?" in *Satori in Paris* and some correspondence.) [Tr. note]

220.9 *Holy Batchism*] In the French, *Eh batêge*; I have adopted the translation used by Kerouac in *Doctor Sax*. [Tr. note]

220.29 naborhoods] The word appears thus in the French text. [Tr. note]

223.24–224.7 "W d is it?" . . . at the window.] I have relied on a revised version of this passage—which is problematic and confusing in the French text—translated by Kerouac on a separate sheet in his archive. [Tr. note]

224.8 dope] The word is used here in the sense of "varnish" or "any thick liquid." [Tr. note]

225.10 hangjawed] See Kerouac's description, in *Visions of Gerard*, of Canucks having the "hungjawed dull faces of grown adults." [Tr. note]

226.33–34 Leo cried, throwing out his arms."] In English in the original. [Tr. note]

228.15–16 crazy as a broom] See note 70.40–71.1. [Tr. note]

228.18 bastat] Kerouac uses this translation for a corresponding expletive in *Visions of Gerard*. [Tr. note]

230.24 "Ah'm from Nawth Ca lina my self,"] Thus in the original manuscript. [Tr. note]

231.10 Hot Lips] See note 23.10.

231.15–27 "There's always gotta be . . . man, he's *high*!"] All dialogue in English in the original. [Tr. note]

232.17–20 "They didn't wanta . . . lost the man's hole."] Dialogue in English in the original. [Tr. note]

232.38–233.4 "Man, we rolled . . . stretched myself *out*.] In English in the original. [Tr. note]

233.9 Charley St. Christian] Charlie Christian (1916–1942), jazz guitarist of the swing era.

234.10 doawns!] Thus in the original manuscript. [Tr. note]

235.11 Gaby] Leo's wife, Ti Jean's mother; Kerouac's mother's name was Gabrielle-Ange Lévesque. [Tr. note]

237.4 roundifilated] In French, *enroudanfola*, a coinage of Kerouac, who also provided the equivalent English neologism in parentheses. [Tr. note]

237.9 *Brigash, cass mi gass*] This phrase at the bottom of the manuscript remains cryptic; it also appears in the novel *Maggie Cassidy*, which Kerouac composed immediately after *Sur le chemin*. Though its exact meaning is uncertain, it pertains to Kerouac's childhood in Lowell. [Tr. note]

TICS

241.17 crummy] Caboose.

241.22 Zulueta & Persley] On July 8, 1953, Orlando Zulueta defeated Arthur Persley in a lightweight boxing match at Madison Square Garden.

242.9 Morning Telegraph] Daily newspaper published in New York 1839–1972, strongly focused on horse racing news.

243.27 Mardou] Alene Lee (1931–1991); her 1953 love affair with Kerouac served as the basis for *The Subterraneans* (1958), with Lee cast as Mardou Fox.

245.19 Julien Green] French-born American writer (1900–1998) whose books were mostly written in French; his novels include *The Closed Garden* (1927) and *The Dark Journey* (1929).

246.35–36 *que hora es . . . Grande Baile del Mundo!*] The somewhat garbled Spanish translates roughly as: "What time is it, mister, at four in the morning? Today! Only today! The biggest dance in the world."

248.10–11 *Au typewriter / toujours!*] At the typewriter always! [Tr. note]

MEMORY BABE

255.33 Tom Mix] Cowboy star of the silent and early sound era (1880–1940) whose many films included *The Last Trail* (1927), *A Horseman of the Plains* (1928), and *Destry Rides Again* (1932).

257.26 *Shadow* magazines] The Shadow, originally a radio character, became the masked, crime-fighting hero of a long-running pulp magazine, 1931–49.

257.30–31 *Phantom Detective . . . Star Western*] *The Phantom Detective*, pulp magazine published 1933–53; *Star Western*, pulp magazine published by Popular Publications beginning in the 1930s.

258.27–28 "Portia Faces Life"] The radio soap opera "Portia Faces Life," starring Lucille Wall as a crusading woman lawyer in a small town, was broadcast from 1940 to 1953.

262.12 "*Tannant d'voleur*] "You obnoxious crook. [Tr. note]

265.21–22 Vicoan circumlocution] The allusion is to Giambattista Vico (1668–1744), Italian political philosopher whose notion of history as cyclical influenced James Joyce's *Finnegans Wake* (1939).

267.14 "Dardanella,"] Song (1919) with music by Felix Bernard and Johnny S. Black and lyrics by Fred Fisher, recorded by Ben Selvin.

267.15 Al Jolson . . . Rudy Vallee] Jolson (1886–1950), singer and film actor, star of *The Jazz Singer* (1928); Vallée (1901–1986), popular singer of French-Canadian ancestry whose hits include "Deep Night" and "I'm Just a Vagabond Lover," both 1929.

268.15   *J peu tu alez . . . ti loup.*] Can I go play outside? If you want lil wolf. [Tr. note]

268.27   Cy Young or Honus Wagner] Young (1867–1955), major league baseball pitcher; Wagner (1874–1955), major league shortstop.

268.25   Warren Spahns . . . Mazeroskis] Spahn (1921–2003), major league pitcher; Bill Mazeroski (b. 1936), second baseman for the Pittsburgh Pirates.

269.37   *Ti Jean pourquoi tu jou tuseul*] Ti Jean, why are you playing by yourself? [Tr. note]

270.2–3   "*Rente dans maison . . . pi du la.*"] "Get in the house and come eat some Ritz crackers and peanut butter and some milk." [Tr. note]

270.19–20   "*Allo Kewpie, ta tu faim la?*"] "Hello Kewpie, are you hungry there?" [Tr. note]

270.26   *C'est tu bon? cest tu bon?*] Is it good? Is it good? [Tr. note]

270.37   "*Ah ca c'est bon, ah?*"] "Ah now that's good, ah?" [Tr. note]

271.26–28   *Ma allez were . . . va achetez laubre.*"] "I'm going to see my chums, ma." "Okay and get back at 6 o'clock for your supper, me and you and Ti Nin we're gonna go to Lambert's to pick up the groceries and after that we're gonna buy the tree." [Tr. note]

271.38   Big-Parade war battles] King Vidor's enormously successful movie *The Big Parade* (1925) featured extensive scenes of World War I combat.

276.5   Zorro] Masked swordsman fighting for justice in California under Mexican rule, created by Johnston McCulley in the novella "The Curse of Capistrano" (1919).

277.8   "*Ten, l Ti Pousse*"] "Here, there's Ti Pousse." [Tr. note]

277.10–11   "*Cosse qui fat . . . va l'arrangez.*"] "What's he up to today?" "We're gonna buy the Xmas tree tonight and we'll set it all up."

277.23–24   "*Ah ti Kewpie, i veu du hamburg?*"] "Ah Lil Kewpie, he wants some hamburg?" [Tr. note]

277.27–28   "*Eh twe, j'ai faite . . . encore asoir*"] "Eh you, I had these pants cleaned just yesterday. Gonna have to completely change again tonight." [Tr. note]

278.3   "*Ya tu encore d la date pie?*" "*Ben oui.*"] "Is there any of that date pie left?" "Yeah sure." [Tr. note]

278.19   "*I neige!*"] "It's snowing!" [Tr. note]

278.25   "*Fe!*" . . . "*La marde!*"] "Phooey!" . . . "Bullshit!" [Tr. note]

278.26–27   "*Leo, parle pa . . . de les enfants!*"] "Leo, don't talk like that in front of the children!" [Tr. note]

279.24–27   *j men a d lecole . . . Estamac flasse*"] "I was leaving school, for a glass of water." "Poor Joe. What did he have to say?" "Nothing . . . he wanted you to come see him. He said that you stay on the other side of the river and you never come to see him." "Ah well, one fine day there . . ." "Flabby stomach." [Tr. note]

279.32–33   "*j'ai lestmac . . . je peu avoire . . . ?*"] "I got a flabby stomach . . . is there a lil something to eat that I could have . . . ?" [Tr. note]

280.5–6   "*Ah l bonhomme,*" . . . "*s pa que'l ti bon homme ca.*"] "Ah that man,". . . "If it ain't just the old man right there." [Tr. note]

280.9   Edgar Cayce] Self-proclaimed clairvoyant and faith healer (1877–1945), founder of the Association for Research and Enlightenment.

280.29   Hugh Herbert] Comic actor (1887–1952) noted for playing fatuous or eccentric characters in many films, including *Million Dollar Legs* (1932), *Footlight Parade* (1933), and *Dames* (1934). "Woo woo!" was one of his catchphrases.

281.3–4   "*l bonhomme Zagg . . . boeu comme ca.*"] "That Zagg character he's always drunk. Will you ask me why a man drinks like that." [Tr. note]

281.7   "*I pourra seulement . . . chez eux.*"] "He won't even be able to drag himself home." [Tr. note]

281.26–27   "*Vien t en . . . maudit foulla?*"] "Come on Ti Jean, what are you looking at on that damn crazy fool there?" [Tr. note]

281.32–33   "*Ont lara . . . Ti Nin.*"] "We might not get any snow for Christmas, Ti Nin." [Tr. note]

282.21   Hank Greenberg] Baseball player (1911–1986) mostly for the Detroit Tigers.

283.13   "*S lui la ye trop skinny*"] "This one's too skinny." [Tr. note]

283.26   "*Leve les un peu, tu l drag dans rue.*"] "Lift it up a bit, you're dragging it in the street." [Tr. note]

283.31–33   "*T S tanne mon fair . . . un tite chandelle.*"] "Now this year I'm gonna make a nice lil corner for Gerard in the parlor, right against the tree, with flowers and a lil candle." [Tr. note]

283.37–38   "*On peu mettre . . . ta right la.*"] "We can put that next to his portrait. Well alright, it's all right there." [Tr. note]

284.14   *Un beau arbre fattez pis rond.*] A beautiful tree fatted up and round. [Tr. note]

284.22–23   *Ma Ste Terese . . . anyway la.*] Put St. Theresa next to him there, I said. But why St. Theresa, there's no room there anyway. [Tr. note]

284.26–29 *"Ten garde . . . Ouit ti bi di!"*] "Here look at your little sister Ti Nin, there, you see how nice she is?" "Yes." "She's making it all beautiful, all for you that. Don't get angry with her anymore." "Yes and don't steal my caramel anymore." "Yessereedoo!" [Tr. note]

284.35 *I neige tu encore?*] Is it still snowing? [Tr. note]

285.3 *Roll River* by James Boyd] Novel set in Pennsylvania, published in 1935; Boyd's other novels include *Drums* (1925) and *Marching On* (1927).

285.14–15 *"Ten, gard Ti Nin . . . pi i lit."*] "Here, Ti Nin, look at Ti Jean, he loves his portrait of Gerard so much that he sits around it and he reads." [Tr. note]

285.35 "Ah Sweet Mystery of Life,"] "Ah, Sweet Mystery of Life" (1910), song from Victor Herbert's operetta *Naughty Marietta*, with lyrics by Rida Johnson Young; it enjoyed renewed success as sung by Jeanette MacDonald in the 1935 film version.

292.12–13 Jack Holt . . . Buck Jones] Holt (1888–1951), actor who appeared in many Westerns, including *The Thundering Herd* (1925) and *The Border Legion* (1930); Jones (1891–1942), Western star of films, including *Just Pals* (1920), *The Texas Ranger* (1931), and *Range Feud* (1931).

292.14–15 *"Ten, Ti Jean yest arrivez!"*] "Look, Ti Jean is here!" [Tr. note]

294.11 Errol Flynn] Australian-born actor (1909–1959) known for swash-buckling roles in such films as *Captain Blood* (1935) and *The Sea Hawk* (1940).

294.30–31 'Dodge brothers, late 29'] In *A Day at the Races* (1936).

297.30 *"Va t couchez la Ti Jean, yest tard."*] "Go to bed now Ti Jean, it's late." [Tr. note]

299.2–7 *"Ti Jean? Comment . . . moi je bu plus."*] "Ti Jean? How come? You're not up yet?" "I went out the upstairs window." "Bad boy . . . you're gonna break your legs." "Don't be scared, I know how to jump." "I made some good oatmeal for your breakfast. Do you want some toast now to start?" "Yes." "O boy, I have a big headache after all that last night, O boy me I'm not drinking anymore." [Tr. note]

303.24 *Monkey Business*] Film (1931) directed by Norman McLeod, in which the Marx Brothers stow away on a luxury liner.

304.11–12 Una Merkel] Comic actress (1903–1986) who appeared in *Private Lives* (1931), *Red Headed Woman* (1932), and other films.

304.15–16 Rintintin . . . Lon Chaney] Rin Tin Tin (1918–1932), German Shepherd who became a popular attraction in such films as *A Race for Life* (1928) and *On the Border* (1930); Chaney (1883–1930), actor whose films include *The Hunchback of Notre Dame* (1923), *The Phantom of the Opera* (1925), and *The Unholy Three* (1925).

DOING LITERARY WORK

307.2 *Nothing More to Declare*] Holmes's book was published in 1967 by E. P. Dutton. The chapter on Kerouac is called "The Great Rememberer."

307.28 Alphonse & Gaston] Protagonists of the comic strip of the same name, created by Frederick Burr Opper in 1901; their hallmark was absurd and overelaborate mutual deference.

308.37 Oswald Spengler] German historian (1880–1936) best known for his multivolume work *The Decline of the West* (1918–22).

309.12–13 Nietzsche . . . turning brown."] See note 117.32–33.

310.37 "The pathway . . . through excess"] See William Blake, *The Marriage of Heaven and Hell*: "The road of excess leads to the palace of wisdom."

311.1–2 *The derangement of the senses*] See Arthur Rimbaud, letter to Paul Demeny, May 15, 1871: "The poet makes himself a *seer* by an immense, long, deliberate *derangement* of all the senses."

312.3 Gregory Corso] American poet (1930–2001), author of *Gasoline* (1958), *The Happy Birthday of Death* (1960), and other books.

314.6 Malcolm Cowley] Memoirist and literary critic (1898–1989); an editor at Viking Press from the 1940s on.

314.23 movie of *Alice in Wonderland*] The Walt Disney animated feature was released in 1951.

316.28 "Why Was I Born?"] Song (1929) with music by Jerome Kern and lyrics by Oscar Hammerstein II, which enjoyed renewed currency through Billie Holiday's 1937 recording.

317.28 Alan Watts] British writer (1915–1973) known for such books as *The Way of Zen* (1957) and *The Joyous Cosmology* (1962).

317.33 *Leuconostoc mesenterioides*] Class of bacteria involved in the manufacture of sugar.

318.23 Lipschitz] Modernist sculptor (1891–1973).

321.14–15 von Braun] Wernher von Braun (1912–1977), German aerospace engineer who helped develop the V-2 rocket for Nazi Germany and later played a major role in the United States space program.

321.26–35 Lenny Bruce . . . Lawrence] Lenny Bruce (1925–1966), stand-up comedian and satirist; Norman Mailer (1923–2007), novelist and journalist; James Baldwin (1924–1987), novelist, essayist, and social critic; Jean Genet (1910–1986), French playwright and novelist; Jack Gelber (1932–2003), playwright known primarily for *The Connection* (1959); Thelonious Monk (1917–1982), jazz pianist and composer; Nelson Algren (1909–1981), novelist whose works include *The Man with the Golden Arm* (1949); Robert Rauschenberg

(1925–2008), painter and assemblage artist; J. D. Salinger (1919–2010), novelist; James Jones (1921–1977), novelist, author of *From Here to Eternity* (1951); Ornette Coleman (1930–2015), pioneering free jazz saxophonist and composer; John Rechy, novelist and essayist, author of *City of Night* (1963); Yevgeny Yevtushenko (b. 1933), Russian poet; Ray Charles (1930–2004), pianist and composer; William Styron (1925–2006), novelist; Gary Snyder (b. 1930), poet, depicted by Kerouac as Japhy Ryder in *The Dharma Bums*; Mort Sahl (b. 1927), stand-up comedian; Jean-Paul Sartre (1905–1980), French philosopher, novelist, and playwright; Marquis de Sade (1740–1814), French writer and exponent of libertinism; D. H. Lawrence (1885–1930), English novelist and poet.

323.30–31 *The Counterfeiters . . . The Idiot*] *The Counterfeiters* (1925), novel by André Gide; *The Idiot* (1868–69), novel by Fyodor Dostoevsky.

324.39 Something more may come of this] See the last sentence of Herman Melville's *The Confidence-Man* (1857): "Something further may follow of this Masquerade."

327.4–5 William S. Hart, Conway Tearle, Theda Bara] Hart (1864–1946), star of silent Westerns, including *Hell's Hinges* (1916) and *The Toll Gate* (1920); Tearle (1878–1938), actor who appeared in *Bella Donna* (1923), *The Dancer of Paris* (1926), and other films; Bara (1885–1955), silent star nicknamed "The Vamp" whose films include *A Fool There Was* (1915) and *East Lynne* (1916).

328.3–4 "What did your face . . . you were born?"] See Case 23 in the *Mumon-kan (The Gateless Gate)*.

328.31 "draw breath in pain"] *Hamlet*, V.ii.346.

330.30 Ciacco] See Dante, *Inferno*, canto 6, 52–54.

I WISH I WERE YOU

343.11–12 *Nigger of the Narcissus*] *The Nigger of the "Narcissus"* (1897), novel by Joseph Conrad; the Russian Finn Wamibo is a crew member on board the *Narcissus*.

360.12–13 "You Always Hurt the One You Love."] Song with words by Allan Roberts and music by Doris Fisher, popularized by The Mills Brothers in 1944.

371.4 Madame de Castaing] Madeleine Castaing (1894–1992), interior designer and patron of the arts.

372.18 Spengler's book] See note 308.37.

374.20–21 Tchelitchev's *Cache-Cache*] Painting (1940–42) by Pavel Tchelitchev (1898–1957), also known as "Hide and Seek."

379.6–7   Rimbaud's *Season in Hell*] *Une saison en enfer* (1893), visionary prose poem.

387.20   'The Wound and the Bow'] The essay originally appeared in *The New Republic*, April 21, 1941, and was reprinted (under the title "Philoctetes: The Wound and the Bow") in *The Wound and the Bow: Seven Studies in Literature* (1941).

399.35–36   *Plonger au fond du gouffre . . . ciel ou enfer, qu'importe?*] See the final lines of Charles Baudelaire, "Le Voyage," *Les Fleurs du Mal* (1857): "*Plonger au fond du gouffre, Enfer ou Ciel, qu'importe? / Au fond de l'Inconnu pour trouver du* nouveau!" ("To plunge into the depths of the abyss, Hell or Heaven, what difference? In the depths of the unknown to find something *new!*)

400.2   *bateau ivre*] *Le Bateau Ivre* (*The Drunken Boat*), poem (1871) by Arthur Rimbaud.

401.15–16   "It is a violent Paradise . . . this savage parade!"] See Arthur Rimbaud, "Parade" (translated by Louise Varèse, in the version quoted here, as "Side Show"), in *Les Illuminations* (1886).

403.1   *acte gratuite*] *Acte gratuit*, a gratuitous action committed with no apparent motive or incitement; it is used by André Gide to describe the murder committed by the protagonist of his novel *Les Caves du Vatican* (*Lafcadio's Adventure*, 1914).

408.20   Appassionata Sonata] Ludwig van Beethoven's Piano Sonata No. 23 in F Minor, Op. 53, published in 1807.

418.8–9   *The Port of Shadows*] *Quai des Brumes* (1938), film directed by Marcel Carné and starring Jean Gabin, Michel Simon, and Michèle Morgan.